THE CRITICS APPLAUD
ROSAMUNDE PILCHER

Rosamunde Pilcher

A New Collection of
Three Complete Books

ROSAMUNDE PILCHER

A *New Collection of*
Three Complete Books

SNOW IN APRIL

WILD MOUNTAIN THYME

FLOWERS IN THE RAIN
AND OTHER STORIES

Wings Books
New York

This edition contains the complete and unabridged texts of the original editions. They have been completely reset for this volume.

This 1997 edition is published by Wings Books,
a division of Random House Value Publishing, Inc.,
201 East 50th Street, New York, New York 10022,
by arrangement with St. Martin's Press, Inc.

Wings Books and colophon are trademarks of Random House Value Publishing, Inc.

Random House
New York • Toronto • London • Sydney • Auckland
http://www.randomhouse.com/

Printed and bound in the United States of America

Library of Congress Cataloging-in-Publication Data

Pilcher, Rosamunde.
 [Novels. Selections]
 A new collection of three complete books / Rosamunde Pilcher.
  p. cm.
 Contents: Snow in April — Wild mountain thyme — Flowers in the Rain and other stories.
  ISBN 0-517-18237-8
  1. Love stories, English. I. Title.
 PR6066.I38A6 1996
 823'.914—dc20   96-27249
                                                      CIP

8 7 6 5

Contents

SNOW IN APRIL
1

WILD MOUNTAIN THYME
133

FLOWERS IN THE RAIN
AND OTHER STORIES
373

SNOW IN APRIL

1

Banked in scented steam, with her hair wound up in a bathcap, Caroline Cliburn lay supine in the bath and listened to the radio. The bathroom was large—as all the rooms in this generous house were large. It had once been a dressing-room, but long ago Diana had decided that people neither used nor needed dressing-rooms any longer, and she had stripped it naked, and called in plumbers and carpenters, and fitted it out with pink porcelain and a thick white carpet and hung floor-length chintz curtains at the window. There was a low glass-topped table, for bath salts and magazines and large eggs of pink soap, smelling of roses. There were roses, too, on the French bath-towels and the bathmat, on which now reposed Caroline's dressing-gown, her slippers, the radio and a book which she had started to read and then abandoned.

The radio played a waltz. One-two-three, one-two-three went the sighing violins, conjuring up visions of palm courts and gentlemen in white gloves and elderly ladies sitting on gilt chairs and nodding their heads in time to the pretty tune.

She thought, *I'll wear the new trouser suit*. And then remembered that one of the gilt buttons had fallen off the jacket and was now, in all probability, lost. It would, of course, be perfectly possible to look for the button, to thread a needle, to sew it on. The operation would take no more than five minutes, but it would be far simpler not to. To wear instead the turquoise caftan, or the black velvet midi dress that Hugh said made her look like Alice in Wonderland.

The water was growing cold. She turned on the hot tap with her toe and told herself that at half past seven she would get out of the bath, get dried, put on a face and go downstairs. She would be late, but it wouldn't matter. They would all be waiting for her, grouped around the fireplace, Hugh in the velvet dinner jacket that she secretly disliked and Shaun girthed in his scarlet cummerbund. And the Haldanes would be there, Elaine well into her second martini, and Parker with his knowing, suggestive eyes, and the guests of honour, Shaun's business associates from Canada, Mr. and Mrs. Grimandull, or some such name. And, after a reasonable delay, they would all troop in to dinner, turtle soup and the cassoulet Diana had spent the morning concocting, and a sensational pudding which would probably be brought in flaming, to the accompaniment of oohs and aahs and "Darling Diana, how do you do it?"

The thought of all that food made her feel, as usual, nauseated. It was puzzling. Indigestion was surely the prerogative of the very old, the greedy, or possibly, the pregnant, and Caroline, at twenty, could qualify for none of these. She didn't exactly feel ill, she just never felt well. Perhaps before next Tuesday—no, next Tuesday week—she should go to a doctor. She imagined trying to explain. *I'm going to be married and I feel sick all the time.* She saw his smile, paternal and understanding. *Pre-wedding nerves, natural enough, I'll give you a sedative . . .*

The waltz faded discreetly out, and the announcer came in with the seven-thirty news bulletin. Caroline sighed and sat up, pulled out the plug before she could succumb to the temptation of further basking, and climbed out on to the bath-mat. She turned off the radio, dried herself in a cursory fashion, pulled on the dressing-gown and padded through to her bedroom, leaving wet footmarks on the pale white carpet. She sat at her skirted dressing-table, pulled off the bath-cap, and observed, without enthusiasm, her triply-reflected image. Her hair was long and straight and pale as milk, and hung, on either side of her face, like two silk tassels. It was not a pretty face in the accepted sense of the word. The cheekbones were too high, the nose blunt, the mouth wide. She knew that she could look either hideous or beautiful, and only her eyes, wide-set, dark brown and thickly-lashed, were consistently remarkable, even now when she was plain with tiredness.

(She remembered Drennan, and something he had once said, long ago, holding her head between his hands and turning her face up to his. "How is it that you have a boy's grin and a woman's eyes? And the eyes of a woman in love, at that?" They had been sitting in the front of his car, and outside it had been very dark and raining. She remembered the sound of the rain, the ticking of the car clock, the feel of his hands encircling her chin, but it was like remembering an incident in a book or a film, an incident that she had witnessed, but taken no part in. It had happened to another girl.)

She reached, abruptly, for her brush, disposed of her hair in a twist of rubber band, and began to make up her face. While she was in the middle of this, footsteps came down the passage, soft on the thick carpet, and stopped at her door. The door was lightly tapped.

"Hallo?"

"Can I come in?" It was Diana.

"Of course."

Her stepmother was already dressed in white and gold, her grey-blonde hair wound like a shell, speared with a gold pin. She looked, as always, beautiful, slender, tall, immaculately groomed. Her eyes were blue, accentuated by a tan which was maintained by regular sessions with a sunlamp, and one of the reasons why she was so often mistaken for a Scandinavian. And indeed, she possessed that happy ability to look as good in casual ski-clothes or tweeds as she did now, dressed and ready for an evening of the utmost formality.

"Caroline, you aren't nearly ready!"

Caroline began to do complicated things with her eye-lash brush.

"I'm half-way there. You know how quick I can be once I start." She added, "It's perhaps the only thing I learned at Drama School that's going to be of lasting use to me. You know, putting on a face in one minute flat."

This was a remark thoughtlessly made and instantly regretted. Drama School was still forbidden territory as far as Diana was concerned and her hackles went up at the very mention of the words. She said coolly, "In that case, perhaps the two years you spent there weren't entirely wasted," and when Caroline, crushed, made no reply, she went on, "Anyway, there's no hurry. Hugh's here, Shaun's giving him a drink now, but the Lundstroms will be a little late. She telephoned from the Connaught to say that John has been held up at a conference."

"Lundstrom. I couldn't remember their name. I've been calling them the Grimandulls."

"That's very unfair. You've not even met them."

"Have you?"

"Yes, and they're very nice."

She began, in a pointed fashion, to tidy up after Caroline, moving about her bedroom, pairing shoes, folding a sweater, gathering up the damp bath-towel which lay in the middle of the floor. This she folded and carried back to the bathroom, where Caroline could hear her making efforts to clean the basin, opening and shutting the door of the mirrored cupboard, doubtless putting back the lid on a jar of cold cream.

She raised her voice. "Diana, what does Mr. Lundstrom confer about?"

"Um?" Diana re-appeared and Caroline repeated her question.

"He's a banker."

"Is he involved in this new deal of Shaun's?"

"Very much so. He's backing it. That's why he's in this country, to get the last few details finalized."

"So, we'll all have to be very charming and well-behaved."

Caroline stood up, dropped off her dressing-gown and went naked, in search of clothes.

Diana sat on the end of the bed. "Is that such an effort? Caroline, you're dreadfully thin. Really too thin, you ought to try and put on a little weight."

"I'm all right." She picked some underclothes out of an over-flowing drawer and began to put them on. "Just made this way."

"Rubbish. All your ribs are showing. And you don't eat enough to keep a fly alive. Even Shaun noticed the other day and you know how unobservant he usually is." Caroline pulled on a pair of tights. "And your colour's so bad, so pale. I noticed it just now when I came in. Perhaps you should start taking iron."

"Doesn't that turn your teeth black?"

"Now, where did you hear that old wives' tale?"

"Perhaps it's something to do with getting married. Having to write one hundred and forty-three thank you letters."

"Don't be ungrateful . . . oh, incidentally, Rose Kintyre was on the telephone, wondering what you wanted for a present. I suggested those goblets you saw in Sloane Street, you know, the ones with the engraved initials. What are you going to wear this evening?"

Caroline opened her wardrobe and took down the first dress which came to hand, which happened to be the black velvet. "This?"

"Yes. I love that dress. But you should wear dark stockings with it."

Caroline put it back, took out the next. "Then this?" The caftan, luckily not the trouser suit.

"Yes. Charming. With gold ear-rings."

"I've lost mine.'

"Oh, *not* the ones that Hugh gave you."

"Not really lost, just mislaid. I've put them somewhere but I can't remember where. Don't bother." She tossed the turquoise silk, soft as thistledown over her head. "Earrings don't show on me, anyway, unless my hair's been properly done." She began to do up the tiny buttons. She said, "What about Jody? Where's he having dinner?"

"With Katy, in the basement, I said he could have it with us, but he wants to watch the Western on television."

Caroline loosened her hair and brushed it smooth. "Is he there now?"

"I think so."

Caroline sprayed herself at random with the first bottle of scent that came to hand. "If you don't mind," she said, "I'll go down first and say good night to him."

"Don't be too long. The Lundstroms will be here in about ten minutes."

"I won't."

They went downstairs together. As they descended into the hall the door of the drawing-room opened and Shaun Carpenter emerged, carrying a red ice-jar which was shaped like an apple and had a gilt stalk sticking up from its lid to form a handle. He looked up and saw them.

"No ice," he said by way of explanation and then was diverted, like a stage comedian doing a double-take, by their appearance, and stood still, in the middle of the hall, to witness their descent.

"Well, don't you both look beautiful? What a pair of gorgeous women."

Shaun was Diana's husband, and Caroline's . . . her mode of reference varied. My step-mother's husband she sometimes called him. Or, my step-step-father. Or, simply, Shaun.

He and Diana had been married for three years, but, as he was fond of telling people, he had known her and adored her for far longer than that.

"Knew her in the old days," he would say. "Thought I had the whole business neatly buttoned up, and then she went off to the Greek Islands to buy a piece of property, and the next thing I knew, she was writing to tell me she'd met and got herself married off to this architect fellow—Gerald Cliburn. Not a bean to his name, a ready-made family and as Bohemian as hell. You could have knocked me down with a feather."

He had remained faithful to her memory, however, and being a naturally successful man, had made an equal success of his role as professional bachelor, the older, more sophisticated man, much in demand by London hostesses and never without a diary packed with engagements for months to come.

Indeed, his single life was so remarkably well-organized and pleasant that when Diana Cliburn, widowed and with two stepchildren in tow, returned to London to move back into her old house, pick up the old threads and start life anew, there was certain speculation about what Shaun Carpenter would do now. Had he dug himself too deeply into his comfortable bachelor rut? Would he—even for Diana—give up his independence and settle for the humdrum life of an ordinary family man? Gossip doubted it very much.

But gossip had reckoned without Diana. She returned from Aphros if anything more beautiful and desirable than ever. She was now thirty-two and at the height of her attraction. Shaun, cautiously renewing their friendship, was bowled over in a matter of days. Within a week he had asked her to marry him and repeated himself at regular seven-day intervals until she finally agreed.

The first thing she made him do was to break the news, himself, to Caroline and Jody. "I can't be a father," he had told them, pacing the drawing-room carpet and going warm round the collar beneath their clear and oddly identical gazes. "Wouldn't know how to, anyway. But I'd like you to feel that you can always make use of me, as a confidant or possible financier . . . after all, this is your home . . . and I'd like you to feel . . ."

He floundered on, cursing Diana for having put him in this awkward situation and wishing that she had let well enough alone and allowed his relationship with Caroline and Jody to develop slowly and naturally. But Diana was impatient by nature, she liked everything cut and dried and she liked it cut and dried now.

Jody and Caroline watched Shaun, sympathetic, but saying and doing nothing to help him out. They liked Shaun Carpenter, but saw, with the clear eyes of youth, that already Diana had him in the palm of her hand. And he spoke about Milton Gardens as their home, whereas home, to them, was and always would be, a white cube like sugar loaf, perched high above the navy-blue Aegean Sea. But that was gone, sunk without a trace into the confusion of the past. What Diana chose to do, whom she chose now to marry, could be none of their business. However, if she had to marry anyone, they were glad it was the large and kindly Shaun.

Now, as Caroline moved to go past him, he stood aside, courtly and starched and faintly ridiculous with the ice bucket held like an offering in his hands. He smelt of "Brut" and the clean smell of fresh linen, and Caroline remembered her father's frequently stubbly chin and the blue work-shirts that he preferred to wear straight from the washing line without so much as a touch of the iron. She remembered, too, the fights and arguments that he and Diana had cheerfully indulged in and which her father almost always won! and she was newly amazed that one woman could find it possible to marry two men who were so remotely different.

Descending to the basement and Katy's domain was like going from one world to another. Upstairs were the pastel carpets, the chandeliers, the heavy velvet curtains. Downstairs, all was cluttered, uncontrived and cheerful. Checked linoleum vied with vivid rugs, curtains were patterned with zig-zags and leaves, every horizontal surface bore its burden of photographs, china ash-trays from forgotten seaside resorts, painted shells and vases of plastic flowers. A proper fire burned redly in the fireplace and in front of it, curled up in a sagging armchair and with his eyes glued to the quivering television screen, was Caroline's brother Jody.

He wore jeans and a navy polo-necked sweater, battered chukka boots, and for no particular reason, a ramshackle yachting cap, several sizes too large for him. He looked up as she came in, and then went immediately back to the screen. He didn't want to miss a single shot, a single second of the action.

Caroline edged him over in the chair and let herself down beside him. After a little she said, "Who's the girl?"

"Oh, she's stupid. She's always kissing. It's one of those."

"Turn it off then."

He considered this, decided that perhaps it was a good idea; and climbed out of the chair to turn off the set. The television died with a small moan. He stood on the hearthrug, looking down at her.

He was eleven, a good age, out of babyhood, but not yet tall and scrawny and bad-tempered and troubled by spots. His features were so like Caroline's own that strangers, seeing them for the first time, knew that they could be nothing but brother and sister, but while Caroline was fair, Jody had hair of so bright a brown that it verged on red, and while her freckles confined themselves to a smattering across the bridge of her nose, Jody's were all over, scattered like confetti across his back and his shoulders and down his arms. His eyes were grey. His smile, which was slow, but disarming when it did appear, revealed second teeth too big for his face and a little crooked, as though they jostled to make space for themselves.

"Where's Katy?" Caroline asked.

"Upstairs in the kitchen."

"Have you had dinner?"

"Yes."

"Did you get what we're having?"

"I had some soup. But I didn't want the other thing so Katy cooked bacon and eggs."

"I wish I could have had it with you. Did you see Shaun and Hugh?"

"Yes. I went up." He made a face. "The Haldanes are coming, bad luck on you."

They smiled in conspiracy. Their views on the Haldanes had a certain sameness. Caroline said, "Where'd you get the hat?"

He had forgotten about the hat. Now he took it off, looking bashful. "I just found it. In the old dressing-up box in the nursery."

"It was Poppa's."

"Yes. I thought it probably was."

Caroline leaned over and took it from him. The hat was dirty and bent, stained with salt, the badge beginning to come loose from its stitches. "He used to wear it when he went sailing. He used to say that being properly dressed gave him confidence so that when someone swore at him for doing the wrong thing, he just used to swear right back." Jody grinned. "Do you remember him saying things like that?"

"Some," said Jody. "I remember him reading Rikki Tikki Tavi."

"You were just a little boy. Six years old. But you remember that."

He smiled again. Caroline got up and put the old hat back on his head. The peak obliterated his face so that she had to stoop to reach beneath it to kiss him.

"Good night," she said.

"Good night," said Jody, not moving.

She was reluctant to leave him. At the foot of the stairs she turned back. He was watching her intently from beneath the peak of the ridiculous cap and there was something in his eyes that made her say, "What's wrong?"

"Nothing."

"I'll see you tomorrow then."

"Yes," said Jody. "Sure. Good night."

Upstairs again she found the drawing-room door shut, a hum of voices coming from beyond, and Katy putting a dark fur coat on to a hanger and disposing of it in the cupboard by the front door. Katy wore her maroon dress and a flowered apron, her concession to the formality of a dinner party, and she started dramatically when Caroline suddenly appeared.

"Ooh, you didn't arf give me a start."

"Who's come?"

"Mr. and Mrs. Aldane." She jerked her head. "They're in there now. You'd better get a move on, you're late."

"I just saw Jody." Reluctant to join the party, she stayed with Katy, leaning against the bottom on the banister. She imagined the bliss of going back upstairs, climbing into bed, being brought a boiled egg.

"Still watching those Indians?"

"I don't think so. He said there was too much kissing."

Katy made a face. "Better watch kissing than all that violence, that's what I say." She shut the cupboard door. "I'd rather have them wondering what it's all about, than going out and coshing old ladies with their own umbrellas."

And with this telling observation she went back to her kitchen. Caroline, left alone and with no further excuse for delay, crossed the hall, put a smile on her face and opened the drawing-room door. (Another thing that she had learned at Drama School was how to make an entrance.) The buzz of chatter ceased and somebody said, "Here's Caroline."

Diana's drawing-room, at night, lit for a party, was as spectacular as any stage set. The three long windows which faced out over the quiet square were draped in pale, almond-green velvet. There were huge, squashy sofas in pink and beige, a beige carpet, and, blending marvelously with the old pictures, walnut cabinets and Chippendale, a modern coffee table, Italian in steel and glass. There were flowers everywhere and the air was pervaded with a variety of delicious and expensive smells; hyacinths and "Madame Rochas" and Shaun's Havana cigars.

They stood, just as she had imagined them, grouped around the fireplace, with drinks in their hands. But before she had even closed the door behind her, Hugh had detached himself from the group, laid down his glass and come across the room to meet her.

"Darling." He took her shoulders between his hands and bent to kiss her. Then he glanced at his wafer-thin gold wrist-watch, displaying as he did so an expanse of starched white cuff caught with links of knotted gold. "You're late."

"But the Lundstroms haven't even come yet."

"Where've you been?"

"With Jody."

"Then you're forgiven."

He was tall, much taller than Caroline, slim, swarthy, beginning to go bald. This made him look older than his actual age, which was thirty-three. He wore the midnight blue velvet dinner jacket and an evening shirt lightly touched with bands of embroidered lace, and his eyes, beneath the strongly marked brows, were a very dark brown and held, at this moment, an expression which contained amusement, exasperation, and a certain amount of pride.

Caroline saw the pride and was relieved. Hugh Rashley took a certain amount of living up to and Caroline spent half her time struggling with sensations of gross inadequacy. Otherwise he was, as a future husband, eminently satisfactory, successful in his chosen career of stockbroking and marvelously thoughtful and considerate even if his standards did sometimes reach unnecessary heights. But this, perhaps, was only to be expected, for it was a characteristic which ran in his family, and he was, after all, Diana's brother.

Because Parker Haldane was unrepentantly attracted to pretty young women and Caroline was one of them, Elaine Haldane's manner towards Caroline was habitually cool. This did not worry Caroline unduly; for one thing, she seldom met Elaine, for the Haldanes lived in Paris, where Parker was in charge of the French department of a big American advertising agency, and only came to London for important meetings, every two or three months. This visit was just such an occasion.

For another, she did not particularly like Elaine, which was unfortunate, for Elaine and Diana were the best of friends. "Why do you always have to be so off-hand with Elaine?" Diana would demand and Caroline had learned to shrug and say "I'm sorry," for any more detailed explanations could only cause the greatest offence.

Elaine was a handsome, distinguished woman, with a tendency to over-dress which even living in Paris had done nothing to cure. She could also be extremely amusing, but Caroline had learned, through bitter experience, that, buried in her witticisms were sharp barbs of verbal cruelty, directed at friends and acquaintances who did not happen, at the time, to be present. It was daunting to listen to her, because you could never be sure what she was planning to say about you.

Parker, on the other hand, was not to be taken seriously.

"You beautiful creature." He stooped to sketch a continental kiss over the back of Caroline's hand. She half expected him to click his heels. "Why do you always have to keep us waiting?"

"I was saying good night to Jody." She turned to his wife. "Good evening, Elaine." They touched cheeks, making kissing sounds in the air.

"Hallo, dear. What a pretty dress!"

"Thank you."

"They're so easy to wear, those loose things . . ." She took a pull at her cigarette, exhaled a huge cloud of smoke. "I've just been telling Diana about Elizabeth."

Caroline's heart sank, but she said, politely, "What about Elizabeth?" waiting to be told that Elizabeth was engaged; that Elizabeth had been staying with the Aga Khan; that Elizabeth was in New York modelling for *Vogue*. Elizabeth was Elaine's daughter, by a previous marriage, and a little older than Caroline, but, despite the fact that Caroline sometimes felt she knew more about Elizabeth than she did about herself, they had never met. Elizabeth divided her time between her parents—mother in Paris and father in Scotland—and on the rare occasions when she turned up in London, Caroline was invariably away.

Now she tried to remember the latest news on Elizabeth. "Hasn't she been in the West Indies, or something?"

"Yes, my dear, staying with an old school-friend, having the most wonderful time. But she flew home a couple of days ago and was met at Prestwick by her father with this ghastly news."

"What news?"

"Well, you know, ten years ago, when Duncan and I were still together, we bought this place in Scotland . . . at least Duncan bought it, in the face of violent opposition from me . . . Marriage-wise, it was just the last straw." She stopped, a confused expression on her face.

"Elizabeth," Caroline prompted gently.

"Oh, of course. Well, the first thing Elizabeth did was to make friends with the two boys who lived on the neighbouring estate . . . well, not boys exactly, they were already grown-up when we first met them, but completely charming, and they just took Elizabeth under their wing like a little sister. Before you could snap your fingers she was in and out of their house as though she'd lived there all her life. They adored her, but she was always the special pet of the older brother, and my dear, just before she came home, he killed himself in the most terrible car smash. Too ghastly, icy roads, the car went straight into a stone wall."

Despite herself, Caroline was truly shocked. "Oh, how awful!"

"Oh, ghastly. Only twenty-eight. A wonderful farmer, marvellous shot, such a darling person. You can imagine what sort of a home-coming the poor darling had, she rang me up in tears to tell me, and I longed to get her to London and meet us here, and let us cheer her up, but she says she's needed up there . . ."

"I'm sure her father will love having her . . ." Parker chose this moment to materialize at Caroline's elbow, and handed her a Martini so cold that it nearly froze her fingers. He said, "Who are we waiting for?"

"The Lundstroms. They're Canadians. He's a banker from Montreal. It's all to do with this new project of Shaun's."

"Does that really mean that Diana and Shaun are going out to Montreal to live?" asked Elaine. "But what are we going to do without them? Diana, what are we going to do without you?"

Parker said, "How long are they going to be away?"

"Three, four years. Less perhaps. They leave as soon after the wedding as they can."

"And this house? Are you and Hugh going to live here?"

"It's much too big. Anyway, Hugh's got a perfectly adequate flat of his own. No, Katy's going to stay in the basement as a sort of care-taker, and Diana thought that she might let it if she could find the right sort of tenant."

"And Jody?"

Caroline looked at him, and then down at her drink.

"Jody's going with them. To live."

"Won't you mind that?"

"Yes, I'll mind. But Diana wants to take him."

And Hugh doesn't want to be saddled with a little boy. Not just yet, at any rate. A baby, perhaps, in a couple of years, but not a little boy of eleven. And Diana's already got him into a private school and Shaun says he'll have him taught how to ski and play ice hockey.

Parker was still watching her. She smiled wryly. "You know Diana, Parker. She makes plans, and bang, they happen."

"You'll miss him, won't you?"

"Yes, I'll miss him."

The Lundstroms arrived at last, were introduced, given drinks and drawn, politely, into the conversation. Caroline, moving aside on the pretence of finding a cigarette, watched them curiously and thought that they looked alike, as married people so often do, both tall and angular, rather sporty. She imagined them playing golf together at the week-ends or sailing—perhaps ocean racing—in the summer. Mrs. Lundstrom's dress was simple, her diamonds sensational, and Mr. Lundstrom had that certain colourless nonentity that often blurs the outline of a spectacularly successful man.

She thought, quite suddenly, that it would be wonderful, like a breath of fresh air, for someone to come into this house who was poor, a failure, without morals, or even drunk. An artist, perhaps, starving in a garret. An author who wrote stories that no one would buy. Or some cheerful beachcomber with a three-day growth of beard and an inelegant belly bulging over the belt of his trousers. She thought of her father's friends, ill-assorted and usually disreputable, drinking red wine or retsina well into the night, sleeping where they found themselves, on the sagging sofa, or with their feet propped on the low wall of the terrace. And she thought of the house on Aphros, at night, painted by moonlight in blocks of black and white, and always the sound of the sea.

". . . we're going in for dinner."

It was Hugh. She realized that he had already told her this and been forced to repeat himself. "You're dreaming, Caroline. Finish your drink, it's time to go and have something to eat."

At the dinner table, she found herself between John Lundstrom and Shaun. Shaun was busy with the wine decanter, and so she fell naturally into conversation with Mr. Lundstrom.

"Is this your first visit to England?"

"Oh, by no means. I've been here many times before." He straightened his knife and fork, frowning slightly. "Now, I haven't got this quite straight. This family relationship, I mean. You're Diana's stepdaughter?"

"Yes, that's right. And I'm going to marry Hugh, who is her brother. Most people seem to think it's practically illegal, but it isn't really. I mean, there's nothing about it in the back of the prayer-book."

"I never thought for a moment that it was illegal. Simply very tidy. It keeps all the right people in the same family."

"Isn't that a little narrow minded?"

He looked up and smiled. He looked younger, gayer, and less rich when he smiled. More human. Caroline warmed to him.

"You could call it practical. When are you going to be married?"

"On Tuesday week. I can hardly believe it."

"And will you both come out to visit Shaun and Diana in Montreal?"

"I expect we shall later on. Not just yet."

"And then there's the little boy . . ."

"Yes. Jody, my brother."

"He's coming with them."

"Yes."

"He'll take to Canada like a duck to water. It's a great place for a boy."

"Yes," said Caroline again.

"There are just the two of you?"

"Oh, no," said Caroline. "There's Angus."

"Another brother?"

"Yes. He's nearly twenty-five."

"And what does he do?"

"We don't know."

John Lundstrom raised polite but surprised eyebrows. Caroline said, "I mean that. We don't know what he does and we don't know where he is. You see, we used to live on Aphros in the Aegean. My father was an architect, a sort of agent for people who wanted to buy property and build out there. That was how he met Diana."

"Now hold it. You mean, Diana came out to buy some land?"

"Yes, and build a house. But she didn't do either. She met my father and married him instead and she stayed out in Aphros with us all and lived in this house we'd always had . . ."

"But you came back to London?"

"Yes, my father died, you see, so Diana brought us back with her. But Angus said he wasn't coming. He was nineteen then, with hair down to his shoulders and not a pair of shoes to his name. And Diana said that if he wanted to stay in Aphros he could, but he said she might as well sell the house, because he'd acquired a secondhand Mini Moke and he was going to drive to India through Afghanistan. And Diana asked him what he was going to do when he got there, and Angus said, find himself."

"He's just one of thousands. You know that, don't you?"

"It doesn't make it any easier when he's your brother."

"Haven't you seen him since?"

"Yes. He came back soon after Diana and Shaun were married, but you know how these things go. We all thought he'd at least have a pair of shoes on his feet, but he was unchanged and unrepentant and everything Diana suggested just made him worse, so he went back to Afghanistan again, and we haven't heard from him since."

"Not at all?"

"Well . . . once. A picture postcard of Kabul or Srinagar or Tehran or somewhere." She smiled, trying to make a joke of it, but before John Lundstrom could think up any sort of a reply, Katy leaned over his shoulder to set down a bowl of turtle soup, and, with the conversation broken, he turned away from Caroline and started instead to talk to Elaine.

The evening wore on, formal, predictable and, to Caroline, boring. After coffee and brandy they all foregathered once more in the drawing-room. The men gravitated into one corner to talk business, the women gathered by the fire, gossiped, made plans for Canada, admired the tapestry on which Diana was currently working.

After a little, Hugh detached himself from the group of men, ostensibly to refill John Lundstrom's glass. But when he had done this, he came over to Caroline's side, sat on the arm of her chair and said, "How are you?"

"Why do you ask?"

"Are you well enough to go to Arabella's?"

She looked up at him. From the depth of the armchair his face appeared almost upside down. It looked odd.

"What time is it?" she asked.

He glanced at his watch. "Eleven. Perhaps you're too tired?"

Before she could reply, Diana, overhearing the conversation, looked up from her tapestry and said, "Off you go, the two of you."

"Where are they off to?" asked Elaine.

"Arabella's. It's a little club Hugh belongs to . . ."

"Sounds intriguing . . ." Elaine smiled at Hugh, looking as though she knew all about intriguing night clubs. Hugh and Caroline excused themselves, said good night to the company and left. Caroline went upstairs to fetch a coat, paused to comb her hair. At Jody's door she stopped, but the light was off and no sound came from within, so she decided not to disturb him, and went downstairs again to where Hugh waited for her in the hall. He opened the door for her and they went out together into the soft, windy darkness, and walked down the pavement to where he had parked his car, and drove around the Square and out into Kensington High Street, and she saw that there was the beginnings of a moon, and rags of cloud were being driven across its face by the wind. The trees in the park tossed their bare branches; the orange glow of the city was reflected in the sky, and Caroline rolled down the window and let the cool air blow her hair and thought that on such a night, one should be in the country, walking along dark, unlighted roads, with the wind soughing in the trees and only the fitful moonlight to show the way.

She sighed. "What's that for?" asked Hugh.

"What's what for?"

"The sigh. It sounded like tragedy."

"It's nothing."

After a little, "Everything's all right?" Hugh asked. "You're not worried about anything?"

"No." There was, after all nothing to be worried about. Nothing, and everything. Feeling ill all the time was one of them. She wondered why it was impossible to talk to Hugh about this. Perhaps because he was always so fit himself. Energetic, active, full of energy and apparently never tired. At any rate, it was boring to be in ill-health, doubly boring to talk about it.

The silence between them grew. At last, waiting for traffic lights to change from red to green, Hugh said, "The Lundstroms are delightful."

"Yes. I told Mr. Lundstrom about Angus and he listened."

"What else did you expect him to do?"

"Just what everybody else always does. Look shocked and horrified and delighted—or change the subject. Diana hates us to talk about Angus. I suppose because he was her one failure." She corrected herself. "*Is* her one failure."

"You mean because he didn't come back to London with you all."

"Yes, and learn how to be a chartered accountant or whatever career it was she had planned for him. Instead, he did exactly what he wanted to do."

"At the risk of being told that I am taking Diana's part in this argument, I would say, so did you. In the teeth of all opposition you got yourself to Drama School and even managed to hold down a job . . ."

"For six months. That was all."

"You were ill. You had pneumonia. That wasn't your fault."

"No. But I got better and if I'd been worth my salt, I'd have gone back and tried again. But I didn't, I chickened out. And Diana had always said that I hadn't got the staying power, so in the end, inevitably, she was right. The only thing she didn't say was 'I told you so.' "

"But if you'd still been on the stage," said Hugh gently, "you probably wouldn't be getting married to me."

Caroline glanced at his profile, strangely lit by overhead street lights and the glow from the dashboard. He looked saturnine, slightly villainous.

"No. I don't suppose I would."

But it wasn't as simple as that. The reasons she had for marrying Hugh were legion and so bound up with each other that it was hard to disentangle them. But gratitude seemed the most important. Hugh had come into her life when she had returned from Aphros with Diana, a stringy fifteen-year-old. But even then, sullen and inarticulate with unhappiness, watching Hugh cope with luggage and passports and a tired and weeping Jody, she had recognized his qualities. He was just the sort of reliable male relation she had always needed but never known. And it was pleasant to be ordered about and taken care of, and his protective attitude—not paternal, exactly, but certainly avuncular—had endured through the difficult years of growing up.

Another force to be reckoned with was Diana herself. From the very beginning, she seemed to have decided that Hugh and Caroline were the perfect match. The very orderliness of the arrangement appealed to her. Subtly, for she was too clever to indulge in any obvious action, she encouraged them to be together. *Hugh can drive you to the station. Darling, will you be in for dinner, Hugh's coming and I want you to make up the numbers.*

But even this relentless pressure would have been of no avail if it had not been for the affair that Caroline had with Drennan Colefield. After that . . . after loving that way, it seemed to Caroline that nothing could ever be quite the same again. When it was all over, and she could look around without her eyes filling with tears, she saw that Hugh was still there. Waiting for her. Unchanged—except that now he wanted to marry her, and now there seemed no reason on earth why she shouldn't.

He said, "You've been quiet all evening."

"I thought I was talking too much."

"You'd tell me if anything was worrying you?"

"Only that things are happening too quickly, and there's so much to do, and meeting the Lundstroms makes me feel as though Jody's already gone to Canada and I'm never going to see him again."

Hugh fell silent, reaching for a cigarette, and lighting it from the gadget on the dashboard. He replaced the lighter, and said, "I'm fairly certain that what you're suffering from is Bridal Depression or whatever it is the Women's Page always calls it."

"Caused by what?"

"Too many things to think about; too many letters to write; too many presents to unpack. Clothes to try on, curtains to choose, caterers and florists beating at the door. It's enough to drive the sanest girl off her nut."

"Then why did you let us be railroaded into this huge wedding?"

"Because we both mean a lot to Diana, and to have slunk off to a Registry Office and then spent two days at Brighton would have done her out of endless pleasure."

"But we're people, not sacrificial lambs."

He put a hand over hers. "Cheer up. It'll soon be Tuesday and then it'll be over and we'll be flying to the Bahamas and you can lie in the sun all day and not write a single letter to anybody and eat nothing but oranges. How does that appeal to you?"

She said, knowing she was being childish, "I wish we were going to Aphros."

Hugh began to sound impatient. "Caroline, you know we've been over this a thousand times . . ."

She stopped listening to him, her thoughts jerked back to Aphros like a fish on a line. She remembered the olive orchards, ancient trees knee-deep in poppies, against a back-drop of azure sea. And fields of grape-hyacinths and pale scented pink cyclamen. And the sound of bells from the herds of goats and the scent in the mountains, of pine, running warm, dripping with resin.

". . . anyway, it's all been arranged."

"But, one day, shall we go to Aphros, Hugh?"

"You haven't been listening to a single word I've said."

"We could rent a little house."

"No."

"Or hire a yacht."

"No."

"Why don't you want to go?"

"Because I think you should remember it the way it was, not the way it may be now, spoiled by developers and sky-scraper hotels."

"You don't know it's like that."

"I have a very shrewd idea."

"But . . ."

"No," said Hugh.

After a pause, she said, stubbornly, "I still want to go back."

2

The clock in the hall was striking two when they at last got home. The chimes rang out, stately and mellow, as Hugh put Caroline's key into the lock and pushed open the back door. Inside, the hall light burned, but the staircase rose to darkness. It was very quiet, the party was long since over and everybody had gone to bed.

She turned to Hugh. "Good night."

"Good night, darling." They kissed. "When shall I see you again? I'm out of town tomorrow evening . . . perhaps Tuesday?"

"Come round for dinner. I'll tell Diana."

"You do that."

He smiled, went out, began to close the door. She remembered to say "Thank you for the lovely evening" before the door clicked shut and then she was alone. She waited, listening for his car.

When the sound of the engine had died away, she turned and went upstairs a step at a time, holding the banister rail. At the top of the stairs, she turned off the hall light and went along the passage to her bedroom. The curtains were drawn, the bed turned down, her night-dress laid across the foot of the quilt. Shedding shoes, bag, coat and scarf in her progress across the carpet, she reached the bed at last and flopped across it, careless of any damage that she might do to her dress. After a little she put up a hand and began, slowly, to undo the tiny buttons, pulled the caftan over her head and then the rest of her clothes; she put on her nightdress, and it felt cool and light against her skin. Barefoot, she padded through to the bathroom, washed her face in a cursory fashion and scrubbed her teeth. This refreshed her. She was still tired, but her brain was as active as a squirrel in its cage. She went back to her dressing table and picked up her brush, and then, deliberately, laid down the brush and opened the bottom drawer of the dressing-table and took out the letters from Drennan, the bundle still tied in red ribbon, and the photograph of them both, feeding the pigeons in Trafalgar Square; and the old theatre programmes and the menus and all the little worthless scraps of paper that she had collected and treasured simply because they were the only tangible way of pinning down the memories of the time they had spent together.

You were ill, Hugh had said this evening, making excuses for her. *You had pneumonia.*

It sounded so obvious, so straightforward. But none of them, not even Diana, had known about Drennan Colefield. Even when it was all over and Diana and Caroline were alone together in Antibes where Diana had taken her to convalesce, Caroline never told her what had really happened, although she longed sometimes for the comfort of old clichés. *Time is the great healer. Every girl has to have at least one unhappy love affair in her life. There's better fish in the sea than ever came out of it.*

Months later, his name had come up at breakfast. Diana was reading the paper, the theatre page, and she looked up and said to Caroline, across the sunlight and the marmalade and the smell of coffee, "Wasn't Drennan Colefield at Lunnbridge Repertory when you were down there?"

Caroline, very carefully, laid down her cup of coffee and said, "Yes. Why?"

"It says here he's going to play Kirby Ashton in the film of *Bring Out Your Gun.* I should think that would be a pretty meaty part, the book was all sex and violence and gorgeous girls." She looked up. "Was he good? I mean as an actor?"

"Yes, I suppose he was."

"There's a photo of him here with his wife. Did you know he'd married Michelle Tyler? He looks terribly handsome."

And she had handed the paper over, and there he was, thinner than

Caroline remembered, and the hair longer, but still the smile, the light in the eye, the cigarette between his fingers.

"What are you doing tonight?" he had asked the first time they had ever met. She had been making coffee in the Green Room and was covered in paint from working on the scenery. And she had said "Nothing," and Drennan said "So am I. Let's do nothing together." And after that evening the world became an unbelievably beautiful place. Each leaf on every tree was suddenly a miracle. A child playing with a ball, an old man sitting on a park bench, were filled with a meaning that she had never recognized. The dull little town was transformed, the people who lived in it smiled and looked happy and the sun always seemed to be shining, warmer and brighter than ever before. And all this because of Drennan. *This is how it is to love,* he had told her and showed her. *This is how it is meant to be.*

But it was never like that again. Remembering Drennan and loving him; knowing that in a week she was going to marry Hugh, Caroline began to cry. There were no sobs or disturbing sounds, simply a flood of tears that filled her eyes and streamed down her cheeks, unchecked and unheeded.

She might have sat there till morning, staring at her reflection, wallowing in self-pity and coming to no worthwhile conclusion if she had not been disturbed by Jody. He came soundlessly down the passage which separated his room from hers and tapped at the door, and then, when she did not reply, opened the door and put his head round.

"Are you all right?" he asked.

His unexpected appearance was as good as a douche of cold water. Caroline at once made an effort to pull herself together, wiped at her tears with the flat of her hand, reached for a dressing-gown to pull over her nightdress.

"Yes . . . of course I am . . . what are you doing out of bed?"

"I was awake. I heard you come in. Then I heard you moving around and I thought you might be feeling sick." He closed the door behind him and came over to where she sat. He wore blue pyjamas and his feet were bare, and his red hair stuck up in a crest at the back.

"What were you crying about?"

It was useless to say "I wasn't crying." Caroline said "Nothing" which was just about as useless.

"You can't say 'nothing.' It isn't possible to cry about nothing." He came close, his eyes on a level with hers. "Are you hungry?"

She smiled, and shook her head.

"I am. I thought I'd go downstairs and find something."

"You do that."

But he stayed where he was, his eyes moving around, searching for clues as to what had made her unhappy. They fell on the bundle of letters, the photograph. He reached out and picked this up. "That's Drennan Colefield. I saw him in *Bring Out Your Gun*. I had to get Katy to take me because it was an A Certificate. He was Kirby Ashton. He was super." He looked up at Caroline. "You knew him, didn't you?"

"Yes. We were at Lunnbridge together."

"He's married now."

"I know."

"Is *that* why you were crying?"

"Perhaps."

"Did you know him as well as that?"

"Oh, Jody, it was all over a long time ago."

"Then why does it make you cry?"

"I'm just being sentimental."

"But you . . ." He stumbled over the use of the word "Love." "You're going to marry Hugh."

"I know. That's what being sentimental means. It means crying over something that's finished, over and done with. And it's a waste of time."

Jody stared at her intently. After a little, he laid down the photograph of Drennan and said, "I'm going down to find a piece of cake. I'll come back. Do you want anything?"

"No. Go quietly. Don't wake Diana."

He slipped away. Caroline put the letters and the photograph back into the drawer, closed it firmly. Then she went to collect the clothes she had discarded, hung up her caftan, treed her shoes, folded the other things and laid them over a chair. By the time Jody returned, bearing his snack on a tray, she had brushed her hair, and was sitting up in bed, waiting for him. He came to settle himself beside her, edging the tray on to her bedside table.

He said, "You know, I've got an idea."

"A good one?"

"I think so. You see, you think I don't mind going to Canada with

Diana and Shaun. But I do. I don't want to go in the very least. I'd rather do anything than go."

Caroline stared at him. "But, Jody, I thought you wanted to go. You seemed so keen on the idea."

"I was being polite."

"For heaven's sake, you can't be polite when it's a question of going to Canada."

"I can. But now I'm telling you that I don't want to go."

"But Canada will be fun."

"How do you know it'll be fun? You've never been there. Besides I don't want to leave this school and my friends and the football team."

Caroline was mystified. "But why didn't you tell me this before? Why are you telling me now?"

"I didn't tell you *before* because you were always so busy with letters and toast-racks and veils and things."

"But never too busy for *you* . . ."

He went on as though she had never spoken. "And I'm telling you *now* because if I don't tell you now it'll be too late. There just won't be time. So do you want to hear about my plan?"

She was suddenly apprehensive. "I don't know. What is your plan?"

"I think I should stay here in London, and not go to Montreal . . . no, not stay with you and Hugh. With Angus."

"*Angus*?" It was almost funny. "Angus is in the back of beyond. Kashmir, or Nepal or somewhere. Even if we knew how to get hold of him, which we don't, he'd never come back to London."

"He's not in Kashmir, or Nepal," said Jody taking a large mouthful of cake. "He's in *Scotland*."

His sister stared at him, wondering if she had heard aright through all the cake crumbs and sultanas. "*Scotland*?" He nodded. "What makes you think he's in *Scotland*?"

"I don't think. I know. He wrote me a letter. I got it about three weeks ago. He's working at the Strathcorrie Arms Hotel, Strathcorrie, Perthshire."

"He wrote you a letter? And you never told me?"

Jody's face closed up. "I thought it better not to."

"Where is the letter now?"

"In my room." He took another maddening bite of his cake.

"Will you show it to me?"

"All right."

He slipped off the bed and disappeared, to return carrying the letter in his hand. "Here," he said and gave it to her, and climbed back on to the bed, and reached for his milk. The envelope was a cheap, buff-coloured one, the address typewritten. "Very anonymous," said Caroline.

"I know. I found it one day when I came back from school and I thought it was someone trying to sell me something. It looks like that, doesn't it? You know, when you write away for things . . ."

She took the letter out of the envelope, a single sheet of airmail paper, which had obviously been much handled and many times read, and felt as if it were about to fall apart.

Strathcorrie Arms Hotel,
Strathcorrie,
Perthshire.

My dear Jody,

This is one of those messages you burn before reading because it is so secret. So don't let Diana get her peepers on it, otherwise my life won't be worth living.

I returned from India about two months ago, finished up here with a chap I met in Persia. He has now departed and I managed to get myself a job in the hotel as boot boy and filler of coal buckets and log baskets. The place is full of old people up for the fishing. When they aren't fishing they sit about in chairs looking as though they had been dead for six months.

I was in London for a couple of days after my ship docked in. Would have come to see you and Caroline, but terrified that Diana would corral me, halter me (in starched collars), shoe me (in black leather) and groom me (cut my hair). Then it would only be a matter of time before I was broken to harness and a nice safe ride for a lady.

Send C. my love. Tell her I am well and happy. Will let you know next move.

I miss you both.
Angus.

"Jody, why didn't you show me this before?"

"I thought perhaps you'd feel you had to show Hugh and then he would tell Diana."

She re-read the letter. "He doesn't know I'm getting married."

"No, I don't suppose he does."

"We can ring him up."

But Jody was against this. "There's no phone number. And anyway, someone would hear. And anyway, phoning's no good, you can't see the other person's face, and you always get cut off." She knew that he hated the telephone, was even frightened of it.

"Well, we could write him a letter."

"He never replies to letters."

This was too true. But Caroline was uneasy, Jody was driving at something and she didn't know what it was. "And so?"

He took a deep breath. "You and I must go to Scotland and find him. Explain. Tell him what's happening." He added, his voice raised as though she were slightly deaf, "Tell him that I don't want to go to Canada with Diana and Shaun."

"You know what he'll say to that, don't you? He'll say what the hell's it got to do with him."

"I don't think he'll say that . . ."

She felt ashamed. "All right. So we go to Scotland and we find Angus. And what do we tell him?"

"That's he got to come back to London and look after me. He can't run away from responsibilities for the rest of his life—that's what Diana's always saying. And I'm a responsibility. That's what I am, a responsibility."

"How could he look after you?"

"We could have a little flat, and he could get a job . . ."

"Angus?"

"Why not? Other people do. The only reason he's stuck out against it all this time is because he doesn't want to do anything that Diana wants."

Despite herself Caroline had to smile. "I must say, that fits."

"But for *us* he would come. He says he misses us. He'd like to be with us."

"And how would we get to Scotland? How could we get out of the house without Diana missing us? You know she'd be on the telephone to every airport and railway station. And we can't borrow her car, we'd be flagged down by the first policeman we came to."

"I know," said Jody. "But I've thought it all out." He finished his milk and moved in closer. "I've got a plan."

* * *

Although, in a day or so it would be April, the bitter black afternoon was already sinking into darkness. Indeed it had scarcely been light all day. Since morning, the sky had been filled with low and leaden clouds which spilled, every now and then, into thin freezing showers of rain. The countryside was equally bleak. What could be seen of the hills were dark with the last brown grass of the winter. Snow, left over from the last fall, covered most of the high ground and lay deep in haphazard corries and sunless crannies, looking like ineptly applied icing sugar.

Between the hills, the glen took its shape from the twists and turns of the river and down this the wind blew, straight from the north— from the Arctic, possibly—hard and cold and without mercy. It dragged at the bare branches of the trees; tore old dried leaves out of ditches, to fly about, demented, in the bitter air; made a sound in the tall pines that was like the distant thundering of sea.

In the churchyard, it was exposed and without shelter, and the black-clad groups of people stood, hunched against the blast. The starched surplice of the rector flapped and bellied like an ill-set sail, and Oliver Cairney, bare-headed, felt that his cheeks and ears no longer belonged to him and wished that he had thought to wear a second layer of overcoat.

He found that his mind was in a curious state, partly blurred and partly clear as crystal. The words of the service, which should have been meaningful, he scarcely heard, and yet his attention was caught and held by the bright yellow petals of a great bunch of daffodils, flaming on that sombre day like a candle in a dark room. And although most of the mourners who stood about him, just beyond the perimeter of his vision, were as anonymous as shadows, one or two of them had caught his notice, like figures in the foreground of a painting. Cooper, for one, the old keeper, in his best tweed suit and a black knitted tie. And the comforting bulk of Duncan Fraser, neighbour to Cairney. And the girl, the strange girl, incongruous in this homely gathering. A dark girl, very slender and tanned, a black fur hat deep over her ears and her face almost obliterated behind a huge pair of dark glasses. Quite glamorous. Disturbing. Who was she? A friend of Charles? It seemed unlikely . . .

He found himself lost in unworthy speculations, jerked his mind free of them and tried once more to concentrate on what was happening. But the malicious wind, as though taking sides with Oliver's own personal Satan, rose, howling, in a sudden gust, tore a flurry of dead leaves from the ground at his feet and sent them flying. Disturbed, he turned his head, and found himself looking straight at the unknown girl. She had taken off the glasses, and he saw with astonishment that it was Liz Fraser. Liz, unbelievably elegant, standing beside her father. For an instant, his eyes met hers, and then he turned away, his thoughts in a turmoil. Liz, whom he had not seen for two years or more. Liz, grown up now and for some reason, at Rossie Hill. Liz, whom his brother had so adored. He found time to feel grateful to her for coming today. It would have meant everything to Charles.

And then, at last, it was over. People began to move, thankfully, away from the cold, turning their backs on the new grave and the piles of shivering spring flowers. They walked in twos and threes out of the churchyard, blown by the gale, swept through the gate like dust before a broom.

Oliver found himself out on the pavement, shaking hands and making appropriate noises.

"So good of you to come. Yes . . . a tragedy . . ."

Old friends, village people, farmers from the other side of Relkirk, many of whom Oliver had never seen before. Charles's friends. They introduced themselves.

"So good of you to come so far. If you have time on your way home, drop in at Cairney. Mrs. Cooper's got a big tea ready . . ."

Now, only Duncan Fraser waited. Duncan, large and solid, buttoned into his black overcoat and mufflered in cashmere, his grey hair blown into a coxcomb. Oliver looked for Liz.

"She's gone," said Duncan. "Went home by herself. Not much good at this sort of thing."

"I'm sorry. But you'll come back to Cairney, Duncan. Have a dram to warm you up."

"Of course I'll come."

The rector materialized at his side. "I won't come to Cairney, Oliver, thank you all the same. My wife's in bed. 'Flu, I think." They shook hands, a silent acknowledgement of thanks on one hand and sympathy on the other. "Let me know what you eventually plan to do."

"I could tell you now only it would take too long."

"Later then, there's plenty of time."

The wind filled his cassock. His hands, holding the prayer book, were swollen and red with cold. Like beef sausages, thought Oliver. He turned and went away from Oliver, up the church path between the leaning gravestones, his white surplice bobbing away through the gloom. Oliver watched until he had gone back into the church and closed the great door behind him, and then he went down the pavement to where his car waited, solitary. He got in and closed the door and sat, glad to be private and alone. Now that the ordeal of the funeral was over, it was possible to accept the idea that Charles was dead. Having accepted this, it seemed likely that things, now, would get easier. Already Oliver felt—not happier, exactly—but calm and able to feel pleased that so many people had come today, and pleased, especially, that Liz had been there.

After a little, he reached awkwardly into his coat pocket, found a pocket of cigarettes, took one and lit it. He looked at the empty street and told himself that it was time to go home, there were still the last small social obligations to be met. People would be waiting. He turned on the ignition, put the car into gear and moved out into the street, the frozen gutters crunching beneath the heavy treads of the snow tyres.

By five o'clock the last visitor had gone. Or, at least, the second last visitor. Duncan Fraser's old Bentley still stood by the front door, but then Duncan scarcely qualified as a visitor.

Oliver, having seen the final car away, came back indoors, shut the front door with a slam and returned to the library and the comfort of a roaring fire. As he did this, Lisa, the old Labrador, roused herself and came across the room to his side, and then, realizing that the one for whom she waited had still not come, returned slowly to the hearthrug and settled down once more. She was—had been— Charles's dog, and somehow her air of being lost and abandoned was the most unbearable thing of all.

He saw that Duncan, left alone, had drawn up a chair to the blaze and made himself comfortable. His face was ruddy, perhaps from the heat of the fire, but more likely from the central heating of the two large whiskies which he had already drunk.

The room, always shabby, bore witness to the remains of Mrs. Cooper's excellent tea. Crumbs of fruit-cake littered the white damask cloth spread over the table which had been pushed to the far side of the room. Empty teacups stood about, interspersed with tumblers which had contained something a little stronger than tea.

As he appeared, Duncan looked up and smiled and stretched his legs and said, in a voice still rich with the accents of his native Glasgow, "I should be on my way." He made, however, no move to go, and Oliver, stopping at the table to cut himself a slice of cake, said, "Stay for a bit." He did not want to be left alone. "I want to hear about Liz. Have another drink."

Duncan Fraser eyed his empty glass as though debating the proposition. "Well," he said at last, as Oliver had known that he would; he let Oliver relieve him of the glass. ". . . Maybe a very small one. But you've not had a drink yourself. It would be companionable if you'd join me."

"Yes, I will now."

He took the glass over to the table, found a second, clean one, poured the whisky and added, not too generously, water from a jug. "I didn't recognize her, do you know that? I couldn't think who she was." He carried the glasses back to the fire.

"Yes, she's changed."

"Has she been with you long?"

"A couple of days. Staying in the West Indies with some girl-friend or other. I went over to meet the plane at Prestwick. I hadn't intended going over, but, well . . . I thought it would be better to tell her myself about Charles." He gave the ghost of a grin. "You know, women are a funny lot, Oliver. Hard to know what they're thinking. They bottle things up, seem to be afraid to let go."

"But she came today."

"Oh yes, she was there. But this is the first time Liz has ever had to face up to the fact that dying is a thing that happens to people you know, not just names in newspapers and obituary columns. Friends die. Lovers. She'll maybe be down to see you tomorrow or the next day . . . I couldn't say for sure . . ."

"She was the only girl Charles ever looked at. You know that, don't you?"

"Yes. I knew. Even when she was a little girl . . ."

"He was only waiting for her to grow up." Duncan made no reply to this. Oliver found himself a cigarette and lit it, and then let himself down on to the edge of the chair that stood on the other side of the hearth. Duncan eyed him.

"And what are you going to do now? With Cairney I mean?"

"Sell it," said Oliver.

"Just like that."

"Just like that. I have no alternative."

"It's a shame to let a place like this go."

"Yes, but I don't live here. My job and roots are in London. And I was never cut out to be a Scottish laird. That was Charles's job."

"Doesn't Cairney mean anything to you?"

"Of course. The house where I grew up."

"You were always a cool-headed fellow. What do you do with yourself in London? I could never stand the place."

"I love it."

"Are you making money?"

"Enough. For a decent flat, and a car."

Duncan's eyes narrowed. "What about your love life?"

If anyone else had asked Oliver that question he would have thrown something at them for sheer bloody interference. But this was different. *You wily old coot,* thought Oliver, and told him, "Satisfactory."

"I can imagine you, running around with a lot of glamorous women . . ."

"From your tone I can't tell whether you are disapproving or merely envious . . ."

"I never worked it out," Duncan said drily, "how Charles ever got himself a young brother like you. Have you never thought of getting married?"

"I'm not getting married until I'm too old to do anything else."

Duncan gave a wheeze of a laugh. "That puts me in my place. But let's get back to Cairney. If you mean to sell it, will you sell to me?"

"I'd rather sell to you than anyone else. You know that."

"I'll take the farm in with mine, and the moor and the loch. But there'd still be the house. You could maybe sell that separately. After all, it's not too large, nor too far from the road, and the garden is perfectly manageable."

It was comforting to hear him speak this way, putting emotional decisions into practical language, cutting Oliver's problems down to size. But this was the way that Duncan Fraser worked. This was how he had made his money at a comparatively early age, been able to sell up his London business for an astronomical figure and done what he had always wanted to do, which was to return to Scotland, buy some land and settle down to the pleasant life of a country gentleman.

However, this fulfilment of his ambition had its ironic aspect, for Duncan's wife, Elaine, never particularly anxious to leave her native

South and put down roots in the wilds of Perthshire, soon became bored with the slow pace of life at Rossie Hill. She missed her friends and the weather got her down. The winters, she complained, were long, cold and dry. The summers, short, cold and wet. Accordingly her flying visits to London became more frequent and of longer duration until the inevitable day came when she announced that she was never going to return, and the marriage broke up.

If Duncan was distressed by this, he managed to hide it very well. He enjoyed having Liz to himself and when she went off to visit her mother, he was never lonely, for his interests were legion. When he had first come to Rossie Hill, local people had been sceptical of his capabilities as a farmer, but he had proved himself—now he was accepted, a member of the club in Relkirk and a J.P. Oliver was very fond of him.

He said, "You make it all sound so reasonable and easy, not like selling one's home at all."

"Well, that's the way things are." The older man finished his drink in a single enormous gulp, laid the glass on the table by his chair and abruptly stood up. "Think about it, anyway. How long are you up for?"

"I've two weeks' leave of absence."

"Suppose we meet on Wednesday in Relkirk? I'll give you lunch and we'll have a chat with the lawyers. Or is that pushing things too fast?"

"Not at all. The sooner it's buttoned up, the better."

"In that case, I'll be taking myself home."

He started for the door and at once Lisa got up and, at a distance, followed them out into the chilly hall, her claws scratching on the polished parquet floor.

Duncan glanced back at her over his shoulder. "It's a sad thing, a dog without a master."

"The worst thing of all."

Lisa watched while Oliver helped Duncan on with his coat and then accompanied them both out to where the old black Bentley waited. The evening was, if possible, colder than ever, black dark and torn with wind. The puddled driveway, beneath their shoes, rang hard with ice.

"We'll have more snow yet," said Duncan.

"Looks like it."

"Any message for Liz?"

"Tell her to come and see me."

"I'll do that. See you Wednesday, then, at the club. Twelve-thirty."

"I'll be there." Oliver shut the car door. "Drive carefully."

When the car had gone he went back indoors with Lisa at his heels and shut the door and stood for a moment, his attention caught by the extraordinary emptiness of the house. This had struck him before—had been striking him at intervals ever since he arrived from London two days before. He wondered if he would ever get used to it.

The hall was cold and quiet. Lisa, worried by Oliver's stillness, pushed her nose into his hand, and he stooped to fondle her head, winding her silky ears over his fingers. The wind buffeted, a draught caught the curtain which hung across the front door, and sent it billowing, a swirling skirt of velvet. Oliver shivered and went back to the library, putting his head around the kitchen door on the way. Presently he was joined by Mrs. Cooper with her tray. Together they piled cups and saucers, stacked glasses, cleared the table. Mrs. Cooper folded the starched damask cloth and Oliver helped her pull the table back into the middle of the room. Then he followed her back into the kitchen, held the door open so that she could carry through the laden tray, and followed her, with the empty teapot in one hand and the nearly empty whisky bottle in the other.

She began to wash the dishes. He said, "You're tired. Leave them."

She kept her back turned towards him. "Oh, no, I canna leave them. I've never left a single dirty cup for the morning."

"Then go home when you've finished that lot."

"What about your supper?"

"I'm full of fruit cake. I don't want any supper." Her back remained stiff and unrelenting, as though she found it impossible to show any grief. She had adored Charles. Oliver said, "It was good cake." And then he said, "Thank you."

Mrs. Cooper did not turn around. Presently, when it became obvious that she was not going to, Oliver went out of the kitchen and back to the library fire, and left her on her own.

3

━━◦⦿◦━━

*B*ehind Diana Carpenter's house in Milton Gardens was a long narrow garden which backed on to a cobbled mews. Between the garden and the mews was a high wall with a gate in it and what had once been a large double garage, but when Diana returned to London from Aphros, she decided that it would be a sound investment to turn the garage into a paying property, and accordingly built over it a small flat for letting. This diversion had kept her busy and happy for a year or more and when it was finished and furnished and totally decorated, she let it at a thumping rent to an American diplomat, posted to London for two years. He was the perfect tenant, but when he was returned to Washington and she started casting about for someone to take his place, she was not so fortunate.

For, out of the past, Caleb Ash turned up with his girlfriend Iris, two guitars, a Siamese cat and nowhere to live.

"And who," asked Shaun, "is Caleb Ash?"

"Oh, he was a friend of Gerald Cliburn's in Aphros. One of those people who are always just on the verge of doing something, like writing a novel or painting a mural, or starting in business or building a hotel. But they never do. Anyway, Caleb's the laziest man in the world."

"And Mrs. Ash?"

"Iris. And they're not married."

"Don't you want to have them in the flat?"

"No."

"Why not?"

"Because I think they'll be an unsettling influence on Jody."

"Will he remember them?"

"Of course. They were always in and out of our house."

"And you didn't like him?"

"I didn't say that, Shaun. You can't help liking Caleb Ash, he has all the charm in the world. But I don't know, living at the bottom of the garden like that . . ."

"Can they pay the rent?"

"He says so."

"Will they turn the place into a pigsty?"

"Not at all. Iris is very house-proud. Always polishing floors and stirring stews in great copper pots."

"You make my mouth water. Let them have the place. They're friends from the old days, you shouldn't lose all your links, and I don't see how his being there can do Jody any harm at all . . ."

And so Caleb and Iris and the cat and the guitars and the cooking-pots moved into the Stable Cottage, and Diana gave them a little bit of ground to make a garden, and Caleb paved it and grew a camellia in a pot and thus managed, out of nothing, to create a nostalgic Mediterranean ambience.

Jody, naturally enough, adored him, but from the start he was warned by Diana that he must visit Caleb and Iris only when he was invited, otherwise there was the danger that he would make a nuisance of himself. And Katy came out strongly anti-Caleb, especially when, by means of the local grapevine, she latched on to the fact that Caleb and Iris were not married and never likely to be.

"You're not going down the garden to see that Mr. Ash again, are you?"

"He asked me, Katy. Sukey the cat's had kittens."

"More of them Siamese things?"

"Well, they aren't, actually. She had an affair with the tabby who lives at number eight in the mews, and they're a sort of mixture. Caleb says they'll stay that way."

Katy busied herself with a kettle. She was put out. "Well, I don't know, I'm sure."

"I thought we might have had one."

"Not one of them nasty yawling things. Anyway, Mrs. Carpenter doesn't want no animals around this house. You've heard her often enough. No animals. And a cat is animals so that's that."

The morning after the dinner-party, Caroline and Jody Cliburn emerged from the garden door at the back of the house, and walked down the flagged path towards the Stable Cottage. They made no pretence of concealing themselves. Diana was out and Katy in the kitchen . . . which faced out over the street . . . preparing lunch. They knew, moreover, that Caleb was in, for they had telephoned to ask if they could come over and he had said that he would be waiting for them.

The morning was cold, windy, very bright. The blue sky was reflected in puddles which had collected on the damp paving stones, and the sun was dazzling. It had been a long winter. Now, only the first green stumps of bulbs protruded from the black flowerbeds. All else was brown and withered and seemingly dead.

"Last year," said Caroline, "at this time, there were crocuses. All over the place."

But Caleb's little patch of garden was more sheltered and sunny and there were already daffodils bobbing in his green-painted troughs, and some snowdrops clustered around the base of the sooty-barked almond tree in the middle of the patio.

Access to the flat was by an outside staircase which rose to a wide, decked terrace, rather like the balcony of a Swiss chalet. Caleb had heard their approaching voices, and when they ran up the steps was already out on the balcony to greet them, his hands on the wooden rail, looking like the skipper of some island caique, welcoming guests aboard.

And indeed, he had lived for so many years on Aphros that his features had taken on a strongly Greek cast, much as the faces of people who have been married for many years will grow alike. His eyes were so deep set that it was almost impossible to guess their colour, his face was brown, much lined, his nose a jutting prow, his hair thick and grey and curly. His voice was deep and rich. It always made Caroline think of rough wine and fresh new bread and the smell of garlic in a salad.

"Jody. Caroline." He embraced them, one in each arm, and kissed them both with a wonderfully Greek lack of restraint. No one ever kissed Jody except, sometimes, Caroline. Diana, with her usual perception, guessed how much he hated it. But with Caleb it was different, a respectful salute of affection, man to man.

"What a pleasant surprise! Come along in. I've put the coffee-pot on."

In the days of the American diplomat the little flat had had an air of New England neatness, cool and polished. Now, under Iris's unmistakable influence, it was uncontrived, and colourful; unframed canvases lined the walls, a mobile of coloured glass hung from the ceiling, a Greek shawl had been flung over Diana's carefully chosen chintzes. The room was very warm and smelled of coffee.

"Where's Iris?"

"Out shopping." He pushed up a chair. "Sit down. I'll get the coffee."

Caroline sat down. Jody followed Caleb and presently they returned, Jody carrying a tray with three mugs and the sugar bowl, and Caleb with his coffee-pot. Room was found for all this on a low table in front of the fire, and they settled themselves around it.

"You're not in trouble?" Caleb asked cautiously. He was always wary of getting on the wrong side of Diana.

"Oh, no," said Caroline automatically. But, on thought, she amended this. "At least not really."

"Tell me," said Caleb. So Caroline told him. About the letter from Angus and Jody not wanting to go to Canada, and the ideas he had for finding his brother again.

"So we've decided to go to Scotland. Tomorrow. That's Tuesday."

Caleb said. "Are you going to tell Diana?"

"She'd talk us out of it. You know she would. But we'll leave her a letter."

"And Hugh?"

"Hugh would talk me out of it as well."

Caleb frowned. "Caroline, you're meant to be marrying the man in a week."

"I am marrying him."

Caleb said "Hmm" as though he scarcely believed her. He looked down at Jody, sitting beside him. "And you. What about you? What about school?"

"School finished on Friday. This is holidays."

Caleb said "Hmm" again. Caroline became apprehensive. "Caleb, don't you dare to say you don't approve."

"Of course I don't approve. It's an insane idea. If you want to talk to Angus, why don't you telephone?"

"Jody doesn't want to. It's too complicated trying to explain something like this over the telephone."

"And anyway," said Jody, "you can't *persuade* people on the telephone."

Caleb grinned wryly. "You mean you think Angus will take some persuading? I agree with you. You're going to ask him to come to London, set up house, change his entire life style."

Jody ignored this. "So we can't telephone," he said stubbornly.

"And I suppose writing a letter would take too long?"

Jody nodded.

"Telegram?"

Jody shook his head.

"Well, that seems to have taken care of the alternatives. Which brings us to the next point. How are you going to get to Scotland?"

Caroline said, in what she hoped was a winning fashion, "That's one of the reasons, Caleb, we wanted to talk it over with you. You see, we have to have a car, and we can't take Diana's. But if we had your little car, the Mini van, if you could spare it . . . You and Iris? I mean, you don't use it that much and we'll take the most tremendous care of it."

"*My* car? And what am I meant to say when Diana comes storming down the garden with a long string of uncomfortable questions?"

"You could say it had gone to be serviced. It's only a tiny white lie."

"It's more than a white lie, it's tempting Providence. That car's not been serviced since I bought it seven years ago. Suppose it breaks down?"

"We'll risk it."

"And money?"

"I've got enough."

"And when do you reckon on getting back?"

"Thursday, or Friday. With Angus."

"You're hopeful. What if he won't come?"

"We'll cross that bridge when we get to it."

Caleb stood up, restless and undecided. He went to the window to see if Iris was coming, to help him extricate himself from this hideous dilemma. But there was no sign of her. He told himself that these were the children of his best friend. He sighed. "If I agree to help you and if I do lend you my car, it's only because I think it's time for Angus to shoulder a few responsibilities. I think he should come back." He turned to face them. "But I have to know where you're going. The address. How long you'll be . . ."

"The Strathcorrie Arms, Strathcorrie. And if we aren't back by Friday, you can tell Diana where we've gone. But not before."

"All right." Caleb nodded his great head and looked as though he were about to put it into a noose. "It's a deal."

They composed a telegram to Angus.

WE WILL BE AT STRATHCORRIE ON TUESDAY
EVENING TO DISCUSS IMPORTANT PLAN WITH
YOU LOVE JODY AND CAROLINE

This done, Jody wrote a letter which would be left behind for Diana.

Dear Diana.
  I had a letter from Angus and he is in Scotland so Caroline and I have gone to look for him. We will try to be home by Friday. Please don't worry.

But the letter for Hugh was not so easy and Caroline struggled over its composition for an hour or more.

Dearest Hugh.
  As Diana will have told you, Jody had a letter from Angus. He came home from India by sea, and is now working in Scotland. We both feel it is important that we should see him before Jody goes to Canada and so by the time you get this we will be on our way to Scotland. We hope to be back in London on Friday.
  I would have discussed it with you but you would have been duty bound to tell Diana and then we should have been talked out of going and would never have seen him. And it is important to us that he knows what is going to happen.
  I know it is a terrible thing to do, going off like this the week of our wedding without telling you. But all being well, we'll be home on Friday.

My love,
Caroline.

By the Tuesday morning, the first fine flurry of snow had fallen and then stopped, leaving the ground speckled like the feathers of a hen. The wind, however, had not let up at all, the cold was still extreme and from the look of the lowering, khaki-coloured sky, there was worse weather to come.

Oliver Cairney took one look at it, and decided that it was a good day to stay indoors and try and sort out some of Charles's affairs. It proved a poignant business. Charles, efficient and painstaking, had neatly filed every letter and document relevant to the working of the farm. Tying up the estate was going to be simpler than he had feared.

But there were other things as well. Personal things. Letters and invitations, an out-of-date passport, hotel bills and photographs, Charles's address book, his diary, the silver fountain pen he had been given for his twenty-first, a bill from his tailor.

Oliver remembered his mother's voice, reading aloud a poem to them; Alice Duer Miller.

> *What do you do with a woman's shoes.*
> *After a woman is dead?*

Steeling himself, he tore up the letters, sorted the photographs, threw away stubs of sealing wax, ends of string, a broken lock without a key, a dried-up bottle of India ink. By the time the clock struck eleven, the wastepaper basket was overflowing and he had just got up to collect the rubbish and cart it out into the kitchen when he heard the slam of the front door. It was half-glassed and made a cavernous sound which echoed around the panelled hall. Carrying the wastepaper basket, he went out to see who it was, and came face to face with Liz Fraser walking down the passage towards him.

"Liz."

She wore trousers and a short fur coat; the same black hat that she had worn yesterday, pulled deep over her ears. As he watched, she took it off and with the other hand ruffled up her short dark hair. It was an oddly nervous, uncertain gesture, entirely at odds with her sleek appearance. Her face was rosy from the cold and she was smiling. She looked marvellous.

"Hallo, Oliver."

She reached his side, leaned over the mound of crumpled paper to kiss his cheek. She said, "If you don't want to see me, say so, and I'll go away again."

"Who said I didn't want to see you?"

"I thought maybe—"

"Well, don't think maybe. Come and I'll make you a cup of coffee. I need one myself and I'm tired of being on my own."

He led the way towards the kitchen, pushing the swing-door open with the seat of his pants, letting her go ahead of him, with her long legs and her fresh, open-air smell all mingled up with Chanel No. 5. "Put the kettle on," he told her. "I'll go and get rid of this lot."

He went through the kitchen, out of the back door and into the bitter cold, managed to get his load out of the wastepaper basket and into the dustbin without too much of it blowing away, crammed the lid back on the dustbin and returned thankfully to the warmth of the kitchen. Liz, looking incongruous, was at the sink, filling the kettle from the tap.

Oliver said, "My God, it's cold!"

"I know and this is meant to be spring. I walked over from Rossie Hill and I thought I would die." She carried the kettle over to the Aga, lifted the heavy lid, and placed the kettle on the hob. She stayed by the stove, turning to lean against its warmth. Across the room they faced each other. Then they spoke at the same time.

"You've had your hair cut," said Oliver.

"I'm sorry about Charles," said Liz.

They both stopped, waiting for the other to go on. Then Liz said, looking confused, "I had it done for swimming. I've been staying with this friend in Antigua."

"I wanted to thank you for coming yesterday."

"I . . . I've never been to a funeral before."

Her eyes, ringed with eye-liner and black mascara, were suddenly bright with unshed tears. The short, elegant haircut exposed the length of her neck and the clear line of the determined chin that she had inherited from her father. As he watched, she began to undo the buttons of her fur coat, and her hands were brown too, the almond-shaped nails painted a very pale pink, and she wore a thick gold signet ring and a cluster of find gold bracelets on one slender wrist.

He said, inadequately, "Liz, you've grown up."

"Of course. I'm twenty-two now. Had you forgotten?"

"How long is it since I've seen you?"

"Five years? It's five years at least."

"What's happened to the time?"

"You were in London. I went to Paris, and every time I came back to Rossie Hill, you were always away."

"But Charles was here."

"Yes. Charles was here." She fiddled with the lid of the kettle. "But if Charles ever noticed my appearance, he certainly never remarked on it."

"He noticed all right. He was just never very good at saying what he felt. Anyway, to Charles, you were always perfect. Even when you were fifteen with pigtails and bulging jeans. He was only waiting for you to grow up."

She said, "I can't believe he's dead."

"I couldn't either, until yesterday. But I think I've accepted it now." The kettle began to sing. He left the side of the stove and went to find mugs and a jar of instant coffee and a bottle of milk from the fridge. Liz said, "Father told me about Cairney."

"You mean about selling up?"

"How can you bear to, Oliver?"

"Because there's no other choice."

"Even the house? Does the house have to go?"

"What would I do with the house?"

"You could keep it. Use it for week-ends and holidays, just to keep a root in Cairney."

"That sounds like an extravagance to me."

"Not really." She hesitated slightly and then went on in a rush. "When you're married and have children, you can bring them here, and they can do all the lovely things you used to do. Run wild, and build houses in the beech tree, and have ponies . . ."

"Who said I was thinking of getting married?"

"Father said that you said that you weren't going to get married until you were too old to do anything else."

"Your father tells you a lot too much."

"And what's that supposed to mean?"

"He always did. He indulged you and let you in on all his secrets. You were a spoiled little brat, did you know that?"

She was amused. "Them's fighting words, Oliver."

"I don't know how you've survived. An only child with two doting parents who didn't even live together. And if that wasn't enough, you always had Charles, spoiling you rotten."

The kettle boiled, and he went over to pick it up. Liz lowered the lid back on to the hotplate. She said, "But you never spoiled me, Oliver."

"I had more sense." He poured the water into the mugs.

"You never took any notice of me at all. You were always telling me to get out from under your feet."

"Ah, but that was when you were a little girl, before you became so glamorous. Incidentally, you know, I didn't recognize you yesterday. It was only when you took off your dark glasses that I realized who it was. Gave me quite a turn."

"Is that coffee ready?"

"Yes, it is. Come and drink it up before it gets cold."

They sat, facing each other across the scrubbed kitchen table. Liz held the mug in her hands as though her fingers were still cold. Her expression was provocative.

"We were talking about you getting married."

"I wasn't."

"How long are you staying at Cairney?"

"Until everything's been tied up. And you?"

Liz shrugged. "I'm meant to be south now. My mother and Parker are in London for a few days on business. I called her when I got back from Prestwick—to tell her about Charles. She tried to make me say I'd go back to them, but I explained that I wanted to be at the funeral."

"You still haven't told me how long you're staying at Rossie Hill."

"I haven't any plans, Oliver."

"Then stay for a little."

"Do you want me to?"

"Yes."

To have this settled and said somehow broke down the last of the tension between them. They sat on, talking, time forgotten. It wasn't until the clock in the hall struck twelve that Liz's attention was distracted. She looked at her watch. "Heavens, is that really the time? I must go."

"What for?"

"Lunch. Remember that quaint old-fashioned meal or have you stopped eating it?"

"Not at all."

"Come back with me now and you can eat it with my father and me."

"I'll drive you home but I won't stay for lunch."

"Why not?"

"I've wasted half the morning already, gossiping with you, and there's the hell of a lot to be done."

"Dinner, then. Tonight?"

He considered this and then, for various reasons, rejected the invitation. "But would tomorrow do?"

She shrugged, easy, the epitome of feminine pliancy. "Whenever."

"Tomorrow would be great. About eight o'clock?"

"A little earlier if you want a drink."

"OK. A little earlier. Now, put your hat and coat on and I'll drive you home."

His car was dark green, small, and low and very fast. She sat beside him with her hands deep in the pockets of her coat, staring ahead at the bleak Scottish countryside and so physically aware of the man beside her that it almost hurt.

He had changed, and yet he had not changed. He was older. There were lines on his face that had not been there before, and an expression in the back of his eyes that made her feel as though she was embarking on an affair with a total stranger. But it was still Oliver; offhand, refusing to commit himself, invulnerable.

For Liz, it had always been Oliver. Charles had merely been the excuse to haunt Cairney, and Liz had shamelessly used him as such, because he had encouraged her constant visits, had always been glad to see her. But it was because of Oliver that she had gone.

Charles was the homely one, stringy and sandy and freckled. But Oliver was glamour. Charles had time and patience for a gawky teenager; time to teach her how to cast a line, serve at tennis; time to nurse her through the agonies of her first grown-up dance, show her how to dance the reels. And all the time she had eyes for no one but Oliver, and had prayed that he would dance with her.

But of course he hadn't. There was always someone else, some strange girl or other invited up from the south. *I met her at University, at a party, staying with old so-and-so.* Over the years there were a great many of them. Oliver's girls were a local joke, but Liz did not think it was funny. Liz had watched from the side-lines and hated them all, mentally making wax images of them and spearing them with pins, wracked as she was with the miseries of teenage jealousy.

And after her parents' separation, it was Charles who wrote to Liz, giving her all the news of Cairney and keeping her in touch. But it was Oliver's photograph, a tiny crooked snapshot she had taken herself, which lived in the secret pocket of her wallet and went everywhere with her.

Now, sitting beside him, she allowed her gaze to move fractionally sideways. Oliver's hands on the leather-bound driving-wheel were long-fingered, square-nailed. There was a scar near his thumb, and she remembered how he had torn his hand open on a new barbed-wire fence. Her eyes moved casually up the length of his arm. His sheepskin collar was turned up and around his neck, touching the dark, thick hair. And then he felt her gaze and turned his head to smile at her, and his eyes, beneath the dark brows, were as blue as speedwells.

He said, "You'll know me next time," but Liz did not reply. She remembered flying in to Prestwick, her father waiting to meet her. *Charles has been killed.* There had been a terrible moment of disbelief, as though firm ground had fallen away, and she was left staring down into a huge, gaping hole. And then, "Oliver?" she had asked faintly.

"Oliver's at Cairney. Or should be by now. Driving up from London today. The funeral's on Monday . . ."

Oliver's at Cairney. Charles, dear, kind, patient Charles, was dead, but Oliver was alive and Oliver was at Cairney. After all these years she would see him again . . . Driving back to Rossie Hill, this thought was never out of her mind. *I'll see him. Tomorrow I'll see him and the next day and the day after that.* And she had called her mother in London and told her about Charles, but when Elaine had tried to persuade her to leave all the sadness behind and come south, to be with her, Liz had refused. The excuse came pat.

"I must stay. Father . . . and the funeral . . ." But all the time she knew, and revelled in the fact, that she was only staying for Oliver.

And, miraculously, it had worked out. She had known that it would from the moment that Oliver, for no apparent reason, had suddenly turned in the churchyard and looked straight into her face. She had seen it then, first surprise, and then admiration. Oliver was no longer in a position of superiority. Now they were equals. And . . . which was sad, but made everything a great deal simpler . . . there was no longer Charles to be considered. Kind Charles, maddening Charles, always there, like a rusty old dog, waiting to be taken for a walk.

She let her busy, practical mind speed ahead, allowed herself the luxury of indulging in one or two pretty images of the future. It all worked out so neatly that it might have been pre-contrived. A wedding at Cairney, perhaps, a little country wedding in the local church, with just a few friends. Then a honeymoon in . . . ? Antigua would be perfect. Then back to London—he already had a flat in London so they could use that as a base for further house-hunting. And, brilliant idea, she would get her father to give her Cairney house as a wedding present, and the casual suggestions she had put in Oliver's way this morning would, after all, come true. She saw them driving up for long weekends, spending summer holidays here, bringing children, having house-parties . . .

Oliver said, "You're very quiet all of a sudden."

Liz came back to reality with a bang, saw that they were already nearly home. The car swept up the drive beneath the beeches. Above, bare branches creaked in the cruel wind. They swung around the curve of the gravel to come to a halt in front of the big door.

"I was thinking," said Liz. "Just thinking. Thank you for bringing me home."

"Thank you for coming over to cheer me up."

"And you're coming for dinner tomorrow? Wednesday."

"I shall look forward to it."

"A quarter to eight?"

"A quarter to eight."

They smiled, conveying their mutual pleasure with the arrangement. Then he leaned across to open her door, and Liz got out of the car, and ran up the icy steps and into the shelter of the porch. Here, she turned to wave him away, but Oliver had already departed, and only the back end of his car could be seen, disappearing down the drive, on its way back to Cairney.

That evening, when Liz was in her bath, she was interrupted by a telephone call from London. Wrapped in a bath-towel she went to take it, and heard her mother's voice on the other end of the line.

"Elizabeth?"

"Hallo, Mummy."

"Darling, how are you? How is everything?"

"It's fine. Perfect. Wonderful."

This lilting reply was not exactly what Elaine had expected. She sounded puzzled. "But did you go to the funeral?"

"Oh, yes, that was ghastly, I hated every moment of it."

"Then why not come south ... we're here for a few more days ..."

"I can't come yet ..." Liz hesitated. Usually she behaved like a clam over her own affairs. Elaine continually complained that she never knew what was going on in her only daughter's life. But all at once Liz felt expansive. The excitement of what had happened today and what might be going to happen tomorrow was getting the better of her, and she knew that if she did not talk about Oliver to someone, then she was going to burst.

She finished the sentence in a burst of confidence.

". . . the thing is, Oliver's here for a bit. And he's coming over for dinner tomorrow night."

"Oliver? Oliver Cairney?"

"Yes, of course Oliver Cairney. What other Oliver do we know?"

"You mean . . . ? Because of Oliver . . ."

"Yes. Because of *Oliver*." Liz laughed. "Oh, Mummy, don't be so dense."

"But I always thought it was Ch . . ."

"Well, it wasn't," said Liz quickly.

"And what has Oliver got to say to all this?"

"Well, I don't think he's exactly displeased."

"Well, I don't know . . ." Elaine sounded confused. "It's the last thing I ever expected, but if you're happy . . ."

"Oh, I am. I am happy. Believe me, I've never been so happy."

Her mother said, faintly, "Well, let me know what happens."

"I will."

"And let me know when you come south . . ."

"We'll probably come together," said Liz, already imagining it. "Perhaps we'll drive down together."

Her mother rang off at last. Liz laid down the receiver, wrapped the bath-towel more firmly around herself and padded back to the bathroom. Oliver. She said his name, over and over. Oliver Cairney. She got back into the bath and turned on the hot tap with her toe. Oliver.

Driving north was like driving backwards in time. Spring was late everywhere, but in London there had at least been traces of green, an incipient leafiness on the trees in the park, the first stars of yellow crocus in the park. Daffodils and purple iris flowered from pavement stalls, and there were displays of mouth-melting summer clothes in the big shop windows, making one think of holidays and cruises and blue skies and sun.

But the motorway cut north like a ribbon through flat country that grew progressively more grey and cold and apparently unproductive. The roads were wet and dirty. Every passing lorry—and Caleb's old car was passed by practically everything—threw up blinding showers of wet brown mud that smothered the windscreen and forced the wipers to work overtime. To add to their discomfort, none of the windows seemed to fit properly and the heater was either faulty or needed some secret adjustment which neither Jody nor Caroline could master. Whatever the reason, it did not work.

Despite all this, Jody was in the highest of spirits. He read the map, sang, did complicated sums to work out their speed average (sadly low) and their mileage.

We're a third of the way there. We're halfway there. And then, "In another five miles we'll be at Scotch Corner. I wonder why it's called Scotch Corner when it's not even in Scotland?"

"Perhaps people get out there, and buy themselves scotches?"

Jody thought this very funny. "We've never been to Scotland, any of us. I wonder why Angus came to Scotland?"

"When we find him we'll ask him."

"Yes," said Jody cheerfully, thinking about seeing Angus. He leaned back for the rucksack that they had prudently filled with food. He opened it and looked inside. "What would you like now? There's a ham sandwich left and a rather bruised-looking apple and some chocolate biscuits."

"I'm all right. I don't want anything."

"Do you mind if I eat the ham sandwich?"

"Not at all."

After Scotch Corner they took the A68, the small car grinding up over the bleak moors of Northumberland, through Otterburn and so on to Carter Bar. The road wound upwards, looping to and fro against the steep gradient, and then they crested the final hill and passed the border stone, and Scotland lay before them.

"We're there," said Jody in tones of the greatest satisfaction. But Caroline saw only a spread of undulating grey country, and in the distance hills that were white with snow.

She said, in some apprehension, "You don't suppose it's going to snow, do you? It's terribly cold."

"Oh, not at this time of the year."

"What about those hills?"

"That'll be left over from the winter. It's just not melted."

"The sky looks terribly dark."

It did. Jody frowned. "Would it matter if it snowed?"

"I don't know. But we haven't got snow tyres and I've never driven in really bad weather."

After a little, "Oh, it'll be all right," said Jody, and took up his map again. "Now the next place we've got to get to is Edinburgh."

By then it was nearly dark, the windy city spangled with street lights. Inevitably, they got lost, but finally found the correct one-way street and headed out on the motorway towards the bridge. They stopped, for the last time, for petrol and oil. Caroline got out of the car to stretch her legs while the garage attendant checked the water and then attacked the dirty windscreen with a damp sponge. As he did this, he observed the worn, travelled little car with some interest, and then turned his attention to its occupants.

"Have you come far?"

"From London."

"Are you going on?"

"We're going to Strathcorrie. In Perthshire."

"You've a long way to go."

"Yes. We know."

"You'll be driving into some dirty weather." Jody liked the way he said dirty. Durrty. He practised saying it, under his breath.

"Will we?"

"Aye. I just heard the weather forecast. More snow. You'll need to watch. Your tyres . . ."—he kicked them with the toe of his boot— "your tyres are no' all that good."

"We'll be all right."

"Well, if you get stuck in the snow, remember the golden rule. Don't get out of the car."

"We'll remember."

They paid him and thanked him and set off once more. And the garage man watched them go, shaking his head at the irresponsibility of all Sassenachs.

The Forth Bridge reared ahead of them, with warning lights flashing. SLOW. STRONG WINDS. They paid their toll and drove out and over it, slammed and battered by the wind. On the far side, the motorway cut north, but it was so dark and stormy that, beyond the headlights' feeble beam, they could see nothing.

"What a shame," said Jody. "Here we are in Scotland and we can't see a thing. Not so much as a haggis."

But Caroline couldn't even rustle up a laugh. She was cold and tired and anxious about the weather and the threatened snow. Suddenly the adventure was an adventure no longer, but simply an act of the greatest possible folly.

The snow began to fall as they left Relkirk behind them. Blown by the wind it came at them out of the darkness in long streaks of blinding white.

"Like flak," said Jody.

"Like what?"

"Flak. Anti-aircraft fire. In war films. That's what it looks like."

At first, it did not lie on the road. But later, climbing up into the hills, it became quite deep, piled in ditches and on dykes, blown by the wind into great pillow-like drifts. It stuck to the windscreen, and piled up beneath the wipers until they stopped working altogether and Caroline had to stop the car, and Jody got out and, with an old glove, wiped the snow from the glass. He got back into the car, wet and shivering.

"It's all in my shoes. It's freezing."

They moved forward again. "How many more miles?" Her mouth was dry with fright, her fingers clamped to the steering-wheel. They appeared to be in a country quite empty of any sort of habitation. Not a light showed, not another car, not even a track on the road.

Jody turned on the torch and studied his map. "About eight, I would say. Strathcorrie's about eight miles."

"And what time is it?"

He looked at his watch. "Half past ten."

Presently they topped a small rise and the road ran downhill, narrow between high dykes. Caroline changed down and as they gathered speed, braked gently, but not gently enough, and the car lurched into a skid. For a terrible instant she knew that she was out of control. A dyke reared up before them, and then the front wheels thumped into a bank of snow and the car came to a dead stop. In trepidation Caroline started up the engine again, managed to turn the wheels out of the drift, and back the car on to the road. They moved on at a snail's pace.

"Is it dangerous?" asked Jody.

"Yes. I think it probably is. If only we had snow tyres."

"Caleb wouldn't have snow tyres, even if he lived in the Arctic."

They were now in a deep glen, tree-lined and running alongside a steep gorge. From this came the sound of a river, purling and splashing above the sound of the wind. They came to a hump-backed bridge, very steep and blind, and, frightened of sticking on its slope, Caroline took it in a small burst of speed, and then saw, too late, that beyond it the road took a sharp turn to the right. Ahead were drifts, and the blank face of a stone wall.

She heard Jody gasp. She spun the wheel, but it was too late. The little car, suddenly with a mind of its own, headed straight for the wall, and then plunged nose-first into a deep ditch full of snow. The engine stalled instantly, and they finished up at an angle of forty-five degrees with the back wheels still on the road, and the headlights and the radiator buried deep in snow.

It was dark without the headlights. Caroline put out a hand to switch them off and then turn off the ignition. She was shaking. She turned to Jody. "Are you all right?"

"I bumped my head a bit, that's all."

"I'm sorry."

"You couldn't help it."

"Perhaps we should have stopped before now. Perhaps we should have stayed in Relkirk."

Jody peered at the swirling darkness. He said, bravely, "You know, I think this is a blizzard. I've never been in a blizzard. The man at the garage said we had to stay in the car."

"We can't. It's much too cold. You wait here, I'm going to look."

"Don't get lost."

"Give me the torch."

She buttoned up her coat, and gingerly got out of the car, falling knee-deep into a snow drift, and then clambering up on to the firm surface of the road. It was wet and bitterly cold and even with the torch to guide her, the snow was blinding, confusing. It would be easy to lose all sense of direction.

She took a few paces down the road, shining the torch along the stone wall which had proved their undoing. It carried on for about ten yards and then curved inwards to form some sort of an entrance. Caroline followed it, and came to a gate post and a wooden gate, open. There was a notice. Screwing her eyes against the snow she turned the beam of the torch upwards and read, with difficulty, CAIRNEY HOUSE. PRIVATE.

She switched off the torch and stared up into the darkness which lay beyond the gate. There seemed to be an avenue of trees, she could hear the thunder of wind in bare branches, high above, and then through the swirl of snowflakes, glimpsed, distantly, a single light.

She turned and went hurrying, floundering back to Jody. She pulled the car door open. "We're in luck."

"How?"

"This wall, it's an estate, or a farm or something. There's a sort of entrance and a gate and a drive. And you can see a light. It can't be more than half a mile."

"But the man at the garage said we had to stay in the car."

"If we stay, we'll die of cold. Come on, the snow's thick, but we can make it. It shouldn't be too long a walk. Leave the rucksack, just get our bags. And button up your jacket. It's cold and we're going to get wet."

He did as she told him, struggling out of the car against its awkward angle. She knew that the important thing was to waste no time. Dressed for London in the spring, they were neither of them prepared for these Arctic conditions. Both were in jeans and thin shoes, Caroline had a suède jacket and a cotton scarf to tie around her head, but Jody's blue anorak was sadly inadequate and his head was bare.

"Do you want the scarf for your head?" The words were torn from her mouth by the wind.

He was furious. "No, of course not."

"Can you carry your bag?"

"Yes, of course I can."

She shut the door. Already the car had collected a considerable coating of snow, its outlines were blurred, soon it would be buried and hidden completely.

"Will anyone drive into it?" Jody asked.

"I don't think so. Anyway, there's nothing we can do. If we left a light on, the snow would simply cover it." She took his hand. "Now come along, we mustn't talk, we've got to hurry."

She led him back to the gate, following the wavering track of her own footprints. Beyond the gate the darkness swept ahead into a black tunnel shimmering with snow. But the light was there still, a pin prick, no more. Far ahead. Hand in hand, heads bent against the wind, they started to walk towards it.

It was a frightening business. All the elements were against them. In moments they were both soaked to the skin and very cold. The overnight bags, which had seemed so light, became heavier with every step. Snow cascaded on to them, wet, sodden, clinging like paste. Overhead, high above the snow, the arched branches of leafless trees soughed and creaked ominously, flayed by the wind. Every now and then came the sound of a branch breaking, followed by the crash and splinter of its fall.

Jody was trying to say something. "I hope . . ." His lips were frozen, his teeth chattered, but he struggled to get the words out. "I hope a tree doesn't fall on us."

"So do I."

"And my coat's supposed to be shower-proof." His voice was testy. "I'm wet right through."

"This is a blizzard, Jody, not a shower."

The light still shone, perhaps a little brighter, and a little closer to hand, but by now Caroline felt as if they had been walking for ever. It was like an endless journey in a nightmare, with the will-o'-the-wisp light dancing ahead of them, always just out of reach. She had begun to give up hope of ever getting anywhere, when all at once the darkness became a little less dense, the sound of the creaking branches fell behind them, and she realized that they had reached the end of the avenue. At this moment the light disappeared, behind a looming bulk of what was probably a clump of rhododendrons. But as they picked their way around this, the light appeared once more, and now it was quite close. They went forward and stumbled over the edge of a bank. Jody nearly fell and Caroline pulled him to his feet.

"It's all right. We're on a lawn, or grass. Perhaps part of a garden."

"Let's go on," said Jody. It was all he could manage.

Now, the light took shape, shining from an upstairs, uncurtained window. They were walking across an open space towards a house. It reared up ahead of them, made shapeless by the blurring edges of the snow, but they could make out other lights, faintly glowing behind thickly drawn curtains in the downstairs rooms.

"It's a big house," whispered Jody.

It was, too. "All the more room for us," said Caroline, but she did not know if Jody heard. She let go of his hand and fumbled clumsily, frozen fingered, in her pocket for the torch. She turned it on, and the faint beam picked out a flight of stone steps, cushioned in snow, leading to the dark recesses of a square porch. They went up the steps and found themselves in cover, out of the snow. The torch's beam played over the panels of the door, and picked out a long, wrought-iron bell-pull. Caroline put down her bag and reached out to pull it. It was stiff and heavy and apparently produced no result at all. She tried again, lending a little more weight to her efforts, and this time a bell rang, distantly, hollowly, from the back of the house.

"That's working, at any rate." She turned to Jody and inadvertently the torch's beam caught his face and she saw that he was grey with cold, his hair plastered to his skull, his teeth chattering. She switched off her torch and put an arm around him and drew him close. "It'll be all right."

"I hope," said Jody in a distinct voice that shook with nerves. "I hope that a horrible butler doesn't come and say 'You rang, sir?' like they do in horror films."

Caroline hoped so too. She was about to ring the bell again, when she heard the footsteps. A dog barked and a deep voice told it to be quiet. Lights sprang from the narrow windows on either side of the entrance, the footsteps came closer and the next moment the door was flung open and a man stood, just inside, with a yellow labrador, bristling, at his heels.

He said to the dog, "Be quiet, Lisa," and then looked up. "Yes?"

Caroline opened her mouth to speak, but could think of nothing to say. She simply stood there, with one arm around Jody, and perhaps it was the best thing she could have done, for without another word being uttered, her bag had been picked up off the flagged floor, the pair of them had been swept indoors, and then the great door was closed against the stormy night.

The nightmare was over. The house felt warm. They were safe.

4

*I*n his state of astonishment, the thing that struck Oliver more forcibly than anything else was their extreme youth. What were two children doing, at half past eleven, out on a night like this? Where had they come from with their little overnight bags, and where on God's earth were they going? But as the questions crowded into his mind, he realized that they would have to be shelved till later. The only important thing now, was to get them out of their wet clothes and into a hot bath before they both died of exposure.

Without wasting time on explanations he said, "Come along. Quickly." And turned and headed, two at a time, up the stairs. After an instant's hesitation he heard them follow him, hurrying to keep up. His mind raced ahead. There were two bathrooms. He went first to his own, snapped on the light, put the plug in the bath, turned on the hot tap, took time to be thankful that one of the things that really worked in this old house was the hot water system, for almost immediately the steam rolled up in comforting clouds.

"You go in here," he told the girl. "Get in as fast as you can, and stay there till you're warm again. And you—" he took hold of the boy's arm, passive beneath the soggy chill of his clothes—"you come this way." He jostled him back down the long passage to the old nursery bathroom, turning on lights as he went. This bathroom had not been used for some time, but the hot pipes kept it cosy and he drew the old faded curtains, with their pattern of Beatrix Potter characters, and turned on the second set of taps.

The boy was already fumbling with the buttons of his jacket. "Can you manage?"

"Yes, thank you."

"I'll be back."

"All right."

He left the boy to his own devices. Outside the door he stood for a moment, trying to decide what had to be done next. It was obvious that at this time of night they would have to stay until morning, so he went back down the passage to the big old spare bedroom. It was bitterly cold, but he drew the heavy curtains and turned on both bars of the electric fire and then turned down the bedspread and saw with relief that Mrs. Cooper had left the double bed made up, with the best linen sheets and hemstitched pillowcases. A door from this room led into a smaller one, once a dressing-room, which contained a single bed, and this too was ready for an occupant, although again the atmosphere was frigid. When he had drawn the curtains and turned on another fire, he returned downstairs, picked up the two small pieces of luggage which had been abandoned in the hall, and carried them along to the library. The fire was dying. He had been on the point of going to bed when the bell disturbed him. But now he built this up, piling on the logs, and then placed a brass-railed fireguard in front of the spitting sparks.

He unzipped the first bag and took out a pair of blue and white striped pyjamas, some slippers, a grey woollen dressing-gown. Everything was slightly damp, so feeling like a conscientious Nanny, he draped them over the fireguard to dry. The other bag produced nothing so practical as blue and white pyjamas. There were bottles and jars, a hairbrush and comb, a pair of little gold slippers, and finally, a nightdress with a matching negligee; pale blue, very lacy, entirely useless. Oliver laid the nightdress alongside the pyjamas. It struck him as looking both suggestive and sexy and he found time to grin at the idea before heading for the kitchen and the business of finding something sustaining for his visitors to eat.

Mrs. Cooper had made a pot of scotch broth for Oliver's supper and there was still half of this left. He put it on the Aga to heat, and then remembered that small boys did not always like scotch broth, so he found a tin of tomato soup, and opened that and put it in another saucepan. He took out a tray, cut bread and butter, found some apples, a jug of milk. He considered this homely repast, and then added a whisky bottle (for himself if no one else) and a soda syphon and three tumblers. Finally, he boiled up the big kettle and after a search ran a couple of hot water bottles to earth in an unsuspected drawer. With these, fatly-filled, held under his arm, he went to collect the night-things, which were dry now, and warm, and smelt comforting, like an old-fashioned nursery. He put the bottles in the bed, and then went to his own room and took a shetland sweater from a drawer and a Viyella dressing-gown from the back of the door. Then he found a couple of bath-towels.

He thumped at the bathroom door with his fist. "How are you getting on?"

"I'm warm. It's marvellous," came the girl's voice.

"Well, I'll leave a towel and some things to put on, outside the door. You get dressed when you're good and ready."

"All right."

He did not bother to knock on the door of the other bathroom, but simply opened it and went in. The boy lay in the deep water, slowly moving his legs to and fro. He looked up, unembarrassed by Oliver's abrupt appearance.

"How do you feel now?" asked Oliver.

"Much better, thank you. I'd never been so cold in my life."

Oliver pulled up a chair, and settled himself companionably.

"What happened?" he asked.

The boy sat up in the bath. Oliver saw the freckles, across his back, down his arms, spattered all over his face. His hair was damp and tousled and the colour of copper beech leaves. He said, "The car went into a ditch."

"In the snow?"

"Yes. We came over the little bridge and we didn't know the road turned so quickly. We couldn't see in the snow."

"It's a bad corner at the best of times. What happened to the car?"

"We left it there."

"Where were you going?"

"Strathcorrie."

"And where have you come from?"

"London."

"London?" Oliver could not keep the astonishment out of his voice. "From London? Today?"

"Yes. We left early this morning."

"And the girl? Is she your sister?"

"Yes."

"Was she driving?"

"Yes, she drove all the way."

"Just the two of you."

The boy looked dignified. He said, "We were all right."

"Yes, of course," Oliver assured him hastily. "It's just that your sister doesn't look old enough to drive a car."

"She's twenty."

"Well, in that case of course she is old enough."

A small silence followed. Jody took up a sponge, thoughtfully squeezed it and then dabbed at his face, pushing a crest of wet hair off his forehead. He emerged from behind the sponge and said, "I think I'm hot enough now. I think I'll get out."

"Out you come then." Oliver reached for the bath-towel, shook out its folds, and as the boy stepped out on to the bath-mat, wrapped him in it. The boy faced him. Their eyes were level. Oliver gently rubbed at him with the towel.

"What's your name?" he asked.

"Jody."

"Jody what?"

"Jody Cliburn."

"And your sister?"

"She's Caroline."

Oliver took up a handful of towel and rubbed at Jody's hair. "Did you have any particular reason for going to Strathcorrie?"

"My brother's there."

"Is he called Cliburn, too?"

"Yes. Angus Cliburn."

"Ought I to know him?"

"I don't suppose so. He's only been there a little while. He's working in the hotel."

"I see."

"He's going to be rather worried," Jody said.

"Why?" Oliver reached for the pyjamas, held the jacket out for Jody.

"These are all warm," said Jody.

"They've been in front of the fire. Why is your brother going to be worried?"

"We sent him a telegram. He'll be expecting us. And now we aren't there."

"He'll know about the blizzard. He'll guess something like this has happened."

"We never thought it would snow. In London there are crocuses and things and buds on the trees."

"This is the far, frozen North, my boy. You can never depend on the weather."

"I've never been to Scotland before." Jody pulled on his pyjama trousers and tied the cord around his waist. "Neither has Caroline."

"It was bad luck, the weather doing this to you."

"It was rather exciting, really. An adventure."

"Adventures are all very well when they're safely over. But they're not so funny when they're going on. I think you've come out of yours very well."

"We were lucky to find you."

"Yes, I think you were."

"Is this your house?"

"Yes."

"Do you live here all alone?"

"At the moment I do."

"What's it called?"

"Cairney."

"And what's your name."

"The same. Cairney. Oliver Cairney."

"Goodness."

Oliver grinned. "Muddling, isn't it? Now, if you're ready we'll go and find your sister and then get something to eat." He opened the door. "Incidentally, would you rather have scotch broth or tomato soup?"

"Tomato, if you've got it."

"I thought you would."

As they came down the passage, Caroline emerged from the other bathroom. In Oliver's dressing-gown she was submerged. She looked even smaller and thinner than his first impression of her. Her long hair was damp, and the high collar of his sweater appeared to be supporting her fragile head.

"I feel quite different now . . . thank you so much . . ."

"We're going to find something to eat . . ."

"I'm afraid we're being the most terrible nuisance."

"You'll only be a nuisance if you catch colds on me and I'm forced to look after you."

He went on downstairs, and behind him, heard her brother say to Caroline in tones of the greatest satisfaction, "He says it's *tomato* soup."

At the kitchen door he stopped. "That's the library door down there. You go and wait and I'll bring you your supper. And put more logs on the fire, get a good blaze going."

The soup was bubbling gently. He ladled out two bowls, and then carried the laden tray along to the library where he found them by the fire, Jody sitting on a footstool and his sister kneeling on the hearthrug trying to dry her hair. Lisa, Charles's dog, sat between them, her head resting on Jody's knee. The boy stroked her ears. He looked up as Oliver appeared.

"What's the dog's name?"

"Lisa. Has she made friends with you?"

"I think so."

"She doesn't usually make friends as quickly as that." He put the tray down on a low table, shoving aside some magazines and old newspapers to make room for it.

"Is she your dog?"

"At the moment she is. Have you got a dog?"

"No." His voice was bleak. Oliver decided to change the subject. "Why not have the soup before it gets cold?" And while they started in on their meal, he took away the fireguard, put on another log, poured himself a whisky and soda, and settled in the old sagging armchair by the side of the hearth.

They ate in silence. Jody had soon finished his soup, eaten all the bread and butter, drunk a couple of tumblers of milk and then started in on the apples; but his sister only ate a little of her broth and then laid down the spoon as if she were no longer hungry.

"Not nice?" Oliver asked.

"Delicious. But I couldn't eat any more."

"Aren't you hungry? You have to be hungry."

Jody chipped in. "She never is."

"A drink, perhaps?"

"No, thank you."

The subject was closed. Oliver said, "Your brother and I had a talk when he was having a bath. You're Jody and Caroline Cliburn."

"Yes."

"And I'm Oliver Cairney. Did he tell you?"

"Yes, he did. He just did."

"You've come from London?"

"Yes."

"And you ditched the car at the bottom of my drive."

"Yes."

"And you were heading for Strathcorrie?"

"Yes. Our brother works there. In the hotel."

"And he's expecting you?"

"We sent him a telegram. He'll be wondering what's happened to us."

Oliver looked at his watch. "It's nearly midnight. But if you like I can try and get through on the telephone. There may be a night porter on duty."

She looked grateful. "Oh, would you do that?"

"I can always try." But the telephone was dead. "The lines must be down. It's the storm."

"But what shall we do?"

"There's nothing you can do except stay here."

"But Angus . . ."

"As I said to Jody, he'll realize what's happened."

"And tomorrow?"

"If the road isn't blocked we can get to Strathcorrie by some means or other. I've a Land-Rover if the worse comes to the worst."

"And if the road is blocked?"

"Let's worry about that when it happens."

"The thing is . . . well, we haven't got an awful lot of time. We're meant to be back in London on Friday."

Oliver looked down at his drink, gently rocking the glass in his hand. "Is there anyone in London we should get in touch with? Let them know that you are safe?"

Jody looked at his sister. After a little she said, "But there's no telephone."

"But when we do have a telephone?"

She said, "No. We don't have to get in touch with anyone."

He was sure she was lying. He watched her face, saw the high cheekbones, the short blunt nose, the wide mouth. She had dark smudges beneath her eyes, and her hair was very long, pale, straight as silk. For an instant her eyes met his, and then she turned away. Oliver decided not to pursue the subject. "I only wondered," he said mildly.

In the morning, when Caroline awoke, the snow light was reflected on the white ceiling of the big bedroom. She lay, drowsy, pillowed in goose-down and linen; heard a dog bark, and presently the grinding sound of an approaching tractor. She reached for her watch and saw that it was already past nine o'clock. She got out of bed and padded to the window and drew back the pink curtains, and was assailed by a blast of light so blinding that she blinked.

The world was white. The sky clear, and blue as a robin's egg. Long shadows lay like bruises on the sparkling ground, everything was softened and rounded by the snow. It lay along the branches of pines, and piled in white hats on the top of fence posts. Caroline threw open the window and leaned out and the air was cold and fragrant and stimulating as iced wine.

Remembering the horrors of the night before, she tried to get her bearings. In front of the house was a large open space, probably a lawn, ringed by the driveway. She saw the tall avenue up which she and Jody had struggled, leading away, down over the crest of a hill. In the distance, between folds of sloping pastures, the main road wound between dry stone walls. A car was moving, very slowly.

The tractor she had heard was coming up the avenue. As she watched, it appeared from behind a huge clump of rhododendrons, and churned carefully around the perimeter of the lawn and so out of sight behind the house.

It was too cold to be out. She drew back into her bedroom and shut the window. She thought of Jody and went to open the door that led into his room. Inside, it was dark and quiet, only his breathing stirred the silence. He was still fast asleep. She closed the door, and looked for something to put on. But there was only the sweater and the borrowed dressing-gown, so wearing these, but barefoot, she went out of the bedroom and down the passage in the hope of finding someone to help her.

She realized then that it was an enormous house. The passage came out on to a great landing, furnished with carpets and a walnut tallboy, and chairs and a table where someone had laid down a pile of clean shirts, neatly ironed. At the top of the stair, she listened and discerned distant voices. She went downstairs, and following the murmur of voices, found herself at the door of what was presumably the kitchen. She put her hands against the door and pushed, and it swung open and immediately the two people inside stopped talking, and turned to see who it was.

Oliver Cairney, in a thick cream coloured sweater, sat at the kitchen table with a mug of tea in his hand. He had been talking to the woman who stood, peeling potatoes at the sink. Middle-aged, she was, grey-haired, and with her sleeves rolled up, and a flowered pinafore tied in a bow at the back of her waist. The kitchen was warm and smelled of baking bread. Caroline felt like an intruder. She said, "I'm sorry . . ."

Oliver, who had been momentarily surprised into inactivity, put down the mug and got to his feet.

"Nothing to be sorry about. I thought you'd sleep till lunchtime."

"Jody's still asleep."

"This is Mrs. Cooper, Mrs. Cooper, this is Caroline Cliburn. I've just been telling Mrs. Cooper what happened to you."

Mrs. Cooper said, "It was a terrible night and no mistake. All the telephone lines are down."

Caroline looked at Oliver. "You mean we still can't get through?"

"No, and won't be able to for some time. Come and have a cup of tea. Come and have some breakfast. What would you like? Bacon and egg?"

But she didn't want anything. "Some tea, that would be lovely." He pulled out a chair for her and she sat at the scrubbed table. "And are we snowed up?"

"Partially. The Strathcorrie road's blocked, but we can get down to Relkirk."

Caroline's heart sank. "And . . . the car?" She was almost frightened to ask.

"Cooper's been down on the tractor to investigate."

"Is it a red tractor?"

"Yes."

"I saw it coming back up the road."

"In that case, he'll be here any moment to let us know what's going on." He had found a cup and saucer, and now poured Caroline a cup of tea from the brown teapot which sat, stewing happily, on the Aga. It was very strong, but also very hot and she drank it gratefully. She said, "I can't find my clothes."

"That'll be me," said Mrs. Cooper. "I put them to dry in the hot cupboard. They should be ready by now. But, my word—" she shook her head—"you two must have got a drenching."

"They did," said Oliver. "They were like drowned rats."

By the time Caroline was dressed and downstairs again, the party had been joined by Mr. Cooper, with news of the ditched car. He was a country man and his accent so strong that Caroline had difficulty in understanding what he said.

"Oh, aye, we'll get it oot o' the ditch richt enough, but there'll be no life in the engine."

"Why not?"

"Frozen stiff, I wouldna be surprised."

Oliver looked at Caroline. "Didn't you have any antifreeze?"

Caroline looked blank.

"Anti-freeze," he said again. "It doesn't mean anything to you?"

She shook her head and he turned back to Cooper. "You're quite right. Frozen stiff."

"*Should* I have had anti-freeze?"

"Well, it's a good idea."

"I didn't know. You see, it isn't my car."

"Perhaps you stole it?"

Mrs. Cooper made a small sound of disapproval, a drawing-in of the breath between pursed lips. Caroline was not sure whether the disapproval was aimed at Oliver or herself. She said, with dignity, "No, of course not. We were lent it."

"I see. Well begged, borrowed, or stolen, I suggest we go down and see what can be done with it."

"Well," said Cooper, putting his old bonnet back on his head with a large red hand, and heading for the door, "If you take the Land-Rover, I'll go and find a tow-rope and maybe young Geordie to give me a hand, and we'll see if we can get it out with the tractor."

When he had gone, Oliver looked at Caroline. "Are you coming?"

"Yes."

"You'll need boots."

"I haven't got any."

"There are some here . . ."

She followed him into an old wash-house, now used as a catch-all for raincoats, rubber boots, dog-baskets, a rusty bicycle or two and a brand-new washing machine. After some searching, Oliver produced a pair of rubber boots which more or less fitted and a black oil-skin coat. Caroline put this on and flipped her hair free of the collar, and then, suitably attired, followed him out into the glittering morning.

"Winter snow, spring sun," said Oliver, with satisfaction as they trod across the pristine snow towards the closed doors of the garage.

"Will the snow last?"

"Probably not. Though it'll take a bit of melting. Nine inches fell last night."

"It was spring in London."

"That's what your brother said."

He reached up to unsnib bolts, and opened the wide double doors of the garage. Inside were two cars, the dark green sports saloon and the Land-Rover. "We'll take the Land-Rover," he said, "and then we won't get stuck."

Caroline climbed in. They backed out of the garage, drove around the house and down the avenue, cautiously following the dark tracks that Mr. Cooper's tractor had already made. The morning was completely quiet, all sound muffled by the snow, and yet there was life about . . . here tracks ran beneath the trees, and the small starred footprints of random birds. High above, the branches of the beeches met in a soaring arch, a lace-like tangle silhouetted against the pale, bright morning sky.

They came out through the gate, and on to the road and into blinding sunshine. Oliver stopped the Land-Rover by the verge and they both got out. Caroline saw now the hump-backed bridge which had been their downfall, and the disconsolate shape of Caleb's car, muffled in snow, all askew in the ditch, the ground about it patterned with Mr. Cooper's large-booted footprints. It looked finished, mummified, as though it would never move again. Caroline felt dreadfully guilty.

Oliver got the door open and with care inserted half of himself into the driving-seat, leaving one long leg outside. He turned the key which Caroline had carelessly left in the ignition and there was an agonized sound from the engine and a strong smell of burning. Without saying a word, he got out of the car again and slammed the door shut. "Hopeless," she heard him mutter, and felt not only guilty but a fool as well.

She said, with some vague notion of defending herself, "I didn't know about the anti-freeze. I told you it wasn't my car."

He made no reply to this, but went around the car, kicking the snow from the back tyres, then crouching on the snowy road to see if the back axle had become wedged against the edge of the ditch.

She found this all very depressing, and all at once, felt near tears. Everything was going wrong. She and Jody were stuck here, with this unsympathetic man. Caleb's car was useless, there were no telephones to Strathcorrie and the road was blocked. Blinking back tears, she turned to look up the road, which wound on, up and over the crest of a small hill. The snow lay thick and white between the dry stone dykes, a breeze moved, a baby sister of the gale last night, and blew a soft drift of snow, like smoke, off the fields and on to the drifts which were already piled, like glistening sculptures, in the angles of the dykes. Somewhere in the still morning, a curlew dropped from the sky, calling his long liquid cry. And then the air was motionless again.

Behind her, Oliver's footsteps squeaked across the snow. She turned to face him, hands buried deep in the pockets of the borrowed oilskin.

"It's had it, I'm afraid," he told her.

Caroline was horrified. "But can't it be mended?"

"Oh, yes. Cooper'll get it out with the tractor, and along to the garage down the road. He's a good man there. The Mini'll be ready for you tomorrow, or maybe the day after." Something in her face made him add, as though trying to bolster her spirits, "Even if you had a car, you can see you'd never be able to drive it to Strathcorrie. The road's impassable."

She turned again to look. "But when do you think it'll be clear?"

"As soon as the snow-plough gets around to it. A fall like this, at the very tail end of the winter, is inclined to disrupt everything. We just have to be patient."

He opened the door of the Land-Rover for her, and stood, waiting for her to get in. Slowly, Caroline did so. He shut the door and came around and got in behind the wheel. She thought that he would drive her back to the house, but instead he lit a cigarette, and sat smoking it, apparently deep in thought.

Caroline felt apprehensive. Cars were good places to be with a person you liked. But not good if the person was going to ask a lot of questions you didn't feel like answering.

And the moment he spoke, her fears were justified.

"When did you say you had to be back in London?"

"Friday. That's when I *said* we'd be back."

"Who did you say it to?"

". . . Caleb. The man who lent us the car."

"What about your parents."

"Our parents are dead."

"Isn't there anyone? There must be someone. I can't believe the pair of you keep house together, on your own." Despite himself, Oliver grinned at the thought. "The situation would be fraught with the most appalling disasters."

Caroline did not think this was particularly funny. She said, coldly, "If you must know, we live with my stepmother."

Oliver looked knowing. *"I see."*

"What do you see?"

"A wicked stepmother."

"She's not wicked at all. She's very nice."

"But she doesn't know where you are?"

". . . yes," said Caroline, hardly hesitating over the half-truth. And then, more convincingly, "Yes, she does. She knows we're in Scotland."

"Does she know why? About brother Angus?"

"Yes. She knows that too."

"And . . . coming all this way to find Angus. Was that for any particular reason or just to say hallo?"

"Not entirely."

"That's not an answer."

"Isn't it?"

This was followed by a long pause. After a little Oliver said, with deceptive mildness, "You know, I have the strongest feeling that I'm skating on very thin ice. I think you should know that I don't give a damn about what you're up to, but I do feel, very slightly, that I should be responsible for your brother. After all, he's only . . . eleven?"

"I can be responsible for Jody."

His voice was quiet. "You might both have died last night. You know that, don't you?" Caroline stared at him, and saw, to her astonishment, that he meant what he said.

"But I saw the light before I left the car behind. Otherwise, we'd have stayed, and just sat the storm out."

"Blizzards are something to be reckoned with in this part of the world. You were lucky."

"And you were kind. More than kind. And I haven't thanked you properly. But I still feel that the sooner we get to Angus and out from under your feet, the better."

"We'll see how it goes. And incidentally, I have to go out today, I have a lunch appointment in Relkirk. But Mrs. Cooper will feed you and Jody, and by the time I'm back, perhaps the Strathcorrie road will be open and I can drive you both up and deliver you to your brother."

Caroline considered this, and found that for some reason, the idea of Oliver Cairney and Angus Cliburn meeting, was not a good one.

"Surely there's some way I could . . ."

"No." Oliver leaned forward and stubbed out his cigarette. "No, there is no other way of getting to Strathcorrie, short of flying. So you just sit tight and wait for me at Cairney. Understood?"

Caroline opened her mouth to argue, caught his eye, and shut her mouth again. She nodded reluctantly. "All right."

For a moment she thought he was going to continue the discussion, but his attention was mercifully diverted by the arrival of the tractor, with Mr. Cooper at the wheel and a young boy in a knitted hat, perched up on the seat behind him. Oliver got out of the Land-Rover and went to assist them; but it was a tedious business, and by the time Caleb's car had been swept clear of snow, grit shovelled beneath its wheels, ropes attached to the back axle and two or three abortive attempts made to drag it clear before it finally, protestingly came, it was nearly eleven o'clock. Caroline watched the small cavalcade set off in the direction of the garage, Cooper at the wheel of the tractor, and Geordie in the Mini, steering an unsteady course at the end of the tow rope. She felt terrible.

"I do hope it will be all right," she told Oliver as he climbed back beside her. "It wouldn't be so bad if it were my car, but I promised Caleb I'd take such care of it."

"It wasn't your fault. It could have happened to anybody. By the time the garage have finished with it, it'll probably be better than ever." He looked at his watch. "We must move, I've got to get changed and into Relkirk by twelve-thirty."

They returned to the house in silence, parked at the door and went indoors. At the foot of the stairs Oliver stopped and looked at Caroline.

"You'll be all right?"

"Of course."

"I'll see you later then."

Caroline watched him go upstairs, his long legs taking the stairs two at a time. Then she shed herself of the oilskin and the large boots and went in search of Jody. The kitchen was empty, but she found Mrs. Cooper vacuuming the enormous turkey-carpeted wastes of a little-used dining-room. She switched off the machine when Caroline appeared at the door.

"Did you get your motor sorted?" she asked.

"Yes. Your husband's very kindly taken it to the garage. Have you seen Jody?"

"Yes, he's up and about, the dear wee soul. Came downstairs, and had his breakfast with me in the kitchen, right as rain. Two boiled eggs he had and toast and honey and a glass of milk. Then I showed him the boys' old nursery and he's there now, up to high doh with all the bricks and cars and goodness knows what."

"Where is the nursery?"

"Come away and I'll show you."

She abandoned her cleaning and led the way up a small back stair-case and through a door into a white-painted, blue-carpeted passage. "This was the nursery wing in the old days, the children had it all to themselves. It's not used now, of course, hasn't been for years, but I lit a wee fire, so it's nice and warm." She opened a door and stood aside for Caroline to go in. It was a big room, with a bay window looking out over the garden. A fire burned behind a tall fender, there were old armchairs and a sagging couch, bookshelves, an ancient tail-less rocking horse, and on the floor, in the middle of the threadbare carpet, Jody, surrounded by a fortification of wooden bricks which spread to the corners of the room, all set about with model cars, toy soldiers, cowboys, knights-in-armour and farmyard animals. He looked up as she came in, his concentration so intent that he didn't even look embarrassed at being caught in such a babyish occupation.

"Heavens," said Caroline. "How long has it taken you to build this lot?"

"Since breakfast. Don't knock that tower over."

"I wasn't going to." She stepped carefully over it and made for the fireplace where she stood, leaning against the fender.

Mrs. Cooper was full of admiration. "I've never seen anything so neat! And all the wee roads! You must have used up every brick in the place."

"I have, just about." Jody smiled at her. They were obviously already the best of friends.

"Well, I'll leave you then. And lunch is at half past twelve. Apple pie I've made and there's a wee bit of cream. Do you like apple pie, pet?"

"Yes, I love it."

"That's good." She went away. They heard her humming to herself. "Isn't she nice?" said Jody, aligning two tall bricks to make a ceremonial gateway into his fort.

"Yes, isn't she? Did you sleep all right?"

"Yes, for hours. It's a super house." He piled on another couple of bricks to make a really high gateway.

"The car's gone to the garage. Mr. Cooper took it. It didn't have any anti-freeze."

"Silly old Caleb," said Jody. He chose an arched brick and placed it carefully, crowning his masterpiece. He put his cheek to the carpet, looking through the archway, thinking himself tiny, pretending that he would be able to ride through it on a great white charger, with the plume on his helmet fluttering in the breeze and his quartered banner held high.

"Jody, last night, when you were talking in your bath, you didn't say anything about Angus, did you? To Oliver Cairney?"

"No. Just that we were going to find him."

"Or about Diana? Or Hugh?"

"He never asked."

"Don't say anything."

Jody looked up. "How much longer are we going to stay here?"

"Oh, no time. We'll find Angus this afternoon, we'll go to Strathcorrie when the roads have been cleared."

Jody made no comment on this. She watched him take a little horse from an open box, then search for the knight that would fit into its saddle. He selected one, fitted the two together, held them off for a moment to gauge the effect. He placed the rider, with the utmost precision, beneath his archway.

He said, "Mrs. Cooper told me something."

"What did she tell you?"

"This isn't his house."

"What do you mean, it isn't his house? It has to be his house."

"It belonged to his brother. Oliver lives in London, but his brother used to live here. He used to farm. That's why there are dogs and tractors and things about the place."

"What happened to his brother?"

"He was killed," said Jody. "In a car crash. Last week."

Killed in a car crash. Something, some memory, stirred in the back of Caroline's subconscious, but was almost at once lost in horror, as the implication of Jody's cool statement made itself felt. She found that she had put a hand over her mouth as though to choke back the word. Killed.

"That's why Oliver's here." Jody's voice was off-hand, a sure sign that he was distressed. "For the funeral and everything. To tie things up, Mrs. Cooper says. He's going to sell this house and the farm and everything and never come back." He stood up carefully, trod his way over to Caroline's side, and stood close, and she knew that for all his apparent coolness, he was, all at once, in need of comfort.

She put her arm around him. She said, "And in the middle of it all, we had to turn up. Poor man."

"Mrs. Cooper says it was a good thing. She says it keeps his mind off his sorrow." He looked up at her. "When will we get to Angus?"

"Today," Caroline promised him without any hesitation. "Today."

Besides the apple pie and cream, there was mince for lunch, baked potatoes and mashed swedes. "Chappit neeps" Mrs. Cooper called them, ladling them on to Jody's plate. Caroline, who had thought she was hungry, discovered that she was not, but Jody ate his way through the lot and then attacked with relish a bar of home-made "taiblet."

"And now, what are you ones going to do with yourselves for the rest of the day? Mr. Cairney won't be back till tea-time."

"Can I go on playing in the nursery?" Jody wanted to know.

"Of course, pet." Mrs. Cooper looked at Caroline.

Caroline said, "I shall go for a walk."

Mrs. Cooper seemed surprised. "Have you not had enough fresh air for one day?"

"I like being out. And it's so pretty with the snow."

"It's clouding over now, though, it won't be such a fine afternoon."

"I don't mind."

Jody was torn. "Do you *mind* if I don't come with you?"

"Of course not."

"I rather thought I might build a grandstand. You know, to watch the jousting."

"You do that."

Taken up with his plans, Jody excused himself and disappeared upstairs to put them into action. Caroline offered to help Mrs. Cooper with the dishes but was told no, away out with you, before the rain comes on. So she went out of the kitchen and across the hall, put on the oilskin and the rubber boots she had worn that morning, tied a scarf around her head and let herself out of the house.

Mrs. Cooper had been right about the day. Clouds had rolled in from the west, there was a mildness in the air, the sun had disappeared. She drove her hands deep into the pockets of the coat and set off, across the lawn, down the avenue, and through the gates on to the road. She turned left, in the direction of Strathcorrie, and started to walk.

You sit tight and wait for me at Cairney, Oliver had said, and if she wasn't there by the time he returned he would probably be furious, but taking the long view, Caroline could not see that this would matter very much. After today, they would probably never see him again. She would write, of course, to thank him for his kindness. But she would never see him again.

And, somehow, it was important that when she and Angus met up once more, after all these years, they did not do so beneath the eyes of some critical stranger. The worst thing about Angus was that you could never depend on him. He had always been the most unpredictable person in the world, vague, elusive and utterly maddening. From the very beginning she had had reservations about this wild scheme of coming to Scotland to find him, but somehow Jody's enthusiasm had been infectious. He was so sure that Angus would be waiting for them, delighted to see them, anxious to help, that, from the safe distance of London, he had managed to convince Caroline as well.

But now, in the chill light of a Scottish afternoon, her doubts returned. Angus would of course *be* at the Strathcorrie Hotel because that was where he was working, but the fact that he cleaned shoes and carried logs was no insurance that he would not have long hair, a beard, bare feet and no intention whatsoever of doing anything to help his brother and sister. She imagined Oliver Cairney's reaction to such an attitude and knew that she could not have borne him to be present to witness the great reunion.

Besides, there was the new knowledge of his brother's recent death, and a sensation of the most acute embarrassment that they had encroached on Oliver's kindness and taken advantage of his unquestioning hospitality at such a totally inopportune time. There was no doubt that the sooner he was shed of them the better. There was no doubt that coming to find Angus now, on her own, was the only possible course to take.

Trudging down the long, snow-packed road, she filled the time convincing herself that this was really so.

She had been walking for over an hour, without any idea of how many miles she had covered, when a lorry overtook her, slowly grinding up the slope behind her. It was the County snow-plough, its huge steel plough cutting through the snow like the bows of a ship through water, sending out a spuming wake of slush on either side of the road.

Caroline got out of the way, clambering up on to the top of the wall, but the snow-plough stopped, and the man inside opened the door and called down to her.

"Where are you going?"

"Strathcorrie."

"That's another six miles. Do you want a ride?"

"Yes, please."

"Come away then." She scrambled down off the wall, and he put down a horny hand and helped her up, moving across to make space for her. His mate, a much older man driving the lorry, said dourly, "I hope you're no' in a hurry. The snow's lying deep on the brow of the hill."

"I'm in no hurry. Just so that I don't have to walk."

"Aye, it's durrty weather."

He crashed the heavy gears, threw off the handbrake, and they moved on, but it was, in truth, a slow progress. At intervals the two men got down and did a bit of strenuous shoveling, clearing the grit piles that had been left, strategically, at the sides of the road. Damp oozed its way through the windows of the cab, and Caroline's feet, in her ill-fitting boots, became like two lumps of ice.

But at last they crested the final hill and the kindly roadman said, "There's Strathcorrie now," and she saw the white and grey country-side drop before them, into a deep glen, and a long meandering loch, quite still, and steel-grey with reflected sky.

On the far side of the water the hills climbed again, patterned black with stands of fir and pine, and beyond their gentle summits could be seen other peaks, a range of distant, northern mountains. And directly below, clustered around the narrow end of the loch, lay the village. She saw the church and little streets of grey houses, and there was a small boat yard, with jetties and moorings and small craft pulled up on the shingle for the winter.

"What a pretty place!" said Caroline.

"Aye," said the roadman. "And they get a gey lot of visitors in the summer months. Sailing boats for hire, bed and breakfast, caravans . . ."

The road ran downhill. The snow here, for some reason, lay not so thick and they were making better time. "Where do you want us to leave you?" the driver asked.

"The hotel. The Strathcorrie Hotel. Do you know where that is?"

"Oh, aye, I ken it fine."

In the village, the grey streets were wet, snow melting in the gutters, dropping, with soft plopping sounds, from sloping eaves. The snow-plough drove down the main street, passed under an ornamental Gothic archway, built to commemorate some long-forgotten Victorian occasion, and came to a halt before a long white-washed building, fronted by a cobbled pavement and with a sign swinging over the door.

Strathcorrie Hotel. Visitors Welcome.

There was no sign of life. "Is it open?" Caroline asked doubtfully.

"Aye, it's open right enough. It's just no' very busy."

She thanked them for their kindness and climbed down from the snow-plough. As it moved away, she crossed the road, and the cobbled pavement, and went in through the revolving door. Inside it smelled of stale cigarette smoke and boiled cabbage. There was a sad picture of a roe deer on a wet hill, and a desk with a notice, *Reception,* but no one to do any receiving. There was, however, a bell, which Caroline rang. In a moment a woman appeared from an office. She wore a black dress and spectacles trimmed with diamanté, and did not look too pleased at being interrupted in the middle of the afternoon, especially by a girl in jeans and an oilskin with a red cotton handkerchief tied around her head.

"Yes?"

"I'm so sorry to bother you, but I wondered if I could speak to Angus Cliburn."

"Oh," said the woman immediately. "Angus isn't here." She looked quite pleased to be able to impart this information.

Caroline simply stared at her. Overhead a clock ticked sonorously. Somewhere, in the back regions of the hotel, a man started to sing. The woman re-adjusted her spectacles.

"He *was* here, of course," she enlarged, as though conceding a point to Caroline. She hesitated and then said, "Did you by any chance send him a telegram? There is a telegram for him, but of course he'd gone by the time it arrived." She opened a drawer and took out the orange envelope. "I had to open it, you see, and I'd have let you know he wasn't here, only there wasn't any address."

"No, of course . . ."

"He was here, mind you. He worked here for a month or more. Helping out. We were a little short-staffed, you see."

"But where is he now?"

"Oh, I couldn't say. He went with an American lady, driving her car for her. She was staying here, and hadn't anyone to drive her, so as we had a replacement for Angus by then, we let him go. A chauffeur," she added as though Caroline would never have heard of the word.

"But when are they coming back?"

"Oh, in a day or so. The end of the week Mrs. Mcdonald said."

"Mrs. Mcdonald?"

"Yes, the American lady. Her husband's ancestors came from this part of Scotland. That's why she was so keen to go sight-seeing, hired the car and got Angus to drive her."

Back at the end of the week. That meant Friday, or Saturday. But Caroline and Jody had to be back in London by Friday. She couldn't wait until the week-end. She was getting married on Tuesday. On Tuesday she was getting married to Hugh, and she had to be there, because there was a wedding rehearsal on Monday, and Diana would be frantic, and all the presents.

Her thoughts galloped uselessly, to and fro, like a distracted run-away horse. She pulled herself up and told herself that she must be practical. And then realized that she could not think of one practical thing to say or to do. *I am at the end of my tether*. This was how it felt. Now, when people said *I am at the end of my tether*, she, Caroline, would understand.

The woman behind the desk was becoming a little impatient with all this waiting about. "Did you particularly want to see Angus?"

"Yes. I'm his sister. It's rather important."

"Where did you come from today?"

Without thought Caroline told her. "From Cairney."

"But that's eight miles. And the road's blocked."

"I walked a bit, and then I got a lift with the snow-plough."

They would have to wait for Angus. Perhaps they could stay here, at the hotel. She wished she had brought Jody with her.

"Would you have two rooms vacant that we could have?"

"We?"

"I have another brother. He's not with me just now."

The woman looked doubtful, but she said "Just a moment" and went back to her office to consult some book. Caroline leaned against the counter and decided that it was no good getting into a panic, it only made you feel ill. It made you feel sick.

And then she knew it was back again, the old nausea, the knife-like pain in her stomach. It had taken her completely by surprise, like some horrible monster waiting around the corner to pounce. She tried to ignore it, but it was not to be ignored. It grew, with frightening speed, like a huge balloon being pumped up with air. Enormous, and so intensely agonizing that it left no room in her consciousness for anything else. She was made of pain, pain stretched to the most distant horizon, she closed her eyes and there came a sound like the screaming of a distant alarm bell.

And then, when she thought she could bear it no longer, it began to die away, slipping down and off her, like some discarded garment. After a little, she opened her eyes, and found herself looking straight into the horrified face of the receptionist. She wondered how long she had been standing there.

"Are you all right?"

"Yes." She tried to smile. Her face was wet with sweat. "Indigestion, I think. I've had it before. And then the walk . . ."

"I'll get you a glass of water. You'd better sit down."

"I'm all right."

But something was wrong with the woman's face; in a strange blur it was approaching and receding. She was speaking, Caroline could see her mouth open and shut, but she made no sound. Caroline put out a hand and took hold of the edge of the counter, but it did no good, and the last thing she remembered was the brightly patterned carpet swinging up to hit her with a resounding clout on the side of the head.

5

Oliver did not get back to Cairney until half past four. He was tired. Duncan Fraser, besides standing him a heavy luncheon, had insisted on discussing every aspect of the financial and legal details of the taking over of Cairney. Nothing had been left out and Oliver's head swam with facts and figures. Acreages, yields, heads of cattle, the value of cottages, the condition of steadings and barns. It was necessary, of course, and right, but he had found it distressing, and he made the long drive home through the darkening afternoon in a state of black depression, trying to accept the truth; that, by giving up Cairney, even to Duncan, it was inevitable that he was giving up something of himself, and cutting away the last of the connections that held him to his youth.

The conflict within himself had left him drained of energy. His head ached, and he could think of nothing but the sanctuary of his home, the comfort of his own armchair, his own fireside, and possibly, a soothing cup of tea.

The house had never looked so secure, so welcoming. He took the Land-Rover around to the garage, parked it there, and went indoors, through the kitchen. He found Mrs. Cooper, at her ironing board, but with her eyes on the door. When he appeared, she gave a sigh of relief, and set the iron down with a thump.

"Oh, Oliver, I hoped it was you. I heard the car, and I hoped it was you."

Something in her face made him say, "What's wrong?"

"It's just the boy's sister went out for a walk, and she's not back yet, and it's nearly dark."

Oliver stood there, in his overcoat, and slowly digested this unwelcome piece of information.

"When did she go?"

"After lunch. Not that she ate anything, just picked away, didn't take enough to keep a flea alive."

"But it's . . . half past four."

"That's just it."

"Where's Jody?"

"He's in the nursery. He's fine and not worried. I took him his tea, the wee lamb."

Oliver frowned. "But where did she go?"

"She didn't say. 'I'm just going for a wee walk,' she said." Mrs. Cooper's face was drawn with anxiety. "You don't think something could have happened?"

"I shouldn't be surprised," said Oliver, bitterly. "She's such a fool, she could drown herself in a puddle."

"Oh, poor wee soul . . ."

"Poor wee soul nothing, she's a bloody nuisance," said Oliver brutally.

He was headed for the back staircase, meaning to go and find Jody and pick his brains, but at that moment the telephone started ringing. Oliver's first reactions were that at last the lines had been repaired, but Mrs. Cooper slapped her hand over her heart and said, "Perhaps that's the police now."

"Probably nothing of the sort," said Oliver, but for all that he went, more swiftly than usual, out of the kitchen and along to the library to answer the call.

"Cairney," he barked.

"Is that Cairney House?" A female voice, very refined.

"Yes it is, Oliver Cairney speaking."

"Oh, Mr. Cairney, this is Mrs. Henderson speaking from the Strathcorrie Hotel."

Oliver braced himself. "Yes?"

"There's a young lady here, she came to inquire for her brother, who used to work here . . ."

Used to work? "Yes?"

"She said she'd been staying at Cairney."

"That's right."

"Well, I think perhaps you should come and fetch her, Mr. Cairney. She doesn't seem to be at all well, and she fainted and then she was very . . . sick." She brought the word out reluctantly as though it were rude.

"How did she get to Strathcorrie?"

"She walked part of the way she said, and then she got a lift with the snow-plough."

That meant that at least the road would be open. "And where is she now?"

"I put her to lie down . . . she seemed so unwell."

"Does she know you've called me?"

"No. I thought better not to say."

"Don't say. Don't say anything. Just keep her there till I come."

"Yes, Mr. Cairney. And I'm so sorry."

"Not at all. You were quite right to call. We were worried. Thank you. I'll be there as soon as I can."

Caroline was asleep when he came. No, not asleep, but suspended in that delicious state between sleeping and waking; warm, and comforted by the touch of blankets. Until the sound of his deep voice cut through her drowsiness like a knife and she was instantly wide awake, alert and clear-headed. She remembered saying that she had come from Cairney and cursed her own careless tongue. But the pain was gone, and the sleep refreshed her, so when, without so much as a cursory knock, Oliver Cairney threw open her door and marched in, Caroline was ready for him, with all her defences up.

"Oh, what a shame, you've come all this way, and there's really nothing wrong at all. Look." She sat up. "I'm perfectly all right." He wore a grey overcoat and a black tie and this reminded her of his brother and she went on in a rush. "It's just that it was rather a long walk, at least it wasn't all that long because I got a lift from the snow-plough." He slammed the door shut and came to lean against the brass rail at the end of the bed. "Did you bring Jody?" she asked brightly. "Because we can stay here. They've got rooms, and we'd be better to wait here till Angus gets back. He's away you see, just for another couple of days, with an American lady . . ."

Oliver said, "Shut up."

No one had ever spoken to Caroline in that voice before and she was utterly silenced. "I told you to stay at Cairney. To wait."

"I couldn't."

"Why not?"

"Because Jody told me about your brother. Mrs. Cooper told Jody. And it was so terrible us turning up, just then. I was so sorry . . . I didn't know . . ."

"How could you know?"

". . . but at such a time."

"It makes no difference one way or the other," said Oliver bluntly. "How do you feel now?"

"I'm perfectly all right."

"You fainted." It sounded like an accusation.

"So silly, I never faint."

"The trouble is, you never eat anything. If you choose to be so moronic you deserve to faint. Now get your coat on and I'll take you home."

"But I told you, we can stay here. We'll wait for Angus here."

"You can wait for Angus at Cairney." He went over to the chair and picked up the black oilskin.

Caroline frowned. She said, "Suppose I don't want to come? I don't have to "

"Suppose for once you do what you're told. Suppose you think about someone other than yourself? Mrs. Cooper was grey in the face when I got back, imagining every sort of ghastly disaster that might have happened to you."

She felt a pang of guilt. "And Jody?"

"He's all right. I left him watching television. Now, are you coming?"

There was nothing else to do. Caroline got off the bed, let him help her into the oilskin, trod her feet into the rubber boots, and then followed him meekly downstairs.

"Mrs. Henderson!"

She appeared from her office, standing behind her desk like an obliging shop-assistant.

"Oh, you found her, Mr. Cairney, that's good." She lifted the flap of the counter and came out to join them. "How are you feeling, dear?" she said to Caroline.

"I'm all right." She added on an afterthought, "Thank you,"

although it was hard to forgive Mrs. Henderson for having telephoned for Oliver.

"It was no trouble. And when Angus gets back . . ."

Oliver said, "Tell him his sister's at Cairney."

"Of course. And I'm glad you're feeling better."

Caroline made for the door. Behind her Oliver thanked Mrs. Henderson once again, and then they were both out in the cold, soft,
windy twilight, and she was clambering defeatedly back into the
Land-Rover.

They drove in silence. The promised thaw had turned the snow to
slush and the road over the hill was comparatively clear. Above, grey
clouds were being bowled aside by a west wind leaving spaces of
shining sky the colour of sapphires. Through the open window of the
Land-Rover came the smell of turf and damp peat. Curlews rose from
the margins of a small reed-fringed loch, and all at once it seemed
possible that the empty trees would soon be in bud and the long-
awaited spring almost upon them.

And Caroline was reminded of that evening in London, driving to
Arabella's with Hugh. She remembered the city's lights reflected
orange in the sky, and how she had rolled down the window and let
the wind blow her hair and wished that she was in the country. It was
only three–four days ago, and yet now it felt like a lifetime. As though
it had happened to another girl in another time entirely.

An illusion. She was Caroline Cliburn with a hundred unsolved
problems sitting on her plate. She was Caroline Cliburn and she was
going to have to get back to London before all hell broke loose. She
was Caroline Cliburn and she was going to marry Hugh Rashley. On
Tuesday.

That was real. To make it more real she thought of the house in
Milton Gardens awash with wedding presents. The white dress,
hanging in her cupboard, the caterers coming in with their trestle-
tables and their stiff white damask tableclothes. She thought of champagne glasses massed like soap bubbles, gardenias in a bouquet, the
pop of corks and the cliché of speeches; and she thought of Hugh,
considerate, organized Hugh, who had never so much as raised his
voice to Caroline, let alone tell her to shut up.

This rankled still. Indignant at the memory, she let her resentments
swell. Resentment at Angus, for letting her down just when she

needed him most; swanning off in a car with some old American dowager, leaving no address, no date of return, nothing definite. Resentment at Mrs. Henderson, with her diamanté spectacles and her air of humble efficiency, telephoning Oliver Cairney when the last thing Caroline wanted was his renewed interference. And finally resentment at Oliver himself, this overbearing man who had taken on more than could possibly be justified in the name of hospitable concern.

The Land-Rover ground its way over the crest of the hill and the road sloped away from them, leading back to Cairney. Oliver changed gear and the tyres bit deep into the slushy snow. The silence between them was thick with his disapproval. She wished that he would say something. Anything. All her resentments capsuled into an irritation that was directed solely at him. It grew until it could no longer be contained, and she said at last, frostily, "This is ridiculous."

"What is ridiculous?" His chill voice matched her own.

"The whole situation. Everything."

"I don't know enough about the situation to comment on that. In fact, apart from knowing that you and Jody appeared at Cairney out of a snow storm, I am completely in the dark."

"It isn't your business," said Caroline, sounding ruder than she had meant to.

"But what is my business is seeing that your brother doesn't have to suffer from any more of your idiocies."

"If Angus had been at Strathcorrie . . ."

He did not let her finish. "That's hypothetical. He wasn't. And I have a strange feeling that you weren't too surprised. What sort of a guy is he, anyway?" Caroline maintained what she hoped was a dignified silence. Oliver said "I see" in the smug voice of one who understands all.

"No, you don't. You don't know a thing about him. You don't even understand."

"Oh, shut up," said Oliver, unforgivably, for the second time, and Caroline turned away from him and stared out of the darkened window, so that he would neither see nor guess at the smarting prick of tears that suddenly stung her eyes.

In the dusk the house stood foursquare, yellow lights suffused from behind drawn curtains. Oliver stopped the Land-Rover at the door and got out, and slowly, reluctantly, Caroline climbed down too, and followed him up the steps and passed him as he stood aside, holding the odor open, letting her go ahead. Feeling like a naughty child, brought to book, she would not even look at him. The door slammed shut behind them, and at once, as though this sound were a signal, there came the sound of Jody's voice. A door opened, his footsteps came up the passage from the kitchen. He appeared at a run, then stopped dead when he saw that only two people stood there. His eyes went to the door behind Caroline and then back to her face. He was very still.

"Angus?" he said.

He had been expecting her to bring Angus back with her. She said, hating having to tell him, "Angus wasn't there."

There was a silence. Then Jody said casually, "You didn't find him."

"He's been there, working there. But he's gone away for a few days." She went on, trying to sound confident. "He'll be back. In a day or so. There's nothing to worry about."

"But Mrs. Cooper said you were ill."

"I'm not," said Caroline quickly.

"But she said . . ."

Oliver interrupted. "All that's wrong with your sister is that she never does what she's told and she never eats anything." He sounded thoroughly put out. Jody watched as he unbuttoned his tweed overcoat and slung it over the end of the banister. "Where's Mrs. Cooper?"

"In the kitchen."

"Go and tell her everything's all right. I've brought Caroline back and she's going to bed and to have some supper and tomorrow she'll be as right as rain." And when Jody still hesitated, Oliver went over and turned him and gave him a gentle shove in the direction from whence he had appeared. "Go on. There's nothing to worry about. I promise you."

Jody departed. The kitchen door swung shut; distantly, they heard his voice, relaying the message. Oliver turned to Caroline.

"And now," he said with deceptive pleasantness, "you are going upstairs to bed, and Mrs. Cooper will bring you some supper on a tray. It's as simple as that."

The tone of his voice kindled an old, rare stubbornness. A stubbornness that had, from time to time, won Caroline her own way in childhood; had finally broken down her stepmother's objections to the Drama School. Hugh, perhaps, had early recognized this streak in her character, for his handling of her had always been tactful to a degree, coaxing, suggesting, leading her by a string when she would have refused to be driven.

Now, she pondered on the idea of making a final terrible scene, but, as Oliver Cairney continued to stand, waiting, politely implacable, her resolution faded. Finding excuses for her surrender, she told herself that she was tired, too tired for any further arguments. And the thought of bed and warmth and privacy was suddenly very appealing. Without a word, she turned away from him and went upstairs, a step at a time, her hand running the length of the long, polished banister rail.

When she had gone Oliver made his way back to the kitchen where he found Mrs. Cooper preparing supper and Jody at the scrubbed table, struggling with an elderly jigsaw which, when completed, would be a picture of an old-fashioned steam engine. Oliver remembered the jigsaw, remembered doing it with his mother and Charles to help. Whiling away long wet afternoons, waiting for the rain to stop so that they could get out of doors again to play.

He leaned over Jody's shoulder. "You're doing very well," he told him.

"I can't find that bit. With the sky and the bit of branch. If I could find that bit, I could join this other chunk up."

Oliver started to search for the elusive piece. From the stove Mrs. Cooper said, "Is the young lady all right?"

Oliver did not look up. "Yes, she's all right. She's gone to bed."

"What happened to her?" Jody asked.

"She fainted and then she was sick."

"I hate being sick."

Oliver grinned. "So do I."

"I'm sieving a nice wee bowl of broth," said Mrs.. Cooper. "When you're not well, the last thing you want is a supper that lies heavy on your stomach."

Oliver agreed that indeed you didn't. He ran the missing piece of jigsaw to earth and handed it to Jody.

"How's that?"

"That's it." Jody was delighted at Oliver's cleverness. "Oh, thank you, I've been looking and looking at that bit and never even saw it was the right one." He looked up to smile. "It helps having two people to do it, doesn't it? Will you go on helping?"

"Well, right now I'm going to have a bath and then I'm going to have a drink, and then we'll have supper together, you and I. But after supper, we'll see if we can finish the jigsaw."

"Was it yours?"

"Mine, or Charles's, I can't remember."

"It's a funny sort of train."

"Steam engines were splendid. They made such a magnificent noise."

"I know. I've seen them on films."

He had his bath and dressed and was on his way downstairs, headed for the library and the drink he had promised himself when he remembered, out of the blue, that he was due to dine, that very evening, at Rossie Hill. The shock of this, however, was not so great as the sense of surprise that he had forgotten the appointment at all. But, despite the fact that he had seen Duncan Fraser at lunchtime, and had even spoken of the projected dinner, the frantic events of the afternoon and evening had succeeded in driving it clean out of his head.

And now it was half past seven and he was dressed not in a dinner-suit, but in an old polo-necked sweater and a pair of washed-out corduroys. For a moment he hesitated, pulling at his lower lip, and trying to decide what to do, but his mind was finally made up by the image of Jody, who had spent a lonely and distressing afternoon, and whom Oliver had promised company for the evening, and assistance with the jigsaw puzzle. That settled it. He went along to the library, picked up the receiver and dialled the Rossie Hill number. After a moment Liz herself answered the call.

"Hallo."

"Liz."

"Oh, Oliver, are you ringing to say you'll be late? Because if so it doesn't matter, I forgot to put the pheasant in and besides . . ."

He interrupted her. "No, I didn't ring for that. I rang to call off. I can't make it."

"But . . . I . . . Father said . . ." and then in quite a different voice, "Are you all right?" She sounded as though he might suddenly have gone mad. "Not ill, or anything?"

"No. It's just that I can't make it . . . I'll explain . . ."

She said, her voice cool, "It wouldn't have anything to do with the girl and the boy you've got staying at Cairney?"

Oliver was astonished. He had said nothing to Duncan about the Cliburns, not with any intention of concealment, but simply because there had been other and more important subjects to discuss. "How did you know?"

"Oh, the old glen grapevine. Don't forget, our Mrs. Douglas is Cooper's sister-in-law. You can't keep any secrets living up here, Oliver. You should know that by now."

He felt vaguely nettled, as though she were accusing him of being deceitful.

"It's no secret."

"Are they still there?"

"Yes."

"I shall have to come and investigate. It's intriguing."

He ignored the innuendo in her voice, and dropped the subject. "Do you forgive me for being so mannerless this evening, and crying off at such short notice?"

"It doesn't matter. These little things crop up from time to time. It just means all the more pheasant for Father and me. But come another night."

"If you'll ask me."

"I'm asking you now." But her voice was still crisp. "All you have to do, once your social life has sorted itself out, is to give me a ring."

"I'll do that," said Oliver.

" 'Bye, then."

"Goodbye."

But before the word was out of his mouth, she had already put down her receiver and cut him off.

She was annoyed with him and with some reason. He thought wistfully of the carefully set dinner-table, the candles, the pheasant and the wine. Dinner at Rossie Hill was never, at any time, an occasion to be sneezed at. He swore softly, hating the whole day, wishing for it to be over. He poured himself a drink, stronger than usual, added a splash of soda, poured some of it mindlessly down his throat, and then, feeling remotely comforted, went to look for Jody.

But he never got that far. Instead, in the passage he met Mrs. Cooper, carrying a tray. There was a strange expression on her face, almost furtive, and when she saw him, her pace quickened so that she could get through the kitchen door before he reached her side.

"What's wrong, Mrs. Cooper?"

With her back against the swing-door she stopped, looking anguished.

"She won't eat a mouthful, Oliver." He looked at the tray, then took the lid off the soup bowl. Steam rose in a fragrant cloud. "I did my best, I told her what you said, but she won't eat a mouthful. She says she's frightened of being sick again."

Oliver put the lid back on the soup bowl, the whisky glass on the tray, then took the lot from Mrs. Cooper's hands.

He said, "We'll see about that."

He was tired and depressed no longer, simply marvellously angry. Exasperated beyond words. He marched upstairs, two at a time, went down the passage and burst into the Cairney guest room without so much as a knock on the door. She lay in the middle of the huge, pink-quilted double bed, pillows scattered on the floor, ringed by the small light of a pink-shaded bedside lamp.

Seeing her thus only increased his irritation. She was a bloody girl, she walked into his house, turned everything upside down, ruined his evening and finally lay in his own spare bed refusing to eat and driving everybody up the wall. He strode across the room and dumped the tray with some force down upon the bedside-table. The lamp shook slightly, his whisky danced and splashed.

She watched him flatly from the bed, her eyes enormous, her hair spread and tangled like skeins of creamy silk. Without a word he began gathering up the pillows, then pulled her into a sitting position and stuffed them behind her, as though she were a rag doll incapable of sitting up on her own.

Her expression was mutinous, her underlip swollen as a spoiled child's. He picked the napkin off the tray and tied it around her neck as though he had intentions of throttling her. He took the lid off the soup bowl.

She said, clearly, "If you make me eat that, I shall be sick."

Oliver reached for the spoon. "And if you are sick I shall beat you."

The lower lip trembled at the injustice of such a threat. "Now, or when I'm well again?" she inquired bitterly.

"Both," said Oliver brutally. "Now open your mouth."

When she did, more out of astonishment than anything else, he poured in the first spoonful. As she swallowed it, she gagged slightly, and sent him a look of reproachful appeal, to which he simply raised a cautionary eyebrow. The second spoonful went down. And the third. And the fourth. By now she had started to cry. Silently her eyes filled with tears, over-spilled, poured down her cheeks. Oliver ignored them, relentlessly feeding her the broth. By the time it was finished she was awash with weeping. He set down the empty bowl on the tray, and said, without sympathy, "You see, you weren't sick."

Caroline gave a great sob, incapable of comment. All at once his temper died, he wanted to smile, he was filled with a ridiculous and tender amusement. His final burst of rage, like a thunderstorm, had cleared his own personal air, and he was suddenly quite calm and relaxed, with all the troubles and frustrations of the day slotted away in their correct perspectives. All that remained was this peaceful, pretty room, the glow of the pink-shaded light, the remains of his whisky in its glass, and Caroline Cliburn, finally fed and subdued.

He pulled the napkin gently free of her neck and handed it to her. "Perhaps," he suggested, "you could use this as a handkerchief."

She sent him a grateful look and took it, wiped at cheeks, at eyes, and finally, lustily, blew her nose. A strand of hair lying close to her cheek was wet from her tears, and he put out a finger to smooth it back, away behind her ear.

It was a small, instinctive action of comfort, unpremeditated, but the unexpected physical contact sparked off a chain reaction. For an instant Caroline's face was suffused with astonishment, and then an overwhelming relief. As though it were the most natural thing in the world, she leaned forward and pressed her forehead against the rough wool of his sweater, and without thinking about it, he wrapped his arms around her thin shoulders and pulled her close, the top of her silky head tight beneath his chin. He could feel her fragility, her very bones, the beating of her heart. After a little he said, "You'll really have to tell me what it's all about, won't you?"

And Caroline nodded, thumping her head against his chest. "Yes," came her muffled voice. "I really think I will."

She started, where it had all started, on Aphros. "We went to live there after my mother died. Jody was just a baby, he could speak Greek before he spoke English. My father was an architect, he went out there to design houses, but English people started discovering Aphros and wanting to live there, and he ended up as a sort of property agent, buying houses and overseeing while they were converted and that sort of thing. Perhaps if Angus had been brought up in

England he would have been different. I don't know. But we went to local schools because my father couldn't afford to send us home."

She broke off, and started trying to explain about Angus. "He'd always lived such a free life. My father never bothered about us or where we were. He knew we were safe. Angus spent most of his time with the fishermen and when he left school, he just stayed on Aphros and it never seemed to occur to anybody that he might get a job. And then Diana came."

"Your stepmother."

"Yes. She came to the island to buy a house, she came to my father to ask him to act as her agent. But she never bought the house, because she married him instead and lived with us."

"Did that make a lot of difference?"

"To Jody it did. And to me. But not to Angus. Never to Angus."

"Did you like her?"

"Yes." Caroline pleated the edge of the sheet, carefully, precisely, as though it were a finicky task directed by Diana and to be accomplished to her own exact standards. "Yes, I liked her. And so did Jody. But Angus was too old to be influenced by her and she . . . she was too wise to try to influence him. But then my father died, and she said that we must all come back to London, but Angus didn't want to come. He didn't want to stay on Aphros either. He bought a second-hand Mini Moke and he went to India, through Syria and Turkey, and we used to get postcards from him of outlandish places and nothing much else."

"But you came back to London?"

"Yes. Diana had a house in Milton Gardens. That's where we still live."

"And Angus?"

"He came there once, but it didn't work. He and Diana had a terrible row because he wouldn't conform or cut his hair or shave his beard or put on a pair of shoes. You know. And anyway, by that time Diana had married again, an old boy-friend called Shaun Carpenter. So now she's Mrs. Carpenter."

"And Mr. Carpenter?"

"He's nice, but he's not a strong enough character for Diana. She gets her own way, she manipulates people, all of us, really. But in the most tactful possible way. It's hard to describe."

"And what were you doing all this time?"

"Oh, I finished school and then I went to Drama School." She looked at Oliver with the ghost of a smile. "Diana didn't want that. She was frightened I'd turn into a hippie or go on to drugs or get like Angus."

Oliver grinned. "And did you?"

"No. But she also said I wouldn't stay the course and she was right. I mean, I got through Drama School all right, and I even got a job in a Repertory theatre, but then . . ." She stopped. Oliver's face was oddly gentle, his eyes very understanding. He was easy to talk to. She had not realized how easy he would be to talk to. He had done nothing, all day, but indicate in every possible way that he thought she was a fool, but instinctively, she knew that he would not call her a fool, simply because she had fallen in love with the wrong man. ". . . well, I got involved with this man. And I was stupid, I suppose, and innocent, and I thought that he wanted to go on being involved with me. But actors are single-minded creatures, and he was very career-minded and ambitious and he moved on and left me behind. He was called Drennan Colefield and he's quite famous now. You've maybe heard of him . . ."

"Yes, I have."

". . . he married a French actress. I think they live in Hollywood now. He's going to make a string of films. Anyway, after Drennan everything went wrong, and then I got pneumonia, and in the end I just gave it all up."

She began to pleat the sheet again. "And Angus?" Oliver prompted gently. "When did he turn up in Scotland?"

"Jody got a letter from him, a week or two ago. But he didn't tell about it until last Sunday night."

"And why was it so important to see him again?"

"Because of Diana and Shaun going to Canada. Shaun's got this posting to Canada, and they're going as soon as . . . well, very soon. And they're taking Jody with them. And Jody doesn't want to go, although Diana doesn't know that. But he told me and he asked me to come to Scotland with him and find Angus. He thought Angus might come to London and make a home for Jody so that Jody doesn't have to go."

"Is that likely to happen?"

Caroline said, with bleak truth, "Not particularly. But I had to try. For Jody's sake I had to try."

"Couldn't Jody stay with you?"

"No."

"Why not?"

Caroline shrugged. "It just wouldn't work out. Anyway, Diana would never agree to it. But Angus is different. Angus is twenty-five now. If Angus wanted to keep Jody, Diana couldn't stop him."

"I see."

"And so we came to find him. And we borrowed the car from Caleb Ash, he's a friend of my father's but he lives in London, in the flat at the other end of Diana's garden. He likes Diana, but I don't think he approves of the way she organizes us all and runs our lives. That's why he lent us his car, on condition we told him where we were coming."

"But you didn't tell Diana?"

"We said we were coming to Scotland. That was all. We left a letter. If we'd told her more, she'd have caught up with us long before we got here. She's that sort of person."

"Isn't she going to be very worried about you?"

"I expect so. But we said we'd be back on Friday . . ."

"But you won't. Not if Angus doesn't get back."

"I know."

"Don't you think it might be a good idea to telephone her?"

"No. Not yet. For Jody's sake, we mustn't."

"She'd understand, surely."

"In a way, but not entirely. If Angus were a different sort of person . . ." Her voice tailed hopelessly away.

"So what are we going to do?" asked Oliver.

The "we" disarmed her. She said "I don't know" but the desperate expression had gone from her face. And then, hopefully, "Wait?"

"For how long?"

"Till Friday. And then, I promise you, we'll call Diana and we'll go back to London."

Oliver considered this, and finally, with some reluctance, agreed. "Not that I approve," he added.

Caroline smiled. "That's nothing new. You've been radiating disapproval ever since we walked in through your door."

"With, you must admit, some justification."

"The only reason I went to Strathcorrie today was because of learning about your brother. I wouldn't have gone if it hadn't been for that. I felt so terrible, embarrassed, knowing we'd turned up at such a desperate time."

"It's not desperate now. It's all over."

"What are you going to do?"

"Sell Cairney and go back to London."

"Isn't that very sad?"

"Sad, but not the end of the world. Cairney, the way I remember it, is inside my head, indestructible. It's not so much the house as all the good things that happened in it. The underpinnings of a very happy life. I won't lose any of that even if I live to be an old man with white hair and no teeth."

"Like Aphros," said Caroline. "Aphros is like that for Jody and me. All the nice things that happen to me are nice because they remind me of Aphros. Sun and white houses and blue skies and winds blowing off the sea, and the smell of pine trees, and geraniums in pots. What was your brother like? Was he like you?"

"He was nice, the nicest guy in the world and he wasn't like me."

"How was he?"

"Red-headed and hard working and up to his ears in Cairney. He was a good farmer. He was a good man."

"If Angus had been like that, things would have been so different."

"If Angus had been like my brother Charles you would never have come to Scotland to look for him, never come to Cairney, and then I should never have met you both."

"That surely can't be such a good thing."

"But undoubtedly what Mrs. Cooper would call an 'experience.' "

They laughed together. Their laughter was interrupted by a knock on the door, and when Caroline said "Come in," the door opened and Jody put his head around its edge.

"Jody."

He came slowly into the room. "Oliver, Mrs. Cooper says to tell you supper's ready."

"Good heavens, is it that time already?" Oliver looked at his watch. "All right. I'm on my way."

Jody came to his sister's side. "Are you feeling better now?"

"Yes, much better."

Oliver stood up, picked up the empty tray and started for the door. "How's the jigsaw going?" he asked.

"I've done a bit more, but not much."

"We'll sit up all night, till it's finished." He said to Caroline, "You go to sleep now. We'll see you in the morning."

"Good night," said Jody.

"Good night, Jody."

When they had gone, she turned off the bedside lamp. Starlight shone from beyond the open window and the half-drawn curtains. A curlew called and a stirring of wind moved in the tall pines. Caroline was already on the edge of sleep, but before she finally dropped off there were two important and puzzling thoughts which occurred to her.

The first was that, after all this time, her affair with Drennan Colefield was finally over. She had talked about him, spoken his name, but the magic had gone. He was in the past now, finished and done with, and it was as though a great weight had been lifted from her shoulders. She was free again.

The second thought was even more confusing. For, although she had told Oliver everything else, she had somehow not been able to bring herself to mention Hugh. She knew that there had to be a reason for this . . . there was a reason for everything . . . but she was asleep before there was time to start working it out.

6

The next morning, it was April and it was spring. Just like that, spring had arrived. The wind dropped, the sun rose into a cloudless sky, the barometer soared and the temperature with it. The air was balmy, soft, smelling of newly-turned earth. The snow melted to nothing, revealing drifts of snowdrops and tiny, early crocuses, and under the beech trees carpets of shiny yellow aconites. Birds sang, doors stood open to the welcome warmth, washing lines billowed with curtains and blankets and other evidence of spring cleaning.

At Rossie Hill, at about ten o'clock in the morning, the telephone began to ring. Duncan Fraser was out, but Liz was in the flower pantry, arranging a vase of pussy-willow sprigs and tall King Alfred daffodils. She put down her secateurs, dried her hands and went to answer the call.

"Hallo?"

"Elizabeth!"

It was her mother from London, sounding expectant, and Liz frowned. She was still smarting from Oliver's abrupt rejection of the night before, and consequently not in the best of moods.

Elaine Haldane, however, was not to know this. "Darling, so extravagant ringing in the morning, but I simply had to know how everything went. I knew you'd never call me. How did the dinner-party go?"

Liz, resigned, pulled up a chair and slumped into it.

"It didn't," she said.

"What do you mean?"

"At the last moment Oliver couldn't come. The dinner-party never happened."

"Oh, dear, how disappointing, and I was longing to hear all about it. You sounded so excited." She waited, and then when her daughter was forthcoming with no more information, added tentatively, "You haven't had a row or anything?"

Liz laughed softly. "No, of course not. He just couldn't make it. He's busy, I guess. Dad gave him lunch yesterday and they talked business the entire time. Incidentally, Dad's going to buy Cairney."

"Well, that'll keep *him* busy at any rate," Elaine said, in a waspish fashion. "Oh, poor Oliver, what a prospect for him. He's going through a very thin time. You must be very patient, darling, and *very* understanding."

Liz did not want to talk about Oliver any more. To change the subject she said, "What's happening in the great city?"

"All sorts of things. We're not going back to Paris for another week or two. Parker's involved with some visiting firemen from New York, so we're staying here. It's fun seeing people, hearing all the news. Oh, I know what I *must* tell you. The *most* extraordinary thing has happened."

Liz recognized the gossipy tone in her mother's voice, knew that the telephone call would last for at least another ten minutes. She reached for a cigarette and settled down to listen.

"You know Diana Carpenter, and Shaun? Well, Diana's step-children have disappeared. Yes, literally, disappeared. Off the face of the earth. All they left was a letter saying they'd gone to Scotland—of all places—to find their brother Angus. And of course he's the most terrible hippie-type, Diana's had a terribly worrying time with him. Spends his time seeking the truth in India or wherever it is these people think they're going to find it. I would have thought Scotland would be the last place he'd come to, nothing but down-to-earth tweeds and haggis. I must say I always thought Caroline was rather an *odd* girl. She tried to go on the stage once, and it was the most terrible failure, but I never thought she'd do anything so bizarre as simply *disappear*."

"What's Diana doing about it?"

"My dear, what can she do? And the last thing she wants is to call the police in. After all, although the boy is only a child, the girl *is* supposed to be adult . . . she should be able to look after him. And Diana's terrified of the papers getting on to the story and splashing it all over the front pages of the evening editions. And if that wasn't enough, the wedding's on Tuesday, and Hugh does have a certain professional reputation to maintain."

"Wedding?"

"Caroline's wedding." Elaine sounded exasperated as though Liz was being very stupid. "Caroline is marrying Diana's brother, Hugh Rashley. On Tuesday. The wedding rehearsal's on Monday and they don't even know where she is. It's all too distressing. I always thought she was an odd girl, didn't you?"

"I don't know. I never met her."

"No, of course you haven't. I always forget. Silly of me. But you know I always thought she was rather fond of Diana, I never thought she'd do this to her. Oh, darling, you won't do it to me, will you, when you eventually do get married? And let's hope it's very soon now and to the Right Man. No mentioning names, but you know who I mean. And now I simply must go. I've got a hair appointment and I'm going to be late as it is. And, darling, don't fret about Oliver, just go and see him and be cosy and understanding. I'm sure everything will be all right. And I'm longing to see you. Come back soon."

"I will."

"Goodbye, darling." And then an unconvincing afterthought: "My love to your father."

Later still in the morning Caroline Cliburn lay, supine on a bed of heather, the sun's warmth like a cloak on the length of her body, her arm flung across her eyes against its dazzling brightness. Thus blinded, her other senses became twice as sharp. She heard curlews, the distant cawing of a crow, the lap of water, the tiny sough of some mysterious, unfelt breeze. She smelt the pure sweetness of snow and clear water and earth, mossy and damp and dark with peat. She felt the cool nose of Lisa, the old labrador, who lay beside her, and pressed her nose into Caroline's hand.

Beside her, Oliver Cairney sat, smoking a cigarette, his hands loose between his knees, watching Jody's exertions as the boy struggled, out in the middle of the little loch, with a bulky rowboat and a pair of oars too long for him. Every now and then came an ominous splash, and Caroline would raise her head to investigate, see that he had merely caught a crab, or was driving the rowboat around in small circles, and satisfied that he was not on the point of drowning himself, lie back in the heather and cover her eyes once more.

Oliver said, "If I hadn't tied him up in that life-jacket, you'd be running up and down the bank like a demented hen."

"No, I wouldn't. I'd be out there with him."

"Which would make two of you ripe for drowning." The heather pricked through her shirt, a nameless bug walked up her arm. She sat up, brushing the bug away, screwing her face up into the sunshine.

"You could hardly believe it, could you? Two days ago and Jody and I were in the middle of a blizzard. And now this." The surface of the loch was still and clear, blue as summer with reflected sky. Beyond the distant reed-fringed bank, the moor rose in a series of swelling, heathery slopes, crested at the peak by an out-crop of rock, like a beacon on the top of a mountain. She could see the distant shapes of a flock of grazing sheep, hear in the still morning, their plaintive baa-ing. The rowboat, so manfully oared, creaked slowly across the surface of the water. Jody's hair stood up on end, and his face was beginning to turn pink.

She said, "It *is* a lovely place. I hadn't realized how lovely it was."

"This is the best time. Now and for another month or two when the beech leaves open and the daffodils come out and all of a sudden it's summer. And then in October, it's beautiful again, the trees flaming out, the sky deep blue and all the heather turned purple."

"Won't you miss it terribly?"

"Of course I will, but there's nothing to be done about it."

"You're going to sell it?"

"Yes." He dropped the stub of his cigarette, stamped it out with the heel of his shoe.

"Have you got a buyer?"

"Yes. Duncan Fraser. My neighbour. He lives across the glen, you can't see his house, because it's hidden by that stand of pines, but he wants the land to take in with his own. It's simply a question of doing away with the march fences."

"And your house?"

"That'll have to go separately. I've got to talk to the lawyers about that. I said I'd go down to Relkirk this afternoon and see them, see if we can thrash something out."

"Won't you keep *any* of Cairney?"

"How you do harp on a subject."

"Men are usually sentimental about tradition, and land."

"Perhaps I am."

"But you don't mind living in London?"

"Good God, no. I love it."

"What do you do?"

"I work for Bankfoot and Balcarries. And if you don't know what they do, they're one of the largest engineering consultants in the country."

"And where do you live?"

"In a flat, just off the Fulham Road."

"Not very far from us." She smiled to think how close they had lived, without ever meeting each other. "It's funny, isn't it? London's so big, and yet you can come to Scotland and meet your next-door neighbour. Is it a nice flat?"

"I like it."

She tried to picture it, but failed utterly because it was impossible to imagine Oliver away from Cairney.

"Is it big or small?"

"Quite big. Big rooms. It's the ground floor of an old house."

"Have you got a garden?"

"Yes. Rather overrun by my neighbour's cat. And a big sitting-room and a kitchen where I eat, and a couple of bedrooms and a bathroom. All mod. cons. in fact, except that my car has to moulder at the pavement's edge in all weathers. Now what else do you want to know?"

"Nothing."

"The colour of the curtains? Crushed elephant's breath." He cupped his hand to his mouth and shouted out across the water. "Hey, Jody!"

Jody paused and looked around, the oars held high and dripping. "I think you've had enough. Come along in now."

"All right."

"That's it. Pull with the left oar. No, the *left*, you idiot! That's the way." He got to his feet and walked down to the end of the wooden jetty and stood waiting for the rowboat's slow, splashy progress to bring it within reach. Then he crouched down to reach for the painter and draw it alongside. Beaming, Jody unshipped the heavy oars, and Oliver took them and tied up the boat while Jody clambered out. He came back up the jetty towards his sister, and she saw that his sneakers were soaking and his jeans wet to the knee. He was delighted with himself.

"You did very well," Caroline told him.

"I'd have done better if the oars hadn't been so big." He struggled with the knots on the life-jacket and pulled it off over his head. "I've been thinking, Caroline, wouldn't it be nice if we could stay here for ever? It's got everything anybody could want."

Caroline had been thinking this at intervals throughout the morning; and then telling herself, at equal intervals, not to be such a fool. Now, she told Jody not to be a fool, and his face was surprised at the impatience in her voice.

Oliver tightened the rope on the wooden bollard, shouldered the heavy oars and carried them over to the ramshackle boat house to put them away. Jody picked up the life-jacket and went to put that away as well, and they shut the sagging door and came back to Caroline over the springy turf, the tall young man and the freckled boy, with the sun behind them and the dazzle of water.

They reached her side. "Up you get," said Oliver and reached out a hand to pull her to her feet. Lisa scrambled up as well, and stood waving her tail, as if anticipating some pleasant excursion.

"This was meant to be a walk of an exploration or something," Oliver went on. "And all we've done is sit in the sun and watch Jody take all the exercise."

Jody asked, "Where shall we go now?"

"There's something I want to show you . . . it's just round the corner."

They followed him, Indian file, trailing the small sheep tracks that netted the margins of the loch. They crested a rise and the loch took a sharp turn and at its end stood a small, derelict cottage.

"Is that what you wanted to show us?" asked Jody.

"Yes."

"It's a ruin."

"I know. It hasn't been lived in for years. Charles and I used to play here. Once we were even allowed to sleep out."

"Who used to live here?"

"I don't know. A shepherd. Or a crofter. Those little walls are old sheep pens and there's a rowan in the garden. In the old days, country people used to plant rowans at their doors because they thought they brought good fortune."

"I don't know what a rowan looks like."

"In England they call them Mountain Ash. They have feathery leaves and bright red berries, rather like holly."

As they came closer to the house Caroline saw that it was not as derelict as it had first appeared. Stone built, it had retained a certain air of solidity, and although the corrugated iron roof had fallen into disrepair, and the door hung from its hinges, it was clear that it had once been an entirely respectable dwelling, snug in the fold of the hill, with the traces of a garden still visible between the drystone walls. They went up the ghost of the path, and in through the door, Oliver prudently ducking his head beneath the low lintel, and there was one big room, with a rusty iron stove at one end, and a broken chair, and on the floor, the remains of a swallow's nest. The floor was cracked and gaping and stained with bird droppings, and the slanting sun rays danced with motes of dust.

In the corner a rotted ladder led to an upper floor.

"Desirable, detached, two-storey dwelling house," said Oliver. "Who wants to go up?"

Jody wrinkled his nose. "I don't." He was secretly afraid of spiders. "I'm going back to the garden. I want to look at the rowan tree. Come along, Lisa, you come with me."

So Oliver and Caroline were left alone to mount the rotting ladder, which was missing more rungs than it had kept. They climbed into a loft that was splashed with sunlight that poured through the holes in the gaping roof. The floor planks were rotten and breaking, but the crossbeams beneath them sound, and there was just space for Oliver to stand erect, in the very centre of the room, with the top of his head only half an inch from the ridgepole.

Caroline stuck her head cautiously out of one of the holes in the roof and saw Jody in the garden below, swinging like a monkey from a branch of the rowan. She saw the curving length of the loch, the green of the first of the farm fields, cattle grazing, brown and white like toys, and in the far distance, the line of the main road. She withdrew her head and turned to Oliver. He had a cobweb on his chin and he said in Cockney, "How about it, lidy? With a lick of paint you won't know the place?"

"But you couldn't do anything with it, could you? Seriously."

"I don't know. It just occurred to me that perhaps it would be possible. If I can sell Cairney House then I could maybe afford to spend some money on this place."

"But there's no running water."

"I could fix that."

"Or drains."

"Septic tank."

"Or electricity."

"Lamps. Candles. Much more flattering."

"And what would you cook on?"

"Calor gas."

"And when would you use it?"

"Week-ends. Holidays. I could bring my children here."

"I didn't know you had any."

"I haven't yet. That I know of. But when I get married, it would be a desirable little property to have under my belt. It would also mean that I still owned a little bit of Cairney. Which should set your sentimental heart at rest."

"So it does matter to you."

"Caroline, life is too short to look back over your shoulder. You only lose the way and stumble and probably fall flat on your face. I'd rather look forward."

"But this house . . ."

"It was just an idea. I thought it might amuse you to see it. Come on now, we must get back or Mrs. Cooper will think we're all drowned."

He went first down the ladder, cautiously feeling for each surviving rung before he put his weight on it. At the bottom he waited for Caroline, holding the ladder steady between his hands. But half-way down, she became stranded, unable either to go up or down. She started to laugh and he told her to jump, and she said that she couldn't jump, and Oliver said any fool could jump, but by then Caroline was laughing too much to do anything constructive, and finally, inevitably, she slipped, there was the ominous crack of rotted wood, and her descent finished in an undignified slither before Oliver finally caught her in his arms.

There was a sprig of heather in her pale hair, her sweater felt warm from the sunshine, and the long sleep of the night before had wiped the smudges from beneath her eyes. Her skin was smooth and faintly pink, her face turned up to his, her mouth open in laughter. Without thought, without hesitation, he bent and kissed her. Suddenly, it was very quiet. For an instant she stayed still, and then she put the palms of her hands against his chest and pushed him gently away. The laughter had gone from her face, and there was an expression in her eyes that he had never seen there before.

She said at last, "It was just the day."

"What's that meant to mean?"

"Part of a nice day. The sunshine. Spring."

"Does that make any difference?"

"I don't know."

She moved away from him, out of his arms, turned and went towards the door. She stood there, leaning a shoulder against the doorpost, silhouetted against the light, her tangled hair an aureole about the neat shape of her head.

She said, "It's a darling house. I think you should keep it."

Jody had abandoned the rowan, had been lured back to the water's edge, was skimming stones trying to make them jump, and driving Lisa insane because she didn't know whether she was meant to plunge in and retrieve them, or stay where she was. Caroline picked up a flat pebble and threw it and it jumped three times before it sank out of sight.

Jody was furious. "I wish you'd show me. Show me how you do it," but Caroline turned away from him because she couldn't reply, and she didn't want him to see her face. Because all at once she knew why she had fallen out of love with the memory of Drennan Colefield. And, which was much more frightening, she knew why she had not told Oliver that she was going to marry Hugh.

Liz, coming to Cairney, found it quiet and apparently deserted. She stopped her car at the door, killed the engine and waited for someone to come out and greet her. Nobody did. But the door stood open, so she got out of the car and went indoors and stood in the middle of the hall and said Oliver's name. Still no response, but domestic noises came from the direction of the kitchen, and familiar as she was with the house, Liz took herself down the passage and through the swing door, and surprised Mrs. Cooper who had just come indoors from hanging out a line of clothes.

She started elaborately, and placed her hand over her heart. "Liz!" She had known Liz since she was a child and would never have thought of calling her Miss Fraser.

"Sorry. I didn't meant to frighten you. I thought the house was deserted."

"Oliver's out. He took . . . the others with him." There was only the slightest hesitation but Liz latched on to it at once. She raised her eyebrows.

"You mean your unexpected visitors? I've been hearing all about them."

"Och, they're just a couple of youngsters. Oliver took them down to the loch, the wee boy wanted to see the boat." She looked up at the kitchen clock. "But they'll be back any time, they're having an early dinner, for Oliver has to get back to Relkirk this afternoon to have another wee chat with the lawyer. Will you wait? Will you stay for lunch?"

"I won't stay for lunch, but I'll wait a moment, and if they don't come, I'll go home. I only came to see how Oliver was getting on."

"He's really been great," Mrs. Cooper told her. "In a way all this happening has been a good thing, taken his mind off his loss."

"All this?" Liz prompted gently.

"Well, the young ones turning up like that, with their car broken down and nowhere to go."

"They came by car?"

"Yes, drove from London seemingly. The car was in a terrible mess, right in the ditch, and on top of that frozen solid after a night in the open. But Cooper took it down to the garage, and they phoned early this morning and he went to pick it up and bring it back. It's in the shed at the back of the house now, all ready for when they want to go away again."

"When are they going?" Liz kept her voice casual and very cool.

"I couldn't be sure. Nothing's been said to me. There's some talk about their brother staying in Strathcorrie, but he's away just now, and I think they're hoping to wait until he gets back." She added, "But if you see Oliver, he'll give you all the news himself. They're just down at the loch. If you wanted, you could start off and meet them half way."

"Maybe I'll do that," said Liz.

But she didn't. She went back outside and settled herself on the stone bench outside the library window, put on her dark glasses, lit a cigarette and stretched out her body to the sun.

It was very quiet, so that she heard their voices in the still morning air long before they actually appeared. The garden path curved away around the perimeter of a beech hedge, and as they came around this, into view, they seemed engrossed in conversation and did not immediately see Liz sitting there, waiting for them. The small boy led the way, and a pace or two behind him, Oliver, in an ancient tweed jacket and with red cotton handkerchief knotted at his throat, pulled the girl along by the hand, as though she had become tired from the walk and started to lag behind.

He was talking. Liz heard the deep tones of his voice without being able to catch the words. Then the girl halted, and bent over, as if to ease a stone out of her shoe. A long curtain of pale hair fell across her face, and Oliver stopped, too, to wait for her, patient, his dark head bent down, her hand still in his. And Liz saw this and all at once she was afraid. She felt she was being shut out of something, as though the three of them were in some sort of a conspiracy against her. The stone was finally removed. Oliver turned to resume the climb, and then caught sight of the dark blue Triumph parked in front of the house. He saw Liz. She dropped her cigarette and stubbed it out under the heel of her shoe and stood up and went to meet them, but Oliver had let go of the girl's hand and strode out ahead of the others, taking the steep grassy bank at a run, and meeting Liz at the top.

"Liz."

"Hallo, Oliver."

He thought that she looked better than ever, in tight buff pants and a fringed leather jacket. He took her hands and kissed her. He said, "Have you come to give me hell about last night?"

"No," said Liz frankly, and her eyes looked over his shoulder to where Caroline and Jody, more slowly, were coming over the grass. "I told you I was intrigued by your sudden rash of house guests. I've come to say how do you do."

"We went down to the loch." He turned towards the others. "Caroline, this is Liz Fraser, she and her father are my nearest neighbours and she's been in and out of Cairney since she was knee-high to a grasshopper. I showed you their house this morning, through the trees. Liz, this is Caroline Cliburn, and this is Jody."

"How do you do," said Caroline. They shook hands. Liz took off her dark glasses, and it was something of a shock that Caroline saw the expression in the other girl's eyes.

"Hallo," said Liz. And then, "Hallo, Jody."

"How do you do," said Jody.

Oliver asked, "Have you been here long?"

She turned to him, away from the other two. "Ten minutes, perhaps. No longer."

"You'll stay for lunch?"

"Mrs. Cooper very sweetly asked me, but I'm expected home."

"Then come in and have a drink."

"No, I must get back. I only dropped by to say hallo." She smiled at Caroline. "Mrs. Cooper's been telling me all about you. She says you've got a brother staying at Strathcorrie."

"He's not been there long . . ."

"Perhaps I've met him. What's his name?"

Without knowing why, Caroline hesitated, and Jody, catching the hesitation, answered the question for her.

"He's called Cliburn, like us," he told Liz. "Angus Cliburn."

After lunch Oliver, swearing at the necessity, on such a beautiful afternoon, of having to change into a respectable suit and a collar and tie, get into his car, drive to the town and spend the rest of the day incarcerated in a stuffy lawyer's office, duly departed.

Caroline and Jody saw him away, waving him down the drive. When the car had gone out of sight, they still stood there, listening to the sound of his engine as it paused at the main road, and then swung out, changed up, and roared up and away over the hill.

He was gone, and they found themselves slightly at a loss. Mrs. Cooper, her dishes washed and wiped, had gone home to look after her own house and get a load of washing out on to the line before the warmth went out of the day. Jody kicked disconsolately at the gravel. Caroline watched him in sympathy, knowing just how he felt.

"What do you want to do?"

"I don't know."

"Do you want to go back to the loch?"

"I don't know." He was any small boy, suddenly bereft of his best friend.

"We could do another jigsaw."

"Not indoors."

"We could bring it out and do it in the sun."

"I don't feel like doing jigsaws."

Defeated, Caroline went to sit on the bench where they had found Liz Fraser waiting for them this morning. She found that her thoughts instinctively shied from the memory of the encounter, and so, deliberately, she made herself go back, go over it, try to decide why she had found the other girl's sudden appearance so disturbing.

It was, after all, entirely natural. She was obviously a very old friend, a close neighbour, she appeared to have known Oliver all his life. Her father was buying Cairney. What could be more normal than she should drive over to make a friendly call and meet Oliver's guests?

But still, there was something there. A violent antipathy which Caroline had felt the moment Liz took off her dark glasses and looked her straight in the eye. Jealousy, perhaps? But, surely she had nothing to be jealous of. She was a hundred times more attractive than Caroline and Oliver was obviously devoted to her. Or perhaps she was simply possessive, as a sister might be? But this still did not account for the fact that standing, talking to her, Caroline had been left with the impression that, layer by layer, she was being slowly stripped of every garment she wore.

Jody was squatting, scooping gravel into small mounds with hands that were grey with dust. He looked up.

"Someone's coming," he said.

They listened. He was right. A car had turned in at the foot of the avenue, was now approaching the house.

"Perhaps Oliver's forgotten something."

But it wasn't Oliver. It was the same dark blue Triumph that had stood outside the house this morning; its hood down, and Liz Fraser, with her glinting hair and her dark glasses, and a silk scarf around her neck, was at the wheel. Instinctively, both Caroline and Jody stood up, and the car rammed to a stop not two yards from where they waited, a cloud of dust flying from the back wheels.

"Hallo again," said Liz and switched off the engine.

Jody said nothing. His face was blank. Caroline said "Hallo" and Liz opened the door and got out and slammed the door shut behind her. She took off her glasses and Caroline saw that her eyes were not smiling although her mouth was. "Oliver gone?"

"Yes, about ten minutes ago."

Liz smiled at Jody and reached over into the back of her car. "I brought you a present. I thought you might be running out of things to do." She produced a small-size putter and a golf ball. "There used to be a putting-green on that flat bit of lawn. I'm sure if you look you'll find the hole and some of the markers. Do you like putting?"

Jody's face lit up. He adored presents. "Oh, thank you. I don't know. I've never done it."

"It's fun. Very tricky. Why don't you go and see how good you are?"

"Thank you," he said again, and started off. Half-way down the bank he turned. "When I've learned how, will you come and have a game with me?"

"Of course I will. We'll have a little bet and see who wins the prize."

He went, running down the last of the slope on to the level lawn. Liz turned to Caroline and let her smile die. She said, "I really came to have a little talk with you. Shall we sit down? It's so much more restful."

They sat, Caroline wary, Liz very much at ease, reaching for a cigarette, lighting it with a tiny gold lighter. She said, "I had a telephone call from my mother."

Caroline had nothing to say to this bit of gratuitous information. Liz went on, "You don't know who I am, do you? I mean, apart from being Liz Fraser who lives at Rossie Hill?" Caroline shook her head. "But you know Elaine and Parker Haldane." Caroline nodded. "My dear, don't look so blank. Elaine's my mother."

Looking back, Caroline could not imagine how she had been so dense. Elizabeth. Liz. Scotland. She remembered at that last dinner-party in London, Elaine talking about Elizabeth. *Well, you know, ten years ago when Duncan and I were still together, we bought this place in Scotland.* Duncan, Liz's father, who was going to buy Cairney from Oliver. *And the first thing Elizabeth did was to make friends with the two boys who lived on the neighbouring estate ... the older brother ... killed himself in a terrible car smash.*

And she remembered Jody telling her about Charles being killed, and how a memory had stirred in her subconscious, and yet been forgotten before it had come to conscious light.

The pieces had been scattered, like the pieces of Jody's undone jigsaw, but they had been there, right in front of her nose, only she had been too stupid, or perhaps too involved in her own problems, to fit them all together.

She said, "I've always known you as Elizabeth."

"My mother and Parker call me that, but here I've always been Liz."

"I never realized. I simply never realized."

"Well, there it is. Coincidence and a small world and all that. And, as I say, my mother phoned this morning."

Her eyes were knowing. "What did she tell you?" asked Caroline.

"Well, everything, I suppose. About you and ... Jody, it is? ...

disappearing. Diana frantic with worry, knowing merely that you are in Scotland, nothing else. And a big wedding next Tuesday. You're marrying Hugh Rashley."

"Yes," said Caroline flatly, for there seemed nothing else to say.

"You appear to have got yourself in something of a mess."

"Yes," said Caroline. "I think I probably have."

"My mother said you'd come to Scotland to find Angus. Wasn't that rather a wild-goose chase?"

"It didn't seem so at the time. It was just that Jody wanted to see Angus again. Because Diana and Shaun want to take Jody to Canada with them and Jody doesn't want to go. And Hugh doesn't want Jody living with us, so that only leaves Angus."

"I thought Angus was a hippie?"

All Caroline's instincts urged her to spring to her brother's defence, but in truth it was hard to think of anything to say. She shrugged. "He is our brother."

"And living at Strathcorrie?"

"Working there. In the hotel."

"But not at the moment?"

"No, but he should be back by tomorrow."

"And you and Jody are going to wait here until he comes?"

"I . . . I don't know."

"You sound uncertain. Perhaps I can help you, make up your mind for you. Oliver's going through a bad time. I don't know whether you realized this. He was devoted to Charles, there were only the two of them. And now Charles is dead and Cairney has to go and this is the end of the line for Oliver. Don't you think, under the circumstances, it would perhaps be . . . considerate if you and your brother were to go back to London? For Oliver's sake. And Diana's. And Hugh's."

Caroline was not deceived. "Why do you want us out of the way?"

Liz was unperturbed. "Perhaps because you're an embarrassment to Oliver."

"Because of you?"

Liz smiled. "Oh, my dear, we've known each other so long, we're very close. Closer than you could imagine. That's one of the reasons my father's buying Cairney."

"You're going to marry him?"

"Of course."

"He never said."

"Why should he? Did you tell him that you were going to be married? Or perhaps it's a secret? I notice you don't wear an engagement ring."

"I . . . I left it in London. It's too big for me and I'm always afraid of losing it."

"But he doesn't know, does he?"

"No."

"That's funny, not telling Oliver. After all, according to my mother, it's going to be a very large affair. I suppose a well-to-do stockbroker like Hugh Rashley would consider it part and parcel of his successful image. You are still going to marry him? But for some reason you don't want Oliver to know?" And then when Caroline did not reply to any of these queries, she began to laugh. "My dear child, I do believe you've fallen in love with him. Well, I don't blame you at all. I'm very sorry for you. But I'm on your side, so I'll make a little bargain. You and Jody go back to London, and I shan't breathe a word to Oliver about your wedding. He won't know a thing about it until he sees the newspapers on Wednesday morning, which will doubtless carry the whole story, with a picture of the pair of you at the church door, looking like something that came off the top of a wedding cake. How's that? No explanations, no excuses. Just a clean break. Back to your Hugh who obviously adores you, and leave hippie Angus to his own devices. Now, doesn't that make sense?"

Caroline said, helplessly, "There's Jody . . ."

"He's a child. A little boy. He'll adapt. He'll go to Canada and love it, be captain of the ice hockey team in no time. Diana's the best person to take care of him, you can surely see that? Someone like Angus could be nothing but the worst possible influence. Oh, Caroline, come off your cloud and face facts. Throw the whole thing over and go back to London."

From the lawn below them came a triumphant yell as Jody finally got the golf ball into the hole. He appeared up the bank, running, brandishing his new club. "I've got the hang of it. You have to hit it quite slowly and not too hard, and . . ." He stopped. Liz was on her feet, was pulling on her gloves. "Aren't you going to play with me?"

"Another time," said Liz.

"But you said."

"Another time." She got into her car, neatly stowing her long legs. "Right now your sister has something she wants to tell you."

* * *

Oliver drove home through the blue dusk of the perfect day, his mood quite different from that of the day before. Now, he was relaxed, and for some reason, oddly content. Not exhausted by the long legal interview; clear-headed and much happier now that he had actually taken the final step of putting Cairney House up for sale. He had spoken, too, to the lawyer, about keeping the Loch Cottage, renovating it and converting it to a small holiday house, and the lawyer had raised no objections, provided Oliver could make arrangements with Duncan Fraser for an access road through what would become, in the course of time, Duncan's land.

Oliver did not imagine that Duncan would raise any objections to this. The thought of the house, raised square and sturdy again, filled him with satisfaction. He would take the garden down to the water's edge, open up the old hearth, re-build the chimney, put dormer windows in the loft. Planning, he began to whistle to himself. The leather wheel felt firm and pleasant beneath his hands and the car took the curves of the familiar road easily, sweetly, like a steeplechaser. As though, like Oliver, it knew it was coming home.

He turned in at the gates and roared up the drive beneath the trees, coming around the sweep by the rhododendrons with a flourish on his horn to let Jody and Caroline know that he was safely back. He left the car by the front door and went indoors taking off his coat, and waiting for Jody's footsteps.

But the house was silent. He put his coat down across a chair and called, "Jody!" There was no reply. "Caroline!" Still nothing. He went down to the kitchen but it was dark and empty. Mrs. Cooper had not yet come in to start cooking supper. Puzzled, he let the door swing shut and went along to the library. This, too, he found dark, the fire dying in the hearth. He switched on the light and went over to throw on some fresh logs. He straightened and saw the envelope on his desk, a square of white propped against the telephone. One of the best envelopes out of the top drawer in his desk, and on it was written his name.

He opened it and saw, to his surprise, that his hands were shaking. He unfolded the single sheet and read Caroline's letter.

Dear Oliver,
   After you had gone Jody and I talked things over and we have decided that it would be best if we go back to London. It isn't any good waiting for Angus, we don't know when he will be

back and it isn't fair on Diana to stay longer when she doesn't even know where we are.

Please don't worry about us. The car is working beautifully and your kind garage filled it up with petrol for us. I don't think there will be any more blizzards and I'm sure we shall get back safely.

There isn't any way of saying thank you, to you and Mrs. Cooper, for all you have done. We loved being at Cairney. We shall never forget it.

> With love from us both,
> Caroline.

7

The next morning, pretending to himself that he wanted to square off one or two problems with Duncan Fraser, Oliver drove himself over to Rossie Hill. It was another beautiful day, but colder; over the night there had been the lightest of frosts, and the sun had not yet enough warmth to melt this away, but still the Rossie Hill drive was lined with the bobbing heads of the first early daffodils and when he went into the house it smelt of the great bowl of blue hyacinths which stood in the middle of the table in the hall.

As familiar with this house as Liz was with Cairney, he searched for occupants, running Liz to earth at last in her father's study, where she sat on the desk and conducted a telephone conversation. To the butcher by the sound of it. When he opened the door she looked up, saw him, raised her eyebrows in a silent message to tell him to wait. He came into the room and went to stand by the fire, wanting a cigarette and yet not wanting one, comforted by the warmth of the flames against the front of his legs.

She finished the phone call and hung up, but stayed by the telephone, very still, one long leg swinging thoughtfully. She wore a pleated skirt, a skinny sweater, a silk scarf knotted round the base of her throat. The skin of her arms and her face still glowed from the Antigua sun, and for a long moment her dark eyes met his across the room.

Then she said, "Looking for somebody?"

"Your father."

"He's out. Gone to Relkirk. Won't be back till lunchtime." She reached for a silver cigarette-box and held it out to him. Oliver shook his head, so she took one for herself and lit it from the heavy desk lighter. She surveyed him thoughtfully through a drift of blue smoke. She said, "You look a little distrait, Oliver. Is anything wrong?"

He had been trying all morning to tell himself that nothing was wrong, but now he said bluntly, "Caroline and Jody have gone."

"Gone?" Her voice was mildly surprised. "Where have they gone?"

"Back to London. I got back last night and found a letter from Caroline."

"But surely that's quite a good thing."

"After all that, they never got to find their brother."

"From what I could gather, that doesn't sound as though it'll make much difference either way."

"But it mattered to them. It mattered to Jody."

"Provided you think they're capable of getting themselves back to London I shouldn't worry too much about them. You've got enough on your plate without acting as Nanny to a couple of lame dogs you'd never even seen before." She changed the subject, as though it were of little importance. "What did you want to see my father about?"

He could scarcely remember. ". . . an access road. I want to keep the Loch Cottage if I can, but I'll need access up the glen."

"Keep the Loch Cottage? But it's a ruin."

"Basically, it's sound enough. Just needs a bit of tidying up, a new roof."

"And what do you want the Loch Cottage for?"

He said, "To keep. A holiday house, perhaps. I don't know. Just to keep."

"Was it I who put that idea into your head?"

"Perhaps it was."

She slipped off the desk then, and came across the room to stand beside him. "Oliver, I have a better idea."

"And what is that?"

"Let my father buy Cairney House."

Oliver laughed. "He doesn't even want it."

"No, but I do. I would like to have it for . . . what was it you said? Holidays. Week-ends."

"And what would you do with it?"

She tossed her cigarette on the fire. "I would bring my husband here, and my children."

"Would they like that?"

"I don't know. You tell me."

Her eyes were clear, honest, unblinking. He was astonished by what she was saying and yet flattered too. And amazed. Little Liz, leggy, gawky Liz, all grown up and composed as hell and asking Oliver to . . .

He said, "Forgive me if I'm all wrong, but oughtn't I to be the one who comes up with these sorts of ideas?"

"Yes, I suppose you should. But I've known you too long to indulge in coy dishonesties. And I have this feeling that our coming together again like this, when neither of us expected to find each other, is meant. Part of a pattern. I have this feeling that Charles meant it to happen."

"But it was always Charles who loved you."

"That's what I mean. And Charles is dead."

"Would you have married him, if he'd lived?"

Her answer was to put her arms round his neck and pull down his head and kiss him on the mouth. For a second he hesitated, taken off his guard, but only for a second. She was Liz, scented, dazzling, marvellously attractive. He put his arms round her and drew her close, her slender body pressed against his, and told himself that perhaps she was right. Perhaps this was the direction his life was meant to go, and perhaps this was what Charles had always meant to happen.

He was, not unnaturally, late home for lunch. The kitchen was reproachfully empty, his single place laid at the table, a good smell of cooking coming from the stove. Searching for Mrs. Cooper he found her in the nursery, stacking away all the old toys that Jody had left disarranged, and looking like a mother who has been bereft of her children.

He put his head around the door and said, "I'm late, I'm sorry."

She looked up from the box of bricks which she was meticulously packing. "Och, it doesn't matter." She sounded listless. "It's only a shepherd's pie. I left it in the cool oven, you can eat it when you feel like it."

She had been shocked and much distressed last night when he told her that the Cliburns had gone. From her expression now he knew that she had not got over this. He said, robustly, trying to cheer her, "They should be well on their way by now. In London by this evening, if there's not too much traffic on the roads."

Mrs. Cooper sniffed. "I just can't bear the feel of the house without them. It's as though that wee boy had lived here the whole of his life. It was like Cairney coming alive again, having him here."

"I know." Oliver was sympathetic. "But they'd have had to go in a day or two anyway."

"And it wasn't even as though I had the chance to say goodbye to them." She made it sound as though it were all Oliver's fault.

"I know." He could think of nothing else to say.

"And he never got to see his brother. He talked so much about his brother Angus, and then he never even got to see him. It just makes me heart sick."

This, from Mrs. Cooper, was strong language. All at once Oliver felt as depressed as she was. He said, feebly, "I . . . I'll go and eat that shepherd's pie," and then, at the door, remembered why he had originally come in search of her. "Oh, Mrs. Cooper, don't bother to come in this evening. I've been asked to dinner at Rossie Hill . . ."

She acknowledged this with a nod, as though too distressed to say another word. Oliver left her to her disconsolate tidying and went downstairs again, and felt the house watchful and silent, as though, bereft of Jody's noisy presence, it had sunk into a gloom as thick as Mrs. Cooper's own.

Rossie Hill, made ready for a dinner-party, was as bright and glowing as the inside of a jewel-box. When Oliver let himself into the house, he smelt the hyacinths, saw the flickering of logs in the grate, was immediately soothed by warmth and comfort. As he took off his coat and dropped it over the chair in the hall, Liz emerged from the kitchen, carrying a bowl of ice-cubes in her hand. She stopped when she saw him, her smile sudden and brilliant.

"Oliver."

"Hallo."

He took her shoulders between his hands and kissed her carefully, cautious about blurring the clear line of her lipstick. She both smelt and tasted delicious. He held her off, the better to admire her. She wore red, a silk trouser dress with a high collar, and diamonds sparked from her neatly-set ears. She reminded him of a parakeet, a bird of paradise, all bright eyes and glittering plumage.

He said, "I'm early."

"Not early. Just right. The others haven't come yet."

He raised his eyebrows. "Others?"

"I told you it was a dinner-party." He followed her through to the drawing-room where she set down the ice-bowl on a meticulously prepared drink table. "The Allfords. Do you know them? They've come to live in Relkirk. He's something to do with whisky. They're longing to meet you. Now, shall I pour you a drink or would you rather do it yourself? I do mix a very special martini."

"Where did you learn to do that?"

"Oh, I picked it up on my travels."

"Would I be ungracious if I opted for a whisky and soda?"

"Not ungracious at all, just typically Scottish."

She poured it for him, just the way he liked it, not too dark, bubbling, bobbing with ice. She brought it over and he took it, and he kissed her again. She detached herself reluctantly, and went back to the drink table and began to mix a jug of martinis.

While she did, they were joined by Duncan, and then the front-door bell rang, and Liz went out to greet her other guests.

When she was out of the room Duncan said to Oliver, "Liz has told me."

Oliver was surprised. Nothing definite had been settled this morning. Nothing discussed. His talk with Liz, though filled with delight, had been more of the past, remembering, than of the future. It had seemed to Oliver that there was all the time in the world to decide about the future.

He said, carefully, "What did she say?"

"Nothing very much. Just put one or two ideas in my way, as it were. But you have to know, Oliver, that nothing would make me a happier man."

"I . . . I'm glad."

"And as for Cairney . . ." Voices approached the half open door, and he broke off abruptly. "We'll talk about it later."

The Allfords were middle-aged, the husband large and ponderous, the wife very slender, pink-and-white with the soft, fluffy blonde hair that looks so colourless when it starts to go grey. Everybody was introduced, and Oliver found himself sitting by Mrs. Allford on the sofa, hearing about her children who hadn't wanted to come and live in Scotland but now loved it. About her daughter who lived for the local Pony Club, and her son who was in his first year at Cambridge.

"And you . . . now you live next door, if that's the right term to use."

"No. I live in London."

"But . . ."

"My brother, Charles Cairney, lived at Cairney but he was killed in a car smash. I'm just up here trying to get all his affairs sorted out."

"Oh, of course." Mrs. Allford put on a face suitable for tragedy. "I did know. I am sorry. It's so difficult to keep track of everybody when you're meeting them all for the first time."

His attention wandered back to Liz. Her father and Mr. Allford were standing, deep in business talk. She stood beside them, holding her drink and a small dish of salted nuts from which Mr. Allford, absently, helped himself from time to time. She felt Oliver's gaze and turned towards him. He winked with the eye farthest from Mrs. Allford and Liz smiled.

Finally, they went in to dinner, the dining-room softly lit, velvet curtains drawn against the night. There were lace mats on dark shining wood, crystal and silver, a mass of scarlet tulips, the same red as Liz's dress, in the middle of the table. Then smoked salmon, pink and delectable, white wine, escalopes de veau, tiny brussels sprouts cooked with chestnuts, a pudding that was simply a froth of lemon and cream. Then coffee and brandy, the smell of Havana cigars. Oliver pushed back his chair, replete and sleek with the comforts of good living, and settled down to the after-dinner conversation.

Behind him the clock on the mantelpiece struck nine o'clock. Some time during the day he had pushed the thought of Jody and Caroline into the back of his mind, and had had no bother with them since. But as the chimes gently rang out he was, all at once, no longer at Rossie Hill, but in London with Cliburns. By now they would be home, tired and weary, trying to explain to Diana, trying to tell her all the things that had happened; Caroline would be exhausted and pale after the long drive, Jody still consumed with disappointment. *We went to find Angus. We went all the way to Scotland to find Angus but he wasn't there. And I don't want to go to Canada.*

And Diana, frantic, scolding, finally forgiving, heating milk for Jody and getting him to bed; and Caroline going upstairs, a step at a time, her face curtained by her long hair, her hand trailing on the banister.

". . . what do you say, Oliver?"

"Uh?" They were all looking at him. "I'm sorry, I wasn't paying attention."

"We were talking about the salmon fishing rights on the Corrie, there's some talk of . . ."

Duncan's voice trailed away. Nobody else spoke. It was suddenly very quiet, and through the stillness they heard what Duncan's sharp ears had heard already. The sound of a car, not on the road, but coming up the hill towards the house. A van, or a lorry; gears crashing down as the incline steepened, and then a flash of headlights against the outside of the drawn curtains, and the steady throb of an ancient engine.

Duncan looked at Liz. "It sounds," he said, making a joke of it, "as though you're expecting the coalman."

She frowned. "I expect it's someone lost the way. Mrs. Douglas will go to the door," and smoothly she turned once more to Mr. Allford, intending to carry on with the conversation, ignoring the unknown caller who waited outside. But Oliver's attention was drawn as tight as a rubber band, his ears pricked like a dog's. He heard the ringing of the front-door bell, and slow footsteps go to answer the summons. He heard a voice, high and excited, interrupted by Mrs. Douglas's mild objects. ". . . canna go in there, there's a dinner-party . . ." And then an exclamation, "Ah, ye wee divil . . ." and the next moment the dining-room door was flung open and outside, poised, his eyes searching the room for the only person he wanted to find, was Jody Cliburn.

Oliver was on his feet, his napkin flung on the table.

"Jody!"

"Oh, *Oliver.*"

He came across the room like a bullet, like a homing pigeon, straight into Oliver's arms.

The urbane formality of the dinner-party collapsed instantly, like a pricked balloon. The shambles that resulted would have been funny had it not been tragic. For Jody was in tears, bawling like a baby, with his head butted into Oliver's stomach and his arms clutched tight about Oliver's waist as though he had no intention of ever letting him go. Mrs. Douglas, harassed in her pinafore, hovered in the doorway, undecided as to whether or not she should come into the dining-room and bodily haul the intruder away. Duncan was on his feet, with no idea of what was happening or who this child could be. From time to time he said, "What the devil is all this about?" but nobody was in a position to give him any sort of a reply. Liz was also on her feet, but saying nothing, simply staring at the back of Jody's head as though, given half a chance, she would like to have smashed it, like some rotten fruit, against the nearest stone wall. Only the Allfords, conventional to the last, stayed where they were, Mr. Allford saying, "Extraordinary thing to happen," between puffs of his cigar. "Do you mean to say he's come in the coal lorry?" While Mrs. Allford smiled sociably, giving the impression that unknown children had disrupted every memorable dinner-party she had ever been to.

From the depths of Oliver's waistcoat came sobs and snuffles and garbled sentences of which he could neither hear nor understand one word. It was obvious that the situation could not be allowed to continue, but Jody clung so tightly that it was impossible for Oliver to move.

"Now come along," he said at last, raising his voice to make himself heard above the sobs. "Loosen off. We'll go outside and you can tell me what this is about . . ." His words somehow got through to Jody, who loosened his stranglehold slightly and allowed himself to be led towards the door. "So sorry," said Oliver as he went. "Please excuse me for a moment . . . rather unexpected."

Feeling as though he had accomplished a brilliant escape he found himself out in the hall, and Mrs. Douglas, bless her good heart, was closing the door behind them.

"Will you be all right?" she whispered.

"We're fine."

She went back to her kitchen, muttering away under her breath, and Oliver sat on a carved wooden chair that had never been built for sitting in and pulled Jody close between his knees. "Stop crying. Try to stop crying. Here, blow your nose and stop crying." Scarlet-faced, swollen, Jody made a valiant effort, but the tears still came.

"I c-can't."

"What's happened?"

"Caroline's ill. She's really ill. She's sick like she was before, and she's got a terrible pain here." Jody laid his own grubby hands over his stomach. "And it's getting worse."

"Where is she?"

"At the Strathcorrie Hotel."

"But she said you were going back to London."

"I wouldn't let her." Tears filled his eyes again. "I w-wanted to find Angus."

"Has Angus come back yet?"

Jody shook his head. "No. There wasn't anybody but you."

"Have you told a doctor?"

"I . . . I didn't know what to do. I c-came to find you . . ."

"You think she's really sick?"

Speechless with crying Jody nodded again. Behind Oliver, the dining-room door quietly opened and shut again. He turned and saw Liz standing there. She said to Jody, "Why didn't you go back to London?" but he saw the anger in her face and he wouldn't answer. "You said you were going back. Your sister said she was taking you back." Her voice was suddenly shrill. "She said . . ."

Oliver stood up, and Liz stopped, as though he had turned off a tap. He turned back to Jody. "Who brought you here?"

"A m-man. A man in a van."

"Go out and wait with him. Tell him I'll be out in a moment . . ."

"But we have to *hurry*."

Oliver raised his voice. "I said I'd be out in a moment." He turned Jody round, gave him a push. "Go on, scoot. Tell him you've found me."

Dejected, Jody went, struggling with the handle of the big door and slamming it shut behind him. Oliver looked at Liz. He said, "The reason they didn't go to London was because Jody wanted a last chance of finding his brother. And now Caroline's ill. That's all there is to it, I'm sorry." He crossed the hall to collect his coat. Behind him Liz said, "Don't go."

He turned, frowning. "But I have to."

"Phone the doctor in Strathcorrie, he'll take care of her."

"Liz, I must go."

"Is she that important to you?"

He started to deny this and then found that he didn't want to. "I don't know. Perhaps she is." He began to put on his coat.

"And what about us? You and I?"

He could only repeat himself. "I have to go, Liz."

"If you walk out on me now, you don't ever need to come back."

It sounded like a challenge—or a bluff. Either way it did not seem to be very important. He tried to be gentle. "Don't start saying things you'll only regret."

"Who says I'll regret them?" She wrapped her arms across her chest, holding her upper arms so tightly that the knuckles on her brown hands showed white. She looked as though she were suddenly very cold, as though she were trying to hold herself together. "If you don't watch out, you're going to be the one with the regrets. She's going to be married, Oliver."

He had put on his coat. He said, "Is she, Liz?" and started to do up the buttons and his calm drove her over the edge of her own control.

"She didn't tell you? How extraordinary! Oh, yes, she's getting married on Tuesday. In London. To a very up-and-coming young stockbroker called Hugh Rashley. It's funny you never guessed. But of course she didn't wear an engagement ring, did she? She said it was too big and that she was frightened of losing it, but that seems a little farfetched to me. Aren't you going to ask me how I know all this, Oliver?"

Oliver said, "How do you know it?"

"My mother told me. On the telephone yesterday morning. You see, Diana Carpenter is just about her dearest friend, so of course my mother knows it all."

He said, "Liz, I have to go."

"If you have already lost your heart," she told him sweetly, "take my advice and don't lose your head as well. There's no future in it. You'll only make a fool of yourself."

He said, "Explain to your father for me. Tell him what's happened. Tell him how sorry I am." He opened the door. "Goodbye, Liz."

She could not believe that he wouldn't turn and come back to her, and take her in his arms and tell her that none of this had happened, that he would love her as Charles had loved her, that Caroline Cliburn could take care of herself.

But he didn't. And then he had gone.

The man in the van was a large, red-faced individual in a checked cloth "bonnet." He looked like a farmer and his van smelt of pig manure but he had waited patiently for Oliver to emerge and kept Jody company into the bargain.

Oliver put his head in at the window. "I am sorry to have kept you waiting."

"Nae bother, sir, I'm no' in any hurry at all."

"It was very good of you to bring the boy, I'm most grateful. I hope you didn't have to come far out of your way."

"Not at all. I was on my way down the glen from Strathcorrie in any case. I'd just dropped in for a dram when the wee boy asked me to bring him to Cairney. He seemed a wee bittie upset, and I didna like to leave him there on the roadside." He turned to Jody, patted his knee with a large hamlike hand. "Ach, but you'll be fine now, laddie, now you've found Mr. Cairney."

Jody got out of the van. "Thank you *so* much. I don't know what I would have done if you hadn't been there and been so kind."

"Oh, think nothing of it. Maybe someone'll do the same for me one day, when I'm on shank's pony. I just hope you'll find your sister weel. I'll say good night, sir."

"Good night," said Oliver. "And thank you again." And, as the tail-light of the van disappeared around the curve of the drive he took Jody's hand in his and said, "Come along now. We've no more time to lose."

Out on the road, with the headlights probing the racing darkness and every turn and curve a familiar one, he said to Jody, "Now tell me."

"Well. Caroline was sick again, and then she said she had a pain, and she's all pale and sweaty and I didn't know . . . the telephone . . . and then . . ."

"No. From the beginning. From the letter Caroline wrote. The one she left on my desk."

"She told me we were going back to London. But I said she'd *promised* to wait till Friday, that Angus would maybe be back on Friday."

"That's today."

"That's what I said. Just wait until today. And she said that it was better for everybody if we went back to London and she wrote you that letter, but then at the last moment she . . . gave in. And she said we'd go to the Strathcorrie Hotel just for one night, just last night, and then today we would have to drive back to London. So I said all right, and we went to Strathcorrie and Mrs. Henderson gave us rooms and everything was all right until breakfast, because she felt awful and said she couldn't possibly drive. So she stayed in bed, and then she tried to eat lunch, but she said she was going to be sick, and she was, and then this awful pain started."

"Why didn't you tell Mrs. Henderson?"

"I didn't know what to do. I kept thinking maybe Angus would get back and everything would be all right. But he didn't come and Caroline just got worse. And then I had to go and have supper by myself because she said she didn't want any, and when I went upstairs she was all sweaty and she looked as though she was asleep but she wasn't and I thought she was going to die . . ."

His voice was becoming hysterical. Oliver said levelly, "You could have phoned me. You could have looked up the telephone number."

"I'm frightened of telephones," said Jody and it was some measure of his distress that he would admit to this. "I can never hear what people are saying and I always put my finger into the wrong hole."

"So what did you do?"

"I ran downstairs and I saw that kind man coming out of the bar and he said he was going home and went outside, and I went after him and told him my sister was sick and told him about you and said would he take me to Cairney."

"And I wasn't there?"

"No. And the kind man got out of his car and rang bells and things and then I thought of Mrs. Cooper. So he took me round to her house and she gave me a huge hug when she saw me and she told me you were at Rossie Hill. And Mr. Cooper said he would take me, though he was in his braces and slippers, but the kind man said no, he would, he knew the way. So he did. And I came. And I'm sorry about spoiling the party."

"That didn't matter," said Oliver.

By now Jody had stopped crying. He sat forward on the edge of his seat as though his very attitude would make them go faster. He said at last, "I don't know what I would have done if you hadn't been there."

"But I was. I am here." He put out his left arm and pulled Jody close. "You did very well. You did everything right."

The road poured away. Up and over the hill they went. The lights of Strathcorrie twinkled far below, tucked into the folds of the dark, quiet mountains. *We're coming,* he told Caroline. *We're coming, Jody and I.*

"Oliver."

"Yes."

"What do you think is wrong with Caroline?"

"At a rough layman's guess," said Oliver, "I would say that she has an appendix that needs to be removed."

8

His diagnosis proved perfectly accurate. Within ten minutes the Strathcorrie doctor, hastily summoned by Mrs. Henderson, arrived, confirmed the appendicitis, gave Caroline a shot to ease the pain, and went downstairs again to call the local Cottage Hospital and ring for an ambulance. Jody, with what might have been a rare display of tact in one so young, went with him. But Oliver stayed with Caroline, sitting on the edge of the bed, and holding one of her hands in both of his.

She said, already sounding faintly dopy, "I didn't know where Jody had gone. I didn't know he'd come to find you."

"You could have knocked me over with a feather when he suddenly appeared. I had you both safe and sound and back in London."

"We didn't go. At the last moment I knew I couldn't go. Not when I'd promised Jody."

"Just as well you didn't. An appendix blowing up halfway down the Motorway wouldn't have been much of a joke."

"No, it wouldn't, would it?" She smiled. "I suppose that's what's been wrong all this time, feeling so sick, I mean. I never thought of an appendix." She said, as though the idea had just occurred to her, "I'm meant to be getting married on Tuesday."

"That's one appointment you won't be able to keep."

"Did Liz tell you?"

"Yes."

"I should have told you. I don't know why I didn't." She amended this to, "I didn't know why I didn't."

"But you know now?"

She said, hopelessly, "Yes."

Oliver said, "Caroline, before you say anything more, I think you should know that when you do get married, I don't want it to be to anybody but me."

"But aren't you going to marry Liz?"

"No."

She considered this, her face grave. "Everything's such a muddle, isn't it? I always make such a muddle of everything. Even getting engaged to Hugh seems to be part of the muddle."

"I wouldn't know, Caroline. I don't know Hugh."

"He's nice. You'd like him. He's always around, and organized and very kind and I've always been so fond of him. He's Diana's younger brother. Did Liz tell you that? He met us off the plane when we got back from Aphros, and took charge of everything, and somehow he seems to have been taking charge ever since. And of course Diana encouraged the idea of our getting married. It appealed to her sense of order, having me marry her brother. It kept everything all neat and tidy in the family. But still I'd never had said I'd marry him except for that miserable business with Drennan Colefield. But when Drennan walked out on me I felt as though I would never properly fall in love again, and so it didn't matter whether I truly loved Hugh or not." She frowned. "Does that make sense?" she asked him, muzzy and confused.

"Perfect sense."

"Then what am I going to do?"

"Do you love Hugh?"

"In a way, but not that way."

"Then it's no problem. If he's a nice guy, and he has to be or you'd never have said you'd marry him, then it would be very wrong to saddle him, for the rest of his life, with a half-hearted wife. In any case, you won't be able to marry him on Tuesday. You'll be far too busy sitting up in bed, eating grapes and smelling flowers and reading large, glossy magazines."

"We'll have to tell Diana."

"I'll do that. As soon as they've taken you off in the Black Maria, I'll call her."

"You're going to have an awful lot of explaining to do."

"That's what I'm best at."

She moved her hand, lacing her fingers into his. She said, contentedly, "We only met just in time, didn't we?"

There was a sudden, unaccountable lump in Oliver's throat. He leaned over and kissed her. "Yes," he said, gruffly. "We ran it pretty close. But we made it."

By the time they had seen her off, accompanied by the ambulance men and a plump and kindly nurse, he felt as though he had already lived through a lifetime of days. He watched the taillight of the ambulance away, down the empty street and under the little stone archway, and so out of sight, and he breathed a silent prayer. At his side, Jody put a hand into his.

"She'll be all right, won't she, Oliver?"

"Of course she will."

They went back into the hotel, two men with much accomplished.

"What do we do now?" asked Jody.

"You know as well as I do."

"Ring Diana."

"Right."

He bought Jody a Coca-Cola, installed the boy at a table just outside the telephone booth, incarcerated himself in its stuffy interior, and put the call through to London. Twenty minutes later, with long, involved and exhausting explanations over, he opened the door and called Jody in and handed him the receiver.

"Your stepmother wants to talk to you."

Jody said, in a whisper, "Is she angry?"

"No. But she wants to say hallo."

Jody, gingerly, put the dreaded instrument to his ear. "Hallo? Hallo, Diana." Slowly a smile spread over his face. "Yes, I'm fine . . ."

Leaving him, Oliver went to order himself the largest whisky and soda the hotel could muster. By the time it arrived Jody had said goodbye to Diana and rung off. He emerged, beaming, from the booth. "She isn't a bit cross and she's flying up to Edinburgh tomorrow."

"I know."

"And she says I'm to stay with you until then."

"Is that all right?"

"All right? It's fantastic." He saw the long glass in Oliver's hand.

"I'm suddenly feeling terribly thirsty. Do you think I could have another Coke?"

"Of course you can. Go and ask the barman."

He had imagined that they had reached the end of the road. That there was nothing more to be done, that the day could not possibly turn up any more surprises. But he was wrong. For, as Jody went in search of his drink, there came the sound of a car driving up the street and stopping outside the hotel. Doors opened and were slammed shut; there was a blur of voices, footsteps, and the next moment the half-glassed doors from the street flew open, and in came a small grey-haired lady, very chic in a pink-and-white suit, like icing sugar, and shiny crocodile shoes. She was immediately followed by a young man, hung about with tartan covered suitcases, bumping his way through the swinging door, because he hadn't a free hand with which to hold it open. He was tall and fair, his hair worn long, his face strangely slavonic, with high, bumpy cheekbones and a wide curving mouth. He wore pale blue corduroy trousers and a large shaggy coat, and as Oliver watched he carried the suitcases over to the reception desk, dumped them on to the floor and reached out a hand to ring the bell.

But he never rang it. For just then Jody came back from the bar. It was like a film, stopping in its tracks. Their eyes met and they were both still, quite motionless, staring at each other. And then, with a click and a whirr, the film moved again. The young man shouted "Jody!" at the top of his considerable voice, and before anyone could say another word, Jody had catapulted himself across the hall and into his brother's arms.

That night, they all went back to Cairney. The next afternoon Oliver left the brothers together, and drove, on his own, to Edinburgh, to meet Diana Carpenter off the London plane. He stood in the glass-walled arrivals lounge at Turnhouse Airport, watching the passengers come down the gangways, and as soon as she appeared, knew that it was she. Tall, slender, dressed in a loose tweed overcoat, with a little tie of mink at her neck. As she came across the tarmac, he moved forward so that he would be there to greet her. He saw the frown between her eyebrows, the anxious expression. She came through the glass doors and he said, "Diana."

She had blonde hair wound up in a thick knot at the back of her head and very blue eyes. She at once looked relieved, some of the anxiety went out of her face.

"You're Oliver Cairney." They shook hands, and then, for some unknown but obviously good reason, he kissed her.

She said, "Caroline?"

"I saw her this morning. She's all right. She's going to be fine."

He had told her everything last night on the telephone, but now, roaring northwards over the Forth Bridge, he told her about Angus.

"He arrived last night, just when he said he was going to. With this American woman he's been chauffeuring around the Highlands. He walked into the hotel and Jody saw him and there was a tremendous reunion."

"It's marvellous that they even recognized each other. They haven't seen each other for years."

"Jody's very fond of Angus."

Diana said, in a small voice, "I realize that now."

"But you hadn't before?" He was careful not to sound reproachful.

She said, "It's difficult . . . it was difficult, being a stepmother. You can't be a mother and yet you have to try to be more than just a friend. And they weren't like other children. They'd virtually brought themselves up, running wild, barefoot, entirely free. And while their father was alive, it worked, but it was different after he died."

"I can understand."

"I wonder if you can. It was like being on a razor's edge, not wanting to suppress their natural instincts and yet feeling that I had to give them some sort of a sound basis for living their separate lives. Caroline was always so vulnerable. That's why I tried to talk her out of going to Drama School and trying to get a job in the theatre. I was so afraid she would get discouraged, and disappointed, and hurt. And then, when all my fears were realized, it was so marvellous when she started to be fond of Hugh, and I thought that, with Hugh to look after her, she wouldn't ever have to be hurt again. Perhaps I did . . . manipulate it a little, but I do promise you it was only with the best intentions in the world."

"Did you tell Hugh, what I told you last night on the telephone?"

"Yes. I got out the car and went round to his flat, because I hadn't the heart to tell him on the telephone."

"How did he take it?"

"You never know, with Hugh. But I got the idea, in a funny way, he'd been expecting something like this to happen. Not that he said anything. He's a very self-sufficient sort of person, very civilized. The fact that Caroline's in hospital takes some of the sting out of having to postpone the wedding, and by the time the engagement is formally broken off, people will have got used to the idea."

"I hope so."

Diana's voice changed. "And after I'd seen Hugh, I went round and saw Caleb, the stupid old goat. Of all the irresponsible things to do, lending the children his car like that. It's a wonder it got as far as Bedfordshire without blowing up. And never saying a word to me. I really could have strangled him."

"He did it with the best motives in the world."

"He could at least have made sure the car was serviced first."

"He's obviously very fond of Jody and Caroline."

"Yes, he was fond of them all. Their father, and Jody, and Caroline, and Angus. You know, I wanted Angus to stay with us after his father died, but he didn't want my sort of a life, or any of the things I could offer him. And he was nineteen and I would never have thought of trying to stop him going off on that mad excursion to India. I just hoped that eventually he'd get it all out of his system and then he'd come back to us and start living a normal life. But he didn't. I expect Caroline told you. He never did."

"He told me," said Oliver. "Last night. We talked until the small hours of the morning. And I told him what Jody wanted him to do . . . come back to London and make a home for Jody. And Angus told me what he wants to do. He's been offered a job with a yacht chartering firm in the Mediterranean. He's going back to Aphros."

"Does Jody know this?"

"I didn't tell him. I wanted to discuss it with you first."

"What is there to discuss?"

"This," said Oliver and told her, and click, click went the pieces, dove-tailed, fitting together as cleanly as if they had been planned. "I'm going to marry Caroline. Just as soon as she's better I'm going to marry her. My job's in London, and I already have a flat there where we can live. And, if you and your husband will agree to it, Jody too. There's plenty of room for the three of us."

It took some time for this to sink in. Then Diana said, "You mean, *not* take him to Canada with us?"

"He likes his school, he likes living in London, he likes being with his sister. He doesn't want to go to Canada."

Diana shook her head. "I wonder why I never guessed."

"Perhaps because he didn't want you to know. He didn't want to hurt your feelings."

"I . . . I shall miss him dreadfully."

"But you'll let him stay?"

"Is that what you really want?"

"I think it's what we all want."

She laughed. "Hugh wouldn't have done that. He wasn't prepared to take Jody on."

"I am," said Oliver. "If you'll let me. I only had one brother and I miss him very much. If I'm going to have another, I'd like it to be Jody."

They came up the avenue at Cairney and Angus and Jody were waiting for them, sitting on the front-door step, a patient reception committee of two. Almost before the car had stopped, Diana was out of it, scrambling, not dignified at all, stooping to gather the excited Jody into her arms, and then, over his bright head, looking up into Angus's face. His expression was wary, but unresentful. They had never seen eye to eye but he had grown beyond her, and now, whatever he chose to do could be none of her concern and for this she was very grateful.

She smiled and straightened, and went into his huge, bear-like embrace. "Oh, Angus," she said, "you impossible creature. How wonderful to see you again."

All Diana wanted was to see Caroline, so Oliver unloaded her luggage, handed Angus the car keys and told him to take her.

"But I want to go too," said Jody.

"No. We're staying here."

"But why? I want to see Caroline."

"Later."

They watched the car drive away. Jody said again, "Why didn't you let me go?"

"Because it's nice for them to be together. They haven't seen each other for a long time. Besides, I want to talk to you. I've got a whole lot of things I want to tell you."

"Nice things?"

"I think so." He put his hand around the back of Jody's neck and turned him gently, and they went indoors. "The best."

WILD MOUNTAIN THYME

For Robin and Kirsty and Oliver

CONTENTS

1
FRIDAY

Once, before the bypass had been built, the main road ran through the heart of the village, a constant stream of heavy traffic that threatened to rattle the heart out of the gracious Queen Anne houses and the small shops with their bulging windows. Woodbridge had been, not such a long time ago, simply a place you drove through in order to reach some other place.

But since the opening of the bypass, things had changed. For the better, said the residents. For the worse, said the shopkeepers and the garage proprietors and the man who had run the lorry-drivers' restaurant.

Now, the people of Woodbridge could go shopping and cross the road without taking their lives into their hands or having their pet dogs securely leashed. At weekends, children with brown velvet caps jammed down over their eyebrows, and mounted on a variety of shaggy steeds, trotted off to their local pony club meets, and already there had been a positive flowering of open-air events, garden parties and charity fetes. The lorry-drivers' cafe became an expensive delicatessen, a ramshackle tobacconist sold out to a precious young man who dabbled in antiques, and the vicar had begun to plan a festival for next summer, in order to celebrate the tricentenary of his small, perpendicular church.

Woodbridge had come into its own again.

The clock on the church tower was pointing to ten minutes to twelve on a chill February morning when a big shabby Volvo turned the corner by the saddlers, and came slowly down the main street between the wide cobbled pavements. The young man at the wheel saw the whole long empty curve of it, his eye undeflected by thundering streams of traffic. He saw the charming irregularity of houses and bow-fronted shops, the beckoning perspective, and a distant glimpse of willow-fringed meadows. Far above, in a wintry sky full of sailing clouds, a plane droned in towards Heathrow. Otherwise it was very quiet, and there seemed to be scarcely anybody about.

He passed a pub, newly painted and with tubs of bay trees at either side of the door; a hairdresser, Carole Coiffures. The wine merchant with his bow-fronted bottle-glass window, and an antique shop stuffed with over-priced relics of better days.

He came to the house. He drew the car into the pavement's edge and switched off the engine. The sound of the plane died, thrumming, into the morning quiet. A dog barked, a bird sang hopefully from a tree, as though deluded that the thin sunshine meant that spring had come. He got out of the car, slammed the door shut, and stood looking up at the flat, symmetric face of the house, with its fan-lighted door and pleasing proportions. Flush on the pavement it stood, a flight of stone steps leading up to the front door and tall sash windows discreetly veiled in filmy curtains.

It was, he thought, a house that had never given anything away.

He went up the steps and rang the doorbell. The surround of the bell was brass and brightly polished, as was the lion's head knocker. The door was painted yellow, new and bright looking, without a sun-blister or a scratch upon it. In the lea of the house, out of the sun, it was cold. He shivered inside his thick donkey jacket and rang the bell again. Almost at once there were footsteps, and the next instant the yellow front door opened for him.

A girl stood there, looking rather cross, as though she had been interrupted, disturbed by the bell, and wanted to put off for as little time as possible. She had long, milk-fair hair, and she wore a tee shirt bulging with puppy fat, an apron, knee stockings and a pair of scarlet leather clogs.

"Yes?"

He smiled and said, "Good morning," and her impatience instantly melted into quite a different expression. She had realized that it wasn't the man about the coal, or someone collecting for the Red Cross, but a tall and personable young man, long-legged in his well-scrubbed jeans, and bearded like a Viking. "I wondered if Mrs. Archer was in?"

"I'm so sorry." She looked quite sorry, too. "But I'm afraid not. She is gone to London today. To shop."

She was, he reckoned, about eighteen, and from her accent, some sort of Scandinavian. Swedish, probably.

He said, with what he hoped was engaging ruefulness, "Isn't that just my luck? I should have phoned or something, but I thought I'd take the chance of catching her at home."

"Are you a friend of Mrs. Archer's?"

"Well, I used to know the family, some years ago. But we've been . . . well, sort of out of touch. I was passing, on my way up to London from the West Country. I thought it would be nice to come and say hello. Just an idea I had. It doesn't matter."

He began, diffidently, to back away. As he had hoped, the girl delayed him.

"When she comes back, I could tell her that you have been here. She will be back in time for tea."

At that moment, with splendid timing, the church clock began to chime for midday.

He said, "It's only twelve o'clock now. I can scarcely hang around till then. Never mind, I'll maybe be down this way again some time." He looked up and down the street. "There used to be a little café here . . ."

"Not any more. It is a delicatessen now."

"Well, perhaps I can get a sandwich in the pub. It seems a long time since breakfast." He smiled down at her from his great height. "Goodbye, then. It's been nice meeting you." He turned as though to leave. He could feel her hesitation, her decision, as though he had directed them himself. She said, "I could . . ."

With one foot already on the upper step, he turned back.

"What could you do?"

"Are you really an old friend of the family?" She longed to be put out of her doubt.

"Yes, I really am. But I have no way of proving it to you."

"I mean, I was just going to get the lunch for myself and the baby. I could get it for you, too."

He looked reproachful, and she began to blush. "Now, that's very foolhardy of you. I'm sure you've been warned, time and time again, about strange men coming to the door."

She looked distressed. She obviously had. "It is just that, if you are a friend of Mrs. Archer's, Mrs. Archer would want me to ask you in." She was lonely and probably bored. All au pair girls seemed to be lonely and bored. It was an occupational hazard.

He said, "You mustn't get yourself into trouble."

Despite herself, she began to smile. "I don't think I will."

"Supposing I steal the silver? Or start trying to make violent love to you?"

For some strange reason this possibility did not alarm her in the least. Rather, she seemed to regard it as a joke, and so to be reassured. She even gave a small, conspiratorial giggle. "If you do, I shall scream and the whole village will come to my rescue. Everybody knows what everybody does in Woodbridge. Everybody talks all the time. Chat, chat. Nobody has a secret." She stepped back, opening the yellow door wide. The long, pretty hallway was invitingly revealed.

He hesitated for just long enough to make it seem genuine and then shrugged, said, "All right," and followed her over the threshold, wearing the expression of a man who has been finally, reluctantly, persuaded. She closed the door. He looked down into her face. "But you may have to take the consequences."

She laughed again, excited by the little adventure. She said, in hostess-like tones, "Would you like to take off your coat?"

He did so, and she hung it up for him.

"If you would like to come to the kitchen, perhaps you would like a glass of beer?"

"Well, thank you."

She led the way, down the passage that led to the back of the house, to the modern kitchen, built out into the south-facing garden and flooded now with pale sunlight. Everything shone with cleanliness and order; bright surfaces, a gleaming cooker, stainless steel and polished teak. The floor was blue and white tiles, which looked Potuguese. There were plants along the windowsill, and a table at the window was laid for lunch. He saw the high chair, the bright plastic table mat, the small spoons, the Beatrix Potter mug.

He said, "You've got a baby to look after."

She was at the fridge, getting him a can of beer. "Yes." She closed the fridge door and went to take a pewter mug from a hook on the scrubbed pine dresser. "He's Mrs. Archer's grandchild."

"What's he called?"

"Thomas. He's called Tom."

"Where's he now?"

"In his cot, having his morning rest. In a moment, I'll go up and get him, because he'll be ready for his lunch."

"How old is he?"

"Two." She handed him the can and the mug, and he opened the can and poured it carefully, without a head.

"I suppose he's staying here, is he? I mean, his parents are away, or something."

"No, he lives here." Her smiling, dimpled face took on an expression of woe. "It's very sad. His mother is dead." She frowned. "It is funny that you do not know that."

"I told you. I've been out of touch since I last saw the Archers. I had no idea. I *am* sorry."

"She was killed in a plane crash. She was coming home from a holiday in Yugoslavia. She was their only child."

"So they look after the grandchild?"

"Yes."

He took a mouthful of beer, cool and delicious. "What about the father?"

The girl had turned her rounded back on him, was stooping to investigate something in an oven. A fragrant smell filled the kitchen, and his mouth watered. He had not realized how hungry he was.

She said, "They were separated. I don't know anything about him." She closed the oven and straightened up. She gave him another searching look. "I thought you would have known about that, too."

"No, I don't know about anything. I was out of this country for a bit. I was in Spain and I was in America."

"Yes. I see." She looked at the clock. "If I leave you, will you be all right? I have to go up and get Thomas."

"If you're sure you can trust me not to help myself to the spoons." He was teasing her, and she cheered up and smiled again. "I don't think you'll do that." She was wholesome, creamy as a tumbler of milk.

He said, "What's your name?"

"Helga."

"Are you Swedish?"

"Yes."

"They're lucky, the Archers. I mean, having someone like you."

"I'm lucky, too. It is a good job, and they are very kind. Some girls get terrible places. I could tell you some stories."

"Do you go to classes in the afternoons?"

"Yes. English and history."

"Your English sounds perfect to me."

"I am doing literature. Jane Austen."

She looked so pleased with herself that he laughed. He said, "Run along, Helga, and get that baby. I'm starving, even if he isn't." For some reason she blushed again, and then went away and left him alone in the shining, sunny kitchen.

He waited. Heard her go upstairs, her footsteps cross the floor of the room above. He heard her voice, speaking quietly; curtains being drawn back. He laid down his beer and went, soft-footed, rubber-soled, back down the hall and opened the door at the bottom of the staircase. He went in. There were the chintzes, the grand piano, the orderly bookshelves, the unassuming water colors. A fire had been laid in the Adam grate, but was, as yet, unlit. Even so, the room was warm with central heating and heavy with the scent of hyacinths.

Its neatness, its order, its air of well-bred, well-moneyed smugness, enraged him, as it always had. He longed for muddled knitting, strewn newspapers, a dog or a cat on some familiar cushion. But there was nothing. Only the slow ticking of the clock on the mantelpiece bore witness to any sort of activity.

He began to prowl around. The grand piano was a repository of photographs. Mr. Archer in a top hat, proudly displaying some minor order bestowed upon him by the queen at Buckingham Palace; his moustache like a toothbrush, his morning coat strained across his spreading stomach. Mrs. Archer as a misty girl, dressed for her wedding. The baby, propped up on a fur rug. And Jeannette.

He picked up the stylized portrait and stood, looking down at it. Pretty, as she had always been pretty. Sexy even, in her extraordinary, fastidious way. He remembered her legs, which were sensational, and the shape of her well-manicured hands. But nothing much else. Not her voice, not her smile.

He had married her because the Archers hadn't wanted their daughter to be the mother of an illegitimate baby. When the disastrous news had been broken to them that their precious only child had been having an affair with, actually living with, that dreadful Oliver Dobbs, their tidy little world had fallen apart. Mrs. Archer had taken to her bed with a *crise de nerfs,* but Mr. Archer, harking back to his brief years as a soldier, had straightened his tie and his back and taken Oliver out to lunch at his London club.

Oliver, unimpressed and not a little amused, had recorded the subsequent discussion with the detachment of a totally impartial observer. Even at the time it had seemed as unreal as a scene from an old-fashioned play.

Only daughter, Mr. Archer had said, plunging in at the deep end. Always had great plans for her. No question of recriminations, hindsight never did a man any good, but the question was, what was Oliver going to do about this baby?

Oliver said that he didn't think he could do anything. He was working in a fish-and-chips shop, and he couldn't afford to marry anyone, let alone Jeannette.

Mr. Archer cleared his throat, and said that he didn't want to tread on toes, or to appear curious, but it was obvious to him that Oliver came from a good family, and he knew for a fact that Oliver had been to a well-known school, was there any reason that he had to work in a fish-and-chips shop?

Oliver said that yes, there was a reason. The reason was that he was a writer, and the fish-and-chips shop job was the sort of undemanding occupation he needed to keep himself alive in order to be able to write.

Mr. Archer cleared his throat again and began to talk about Oliver's parents, and Oliver told Mr. Archer that his parents, who lived in Dorset, were not only penniless, but unforgiving. Living on an army pension, they had denied themselves everything in order to be able to scrape up enough money to send Oliver to that exclusive school. When he had finally walked out of it at the age of seventeen, they had tried, in a broken-hearted sort of way, to persuade him to follow some sensible, conventional course. To join the army, the navy, perhaps. To become a chartered accountant, a banker, a lawyer. But he could only be a writer, because by then he already was a writer. Defeated at last, they washed their hands of their son, cutting him without the proverbial shilling, and remaining sulkily and stubbornly incommunicado.

This obviously disposed of Oliver's parents. Mr. Archer tried another tack. Did Oliver love Jeannette? Would he make her a good husband?

Oliver said that he didn't think he would make her a good husband, because he was so terribly poor.

Mr. Archer then cleared his throat for the third and last time and came to the point. If Oliver agreed to marry Jeannette and provide the baby with a legitimate father, then he, Mr. Archer, would see to it that . . . er . . . financially, the young couple would be all right.

Oliver asked, how all right? And Mr. Archer elucidated, his eyes steadily holding Oliver's across the table, but his anxious hands shifting his wineglass, straightening a fork, crumbling a roll. By the time he was done, his place setting was in chaos, but Oliver realized that he was onto a good thing.

Living in Jeannette's flat in London, with a steady income coming in each month to his bank account, he could give up the job in the fish-and-chips shop and get down to finishing his play. He already had a book under his belt, but that was still with an agent, and the play was something else, something that he had to get down, before it ate his soul out like some ghastly cancer. That was how it was with writing. He was never happy unless he was living two lives. A real life with women and food and drinking in pubs with friends; and the other life, teeming with his own people, who were more vital and sympathetic than anyone he ever met in the normal course of events. And certainly, he thought, more interesting than the Archers.

Over the lunch table, the two men had come to an agreement. Later, it was consolidated by lawyers' letters and drafts and signatures. Oliver and Jeannette were duly married in a registry office, and this seemed to be all that mattered to the Archers. The alliance lasted no more than a few months. Even before the child was born, Jeannette had gone back to her parents. Boredom she could stand, she said, and loneliness too, but abuse and physical violence were more than she was prepared to endure.

Oliver scarcely noticed her going. He stayed in her flat and peacefully, without any sort of interruption, finished the play. When it was done, he left the flat, locked the door and posted Jeannette the key. He took himself off to Spain. He was in Spain when the baby was born, and still there when he read, in some week-old paper, of his wife's death in the Yugoslavian air disaster. By then Jeannette had become a person who had happened to Oliver a long time ago, and he discovered that the tragedy aroused little emotion in him. She belonged to the past.

Besides, by then he was well into his second novel. So he thought

about Jeannette for perhaps five minutes and then plunged thankfully
back into the company of the infinitely more compelling characters
who were now going about their business within the confines of his
own head.

When Helga came downstairs again, he was back in the kitchen sitting on the window seat, with his back to the sun, and enjoying his
beer. The door opened, and she appeared, carrying the child in her
arms. He was larger than Oliver had imagined, dressed in red overalls
with a bib and a white sweater. His hair was a sort of reddish gold,
like new pennies, but Oliver couldn't see his face, which was buried in
Helga's delectable neck.

Helga smiled at Oliver over Thomas's shoulder.

"He's shy. I have told him that there is a visitor, and he doesn't
want to look at you." She bent her head to say to the little boy,
"Look, you silly. He is a nice man. He has come to have lunch
with us."

The child made a mooing, negative sound and buried his face still
deeper. Helga laughed and brought him over to his high chair and
inserted him into it, so that at last he had to let go of her. He and
Oliver looked at each other. The child had blue eyes and seemed
sturdy. Oliver didn't know much about children. Nothing, in fact.
He said, "Hi."

"Say hello, Thomas," Helga prompted. She added, "He does not
like to talk."

Thomas stared at the stranger. One-half of his face was red from
being pressed into a pillow. He smelled of soap. Helga clipped a
plastic bib around his neck, but he didn't take his eyes off Oliver.

Helga went to the stove to collect their meal. From the oven she
took a shepherd's pie, a dish of brussels sprouts. She put a little into
a round dish, mashed it up with a fork and set it down on the tray of
Thomas's high chair. "Now, eat it up," and she put his spoon into
his hand.

"Does he feed himself?" asked Oliver.

"Of course. He's two now, not a baby anymore. Are you, Thomas?
Show the man how you can eat up your dinner." Thomas responded
by laying down his spoon. His blue eyes fixed, unwinking, on Oliver,
and Oliver began to feel self-conscious.

"Here," he said. He set down his glass of beer, and reaching over,
took up the spoon, filled it with squashed meat and potato, and

steered it towards Thomas's mouth. Thomas's mouth opened, and it all disappeared. Thomas, munching, continued to stare. Oliver gave him back the spoon. Thomas finished his mouthful and then smiled. A good deal of the smile was shepherd's pie, but there was, as well, the glimpse of an engaging double row of small pearly teeth.

Helga, putting down Oliver's plate in front of him, caught sight of the smile.

"There now, he has made a friend." She brought another plate and sat herself at the head of the table, so that she could help Thomas. "He's a very friendly little boy."

"What does he do all day?"

"He plays, and he sleeps, and in the afternoons he goes for a walk in his push chair. Usually Mrs. Archer takes him, but today I will take him."

"Does he look at books and things?"

"Yes, he likes picture books, but sometimes he tears them."

"Does he have toys?"

"He likes little cars and blocks. He doesn't like teddies or rabbits or things like that. I don't think he likes the feel of fur. You know what I mean?"

Oliver began to eat the shepherd's pie, which was very hot and delicious. He said, "Do you know a lot about babies?"

"At home in Sweden I have younger brothers and sisters."

"Are you fond of Thomas?"

"Yes, he is nice." She made a face at the child. "You are nice, aren't you, Thomas? And he doesn't cry all the time like some children do."

"It must be rather . . . dull for him, being brought up by his grandparents."

"He is too little to know whether it is dull or not."

"But it'll be dull when he's older."

"A child on his own is always sad. But there are other children in the village. He will make friends."

"And you? Have you made friends?"

"There is another au pair girl. We go to classes together."

"Haven't you got a boyfriend?"

She dimpled. "My boyfriend is at home in Sweden."

"He must miss you."

"We write to each other. And it is only for six months. At the end of six months, I shall go back to Sweden."

"What will happen to Thomas then?"

"I expect Mrs. Archer will get another au pair girl. Would you like some more shepherd's pie?"

The meal progressed. For dessert there was fruit or yoghurt or cheese. Thomas ate yoghurt. Oliver peeled an orange. Helga, at the stove, made coffee.

She said to Oliver, "Do you live in London?"

"Yes, I've got a basement flat just off the Fulham Road."

"Is that where you are going now?"

"Yes. I've been in Bristol for a week."

"On holiday?"

"Who'd go to Bristol for a holiday in February? No, I have a play being put on at the Fortune Theatre there. I went down to do a small rewrite. The actors complained they couldn't get their tongues round some of my lines."

"A writer?" She turned wide-eyed. "You write *plays*? And get them *performed*? You must be very good."

"I like to think so." He filled his mouth with sections of orange. Their taste, and the bitter tang of the peel, reminded him of Spain. "But it's what other people think that really matters. The critics, and the people who pay to come to the theatre."

"What is the play called?"

"*Bent Penny*. And don't ask me what it's about, because I haven't got time to tell you."

"My boyfriend writes. He writes articles on psychology for the university journal."

"I'm sure they're fascinating."

"But it isn't the same as writing plays."

"No. Not quite the same."

Thomas had finished his yoghurt. Helga wiped his face and took off his bib and lifted him out of his high chair. He came to stand by Oliver, balancing himself by placing his hands on Oliver's knee. Through the worn denim, Oliver could feel their warmth, the grip of the little fingers. Thomas gazed up at Oliver and smiled again, a grin with dimples and that row of little teeth. He put up a hand to touch Oliver's beard, and Oliver stooped so that he could reach it. Thomas laughed. Oliver picked him up and held him on his knee. He felt solid and warm.

Helga seemed gratified by all these friendly advances. "Now he has made friends. If I got a book, you could show him the pictures while I put the plates in the dishwasher. Then I have to take him for a walk."

Oliver had already decided that it was time to leave, but he said, "All right" so Helga went to find a book, and he and Thomas were left alone.

Thomas was fascinated by his beard. Oliver hoisted him up so that he stood on Oliver's knee and their eyes were on a level. Thomas tugged his beard. Oliver yelped. Thomas laughed. He tried to tug it again, but Oliver caught his hand and held it in his own. "That hurts, you brute." Thomas stared into his eyes. Oliver said softly, "Do you know who I am?" and Thomas laughed again, as though the question were a great joke.

Helga came back with the book and laid it on the table, a large and brightly colored book with farm animals on the shiny cover. Oliver opened it at random and Thomas sat down again on his knee, leaning forward on the table, to peer at the pictures. As Helga went about her work putting plates away and scrubbing out the dish that had contained the shepherd's pie, Oliver turned the pages, and said the names of the animals, and pointed to the farmhouse and the gate and the tree and the haystack. And they came to a picture of a dog, and Thomas barked. And then to a picture of a cow, and he made mooing sounds. It was all very companionable.

Then Helga said it was time for Thomas to come upstairs and be dressed in his outdoor clothes, so she gathered him up and bore him away. Oliver sat and waited for them to come down again. He looked at the immaculate kitchen, and out into the immaculate garden, and he thought of Helga leaving and the next au pair girl coming, and the pattern repeating itself until Thomas was eight years old, and of an age to be sent to some well-established and probably useless prep school. He thought of his son, slotted, labeled, trapped on the conveyor belt of a conventional education, expected to make the right friends, play the accepted games, and never question the tyranny of meaningless tradition.

Oliver had escaped. At seventeen he had cut and run, but only because he had had the twin weapons of his writing and his own single-minded, rebellious determination to go his own way.

But how would Thomas fare?

The question made him feel uncomfortable, and he rejected it as being hypothetical. It was none of Oliver's business what school

Thomas went to, and it didn't matter anyway. He lit another cigarette, and idly opened Thomas's picture book again, lifting the front
cover. He saw on the white fly sheet, written in Mrs. Archer's neat
black-inked script,

Thomas Archer
For his Second Birthday
From Granny.

And all at once it did matter. A sort of rage rose within Oliver, so
that if Jeannette's mother had been standing nearby, he would have
attacked her; with words that only he knew how to use; with his fists
if necessary.

*He is not Thomas Archer, you sanctimonious bitch. He is Thomas
Dobbs. He is my son.*

When Helga came downstairs, carrying Thomas dressed in a sort of
ski suit and a woolen hat with a bobble on it, Oliver was already
waiting for her in the hall. He had put on his coat, and he said, "I
have to go now. I have to get back to London."

"Yes, of course."

"It was very kind of you to give me lunch."

"I will tell Mrs. Archer that you were here."

He began to grin. "Yes. Do that."

"But . . . I don't know your name. To tell her, I mean."

"Just say Oliver Dobbs."

"All right, Mr. Dobbs." She hesitated, standing at the bottom of
the stairs, and then said, "I have to get the pram and my coat from
the cloakroom. Will you hold Thomas for a moment?"

"Of course."

He lifted the child out of her arms, hoisting him up against one
shoulder.

"I won't be long, Thomas," Helga assured him, and she turned
and went down the passage beneath the staircase, and disappeared
through a half-glassed door.

A pretty, trusting, stupid little girl. He hoped they would not be
too hard on her. *You can be as long as you like, my darling.* Carrying
his son he went down the hall, let himself out through the yellow
front door, went down the steps and got into his waiting car.

Helga heard the car go down the street, but she did not realize it was Oliver's. When she returned with the push chair, there was no sign of either the man or the child.

"Mr. Dobbs?"

He had left the front door open, and the house was invaded by the bitter cold of the afternoon.

"Thomas?"

But outside was only the empty pavement, the silent street.

2

FRIDAY

*T*he most exhausting thing in the world, Victoria Bradshaw decided, was not having enough to do. It was infinitely more exhausting than having far too much to do, and today was a classic example.

February was a bad time for selling clothes. She supposed it was a bad time, really, for selling anything. Christmas was forgotten, and the January sales just a gruesome memory. The morning had started hopefully, with thin sunshine and a light icing of frost, but by early afternoon it had clouded over, and now it was so cold and wet that people with any sense at all were staying at home by fires or in centrally heated flats, doing crosswords or baking cakes or watching television. The weather gave them no encouragement to plan wardrobes for the spring.

The clock edged around to five o'clock. Outside, the bleak afternoon was darkening swiftly into night. The curved shop window had SALLY SHARMAN written across it. From the inside of the shop this presented itself backwards, like writing seen in a mirror, and beyond these hieroglyphics Beauchcamp Place was curtained in rain. Passersby, umbrellaed and gusted by wind, struggled with parcels. A stream of traffic waited for the Brompton Road lights to change. A figure, camouflaged by rainproof clothing, ran up the steps from the street and burst through the glass-paneled door like a person escaping, letting in a gust of cold air before the door was hastily slammed shut again.

It was Sally, in her black raincoat and her huge red fox hat. She said, "God, what a day," furled her umbrella, took off her gloves and began to unbutton her coat.

"How did it go?" Victoria asked.

Sally had spent the afternoon in the company of a young designer who had decided to go into the wholesale trade.

"Not bad," she said, draping her coat over the umbrella stand to drip. "Not bad at all. Lots of new ideas, good colors. Rather mature clothes. I was surprised. I thought his being so young, it would have been all jeans and workmen's shirts, but not at all."

She pulled off her hat, shook it free of raindrops, and finally emerged as her usual, lanky, elegant self. Narrow trousers tucked into tall boots, and a string-like sweater that on anyone else would have looked like an old floor-cloth, but on Sally was sensational.

She had started life as a model and had never lost her beanpole shape or the ugly, jutting, photogenic bones of her face. From being a model, she had gravitated to the editorial pages of a fashion magazine, and from there, using her accumulated know-how, her many connections, and a natural flair for business, had opened her own shop. She was nearly forty, divorced, hard-headed, but far more tenderhearted than she liked anybody to suspect. Victoria had worked for her for nearly two years and was very fond of her.

Now, she yawned. "I really hate business lunches. I always feel hung over by the middle of the afternoon, and somehow that throws me for the rest of the day."

She reached into her immense handbag and took out cigarettes and an evening paper, which she tossed down onto the glass counter. "What's been happening here?"

"Practically nothing. I sold the beige overdress, and some female came in and dithered for half an hour over the paisley coat, and then she went out again and said she'd think it over. She was put off by the mink collar. She says she's a wildlife supporter."

"Tell her we'll take it off and put on plastic fur instead." Sally went through the curtained doorway into the small office at the back of the shop, sat at her desk and began to open the mail.

She said, "You know, Victoria, I've been thinking, this would be a terribly good time for you to take a couple of weeks off. Things'll start livening up soon, and then I shan't be able to let you go. Besides, you haven't had a holiday since goodness knows when. The only thing is, February isn't very exciting anywhere. Perhaps you could go and ski, or stay with your mother in Sotogrande. What's Sotogrande like in February?"

"Windy and wet, I should think."

Sally looked up. "You don't want to take two weeks off in February," she announced resignedly. "I can tell by your voice." Victoria did not contradict her. Sally sighed. "If I had a mother who had a gorgeous house in Sotogrande, I'd stay with her every month of the year if I could. Besides, you look as though you need a holiday. All skinny and pale. It makes me feel guilty having you around, as though I worked you too hard." She opened another envelope. "I thought we'd paid that electricity bill. I'm sure we paid it. It must be the computer's fault. It must have gone mad. Computers do, you know."

To Victoria's relief the question of her suddenly taking a holiday at the end of February was, for the moment, forgotten. She picked up the newspaper that Sally had tossed down, and for lack of anything better to do, leafed idly through it, her eye skimming the usual disasters, both great and small. There were floods in Essex, a new conflagration threatened in Africa. A middle-aged earl was marrying his third wife, and in Bristol rehearsals were under way at the Fortune Theatre for Oliver Dobbs' new play, *Bent Penny.*

There was no reason why she should have noticed this little scrap of news. It was tucked in at the end of the last column on the entertainments page. There was no headline. No photograph. Just Oliver's name, which leapt out at her, like a shout of recognition, from the small print.

". . . . it's a final demand. What a nerve, sending a final demand. I know I wrote a cheque last month." Victoria said nothing, and Sally looked at her. "Victoria . . . ? What are you staring at?"

"Nothing. Just this bit in the paper about a man I used to know."

"I hope he's not being sent to jail."

"No, he writes plays. Have you ever heard of Oliver Dobbs?"

"Yes, of course. He writes for television. I saw one of his short plays the other night. And he did the script for that marvelous documentary on Seville. What's he been doing to get himself in the news?"

"He's got a new production coming off in Bristol."

"What's he like?" Sally asked idly, half her mind still on the iniquities of the London Electricity Board.

"Attractive."

This caught Sally's attention. She was all in favor of attractive men. "Did he attract you?"

"I was eighteen and impressionable."

"Weren't we all, darling, in the dim days of our youth. Not that that applies to you. You're still a blooming child, you fortunate creature." Suddenly she lost interest in Oliver Dobbs, in the final demand, in the day, which had already gone on far too long. She leaned back and yawned. "To hell with it. Let's shut up shop and go home. Thank the Lord for weekends. All at once the prospect of nothing to do for two days is total paradise. I shall spend this evening sitting in a hot bath and watching television."

"I thought you'd be going out."

Sally's private life was both complicated and lively. She had a string of men friends, none of whom seemed to be aware of the others' existence. Like an adroit juggler, Sally kept them all on the go, and avoided the embarrassment of inadvertently muddling their names by calling them all "darling."

"No, thank God. How about you?"

"I'm meant to be going out to have a drink with some friends of my mother's. I don't suppose it will be very thrilling."

"Oh, well," said Sally, "you never know. Life is full of surprises."

One of the good things about working in Beauchamp Place was that it was within walking distance of Pendleton Mews. The flat in Pendleton Mews belonged to Victoria's mother, but it was Victoria who lived there. Most of the time she enjoyed the walk. Down shortcuts and narrow back roads, it only took half an hour and provided a little pleasant exercise and fresh air at the beginning and the end of the day.

But this evening it was so cold and wet that the prospect of a trudge through icy wind and rain was almost more than she could bear; so, breaking her own rule about never taking taxis, she succumbed, without much resistance, to temptation, walked up to the Bromptom Road and finally flagged down a cab.

Because of one-way streets and snarled-up traffic, it took perhaps ten minutes longer to reach the Mews than if she had made the journey on foot, and cost so much that she simply handed the driver a pound note and let him count out the meagre change. He had set her down at the arch that divided the Mews from the road, so there was still a little way to go, across the puddles and the shining wet cobbles before she reached at last the haven of her own blue front door. She opened the door with her latch key, reached inside and switched on the light; climbed the steep, narrow stairs, carpeted in worn beige Wilton, and emerged at the top directly into the small sitting room.

She shed umbrella and basket and went to draw the chintz curtains against the night. The room at once became enclosed and safe. She lit the gas fire and went through to the tiny kitchen to put on a kettle for a cup of coffee; switched on the television and then switched it off again, put a Rossini overture on the record player, went into her bedroom to take off raincoat and boots.

The kettle, competing with Rossini, whistled for attention. She made a mug of instant coffee, went back to the fireside, pulled her basket towards her and took out Sally's evening paper. She turned to the item about Oliver Dobbs and the new play in Bristol.

I was eighteen and impressionable, she had said to Sally, but she knew now that she had also been lonely and vulnerable, a ripe fruit, trembling on its stalk, waiting to fall.

And Oliver, of all men, had been standing at the foot of the tree, waiting to catch her.

Eighteen, and in her first year at art school. Knowing nobody, intensely shy and unsure of herself, she had been both flattered and apprehensive when an older girl, perhaps taking pity on Victoria, had flung a vague invitation to a party in her direction.

"Goodness knows what it'll be like, but I was told I could ask anybody I wanted. You're meant to bring a bottle of something, but I don't suppose it matters if you come empty handed. Anyway, it's a good way to meet people. Look, I'll write down the address. The man's called Sebastian, but that doesn't matter. Just turn up if you feel like it. Any time; that doesn't matter either."

Victoria had never had such an invitation in her life. She decided that she wouldn't go. And then decided that she would. And then got cold feet. And finally put on a pair of clean jeans, stole a bottle of her mother's best claret, and went.

She ended up in a top floor flat in West Kensington, clutching her bottle of claret and knowing nobody. Before she had been there two minutes somebody said "How immensely kind," and removed the bottle of claret, but nobody else said a single word to her. The room was filled with smoke, intense men in beads, and girls with grey faces and long seaweed-like hair. There was even a grubby baby or two. There was nothing to eat and—once she had parted with the claret— nothing recognizable to drink. She could not find the girl who suggested that she come and was too shy to join any of the tight, conversational groups gathered on floor, cushions or the single sagging sofa that had curly wire springs protruding from between arm and seat. She was, as well, too diffident to go and get her coat and leave. The air was filled with the sweet and insidious smell of marijuana, and she was standing in the bay window, lost in nerve-wracking fantasies of a possible police raid, when suddenly somebody said, "I don't know you, do I?"

Startled, Victoria swung round, so clumsily that she almost knocked the drink out of his hand.

"Oh, I am sorry . . ."

"It doesn't matter. It hasn't spilled. At least," he added, generously, "not very much."

He smiled as though this were a joke, and she smiled back, grateful for any friendly overture. Grateful too that out of such woebegone company the only man who had spoken to her was neither dirty, sweaty, nor drunk. On the contrary, he was perfectly presentable. Even attractive. Very tall, very slender with reddish hair that reached to the collar of his sweater, and an immensely distinguished beard.

He said, "You haven't got a drink."

"No."

"Don't you want one?"

She said no again, because she didn't and also because if she said that she did, he might go away to get her one and never come back again.

He seemed amused. "Don't you like it?"

Victoria looked at his glass. "I don't exactly know what it is."

"I don't suppose anybody does. But this tastes like . . ." He took a mouthful, thoughtfully, like a professional taster, rolling it round his mouth, finally swallowing it, ". . . red ink and aniseed balls."

"What's it going to do to the inside of your stomach?"

"We'll worry about that in the morning." He looked down at her, a frown of concentration furrowing his brow. "I *don't* know you, do I?"

"No. I don't suppose you do. I'm Victoria Bradshaw." Even saying her own name made her feel embarrassed, but he did not seem to think that there was anything embarrassing about it.

"And what do you do with yourself?"

"I've just started at art college."

"That explains how you got to this little do. Are you enjoying it?"

She looked around. "Not very much."

"I actually meant art college, but if you're not enjoying this very much, why don't you go home?"

"I thought it wouldn't be very polite."

He laughed at that. "You know, in this sort of company, politeness doesn't count all that much."

"I've only been here for ten minutes."

"And I've only been here for five." He finished his drink, tipping back his remarkable head and pouring the remains of the noxious tumbler down the back of his throat as easily as if it had ben a cold and tasty beer. Then he set the glass down on the window ledge and said, "Come on. We're leaving." And he put a hand under her elbow and steered her expertly towards the door, and without making the vaguest of excuses or even saying good-bye, they left.

At the top of the dingy staircase, she turned to face him.

"I didn't mean that."

"What didn't you mean?"

"I mean that I didn't want *you* to leave. I wanted *me* to leave."

"How do you know I didn't want to leave?"

"But it was a party!"

"I left those sort of parties behind light years ago. Come on, hurry up, let's get out into the fresh air."

On the pavement, in the soft dusk of a late summer's night, she stopped again. She said, "I'm all right now."

"And what is that supposed to mean?"

"I can get a taxi, and go home."

He began to smile. "Are you frightened?"

Victoria became embarrassed all over again. "No, of course not."

"Then what are you running away from?"

"I'm not running away from anything. I simply . . ."

"Want to go home?"

"Yes."

"Well you can't."

"Why not?"

"Because we're going to go and find a spaghetti house or something, and we're going to buy a proper bottle of wine, and you are going to tell me the story of your life."

An empty taxi hove into view, and he hailed it. It stopped, and he bundled her in. After he gave the taxi driver directions, they drove in silence for about five minutes, and then the taxi stopped and he bundled her out again. He paid off the taxi and led her across the pavement into a small and unpretentious restaurant, with a few tables crowded around the walls and the air thick with cigarette smoke and the good smells of cooking food. They were given a table in the corner without enough room for his long legs, but somehow he arranged them so that his feet didn't trip the passing waiters, and he ordered a bottle of wine and asked for a menu, and then he lit a cigarette and turned to her and said, "Now."

"Now what?"

"Now tell me. The story of your life."

She found herself smiling. "I don't even know who you are. I don't know what your name is."

"It's Oliver Dobbs." He went on, quite kindly, "You have to tell me everything, because I'm a writer. A real honest-to-God published writer, with an agent and an enormous overdraft, and a compulsion for listening. Do you know, nobody listens enough. People fall over themselves trying to tell other people things, and nobody ever listens. Did you know that?"

Victoria thought of her parents. "Yes, I suppose I do."

"You see? You suppose. You're not sure. Nobody's ever sure of anything. They should listen more. How old are you?"

"Eighteen."

"I thought you were less when I saw you. You looked about fifteen standing there in the window of that crumby joint. I was about to ring the welfare and tell them that a tiny junior minor was out on the streets at night."

The wine came, uncorked, a liter bottle dumped onto the table. He picked it up and filled their glasses. He said, "Where do you live?"

"Pendleton Mews."

"Where's that?"

She told him and he whistled. "How very smart. A real Knightsbridge girl. I didn't realize they went to art college. You must be immensely rich."

"Of course I'm not rich."

"Then why do you live in Pendleton Mews?"

"Because it's my mother's house, only she's living in Spain just now, so I use it."

"Curiouser and curiouser. Why is Mrs. Bradshaw living in Spain?"

"She's not Mrs. Bradshaw, she's Mrs. Paley. My parents divorced six months ago. My mother married again, to this man called Henry Paley, and he has a house in Sotogrande because he likes playing golf all the time." She decided to get it all over in a single burst. "And my father has gone to live with some cousin who owns a moldering estate in Southern Ireland. He's threatening to breed polo ponies, but he's always been a man of great ideas but little action, so I don't suppose he will."

"And little Victoria is left to live in London."

"Victoria is eighteen."

"Yes, I know, old and experienced. Do you live alone?"

"Yes."

"Aren't you lonely?"

"I'd rather be alone than live with people who dislike each other."

He made a face. "Parents are hell, aren't they? My parents are hell, too, but they've never done anything so definite as divorcing each other. They just molder on in darkest Dorset, and everything—their reduced circumstances, the cost of a bottle of gin, the fact that the hens aren't laying—is blamed on either me or the government."

Victoria said, "I like my parents. It was just that they'd stopped liking each other."

"Have you got brothers or sisters?"

"No. Just me."

"No one to take care of you?"

"I take very good care of myself."

He looked disbelieving. "*I* shall take care of you," he announced, magnificently.

After that evening Victoria did not see Oliver Dobbs again for two weeks, and by that time she knew that she was never going to see him again. And then it was a Friday evening, and she was so miserable that she compulsively spring-cleaned the flat, which did not need it, and then decided to wash her hair.

It was while she was kneeling by the bath with her head under the shower that she heard the bell ring. She wrapped herself up in a towel and went to open the door, and it was Oliver. Victoria was so pleased to see him that she burst into tears, and he came in and shut the door and took her in his arms, then and there, at the foot of the stairs, and dried her face with the end of the towel. After this they went upstairs, and he produced a bottle of wine out of his jacket pocket, and she found some glasses, and they sat by the gas fire and drank wine together. And when they had finished the wine, she went into her bedroom to get dressed, and to comb out her long, fair, damp tresses, and Oliver sat on the end of the bed and watched her. And then he took her out for dinner. There were no apologies, no excuses for his two weeks silence. He had been in Birmingham, he told her, and that was all. It never occurred to Victoria to ask him what he had been doing there.

And this proved to be the pattern of their relationship. He came and went, in and out of her life, unpredictable, and yet strangely constant. Each time he came back, she never knew where he had been. Perhaps Ibiza, or perhaps he had met some man who owned a cottage in Wales. He was not only unpredictable, he was strangely secretive. He never spoke about his work, and she did not even know where he lived, except that it was a basement flat in some street off the Fulham Road. He was moody, too, and once or twice she had seen a terrifying flash of uncontrollable temper, but this all seemed to be an acceptable part of the fact that he was a writer and a true artist. And there was another side to the coin. He was funny and loving and immensely good company. It was like having the kindest sort of older brother who was, at the same time, irresistibly attractive.

When they were not together, she told herself that he was working. She imagined him at his typewriter, writing and rewriting, destroying, starting again, never achieving his own goals of perfection. Sometimes, he had a little money to spend on her. At others, none at all, and then Victoria would provide the food and cook it for him in the Mews flat, and she would buy him a bottle of wine and the small cigars that she knew he loved.

There came a bad period when he went through a slough of despondency. Nothing would go right and nothing seemed to be selling, and it was then that he took the night job in a little café, piling dirty dishes into the automatic washer. After that things began to get better again, and he sold a play to Independent Television, but he still went on washing dishes in order to be able to earn enough money to pay his rent.

Victoria had no other men friends, and did not want them. For some reason, she never imagined Oliver with other women. There was no occasion for jealousy. What she had of Oliver was not much, but it was enough.

The first she heard of Jeannette Archer was when Oliver told her that he was going to be married.

It was early summer, and the windows of Victoria's flat were open to the Mews. Below, Mrs. Tingley from number fourteen was bedding out geraniums in her decorative tubs, and the man who lived two doors down was cleaning his car. Pigeons cooed from rooftops, and the distant hum of traffic was deadened by trees in full leaf. They sat on the window seat, and Victoria was sewing a button onto Oliver's jacket. It hadn't fallen off, but it was going to, and she had offered to sew it on before it did. She found a needle and thread and put a knot in the thread and pushed the needle into the worn corduroy when Oliver said, "What would you say if I told you I was going to be married?"

Victoria pushed the needle right into her thumb. The pain was minute but excruciating. She pulled the needle carefully out and watched the red bead of blood swell and grow. Oliver said, "Suck it, quickly, or it'll drip all over my coat," and when she didn't, he took her wrist and thrust her thumb into his mouth. Their eyes met. He said, "Don't look at me like that."

Victoria looked at her thumb. It throbbed as though some person had hit it with a hammer. She said, "I don't know any other way to look."

"Well say something then. Don't just stare at me like a lunatic."

"I don't know what I'm meant to say."

"You could wish me luck."

"I didn't know . . . that you . . . I mean, I didn't know that you were . . . ." She was trying, even at this ghastly juncture, to be rational, polite, tactful. But Oliver scorned such euphemisms and interrupted brutally.

"You mean, you never realized that there was anybody else? And that, if you like it, is a line, straight from an out-of-date novel. The kind my mother reads."

"Who is she?"

"She's called Jeannette Archer. She's twenty-four, a nicely brought-up girl with a nice flat and a nice little car, and a good job, and we've been living together for the past four months."

"I thought you lived in Fulham."

"I do sometimes, but I haven't just lately."

She said, "Do you love her?" because she simply had to know.

"Victoria, she's going to have a child. Her parents want me to marry her so that the baby will have a father. It seems to matter to them very much."

"I thought you didn't pay regard to parents."

"I don't if they're like mine, complaining and unsuccessful. But these particular parents happen to have a lot of money. I need money. I need money to buy the time to write."

Her thumb still ached. Her eyes were filling with tears, and so that he shouldn't see them, she dropped her head and started to try to sew on the button, but the tears brimmed over and rolled down her cheeks and fell, great drops on the corduroy of his coat. He saw them and said, "Don't cry." And he put a hand under her chin and lifted her streaming face.

Victoria said, "I love you."

He leaned forward and kissed her cheek. "But you," he told her, "don't happen to be having a baby."

The clock on the mantelpiece astonished her by chiming, with silvery notes, seven o'clock. Victoria looked at it, disbelieving, and then at her wristwatch. Seven o'clock. The Rossini had finished long ago, the dregs in her coffee mug were stone cold, outside it was still raining, and in half an hour she was due at a party in Campden Hill.

She was assailed by the usual small panic of one who has lost all trace of time, and all thoughts of Oliver Dobbs were, for the moment, forgotten. Victoria sprang to her feet and did a number of things in quick succession. Took the coffee mug back into the kitchen, turned on a bath, went into her room to open her wardrobe and take out various garments, none of which seemed suitable. She took off some clothes and searched for stockings. She thought about ringing up for a taxi. She thought about calling Mrs. Fairburn and pleading a headache, and then thought better of it, because the Fairburns were friends of her mother's, the invitation was a long-standing one, and Victoria had a horror of causing offense. She went into the steaming bathroom and turned off the taps and splashed in some bath oil. The steam became scented. She disposed of her long hair in a bathcap, slathered cold cream on her face and wiped it all off again with a tissue. She climbed into the scalding water.

Fifteen minutes later she was out once more and dressed. A black silk turtleneck with a peasant-embroidered smock on top of it. Black stockings, black shoes with very high heels. She blackened her thick lashes with mascara, clipped on earrings, sprayed on some scent.

Now, a coat. She drew back the curtains and opened the window and leaned out to gauge the weather. It was very dark and still windy, but the rain, for the moment, seemed to have ceased. Below, the Mews was quiet. Cobbles shone like fish scales, black puddles reflected the light from the old-fashioned street lamps. A car was turning in from the street, under the archway. It nosed down the Mews like a prowling cat. Victoria withdrew her head, closed the windows and the curtains. She took an old fur coat from the back of the door, bundled herself into its familiar comfort, checked for her keys and wallet, turned off the gas fire and all the upstairs lights, and started downstairs.

She had taken one step when the doorbell rang.

She said, "Damn." It was probably Mrs. Tingley come to borrow milk. She was always running out of milk. And she would want to stand and talk. Victoria ran to the foot of the stairs and flung open the door.

On the far side of the Mews, beneath a lamp, the prowling cat was parked. A big old Volvo estate car. But of its driver there was no sign. Puzzled, she hesitated, and was about to go and investigate, when, from the dark shadows at the side of the door, a figure moved soundlessly forward, causing Victoria nearly to jump out of her skin. He said her name, and it was as though she had been taken, very swiftly, down twenty-three stories in a very fast lift. The wind blew a scrap of newspaper the length of the Mews. She could hear the beating of her own heart.

"I didn't know if you'd still be living here."

She thought, these things don't happen. Not to ordinary people. They only happen in books.

"I thought you might have moved. I was sure you'd have moved."

She shook her head.

He said, "It's been a long time."

Victoria's mouth was dry. She said, "Yes."

Oliver Dobbs. She searched for some change in him but could find none. His hair was the same, his beard, his light eyes, his deep and gentle voice. He even wore the same sort of clothes, shabby and casual garments that on his tall, lean frame did not look shabby at all but somehow contrived and distinctive.

He said, "You look as though you're just going out."

"Yes, I am. I'm late as it is. But . . ." She stepped back. ". . . You'd better come in, out of the cold."

"Is that all right?"

"Yes." But she said again, "I have to go out," as if her going out were some sort of an escape hatch from a possibly impossible situation. She turned to lead the way back upstairs. He began to follow her and then hesitated. He said, "I've left my cigarettes in the car."

He plunged back into the outdoors. Halfway up the stairs Victoria waited. He returned in a moment, closed the door behind him. She went up, turning on the light at the head of the stairs, and was going to stand with her back to the unlit gas fire.

Olive followed her, his eyes alert, instantly scanning the pretty room, the pale walls, the chintzes, patterned with spring flowers. The pine corner-cupboard that Victoria had found in a junk shop and stripped herself, her pictures, her books.

He smiled, satisfied. "You haven't changed anything. It's exactly the way I remembered. How marvelous to find something that hasn't changed." His eyes came back to her face. "I thought you'd have gone. I thought you'd have married some guy and moved. I was so certain that the door would be opened by a complete stranger. And there you were. Like a miracle."

Victoria found that she could think of absolutely nothing to say. She thought, I have been struck speechless. Searching for words, she found herself looking around the room. Beneath the bookcase was the cupboard where she kept a meagre collection of bottles. She said, "Would you like a drink?"

"Yes, I'd like one very much."

She laid down her bag and went to crouch by the cupboard. There was sherry, half a bottle of wine, a nearly empty bottle of whisky. She took out the whisky bottle. "There isn't much, I'm afraid."

"That's marvelous." He came to take the bottle from her. "I'll do it." He disappeared into the kitchen, at home in her flat as if he had walked out only yesterday. She heard the chink of glass, the running of the tap.

"Do you want one?" he called.

"No thank you."

He emerged from the kitchen with the drink in his hand. "Where's this party you're going to?"

"Campden Hill. Some friends of my mother's."

"Is it going on for long?"

"I don't suppose so."

"Will you come back for dinner?"

Victoria almost laughed at this, because this was Oliver Dobbs, apparently inviting her to have dinner with him in her own flat.

"I imagine I will."

"Then you go to your party, and I'll wait here." He saw the expression her face and added quickly, "It's important. I want to talk to you. And I want to have time to talk to you."

It sounded sinister, as though someone was after him, like the police, or some Soho heavy with a switch knife.

"There's nothing wrong, is there?"

"How anxious you look! No, there's nothing wrong." He added, in a practical fashion, "Have you got any food in the house?"

"There's some soup. Some bacon and eggs. I could make a salad. Or, if you wanted, we could go out. There's a Greek restaurant around the corner, it's just started up . . ."

"No, we can't go out." He sounded so definite that Victoria began to be apprehensive all over again. He went on, "I didn't want to tell you right away until I knew what the form was with you. The thing is, there's someone else in the car. There are two of us."

"Two of you?" She imagined a girlfriend, a drunken crony, even a dog.

In answer Oliver laid down his glass and disappeared once more down the stairs. She heard the door open and his footsteps crossing the Mews. She went to the head of the stairs and waited for him to return. He had left the door open, and when he reappeared he closed this behind him, carefully with his foot. The reason that he did this was that his arms were otherwise occupied with the weight of a large, mercifully sleeping, baby boy.

3

FRIDAY

*I*t was a quarter past seven, at the end of a grueling day, before John Dunbeath finally turned his car into the relative quiet of Cadogan Place, down the narrow lane between tightly parked cars, and edged it into a meagre gap not too far from his own front door. He killed the engine, turned off the lights, and reached into the back seat for his bulging briefcase and his raincoat. He got out of the car and locked up.

He had left his office, and commenced the daily ordeal of the journey home, in lashing rain, but now, half an hour or so later, it seemed to be easing up a little. Dark and still windy, the sky, bronzed with the reflected low of the city lights, seemed to be full of ominous, racing clouds. After ten hours spent in an overheated atmosphere, the night air smelled fresh and invigorating. Walking slowly down the pavement, his briefcase slapping against his leg, he took one or two deep and conscious lungfuls, and was refreshed by the cold wind.

With his key ring in his hand, he went up the steps to the front door. It was black, with a brass handle and a letter box that the porter polished every morning. The tall old London house had been turned, some time ago, into flats, and the lobby and staircase, although carpeted and neatly kept, always smelled stale and stuffy, unaired and claustrophobic with central heating. This odor greeted him now, as it greeted him every evening. He shut the door with the seat of his pants, collected his mail from its pigeon hole and began to climb the stairs.

He lived on the second floor, in an apartment that had been cunningly contrived from the main bedrooms of the original house. It was a furnished flat, found for him by a colleague when John had left New York and come to work in London at the European headquarters of the Warburg Investment Corporation, and he had arrived at Heathrow off the plane from Kennedy and taken instant possession. Now, six months later, it had become familiar. Not a home, but familiar. A place for a man alone to live.

He let himself in, turned on the lights and saw on the hall table his message from Mrs. Robbins, the daily lady whom the porter had recommended should come in each morning to clean the flat. John had only seen her once, at the very beginning, when he had given her a key and told her more or less what he wanted her to do. Mrs. Robbins had made it clear that this was quite unnecessary. She was a stately person, portentously hatted and wearing her respectability like armor. At the end of the encounter he was fully aware that he had not been interviewing her, but that Mrs. Robbins had been judging him. However, it seemed that he had passed muster, and she duly took him on, along with one or two other privileged persons who also lived in the house. Since then, he had never set eyes on her, but they corresponded by means of notes that they left for each other, and he paid her, weekly, in the same fashion.

He dropped his briefcase, slung his raincoat onto a chair, picked up Mrs. Robbins' letter, and along with the rest of his mail took it into the sitting room. Here all was beige and brown and totally impersonal. Another person's pictures hung upon the wall; another person's books filled the shelves which flanked the fireplace, and he had no wish for it to be any different.

Sometimes, for no particular reason, the emptiness of his personal life, the need for welcome, for love, would overwhelm him, breaking down the careful barriers which he had painfully built. On these occasions, he could not stop the memories flooding back. Like coming home to the shining brilliance of the New York apartment, with its white floors and its white rugs, and a sort of perfection which Lisa had achieved with her eye for color, her passion for detail and her total disregard for her husband's bank balance. And, inevitably, Lisa would be there, waiting for him—for these memories belonged to the beginning of their marriage—so beautiful that she took your breath away, wearing something gauzy by de la Renta, and smelling unbearably exotic. And she would kiss him, and put a martini into his hand, and be glad to see him.

But most times, like this evening, he was grateful for quiet, for peace; for time to read his mail, to have a drink, to reassemble himself after the day's work. He went around the room turning on lights; he switched on the electric fire which instantly became a pile of rustic logs, flickering in the pseudo firebasket. He drew the brown velvet curtains and poured himself a Scotch, and then read the message from Mrs. Robbins.

Her notes were always brief and abbreviated, rendering them as important sounding as cables.

Laundry missing pair sox and 2 hankchfs.
Miss Mansell called says will you ring her this evng.

He leafed through the rest of his mail. A bank statement, a company report, a couple of invitations, an airmail letter from his mother. Putting these aside for later perusal, he sat on the arm of the sofa, reached for the telephone and dialed a number.

She came on almost at once, sounding breathless as she always did, as though perpetually in a tearing hurry.

"Hello?"

"Tania."

"Darling. I thought you'd never call."

"Sorry, I'm only just back. Just picked up your message now."

"Oh, poor sweet, you must be exhausted. Listen, something maddening's cropped up, but I can't make this evening. The thing is, I'm going down to the country *now*. Mary Colville rang up this morning, and there's some dance going on, and some girls got flu, and she's desperate about her numbers, and I simply had to say I'd go. I tried to say no, and explain about this evening, but then she said would *you* come down tomorrow, for the weekend."

She stopped, not because she hadn't got plenty more to say, but because she had run out of breath. John found himself smiling. Her spates of words, her breathlessness, her confused social arrangements were all part of the charm that she held for him, mostly because she was so diametrically different from his ex-wife. Tania had, perpetually, to be organized, and was so scatty that the thought of organizing John never entered her pretty feather-head.

He looked at his watch. He said, "If you're going to be at some dinner party in the country this evening, aren't you running things a little fine?"

"Oh, darling, yes. I'm going to be desperately late, but that's not what you're meant to say at all. You're meant to be desperately disappointed."

"Of course I'm disappointed."

"And you will come down to the country tomorrow?"

"Tania, I can't. I just heard today. I have to go to the Middle East. I'm flying out tomorrow morning."

"Oh, I can't bear it. How long are you going for?"

"Just a few days. A week at the outside. It depends on how things go."

"Will you call me when you get back?"

"Yes, sure."

"I rang Imogen Fairburn and told her I couldn't make it this evening, so she understands, and she says she's looking forward to seeing you even if I can't be there too. Oh, darling, isn't everything grim? Are you furious?"

"Furious," he assured her, mildly.

"But you do understand, don't you?"

"I understand completely, and you thank Mary for her invitation and explain why I can't make it."

"Yes, I will, of course I will, and . . ."

Another of her characteristics was that she could never finish a phone call. He interrupted firmly.

"Look, Tania, you have an appointment this evening. Get off the line and finish your packing and get moving. With luck, you'll arrive at the Colvilles no more than two hours late."

"Oh, darling, I do adore you."

"I'll call you."

"You do that." She made kissing sounds. "Bye." She hung up. He put the receiver back on the hook and sat looking at it, wondering why he couldn't feel disappointed when a charming and engaging female stood him up for a more exciting invitation. He mulled over this problem for a moment or two, and finally decided that it didn't matter anyway. So he dialed Annabel's and cancelled the table he had ordered for this evening and then he finished his drink and went to have a shower.

Just as he was on the point of leaving for the Fairburns' a call came through from his vice president, who had had, on his journey home in the company Cadillac, one or two important thoughts about John's projected trip to Bahrain. Discussing these, getting them collated and noted, had taken a good fifteen minutes, so that by the time John finally arrived at the house in Campden Hill, he was nearly three quarters of an hour late.

The party was obviously in full swing. The street outside was jammed with cars—it took him another frustrating five minutes to find a scrap of space in which to park his own—and light and a steady hum of conversation emanated from beyond the tall, curtained first-floor windows. When he rang the bell the door was opened almost immediately by a man (hired for the occasion?) in a white coat, who said, "Good evening," and directed John up the stairs.

It was a pleasant and familiar house, expensively decorated, thickly carpeted, smelling like an extravagant hothouse. As John ascended, the sound of voices swelled to a massive volume. Through the open door that led into Imogen's drawing room, he could discern an anonymous crush of people, some drinking, some smoking, some munching canapés, and all intent on talking their heads off. A couple was sitting at the head of the stairs. John smiled and excused himself as he stepped around them, and the girl said, "We're just having a tiny breath of air," as though she felt she must apologize for being there.

By the open door was a table set up as a bar, with another hired waiter in attendance.

"Good evening, sir. What'll it be?"

"Scotch and soda, please."

"With ice, sir, naturally."

John grinned. The "naturally" meant that the barman had recognized him for the American that he was. He said, "Naturally," and took the drink. "How am I going to find Mrs. Fairburn?"

"I'm afraid you'll just have to go and look for her, sir. Like a needle in a ruddy haystack, I'd say."

John agreed with him, took a spine-stiffening slug of whiskey and plunged.

It wasn't as bad as it might have been. He was recognized, greeted, almost at once, drawn into a group, offered a smoked salmon roll, a cigar, a racing tip. "Absolute certainty, old boy, three-thirty at Doncaster tomorrow." A girl he knew slightly came and kissed him and, he suspected, left lipstick on his cheek. A tall young man with an old man's balding head swam forward and said, "You're John Dunbeath, aren't you? Name's Crumleigh. Used to know your predecessor. And how are things in the banking world?"

He was nursing his drink, but a waiter nipped up and refilled his glass when he wasn't looking. Somebody trod on his shoe. A very young man wearing a brigade tie materialized at his elbow, trailing a protesting female by the arm. She was perhaps seventeen years old, and her hair looked like dandelion floss. ". . . This girl wants to meet you. Been eyeing you across the room."

"Oh, Nigel, you are *awful*."

Mercifully, he spied his hostess. He excused himself, and edged, with some difficulty, across the room to her side. "Imogen."

"John! Darling!"

She was immensely pretty. Grey-haired, blue-eyed, her skin smooth as a young girl's, her manner unashamedly provocative.

He kissed her politely, because she was obviously expecting to be kissed, with that flower-face turned up to his.

"This certainly is a party."

"So gorgeous to see you. But Tania couldn't come. She telephoned, something about having to go down to the country. So terribly disappointing. I was so looking forward to seeing you *both*. Never mind, you came and that's all that matters. Have you had a word with Reggie? He's longing to have a long, boring chat with you about the stock market or something." A couple hovered, waiting to say good-bye. "Don't go away," Imogen told John out of the corner of her mouth, and then turned from him, all smiles. "Darling. Do you really have to go? Such a sadness. Heavenly to see you. So glad you enjoyed it . . ." She came back to John. "Look, as Tania hasn't come, and you're on your own, there's a girl that perhaps you could go and chat up. She's pretty as paint, so I'm not letting you in for anything gruesome, but I don't think she knows many people. I mean, I asked her, because her mother's one of our greatest friends, but somehow she seems a little out of her depth. Be an angel, and be sweet to her."

John, whose party manners had been rigorously drilled into him by his American mother (Imogen knew this, otherwise she would never have appealed to him for help) said that he would be delighted. But where was the girl?

Imogen, who was not tall, stood tiptoes, and searched with her eyes. "There. Over in the corner." Her little feminine hand closed over his wrist like a vise. "I'll take you over and introduce you."

Which she proceeded to do, shouldering her way across the stifling room without once releasing her grip of him. John tagged along, willy-nilly, feeling like a bulky liner in the tow of a tug. They emerged at last, and it seemed to be a quiet corner of the room, perhaps because it was furthest from the door and the bar, but all at once there was room to stand, or move your elbows or even sit.

"Victoria."

She was perched on the arm of a chair, talking to an elderly man who was obviously going on to some other party, for he was wearing a dinner suit and a black tie. When Imogen said her name, she stood up, but whether this was out of politeness to Imogen, or to escape from her companion, it was impossible to say.

"Victoria, I do hope I'm not interrupting something absolutely riveting, but I do want you to meet John, because his girlfriend hasn't been able to come tonight, and I want you to be terribly kind to him." John, embarrassed both for himself and the girl, continued to smile politely. "He's an American, and he's one of my most favorite people . . ."

With a clearing of the throat, and a small, imperceptible gesture of farewell, the elderly man in the dinner suit also stood up and eased himself away.

". . . and John"—the grip on his wrist had not lessened. Perhaps the blood stream to his hand had already seized up and in a moment his fingers would start falling off—"this is Victoria. And her mother is one of my best friends, and when Reggie and I were in Spain last year, we went and stayed with her. At Sotogrande. In the most heavenly house you've ever seen. So now you've got *lots* to talk about."

She let go of his wrist at last. It was like being freed from handcuffs.

He said, "Hello, Victoria."

She said, "Hello."

Imogen had chosen the wrong words. She was not pretty as paint. But she had a scrubbed, immaculate look to her that reminded him, with some nostalgia, of the American girls he had known in his youth. Her hair was pale and silky, straight and long, cut cunningly to frame her face. Her eyes were blue, her face neatly boned, her head supported by a long neck and narrow shoulders. She had an unremarkable nose, disarmingly freckled, and a remarkable mouth. A sweet and expressive mouth with a dimple at one corner.

It was an out-of-doors sort of face. The sort of face one expected to encounter at the tiller of a sailboat or at the top of some hair-raising ski-slope; not at a London cocktail party.

"Did Imogen say Sotogrande?"

"Yes."

"How long has your mother lived out there?"

"About three years. Have you ever been to Sotogrande?"

"No, but I have friends who golf, and they get out there whenever they can."

"My stepfather plays golf every day. That's why he chose to go and live there. Their house is right on the fairway. He steps out of the garden gate and he's playing the tenth hole. It's as easy as that."

"Do you play golf?"

"No. But there are other things to do. You can swim. Play tennis. Ride, if you want to."

"What do you do?"

"Well, I don't very often go out, but when I do I play tennis mostly."

"Does your mother come back to this country?"

"Yes. Two or three times a year. She dashes round from one art gallery to another, sees about six plays, buys some clothes, and then goes back again."

He smiled at this, and she smiled back. There came a small pause. The subject of Sotogrande seemed to have exhausted itself. Her eyes moved over his shoulder, and then quickly, as though she did not wish to appear ill-mannered, back to his face again. He wondered if she was expecting somebody.

He said, "Do you know many people here?"

"No, not really. Not anybody really." She added, "I'm sorry your girlfriend couldn't come."

"Like Imogen said, she had to go down to the country."

"Yes." She stooped to take a handful of nuts out of a dish that had been placed on a low coffee-table. She began to eat them, putting them into her mouth one at a time. "Did Imogen say you were American?"

"Yes, I think she did."

"You don't sound like an American."

"How do I sound?"

"Sort of halfway between. Mid-Atlantic. Alistair Cooke type American."

He was impressed. "You have a sharp ear. I have an American mother and British father. I'm sorry . . . a Scottish father."

"So you're really British?"

"I have a dual passport. I was born in the States."

"Whereabouts?"

"Colorado."

"Was your mother skiing at the time, or do your parents live there?"

"No, they live there. They have a ranch in Southwest Colorado."

"I can't imagine where that is."

"North of New Mexico. West of the Rockies. East of the San Juans."

"I'd have to have an atlas. But it sounds very spectacular."

"It is spectacular."

"Were you riding a horse before you could walk?"

"Just about."

She said, "I can imagine it," and he had a strange feeling that she probably could. "When did you leave Colorado?"

He told her. "At eleven years old I was sent East to school. And then I came over to this country and I went to Wellington, because that's where my father had been. And after that I went to Cambridge."

"You really do have a dual nationality, don't you? What happened after Cambridge?"

"I went back to New York for a spell, and now I'm back in London. I've been here since the summer."

"Do you work for an American firm?"

"An investment bank."

"Do you get back to Colorado?"

"Sure, whenever I can. Only I haven't been for some time, because things have been pretty busy over here."

"Do you like being in London?"

"Yes, I like it very much." Her expression was very thoughtful. He smiled. "Why, don't you?"

"Yes. But just because I know it so well. I mean I can't imagine, really, living anywhere else."

There came, for some reason, another lull. Once more her eyes strayed, only this time it was to the gold watch strapped to her slender wrist. Having a pretty girl look at her watch while he was chatting her up was an unfamiliar experience for John Dunbeath. He expected to be irritated, but instead found himself mildly amused, although the joke was against himself.

"Are you expecting someone?" he asked her.

"No."

He thought that her face had a private look about it; composed, polite, but private. He wondered if she was always like this, or if their lines of communication were being cut by the murderous impossibility of cocktail party conversation. In order to keep this going, she had asked him a number of friendly questions, but there was no knowing whether she had listened to half of his polite replies. They had talked banalities and found out nothing about each other. Perhaps she wanted it this way. He could not decide whether she was totally disinterested or simply shy. Now, she had started glancing around the crowded room once more as though desperate for a means of escape, and he began to wonder why she had come in the first place. Suddenly exasperated, and ready to cast formalities aside, he was about to ask her this, but she forestalled him by announcing, without preamble, that she ought to be going. ". . . It's getting late, and I seem to have been here for ages." At once she seemed to realize that this remark was perhaps not much of a compliment to him. "I am sorry, I didn't mean it that way. I didn't mean that I seem to have been *here* for ages, I meant that I seem to have been at the party for ages. I . . . I've very much enjoyed meeting you, but I shouldn't be too late." John said nothing. She smiled brightly, hopefully. "I ought to get home."

"Where's home?"

"Pendleton Mews."

"That's very close to where I live. I'm Cadogan Place."

"Oh, how nice." Now she was beginning to sound desperate. "It's so quiet, isn't it?"

"Yes, it's very quiet."

Stealthily, she set down her glass, and hitched the strap of her bag up onto her shoulder. "Well, then, I'll say good-bye . . ."

But all at once he was consumed with an unfamiliar and healthy annoyance, and told himself that he was damned if he was going to be palmed off like this. Anyway, with his Scotch finished and no Tania to attend to, the party had gone sour for him. Tomorrow and the long flight to Bahrain loomed on the edge of his mind. He still had to pack, check his papers, leave messages for Mrs. Robbins.

He said, "I'm going too."

"But you've only just arrived."

He finished his drink and laid down the empty tumbler. "I'll take you home."

"You don't need to take me home."

"I know I don't need to, but I may as well."

"I can get a taxi."

"Why get a taxi, when we're going in the same direction?"

"There's really no need . . ."

He was becoming bored by the tedious argument. "No problem. I don't want to be late either. I have a plane to catch in the early morning."

"To America?"

"No, to the Middle East."

"What are you going to do there?"

He put a hand under her elbow in order to propel her in the direction of the door. "Talk," he told her.

Imogen was torn between astonishment that he had hit it off so swiftly with her dearest friend's daughter, and a certain peevishness that he had stayed at her party for such a short time.

"But, John darling, you've only just come."

"It's a great party, but I'm headed for the Middle East tomorrow; an early flight, and . . ."

"But tomorrow's *Saturday*. It's too cruel having to fly off on a Saturday. I suppose that's what happens if you're a budding tycoon. But I wish you could stay a little longer."

"I wish I could too, but I really must go."

"Well, it's been divine, and sweet of you to come. Have you talked to Reggie? No, I don't suppose you have, but I'll tell him what's happening, and you must come for dinner when you get home again. Good-bye, Victoria. Heaven to see you. I'll write and tell your mother you're looking fabulously well."

On the landing he said, "Have you got a coat?"

"Yes. It's downstairs."

They went down. On a chair in the hall was a mound of coats. She dug from this an unfashionable fur, probably inherited and much worn. John helped her into it. The man in the starched white coat opened the door for them, and they emerged into the windy darkness and walked together up the pavement to where he had parked his car.

Waiting at the end of Church Street for the lights to change, John became aware of pangs of hunger. He had eaten a sandwich for lunch and nothing since. The clock on his dashboard told him that it was nearly nine o'clock. The lights changed, and they moved out and into the stream of traffic that poured east towards Kensington Gore.

He thought about eating dinner. He glanced at the girl beside him. Her closeness, her reserve, was a challenge. It intrigued him, and against all reason he found himself wanting to break it down, to find out what went on behind that private face. It was like being confronted by a high wall, a notice saying No Trespassers, and imagining that beyond lay the promise of enchanting gardens and inviting tree-shaded walks. He saw her profile, outlined against the lights, her chin deep in the fur collar of the coat. He thought, well, why not?

He said, "Do you want to come and have dinner with me someplace?"

"Oh . . ." She turned towards him. "How kind."

"I have to eat, and if you'd like to join me . . ."

"I do appreciate it, but if you don't mind, I really should get back. I mean, I'm having dinner at home. I arranged to have dinner at home."

It was the second time she had used the word "home," and it disconcerted him, with its implication of close relatives. He wondered who waited for her. A sister, a lover, or even a husband. Anything was possible.

"That's all right. I just thought if you weren't doing anything."

"Really so kind of you, but I can't . . ."

A long silence fell between them, broken only by her giving him directions as to how to get most easily to Pendleton Mews. When they reached the archway that separated the Mews from the street, she said, "You can put me down here. I can walk the rest."

But by now he was feeling stubborn. If she would not have dinner with him, at least he would drive her to her door. He turned the car into the narrow angle beneath the arch and let it idle its way down between the garages and the painted front doors and the tubs that would soon be bright with spring flowers. The rain had stopped, but the cobbles were still damp and shone, like some country street, in the lamplight.

"Which number?" he asked.

"It's right at the very end. I'm afraid there's scarcely room to turn. You'll have to back out."

"That's all right."

"It's this one."

The lights were on. They shone from upstairs windows and through the small pane of glass at the top of the blue front door. She peered anxiously upwards as though expecting a window to be flung open and a face to appear, announcing bad news.

But nothing happened. She got out of the car, and John got out too, not because he wanted to be invited in, but because he had been meticulously brought up, and good manners insisted that a girl should not be simply dumped on her doorstep, but that her latchkey should be located, her door politely opened, her safety and well-being assured.

She had found her key. She had opened her door. She was, obviously, anxious to get away and up the stairs.

"Thank you so much for bringing me back. Really kind of you, and you didn't need to bother . . ."

She stopped. From upstairs there came the unmistakable wail of a furious child. The sound rooted them to where they stood. They stared at each other, the girl looking as astonished as John felt. The wails continued, rising in volume and fury. He expected some sort of an explanation, but none came. In the hard light from the staircase, her face was, all at once, very pale. She said in a strained sort of way, "Good night."

It was a dismissal. He thought, damn you. He said, "Good night, Victoria."

"Have a good time in Bahrain."

To hell with Bahrain. "I will."

"And thank you for bringing me home."

The blue front door was closed in his face. The light beyond was turned off. He looked up at the windows, secret behind the drawn curtains. He thought, and to hell with you too.

Getting back into his car he reversed at top speed down the length of the Mews and into the street, missing the side of the archway by inches. There he sat for a moment or two endeavouring to recover his natural good humor.

A baby. Whose baby? Probably her baby. There was no reason why she shouldn't have a baby. Just because she looked such a child herself, there was no reason why she shouldn't have a husband or a lover. A girl with a baby.

He thought, *I must tell Tania that. It'll make her laugh. You couldn't come to Imogen's party, so I went by myself and got hooked up with a girl who had to go home to her baby.*

As his annoyance abated, so did his hunger, and their going left him feeling flat. He decided to skip dinner and instead go back to his flat and make a sandwich. His car moved forward, and deliberately, his thoughts moved with it, ahead to the following day, to the early start, the drive to Heathrow, the long flight to Bahrain.

4

FRIDAY

O liver was on the sofa, holding the child standing up on his knees. As Victoria came up the stairs the first thing she saw was the back of Oliver's head and the round, red, tear-drenched face of his son. He, surprised by her sudden appearance, stopped crying for an instant, and then, realizing that it was no person he knew, at once started up again.

Oliver jigged him hopefully up and down, but it did no good. Victoria dropped her bag and came around to stand in front of them, unbuttoning her coat.

"How long has he been awake?"

"About ten minutes." The child roared furiously, and Oliver had to raise his voice in order to make his voice heard.

"What's wrong with him?"

"I imagine he's hungry." He got to his feet, heaving his burden with him. The little boy wore dungarees and a wrinkled white sweater. His hair was copper-gold, the curls at the nape of his neck tangled and damp. The only information Victoria had managed to elicit from Oliver before she had left for the Fairburns' was that the child was his son, and with that she had had to be content. She had left them together, the baby sound asleep on the sofa and Oliver peacefully downing his whiskey and water.

But now . . . She gazed with sinking apprehension. She knew nothing about babies. She had scarcely held a baby in her life. What did they eat? What did they want when they wept so heartbreakingly?

She said, "What's he called?"

"Tom." Oliver jigged him again, tried to turn him around in his arms. "Hey, Tom. Say hello to Victoria."

Tom took another look at Victoria and then let them know, lustily, what he thought of her. She took off her coat and dropped it onto a chair. "How old is he?"

"Two."

"If he's hungry, we should give him something to eat."

"That makes sense."

He was being no use at all. Victoria left him and went into the kitchen to search for suitable food for a baby. She stared into the cupboard at racks of spices, Marmite, flour, mustard, lentils, stock cubes.

What was he doing, back in her flat, back in her life, after three years of silence? What was he doing with the child? Where was its mother?

Jam, sugar, porridge oats. A packet brought, the last time she had been in London, by Victoria's mother, for the purpose of making some special sort of biscuit.

"Will he eat porridge?" she called.

Oliver did not reply, because over the yells of his son he did not hear the question; so Victoria went to the open door and repeated it.

"Yes, I suppose so. I suppose he'll eat anything, really."

Feeling near exasperation, she went back to the kitchen, put on a pan of water, poured in some oats, found a bowl, a spoon, a jug of milk. When it had started to cook, she turned down the heat and went back into the sitting room and saw that already it had been taken over by Oliver, it was no longer hers. It was filled with Oliver, with his possessions, his empty glass, his cigarette stubs, his child. The child's coat lay on the floor, the sofa cushions were crushed and flattened, the air rang with the little boy's misery and frustration.

She could bear it no longer. "Here," she said and took Thomas firmly in her arms. Tears poured down his cheeks. She said to Oliver, "You make sure the porridge doesn't burn," and she bore Tom into the bathroom and set him down on the floor.

Steeling herself to cope with steaming nappies, she unbuttoned his dungarees and found that he wasn't wearing nappies at all, and was, miraculously, dry. There was, obviously, no pot in this childless establishment, but with a certain amount of contriving she persuaded him to use the grown-up lavatory. For some reason this mild accomplishment stopped his tears. She said, "What a good boy," and he looked up at her, still tear-drenched, and disarmed her with a sudden grin. Then he found her sponge and began to chew it, and she was so thankful that he had stopped crying that she let him. She buttoned up his clothes and washed his face and hands. Then she led him back into the kitchen.

"He's been to the loo," she told Oliver.

Oliver had poured himself another whiskey, thus finishing Victoria's bottle. He had his glass in one hand and a wooden spoon in the other, with which he stirred the porridge. He said, "I think this sort of looks ready."

It was. Victoria put some into a bowl, poured milk over it, sat at the kitchen table with Tom on her knee, and let him get on with it, which he did. After the first mouthful, she hastily reached for a tea towel and wrapped it around his neck. In a moment the bowl was empty and Thomas apparently ready for more.

Oliver eased himself away from the cooker. "I'm going out for a moment."

Victoria was filled with alarm, and suspicions that if he went he would never come back and she would be left with the child. She said, "You can't."

"Why not?"

"You can't leave me alone with him. He doesn't know who I am."

"He doesn't know who I am either, but he seems quite happy. Eating himself to a standstill." He laid the palms of his hands flat on the table and stooped to kiss her. It was three years since this had happened, but the aftereffects were alarmingly familiar. A melting sensation, a sudden sinking of the stomach. Sitting there with his child heavy on her knee, she thought, oh, no. "I shall be gone about five minutes. I want to buy cigarettes and a bottle of wine."

"You'll come back?"

"How suspicious you are. Yes, I'll come back. You're not going to get rid of me as easily as that."

He was, in fact, away for fifteen minutes. By the time he returned, the sitting room was once more neat, cushions plumped up, coats put away, the ashtrays emptied. He found Victoria at the kitchen sink, wearing an apron and washing a lettuce. "Where's Thomas?"

She did not turn around. "I put him into my bed. He isn't crying. I think he'll go to sleep again."

Oliver decided that the back of her head looked implacable. He put down the brown grocery bag containing the bottles and went to turn her to face him.

"Are you angry?" he asked.

"No. Just wary."

"I can explain."

"You'll have to." She turned back to the sink and the lettuce.

He said, "I'm not explaining if you won't listen properly. Leave that and come and sit down."

"I thought you wanted to eat. It's getting terribly late."

"It doesn't matter what time it is. We've all the time in the world. Come on. Come and sit down."

He had brought wine and another bottle of whiskey. While Victoria untied her apron and hung it up, he found ice cubes and poured two drinks. She had gone back to the sitting room, and he joined her there and found her settled on a low stool with her back to the fire. She did not smile at him. He handed her the glass and raised his own.

"Reunions?" he suggested as a toast.

"All right." Reunions sounded harmless enough. The glass was cold to her fingers. She took a mouthful and felt better. More able to deal with what he was about to tell her.

Oliver sat on the edge of the sofa and faced her. There were artistic patches in the knees of his jeans, and his suede boots were worn and stained. Victoria found herself wondering on what he chose to spend the fruits of his considerable success. Whiskey, perhaps. Or a house in a more salubrious part of London than the Fulham back street where he had lived before. She thought of the big Volvo parked in the Mews outside. She saw the gold watch on his long, narrow wrist.

He said again, "We have to talk."

"You talk."

"I thought you'd be married."

"You said that before. When I opened the door."

"But you're not."

"No."

"Why not?"

"I never met anybody I wanted to marry. Or perhaps I never met anybody who wanted to marry me."

"Did you go on with your painting?"

"No, I threw that up after a year. I wasn't good enough. I had a little talent, but not enough. There's nothing more discouraging than having just a little talent."

"So what do you do now?"

"I have a job. In a dress shop in Beauchamp Place."

"That doesn't sound very demanding."

She shrugged. "It's all right." They were not meant to be talking about Victoria, they were meant to be talking about Oliver. "Oliver . . ."

But he did not want her questions, perhaps because he had not yet made up his mind what the answers would be. He quickly interrupted her. "How was the party?"

She knew that this was a red herring. She looked at him, and he met her gaze with watchful innocence. She thought, what does it matter? Like he says, we have all the time in the world. Sooner or later he's going to have to tell me. She said, "The usual. Lots of people. Lots of drink. Everybody talking and nobody saying anything."

"Who brought you home?"

She was surprised that he was sufficiently interested to want to know this, and then remembered that Oliver had always been interested in people, whether he knew them or not; whether he even liked them. He would sit in buses and listen to other people's conversations. He would talk to strangers in bars, to waiters in restaurants. Everything that happened to him was filed away in the retentive storehouse of his memory, mulled over and digested, only to reappear at some later date in something he was writing, a scrap of dialogue or a situation.

She said, "An American."

He was instantly intrigued. "What sort of an American?"

"Just an American."

"I mean bald-headed, middle-aged, hung about with cameras? Earnest? Sincere? Come along now, you must have noticed."

Of course Victoria had noticed. He had been tall, not as tall as Oliver, but more heavily built, with wide shoulders and a flat stomach. He looked as though he played furious squash in his spare time, or jogged round the park in the early mornings, wearing sneakers and a track suit. She remembered dark eyes, and hair almost black. Crisp, wiry hair, the sort that has to be closely cut or it gets out of hand. His had been expertly barbered, probably by Mr. Trumper or one of the more exclusive London establishments, so that it lay on his well-shaped head like a smooth pelt.

She remembered the strong features, the tan, and the marvelous white American teeth. Why did Americans all seem to have such beautiful teeth?

She said, "No, he wasn't any of those things."

"What was his name?"

"John. John something. I don't think Mrs. Fairburn's very good at introductions."

"You mean he didn't tell you himself? He can't have been a true-blooded American. Americans always tell you who they are and what they do, before you've even decided whether you want to meet them or not. 'Hi!' " He put on a perfect New York accent. " 'John Hackenbacker, Consolidated Aloominum. Glad to have you know me.' "

Victoria found herself smiling, and this made her feel ashamed, as though she must stand up for the young man who had brought her home in his sleek Alfa-Romeo. "He wasn't a bit like that. And he's flying to Bahrain tomorrow," she added as though this were a point in the American's favor.

"Ah! An oil man."

She was becoming tired of his teasing. "Oliver, I have no idea."

"You seem to have made remarkably little contact. What the hell did you talk about?" An idea occurred to him, and he grinned. "I know, you talked about me."

"I most certainly didn't talk about you. But I think it's about time you started talking about you. And about Thomas."

"What about Tom?"

"Oh, Oliver, don't fence."

He laughed at her exasperation. "I'm not being kind, am I? And you're simply bursting to know. All right, here it is. I've stolen him."

It was so much worse than she had imagined that Victoria had to take a long, deep breath. When that was safely over, she was calm enough to ask, "Who did you steal him from?"

"Mrs. Archer. Jeannette's mother. My erstwhile mother-in-law. You probably didn't know, but Jeannette was killed in an air crash in Yugoslavia, just a little while after Tom was born. Her parents have looked after him ever since."

"Did you go and see him?"

"No. Never went near him. Never set eyes on him. Today was the first time I ever saw him."

"And what happened today?"

He had finished his drink. He got up and went into the kitchen to pour himself another. She heard the clink of the bottle, the ice going into the glass, the tap being turned on and off. Then he returned and resumed his seat, leaning back on the deep cushions of the sofa, with his long legs stretched out in front of him.

"I've been in Bristol all week. I've got a play coming off at the Fortune Theatre, it's in rehearsal now, but I had to do some work with the producer, rewrite some of the third act. Driving back to London this morning, I was thinking about the play. I wasn't really paying attention to the road, and suddenly I realized I was on the A.30, and there was a signpost to Woodbridge, and that's where the Archers live. And I thought, why not? And I turned the car and went to call. As simple as that. A whim, you might way. The hand of fate stretching out its grubby paw."

"Did you see Mrs. Archer?"

"No. Mrs. Archer was in London, buying sheets at Harrods or something. But there was a choice au pair girl called Helga who needed little encouragement to invite me in for lunch."

"Did she know you were Tom's father?"

"No."

"So what happened?"

"She sat me down at the kitchen table and went upstairs to fetch Tom. And then we had lunch. Good healthy fare. Everything was good and healthy, and so clean it looked as though it had been through a sterilizer. The whole house is one enormous sterilizer. There isn't a dog or a cat or a readable book in the place. The chairs look as though no one ever sat in them. The garden's full of horrible flower beds, like a cemetery, and the paths look as if they've been drawn with a ruler. I'd forgotten its utter soullessness."

"But it's Tom's home."

"It stifled me. It's going to stifle him. He had a picture book with his name written in the front. 'Thomas Archer. From Granny.' And somehow that finished me, because he's not Thomas Archer, he's Thomas Dodds. So then the girl went to get his beastly perambulator, to take him out for a walk, and I picked him up and carried him out of the house and put him in the car and drove him away."

"But didn't Thomas *mind?*"

"He didn't seem to. Seemed quite pleased, in fact. We stopped off somewhere and spent the afternoon in a little park. He played on the swings and in the sandpit, and a dog came up and talked to him. And then it began to rain, so I bought him some biscuits and we got back into the car again and came back to London. I took him to my flat."

"I don't know where your flat is."

"Still in Fulham. Same place. You've never been there I know, but you see, it isn't really a living place, it's a working place. It's a basement and grotty as hell, and I have an arrangement with a large West Indian lady who lives on the first floor, and she's meant to come and clean it up once a week, but it never seems to look any better. Anyway, I took Tom there, and he obligingly fell asleep on my bed, and then I rang the Archers."

He came out quite casually with this. Moral cowardice was something from which Oliver had never suffered, but Victoria felt quite weak at the thought.

"Oh, *Oliver.*"

"No reason why I shouldn't. After all, he's my child."

"But she must have been out of her mind with worry."

"I told the au pair girl my name. Mrs. Archer knew he was with me."

"But . . ."

"You know something? You sound the way Jeanette's mother sounded. As though I had nothing but evil intentions. As though I were going to harm the child, bash his brains out on a brick wall, or something."

"I don't think that at all. It's just that I can't help but be sorry for her."

"Well don't be."

"She'll want him back."

"Yes, of course she wants him back, but I've told her that for the time being I'm keeping him myself."

"Can you do that? Legally, I mean? Won't she get the police, or lawyers, or even high court judges?"

"She's threatened all those things. Litigation, ward of court, in the space of ten minutes she threw everything at my head. But you see, she can't do anything. Nobody can do anything. He's my child. I'm his father. I'm neither a criminal nor otherwise unfit to take care of him."

"But that's just the point. You can't take care of him."

"All that's required of me is to provide a home for Tom with resources and facilities for taking care of him."

"In a basement in Fulham?"

There was a long silence while Oliver, with slow deliberation, stubbed out his cigarette. "That," he told her at last, "is why I am here."

So, it was out. The cards were on the table. This was why he had come to her.

She said, "At least you're being honest."

Oliver looked indignant. "I'm always honest."

"You want me to look after Tom?"

"We can look after him together. You wouldn't want me to take him back to that moldy flat, would you?"

"I can't look after him."

"Why not?"

"I'm working. I have a job. There isn't any room for a child here."

He said, in a false voice, "And what would the neighbors say?"

"It's nothing to do with the neighbors."

"You can tell them I'm your cousin from Australia. You can say that Tom is my aborigine offspring."

"Oh, Oliver, stop joking. This is nothing to joke about. You've stolen that child of yours. Why he isn't howling his head off with misery and fright is beyond my comprehension. Mrs. Archer is obviously distraught, we're going to have the police on the doorstep at any moment, and all you do is make what you think are funny remarks."

His face closed up. "If you feel like that about it, I'll take the child and go."

"Oh, Oliver, it's not that. It's that you have to be sensible."

"All right, I'll be sensible. Look, I've got on my most sensible expression." Victoria refused even to smile at him. "Oh, come along. Don't be angry. I wouldn't have come if I'd thought it would make you angry."

"I don't know why you did come."

"Because I thought of you as being exactly the right sort of person who'd help me. I thought of you, and I thought of telephoning first, but then I imagined some stranger—or worse, some stiff-necked husband—answering the call. And then what was I going to say? This is Oliver Dobbs, the well-known author and playwright, speaking. I have a baby I'd like your wife to look after. Wouldn't that have gone down a treat?"

"What would you have done if I hadn't been here?"

"I don't know. I'd have thought of something. But I wouldn't have taken Tom back to the Archers."

"You may have to. You can't take care of him . . ."

Oliver interrupted her, as though she had never started to speak. "Look, I have a plan. Like I said, the Archers haven't got a leg to stand on, but still there's the chance that they'll try to make trouble. I think we should get out of London. Go away for a little. There's this play of mine coming off in Bristol, but as far as that's concerned I've done all I can do. The first night's on Monday, and after that it's at the mercy of the critics and the general public. So let's go away. You and me and Tom. Let's just take off. We'll go to Wales or the north of Scotland, or down to Cornwall and watch the spring coming. We'll . . ."

Victoria gazed at him in total disbelief. She was shocked, outraged, indignant. Did he imagine—did he really imagine—that she had so little pride? Had he never truly known how much he had hurt her? Three years ago Oliver Dobbs had walked out of her life, shattering everything, and leaving her alone to put the pieces together as best she might. But now he decided that he needed her once more, simply to look after his child. And so here he sat, already making plans, trying to seduce her with words, believing that it was only a matter of time before he wore down her resistance.

". . . no tourists, empty roads. We won't even have to book in at hotels, they'll all be longing for business, desperate to have us . . ." He went on, hatching plans, leading Victoria on to images of blue seas and fields of yellow daffodils; of carefree escape, and winding country lanes. And she listened, marveling at his selfishness. He had helped himself to his son. He wanted, for the time being, to keep his son. He needed someone to take care of his son. And so, Victoria. It was as simple as an elementary mathematical formula.

He stopped at last. His face was alight with enthusiasm, as though he could not envisage any objection to this delightful project. After a little, Victoria said, because she really wanted to know, "Out of interest, what made you think of me?"

"I suppose because you're the sort of person that you are."

"You mean, stupid?"

"No, not stupid."

"Forgiving, then?"

"You could never be unforgiving. You wouldn't know how. Besides, it was a good time we had together. It wasn't a bad time.

And you're pleased to see me again. You have to be, otherwise you'd never have let me into your house."

"Oliver, some bruises don't necessarily show."

"What's that supposed to mean?"

"For my sins, I loved you. You knew that."

"But you see," he reminded her carefully, "I didn't love anybody. And you knew that."

"Except yourself."

"Perhaps. And what I was trying to do."

"I don't want to be hurt again. I'm not going to be hurt again."

A smile touched his mouth. "You sound very determined."

"I'm not coming with you."

He did not reply, but his eyes, pale and unblinking, never left her face. Outside, the wind rattled a window pane. A car started up. A girl's voice called some person's name. Perhaps she was going to a party. From far off came the distant hum of London traffic.

He said, "You can't spend the rest of your life avoiding being hurt. If you do that, then you turn your back on any sort of relationship."

"Just say that I don't want to be hurt by you. You're too good at it."

"Is that the only reason that you won't come with us?"

"I think it's enough of a reason, but there are other things as well. Practical considerations. For one thing, I have a job . . ."

"Selling clothes to idiotic females. Ring up and make some excuse. Say your grandmother's died. Say you've suddenly had a baby . . . now that would be nearly true! Send in your resignation. I'm a rich man now. I'll take care of you."

"You've said that before. A long time ago. But you didn't."

"What a prodigious memory you have."

"Some things really can't be forgotten." From the mantelpiece her little clock chimed. It was eleven o'clock. Victoria stood up and put her empty glass beside the clock, and as she did so, she saw his reflection, watching her through the looking glass which hung on the wall behind it.

He said, "Are you afraid? Is that what it is?"

"Yes."

"Of me, or of yourself?"

"Both of us." She turned from the mirror. "Let's go and have some supper."

It was nearly midnight by the time they finished the makeshift meal, and Victoria was suddenly so tired that she had not even the energy to collect the plates and the empty glasses and wash them up. Oliver was pouring the last of the wine into his glass and reaching for another cigarette, apparently settled for the night, but Victoria stood up, pushing back her chair, and said, "I'm going to bed."

He looked mildly surprised. "That's very unsocial of you."

"I can't help it if it's unsocial. If I don't go to bed I'll fall asleep on my feet."

"What do you want me to do?"

"I don't want you to do anything."

"I mean," he spoke patiently, as though she were being immensely unreasonable, "do you want me to go back to Fulham? Do you want me to spend the night in my car? Do you want me to wake Thomas up and bear him off into the night, never to darken your door again? You only have to say."

"You can't take Thomas. He's sleeping."

"Then I'll go back to Fulham and leave him here with you."

"You can't do that either. He might wake up in the middle of the night and be frightened."

"In that case I'll stay here." He assumed the expression of a man prepared to be accommodating, at whatever cost to himself. "Where would you like me to sleep? On the sofa? On top of some chest of drawers? On the floor outside your bedroom door, like an old dog, or a faithful slave?"

She refused to rise to his teasing. "There's a divan in the dressing room," she told him. "The room's full of suitcases and my mother's London clothes, but the bed's longer than the sofa. I'll go and make it up . . ."

She left him, with his cigarette and his glass of wine and the chaos of unwashed dishes. In the tiny slip of a dressing room, she found blankets and a pillow. She removed dress boxes and a pile of clothes from the divan and made it up with clean sheets. The room smelled stuffy and rather mothbally (her mother's fur coat?) so she opened the window wide, and the curtains stirred in the cold damp air which blew in from the darkness beyond.

From the kitchen now came sounds as if Oliver had decided to stack the supper plates, or possibly wash them. Victoria was surprised, because domesticity had never been his strong suit, but she was touched as well, and tired as she was, knew an impulse to go and help him. But if she went to help him, they would only start talking again.

And if they started talking, then Oliver would start, all over again, trying to persuade her to go away with him and Thomas. So she left him to it, and went into her bedroom. Here, only a small lamp burned on the dressing table. On one side of the double bed, Thomas slumbered, one arm outflung, his mouth plugged by his thumb. She had taken off everything except his vest and pants, and folded clothes lay on a chair, his small shoes and socks on the floor beneath it. She stooped to lift him out of the bed. His weight was warm and soft in her arms. She carried him to the bathroom and somehow persuaded him to use the lavatory again. He scarcely woke: his head lolled, his thumb stayed determinedly in his mouth. She put him back into the bed, and he sighed contentedly and slept once more. She prayed that he would sleep until morning.

She straightened up, and listened. It seemed that Oliver had decided that he had had enough of the supper dishes, and he had returned to the living room, where he had started telephoning. Only Oliver would start telephoning at midnight. Victoria undressed, brushed her hair, put on her nightdress and cautiously slipped into the other side of the bed. Tom never stirred. She lay on her back and stared at the ceiling, and then closed her eyes, waiting for sleep. But sleep would not come. Her brain whirled with images of Oliver, with memories, with a sort of throbbing excitement which maddened her because it was the last thing in the world that she wanted to feel. Finally, in desperation, she opened her eyes again, and reached for a book, intending to read herself to calmness and so to unconsciousness.

From the next room, the telephoning stopped, and the television was switched on. But most of the programs had finished by now anyway, and eventually Oliver apparently decided to call it a day. She heard him moving about, switching off lights. She heard him go to the bathroom. She lay down her book. His footsteps crossed the little landing, and stopped outside her door. The handle turned. The door opened. His tall figure appeared, silhouetted against the bright light beyond.

He said, "Not asleep?"

"Not yet," said Victoria.

They spoke softly, so as not to disturb the sleeping child. Oliver, leaving the door open, crossed the floor and came to sit on the edge of the bed.

"Just a guy. Nothing important."

"I made up the bed for you."

"I know. I saw."

But he made no move to go. "What will you do tomorrow?" she asked him. "With Thomas?"

He smiled. He said, "I'll decide tomorrow." He touched her book. "What are you reading?"

It was a paperback. Victoria held it up for him to see the front cover. She said, "It's one of those books that you read over and over again. About once a year, I take it out, and it's like being with an old friend."

Oliver read the title aloud. *"The Eagle Years."*

"Have you read it?"

"Perhaps."

"It's by this man called Roddy Dunbeath and it's all about being a little boy in Scotland between the wars. I mean, it's sort of autobiography. And he and his brothers were brought up in this beautiful house called Benchoile."

Oliver had laid his hand over her wrist. His palm was warm, his fingers strong, but the caress very gentle.

"It was in Sutherland, somewhere. With mountains all around and their own private loch. And he had a falcon that used to come and take food out of his mouth . . ."

His hand began to move up her bare arm, pressing the flesh beneath his touch, as though he were massaging life back into some limb which had been paralyzed for years.

". . . and a pet duck and a dog called Bertie that liked eating apples."

"I like eating apples," said Oliver. He lifted a long strand of hair away from her neck and laid it on the pillow. She could feel the solid, throbbing beat of her own heart. Her skin, where he had touched her, felt as though it were standing on tip toe. She went on talking, desperately, trying to control these alarming physical manifestations with the sound of her own voice.

". . . and there was a place with a waterfall, where they used to go for picnics. And there was a stream running across the beach, and the hills were filled with deer. He says that the waterfall was the heart of Benchoile . . ."

Oliver leaned down and kissed her mouth and the flow of words was mercifully stopped. She knew that he hadn't been listening anyway. Now, he drew aside the blankets which covered her, and slid his arms beneath her back, and his lips moved away from her mouth and across her cheek and into the warm hollow of her neck.

"Oliver." She said his name, but her voice made no sound. His going had left her frozen, but now the weight and the warmth of his body warmed her own, melting resolution, and stirring to life long-forgotten instincts. She thought, *oh, no,* and laid her hands against his shoulders and tried to push him away, but he was a thousand times stronger than Victoria and the puny resistance was pathetic, pointless as trying to topple some immense tree.

"Oliver. No."

She might not have spoken aloud. He simply continued his gentle love-making, and after a little, her hands, as though of their own voli-tion, slid away from his shoulders, under his jacket, around his back. He smelled clean, of clothes dried in the open air. She felt the thin cotton of his shirt, the rib cage, the hard muscles beneath his skin. She heard him say, "You've stopped pretending."

The last shred of common sense made her say, "But Oliver, Thomas . . ."

She sensed his amusement, his silent laughter. He drew away from her and stood up, towering over her. "That can easily be arranged," he told her, and he stooped and lifted her up into his arms as easily and lightly as he had carried his son. She felt weightless, dizzy, as the walls of her bedroom spun and slid away and he bore her through the open door, across the bright landing, and into the airy darkness of the little dressing room. It still smelled of camphor, and the bed on which he placed her was hard and narrow, but the curtains stirred in the soft wind, and the starched linen of the pillow lay cool beneath her neck.

She said, looking up into the shadowed blur that was his face, "I never meant this to happen."

"I did," said Oliver, and she knew that she should be angry, but by then it was too late. Because by then she wanted it to happen anyway.

Much later—she knew it was much later, because she had heard the clock in the sitting room strike two with its silvery chimes—Oliver hoisted himself up onto one elbow and leaned over Victoria in order to grope for his jacket and take his cigarettes and lighter from the pocket. The flame illuminated the tiny room for a second, and there came the gentle darkness again and the glow of the cigarette tip.

She lay in the curve of his arm, her head pillowed on his naked shoulder.

He said, "Do you want to make plans?"

"What sort of plans?"

"Plans for what we're going to do. You and me and Thomas."

"Am I coming with you?"

"Yes."

"Have I said I'm coming with you?"

He laughed. He kissed her. "Yes," he said.

"I don't want to be hurt again."

"You mustn't be so afraid. There's nothing to be afraid of. Just the prospect of a holiday, an escape. Lots of laughter. Lots of love."

Victoria did not reply. There was nothing to say, and her thoughts were so confused that there was nothing much to think, either. She only knew that for the first time since he had left her, she felt safe again, and at peace. And she only knew that tomorrow, or perhaps the next day, she was going away with Oliver. Once more, she was committed. For better or for worse, but maybe it would work this time. Maybe he had changed. Things would be different. And perhaps, if he felt so strongly about Thomas, he would feel strongly about other things. Permanent things. Like loving one person and staying with her forever. But whatever happened, the die had been cast. Victoria has passed the point of no return.

She sighed deeply, but the sigh was prompted by confusion rather than unhappiness. "Where shall we go?" she asked Oliver.

"Anywhere you like. Is there an ashtray in this benighted cupboard of a room?"

Victoria reached out and groped for the one she knew lay on the bedside table, and handed it to him.

He went on, "What was the name of that place you were babbling about, when you were so patently anxious not to be made love to? The place in the book, *The Eagle Years?*"

"Benchoile."

"Would you like to go there?"

"We can't."

"Why not?"

"It's not a hotel. We don't know the people who live there."

"I do, my darling innocent."

"What do you mean?"

"I know Roddy Dunbeath. I met him about two years ago. Sat next to him at one of those dismal television award dinners. He was there on account of his last book, and I was there because I was given some piddling little statue for a television script I wrote about Seville. Anyway, there we were, surrounded by moronic starlets and shark-like agents, and thankful for each other's company. By the end of the evening we were friends for life, and he gave me a standing invitation to visit him at Benchoile whenever the spirit moved me. So far I haven't taken it up, but if you want to go there, there's no reason on earth why we shouldn't."

"Do you really mean that?"

"Of course I do."

"Are you certain it wasn't just one of those things people say at the end of a good evening and then forget about, or even regret for the rest of their lives?"

"Not at all. He meant it. Even gave me his card in a rather old-fashioned way. I can find out the telephone number and ring him up."

"Will he remember you?"

"Of course he'll remember me. And I shall tell him that I and my wife and my child want to come and spend a few days with him."

"It sounds like an awful lot of people. And I'm *not* your wife."

"Then I shall say my mistress and my child. He'll jump at that. He's rather Rabelasian. You'll love him. He's very fat, and extremely, politely drunk. At least, he was by the end of that dinner. But Roddy Dunbeath, drunk, is ten times more charming than most men are stone cold sober."

"It'll take us a long time to drive to Sutherland."

"We'll take it in stages. Anyway, we have a long time."

He stubbed out his cigarette, and leaned over Victoria once more, in order to put the ashtray on the floor. She found that she was smiling into the darkness. She said, "You know, I think I'd rather go to Benchoile than anywhere else in the world."

"It's better than that. You're going to Benchoile with me."

"And Thomas."

"You're going to Benchoile with me and Thomas."

"I can't think of anything more perfect."

Oliver gently placed his hand on her stomach; slowly, he slid it up her body, over her rib cage, to cup one small, naked breast. "I can," he told her.

5

SUNDAY

—◦◦◦—

In the middle of February, the cold weather arrived. Christmas had
been sunny and the New Year mild and still, and the weeks of winter
crept past, with some rain and a little frost and nothing much else.
"We're going to be lucky," said people who knew no better, but the
shepherds and the hill-farmers were wiser. They eyed the skies and
smelled the wind and knew that the worst was still to come. The
winter was simply waiting. Biding its time.

The real frosts started at the beginning of the month. Then came
the sleet, swiftly turning to snow, and then the storms. "Straight
from the Urals," said Roddy Dunbeath, as the bitter wind whined in
over the sea. The sea turned grey and angry, sullen as the color
of wet slate, and creaming breakers flooded in over the Creagan
sands, depositing a long tidemark of undigested rubbish. Old fish
boxes, ragged nets, knotted twine, plastic detergent bottles, rubber
tires, even a disfigured shoe or two.

Inland, the hills were cloaked in white, their summits lost in the
dark, racing sky. Snow blew from the open fields and piled in steep
drifts, choking the narrow roads. Sheep, heavy in their winter wool,
could survive, but the cattle searched for shelter in the angles of the
drystone dikes, and the farmers tractored fodder to them twice a day.

Accustomed to, and expecting, cruel winters, the local people accepted all this hardship with stoic calm. The smaller hill crofts and isolated cottages were cut off entirely, but walls were thick and peat stacks high, and there was always plenty of oatmeal, and feedstuff for the stock. Life continued. The scarlet post-van made its daily round of the glens, and sturdy housewives, wearing rubber boots and three cardigans, emerged from doorways to feed hens and hang out lines of washing in the freezing wind.

Now, it was Sunday.

> *The Lord's my Shepherd, I'll not want.*
> *He makes me down to lie*
> *In pastures green . . .*

The pipes in the church were faintly warm, but the draughts excruciating. The congregation, thinned to a mere handful by the weather, bravely raised their voices in the last hymn of the morning service, but their efforts were almost drowned by the fury of the wind outside.

Jock Dunbeath, standing alone in the Benchoile pew, held his hymnbook in mittened hands but did not look at it, partly because he had sung this hymn all his life and knew the words by heart and partly because, by some oversight, he had left his reading spectacles at home.

Ellen had fussed over him. "You must indeed be mad thinking you'll get to the kirk today. The roads are blocked. Would you not stop off at Davey's and get him to drive you?"

"Davey has enough to do."

"Then why not sit by the fire and listen to the nice man on the wireless? Would that not do as well or once?"

But he was stubborn, immovable, and she finally sighed and tossed her eyes to heaven and gave in. "But don't be blaming me if you die in a drift on your way."

She sounded quite excited at the thought of such a happening. Disaster was the spice of life to Ellen, and she was always the first to say "I told you so." Irritated by her, in a hurry to get away, he forgot his spectacles, and was then too pigheaded to go back for them. However, his determination was vindicated, and, in the old Land-rover, grinding in bottom gear down the four miles of the glen, he had managed to make it safely and had come to church. Chilled as he was, and blind as a bat without his glasses, he was glad that he had made the effort.

All his life, unless prevented by illness, war, or some other act of God, he had come to church on Sunday mornings. As a child because he had had to; as a soldier because he needed to; as a grown man because he was the Laird of Benchoile and it was important to be involved, to uphold the established traditions, to set a good example. And now, in his old age, he came for comfort and reassurance. The old church, the words of the service, the tunes of the hymns, were some of the very few things in his life that hadn't changed. Perhaps, at the end of the day, the only thing.

> *Goodness and mercy all my days,*
> *Shall surely follow me,*
> *And in God's house for ever more*
> *My dwelling place shall be.*

He closed his hymnbook, bowed his head for the blessing, collected his driving gloves and his old tweed cap from the seat beside him, buttoned up his overcoat, wound himself up in his scarf, started up the aisle.

"Morning, sir." It was a friendly sort of church. People came out with conversation in their ordinary voices—none of those pious whispers as though there were a body dying in the next room. "Terrible weather. Good morning, Colonel Dunbeath, and how are the roads up with you? . . . Well, Jock, and you're a fine one, making the trip to the kirk on a day like this."

That was the minister himself, coming up at Jock from behind. Jock turned. The minister, the Reverend Christie, was a well-set-up man with a pair of shoulders like a rugby player, but still Jock topped him by half a head.

He said, "I thought you'd be a bit thin on the ground this morning. Glad I made the effort."

"I imagined you all cut off up at Benchoile."

"The telephone's dead. There must be a line down somewhere. But I managed the road in the Landrover."

"It's a bitter day. Why don't you come into the Manse for a glass of sherry before you start back?"

His eyes were kind. He was a good man, with a homely and

hospitable wife. For a moment Jock let himself imagine the living room at the Manse. The chair, which would be drawn up for him by an enormous fire, the air fragrant with the smell of roasting Sunday mutton. The Christies had always done themselves very well. He thought of the dark, sweet, warming sherry, the comfortable presence of Mrs. Christie, and for a small instant was tempted.

But, "No," he said, "I think I'd better get back before the weather worsens. Ellen will be expecting me. And I would not want the constable to find me frozen in a snowdrift with the smell of alcohol on my breath."

"Ah, well, that's understandable." The Minister's kindly countenance and robust manner masked his concern. He had been shocked this morning to see Jock sitting solitary in his pew. Most of the congregation, for some reason, gathered themselves at the back of his church, and the laird, isolated like some outcast, had stuck out like a sore thumb.

He looked old. It was the first time that Mr. Christie had seen him looking really old. Too thin, too tall, his tweed hanging loose on the lanky frame, the fingers of his hands swollen and red with the cold. The collar of his shirt was loose on his neck, and there had been a hesitancy in his actions, fumbling for his hymnbook, for the pound note that was his weekly contribution to the offertory plate.

Jock Dunbeath of Benchoile. How old was he? Sixty-eight, sixty-nine? Not old for nowadays. Not old for here-abouts, where the menfolk seemed to go on well into their eighties, sprightly and active, digging their gardens and keeping a few hens, and making small tottery excursions to the village inn for their evening dram. But last September Jock had suffered a slight heart-attack, and since then, thought Mr. Christie, he seemed to have gone visibly downhill. And yet, what could one do to help? If he had been one of the country folk, Mr. Christie would have gone visiting, taking a batch of his wife's scones, perhaps offered to cut a stack of kindling; but Jock was not country folk. He was Lieutenant Colonel John Rathbone Dunbeath, late of the Cameron Highlanders, the Laird of Benchoile and a Justice of the Peace. He was proud, but he was not poor. He was old and lonely, but he was not poor. On the contrary, he was a well-respected landowner with a large house and a farm in hand, twelve thousand or so acres of hill, a thousand or more sheep, some arable land, some stalking, some fishing. In all respects, an enviable property. If the big house was rambling and shabby, and the laird's shirt had a frayed collar, it was not because he was poor. It was because his wife was dead, he was childless, and old Ellen Tarbat, housekeeper to Jock and his brother Roddy, was getting beyond it.

And somewhere, sometime, before the eyes of them all, the old man seemed to have given up.

Mr. Christie searched for some remark that would keep their conversation going. "And how is the family" was a useful starter on most occasions, but not this one, because Jock didn't have a family. Only Roddy. Oh well, thought the minister, any port in a storm.

"And how is your brother keeping?"

Jock responded with a gleam of humor. "You make him sound like a box of herring. I think he's all right. We don't see that much of each other. Keep to ourselves, you know. Roddy in his house and me in mine." He cleared his throat. "Sunday lunch. We have Sunday lunch together. It's companionable."

Mr. Christie wondered what they talked about. He had never known two brothers so different, one so reserved and the other so outgoing. Roddy was a writer, an artist, a raconteur. The books that he had written, some almost twenty years or so ago, were all still in print, and the paperback editions could always be found on station bookstalls and in the racks of the most unlikely country shops. *A classic* said the blurb on the back covers, under the photograph of Roddy that had been taken thirty years ago. *A breath of the outdoors. Roddy Dunbeath knows his Scotland and presents it, with native perception, within the pages of this book.*

Roddy did not come to church unless it was Christmas or Easter or somebody's funeral, but whether this was due to his inner convictions or his inherent idleness, the minister did not know. Roddy did not even appear very often in the village. Jess Guthrie, the shepherd's wife, did his shopping for him. "And how is Mr. Roddy, Jess?" the grocer would inquire, fitting the two bottles of Dewars down the side of the carton of groceries, and Jess would avert her eyes from the bottles and reply, "Oh, he's not so bad," which could have meant anything.

"Is he working on anything just now?" Mr. Christie asked.

"He mentioned something about an article for the *Scottish Field*. I . . . I never really know." Jock ran a diffident hand down the back of his head, smoothing down the thinning grey hair. "He never talks much about his work."

A lesser man might have been discouraged, but Mr. Christie pressed on, and asked after the third Dunbeath brother.

"And what news of Charlie?"

"I had a letter at Christmas. He and Susan were skiing. At Aspen. That's in Colorado, you know," he added in his mannerly way, as though Mr. Christie mightn't.

"Was John with them?"

There was a small pause. Jock put back his head. His eyes, pale and watering a little in the cold, fixed on some distant, unfocused spot beyond the minister's head.

"John doesn't work in New York any longer. Got sent to the London branch of his bank. Works there now. Been working there for six months or more."

"But that's splendid."

The church was nearly empty now. They began to tread, side by side, up the aisle towards the main door.

"Yes. Good thing for John. Step up the ladder. Clever boy. Suppose he'll be president before we know where we are. I mean president of the bank, not president of the United States of America . . ."

But Mr. Christie was not to be diverted by this mild joke. "I didn't mean that, Jock. I meant that if he's living in London, it shouldn't be too hard for him to get up to Sutherland and spend a few days with you and Roddy."

Jock stopped dead and turned. His eyes narrowed. He was suddenly alert, fierce as an old eagle.

Mr. Christie was a little taken aback by that piercing glance. "Just an idea. It seems to me that you need a bit of young company." And someone to keep an eye on you, as well, he thought, but he did not say this aloud. "It must be ten years since John was last here."

"Yes. Ten years." They moved on, slow-paced. "He was eighteen." The old man appeared to be debating with himself. The minister waited tactfully, and was rewarded. "Wrote to him the other day. Suggested he come up in the summer. He was never interested in the grouse, but I could give him a bit of fishing."

"I'm sure he needs no such bait to lure him north."

"Haven't had an answer yet."

"Give him time. He'll be a busy man."

"Yes. The only thing is, these days I'm not quite sure how much time I have to give." Jock smiled, that rare wry smile that warmed the chill from his features and never failed to disarm. "But then, it comes to all of us. You of all men know that."

They let themselves out of the church, and the wind caught the minister's robes and sent the black skirts ballooning. From the porch, he watched Jock Dunbeath clamber painfully up into the old Land-rover and set off on his uncertain journey home. Despite himself he sighed, heavy-hearted. He had tried. But, at the end of the day, what could anybody do?

No more snow had fallen and Jock was glad of this. He trundled through the quiet, shuttered village and over the bridge and turned inland where the road sign pointed to Benchoile and Loch Muie. The road was narrow and single-tracked, with passing places marked by black and white painted posts, but there was no other traffic of any sort. The Sabbath, even in weather like this, cast its gloom over the countryside. Beset by icy draughts, hunched over the wheel, with his scarf up to his ears and his tweed cap pulled down over his beak of a nose, Jock Dunbeath let the Landrover take its own way home, like a reliable horse, up the tracks in the snow that they had made themselves that morning.

He thought about what the minister had said. He was right, of course. A good man. Concerned and trying not to show it. But he was right.

You need a bit of young company.

He remembered Benchoile in the old days when he, and his friends, and his brothers' friends, had all filled the house. He remembered the hall overflowing with fishing boots and creels, tea on the lawn beneath the silver birches, and in August the sunlit purple hills echoing to the crack of guns. He remembered house parties for the Northern Meetings Hunt Ball in Inverness, and girls coming downstairs in long, pretty dresses, and the old station wagon driving off to collect guests off the train at Creagan Halt.

But those days, like everything else, were gone. For the brothers, youth had gone. Roddy had never married; Charlie had found himself a wife, and a sweet one too, but she was an American girl, and he had gone back with her to the States, and made a life for himself as a cattleman, ranching his father-in-law's spread in Southwest Colorado. And although Jock had married, he and Lucy had never had the children they so ardently wanted. They had been so happy together that even this cruel trick of fate could not mar their content. But when she had died, five years ago, he had realized that he had never before known the true meaning of loneliness.

You need a bit of young company.

Funny, the minister bringing John's name up like that, just days after Jock had written him the letter. Almost as though he had known about it. As a child, John had visited Benchoile regularly, in the company of his parents, and then, as he grew older, alone with his father. He had been a quiet, serious little boy, intelligent beyond his years, and with a searching curiosity that manifested itself in a long stream of endless questions. But even in those days, Roddy had been his favorite uncle, and the two of them would go off for hours on end, to search for shells, or watch the birds, or stand, on still summer evenings, casting their trout rods over the deep brown pools of the river. In all respects, a likeable and satisfactory boy, but still, Jock had never been able to get close to him. The main reason for this was that John did not share with Jock his abiding passion for shooting. John would blissfully lure and catch and slay a fish, and very soon became accomplished at the sport, but he refused to go up the hill with a gun, and if he stalked a deer, would carry nothing more deadly than his camera.

And so the letter had not been an easy one to write. For John had not been to Benchoile for ten years, and this gap of time had left a yawning void that Jock had found almost impossible to bridge with words. Not, he assured himself quickly, that he didn't like the boy. He remembered John Dunbeath at eighteen as a composed, reserved young man with disturbingly mature attitudes and opinions. Jock respected these, but he found his coolness and his polite self-confidence a little disconcerting. And since then they had somehow lost touch. So much had happened. Lucy had died and the empty years had slipped away. Charlie had written, of course, giving news. John had gone to Cambridge, played squash and rackets for the University, and left with an honors degree in economics. He had then returned to New York and there joined the Warburg Investment Corporation, a position that he achieved entirely on his own merits and without any assistance from his influential American connections. For some time he had been at the Harvard Business School, and after some time, inevitably, he had married. Charlie was too loyal a father to spell out the details of this misalliance to Jock, but gradually, reading between the lines of his brother's letters, Jock realized that all was not well with the young couple. So he was distressed, but not surprised, when the news came through that the marriage had broken up, divorce proceedings were being taken, and legal settlements made. The only good thing about it was that there were no children.

The divorce, painfully, was finally accomplished, and John's career, apparently untouched by the traumas of his personal life, continued to go from strength to strength. The appointment in London was the latest in a succession of steady promotions. Banking was a world about which Jock Dunbeath knew nothing, and this was another reason why he felt so totally out of touch with his American nephew.

Dear John,
  Your father tells me that you are now back in this country and working in London.

It wouldn't have been so hard if he had felt that he had anything in common with the young man. Some shared interest that would have provided him with a starting point.

If you are able to get a little time off, perhaps you would think about making the journey north and spending a few days at Benchoile.

He had never been much of a letter writer and it had taken him nearly half a day to finally compose this one, and even then the finished result did not satisfy him. But he signed it, and wrote the address on the envelope and stuck down the flap. It would have been so much easier, he thought wistfully, if only John had shown some interest in the grouse.

These reflections had brought him halfway home. The narrow, rutted, snow-filled road took a turn and the length of Loch Muie slid into view, grey as iron beneath the lowering sky. There was a light on in Davey Guthrie's farmhouse, and away at the end of the loch stood Benchoile itself, sheltered by the stand of pines which stood silhouetted, black as ink, against the snow-covered slopes of the hill.

Built of grey stone, long and low, turreted and gabled, it faced south, across a wide sloping lawn, to the loch. Too big, draughty and unheatable, shabby and constantly in need of repair, it was, nevertheless, his home, and the only place, in all his life, that he had ever really wanted to be.

Ten minutes later, he was there. Up the slope and through the gates, over the rattle of the cattle grid, and down the short tunnel of wild rhododendrons. In front of the house the drive opened up into a wide gravel sweep. At the far end of this was an ornate stone arch which attached the house, by one corner, to the old stable block where Jock's brother Roddy lived. Beyond the arch was a spacious cobbled yard, and at the far end of this were the garages, which were originally built to house carriages and shooting brakes but now contained Jock's old Daimler and the aged green MG into which Roddy squeezed his bulk when the spirit moved him to make some excursion into the outside world.

Alongside these two ill-assorted vehicles, in a thick gloom occasioned by the dreariness of the day, Jock Dunbeath finally homed the Landrover, pulled on the brake, and killed the engine. He took the folded wad of Sunday newspapers off the seat beside him, got out of the car, slammed the door shut, and went out into the yard. Snow lay thick on the cobbles. The light was on in Roddy's sitting room. Cautiously, anxious not to slip or fall, he made his way across the yard to Roddy's front door, and let himself in.

Although it was often referred to as a flat, Roddy's house was, in fact, a two-story dwelling, converted out of the old stables at the end of the war, when Roddy had come back to Benchoile to live. Roddy, fired by enthusiasm, had architected the conversion himself. The bedrooms and bathrooms were downstairs, the kitchen and the living room upstairs, and access to these rooms was by an open teak stair, like a ship's ladder.

Jock stood at the foot of these and called, "Roddy!"

Roddy's footsteps creaked across the floorboards over Jock's head. In a moment his brother's bulk appeared, and Roddy peered down at him over the rail of the stairhead.

"Oh, it's you," said Roddy, as though it might be anybody else.

"Brought the papers."

"Come on up. What a bloody awful day."

Jock mounted the stairs, and came out at the top in the living room where Roddy spent his days. It was a marvelous room, light and large, the ceiling gabled to the shape of the roof, and one wall taken up by an enormous picture window. This had been designed to frame a view over the loch to the mountains, which, in fine weather, took the breath away. But this morning what could be seen was enough to chill the soul. Snow and grey water, running before the wind and capped in white; the hills on the far shore were lost in murk.

It was a man's room, and yet a room of taste and even beauty; lined with books and cluttered with a number of objects which, though worth little, were visually pleasing. A carved overmantel; a blue and white jar filled with pampas grasses; a dangling mobile of paper fishes, probably Japanese. The floorboards had been sanded and polished and sparsely scattered with rugs. Elderly armchairs and a sofa sagged invitingly. In the cavern of a fireplace (which had had to be specially constructed at the time of the conversion, and had proved to be the most costly item of all) a couple of birch logs sizzled on a bed of peat. The room had an extraordinary and quite unique smell about it. Compounded of cigar smoke, and peat smoke too, and the sharp aroma of linseed oil.

Roddy's old Labrador, Barney, lay supine on the hearthrug. At Jock's appearance, he raised his grizzled nose, and then yawned and went back to sleep again.

Roddy said, "Have you been to the kirk?"

"Yes." Jock began to unbutton his overcoat with frozen fingers.

"Did you know the telephone's dead? There must be a line down somewhere." He gave his brother a long, measuring look. "You appear to be blue with cold. Have a drink." He moved ponderously towards the table where he kept his bottles and glasses. He had already, Jock noticed, provided himself with a large, dark whisky. Jock did not ever drink in the middle of the day. It was one of his rules. But somehow today, ever since the minister had mentioned that glass of sherry, he had been thinking about it.

"Have you got some sherry?"

"Only the pale kind. Dry as a bone."

"That'll do very nicely."

He took off his coat and went to stand in front of the fire. Roddy's mantelpiece was always littered with undusted bits and pieces. Curling photographs, old pipes, a mug of pheasant quills, and out-of-date invitations, probably unanswered. There was today, however, a sparkling new card propped against the clock, impressively copper-plated, gold-edged and marvelously pretentious.

"What's this? Looks like a royal command."

"Nothing so splendid. A dinner at the Dorchester. Television awards. Best documentary of the year. God knows why I've been invited. I thought I'd been crossed off all the lists. Actually, apart from the tedium of the after-dinner speeches, I used to quite enjoy those occasions. Met a lot of new young writers, new faces. Interesting to talk to."

"Are you going to this one?"

"I'm getting too elderly to travel the length of the country for a free hangover." He had laid down his whisky, located the sherry, found a suitable glass, poured his brother's drink. Now he retrieved a smoldering, half-smoked cigar from an ashtray, picked up the two glasses and came back to the fireside. "If it were to take place somewhere civilized, like Inverness, I might deign to add tone to what will otherwise be a vulgar brawl. As it is . . ." He raised his glass. "Slainthe, old boy."

Jock grinned. "Slainthe."

Roddy was nine years Jock's junior. When they were young, Roddy had been the handsome one of the three brothers, the dallying charmer who had broken more hearts than could be decently counted, and who never lost his own. Women adored him. Men were never quite so sure. He was too good-looking, too clever, too talented at all the sorts of things that it was not considered manly to be talented at. He drew and he wrote and he played the piano. He could even sing.

On shoots he always seemed to get the prettiest girl of the party into his butt, and quite often forgot that the object of the exercise was to slay grouse. No sound, no blast would come from his butt, while the grouse sailed serenely over him in coveys, and at the end of the drive he would be found deep in conversation with his companion, his gun unfired, and his dog wheeking and frustrated at his feet.

Naturally brilliant, he had skimmed through his schooldays without apparently doing a stroke of work, and had gone on to Oxford in a blaze of glory. Trends were started by Roddy Dunbeath and fashions set. Where others sported tweed, he favored corduroy, and soon everybody was wearing corduroy. He was president of the OUDS and a renowned debater. Nobody was safe from his wit, which was usually gentle, but could be barbed.

When the war broke out, Jock was already a regular soldier with the Camerons. Roddy, impelled by a deep patriotism which he had always kept to himself, joined up the day that war was declared. He signed on, to everybody's surprise, with the Royal Marines, on account of, he said, they had such a pretty uniform; but in no time at all, he was training to be a Commando, struggling up precipitous cliffs on the end of a rope and hurling himself from training planes with tightly closed eyes and his hand clenched around the rip cord of his parachute.

When it was all over and the country was at peace again, it seemed to Jock Dunbeath that everyone who wasn't married rushed to rectify the situation.There was a veritable epidemic of matrimony, and Jock himself had fallen prey to it. But not Roddy. Roddy picked up his life where he had left it in 1939 and went on from there. He made himself a home at Benchoile and started to write. *The Eagle Years* came out first, and then *The Wind in the Pines*, and then *Red Fox*. Fame embraced him. He went on lecture tours, he made after-dinner speeches, he appeared on television.

By now he was putting on weight. While Jock stayed thin and spare, Roddy became stout. Gradually his girth spread, his chin doubled, his handsome features were lost in heavy jowls. And yet, he was as attractive as ever, and when the gossip columns in the daily papers ran out of tidbits about the nobility, they would print blurred photographs of Roddy Dunbeath (*The Eagle Years*) dining with Mrs. So-and-So, who was, as everybody knew, a champion of wild life.

But youth had gone, lost somewhere over the years, and at last even his mild fame began to slip away. No longer feted in London, he returned, as he had always returned, to Benchoile. He occupied himself in writing short articles, the scripts for television nature films, even small items for the local newspapers. Nothing changed him. He was still the same Roddy, charming and witty, the engaging raconteur. Still willing to squeeze his bulk into his velvet jacket and drive himself for miles down dark country roads to make up the numbers at some remote dinner party. And—even more astonishing—somehow getting himself home again in the small hours of the morning, half-asleep and awash with whisky.

For he was drinking too much. Not uncontrollably nor offensively, but still he seldom seemed to have a glass out of his hand. He began to slow down. He, who had always been physically indolent, was now becoming chronically idle. He could scarcely make the effort to get himself into Creagan. His life had become encapsulated at Benchoile.

"What are the roads like?" he asked now.

"Passable. You wouldn't have got far in the MG."

"No intention of going anywhere." He took the cigar from his mouth and aimed it at the fireplace. It made a tiny flame. He stooped to lift more logs from the great basket that stood by the hearth, and toss them into the grey ashes of the peat. Dust rose in a cloud. The fresh logs flickered and caught fire. There was a small explosion, and one or two sparks flew out onto the aged hearthrug. The smell of burning wool filled Jock's nostrils, and Roddy trod them out with the sole of his brogue.

"You should have a fireguard," said Jock.

"Can't stand the look of the things. Besides, they keep all the heat in." He gazed thoughtfully down at his fireplace. "Thought I might get one of those chain curtains. Saw one advertised the other day, but now I can't remember where I saw it." He had finished his drink. He began to drift back towards the bottles on the table. Jock said, "You've hardly time for another. It's past one o'clock already."

Roddy looked at his watch. "Well, bless my soul, so it is. It's a wonder Ellen hasn't yet given us her weekly screech. I suppose you couldn't persuade her to use the old gong. She could bring it out into the stable yard and ring it there. It would be so much more in keeping if I could be summoned to Sunday lunch in the big house by the dignified rumble of a gong. Gracious living and all that. We mustn't let ourselves go, Jock. We must keep up appearances even if there is no person to appreciate our efforts. Think of those old empire builders, dining in the jungle in their starched shirts and black ties. There's backbone for you."

The glass of sherry had freed Jock's inhibitions a little. "This morning the minister told me that we need some young company at Benchoile," he told Roddy.

"Well, what a pretty thought." Roddy hesitated over the whiskey bottle, thought better of it, and poured himself a small sherry instead. "Handsome lads and pretty lasses. What happened to all those young relations of Lucy's? The house used to be running with her nephews and nieces. They were all over the place. Like mice."

"They've grown up. Married. That's what happened to them."

"Let's stage a grand reunion and get them all back again. We'll put a notice in the personal column of the *Times*. 'The Dunbeaths of Benchoile require young company. All applications will be given consideration.' We might get some rather amusing replies."

Jock thought of the letter that he had written to John. He had not told Roddy about that letter. Cautiously, he had made up his mind that when a reply came from John, and not before, he would take Roddy into his confidence.

But now, he found that resolution wavering. He and Roddy saw so little of each other, and it was seldom that they found themselves on such easy and companionable terms as they were at this moment. If he brought the business of John up now, then they could discuss it over Sunday lunch. After all, sometime, it all had to be thrashed out. He finished his sherry. He squared his shoulders. He said, "Roddy . . ."

But was interrupted by a banging on the door downstairs, and then a blast of icy air as it was opened. A voice, shrill and cracked, rose from the foot of the stairs.

"It's past one o'clock. Did you know that?"

Roddy looked resigned. "Yes, Ellen, we did."

"Have you got the colonel with you?"

"Yes, he's here."

"I saw the Landrover in the garage, but he's not been near the big house. You'd better both come over now, or the bird'll be ruined." Ellen had never been one for much formality.

Jock laid down his empty glass and went to collect his coat. "We're coming now, Ellen," he told her. "We're coming right away."

6
MONDAY

*T*he fact that the telephone lines were down and the phone not working was of small concern to Roddy Dunbeath. Where others tried six or seven times in a morning to make outside calls, jigged the receiver in empty exasperation, and finally trod out into the snow to the nearest functioning call box, Roddy remained unperturbed. There was no person with whom he wished to get in touch, and he actively enjoyed the sensation of being undisturbed and unreachable.

And so, when the phone on his desk suddenly began to ring at half past eleven on Monday morning, he was at first startled out of his skin and then irritated.

During the night the wind had died, having first blown all the clouds out of the sky, and the morning had dawned, late and clear and still. The sky was a pale, arctic blue. The sun, rising over the foot of the loch, turned the snowclad countryside first pink, and then a dazzling white. The lawn in front of the house was patterned with the random tracks of rabbits and hares. A deer had been there, too, feeding off the young shrubs that Jock had planted at the back end of the year and tree shadows lay like long, smokey blue bruises. As the sun climbed over the rim of the hills, the sky deepened in blue, and this was reflected in the waters of the loch. Frost glittered, and the icy air was so still that when Roddy opened his window to throw out a handful of crusts for his birds, he could hear the baa-ing of the sheep which grazed on the slopes at the far side of the water.

It was not a day for much activity. But, with a certain resolution, and a deadline hanging over his head, Roddy had managed to finish the first draft of his article for the *Scottish Field*. With this behind him, he succumbed once more to idleness and was sitting at his window with a cigar and his binoculars at the ready. He had seen greylags feeding on the worn stubble of the arable fields beyond the pines. Sometimes, in hard weather like this, they would settle in the thousands.

The telephone rang. He said, aloud, "Oh, bloody hell," and at the sound of his voice Barney raised his head from the hearthrug. Thump thump went his tail. "It's all right, old boy, it's not your fault." He laid down his binoculars, got up, and went, reluctantly, to answer it.

"Roddy Dunbeath."

There came strange peeping sounds. For a moment Roddy felt hopeful that the tiresome instrument was still out of order, but then the peeping sounds stopped and a voice came on, and hope died.

"Is that Benchoile?"

"The Stable House, yes. Roddy Dunbeath here."

"Roddy. This is Oliver Dobbs."

After a little, Roddy said, "Who?"

"Oliver Dobbs." It was a pleasant voice, young, deep, vaguely familiar. Roddy dug about, without noticeable success, in his unreliable memory.

"I'm not with you, old boy."

"We met at a dinner in London a couple of years ago. Sat next to each other . . ."

Recollection dawned. Of course, Oliver Dobbs. Clever young man. A writer. Won some prize. They'd had a great crack together. "But of course." He reached behind him for a chair, settled himself for conversation. "My dear boy, how splendid to hear you. Where are you calling from?"

"The Lake District."

"What are you doing in the Lake District?"

"I'm taking a few days off. I'm driving up to Scotland."

"You're going to come here, of course."

"Well, that's what I'm calling about. I tried to ring you yesterday, but they said the phone lines were down. When we met, you issued an invitation to come and see you at Benchoile, and I'm afraid I'm taking it up."

"Nothing to be afraid of. I couldn't be more pleased."

"We thought perhaps we might be able to come and stay for a couple of days."

"Of course you must come." The prospect of a couple of days in the company of that lively and intelligent young man was quite stimulating. But, "Who's we?" asked Roddy.

"Well, there's the rub," said Oliver Dobbs. "We're a sort of family. Victoria and me and Thomas. He's only two, but he's quite undemanding and very well-behaved. Would there be room for us all, because if not Victoria says we can go to a pub if there's such a thing nearby."

"Never heard such rubbish." Roddy was quite indignant. Benchoile hospitality had always been legendary. True, during the last five years, since Lucy died, the entries in the battered leather-bound visitors book, which lived on the hall table in the big house, were few and far between, but that didn't mean that there wasn't still the warmest of welcomes for any person who wished to come and stay. "Of course you must come here. When will you arrive?"

"Perhaps about Thursday? We thought we'd drive up the West Coast. Victoria's never been to the Highlands."

"Come by Strome Ferry and Achnasheen." Roddy knew the Scottish highways like the back of his hand. "And then down Strath Oykel to Lairg. You've never seen such country in your life."

"Have you got snow up there?"

"We've had a lot, but the good weather's back again. By the time you get here, the road should be clear."

"And you're sure you don't mind us coming?"

"Absolutely delighted. We'll expect you Thursday about lunchtime. And stay," he added with the expansiveness of a potential host who has no intention of being involved in the tedious necessities of airing sheets or dusting bedrooms or cooking meals, "stay as long as you like."

The telephone call, coming out of the blue as it had, left Roddy in a pleasurable state of mild excitement. After he had replaced the receiver, he sat for a little, finishing his cigar, and anticipating, with the satisfaction of a boy, the forthcoming visit.

He loved young people. Trapped in the spreading bulk and the balding head of approaching old age, he still thought of himself as young. Inside, he still felt young. He remembered with pleasure the instant rapport that had sprung up between himself and Oliver Dobbs. How they had sat through that dinner, serious-faced and boiling with suppressed laughter at the endless, cliché-ridden speeches.

At one point, Oliver had made some remark, thrown from the corner of his mouth, about the chest measurements of the lady across the table from them, and Roddy had thought. "You remind me of me." Perhaps that was it. Oliver was his alter ego, the young man Roddy had once been. Or perhaps the young man he would like to have been, if circumstances had been different, if he had been born to a different way of life, if there had been no war.

The pleasure had to be shared. Not only that, Ellen Tarbat had to be told. She would put on a face, shake her head, accept the tidings in martyred resignation. This was customary and meant nothing. Ellen always put on a face, shook her head and looked martyred, even if one happened to be the bearer of delightful news.

Roddy stubbed out his cigar, and without bothering to put on a coat, got up out of his chair and started down the stairs. His dog followed him. They went out into the cold morning air together, crossed the icy cobbles of the stableyard, and let themselves in through the back door of the big house.

The passages that lay beyond were stone-floored, cold, and seemingly endless. Doors gave off to coal sheds, woodsheds, laundries, store rooms, cellars, pantries. He came at last through a green-baize-covered door, and emerged into the big hall of the old house. Here, the temperature rose by a few degrees. Sun poured in through long windows and the glassed inner front door. It sent long beams, dancing with dust motes, down the turkey-rugged staircase and quenched the fire, which smoldered in the immense grate, to a bed of dusty ashes. Roddy stopped to replenish this from the basket of peats which stood alongside and then went in search of his brother.

He found Jock, inevitably, in the library, sitting at the unfashionable roll-top desk, which had belonged to their father, and dealing with the endless accounts and paper work related to the management of the farm.

Since Lucy had died, the drawing room had, by wordless consent, been closed and shut away, and this was now the apartment in which Jock spent his days. It was one of Roddy's favorite rooms, shabby and worn, the walls lined with books, the old leather-covered chairs sagging and comfortable as old friends. Today this room too was filled with the pale sunlight of the winter's day. Another fire burned in the hearth, and Jock's two golden Labradors lay, drugged in the warmth.

As Roddy opened the door, Jock looked up, over the spectacles which habitually slid to the end of his long beak of a nose. Roddy said, "Good morning."

"Hello." He took off the spectacles, leaning back in his chair. "And what might you be wanting?"

Roddy came in and shut the door. He said, "I am the bearer of pleasing news." Jock sat politely, waiting to be pleased. "You might even say, I was some sort of a fairy godmother, granting all your wishes."

Jock still waited. Roddy smiled and let his weight cautiously down into the armchair nearest the fire. After his trek across the yard and down the arctic passages of Benchoile, his feet felt cold, so he toed off his slippers and wriggled his stockinged feet in the warmth. There was a hole in one of his socks. He would have to get Ellen to mend it.

He said, "You know, yesterday, you said that the minister at Creagan said that what we needed at Benchoile was some young company. Well, we're going to get it."

"Who are we going to get?"

"A delightful and bright young man called Oliver Dobbs and what he pleases to call his 'sort of family.' "

"And who is Oliver Dobbs?"

"If you weren't such an old reactionary, you'd have heard of him. A very clever young man with a string of literary successes to his name."

"Oh," said Jock. "One of those."

"You'll like him." That was the extraordinary thing, Jock probably would. Roddy had called his brother a reactionary, but Jock was nothing of the kind. Jock was a liberal, through and through. Beneath his chilling, eagle-proud appearance lay concealed the real man, gentle, tolerant, well-mannered. Jock had never disliked a man on sight. Jock had always been willing and ready, in his reserved and diffident way, to see the other man's point of view.

"And what," asked Jock mildly, "does the 'sort of family' consist of?"

"I'm not quite sure, but whatever it is, we may well have to keep it from Ellen."

"When are they coming?"

"Thursday. Lunchtime."

"Where are they going to sleep?"

"I thought over here, in the big house. There's more space."

"You'll have to tell Ellen."

"I am steeling myself to do that very thing."

Jock sent him a long amused look, and Roddy grinned. Jock leaned back in his chair and rubbed his eyes with the gesture of a man who had been up all night. He said, "What time is it?" and looked at his watch. Roddy, who was longing for a drink, said it was twelve o'clock, but Jock didn't notice the hint, or if he did he took no account of it, but said instead, "I'm going out for a walk."

Roddy suppressed his disappointment. He would go back to his own house and pour himself a drink there. He said, "It's a beautiful morning."

"Yes," said Jock. He looked out of the window. "Beautiful. Benchoile at its most beautiful."

They talked for a little and then Roddy departed, with conscious courage, kitchenwards, in search of Ellen. Jock got up from his desk, and with the dogs at his heel, went out of the room and across the hall to the gunroom. He took down a shooting jacket, shucked off his slippers, climbed into a pair of green rubber boots. He took down his cap, pulled it down over his nose. A muffler to wind round his neck. He found knitted mittens in the pocket of the jacket and pulled them on. His fingers protruded from the open ends, swollen and purple as beef sausages.

He found his stick, a long shepherd's crook. He let himself thankfully out of the house. The cold air hit him, the piercing chill of it biting deep into his lungs. For days he had been feeling unwell. He put it down to tiredness and the bitter weather, but all at once, in the meagre warmth of the February sun, he felt a little better. Perhaps he should get out and about more, but one needed good reason to make the required effort.

Tramping over the creaking snow towards the loch, he thought of the young people whom Roddy had invited to stay, and he was not dismayed, as many men of his age would have been, by the prospect. He loved young people as much as his brother, but somehow he had always been shy with them, had never been much good with them. He knew that his manner, and his upright, soldierly appearance, were off-putting, but what could you do about the way you looked? Perhaps, if he had had children of his own, it would have been different.

With children of your own, there would be no necessity to break down the barriers of shyness.

People to stay. They would have to get the rooms ready, light fires, perhaps open the old nursery. He had forgotten to ask Roddy the age of the child who was coming to stay. A pity there would be no fishing, but the boat was laid up anyway, and the boathouse locked for the winter.

His mind strayed back to other house-parties, other children. He and his brothers when they were small. Their friends, and then Lucy's numerous young nephews and nieces. Rabbit's friends and relations he had called them. He smiled to himself. Rabbit's friends and relations.

He had reached the edge of the loch. It stretched before him, edged with ice from which the winter-pale rushes grew in straggling clumps. A pair of peewits flew overhead, and he raised his head to watch their passing. The sun in his eyes was blinding, and he put up a hand as shade from the dazzle. His dogs nuzzled into the snow, scenting exciting smells. They inspected the ice, in small nervous darts, but were not brave, or perhaps foolhardy, enough to venture out onto the shining surface.

It was indeed a beautiful day. He turned back to look at the house. It lay, a little above him, across the snow-covered slope; familiar, loved, secure. Sunlight glinted on windows, smoke issued from chimneys, rising straight up in the still air. There was a smell of moss, of peat, and the resin of the spruces. Behind the house, the hills rose to meet the blue sky. His hills. Benchoile hills. He felt immensely content.

Well, the young company was coming. They would be here on Thursday. There would be laughter, voices, footsteps on the stairs. Benchoile was waiting for them.

He turned away from the house and set out once more upon his walk, his stick in his hand, his dogs at his heel, his spirit untroubled.

When he did not put in an appearance for his midday meal, Ellen became worried. She went to the front door to look for him, but saw only the single line of footprints that led to the edge of the loch. He had been late many times before, but now her Highland instincts were dark and foreboding. She went to find Roddy. He rang Davey Guthrie and in a moment Davey appeared in his van and the two men set out together to look for Jock.

It was not a difficult search, for the prints of him and his dogs lay clear in the snow. They found the three of them in the lea of dry-stone dike. Jock lay quietly, his face serene and turned up to the sun. The dogs were wheeking and anxious, but it was instantly clear that their master would never know anxiety again.

7

TUESDAY

═══◈═══

*T*homas Dobbs, wearing new red rubber boots, squatted at the water's edge, fascinated by this strange new phenomenon that had suddenly come into his life, and staring at it with the mesmerized, unblinking gaze of some old seafarer. It was all bigger and brighter and wetter than anything he had ever before encountered in his short life, and there were, as well, the added diversions of the little choppy waves, so sunlit and cheerful, the screaming of the sea birds which wheeled in the cold air over his head, and the occasional passing boat. Every now and then he dug up a handful of gritty sand and threw it into the sea.

Behind him, a few yards off, Victoria sat on the shingly beach and watched him. She wore thick, corduroy trousers and three sweaters, two of them her own and one borrowed from Oliver, and she sat huddled, with her knees pulled up and her arms wrapped around them for warmth. It was, indeed, extremely cold. But then at ten o'clock on a February morning in the north of Scotland—well, nearly the north of Scotland—it would have been surprising if it had been anything else.

It wasn't even a proper beach, just a narrow strip of shingle between the wall of the hotel garden and the water. It smelt fishy and tarry, and was littered with scraps of debris from the boats that plied up and down the long sea loch on their way to and from the fishing grounds. There were bits of string, an old fish-head or two, and a damp furry object, which on investigation proved to be a rotting doormat.

"The back of beyond," Oliver had said yesterday evening as the Volvo topped the pass and began the long gradual descent to the sea, but Victoria thought that the isolation was beautiful. They were now much further north than they had intended to come, and so far west that if you took another step, you fell into the sea; but the views, the sheer size and grandeur of the country, the colors, and the brilliance of the sparkling air had made the long drive more then worthwhile.

Yesterday morning they had woken to a Lake District streaming in rain, but as they drove up into Scotland a wind had sprung up from the west, and the clouds had been blown away. All yesterday afternoon, and this morning again, the sky was clear, the air piercing cold. Snow-covered peaks of distant hills glittered like glass, and the waters of the sea loch were a dark indigo blue.

The loch, Victoria had discovered, was called Loch Morag. The little village, with its tiny shops and fleet of fishing boats tied up at the sea wall, was also called Loch Morag, and the hotel was the Loch Morag Hotel. (Oliver said that he expected the manager was called Mr. Lochmorag and his wife, Mrs. Lochmorag.) Built for the sole purpose of catering to fisherman—both freshwater and sea fishing, the brochure boasted, was on their doorstep—it was large and ugly, constructed of some strange stone the color of liver, and much crenellated, towered and turreted. Indoors, it was furnished with worn turkey carpets and uninspired wallpaper the color of porridge, but there were peat fires burning in the public rooms and the people were very kind.

"Would the wee boy like high tea?" had asked the comfortable lady in the mauve dress who appeared, in this quiet season, to have taken on the duties not only of head waitress and barmaid, but receptionist as well. "Maybe a boiled egg, or a wee bit of oakcake?" Thomas stared at her, unhelpfully. "Or a jeely. Would you like a jeely, pet?"

In the end they had settled for a boiled egg and an apple, the kind lady (Mrs. Lochmorag?) brought it up to his bedroom on a tray, and sat with Thomas while Victoria had a bath. When she emerged from the bathroom, she found Mrs. Lochmorag playing with Thomas and

the pink and white calico pig that they had bought him in London
before they left, along with a wardrobe of clothes, a toothbrush and a
pot. Victoria had wanted to buy an endearing teddy bear, but Oliver
informed her that Thomas did not like fur, and chose the pig himself.

The pig was called Piglet. He wore blue trousers and red braces.
His eyes were black and beady and Thomas approved of him.

"You've got a lovely wee boy, Mrs. Dobbs. And what age is he?"

"He's two."

"We've made friends, but, mind, he hasn't said a word to me."

"He . . . he doesn't talk very much."

"Oh, he should be talking by now." She heaved Thomas onto her
knee. "What a lazy wee boy, not saying a word. You can say Mummy,
now, can't you? Are you not going to say Mummy? Are you not
going to tell me the name of your pig?" She took Piglet and jigged
him up and down, making him dance. Thomas smiled.

"He's called Piglet," Victoria told her.

"That's a bonny name. Why does Thomas not say Piglet?"

But he did not say Piglet. He did not indeed say anything very
much. But this in no way detracted from his charm. In fact, it added
to it, because he was such a cheerful and undemanding child that four
days of his company had been nothing but pleasure. In the car,
during the long drive north, he sat on Victoria's knee, hugging his
new toy, and gazing out of the window at passing lorries, fields,
towns; obviously enjoying all the new and strange sights, but seeing
no reason to comment upon them. When they stopped for meals or
to stretch their legs, Thomas joined them, eating bacon and eggs or
drinking milk or munching the slices of apple that Oliver peeled and
cut up for him. When he became tired or bored, he plugged his
mouth with his thumb, settled himself with endearing confidence in
Victoria's arms, and either slept or sang to himself, with eyes
drooping and dark lashes silky against his round red cheeks.

"I wonder why he doesn't talk more?" she had said to Oliver once,
when Thomas was safely asleep on her lap and could not overhear the
discussion.

"Probably because nobody's ever talked to him. Probably they
were all too busy sterilizing the house and manicuring the garden,
and boiling his toys."

Victoria did not agree with Oliver. No child, so well-adjusted and
content, could have been neglected in the smallest way. Indeed, his

behavior and his sunny disposition gave every indication that he had spent his short life enveloped in affection.

She said as much and instantly aroused Oliver's ire. "If they were so marvelous with him, then how come he doesn't seem to be missing them? He can't have been particularly fond of them if he hasn't asked for them once."

"He hasn't asked for anything," Victoria pointed out. "And most likely his being so confident and unafraid is all to do with the way he's been brought up. Nobody's ever been unkind to him, so he doesn't expect unkindness. That's why he's being so good with us."

"Balls," said Oliver shortly. He could not stand a single good word being said on the Archers' behalf.

Victoria knew he was being unreasonable. "If Thomas howled for his grandparents all the time, and complained, and wet his pants and generally behaved like most children would under the same circumstances, I suppose you'd have blamed that on the Archers, too."

"You're talking in hypothetical circles."

"I'm not." But she didn't know what a hypothetical circle was, and so couldn't argue further. Instead, she lapsed into silence. *But we must ring up Mrs. Archer,* she thought. Or write to her or something. Oliver must let her know that Thomas is all right. Some time.

It was, perhaps, their only quarrel. Otherwise, the entire undertaking, which could have been, and even deserved to be, disastrous, was proving an unqualified success. Nothing had gone wrong. Everything had proved simple, easy, delightful. The winter roads were fast and empty; the scenery, the open skies, the stunning countryside, all contributed to their pleasure.

In the Lake District it had rained, but they had put on waterproofs and walked for miles, with Thomas, cheerful as ever, atop his father's shoulders. There had been fires burning pleasantly in their bedrooms at the little lakeside hotel, and boats moored at the jetty that lay at the end of the garden, and in the evening a kindly chambermaid had watched over Thomas while Oliver and Victoria dined by candlelight on grilled trout and rare beefsteaks that had never seen the inside of a deep freeze.

That night, lying in the soft darkness, in featherbedded warmth, in Oliver's arms, she had watched the curtains stirring at the open window and felt the cool damp air on her cheeks. From the quiet darkness beyond the window came the sounds of water and the creak of the boats tied up at the jetty, and there had come a distrust of such perfect content. Surely, she told herself, it could not go on. Surely something would happen that would spoil it all.

But her apprehension was unfounded. Nothing happened. The next day was even better, with the road pouring north to Scotland and the sun coming out as they crossed the border. By the afternoon, the great peaks of the Western Highlands lay ahead of them, iced in snow, and at the foot of Glencoe they stopped at a pub for tea and ate homemade scones dripping with butter. And after that the country-side grew more and more magnificent, and Oliver told Victoria that it was called Lochaber, and he began to sing "The Road to the Isles."

"Sure by *Tummel* and Loch *Rannoch* and Loch*aber* we will go . . ."

Today Loch Morag. Tomorrow, or perhaps the next day, Benchoile. Victoria had lost all sense of time. She had lost all sense of anything. Watching Thomas, she hugged herself more tightly and rested her chin on her knees. Happiness, she decided, should be tangible. A thing you could take hold of and put somewhere safe, like a box with a lid or a bottle with a stopper. And then, later, sometime when you were miserable, you could take it out and look at it and feel it and smell it, and you would be happy again.

Thomas was tired of throwing sand into the sea. He straightened up on his small legs and looked about him. He spied Victoria, sitting there, where he had left her. He grinned, and began to stump unsteadily towards her up the littered little beach.

Watching him filled her heart with an almost unbearable tender-ness. She thought, if I can feel like this about Thomas, after only four days, how does Mrs. Archer feel, not even knowing where he is?

It didn't bear thinking about. Basely, cowardly, she pushed the idea to the back of her mind and opened her arms to Thomas. He reached her and she hugged him. The wind blew her long hair across his cheek, and tickled. He began to laugh.

While Victoria and Thomas sat on the beach and waited for him, Oliver was telephoning. The previous night had been the first perfor-mance of *Bent Penny* at Bristol, and he couldn't wait to hear what the critics had said in the morning papers.

He was not exactly on tenterhooks, because he knew that the play was good—his best, in fact. But there were always elements and reactions that were apt to take one unawares. He wanted to know how the show had gone, how the audience had responded, and whether Jennifer Clay, the new little actress getting her first big chance, had justified the faith that the producer and Oliver had put in her.

He was on the telephone to Bristol for nearly an hour, listening while the ecstatic reviews were read aloud to him along six hundred miles of humming wires. The critics from the *Sunday Times* and the *Observer*, he was told, were coming down to see the play at the end of the week. Jennifer Clay was on the brink of being swept to stardom, and there had already come interested noises from a couple of important West End managements.

"In fact, Oliver, I think we've got a hit on our hands."

Oliver was gratified, but he had watched the show in rehearsal, and he was not particularly surprised. The Bristol call finally finished, he rang his agent, and all the good news was confirmed. As well, there had been feelers from New York about his play *A Man In The Dark*, which had done so well in Edinburgh a summer ago.

"Would you be interested?" the agent asked.

"What do you mean, 'interested'?"

"Would you be prepared to go to New York if you have to?"

Oliver loved New York. It was one of his favorite places. "I'd be prepared to go even if I didn't have to."

"How long are you going to be away?"

"Couple of weeks."

"Can I get in touch with you?"

"After Thursday, I'll be at Benchoile, in Sutherland. Staying with a guy called Roddy Dunbeath."

"*Eagle Years* Dunbeath?"

"The very man."

"What's the phone number?"

Oliver reached for his leather diary, thumbed through it. "Creagan two three seven."

"OK, I've got it. If I have any fresh news I'll call you."

"You do that."

"Good luck then, Oliver. And congratulations."

His agent rang off. After a little, as though reluctant to put an end to such a momentous conversation, Oliver replaced his own receiver, and sat looking at it for a moment or two, while slowly, relief flooded through him. It was over. *Bent Penny* was launched, like a child sent out into the world. A child conceived with passion, brought to life in the most agonizing birth pains, nursed and coaxed to maturity, and bludgeoned into shape, it was, at last, no longer Oliver's responsibility.

All over. He thought of the production, the rehearsals, the personality problems, the temperaments, the tears. The chaos, the panics, the rewriting, the total despair.

I think we've got a hit on our hands.

It would make him, probably, a lot of money. It might even make him rich. But this was of small account compared to the easement of his spirit, and the sense of freedom that existed now that it was all behind him.

And ahead . . . ? He reached for a cigarette. There was something waiting for him, but he wasn't sure what. He only knew that the subconscious edge of his imagination, the part that did all the work, was already filling with people. People living in a certain place, a certain style. Voices had conversations. The dialogues had a form and a balance all their own, and the words, and the faces of the individuals who spoke them, swam up, as they always did, out of his prodigious memory.

These first stirrings of life made everyday existence, for Oliver, as intense and dramatic as it is for most men when they fall in love. This, for him, was the best part of writing. It was the same as the anticipation of waiting in a darkened theatre for the curtain to go up on the first act. You didn't know what was going to happen, but you knew that it would be marvelous and tremendously exciting and better— much better—than anything you had ever seen before.

He got up off the bed and went to the window and flung it open to the icy morning air. Gulls wheeled and screamed over the funnel of a weather-beaten fishing boat as she butted her way, against the western wind, out to the open sea.

On the far side of the dark blue water the hills were frosted in white, and below him was the hotel garden and the scrap of a beach. He looked down upon Victoria and his son Thomas. They did not know he was watching. As he observed them, Tom grew tired of his game of throwing sand into the water, and turned and made his way up the beach to Victoria's side. She opened her arms to him and drew him close, and her long fair hair blew all over his red and chubby face.

The combination of this delightful scene and his own euphoric frame of mind filled Oliver with an unfamiliar content. He knew that it was ephemeral; it might last a day or even an hour or two. But all at once it seemed that the world was a brighter and more hopeful place; that the smallest incident could take on immense significance; that affection would turn to love, and love—that humdrum word—to passion.

He closed the window and went downstairs to tell them his good news.

8

THURSDAY

—◦◦◦—

*M*iss Ridgeway, that impeccable private secretary of undetermined years, was already at her desk when, at a quarter to nine in the morning, John Dunbeath emerged from the lift onto the ninth floor of the new Regency House Building and the opulent, elegant offices of the Warburg Investment Corporation.

She looked up as he came through the door, her expression, as always, polite, pleasant, and impassive.

"Good morning, Mr. Dunbeath."

"Hi."

He had never before had a secretary whom he did not call by her Christian name, but sometimes the formality of "Miss Ridgeway" stuck in his throat. They had, after all, worked together for some months. It would have been so much easier to call her Mary or Daphne or whatever her name was, but the truth of the matter was that he hadn't even found this out, and there was something so strictly formal about her manner that he had never plucked up the courage to ask.

Sometimes, watching her as she sat there, with one shapely leg crossed over the other, taking down his letters in her faultless shorthand, he pondered on her private life. Did she care for an aged mother and take an interest in good works? Did she go to concerts at the Albert Hall and spend her holidays in Florence? Or did she, like a secretary in some film, remove her spectacles and shake loose her mouse pale hair, receive lovers and indulge in scenes of unbridled passion?

He knew that he would never know.

She said, "How was the trip?"

"OK. But the plane was late getting in yesterday evening. We got held up in Rome."

Her eyes moved over his dark suit, his black tie. She said, "You got the cable all right? The one from your father?"

"Yes. Thanks for that."

"It came on Tuesday morning. I thought you'd want to know. I sent a copy through to Bahrain right away. The original is on your desk with some personal mail . . ." John moved through to his own office, and Miss Ridgeway rose from her chair and followed him. ". . . and yesterday's *Times* that the announcement was in. I thought you'd like to see it."

She thought of everything. He said, "Thank you," again and opened his briefcase and took out the report, and twelve pages of foolscap, covered with his own neat writing, that he had composed in the airplane during the flight back to London.

"You'd better get one of the typists on to this right away. The vice president will want to see it as soon as possible. And when Mr. Rogerson gets in, tell him to give me a buzz." He glanced at his desk. "And this morning's *Wall Street Journal*?"

"I have it, Mr. Dunbeath."

"And the *Financial Times* as well. I didn't have time to pick one up." She started out of the office, but he called her back. "Hang on a moment." She returned and he dealt out more papers. "I want the file on this. And if you can, find me some information on a Texas company called Albright; they've been drilling in Libya. And this has to be telexed through to Sheikh Mustapha Said, and this . . . and this . . ."

After a little, "Is that all?" asked Miss Ridgeway.

"For the moment." He grinned. "Except that I'd appreciate a large cup of black coffee."

Miss Ridgeway smiled understandingly, becoming quite human. He wished that she would smile more. "I'll get it," she said, and left him, closing the door, without a sound, behind her.

He sat at his gleaming desk and debated for a moment as to what he should do first. His In tray was piled high, letters neatly clipped to their relevant files, and, he knew, arranged in their order of priority, with the most urgent documents on the top. The three personal letters had been placed in the middle of his blotter. The blotting paper was, as it was every day, new and pristine white. There was also the copy of yesterday's *Times*.

He reached for the green telephone to make an internal call.

"Mr. Gardner please."

He tucked the receiver under his chin and opened the newspaper to the back page.

"John Dunbeath here. Is he in yet?"

"Yes, he's in, Mr. Dunbeath, but he's not in the office right now. Shall I get him to call you?"

"Yes, do that." He replaced the receiver.

> DUNBEATH. *Suddenly, on February 16th at Benchoile in Sutherland, Lt. Col. John Rathbone Dunbeath, D.S.O., J.P., late Cameron Highlanders, in his 68th year. Funeral Service in the Parish Church, Creagan, 10:30 a.m. Thursday February 19th.*

He remembered the old boy, tall and lean, every inch a retired soldier; his pale glare and his prow of a nose; his long legs striding easily up the hill through knee-high heather; his passion for fishing, for shooting grouse, for his land. They had never been close, but there was still an empty sense of loss, as there must be when a man, bound close by family and blood, dies.

He laid down the paper and took his father's cable from the envelope in which Miss Ridgeway had protectively placed it. He read what he had already read, in Bahrain, two days previously.

YOUR UNCLE JOCK DIED RESULT OF A HEART ATTACK BENCHOILE MONDAY 16th FEBRUARY STOP FUNERAL CREAGAN 10:30 THURSDAY MORNING 19th FEBRUARY STOP WOULD BE GRATEFUL IF YOU COULD REPRESENT YOUR MOTHER AND MYSELF STOP FATHER

He had sent cables from Bahrain. To his parents in Colorado, explaining why he would not be able to comply with his father's request. To Benchoile, to Roddy, he had sent sympathy and more explanations, and before he left Bahrain, he had found the time to write Roddy a letter of condolence, which he had posted by first-class mail on his arrival at Heathrow.

The other two letters waited for his attention, one envelope hand-written, the other typed. He picked up the first and began to open it, and then stopped, his attention caught by the writing. An old-fashioned pen nib, black ink, the capitals strongly defined. He looked at the postmark and saw "CREAGAN." The date was the tenth of February.

He felt his stomach contract. *A ghost going over your grave* his father used to say when John was a small boy and scared by the unknown. *That's what it is. A ghost going over your grave.*

He slit the envelope and took out the letter. His suspicions were confirmed. It was from Jock Dunbeath.

> Benchoile,
> Creagan,
> Sutherland.
> Wednesday,
> 9th February.

Dear John,

Your Father tells me that you are now back in this country and working in London. I do not know your address, so I am sending this to your office.

It seems a long time since you stayed with us. I looked it up in the visitors' book and it seems to be ten years. I realize that you are a very busy man, but if you are able to get a little time off, perhaps you would think about making the journey north and spending a few days at Benchoile. It is possible to fly to Inverness or to catch a train from Euston in which case either I or Roddy would come to Inverness to meet you. There are trains to Creagan, but they are few and far between and involve several hours delay.

We have had a mild winter, but I think cold weather is on the way. Better now than in the Spring when late frosts play havoc with the young grouse.

Let me know what you think and when it might be convenient for you to visit us. We look forward to seeing you again.

With best wishes,

Affectionately,
Jock

The arrival, out of the blue, of this extraordinary invitation; the coincidence of timing, the fact that it had been written only days before Jock's fatal heart attack, were intensely disturbing. John sat back in his chair and read the letter through again, consciously searching for some inner meaning between the carefully penned and characteristically stilted lines. He could find none.

It seems to be ten years.

It was ten years. He remembered himself at eighteen with Wellington behind him and all the joys of Cambridge ahead, spending part of the summer holidays with his father at Benchoile. But he had never gone back.

Now, it struck him that perhaps he should feel guilty about this lapse. But too much had happened to him. Too much had been going on. He had been at Cambridge, then New York, and then Harvard, spending all his vacations in Colorado, either at his father's ranch, or else skiing at Aspen. And then Lisa had come into his life, and after that all his spare energy had been spent in simply keeping up with her. Keeping her happy, keeping her amused, keeping her in the high style which she was convinced was her due. Being married to Lisa meant the end of vacations in Colorado. She was bored by the ranch and too fragile to ski. But she adored the sun, so they went to the West Indies, to Antigua, the Bahamas, where John missed the mountains and tried to work off his physical needs in scuba diving or sailing.

And after the divorce, he had buried himself so deeply in his work that somehow there didn't even seem to be time to get out of the city. It was his president in New York who had finally read the riot act, and had him posted to London. Not only was it a promotion, he told John, but it would make a vital and necessary change of pace. London was quieter than New York, the rat race was not so frantic, the ambience generally more easy-going.

"You'll be able to get North and see Jock and Roddy," his father had said over the telephone when John had called to give him the news, but somehow with one thing and another John had never got around to doing this. Now, it struck him that he should feel guilty about this lapse. But the truth was that Benchoile, though undoubtedly beautiful, held no irresistible lure for John. Having been brought up in the heart of the Rockies, he had found the hills and glens of Sutherland peaceful, but somehow tame. There was fishing, of course, but fishing in Colorado, in the tributaries of the mighty Uncompahgre, which ran through his father's spread, was unsurpassable. Benchoile had a farm, but again, that seemed small compared to the endless ranges of the ranch, and the grouse shooting, with its rules and shibboleths, its traditions of butt and beat, had left the young John totally cold.

Even as a boy, he had rebelled against slaughtering wildlife, and had never gone hunting, for mule deer or elk, with the other men, and there seemed no reason, just because he was staying in Scotland and it was expected of him, to give up the habits and convictions of a lifetime.

Finally, and this was the most important reason of all, he had never thought that his Uncle Jock liked him very much. "He's just reserved. He's shy," John's father had assured him, but still, try as he could, John had never been able to work up a rapport with his father's eldest brother. Conversations between the two of them, he remembered, had never done more than creak painfully along, like wagon wheels in need of a good greasing.

He sighed, and laid the letter down, and picked up the last envelope. This time he slit it open without inspecting it first, and with his mind still brooding over the letter from Jock, he unfolded the single sheet of paper. He saw the old-fashioned letterhead, the date.

> McKenzie, Leith & Dudgeon,
> Solicitors, Writers to
> The Signet.
> 18 Trade Lane,
> Inverness.
> Tuesday, 17th February.

John Dunbeath, Esq.,
Warburg Investment Corporation,
Regency House,
London.

John Rathbone Dunbeath Deceased

Dear Mr. Dunbeath,

I have to inform you that under the terms of the Will of your Uncle, John Rathbone Dunbeath, you have been bequeathed the Benchoile Estate in Sutherland.

I suggest that you take an early opportunity to come north and see me in order to make practical arrangements for the management and future of the property.

I shall be happy to see you at any time.

Yours sincerely,
Robert McKenzie.

When Miss Ridgeway came back into the room, bearing his black coffee in a fine white Wedgwood cup, she found John sitting, motionless at his desk, an elbow on his blotter, the bottom half of his face covered by his hand.

She said, "Here's your coffee," and he looked up at her, and the expression in his dark eyes was so somber that she was moved to ask if he was all right, if anything had happened.

He did not reply at once. And then he sat back in his chair, letting his hand fall to his lap, and said that yes, something had happened. But after a long pause, during which he showed no signs of wishing to elucidate on this remark, she laid the cup and saucer beside him, and left him alone, closing the door between them with her usual tactful care.

9

THURSDAY

*A*s they drove east, up and away from the mild-mannered sea lochs of the West of Scotland, leaving the farms and villages and the smell of sea wrack behind them, the countryside changed character with dizzying abruptness, and the empty road wound upwards into a wilderness of desolate moorland, apparently uninhabited except for a few stray sheep and the occasional hovering bird of prey.

The day was cold and overcast, the wind from the east. Grey billows of cloud moved slowly across the sky, but every now and then there came a break in the gloom, a ragged scrap of pale blue appeared, and a gleam of thin wintry sunshine, but this only seemed to accentuate the loneliness rather than do anything to alleviate it.

The undulating land stretched in all directions, as far as the eye could see, patchworked in winter-pale grasses and great tracts of dark heather. Sometimes this was broken by a gaping peat-pit or the somber black of bog. Then scraps of snow began to appear, like the white spots of a piebald horse, and lay where it had been trapped in corries and ditches and in the lea of low drystone dikes. As the gradient steepened, the snow grew thicker, and at the head of the moor—the roof-ridge, as it were, of the country—it was all about them, a blanket of white six inches deep or more, and the road was ice-rutted and treacherous beneath the wheels of the Volvo.

It was like finding oneself in the Arctic, or on the moon. Certainly in some place that one had never even remotely imagined visiting. But then, just as abruptly, the wild and desolate moor was behind them. They had crossed the watershed, and, imperceptibly, the road began to slope downhill once more. There were rivers and waterfalls and stands of larch and fir. First appeared isolated cottages, and then hill farms and then villages. Presently they were running alongside an immense inland loch, and there was the great rampart of a hydroelectric dam and beyond this a little town. The main street ran by the water's edge, and there was a hotel and a number of small boats pulled up on the shingle. A signpost pointed to Creagan.

Victoria became excited. "We're nearly there." She leaned forward and took from the cubbyhole on the dashboard the Ordnance Survey map that Oliver had bought. With Thomas's dubious help, she opened it out. One corner spread out over the driving wheel, and Oliver flipped it back. "Watch it, you'll blind me."

"It's only about another six miles to Creagan."

Thomas, using Piglet as a weapon, struck the map a blow and knocked it from Victoria's hands and onto the floor.

Oliver said, "Put it away before he tears it to pieces." He yawned and shifted in his seat. It had been a hard morning's drive.

Victoria rescued the map and folded it up and replaced it. The road ahead of them wound steadily downhill, between steep banks of bracken and copses of silver birch. A small river kept them company, chuckling and sparkling on its way in a series of little pools and waterfalls. The sun, obligingly, came out from behind a cloud; they turned a final corner, and ahead, glinting and silvery, lay the sea.

She said, "It's really amazing. You leave one coast behind you, and you drive up and over the moor and through the snow, and then you come to another sea. Look, Thomas, there's the sea."

Thomas looked, but was unimpressed. He was getting tired of driving. He was getting tired of sitting on Victoria's knee. He put his thumb in his mouth and flung himself backwards, striking her a resounding blow on the chest with the back of his bullet-hard head.

His father snapped, "Oh, for God's sake, sit still."

"He has sat still," Victoria was moved to point out in Thomas's defense. "He's been a very good boy. He's just getting bored. Do you suppose there's a beach at Creagan? I mean a proper sandy one. We haven't found a proper sandy beach yet. All the ones on the West seemed to be covered in stones. If there was one I could take him."

"We'll ask Roddy."

Victoria thought about this. Then she said, "I *do* hope he isn't going to mind us all turning up like this. I hope it isn't going to be difficult." She had never quite got rid of this apprehension.

"You've already said that a dozen times, at regular intervals. Stop being so anxious."

"I can't help feeling that you cornered Roddy. Perhaps he didn't have time to think up an excuse."

"He was delighted. Jumped at the chance of a little lively company."

"He knows you, but he doesn't know Tom and me."

"In that case, you'll both have to be on your best behavior. If I know Roddy, he won't care if you've got two heads and a tail. He'll just say how do you do, very nicely, and then, I hope and believe, will hand me an enormous gin and tonic."

Creagan, when they reached it, proved a surprise. Victoria had expected the usual small Highland township with its single narrow main street, flanked by rows of plain stone houses built flush on the pavement. But Creagan had a wide, tree-lined street, with deep cobbled sidewalks on either side. The houses, which stood back from the road and were separated from it by quite large gardens, were all detached and remarkably attractive, with the simple proportions and elegant embellishments associated with the best period of Scottish domestic architecture.

In the middle of the town the main street opened up into a wide square, and in the center of this, sitting on a sward of grass, rather as though it had been set carefully down in the middle of a green carpet, rose the granite walls and slate-capped tower of a large and beautiful church.

Victoria said, "But it's lovely! It's like a French town."

Oliver, however, had noticed something else. "It's empty."

She looked again, and saw that this was true. A stillness brooded over Creagan, like the pious gloom of a Sabbath. Worse, for there was not even the cheerful clangor of bells. As well, there seemed to be scarcely anybody about, and only a few other cars. And . . . "All the shops are shuttered," said Victoria. "They're closed and all the blinds have been pulled down. Perhaps it's early closing."

She rolled down the window on her side of the car to let the icy air blow in on her face. Thomas tried to put his head out, and she pulled him back onto her knee. She smelled the salt of the sea and the tang of sea wrack. Overhead a gull began to scream from a rooftop.

"There's a shop open," said Oliver.

It was a small newsagent, with plastic toys in the window and a rack of colored postcards at the door. Victoria rolled up the window again, for the blast of cold air was bitter. "We can go and buy postcards there."

"What do you want postcards for?"

"To send to people." She hesitated. Ever since that morning by Loch Morag, her conscience had been constantly troubled by the nagging awareness of Mrs. Archer's anxiety and distress for Thomas. The opportunity to confide in Oliver had not, so far, presented itself, but now . . . She took a deep breath and went on with the bold determination of one intent upon striking while the iron is hot. "We can send one to Thomas's grandmother."

Oliver said nothing.

Victoria took no notice of this lack of response. "Just a line. To let her know he's safe and sound."

Oliver still said nothing. This was not a good sign. "Surely it couldn't do any harm." She could hear the pleading note in her own voice, and despised herself for it. "A postcard, or a letter or *something.*"

"How you do bang on."

"I'd like to send her a postcard."

"We're not sending her a bloody thing."

She could not believe that he could be so blinkered. "But why be like that? I've been thinking . . ."

"Well, stop thinking. If you can come to no conclusion more intelligent than that one, then simply make your mind a blank."

"But . . ."

"The whole point of coming away was to get away from the Archers. If I'd wanted them on my doorstep, hounding me with lawyer's letters and private detectives, I'd have stayed in London."

"But if she *knew* where he was . . ."

"Oh, shut up."

It was not so much what he said as the tone of voice that he used to say it. A silence grew between them. After a little, Victoria turned her head and looked at him. His profile was stony, his lower lip jutted, his eyes narrowed, and staring straight at the road ahead. They had left the town behind them, and the car was picking up speed when they turned a corner and came all at once, upon the signpost, pointing inland, to Benchoile and Loch Muie. Oliver was caught unawares. He braked abruptly, and swung the car around with a screech of tires. They started up the single-track road, heading for the hills.

Unseeing, Victoria gazed ahead. She knew that Oliver was wrong, which was perhaps one of the reasons that he was being so stubborn. But Victoria could be stubborn, too. She said, "You've already told me that she hasn't got a leg to stand on, legally. That she can't do anything to get Thomas back. He's your child, and your responsibility."

Again, Oliver said nothing.

"So if you're so certain of yourself, there can be no reason not to let her know that he's all right."

He still was silent, and Victoria played her final card. "Well, you may not intend telling Mrs. Archer that Thomas is safe and well, but there's nothing to stop me writing to her."

Oliver spoke at last. "If you do," he said quietly, "if you so much as pick up a telephone, I promise you, I'll batter you black and blue."

He sounded as though he actually meant it. Victoria looked at him in astonishment, searching for some sign to put her mind at rest, to convince herself that this was simply Oliver, using words as his strongest weapon. But she found no reassurance. The coldness of his anger was devastating, and she found herself trembling as though he had already struck her. His stony features blurred as her eyes filled with sudden, ridiculous tears. She looked away, quickly, so that he should not notice them, and later, surreptitiously, wiped them away.

So it was, with the sourness of the quarrel between them, and Victoria struggling not to cry, that they came to Benchoile.

Jock Dunbeath's funeral had been a big and important affair, as befitted a man of his position. The church was full and later the graveyard, crowded with somberly clad men, from all walks of life, who had come—some many miles and from all directions—to pay their respects to an old and much-liked friend.

But the wake that followed was small. Only a few close colleagues made the journey to Benchoile, there to gather about the blazing fire in the library and to partake of Ellen's homemade shortbread, washed down with a dram or two of the best malt whiskey.

One of these was Robert McKenzie, not only the family lawyer, but as well a lifetime friend of Jock Dunbeath. Robert had been Jock's best man when Jock married Lucy, and Jock was godfather to Robert's eldest boy. Robert had driven up that morning from Inverness, appeared in the church wearing his long black overcoat that made him look like one of the undertakers, and afterwards had acted as pallbearer.

Now, with his duties behind him, and a drink in his hand, he had become once more his usual brisk and businesslike self. In the middle of the proceedings, he drew Roddy aside.

"Roddy, if it's possible, I'd like a word with you sometime."

Roddy sent him a keen glance, but the other man's long face was set in its usual professional lines, and gave nothing away. Roddy sighed. He had been expecting something like this, but scarcely so soon.

"Anytime, old boy. What do you want me to do, nip down to Inverness? Beginning of next week, maybe?"

"Later, perhaps that would be a good idea. But I'd rather have a moment or two now. I mean, when this is over. It won't take more than five minutes."

'But of course. Stay and have a bit of lunch. It won't be more than soup and cheese, but you're more than welcome."

"No, I won't do that. I have to get back. I've a meeting at three o'clock. But if I could just stay on after the others have gone?"

"Absolutely. No trouble at all . . ." Roddy's eyes wandered away from the lawyer. He spied an empty glass in somebody's hand. "My dear fellow, another dram for the road . . ."

It was not a gloomy gathering. Indeed, there were nothing but happy memories to recall, and soon there were smiles and even laughter. When the guests finally took themselves off, driving away in Range Rovers, or estate cars, or battered farm vans, Roddy stood outside the open front door of Benchoile and saw them on their way, feeling a little as though he were saying good-bye to the guns at the end of an enjoyable day's shoot.

The simile pleased him because it was so exactly the way that Jock would have liked it. The last car made its way down through the rhododendrons, over the cattle grid, and out of sight around the corner. Only Robert McKenzie's old Rover remained.

Roddy went back indoors. Robert waited for him, standing in front of the mantelpiece, with his back to the fire.

"That went very well, Roddy."

"Thank God it didn't rain. Nothing worse than a funeral in a downpour." He had had only two whiskies. Robert still had a bit in his glass, so Roddy poured himself another small one. "What was it you wanted to talk to me about?"

"Benchoile," said Robert.

"Yes, I imagined it was that."

"I don't know if Jock told you what he intended doing with the place?"

"No. We never discussed it. There never seemed to be any pressing need to discuss it." Roddy considered this. "As things have turned out, perhaps we should have."

"He never said anything about young John?"

"You mean Charlie's boy? Never a word. Why?"

"He's left Benchoile to John."

Roddy was in the act of pouring water into his tumbler. A little of it spilled onto the tray. He looked up. Across the room his eyes met Robert's. Slowly he laid down the water jug. He said, "Good God."

"You had no idea?"

"No idea at all."

"I know Jock meant to talk it over with you. Had every intention of doing so, in fact. Perhaps the opportunity never came up."

"We didn't see all that much of each other, you know. More or less lived in the same house, but didn't see that much of each other. Didn't really talk . . ." Roddy's voice trailed off. He was confused, confounded.

Robert said gently, "Do you mind?"

"Mind?" Roddy's blue eyes widened in astonishment. "Mind? Of course I don't mind. Benchoile was never mine, the way it was Jock's. I know nothing about the farm; I have nothing to do with the house or the garden; I was never particularly interested in the stalking or the grouse. I simply roost in her. I'm the lodger."

"Then you didn't expect you'd be taking over?" Robert was considerably relieved. One could never imagine Roddy Dunbeath being disagreeable about anything, but he might well have been disappointed. Now, it appeared, he was not even that.

"To tell you the truth, old boy, I never even thought of it. Never thought of Jock dying. He always seemed such a tough old thing, walking the hill, and bringing the sheep down with Davey Guthrie, and even working in the garden."

"But," Robert reminded him, "he had had a heart attack."

"A very mild one. Nothing to worry about, the doctor said. He seemed to be all right. Never complained. But then, of course, Jock was never a man to complain. . . ." Once more the sentence drifted to silence. Even for Roddy Dunbeath, thought the lawyer, his thought processes seemed more than usually vague.

"But Roddy, since Jock died, surely you must have wondered what was going to happen to Benchoile?"

"To tell you the truth, old boy, I haven't had much time for wondering. Hell of a lot to organize, you know, when something like this happens. I've been waking up in a cold sweat in the middle of the night, trying to remember what it is I've forgotten to do."

"But . . ."

Roddy began to smile. "And of course, half the time I haven't forgotten it at all."

It was impossible. Robert abandoned Roddy's future, and brought the discussion sharply back into line.

"About John, then. I've written to him, but I haven't yet had a reply to my letter."

"He's been in Bahrain. I had a cable from him. That's why he wasn't here this morning."

"I've invited him to come up and see me. The future of the property will have to be discussed."

"Yes, I suppose it will." Roddy thought about this. He said, with some conviction, "He won't want to live here."

"What makes you so certain?"

"Just that I can't imagine he would have the smallest interest in the place."

"Jock didn't seem to think that."

"It was hard to know, sometimes, exactly what Jock was thinking. I never thought he particularly liked Charlie's boy. They were always so intensely polite to each other. It's not a good sign, you know, when people are too polite. Besides, John Dunbeath has a career of his own. He's a clever, cool, successful young man, wheeling and dealing and making a lot of money. Not that he needs to make a lot of money, because he's always had it through his mother. And that's another thing, he's an American."

"Half American." Robert permitted himself a smile. "And I'd have thought you'd be the last man in the world to hold that against him."

"I don't hold it against him. I have nothing against John Dunbeath. I mean that. He was an exceptional boy and extremely intelligent. But I don't see him as the laird of Benchoile. What would he do with himself? He's only twenty-eight." The more Roddy thought about it, the more preposterous the idea became. "I shouldn't think he knows one end of a sheep from the other."

"It doesn't take much intelligence to learn."

"But why *John?*" The two men looked at each other glumly. Roddy sighed. "I know why of course. Because Jock had no children and I had no children and there wasn't anybody else."

"What do you think will happen?"

"I suppose he'll sell it. It seems a pity, but for the life of me, I can't think what else he'd do with the place."

"Let it? Come here for holidays?"

"A weekend cottage with fourteen bedrooms?"

"Well then, keep the farm in hand and sell the house?"

"He'd never get rid of the house unless he let the shooting and the stalking rights go with it, and Davey Guthrie needs that land for his sheep."

"If he does sell Benchoile, what will you do?"

"That's the sixty four thousand dollar question, isn't it? But I've lived here, on and off, all my life, and perhaps that's too long for any man to stay in one place. I shall move away. I shall move abroad. somewhere distant." Robert had visions of Roddy in Ibiza, wearing a panama hat. "Like Creagan," he finished, and Robert laughed.

"Well, I'm glad you know," he said, and finished his drink and set down the empty glass. "And I hope, between us all, we'll be able to sort it all out. I . . . I expect John will want to come here sooner or later. To Benchoile, I mean. Will that be all right?"

"Right as rain, old boy. Anytime. Tell him to give me a ring."

They moved towards the door.

"I'll be in touch."

"You do that. And Robert, thank you for today. And for everything."

"I'll miss Jock."

"We all will."

He drove away, headed for Inverness, and his three o'clock meeting, a busy man with much to think about. Roddy watched the Rover disappear, and then he was all alone, and he knew that now it was really over. And successfully over, which was so surprising. No small mishaps had occurred, and the funeral had passed in an orderly and soldierly fashion, just as if Jock had organized it himself, and not his singularly disorganized brother. Roddy drew a long sigh, part relief and part sadness. He looked up at the sky, hearing the chatter of greylags high above the clouds, but they stayed out of sight. A thin wind moved up the glen from the sea, and the slate grey surface of the water shivered beneath its touch.

Jock was dead and Benchoille now belonged to young John. So perhaps this day was not only the end of the beginning, but also, if John decided to sell it all, the beginning of the end. The idea would take some getting used to, but in Roddy's book, there was only one way to tackle such gargantuan problems, and that was as slowly as possible, a single step at a time. This meant no anticipation and no precipitant action. Life would move quietly on.

He looked at his watch. It was now half past twelve. His thoughts moved ahead to the remainder of the day, and he suddenly remembered the approaching car, and the young family coming to spend a few days at Benchoile. Oliver Dobbs and some female or other and their child. It occurred to Roddy that Oliver was the sort of man who would always have some female or other in tow.

They would be arriving at any moment, and the prospect lifted his spirts. The day was a sad one, but, thought Roddy, where God closes a window, he opens a door. What this old saw had to do with Oliver Dobbs, he couldn't be sure, but it helped one to realize that there could be no time for useless grieving, and Roddy found this comforting.

Thinking of comfort brought him sharply back to an awareness of the physical agony that he had endured all morning.

It was to do with his kilt. He had not worn this garment for two years or more, but for the laird's funeral, it had seemed appropriate to put it on. Accordingly, this morning he had taken it, reeking of camphor, from the cupboard, only to discover that he had put on so much weight that the kilt would scarcely go round him, and after struggling with it for five minutes or more, he had been forced to take himself over to the big house and enroll the aid of Ellen Tarbat.

He found her in the kitchen, dressed in the inky black that she kept for funerals, and with her gloomiest hat—and none of Ellen's hats were very cheerful—already skewered to her head by an immense jet-headed hat pin. Ellen's tears for Jock had been shed privately, decently, behind the closed door of her bedroom at the top of the house. Now, dry-eyed and tight-lipped, she was engaged in polishing the best tumblers before setting them out on the damask-covered table in the library. When Roddy appeared, clutching his kilt about him like a bathtowel, she said, "I told you so," as he had known she would, but she laid down the tea towel and came manfully to his aid, heaving her puny weight on the leather straps of the kilt, like a tiny groom trying to tighten the girth of some enormous, overfed horse.

Finally, by brute force, the pin of the buckle went into the last hole of the leather strap.

"There," said Ellen triumphantly. She was quite red in the face, and a few stray white hairs had escaped from her bun.

Roddy held his breath. Now, he let it out cautiously. The kilt tightened across his belly like a pair of tightly laced stays, but the straps, miraculously, held.

"You've done it," he told her.

Ellen tidied her hair. "If you were to ask me, I'd say it was about time you went on a diet. Or else you'll need to take your kilt into Inverness and get the man to let it out. Otherwise you'll be giving yourself a seizure, and it's yourself we'll be burying next."

Infuriated, Roddy strode from the kitchen. The kilt straps had held, somehow, all morning, but now, gratefully, he realized he need suffer no longer, and accordingly he made his way back to the Stable House, took off his finery and climbed into the most comfortable clothes he owned.

He was just shrugging himself into his old tweed jacket when he heard the approaching car. From his bedroom window, he saw the dark blue Volvo approach up the drive between the rhododendrons and come to a halt at the edge of the grass in front of the house. Roddy gave a cursory glance in the mirror, smoothed down his ruffled hair with his hand, and went out of the room. His old dog Barney hauled himself to his feet and followed. He had spent the morning shut up and alone, and was not going to risk being left behind again. The two of them emerged from the stable yard just as Oliver climbed out from behind the driving wheel of the car. He saw Roddy and slammed the car door shut behind him. Roddy went towards him, feet crunching over the gravel, his hand outstretched in welcome.

"Oliver!"

Oliver smiled. He looked just the same, Roddy thought, with some satisfaction. He did not like people to change. At the television dinner Oliver had worn a velvet jacket and a flamboyant tie. He was now in faded corduroys and a huge Norwegian sweater, but otherwise he seemed just the same. Same coppery hair, same beard, same smile.

Oliver came towards him, and they met in the middle of the gravel. The very sight of him, tall and young and handsome, gave Roddy new heart.

"Hello, Roddy."

They shook hands, Roddy taking Oliver's hand in both his own, so pleased was he to see him.

"My dear fellow, how are you? How splendid you were able to make it. And right on time, too. Did you have any trouble finding us?"

"No trouble at all. We bought an Ordnance Survey map in Fort William and simply followed the red lines." He looked about him, at the house, the slope of the lawn, the grey waters of the loch, the hills beyond. "What a fantastic place."

"Yes, it's lovely, isn't it?" Side by side they regarded the view. "Not much of a day to see it on, though. I'll have to arrange some better weather for you."

"We don't mind about the weather. However cold it is, all Victoria seems to want to do is sit on beaches." This reminded Oliver of the other occupants of his car. He seemed to be about to do something about them, but Roddy stopped him.

"Look . . . just a minute, old boy. I think we should have a word first." Oliver looked at him. Roddy scratched the back of his neck, searching for the right words. "The thing is . . ." But there seemed no way of getting around it, so he brought it straight out. "My brother died at the beginning of the week. Jock Dunbeath. His funeral was this morning. In Creagan."

Oliver was horrified. He stared at Roddy, taking this in, and then he said, "Oh, God," and there was everything in his voice: distress and sympathy and a sort of agonized embarrassment.

"My dear fellow, please don't feel badly about it. I wanted to tell you right away, so that you'd understand the situation."

"We came through Creagan. We saw all the shutters down, but we didn't know the reason."

"Well, you know how it is. People like to pay their respects in this part of the world, 'specially when it's a man like Jock."

"I'm so dreadfully sorry. But, when did this happen?"

"Monday. About midday. Just about this time. He was out with the dogs and he had a heart attack. We found him in the lea of one of the dikes."

"And you couldn't get in touch with me and tell us not to come, because you didn't know where I was. What a ghastly situation for you."

"No, I didn't know where you were, but even if I had, I wouldn't have got in touch with you. I've been looking forward to seeing you, and I should have been most disappointed if you hadn't come."

"We can't possibly stay."

"Of course you can stay. My brother is dead, but the funeral is over, and life must go on. The only thing is, I'd originally planned that you should sleep in the big house. But it struck me that without Jock there, it might be a little depressing for you, so if you don't mind rather close quarters, you'll be staying in the Stable House with me. Ellen, Jock's housekeeper, and Jess Guthrie from the farm have made up the beds and lit the fires, so everything's ready for you."

"Are you sure you wouldn't rather we just took ourselves off again?"

"My dear boy, it would make me miserable. I've been looking forward to a little young company. Don't get nearly enough of it these days . . ."

He glanced across at the car, and saw that the girl, perhaps tiring of sitting there while the two men talked, had got out of it, and now she and the little boy were making their way, hand in hand, down the slope of the grass towards the water's edge. She was dressed more or less as Oliver was dressed, in trousers and a thick sweater. She had tied a red and white cotton scarf around her head, and the red of the scarf was the same as the little boy's dungarees. In such a setting, they made a charming picture, investing the grey, brooding scene with color and a certain innocence.

"Come and meet them," said Oliver, and they began to slowly back towards the car.

"Just one thing more," said Roddy. "I'm taking it for granted that you're not married to this girl?"

"No, I'm not." Oliver's expression was amused. "Do you mind?"

The inference that Roddy Dunbeath's attitudes might well be out of date and out of touch made Roddy feel mildly indignant. "Heavens, no. I don't mind in the very least. Anyway, it's nothing to do with me, it's your affair entirely. There is just one point, though.

It would be much better if the people who work at Benchoile believe you to be married. It sounds old-fashioned, I know, but people are old-fashioned up here, and I wouldn't want to offend them. I'm sure you understand."

"Yes, of course."

"Ellen, the housekeeper, would probably have a heart attack and pass out on me if she knew the wicked truth, and God knows what would happen to Benchoile if that happened. She's been here forever, longer than most people can remember. She arrived in the first instance, fresh from some remote Highland croft, to look after my younger brother, and she's remained, immovable as a rock, ever since. You'll meet her, but don't expect a devoted, smiling, gentle old dear. Ellen is as tough as old boots and can be twice as unpleasant! So you see, it's quite important not to offend her."

"Yes, of course."

"Mr. and Mrs. Dobbs, then?"

"Mr. and Mrs. Dobbs," Oliver agreed.

Victoria, with Thomas's fat hand held firmly in her own, stood by the reedy margins of Loch Muie and struggled with a terrible conviction that she had come to a place where she had no business to be.

It is better to travel hopefully than to arrive. Arrival, it seemed, had brought nothing but a sense of desolation and disappointment. This was Benchoile. But the Benchoile that Victoria had imagined was the Benchoile seen through the eyes of the ten-year-old boy that Roddy Denbeath had been. *The Eagle Years* was a saga of summertime, of blue skies and long golden evenings and hills purple with heather. An idyll that bore no relation to this windswept and foreboding scene. It seemed to Victoria unrecognizable. Where was the little rowing boat? Where was the waterfall where Roddy and his brothers had picnicked? Where the children, running barefoot?

The answer was simple. Gone forever. Shut away between the covers of a book.

This now, was Benchoile. So much sky, so much space, so quiet. Only the sough of the wind in pine branches and the lap of grey water on the shingle. The size and the silence of the hills was unnerving. They enclosed the glen, rose sheer from the opposite shore of the loch. Victoria's eyes followed their slope, upwards, past great bastions of rock and scree, over swelling shoulders dark with heather, to distant summits veiled in the scudding grey sky. Their very size, their watchfulness, had an obliterating effect. She felt shrunk, dwarfed, insignificant as an ant. Incapable of dealing with anything, least of all the sudden deterioration of her relationship with Oliver.

She tried to call it a silly quarrel, but knew that it was more than that, a breach both bitter and unexpected. That it had blown up at all was Victoria's own fault. She should have kept quiet about sending the stupid postcard to Mrs. Archer. But at the time it had seemed important, an issue worth fighting for. And now everything was spoiled, and not a word had either of them spoken since Oliver's last violent outburst. And perhaps that was Victoria's fault too. She should have stood up for herself, given threat for threat, and, if necessary, threatened blow for blow. Proved to Oliver that she had a will of her own instead of sitting mesmerized like a rabbit, and with her eyes so full of tears she couldn't even see the road ahead.

She felt overwhelmed. By the quarrel, by Benchoile, by a physical tiredness that made her ache, by the uncomfortable feeling that she had mislaid her own identity. Who am I? What am I doing in this outlandish place? How did I ever get here?

"Victoria." She had not heard them approaching across the grass, and Oliver's voice startled her. "Victoria, this is Roddy Dunbeath."

She turned to face a man huge and shabby as a much-loved teddy bear. His clothes looked as though they had been thrown at him, his sparse grey hair blew in the wind, his features were lost in fat. But he was smiling at her. His blue eyes were warm with friendliness. Before them, Victoria's depression, her first fearful impressions of Benchoile, abated a little.

She said, "Hello." They shook hands. He looked down at Thomas. "And who's this?"

"This is Tom." She stooped and lifted him up to her shoulder. Tom's cheeks were intensely red, and he had mud on his mouth where he had been tasting pebbles.

"Hello, Tom. How old are you?"

"He's two," Oliver told him, "and you'll be delighted to hear that he scarcely ever utters a word."

Roddy considered this. "Well, he appears to be quite healthy, so I don't suppose you've got anything to worry about." He looked back at Victoria. "I'm afraid Benchoile isn't at its best today. There's too much cloud about."

There was an old black Labrador at his heels. Thomas caught sight of him, and wriggled, wanting to be put down so that he could go and pat the dog. Victoria set him back on his feet, and he and the dog looked at each other. Then Thomas touched the soft, grizzled muzzle.

"What is he called?" asked Victoria.

"Barney. He's very old. Almost as old as I am."

"I thought you'd probably have a dog."

"Victoria," Oliver explained, "is one of your fans, Roddy." He sounded quite cheerful and ordinary again, and Victoria wondered if the quarrel that had blown up that morning was, for the time being, forgotten.

"How splendid," said Roddy. "Nothing I like better than having a fan about the place."

Victoria smiled. "I was looking for the waterfall."

"Even on a fine day you can't see it from here. It's hidden behind an outcrop. There's a little bay. Perhaps if the weather clears and I can find the key to the boathouse, we'll get over one day and you can see it for yourself." A gust of wind, with a cutting edge like a knife, keened down upon them. Victoria shivered and Roddy was galvanized into ghostly action. "Now, come along, we'll all get pneumonia standing here. Let's get your cases out of the car and get you all settled in."

Again, it was like nothing that Victoria had imagined. For Roddy led them, not into the big house, but through the archway into the stableyard, and so on to what was obviously his own little house. The bedrooms were on the ground floor. "This is for you and Oliver," said Roddy, going ahead of them like a well-trained hotel porter. "And there's a dressing room off it, where I thought you could put the child; and here's the bathroom. It's all pretty cramped I'm afraid, but I hope you'll be comfortable."

"I think it's perfect." She set Tom down on the bed, and looked about her. There was a window facing out over the water, and a deep windowsill, upon which stood a little jug of snowdrops. She wondered if it was Roddy who had put them there.

"It's a funny sort of house," he told her. "The living room and the kitchen are upstairs, but I like it that way. Now, when you've unpacked and made yourselves comfortable, come up and we'll have a drink and something to eat. Does Thomas like soup?"

"He likes anything."

Roddy looked suitably amazed. "What an accommodating child," he remarked, and went off and left her.

Victoria sat on the edge of the bed, and lifted Thomas onto her knee and began to divest him of his little jacket. And all the time her eyes went around the room, loving it because it was so right, white-washed and simply furnished, and yet containing all that any person could possibly need. It even had a fireplace, built across one corner of the room, in which a stack of peats was smoldering, and there was a basket containing more peat alongside the hearth, so that one could replenish it oneself, keep it going all night if need be. She thought of going to sleep by firelight, and it seemed, all at once, the most romantic thing in the world. Perhaps, she told herself cautiously, per-haps after all, everything was going to be all right.

Oliver appeared behind her, bearing the last of the suitcases. He put this down and shut the door behind him.

"Oliver . . ."

But, abruptly, he interrupted her. "Something ghastly's happened. Roddy's brother died at the beginning of the week. That was his funeral in Creagan this morning. I mean, that's why all the blinds were down."

Victoria stared at him, over the top of Thomas's head, in horrified disbelief. "But why didn't he let us know?"

"He couldn't. He didn't know where we were. And anyway, he swears he wanted us to come."

"He's just saying that."

"No, I don't think he is. In a way, I think we're probably the best thing that could have happen to him. You know, give him something to think about. Anyway, we're here now. We can't go away again."

"But . . ."

"And there's another thing. We're Mr. and Mrs. Dobbs like in the hotel register. Apparently, there's a string of old retainers who'll all give notice if they know the terrible truth." He began nosing around, opening cupboards and doors, like a great, long cat making itself at home. "What a fantastic setup. Is this where Thomas is sleeping?"

"Yes. Oliver, perhaps we should only stay one night."

"What do you mean? Don't you like it here?"

"I love it, but . . ."

He came to drop a kiss on her open, protesting mouth, and Vic-toria was silenced. The quarrel still lay between them. She wondered if the kiss was meant as an apology, or whether she was going to have to be the first to say she was sorry. But before she was able to make up her mind about this, one way or the other, he had kissed her again, patted Thomas on the head, and left them. She heard him running upstairs, heard his voice mingling with Roddy's. She sighed, and lifted Thomas off the bed and took him to the bathroom.

It was midnight and very dark. Roddy Dunbeath, steeped in brandy, had taken a torch and whistled up his dog, and gone the rounds of the big house, to make sure, he explained to Oliver, that the doors and windows were all securely closed, and that old Ellen, up in her attic bedroom, was safe for the night.

Oliver wondered, safe from what? They had been introduced, formally, to Ellen during the course of the evening, and she had seemed to him not only older than God but just as formidable. Victoria had long since gone to bed. Thomas was sleeping. Oliver lit the cigar that Roddy had given him and took it out of doors.

The silence that greeted him was immense. The wind had dropped and there was scarcely a sound. His footsteps crunched as he went across the gravel, and then fell silent when he reached the grass. He could feel its cold dampness through the soles of his shoes. He reached the loch and began to walk along the edge of the water. The air was icy. His light clothes—the velvet jacket and the silk shirt—were no protection, and the cold washed over his body like a freezing shower. He reveled in the shock of it and felt refreshed and stimulated.

His eyes grew accustomed to the darkness. Slowly, the massive presence of the surrounding hills began to take shape. He saw the translucent shimmer of the loch. From the trees behind the house, an owl hooted. He came to the little jetty. Now, his footsteps sounded hollow on the wooden planking. At the end, he stopped, and threw the butt of the cigar into the water. It sizzled and then was dark.

The voices were there. The old woman. *It's not the way your father would have done it.* She had been living in his head for months, but she was Ellen Tarbat. And yet she was not Ellen from Sutherland. She was called Kate and she came from Yorkshire. *Your father didn't do things that way, not that way at all.* She was embittered, she was worn, she was indestructible. *He was always a man to pay his way. And proud. When I buried him, I did it with ham. Mrs. Hackworth buried her man, but she's that mean, she did it with nobbut buns.*

She was Kate, but she was Ellen too. This was the way it happened. Past and present, fantasy and reality, all spun together like a steel rope, so that he did not know where one ended and the other began.

And this thing inside him would begin to grow, like some tumor, until it took over altogether, and he would become possessed by it, and by the people who fought to get out of the inside of his head; to get down on paper.

And for weeks, perhaps months, he would exist in a shambling vacuum, incapable of anything except the most basic and essential of bodily functions; like sleeping, and ambling around the corner to the pub, and buying cigarettes.

The anticipation of this state filled him with trembling excitement. Despite the cold, he found that the palms of his hands were sweaty. He turned and looked back at the dim bulk of the house. A light burned in the attic, and he imagined old Ellen pottering about, putting her teeth into a tumbler, saying her prayers, getting into bed. He saw her, lying, staring at the ceiling, her nose sticking up over the edge of the sheet, waiting for the fitful sleep of old age.

There were other lights. From Roddy's sitting room, from behind drawn curtains. From the bedroom below it where Victoria slept.

He made his way, slowly, back to the house.

She was asleep, but she woke when he came in and turned on the light by their bed. He sat beside her, and she turned on the pillow and yawned, and saw who it was and said his name. She wore a night-dress of thin white lawn, edged with lace, and her pale hair spread on the pillow like strands of primrose-colored silk.

He pulled off his tie and undid the top button of his shirt, and she said, "Where have you been?"

"Out."

"What time is it?"

He kicked off his shoes. "Late." He leaned across and took her head between his hands. Slowly, he began to kiss her.

He slept at last, but Victoria lay awake in his arms for an hour or more. The curtains were drawn back and the cold night air flowed in through the open window. In the hearth the peat fire burned steadily, and its flicker and glow were reflected in patterns of light on the low, white ceiling. The quarrel of the morning had been dissolved in love. Victoria was reassured. She lay there in the tranquil knowledge—as calming as a sedative—that nothing this perfect could possibly go wrong.

10

FRIDAY

＊＊＊

She was suddenly, intensely, wide awake, disoriented, with no idea where she was meant to be. She saw the wide window, and beyond it, the sky—pale, pristine, cloudless. The outline of the hills was sharp as glass, the topmost peaks touched by the first rays of the rising sun. Benchoile. Benchoile, possibly at its best. It looked as if it were going to be a beautiful day. Perhaps she could take Thomas to the beach.

Thomas. Thomas's grandmother. Mrs. Archer. Today she was going to write to Mrs. Archer.

Just like that, while she slept, her mind, perhaps realizing that Victoria was capable of dithering about this problem indefinitely, had apparently made itself up. The letter would be written this morning, posted at the earliest opportunity. She would find out the address by going to the post office in Creagan and asking for the relevant telephone directory. Woodbridge was in Hampshire. It was only a small place. There would not be many Archers living in such a small place.

The form of the letter began to frame itself. *I am writing to let you know that Thomas is well and very happy.*

And Thomas's father? Beside her Oliver slumbered soundlessly, his head turned away from her, his long arm stretched outside the covers, the palm of his hand turned up, the fingers curled and relaxed. Victoria raised herself on her elbow and looked down at his untroubled face. He seemed, in that moment, defenseless and vulnerable. He loved her. Love and fear could not share the same bed. She was not afraid of Oliver.

And anyway—cautiously she lay back on her pillows—Oliver need never know. *Oliver did not want me to write to you,* she would put, *so perhaps it would be better if you do not acknowledge this letter or try to get in touch.*

She could not think why this harmless deception had not occurred to her before. Mrs. Archer would understand. All she would want was reassurance about her missing grandson. And Victoria would promise, at the end of the letter, to write again, to keep in touch. It would seem that it was going to be quite a correspondence.

From the next room, from beyond the closed door, came sounds of Thomas stirring. A strange sound, "Meh, meh, meh," disturbed the morning quiet. Thomas, singing. She imagined him sucking his thumb, thumping Piglet against the wall by his bed. After a little the singing stopped, there were scuffling sounds, the door opened and Thomas appeared.

Victoria pretended to be asleep, lay with her eyes closed. Thomas climbed up onto the bed and lay on top of her, forcing her eyelids open with a stubby thumb. She saw his face, only inches from her own, the blue eyes alarmingly close, his nose nearly touching her own.

She had not yet written to his grandmother, but today she was going to, and the knowledge freed Victoria of guilt and filled her with tenderness towards Thomas. She put her arms around him and hugged him, and he laid his cheek on hers and thoughtfully kicked her in the stomach. After a little, when it became obvious that he was not going to be still for a moment longer, she got out of bed. Oliver still slept, undisturbed. She took Thomas into his room and dressed him, and then dressed herself. They left Oliver sleeping, and hand-in-hand climbed the stairs to forage for breakfast.

The domestic arrangements at Benchoile appeared to be fluid— the two establishments, the big house and the Stable House running, as it were, in harness. Yesterday they had lunched on soup and cheese in Roddy's cheerful, littered living room, eating off a table drawn up to the window, the meal as informal as a picnic. Dinner, on the other hand, was a quite different affair, served in the immense dining room of the big house. By some unspoken agreement, they had all changed for this occasion. Oliver had put on his velvet jacket, and Roddy wore a straining doublet made of tartan, with a cummerbund filling the gap between his shirt and the dark trousers which would no longer do up around his waist. A fire had burned in the grate, there were candles in the silver candlesticks, and tall, dim portraits of varied Dunbeaths looked down upon them from the paneled walls. Victoria had wondered which was Jock, but didn't like to ask. There was something vaguely unnerving about the empty chair at the head of the table. She felt as though they were all intruding, as though they had walked into another man's house, without permission, and at any moment the owner was going to walk in and find them there.

But she, apparently, was the only one of them troubled by this uneasy guilt. Oliver and Roddy talked incessantly, of their world of writers, publishers, producers, about which Victoria knew nothing. The conversation flowed, well-oiled by an abundance of wine. And even the old woman, Ellen, had seemed to see nothing amiss in such good spirits on the very night of the laird's funeral. To and fro she trod in her worn-down shoes, her best apron over her black dress, handing the heavy ashets through the hatch that led to the kitchen, and taking away the used plates. Victoria had made signs that she would like to help, but Roddy had stopped her. "Jess Guthrie's in the kitchen, giving Ellen a hand. She'll be mortally offended if you so much as rise from your chair," he had told Victoria when Ellen was out of earshot, and so she sat, against all her better instincts, and let herself be waited on with the others.

At one point during the course of the meal Ellen had taken herself off for ten minutes or more. When she returned with the coffee tray, she had announced, without preamble, that the wee boy was sleeping like an angel, and Victoria realized that she had made the journey down the long stone passages and across the stable yard, to check on Thomas, and was touched.

"I was just going to look at him myself," she told Ellen, but Ellen's mouth had bunched up, as though Victoria had said something indecent. "And why should you be getting up from your dinner, when there's me here to see to the child?" Victoria felt reprimanded.

Now, the following morning, she struggled with the inconsistencies of another person's kitchen, but, by the lengthy expedient of opening one door after another, she ran to earth eggs, bread, a jug of milk. Thomas was no help at all, and always seemed to be under her feet.

She found suitable plates and mugs, knives and forks. Some butter and a jar of instant coffee. She laid the small plastic-topped table, set Thomas up on a chair, tied a tea towel around his neck, took the top off his egg. He settled down, silently, to demolish it.

Victoria made herself a cup of coffee and pulled up a chair to face him. She said, "Would you like to go to the beach today?"

Thomas stopped eating and looked at her, the egg yolk running down his chin. She wiped it away. As she did this the door that led into the house from the stable-yard opened and shut. Footsteps came slowly up the stairs. The next moment Ellen appeared at the open kitchen door.

"Good morning," said Victoria.

"Yes, and you're up and about already. You're an early starter, Mrs. Dobbs."

"Thomas woke me."

"I came over to see if you'd like me to give him his breakfast, but I see you've already seen to that yourself."

Her manner was disconcerting, because you could never tell by her voice whether you were doing the right thing or not. And it was no help looking at her face, because her expression was one of constant disapproval, the faded eyes cold and beady and her mouth pursed as though someone had run a string around it and then pulled it tight. Her hair was thin and white, dragged back from her temples and screwed into a tight little bun. Beneath it her scalp gleamed pinkly. Her figure seemed to have shrunk with age, so that all her clothes—her ageless and seemly clothes—appeared to be a size too big. Only her hands were large and capable, red with scrubbing, the joints swollen and twisted like old tree roots. She stood with these folded across her stomach, over the flowered apron, and looked as though, in her long life, she had never once stopped working. Victoria wondered how old she was.

She said, tentatively, "Perhaps you'd like a cup of coffee?"

"I never touch the stuff. It doesn't agree with me at all."

"A cup of tea, then?"

"No, no. I've had my tea."

"Well, why don't you sit down? Take the weight off your feet?"

For a moment, she thought that even this mild overture of friendliness was going to be rejected, but Ellen, perhaps seduced by Tom's unblinking stare, reached for a chair, and settled herself at the head of the table.

"Eat up your egg, then," she said to Thomas, and then to Victoria, "He's a beautiful child." Her Highland voice turned this into, "He's a peautiful chilt."

"Are you fond of children?"

"Oh, yes, and there used to be so many of them at Benchoile, all over the place." She had come, it was obvious, to see Thomas and have a gossip. Victoria waited, and inevitably the old voice rambled on. "I came here to look after Charlie when he was a baby. Charlie was the youngest of the boys. I looked after the others as well, but I had Charlie all to myself. Charlie's in America now, you know. He married an American lady." Casually, as though they could not help themselves, her hands went out to spread Thomas's toast with butter, to cut the toast into fingers for him.

Victoria said, "I feel so badly, us arriving to stay so soon after . . . I mean, we didn't know, you see . . ."

She stopped, lost in confusion and wishing that she had never started, but Ellen was quite unperturbed.

"You mean, the laird dying so suddenly like that, and the funeral only yesterday?"

"Well, yes."

"It was a beautiful funeral. All the grand people were there."

"I'm sure."

"Mind, he was a lonely man. He had no children of his own, you see. It was a great sorrow to Mrs. Jock that she was never able to have any babies. 'There you are Ellen,' she used to say, 'and there's the empty nursery upstairs, waiting for the babies, and it doesn't look as though there's going to be a single one.' And, indeed, there wasn't."

She put another finger of toast into Thomas's hand.

"What happened to her?"

"She died. Five years ago or more. She died. She was a beautiful lady. Always laughing." She told Thomas, "Yes, yes, you are eating a splendid breakfast."

"Didn't your baby . . . didn't Charlie ever have any children?"

"Oh, yes, Charlie had a boy, and what a bright little lad he was. They used to come over for the summers, all three of them, and what good times those were. Picnics up the hill or on the beach at Creagan. 'I've too much to do in the house to come for picnics,' I used to tell him, but John would say, 'But Ellen, you must come too, it'll not be a proper picnic without you."

"He was called John."

"Yes, he was named for the Colonel."

"You must have missed him when he had to go back to America."

"Oh, the place seemed empty after they had gone. Like a tomb."

Victoria, watching Ellen, suddenly liked her very much. She stopped feeling intimidated or even shy. She said, "I knew a little bit about Benchoile before I got here yesterday, because I'd read all Roddy's books."

"Those were the best times of all, when the boys were young. Before that war."

"He must have been a funny little boy with all his strange pets."

Ellen clicked her tongue and held up her hands in horror at the memory. "I sometimes thought he'd be the death of me. Just a wee devil. He looked like an angel, mind, but you never knew what Roddy would be up to next. And when it came to washing his clothes, as likely as not the pockets would be filled with mealy worms."

Victoria laughed. "That reminds me," she said, "I wonder if there's somewhere I could do some washing. We've been traveling for four days and I haven't been able to wash anything, and soon we're all going to run out of clothes."

"You can put them in the washing machine."

"If I brought it all over to the big house after breakfast, perhaps you could show me where the washing machine is, and how to use it."

"Now, you don't worry about that. I'll see to the washing. You don't want to spend your holiday doing washing. And . . ." she added, with cunning innocence ". . . if you should want to be away on a wee outing with your husband, I could keep an eye on the child for you."

She was obviously longing to get her hands on Thomas, to get him to herself. Victoria thought of the letter she was going to write. "I ought to do some shopping, in that case. We seem to have run out of toothpaste, and Oliver's bound to want cigarettes. If I took our car to Creagan this morning, would you really look after Thomas for me? He doesn't like shopping very much."

"And why should he like shopping? It's a dull occupation for a little man." She leaned forward, nodding her head at Thomas as though already they had some sort of conspiracy going between them. "You'll stay with Ellen, won't you, pet? You'll help Ellen with the washing?"

Thomas stared at the small brown wrinkled face bobbing up and down so close to his own. Victoria watched for his reaction to this in some anxiety. It would be embarrassing if he screamed and hurt Ellen's feelings. But Thomas and Ellen recognized each other. They were years apart in age, but they both belonged to the same world. Thomas had finished his breakfast. He got off his chair and rescued Piglet from the floor by the refrigerator and took him to show Ellen.

She took the pig and bounced him up and down on the table as though he were dancing.

> *Kitty Birdy had a pig*
> *She could do an Irish jig*

sang Ellen in her cracked old voice. Thomas smiled. He laid his hand on her knee, and her own gnarled hand came down to close on the fat fingers.

It was amazing how simple, how straightforward, things became as soon as you had reached a decision. Problems ironed themselves out, difficulties dissolved. Ellen bore Thomas and the washing away, thus relieving Victoria, in a single stroke, of two of her most pressing commitments. Roddy and Oliver, probably sleeping off the brandy they had consumed the evening before, had still not appeared. Victoria, in search of writing paper, went into Roddy's living room and found the curtains still undrawn and the atmosphere thick with stale cigar smoke. She drew the curtains and opened the windows and emptied the ashtrays into the remains of last night's fire.

In the letter rack on Roddy's littered desk, she found writing paper both plain and headed. She hesitated for a moment, debating which to use. If she used the plain paper, and wrote no address, then Mrs. Archer would still not know where to find them. But surely this smacked a little of secrecy, as though she and Oliver really had something to hide.

Besides, the headed paper, thickly embossed, had a certain opulence about it, which would in itself be reassuring. "BENCHOILE, CREAGAN, SUTHERLAND." She imagined Mrs. Archer being impressed by the very simplicity of this. So she took a sheet of the headed paper, and found an envelope lined with dark blue tissue. She found, in a tarnished silver mug, a ball-point pen. It was as though some person had arranged it all, ready for her, making it even easier.

Dear Mrs. Archer,

I am writing to let you know that Thomas is well and very happy. Ever since we left London, he has been very good, hardly cried at all, and has never woken up at nights. He is eating well, too.

She paused, chewing the pen, debating whether she should tell Mrs. Archer that not once had Thomas asked for his grandmother. She finally decided that this would not be tactful.

As you can see we are now in Scotland and the sun is shining, so maybe we will be able to take Thomas to the beach.

She paused again, and then went on to the final and most tricky bit of all.

Oliver does not know I am writing to you. We did discuss it, but he was very against the idea. So perhaps it would be better if you do not acknowledge this letter or try to get in touch. I will write later again and let you know how Thomas is.

With best wishes,

Yours sincerely,

Victoria . . . Victoria what? She was not Victoria Dobbs and she no longer felt like Victoria Bradshaw. In the end she wrote just her Christian name and left it at that. She put the letter into its envelope and put the envelope into her cardigan pocket. Downstairs, she crept into the bedroom and collected her handbag with her money in the wallet. Oliver hadn't moved. She let herself out again, and got into the Volvo, and drove herself to Creagan.

Roddy Dunbeath, wearing a large blue-and-white striped apron which made him look like a successful pork butcher, stood at the counter in his little kitchen, chopped vegetables for the lunchtime pot of soup, and tried, at the same time, to disregard the fact that he was suffering from a hangover. At twelve o'clock he was going to pour himself a sustaining, medicinal horse's neck, but it was only now a quarter to twelve, and so he was filling in the time—and so managing to resist jumping the gun—with a little soothing culinary activity. He liked cooking. Was, in fact, an excellent chef, and it made it all the more enjoyable having a little house party to cook for besides himself.

The house party in question, whether by private arrangement, or by chance, was happily living up to Benchoile traditions, and had taken itself off. By the time Roddy had prized himself out of bed this morning, the girl Victoria and the child had disappeared. Roddy was thankful for this. He had a horror of visitors hanging about and looking bored, and he needed peace and quiet in which to attend to his small domestic duties.

But he went through to the big house to make a few polite inquiries, and was told by Ellen that Victoria had taken the Volvo and gone to Creagan. The little boy was with Ellen, helping her to hang washing on the line, and playing with the basket full of pegs.

Oliver, when he finally put in an appearance, seemed unperturbed by all this independent activity on the part of his family. In fact, thought Roddy, if anything he appeared relieved to be shed of them for an hour or two. Together, he and Roddy had eaten an enormous breakfast, and together had hatched a plan to drive, that afternoon, up to Wick. There, a friend of Roddy's, tiring of the rat race in the south, and the endless commuting, had started a small printing business, specializing in limited editions of beautifully hand-bound books. Roddy, interested in anything that smacked of genuine craftsmanship, had been meaning for some time to go and see the presses working, and to be shown around the bindery, and Oliver, when the idea was put to him, was equally enthusiastic.

"What about Victoria?" Roddy asked.

"Oh, she'll probably want to do something with Thomas."

The telephone call to Wick was made, and the visit arranged. Whereupon Oliver, after a bit of restless prowling, admitted that he wanted to do some work, so Roddy lent him a scribbling pad and sent him off to the library in the big house, where, with a bit of luck, Oliver had spent the morning undisturbed.

In the meantime Roddy, left to himself, had lit a roaring fire, written a couple of letters, and was now making soup. The air was filled with the crisp, sharp smell of celery, sunlight streamed through the window, Vivaldi burbled from his transistor. The telephone started to ring.

Roddy swore, and went on cutting celery, as though the telephone would somehow answer itself. But of course it didn't, so he laid down the knife and wiped his hands on a tea towel and went through to the living room.

"Roddy Dunbeath."

"Roddy. It's John Dunbeath."

Roddy sat down. Luckily there was a chair behind him. He could not have been more astonished. "I thought you were in Bahrain."

"No, I got back yesterday morning. Roddy, I'm so dreadfully sorry about Jock. And that I couldn't make the funeral."

"My dear boy, we quite understood. Good of you to send the cable. Where are you calling from? London? You sound as though you're in the next room."

"No, I'm not in London. I'm in Inverness."

"Inverness?" Roddy's thought processes, blunted by last night's cognac, were not working in what you would call top gear. "How you do get around. When did you get to Inverness?"

"I caught the Highlander last night, I was here this morning. I've spent the morning with Robert McKenzie. He said it would be OK if I rang you . . . if I came to Benchoile."

"But of course. How *splendid*. Stay for a few days. Stay for the weekend. When can we expect you?"

"Well, this afternoon sometime. I'm hiring a car. Would it be all right if I came this afternoon?"

"Marvelous . . ." Roddy started to say, and then remembered the complications. He struck his forehead with the heel of his hand, a theatrical gesture of recall, totally wasted when there was no person to observe it. "Oh, damn, except that I won't be here. I've arranged to go up to Wick. I've got a chap staying and we're going to go there and look at a printing press. But that doesn't matter. We'll be back sometime, and Ellen'll be here."

"How is Ellen?"

"Indestructible. Puts us all in the shade. I'll tell her you're coming. I'll tell her to expect you."

"I hope I'm not putting you out."

Roddy remembered that he had always been an intensely well-mannered person. "Not putting us out at all." He added, because there seemed no point in not doing so, "Besides, it's your house now. You don't have to ask yourself to stay."

There was a tiny silence. Then, "Yes," said John and he sounded thoughtful. "Yes. That's one of the things I want to talk to you about. There's an awful lot to discuss."

"We'll have a good old chin-wag after dinner," Roddy promised him. "Anyway, see you later. I'm really looking forward to it. It's been too long, John."

"Yeah," said John, suddenly sounding very American. "I guess it's been too long."

Victoria returned ten minutes or so later, just as Roddy had finished the soup, tidied the kitchen, and poured himself the longed-for brandy and ginger ale. He was sitting by the window, watching a flock of black-and-white shelduck which had settled down to feed by the edge of the loch, when he heard the sound of the returning car. A moment or so later the downstairs front door opened and shut.

He called, "Victoria!"

"Hello."

"I'm up here. All on my own. Come and join me."

Obediently, she came running up the stairs, and saw him at the far end of the room, sitting in solitary state, with only Barney for company.

"Where is everybody?" she asked, coming over to join him.

"Oliver's in the big house, closeted in the library and working. And Thomas is still with Ellen."

"Perhaps I should go and get him."

"Don't be ridiculous. He's perfectly all right. Sit down. Have a drink."

"No, I don't want a drink." But she sat beside him, pulling off her scarf. He thought, all at once, how pretty she was. Yesterday, when he had first seen her, he had not thought her pretty at all. She had seemed to him both shy and colorless; dull, even. At dinner she had scarcely said a word, and Roddy had been hard put to understand what Oliver saw in her. But this morning, she was a different person. Shining eyes, pink cheeks, a mouth all smiles. Now, Roddy found himself wondering why Oliver didn't marry the girl. Perhaps it had something to do with her background. How old was she? Where had he met her? How long had they been together? She looked ridiculously youthful to be the mother of a two-year-old boy, but then young people these days seemed to plunge into relationships when they were scarcely out of school, committing themselves to domesticity in a manner that the young Roddy would have found intensely frustrating. She had, he noticed, beautiful teeth.

He said, "You're looking very bright eyed and bushy tailed. Something good must have happened in Creagan."

"It's just that it's such a beautiful morning. You can see for miles, and everything's all sparkly and bright. I didn't mean to be so long. I only went to buy some toothpaste and cigarettes and things, but Ellen said she didn't mind looking after Thomas, and Creagan is so pretty, I just stayed there and looked around, and I went into the church, and into that house they call The Deanery, but it's a craft shop now."

Her enthusiasm was endearing. "Did you buy anything?"

"No, but I might go back and buy something. They've got beautiful Shetland sweaters. And then I went and looked at the beach. I can't wait to take Thomas. You'd have thought it would be cold, but it wasn't. The sun was quite warm."

"I'm glad you had a good morning."

"Yes." She met his eyes, and some of the brightness went out of her face. "I somehow didn't get the chance to say anything last night, but . . . Well, Oliver told me about your brother, and I was so sorry. I just feel so awful about us all being here."

"You mustn't feel awful. You're good for me."

"It's just something else for you to worry about. I've been feeling guilty all morning because I should have been helping you or Ellen, instead of simply abandoning Thomas."

"Do you good to get away from Thomas for an hour or so."

"Well, as a matter of fact, it was rather nice." They smiled, in complete understanding. "Did you say that Oliver was working?"

"That's what he said."

Victoria made a little face. "I didn't realize that he wanted to work."

"Probably wants to get some idea down on paper before it goes out of his head." He remembered the projected trip to Wick that afternoon and told her about it. "We'll take you with us if you like, but Oliver thought you'd want to do something with Tom."

"I'd rather stay here."

"In that case, you can do something for me. There's a young man arriving some time during the afternoon. He's going to stay for a day or two. So if we're not back, perhaps you could look after him, pour the tea, generally make him feel welcome."

"Yes of course. But where's he going to sleep? We seem to have filled your house."

"He's going into the big house. I've already had a word with Ellen and she's alight with excitement; linen sheets on the bed, everything scoured and polished."

"I'd have thought she already had enough to do without more visitors arriving."

"Ah, but you see, this young man is Ellen's precious baby. In fact, he's my nephew John Dunbeath."

Victoria stared at Roddy in astonishment. "John Dunbeath. You mean your brother Charlie's boy? Ellen told me about him this morning at breakfast. But I thought he was in America."

"No, he's not. In fact, he's just telephoned me from Inverness."

"Ellen must be over the moon."

"She is. Not just because he's coming to stay, but because John is the new laird of Benchoile. My brother Jock has left Benchoile to John."

Victoria was confused. "But I thought you were the new laird."

"Heaven forbid."

She smiled. "But you'd be such a wonderful laird."

"You're very kind, but I'd be a useless one. I'm too old, too set in my evil ways. Better a new young broom to sweep us all clean. When I told Ellen the news a gleam came into her beady eye, but whether it was a tear or a glitter of triumph I wouldn't be able to say."

"Don't be horrid about her. I like her."

"I like her too, but one day she'll drive me into a nuthouse." He sighed and looked down at his empty glass. "Are you *sure* you wouldn't like a drink?"

"Quite sure."

"In that case, be a good girl and go and run Oliver and that little boy of yours to earth, and tell them lunch will be ready in about ten minutes." He heaved himself off the window seat and went to throw more logs onto his dying fire. As usual they sparked violently, and as usual Roddy tramped the glowing embers to death on his long-suffering hearthrug.

Victoria went to do as he had asked. At the top of the stairs, she paused.

"Where did you say I'd find Oliver?"

"In the library."

She left him, clattering down the open treads like an eager child. Alone, Roddy signed again. He debated, and finally succumbed. He poured himself another drink, and took it through to the kitchen where he inspected his fragrant soup.

Victoria put her head around the door. "Oliver."

He was not writing. He sat at the desk in the window, with his arms hanging loose and his legs out-stretched, but he was not actually writing.

"Oliver."

He turned his head. It took a second or two for him to recognize her. Then his blank eyes came to life. He smiled, as though she had just woken him up. He put up a hand to rub the back of his neck.

"Hi."

"It's lunchtime."

She closed the door behind her. He held out a long arm and she went over to him, and he drew her close, burying his face in her thick sweater; nuzzling, like a child, into its warmth. Memories of last night filled her with sweetness. She laid her chin on the top of his head, and looked down at the desk and sheets of paper, covered with scribbles and doodles and Oliver's narrow, tight writing.

She said again, "It's time for lunch."

"It can't be. I've only been here five minutes."

"Roddy says you've been here since breakfast."

"Where did you get to?"

"Creagan."

"What were you doing there?"

"Shopping." He put her away from him, and looked up into her face. Coolly, Victoria met his eyes, and repeated herself. "Shopping. I bought you cigarettes. I thought you'd soon be running out."

"Marvelous girl."

"And there's someone else coming to stay; arriving this afternoon."

"Who's that?"

"John Dunbeath. Roddy's nephew." She put on a spurious Highland accent. "The new young laird of Benchoile."

"Good God," said Oliver. "It's like living in a novel by Walter Scott."

She laughed. "Do you want some lunch?"

"Yes." He pushed the scribbling pad away from him, and stiffly stood up. He stretched and yawned. "But I want a drink first."

"Roddy's longing for someone to have a drink with him."

"Are you coming too?"

"I'll find Thomas first." They moved towards the door. "Ellen's had him all morning."

"Bully for Ellen," said Oliver.

John Dunbeath, driving the hired Ford, came through Eventon, and the road swung east. To his right lay the Cromarty Firth beneath the cloudless winter sky; blue as the Mediterranean and in all the extravagance of a flood tide. Beyond it, the peaceful hills of the Black Isle drew a skyline sharp as a razor in the clear, glittering light. Rich farmland swept down to the edge of the water, sheep grazed on the upper slopes, and scarlet tractors, minimized to toys by the distance, were out ploughing the rick dark earth.

The dazzling brightness of the day came as an unexpected bonus. John had left London cloaked in grey rain, and boarded the Highlander in a state of unrelieved exhaustion. Weary from forty-eight hours of ceaseless activity, suffering from jet lag, and still in a mild state of shock occasioned by Jock Dunbeath's unthought-of bequest, he had drunk two enormous whiskies, and fallen into a sleep so deep that the sleeping car attendant had had to come and shake him awake, and inform him that the train had actually arrived at Inverness Station five minutes before.

Now, on his way to Benchoile, and with nothing but necessarily unhappy news to impart to all who lived there, he could not get rid of the feeling that he was going on holiday.

Part of this was due to association of ideas. The further he got from London and the closer to Benchoile, the clearer and more vivid became the memories. He knew this road. The fact that he had not driven it for ten years did not seem to matter at all. He felt that it could have been yesterday, and the only thing amiss was the fact that his father was not beside him, cheerful with anticipation, and anxious for John not to miss a single familiar landmark.

The road forked. He left the Cromarty Firth behind him and climbed up and over Struie and down to the further magnificence of the Dornoch Firth. He saw the wooded slopes on the distant shore, and behind these the snow-capped ramparts of the hills of Sutherland. Far to the east lay the open sea, still and blue as a day in summer. He rolled down the window of the car and caught the smells, damp and evocative, of moss and peat, and the sharp tang of the sea wrack washed up on the shoreline far below him. The road sloped away, and the Ford idled its way down the smoothly cambered curves.

Forty minutes later, he was through Creagan. He began to slow down in anticipation of the turning to Benchoile. He came upon it and left the main road, and now all was familiar in quite a different way. For he was back on Benchoile land. Here was the path that he had taken one grey day with his father and Davey Guthrie, that led over the distant summit of the hill and down into the desolate glen of Loch Feosaig. There they had fished, and late in the evening, Jock had driven around by the road to collect them and bring them home.

Below him purled the river, and he passed the spot where he had once stood for two hours or more, fighting a salmon. The first line of grouse butts swung into view; the Guthries' farmhouse. The trodden garden was cheerfully bannered with washing, and the tethered sheepdogs raged at the passing car.

He rounded the final bend of the road. Before him lay the long sweep of Loch Muie, and at the end of it, slumbering, solitary in the late afternoon sunshine, the old grey house.

This was the worst of all, but his heart was hardened and his mind made up. *I shall sell it,* he had told Robert McKenzie this morning, because, from the moment he had read the lawyer's letter, he had known that there was nothing else that he could possibly do.

Whether she had been watching for the car or not, John had no idea, but Ellen Tarbat appeared almost instantly. He had only time to open the boot of the Ford and take out his suitcase before she was there, coming out of the front door, down the steps towards him. A little tottery about the legs, smaller than he remembered her, strands of white hair escaping from her bun, her red, knotted old hands flung wide in welcome.

"Well, well, and you are here. And what a delight to see you again after all these years."

He laid down his suitcase and went to embrace her. He had to bend almost double to receive her kiss and her frailness, her lack of substance, was unnerving. He felt that he should urge her indoors before she was caught up by a breath of wind and blown away. And yet she had pounced on his suitcase and had started to try to lug it indoors before he could stop her, and he had to forcibly wrest it from her grasp before she would let it go.

"What do you think you're doing? I'll carry that."

"Well, let's get in, away from the cold."

She led the way back up the steps and into the house, and he followed her and she closed the big doors carefully behind her. He walked into the big hall and was assailed by a smell made up of peat smoke and pipe smoke and floor polish and leather. Blindfolded, or drunk, or dying, he would have known by that smell that he was back at Benchoile.

"And did you have a good journey? What a surprise when Roddy told me this morning that you were coming. I thought you were away with all those Arabs."

"Where's Roddy?"

"He and Mr. Dobbs have gone to Wick. But he'll be back this evening."

"Is he all right?"

"He seems to be bearing up very well. It was a terrible thing your uncle dying, and such a shock to us all . . ." She had begun to lead the way upstairs, very slowly, one hand on the bannister. ". . . but I had a premonition. When he did not come in for his lunch, I was certain that something had happened. As, indeed, it had."

"Perhaps it was a good way for him to go."

"Yes, yes, you are right. Out on a walk, with his dogs. Enjoying himself. But it is a terrible thing for the folk who are left behind.'

She had reached the turn of the stair. She paused, to sigh, to draw fresh breath for the next flight. John shifted his suitcase from one hand to the other. They went on up.

"And now you have come to Benchoile. We wondered, Jess and I, what would happen with the colonel dying so suddenly, but it didn't seem very fitting to start enquiring. So when Roddy came to tell me this morning, you can imagine my delight. 'Why,' I said to him, 'that is the right person for Benchoile. Charlie's boy! There was never anybody like Charlie."

He did not want to continue this line of conversation. He changed the subject firmly. "And how about yourself, Ellen? How have you been keeping?"

"I am not getting any younger, but I manage to keep busy."

Knowing the size of the house, he wondered how she would manage to do anything else. They had now, at last, reached the landing. John wondered where he was sleeping. He had a ghastly suspicion that Ellen might have put him in his uncle's bedroom; it was just the sort of horror she would be capable of springing on him, and he was thankful when she led him towards the best spare bedroom where, before, his father had stayed. She opened the door to a flood of sunlight and a gust of cold, fresh air. "Oh," said Ellen, and went to close the windows, and John, following her into the room, saw the high, wide beds with their white starched cotton covers, the dressing table with the curly framed mirror, the velvet-covered chaise longue. Even the blast of fresh air could not dispel the smell of polish and carbolic. Ellen, it was obvious, had been busy.

"You won't find anything changed." Having closed the windows Ellen pottered about, straightening a starched linen mat, opening the immense wardrobe to check on coat hangers, and letting out a wave of camphor. John laid down his suitcase on the luggage rack at the foot of one of the beds, and went to the window. The sun was beginning to slip out of the sky and a rosy flush stained the hilltops. The mown grass of the lawn spread as far as a shrubbery, and beyond this to a copse of silver birch, and as he stood there, two figures appeared through these trees, making their way slowly towards the house., A girl, and a little boy. Behind them, looking more exhausted than they, an old black Labrador. "And the bathroom's just through that door. I've put clean towels out, and . . ."

"Ellen. Who's that?"

Ellen joined him at the window, peering with her old eyes.

"That is Mrs. Dobbs and her little boy Thomas. The family is staying with Roddy."

They had emerged from the trees and were now out in the open. The child, tagging behind his mother, suddenly spied the water, and began to make for the loch's edge. The girl hesitated, and then resignedly, followed him.

"I thought that you and she could have tea together in the library, and Thomas can have his tea with me." She went on, tempting him, "There's a batch of scones in the oven and heather honey on the tray." When John neither spoke, nor turned from the window, Ellen was a little putout. After all, she had opened the heather honey especially for him. "I've put towels on the rail, so that you can wash your hands," she reminded him, with some asperity.

"Yes. Sure." He sounded abstracted. Ellen left him. He heard her slow descent of the staircase. The girl and the child seemed to be having a small argument. Finally, she stooped and picked him up and started to carry him up towards the house.

John left the window and went out of the room and downstairs, and out of the front door. They saw him at once, and the girl, perhaps startled by his sudden appearance, stood still. He crossed the gravel and started down the slope of the lawn. He could not tell the exact moment of her recognition. He only knew that he had recognized her instantly, as soon as she appeared through the trees.

She wore jeans and a brilliant green sweater with suede patches on the shoulders. Her face, and the child's face, so close, observed his approach. The two pairs of wide blue eyes were ridiculously alike. There were freckles on her nose that had not been there before.

Mrs. Dobbs. With, doubtless, the child who had been making such a hullaballoo the night John drove her home. Mrs. Dobbs.

He said, "Hello, Victoria."

She said, "Hello."

Now, there were four of them around the dinner table, and the empty chair at its head was no longer empty.

Victoria wore a caftan of soft blue wool, the neck and the edges of the sleeves threaded with gold. She had, for the evening, put up her hair, but the arrangement seemed to John Dunbeath to have been ineptly contrived. It trailed one or two pale strands of hair, and served, instead of making her look sophisticated, only to enhance her air of extreme youth. The exposed back of her long neck seemed, all at once, as vulnerable as a child's. Her eyes were darkened, her beautiful mouth very pale. The shut-away, secret expression was still there. For some reason, this pleased John. It came with some satisfaction to realize that if he had not been able to break down the barrier, then neither had Oliver Dobbs.

"They're not married," Roddy had told him over a drink before dinner, when they were waiting for the Dobbses to appear. "Don't ask me why. She seems a charming little thing."

Charming, and reserved. Perhaps in bed, in love, those defenses came down. His eyes moved from Victoria to Oliver, and he was annoyed to discover that from these pretty images his instincts shied like a nervous horse. Firmly, he brought his attention back to what Roddy was saying.

". . . the great thing is to keep investing capital in the land. Not only money, but resources and time. The aim is to make one good blade of grass grow where nothing grew before; to keep up employment for the local people; to stop the endless drift of the country population to the big cities."

This was Roddy Dunbeath, revealing a totally unexpected side to his character. Victoria, helping herself to an orange from the bowl in the middle of the table, wondered how many people had heard him expound thus on a subject that was obviously close to his heart. For he spoke with the authority of a man who had lived in Scotland all his life, who recognized its problems, and was prepared to argue to the hilt against any easy solution that he believed to be inadequate or impractical. People seemed to lie at the root of it all. Everything came back to people. Without people there could be no sort of community. Without communities there could be no sort of future, no sort of life.

"How about forestry?" asked John Dunbeath.

"It depends how you go about it. James Dochart, who farms Glen Tolsta, planted a stretch of hill with woodland, maybe four hundred acres . . ."

She began to peel the orange. He had been at Benchoile for about five hours. She had had five hours in which to get over the shock of his sudden appearance, but she still felt bewildered. That the young American she had met in London, and John Dunbeath, nephew to Roddy and only son of Ellen's beloved Charlie, should be one and the same person, still seemed impossible, unacceptable.

He sat now, at the end of the softly candle-lit table, relaxed and attentive, his eyes on Roddy, his expression somber. He wore a dark suit and a very white shirt. His hand, on the table, slowly turned his glass of port. The candlelight gleamed on the heavy gold of his signet ring.

". . . but he did it in a way that meant those four hundred acres still support some cows and four hundred sheep, and his lambing has improved. But forestry, the way the state goes about it, is no answer to the hill-farmer's problem. A solid mass of stitka spruce, and you're left with a three percent return on capital and another shepherd out of a job."

Mrs. Dobbs. She wondered if Roddy had told him that she wasn't married to Oliver, or whether he had guessed this for himself. Either way, he seemed to take it for granted that Thomas was her child. She told herself that this was a good thing. She and Oliver had come beyond justifications and explanations. This was the way she wanted it to be. She had wanted to belong to somebody, to be needed, and now she belonged to Oliver and she was needed by Tom. She began to break the orange into segments. Juice dripped over her fingers, and onto the delicately trellised Meissen plate.

"How about the tourist industry?" John was asking. "Highlands and Islands."

"Tourism is very tempting, very nice, but it's also dangerous. There is nothing more dismal than a community depending on tourists. You can convert holiday cottages, you can build log-cabin chalets, you can even open your house to summer visitors, but given one bad summer and the wet and the cold frighten the ordinary family man away. All right, if he's a fisherman or a hill walker or a bird watcher, he probably won't object to a bit of rain. But a woman with three children, trapped in a small cottage for a long, wet fortnight, is going to insist on being taken to Torremolinos next summer. No, any population must have jobs for men, and it's their jobs that are being lost."

Oliver sighed. He had had two glasses of port and he was becoming sleepy. He listened to the conversation, not because it was of much interest to him, but because he found himself fascinated by John Dunbeath. The epitome, one would have thought, of the quiet, well-bred, Down-Easter, with his Brooks Brothers shirt, and elusive mid-Atlantic accent. As he talked, Oliver observed him covertly. What made him tick? What were the motivations behind that polite, reserved facade? And what—most intriguing of all—did he think about Victoria?

That they had already met in London, he knew. Victoria herself had told him this evening, while Oliver soaked in a bath, and she brushed her hair, and they talked through the open door.

"So extraordinary," she had said, in her lightest and most casual of voices. He knew that voice. It was Victoria's keep-out sign, and always aroused his avid curiosity. "He was the man who brought me home from the party that evening. Do you remember? When Tom was crying."

"You mean John Hackenbacker of Consolidated Aloominum? Well, I never did. How extraordinary." This was fascinating. He mulled it over, squeezing spongefuls of peat-brown water over his chest. "What did he say when he saw you again?"

"Nothing really. We had tea together."

"I thought he was flying off to Bahrain."

"He was. He's flown back again."

"What a little bird of passage he is. What does he do when he's not flying hither and yon?"

"I think he's in banking."

"Well, why isn't he in London, where he should be, cashing people's cheques?"

"Oliver, he's not that sort of a banker. And he's got a few days leave to try and sort out his uncle's estate."

"And how does he feel about being the new young laird of Benchoile?"

"I didn't ask him." She sounded cool. He knew he was annoying her, and went on with his teasing.

"Perhaps he fancies himself in a kilt. Americans always adore dressing themselves up."

"That's a stupid generalization."

There was now a definite edge to her voice. She was, Oliver realized, sticking up for the new arrival. He got out of the bath and wrapped a towel around himself and came through to the bedroom. Victoria's anxious blue eyes met his through her mirror.

"That's a very long word for you to use."

"Well, he's not that sort of an American at all."

"What sort of an American is he?"

"Oh, I don't know." She laid down her comb and picked up her mascara brush. "I don't know anything about him."

"I do." Oliver told her. "I went and talked to Ellen while she was bathing Tom. Get on the right side of her, and she's a mine of the most delicious morsels of gossip. It seems that John Dunbeath's father married a veritable heiress. And now he's been landed with Benchoile. To him who has shall be given. He's obviously been walking about with a silver spoon sticking out of his mouth since the day he was born." Still wrapped in the bath towel, he began to prowl around the bedroom, leaving wet footmarks on the carpet.

She said, "What are you looking for?"

"Cigarettes."

To he who has shall be given. Roddy had given Oliver a cigar. He leaned back in his chair, and through its smoke, through narrowed eyes, he watched John Dunbeath. He saw the dark eyes, the heavy, tanned features, the closely cut pelt of black hair. He looked, Oliver decided, like a tremendously wealthy young Arab, who had just climbed out of his djellabah and into a Western suit. The malice of the simile pleased him. He smiled. John looked up at that moment and saw Oliver smiling at him, but although there was no antagonism in his face, he did not smile back.

"What about the oil?"

"The oil, the oil." Roddy sounded like Henry Irving intoning "The bells, the bells!"

"Do you reckon it belongs to Scotland?"

"The nationalists think so."

"How about the private millions that British and American companies have invested before the oil could be discovered? If it hadn't been for that, the oil would still be under the North Sea, and nobody would know about it."

"They say this is what happened in the Middle East . . ."

Their voices faded to a soft murmur. Their words became indistinguishable. The other voices moved in, the real voices. Now the girl was there, sullen and pushy.

And where do you think you're going?

I'm going to London. I'm going to get a job.

What's wrong with Penistone? What's wrong with getting a job in Huddersfield?

Oh, Mum, not that sort of a job. I'm going to be a model.

A model. Tarting up and down some street with no knickers on, more like.

It's my life.

And where are you going to live?

I'll find somewhere. I've got friends.

You move in with that Ben Lowry, and I'm finished with you. I tell you straight, I'm finished . . .

". . . soon there won't be any real craftsmen left. And I mean real ones, not the weirdos who come from God knows where and set themselves up in windswept sheds to print silk scarves that no one in their right minds would ever buy. Or to weave tweed that looks like dishcloths. I'm talking about the traditional craftsmen. Kiltmakers and silversmiths, being seduced away by the big money to be earned in the rigs and the refineries. Now, take this man we went to see today. He's got a good business going. He started with two men, and now he's employing ten, and half of them are under twenty."

"What about his markets?"

"This is it. He'd already contacted his market outlets before he came north." Roddy turned to Oliver. "Who was that publisher he worked for before—when he was in London? He told us the name, but I can't remember it."

"Umm?" Oliver was dragged back into the conversation. "Sorry, I wasn't really paying attention. The publisher? Hackett and Hansom, wasn't it?"

"Yes, that's it, Hackett and Hansom. You see . . ."

But then Roddy stopped, suddenly aware that he had been holding forth for far too long. He turned to Victoria to apologize, but at this instant, to her obvious horror, she lost herself in an enormous yawn. Everybody laughed, and she was covered in confusion.

"I'm not really bored, I'm just sleepy."

"And no wonder. We're behaving abominably. I am sorry. We should have saved it for later."

"It's all right."

But the damage was done. Victoria's yawn had broken up and ended the discussion. The candles were burning down and the fire was nearly out, and Roddy looked at his watch and realized that it was half past ten. "Good heavens, is that the time?" He put on an impeccable Edinburgh accent. "How it flies, Mrs. Wishart, when you're enjoying yourself."

Victoria smiled. "It's the fresh air," she said, "that makes you sleepy. Not the lateness of the hour."

Oliver said, "We're not used to it." He leaned back in his chair and stretched.

"What are you going to do tomorrow?" Roddy asked. "What are we all going to do tomorrow? You can choose, Victoria. What would you like to do? It's going to be a good day, if we can rely on the weather forecast. How about the waterfall. Shall we take a picnic over to the waterfall? Or has anybody got a better suggestion?"

Nobody had. Pleased with his notion, Roddy enlarged on the plan. "We'll take the boat across if I can find the key to the boathouse. Thomas would like a boat trip, wouldn't he? And Ellen will pack us a nosebag. And when we get over there we'll light a fire to keep us warm."

This seemed to meet with everybody's approval, and on this note, the evening began to come to an end. Oliver finished his port, stubbed out his cigar, and stood up.

"Perhaps," he said, mildly, "I should take Victoria off to bed."

This suggestion was made to the company in general, but as he said it, he looked at John. John's face remained impassive. Victoria pushed back her chair, and he got to his feet and came around the table to hold it for her.

She said, "Good night, Roddy" and came to kiss him.

"Good night."

"Good night, John." She did not kiss John. Oliver went to open the door for her. As she went through it he turned back to the dusky room, and said with his most charming smile, "See you in the morning."

"See you," said John.

The door closed. Roddy threw more peat on the fire, stirred it to life. Then he and John drew chairs up to its warmth and resumed their discussion.

11
SATURDAY

*T*he weather forecasters had been only partially correct. The sun indeed was shining, but intermittent clouds blew across its face, driven by a western wind, and the very air had a liquidity about it, so that hills, water, sky, all looked as though they had been painted by a huge sodden brush.

The house and the garden were sheltered by the curve of the hills, and only the smallest of breezes had shaken the trees as they waited to embark themselves and an immense amount of equipment into the old fishing boat, but they had no sooner moved forty yards or so from the shore, when the true force of the wind made itself felt. The surface of the beer-brown water was flurried and driven with quite large waves, foam-crested and splashing over the gunwales. The occupants of the boat huddled into the various waterproof garments that had been gleaned from the Benchoile gunroom and handed around at the start of the voyage. Victoria wore an olive drab oilskin with enormous toggle-fastened poacher's pockets, and Thomas had been wrapped in a shooting jacket of immense antiquity, lavishly stained with the blood of some long-defunct bird or hare. This garment restricted him considerably, and Victoria was thankful for this, because it made the task of holding him still less difficult, his one idea apparently being to cast himself bodily overboard.

John Dunbeath, without any spoken agreement, had taken the oars. They were long and heavy, and the sound of creaking rowlocks, the faint piping of the wind, and the splash of breaking waves against the side of the boat were the only sounds. He wore a black oilskin that had once belonged to his uncle Jock, and a pair of green shooting boots, but his head was bare, and his face wet with spray. He rowed expertly, powerfully, the swing of his body driving the prow of the balky old boat through the water. Once or twice he shipped his oars in order to look over his shoulder and judge how far the wind and the run of the water were carrying them off course, and to get his bearings. He looked very much at home, at ease. But then he had done this thing, and come this way, many times before.

Amidships, on the center thwart, sat Roddy and Oliver. Roddy with his back to Victoria, and with his dog Barney secure between his knees; Oliver astride the thwart, leaning back with his elbows propped on the gunwale. Both men had their eyes on the approaching shore, Roddy scanning the hillside through his binoculars. From where she sat, Victoria could see only the outline of Oliver's forehead and chin. He had turned up the collar of his jacket, and his long legs, straddled in their faded jeans, ended in a pair of aged sneakers. The wind caught his hair and blew it back from his face, and the skin, fine-drawn over his cheekbones, was burned russet with the wind.

In the bottom of the boat, pools of water, inevitably, slopped. Every now and then, when he thought about it, Roddy would lower his binoculars on their leather strap and bail absent-mindedly, dipping the water up with an old tin bowl and emptying it overboard. It didn't seem to make much difference. Anyway, the picnic baskets, the box of kindling, the bundles of tarpaulins and rugs had all been stowed with care, out of reach of the puddles. There seemed to be enough food to feed an army, and various vacuum flasks and bottles had a special basket to themselves, with divisions, so that they did not bang together and break.

Roddy, having finished with a little bit of bailing, took up his binoculars again, and began to cover the hill.

"What are you looking for?" Oliver asked.

"Deer. It's amazing how hard they are to see on a hill face. Last week when we had the snow you could pick them out from the house, but there don't seem to be any about today."

"Where will they be?"

"Over the hill, probably."

"Do you get a lot here?"

"Sometimes as many as five hundred. Deer and does. In cold weather they come down and eat the fodder we put out for the cattle. In the summer they bring their young down, after dark, to graze in the pastures and drink from the loch. You can drive up the old cattle road from the foot of the loch. Keep the headlights of the car turned off, and you take them unawares. Then turn the lights onto them, and it's a beautiful sight."

"Do you shoot them?" Oliver asked.

"No. Our neighbor over the hill has the stalking rights. Jock let them to him. However, the deep freeze at Benchoile is full of haunches of venison. You should get Ellen busy on it before you take yourselves off again. It can be dry and tough, but Ellen's a way with venison. It's delicious." He lifted the leather strap over his head and handed the binoculars to Oliver. "Here, you have a look, see if you can spot anything with your young eyes."

Now, in the magical way that such things come about, the other shore, their destination, drew nearer and began to reveal its secrets. No longer was it a landscape blurred by distance, but a place of rocky outcrops, emerald green swards, white pebble beaches. Bracken, dense as fur, coated the lower slopes of the hill. Higher up, this gave way to heather and the occasional lonely Scots pine. The distant skyline was edged by the uneven outline of a drystone dike, the march wall between Benchoile land and the neighboring property. In places this dike had broken, leaving a gap like a missing tooth.

But there was still no sign of the waterfall. Holding Thomas in the circle of her arms, Victoria leaned forward, meaning to ask Roddy about this, but at that moment the boat swept past a great promontory of rock, and the little bay was revealed before them.

She saw the white shingle beach, and purling down the hillside, the burn, tumbling and twisting through heather and bracken, until, twenty feet or so above the beach, it leaped out over a ledge of granite and spouted down into the pool at its base. White as a mare's tail, dancing in the sunlight, fringed with rushes and moss and fern, it lived up to all Victoria's expectations.

Roddy turned to smile at her face of openmouthed delight.

"There you are," he told her. "Isn't that what you came all this way to see?"

Thomas, as excited as she was, lurched forward and escaped from her hold. Before she could catch him, he had stumbled, lost his balance, and fallen forward against his father's knee.

"Look!" It was one of his few words. He banged Oliver's leg with his fist. "Look!"

But Oliver was still engrossed with Roddy's binoculars, and either did not notice Thomas, or else paid no attention. Thomas said, "Look," again, but in the throes of trying to get his father to listen to him, he slipped and fell, bumping his head on the thwart and finishing up in the bottom of the boat, sitting in three inches of icy water.

He began, not unnaturally, to cry, and the first wail was out before Victoria, scrambling forward, could rescue him. As she picked him up, and lifted him back into her arms, she looked up and saw the expression on John Dunbeath's face. He was not looking at her, he was looking at Oliver. He was looking as though, quite happily, he could have punched Oliver in the nose.

The keel ground up onto the shingle. John shipped his oars and climbed overboard, and heaved the prow of the boat up onto the dry beach. One by one they alighted. Thomas was carried to safety by Roddy. Oliver took the forward painter and tied it up to a large, concrete-embedded spike, which was, perhaps, for this very purpose. Victoria handed out picnic baskets and the rugs to John, and finally, herself jumped ashore. The shingle of the beach crunched beneath the soles of her shoes. The sound of the waterfall filled her ears.

There seemed to be a strict protocol for Benchoile picnics. Roddy and Barney led the way up the beach, and the others followed, a straggling, laden procession. Between the waterfall pool and the tumbledown walls of the ruined croft was a sward of grass, and here they set up camp. There was a traditional fireplace, a ring of blackened stones and charred wood bearing witness to previous picnics, and it was very sheltered, although high above, the clouds still raced. The midday sun blinked in and out, but when it shone, it shed a real warmth, and the dark waters of the loch took on the blue of the sky and danced with sun pennies.

The group shed their bulky waterproofs. Thomas set off by himself to explore the beach. John Dunbeath took up a stick and began to scrape together the ashes in the fireplace. From the drink basket Roddy took two bottles of wine, and stood them at the edge of the pool, to cool. Oliver lit a cigarette. Roddy, his wine safely dealt with, stopped to watch a pair of birds, twittering and anxious, circling a rock ledge at the edge of the waterfall.

"What are they?" asked Victoria.

"Dippers. Water ouzels. It's early for them to be nesting." He began to climb the steep bank in order to investigate this. Oliver, with the binoculars still dangling around his neck, watched for a moment, and then followed him. John was already searching for kindling for the fire, gathering handfuls of dry grass and charred heather stalks. Victoria was about to offer her help, when she spied Thomas, heading for the loch and the pretty waves. She ran after him, jumping down onto the beach, and catching him up, just in time, into her arms.

"Thomas!" She held him close and laughed into his neck. "You can't go into the water."

She tickled him and he chuckled, and then arched his back protesting and frustrated. "Wet!" he shouted into her face.

"You're wet already. Come along, we'll find something else to do."

She turned and carried him back up the beach, to where the pool overflowed to a shallow stream that ran over the pebbles to the loch. Beside this she set Thomas, and stooping, picked up a handful of stones, and began to throw them, one by one, into the water. Thomas was diverted by the little splashes they made. After a little he squatted down on his haunches and began to throw pebbles for himself. Victoria left him and went back to the picnic place, and removed the plastic mug from the top of a vacuum flask. She took this back to Thomas.

"Look." She sat beside him and filled the mug with stones. When it was full, she poured them out into a heap. "Look, it's a castle." She gave him the mug. "You do it."

Carefully, one at a time, with starfish hands, Thomas filled the mug. The occupation absorbed him. His fingers, red with cold, were clumsy, his perseverance touching.

Watching him, filled with the tenderness that was by now becoming familiar, Victoria wondered about maternal instincts. Was one meant to have them, if one didn't have a child of one's own? Perhaps, if Thomas had not been such an engaging person, she would never have experienced this basic, unreasonable surge of protective affection. But there it was. Like a child in some sentimental old film, he seemed to have found his way into her heart, made himself snug and was there to stay.

The whole situation was odd to say the least of it. When he had first told Victoria about stealing Thomas from the Archers, Victoria, although shocked at Oliver, had also been moved. That Oliver Dobbs, of all people, should be so aware of his own parenthood as to take this extraordinary step was somehow a marvelous thing.

And to begin with, he had seemed both amused and involved; buying Thomas a toy, carrying him around on his shoulders, even playing with him in the evenings before Victoria put him to bed. But, like a child quickly bored by a new diversion, his interest seemed to have waned, and now he took little notice of Thomas.

The incident in the boat was typical of his attitude. Against all Victoria's better instincts, it was becoming impossible not to suspect that Oliver's impulsive removal of his son had not been prompted by fatherly pride and a real sense of responsibility, but that in his own oblique way he was simply getting back at his parents-in-law. The taking of Thomas from them sprang more from reasons of spite than reasons of love.

It really didn't bear thinking about. Not just because of the slur this cast upon Oliver's motivations and so upon his character, but because it rendered Thomas's future—and indirectly her own—miserably precarious.

Thomas banged her with his fist and said, "Look." Victoria looked, and saw the tumbled pile of pebbles and his beaming, grubby face, and she pulled him up onto her knee and hugged him.

She said, "I love you. Do you know that?" and he laughed as though she had made some tremendous joke. His laughter eased everything. It would all be all right. She loved Thomas and she loved Oliver, and Oliver loved Victoria, and obviously—in his own undemonstrative way—loved Thomas as well. With so much loving around the place, surely nothing could destroy the family that they had become.

Behind her, she heard the crunch of footsteps coming down the beach towards them. She turned and saw John Dunbeath. Beyond him, the fire now blazed, plumed with blue smoke. The other two men had disappeared. She searched for them, and saw their distant figures, more than halfway up towards the march wall, and still climbing.

John said, "I guess we won't get our lunch for another hour. They've gone up to search for the deer."

He reached her side, and stood a moment, looking out across the water, to the distant sunlit blur of the house, half hidden in the trees. From here it looked infinitely desirable, like a house in a dream. Smoke rose from a chimney, a white curtain blew, like a flag, from an open window.

Victoria said, "It doesn't matter. About lunch, I mean. If Thomas gets hungry we can always feed him something to stave off his pangs till the others get back."

He sat beside them, leaning back with his elbows in the shingle. "You're not hungry, are you?" he asked Thomas.

Thomas said nothing. After a bit, he clambered off Victoria's knee and went back to his game with the plastic cup.

Victoria said, "Don't you want to go and look for deer too?"

"Not today. Anyway I've seen them before. And that's quite a climb. I didn't realize Oliver would be so energetic and interested in wildlife."

There was no hint of criticism in his voice, but even so Victoria sprang to Oliver's defense. "He's interested in everything. New experiences, new sights, new people."

"I know it. Last night after you'd gone to bed, Roddy finally got round to telling me that he's another writer. It was funny, because when I was introduced to him, I thought 'Oliver Dobbs, I know that name,' but the associations eluded me. And then when Roddy told me, the penny dropped. I've read a couple of his books, and I saw one of his plays on television. He's a very clever man."

Victoria's heart warmed towards him. "Yes, he is clever. He's just had a new play put on in Bristol. It's called *Bent Penny*. The first night was on Monday, and his agent says he's got a hit on his hands. It's probably going to the West End, just as soon as they can find a theatre."

"That's great."

She went on extolling Oliver, as though praise of him could in some way obliterate the memory of the fleeting expression she had caught on John Dunbeath's face when Thomas fell in the boat. "He hasn't always been successful. I mean, it's a notoriously difficult business to get started in, but he never wanted to do anything else, and I don't think he ever got discouraged or lost faith in himself. His parents practically disowned him because he didn't want to go into the army, or be a lawyer, or do anything like that. So, at the beginning, he really didn't have any security at all."

"How long ago was that?"

"I suppose from the moment he left school."

"How long have you known him?"

Victoria leaned forward and picked up a handful of pebbles. So close to the water's edge they were wet and shining and cold to the touch. "About three years."

"Was he successful then?"

"No. He used to take dreadful, undemanding jobs, just to earn enough money to buy the groceries and pay the rent. You know, like barrowing bricks and mending roads and washing dishes in a fish-and-chips shop. And then a publisher began to take interest in him, and he got a play on television. And since then things have just snowballed, and he's never looked back. He and Roddy met through television. I expect Roddy told you. That's why we came to Benchoile. I read *The Eagle Years* when I was at school, and I've reread it at regular intervals ever since. When Oliver told me he knew Roddy and we were coming here to stay, I could hardly believe it was true."

"Has it lived up to its expectations?"

"Yes. Once you get used to it not being summer all the time."

John laughed. "It certainly isn't that." She thought he looked much younger when he laughed.

The sun had, for the last moment or so, been hidden behind a cloud, but now it came racing out again, and its brightness and warmth were so welcome, that Victoria lay back on the beach, and turned her face up to the sky.

She said, "The only thing that spoiled coming here was being told about your uncle dying. I felt we should have turned right round and gone away again, but Roddy wouldn't hear of it."

"It's probably the best thing in the world that could have happened. A bit of company for him."

"Ellen told me you used to come here when you were a little boy. I mean, when you weren't in Colorado."

"Yes. I used to come with my father."

"Did you love it?"

"Yes. But it was never home. Colorado and the ranch were my real home."

"What did you do when you used to come here? Did you slay deer and grouse and do manly things like that?"

"I used to fish. But I don't like shooting. I never have. It made life a little difficult."

"Why?" It was hard to imagine life for John Dunbeath ever being difficult.

"I suppose because I was the odd man out. Everybody else did it. Even my father. My uncle Jock didn't understand it at all." He grinned. "Sometimes I thought he didn't even like me very much."

"Oh, I'm sure he liked you. He wouldn't have left Benchoile to you if he hadn't liked you."

"He left it to me," John told her flatly, "because there wasn't anybody else."

"Did you guess he was going to leave it to you?"

"It never entered my head. That probably sounds crazy to you, but it's true. I got back from Bahrain and found this lawyer's letter waiting for me on my desk." He leaned forward to pick up a handful of pebbles and started to pitch them, with deadly accuracy, at a lichened rock which jutted from the edge of the loch. He said, "There was another letter as well, from Jock. I guess he wrote it just a couple of days before he died. It's a funny feeling getting a letter from a person who's already dead."

"Are . . . are you going to come and live here?"

"I couldn't, even if I wanted to."

"Because of your job?"

"Yes. That and other reasons. I'm based in London just now, but I may be sent back to New York at the drop of a hat. I have commitments. I have my family."

"Your family?" She was taken by surprise. But, on consideration, why should she be so surprised? She had met John in London, at a party, as a single man, but that did not mean that he had not left a wife and children behind him in the States. Businessmen all over the world were forced to lead such lives. There was nothing unusual about such a situation. She imagined his wife; pretty and chic as all young American women seemed to be, with a space-age kitchen and a station wagon in which to fetch the children from school.

He said, "By family, I mean my mother and father."

"Oh," Victoria laughed, feeling foolish. "I thought you meant you were married."

With immense care, he pitched the last stone. It hit the rock and fell into the water with a miniature splash. He turned to look at her. He said, "I was married. Not any more."

"I'm sorry." There didn't seem to be anything else to say.

"That's all right." He smiled reassuringly and she said, "I didn't know."

"Why should you know?"

"No reason. It's just that people have been talking about you, telling me about you. Roddy and Ellen, I mean. But nobody said anything about your being married."

"It only lasted a couple of years, and they never met her anyway." He leaned back on his elbows and looked out across the loch towards the hills and the old house. He said, "I wanted to bring her to Benchoile. Before we were married I used to tell her about it, and she seemed quite enthusiastic. She'd never been to Scotland and she had all sorts of romantic imaginings about it. You know, skirling pipes and swirling mists and Bonnie Prince Charlie draped in tartan. But after we married . . . I don't know. There never seemed to be time to do anything."

"Was . . . the divorce why you came to live in London?"

"One of the reasons. You know, a clean break, all the rest of it."

"Did you have children?"

"No. Just as well, the way things turned out."

She knew then that she had been wrong about John. Meeting him for the first time, he had impressed her as being self-contained, self-reliant, and totally cool. Now she realized that beneath that smooth veneer was a person just like anybody else; vulnerable, capable of being hurt, probably lonely. She remembered that he had been meant to have a girlfriend with him that evening, but for some reason she had let him down. And so he had asked Victoria to have dinner with him, and Victoria had refused. Thinking of this, she now felt, in some obscure way, as though she had let him down.

She said, "My parents got divorced. When I was eighteen. You'd have thought I'd have been old enough by then to cope with the situation. But it does something to your life. Nothing's ever quite the same again. Security is lost forever." She smiled. "Now, that's something that Benchoile has got and to spare. Security oozes out of the walls. I suppose it's something to do with the people who've lived in the house, and the way people live there now, as though nothing has changed in a hundred years."

"That's right. It certainly hasn't altered in my life time. It even smells the same."

She said, "What will happen to it now?"

He did not answer at once. And then he told her. "I shall sell it."

Victoria stared at him. His dark eyes, unblinking, met hers, and beneath their steady regard, she slowly realized that he meant what he said.

"But, John, you *can't*."

"What else can I do?"

"Keep it on."

"I'm not a farmer. I'm not a sportsman. I'm not even a true-blooded Scot. I'm an American banker. What could I do with a place like Benchoile?"

"Couldn't you run it . . . ?"

"From Wall Street?"

"Put a manager in."

"Who?"

She cast about for some person, and came up, inevitably, with, "Roddy?"

"If I'm a banker, then Roddy is a writer, a dilettante. He's never been anything else. Jock, on the other hand, was the strong pillar of the family and an exceptional man. He didn't just stride around Benchoile with a dog at his heels and a string of instructions. He worked. He went up the hill with Davey Guthrie and brought the sheep down. He helped with the lambing and the dipping. He went to the market in Lairg. As well, it was Jock who kept an eye on the forestry, took care of the garden, mowed the grass."

"Isn't there a gardener?"

"There's a pensioner who cycles up from Creagan three days a week, but keeping the kitchen garden in vegetables and the house in logs seems to take up most of his time."

But Victoria was still unconvinced. "Roddy seems to know so *much* about everything. Last night . . ."

"He knows a lot, because he's lived here all his life, but what he can actually *do* is another matter altogether. I'm afraid that without Jock, supporting him and giving him a shove every now and then, Roddy is in mortal danger of simply sinking into the ground."

"You could give him a chance."

John looked regretful, but he shook his head. "This is a big property. There's twelve thousand acres of hill to be farmed, fences to be kept up, a thousand or more sheep to be reared. There's cattle involved, and crops, and expensive machinery. All that adds up to a lot of money."

"You mean you don't want to risk losing money?"

He grinned. "No banker wants to risk that. But in fact, it isn't that. I could probably afford to lose a bit; but no property is worth holding onto, unless it's a viable proposition and capable, at least, of washing its own face."

Victoria turned away from him, sitting up with her arms wrapped around her knees, looking back across the water to the old house. She thought of the warmth of that house, of its hospitality, of the people who lived there. She did not think of it as a viable proposition.

She said, "What about Ellen?"

"Ellen is one of the problems. Ellen and the Guthries."

"Do they know you're going to sell Benchoile?"

"Not yet."

"Does Roddy?"

"I told him last night."

"What did he say?"

"He wasn't surprised. He said he hadn't expected me to do anything else. And then he poured himself the biggest cognac you've ever seen and changed the subject."

"And what to you suppose will happen to Roddy?"

"I don't know," said John, and for the first time he sounded miserable. She turned her head over her shoulder, and once more their eyes met. His own were bleak and somber, and she was moved to sympathy for him in his dilemma.

She said, impulsively, "He drinks too much. Roddy, I mean."

"I know it."

"I love him."

"I love him, too. I love them all. That's why it's so ghastly."

She felt impelled to try to cheer him. "Perhaps something will turn up."

"Who are you, Mr. Micawber? No, I'm going to sell it. Because I have to. Robert McKenzie, he's the lawyer in Inverness, he's fixing an advertisement for me. It'll go into all the big national newspapers around the middle of the week. Desirable Highland Sporting Property For Sale. So you see, I can't go back now. I can't change my mind."

"I wish I could make you."

"You can't, so don't let's talk about it anymore."

Thomas was getting bored with his game. He was also getting

hungry. He had dropped his plastic mug, and now he came to climb onto Victoria's knee. John looked at his watch. He said, "It's nearly one o'clock. I think you and I and Thomas should go and find something to eat . . ."

They got slowly to their feet. Victoria brushed shingle from the seat of her jeans. She said, "What about the others?" and turned to look up the hill, and saw Oliver and Roddy already on their way down, moving a great deal faster than they had on the way up.

"They're feeling hungry, too, and thirsty as well, no doubt," said John. "Come along . . ." he stooped and hoisted Thomas up into his arms, and led the way back to where his fire smoldered ". . . . let's see what Ellen's put in the picnic baskets."

Perhaps because of the picnic—which had been so successful—and the memories of former happy parties that this had evoked, the conversation that night at dinner did not concern the literary world of London, nor the problems of the future of Scotland, but became instead a feast of reminiscence.

Roddy, sated with fresh air, flushed by wine and good food, and relentlessly prompted by his nephew John, was in his element, carried along on an unstoppable flood of anecdotes that reached far back into the past.

Around the polished, candle-lit table, old retainers, eccentric relations, domineering dowagers, most of them long since defunct, came back to life. There was the story of the Christmas house party when the tree caught fire; the grouse-shoot at which a universally disliked young cousin peppered the guest of honor with shot and was sent home in disgrace; the long-forgotten winter when the blizzards cut the house off for a month or more, and its occupants were reduced to boiling snow to make the porridge and playing endless charades to keep themselves amused.

There were the sagas of the overturned boat; the sheriff's Bentley, which, inadvertently left with its hand brake off, had finished up in the bottom of the loch; and the gentle-woman of reduced circumstances, who had come to stay for a weekend, and remained firmly installed in the best guest room two years later.

It took a long time to run out of stories, and even when he did, Roddy remained inexhaustible. Just as Victoria was about to suggest that perhaps it was time to retire to bed (it was now past midnight) he pushed back his chair, and led them all purposefully away from the table and across the hall to the deserted, dust-sheeted drawing room. There stood the grand piano, draped in an old sheet. Roddy turned this back, pulled up a stool to the keyboard, and started to play.

The room was piercingly cold. The curtains had long since been taken down, and the windows shuttered, and the old melodies echoed like cymbals against the empty walls. High above, descendant from the center of the lavishly decorated ceiling, a crystal chandelier of immense proportions sparkled like a cluster of icicles, and scattered facets of colored light that were reflected in the bars of the brass fender that stood before the white marble fireplace.

Roddy sang songs from before the war. Noel Coward at his most sentimental, and Cole Porter.

> *I get no kick from champagne,*
> *Mere alcohol doesn't thrill me at all,*
> *So tell me, why should it be true . . .*

The rest of the party grouped themselves about him. Oliver, his dramatic senses stirred by the turn that the evening had so unexpectedly taken, leaned against the piano and smoked a cigar, watching Roddy as though he could not bear to miss a single nuance of the other man's expression.

John had crossed to the fireplace, and stood before it, with his hands in his pockets and his shoulders propped against the mantel-piece. Victoria had found a chair in the middle of the room, draped in faded blue gingham, and had perched herself on one of its arms. From where she sat, Roddy had his back to her, but above him, flanking a centrally hung mirror, were two tall portraits, which she knew, without being told, were of Jock Dunbeath and his wife Lucy.

With her ears full of the nostalgic tinkling music, she looked from one to the other. Jock had been painted in the full dress kilt of his regiment, but Lucy wore a tartan skirt and a bracken-brown sweater. She had brown eyes and laughter on her mouth, and Victoria wondered if it was she who had decorated this room, and chosen the pale carpet with its swags of roses, or whether she had inherited it from her mother-in-law, and liked it just the way it was. And then she found herself wondering if Jock and Lucy knew that Benchoile was going to be sold. Whether they were sad about it, or angry, or understood John's dilemma. Looking at Lucy, Victoria decided that she probably understood. But Jock . . . Jock's face above the high collar, the golden epaulettes, was carved into an expression of suitable blankness. The eyes were deep-set and very pale. They would reveal nothing.

She realized that she was slowly freezing. She had put on, that evening, for some reason, a most unsuitable dress, sleeveless and far too light for a winter evening in Scotland. It was the sort of dress meant to be worn with suntanned arms and bare sandals, and in it she knew that she looked thin and colorless and cold.

> *You're the cream in my coffee,*
> *You're the milk in my tea . . .*

Victoria shivered, and rubbed her arms with her hands, trying to warm herself. From across the room, John Dunbeath's voice came quietly, "Are you cold?" and she realized that he had been watching her, and this made her self-conscious. She put her hands back in her lap and nodded, but made a secret face to let him know that she did not want to disturb Roddy.

He took his hands out of his pockets and left the fireplace and came over to her side, on the way gathering up a dustsheet, revealing the French rosewood chair that it had been protecting. He folded the dustsheet like a shawl, and bundled it around her shoulders, so that she was swathed in folds of soft, old cotton, very comforting to the touch.

He did not go back to the fireplace, but settled himself on the other arm of her chair, with his arm lying along its back. His nearness was somehow as comforting as the dustsheet that he had wrapped around her, and after a little she did not feel cold anymore.

Roddy stopped at last for breath, and to refresh himself from the glass that stood on top of the piano. "I think that's probably enough," he told them all. But John said, "You can't stop yet. You haven't played 'Will Ye Go, Lassie, Go.'"

Over his shoulder Roddy frowned at his nephew. "When did you ever hear me play that old song?"

"I suppose when I was about five years old. But my father used to sing it, too."

Roddy smiled, "What a sentimental guy you are, to be sure,"

he told him, but he turned back to the piano, and the old Scottish tune, in the three-four time of a slow waltz, filled the empty, haunted room.

> *O the summer time is coming*
> *And the trees are sweetly blooming*
> *And the wild mountain thyme*
> *Grows around the blooming heather.*
> *Will ye go, lassie, go?*
>
> *I will build my love a tower*
> *Near yon pure crystal fountain*
> *And on it I will pile*
> *All the flowers of the mountain,*
> *Will ye go, lassie, go?*
>
> *If my true love, she were gone,*
> *I would surely find another*
> *Where wild mountain thyme*
> *Grows around the blooming heather*
> *Will ye go, lassie, go?*

12
SUNDAY

*I*t was ten o'clock on the morning of the Sabbath. Once more the wind had come round to the northeast, swirling in from the sea, clean and bitterly cold. The sky, overcast with high, sailing clouds, glimpsed through, blue as a robin's egg, only occasionally, and it was hard to believe that only yesterday they had been picnicking at the waterfall, sitting in the sunshine with pleasant anticipatory thoughts of the approaching spring.

John Dunbeath sat by the fire in the Guthrie's kitchen and drank a cup of tea. The kitchen was snug as a nest. A fire burned redly in the stove, and thick walls and tightly closed windows defied the blustering wind. The air was filled with the smell of burning peat, overlaid by the fragrance of simmering broth, and the table in the center of the room was already laid for the Guthrie's midday dinner.

Jess was going to church. At the sideboard, she took up her hat, and, sagging slightly at the knees, in order to see her reflection in the mirror, put it on. Watching her, and then looking back at Davey, John decided that of all the Benchoile people, the Guthries had changed the least. Jess was still slim, still pretty, with only a trace of grey in her springy fair hair, and Davey looked, if anything, even younger than John remembered him, with his bright blue eyes and tufty, sandy eyebrows.

"Now," Jess picked up her gloves and pulled them on. "I must get away. You'll have to excuse me, but I promised I'd pick up Ellen Tarbat and give her a lift to the kirk." She glanced at the portentous clock in the middle of the mantelpiece. "And if you two are going to be up the hill and home again in time for your dinner, you'd better not be sitting here all day, drinking your tea."

She departed. A moment later there came a great crashing of gears and the revving of a hard-worked engine, and Davey's small grey van bounced down the bumpy path in front of the house and disappeared in the direction of Benchoile.

"She's a terrible driver," Davey observed mildly. He finished his mug of tea, set it down on the table and stood up. "But she's right. We should go." He went through to the little lobby and took down his waterproof jacket from the peg by the door, collected his deer-stalker, his crook, his spyglass. The two golden Labradors, who had been lying, apparently asleep, by the fireside, now sprang into feverish action, scenting walks. They barged to and fro, nuzzling Davey's knees, tails going like pistons. They were, Jess had told John, Jock Dunbeath's dogs.

"Poor creatures, they were with him when he died. And afterwards they wandered about Benchoile like a pair of lost spirits. There was some talk of putting the old one down. She's nearly nine years old now. But we couldn't abide the idea. The colonel had been so fond of her, and she's a great lass to the gun. So they both came to live with us. Mind, we've never had a dog in the house. Davey would never have a dog in the house. But these two had never been in a kennel in their lives, and so he had to relent. They could have stayed at Benchoile, I suppose, but Mr. Roddy has his own dog, and Ellen has enough to do without caring for a couple of great babies like these two."

Now Davey opened the farmhouse door, and the two Labradors escaped into the windswept, scrubby garden, racing like puppies around the blowing grass beneath the washing line. At their appearance, Davey's sheepdogs, shut up in their pen, began dementedly to bark, racing to and fro in the netted run. "Shut your mouths, you silly bitches," Davey told them good-naturedly; but they went on barking, and could still be heard long after the two men and the two dogs had gone through the gate in the wall at the back of the house, and started the long walk up through the heather.

It took them over an hour to reach the march fence that separated the northern boundary of Benchoile from the desolate Glen Feosaig which lay beyond. A long, steady climb, taken at Davey Guthrie's unhurried pace, pausing only to point out some landmark, to scan the hill for deer, to watch the soaring, hovering flight of a kestrel. The dogs were kept well to heel, but even so, every now and then a pair of grouse would explode from the heather at their feet, and go wheeling away, their flight lying close to the slope of the hill; "go-back, go-back," they called.

It was immense country. Slowly, Benchoile sank below them, the loch a long ribbon of pewter grey, the house and trees concealed by the swelling contours of the land. To the north the summits were still snow-clad, and snow lay in deep corries as yet untouched by the low winter sun. As they climbed, Creagan itself came into view, reduced by distance to a cluster of grey houses, a strip of green that was the golf course, the tiny spire of the church. Beyond was the sea, the horizon blanketed in cloud.

"Yes, yes," observed Davey, "it is a dreich sort of a day."

At the crest of the hill there was not even heather underfoot; only pits of peat starred with strange mosses and lichens. The ground was boggy. Black water oozed up around their feet as they trod upwards, and the hoofprints and droppings of deer were everywhere. When they came at last to the straggling dike, the wind pounced on them from the north. It filled ears, nostrils, lungs; whistled through storm-proof clothing and brought tears to John's eyes. He leaned against the wall and looked down into Feosaig. The loch at its foot lay black and deep, and there was no evidence of human habitation. Only the sheep and the kestrels, and showing white against the distant hill, a pair of gulls, working their way inland.

"Are those our sheep?" John asked, raising his voice against the wind.

"Yes, yes," Davey nodded, and then turned and sat himself down, out of the wind, with his back to the wall. After a little John joined him. "But that's not Benchoile land."

"And this is not Feosaig land, either, but we have many Feosaig sheep grazing with ours."

"What happens, do you have a roundup?"

"We start to gather them in, around the end of this month. We bring them down to the sheep folds in the fields by the farmhouse."

"When do the ewes start lambing?"

"About the sixteenth of April."

"Will it still be as cold as this?"

"It may well be colder. Some big storms can blow in April, and they can leave the hills as white as midwinter."

"That can't make your job any easier."

"Indeed, it does not. I have seen myself digging ewes, heavy with lamb, out of the ditches and drifts. Sometimes a mother will desert her lamb, and then there's nothing for it but to take it back to the farmhouse and hand rear it with a bottle. Jess is a great one with the sickly lambs."

"Yes, I'm sure she is, but that doesn't solve the problem of how you're going to cope with all this on your own. Roddy's told me how much my uncle did at the lambing. You're going to need another man, probably two, to help you during the next six weeks."

"Yes, that is indeed a problem," Davey agreed, not looking in the least perturbed. He felt in his pocket and came out with a paper bag. From this he extracted two large bread-and-butter sandwiches. He gave one to John and began to eat the other himself, munching at each mouthful like a ruminating cow. "But I have spoken to Archie Tulloch and he says that this year he will give me a hand."

"Who's he?"

"Archie is a crofter. He farms a few acres down the road to Creagan. But he is an old man—seventy years or more—and he won't be able to carry on with the crofting much longer. He has no son. A month or so before your uncle died, he spoke to me about Archie's croft. He had the idea that he would buy the place from Archie, and take it in with Benchoile. We can always use more land for the arable, and he has a fine cattle pasture down by the river."

"Would Archie be agreeable?"

"Yes, yes. He has a sister in Creagan. He has talked for some time of going to live with her."

"So we'd have more land and another house."

"Your uncle thought we would maybe take on another man, and put him to live in the croft. Your uncle was a fine man, but after that first heart attack he had begun to realize that, like the rest of us, he was not immortal."

He took another mouthful of bread and munched some more. A movement on the side of the hill caught the attention of his blue eyes. He laid down his half-eaten sandwich, drove his crook into the ground, and took out his spyglass. Using his crook and the thumb of his left hand as a steadier, he put the glass to his eye. There was a long silence, broken only by the buffet of the wind.

"A hare," said Davey. "Just a wee hare." He put the spyglass back in his pocket, and reached for the crust of the sandwich. But the old Labrador had already wolfed it. "You are indeed a greedy bitch," he told her.

John leaned back against the wall. Awkward stones dug into his back. His body was warm from the hard exercise, and his face cold. Ahead of them a gap had appeared between the racing clouds. A gleam of sunshine broke across the gloom, and lay like a shaft of gold across the dark waters of Loch Muie. The bracken on the hill turned russet. It was very beautiful, and he realized in that instant, with some shock, that the land, for almost as far as he could see, belonged to him. This was Benchoile. And this . . . he took up a handful of black peaty soil, crumbling it between his fingers.

He was assailed by a sensation of timelessness. This was the way things had stayed for decades; tomorrow they would be no different, nor the weeks, nor the months that lay in the future. Action, of any kind, had all at once become distasteful, and this took him unawares, because apathy was a mood he had never suffered from. He had made his reputation, achieved a considerable personal success in his job, simply by means of swift and shrewd decision, immediate action, and a confidence in his own convictions that left no room for moral shilly-shallying.

He had arranged this morning's expedition with the sole intention of getting Davey on his own, and letting fall the information, as tactfully as possible, that by the middle of next week Benchoile would officially be up for sale. And yet now he found himself discussing its future policies with Davey, as though he had every intention of digging himself in for the rest of his life.

He was procrastinating. But did that matter so much? Was today, this morning, this moment, the right time to bring to an end everything that Davey Guthrie had worked for? Perhaps, he told himself, knowing that he was ducking the issue, it would be better to hold a sort of board meeting in the dining room at Benchoile, thus protecting himself from the human element of the problem by erecting a shield of business-like formality. He would get Ellen Tarbat around the table, and Jess as well, and Roddy, to lend a little moral support. Better still, he would ask Robert McKenzie, the lawyer, to come from

Inverness and take the chair at this meeting. Then he could be given the job of breaking the bad news to them all at one fell swoop.

The sun went in. It was cold and dark again, but the silence between the two men remained companionable and totally unstrained. It occurred to John that the true Highlander like Davey Guthrie had much in common with the ranch hands who worked for his father in Colorado. Proud, independent, knowing that they were as good as any man—and probably better—they found no need to assert themselves, and so were the most straightforward of beings to deal with.

He knew that he must be straightforward with Davey. He said, breaking the silence, "How long have you been at Benchoile, Davey?"

"Nearly twenty years."

"How old are you?"

"Forty-four."

"You don't look it."

"It's the clean living that keeps a man healthy," Davey told him, without a smile. "And the good air. Do you not find working in London and New York and such big cities that the air is very oppressive? Even if Jess and I have a day's shopping in Inverness, I cannot wait to get home and breathe the clean air of Benchoile."

"I suppose if you have a job in a place, you don't think too much about what you're breathing." He added, "Anyway, if I get to feel too stifled, I usually head back to Colorado. There, the air is so rarified that the first gasp is as intoxicating as a jigger of Scotch."

"Yes, yes, that ranch must be a fine place. And a great size, too."

"In fact, not as big as Benchoile. About six thousand acres, but of course we carry more stock. Six hundred acres of that is irrigated hay meadow, the rest is known as open range grazing."

"And what breed of cattle do you rear?"

"No particular breed. They vary from fine Hereford and Black Angus, all the way down to what's known in the West as Running Gear. If the snows have been heavy, and the high meadows are well irrigated and we don't have a killing frost in the late spring, we can graze a thousand head."

Davey ruminated on this, chewing on a blade of grass, and gazing peacefully ahead of him. After a little, he said, "There was a farmer from Rosshire, and he went to the bull-sales in Perth, and there he met one of those big cattlemen from Texas. And they got talking. And the Texan asked the farmer how much land he owned. And the farmer told him, 'two thousand acres.' "

At this point John realized that Davey was not continuing their dissertation on farming, but telling a joke. Anxious not to miss the punch line, or worse, to laugh at the wrong moment, he listened with sharpened attention.

"And then the farmer asked the Texan how much land he owned. And the Texan said to the farmer, 'You would not understand. You could not comprehend, if I told you how much of Texas I own. But I'll tell you this. If I got into my car and drove all day around my boundary fence, I still should not have circled my property.' And the farmer thought a little while, and then he said to the Texan, 'I had a car like that, once upon a time. I got rid of it.' "

There came a long pause. Davey continued to gaze ahead. John stayed straight-faced as long as he could, and then the grin, upstoppable, crept up his face. Davey turned his head and looked at him. His blue eyes held a certain gleam, but otherwise he was as dour as ever.

"Yes, yes," he said, in his gentle Sutherland voice. "I thought that you would enchoy that. It is a very good choke."

Ellen Tarbat, dressed in her good Sunday black, pulled her hat down over her ears and pierced it to her bun with a formidable hat pin. It was a decent hat, only two years old, and trimmed with a buckle. There was nothing like a buckle for lending a bit of dignity to a hat.

She looked at the kitchen clock. It was a quarter past ten, and Ellen was going to church. She was giving them a cold lunch today instead of the usual roast. She had peeled the potatoes, and made a jam tart, and the dining room table was ready and laid. Now, she was ready for Jess to pick her up. Davey was not coming to church with them, because he and John Dunbeath had gone up the hill to look at the sheep. Ellen did not approve of such goings-on on the Sabbath and had said as much to John, but he had pointed out that he had not all the time in the world, and would soon have to go back to London. Ellen could not imagine why he should want to get back to London. She herself had never been to London, but her niece Anne had taken a trip a couple of years ago, and what she had told Ellen about it had left Ellen in no great hurry to follow her example.

Her hat settled, she picked up her coat. She had brought all her things downstairs earlier in the morning so as to save a trip up all those flights of stairs to her attic bedroom. Climbing stairs was one of the things that tired her. She hated being tired. She hated the way her heart thumped when she was tired. Sometimes she hated being old.

She put on her coat and buttoned it up, and adjusted the lapel where she had pinned her best Cairngorm brooch. She took up her bulging handbag, her black gloves. From the front of the house, the telephone rang.

She stood still, waiting, trying to remember who was in the house and who out of it. Mrs. Dobbs had taken the little boy out for a walk. John was with Davey. The telephone continued to ring, and Ellen sighed and laid down her bag and gloves and went to answer it. Out of the kitchen, across the hall, into the library. The telephone stood on the colonel's desk. Ellen picked up the receiver.

"Yes?"

There came a series of clickings and buzzings, distasteful to her ear. The telephone was another thing she hated. "Yes?" she said again, beginning to sound testy.

A final click, and a man's voice. "Is that Benchoile?"

"This is Benchoile."

"I want to speak to Oliver Dobbs."

"He's not here," said Ellen, instantly. Jess Guthrie would be at the door at any moment, and she did not want to keep her waiting.

But the caller was not so easily put off.

"Is there no way you can get hold of him? It's very important indeed."

The word *important* caught her attention.

It was splendid when important people came to stay and important things happened. It gave a body something to talk about that wasn't simply the price of lambs or the weather.

"He . . . he'll maybe be over at the Stable House."

"Could you go and get him?"

"It may take a moment or two."

"I'll hold on."

"The telephone is very expensive," Ellen reminded him sharply. Important or not, it was a sinful thing to waste good money.

"What?" He sounded taken aback, as indeed he might. "Oh. Well, never mind about that. I'd be grateful if you could get him. Tell him it's his agent."

Ellen sighed, and resigned herself to missing out on the first hymn. "Very well."

She laid down the receiver, and made the long journey down through the back of the house to the stableyard. When she opened the back door the wind swirled and gusted and nearly pulled the doorknob out of her grasp. Bent against this, holding on her good hat, she crossed the cobbles and opened Roddy's front door.

"Roddy!" Her voice, raised, cracked a little.

There was a pause, and then footsteps crossed the floor above her, and Mr. Dobbs himself appeared at the head of the stairs, as tall, thought Ellen, as a lamppost.

"He's not here, Ellen. He's gone to Creagan to get the Sunday papers."

"There's a telephone call for you, Mr. Dobbs. The man says he is your agent, and it is very important."

His face lit up. "Oh. Right." And he came helter-skelter down the stairs, so fast that Ellen was obliged to step sideways to avoid being knocked flat. "Thanks, Ellen," he said, as he shot past her.

"He's waiting at the other end of the telephone . . ." she raised her voice to his retreating back ". . . and the Lord himself knows what it's costing him."

But Mr. Dobbs was already out of earshot of her grumblings. Ellen made a face. Some people. She pulled her hat down, and followed him at her own pace. In the kitchen, she saw, through the window, the Guthrie's van, waiting for her, with Jess Guthrie at the wheel. She was flustered and halfway through the door before she realized that she had forgotten her gloves.

Oliver's telephone call from London lasted for more than half an hour, and by the time he got back to the Stable House, Roddy had returned from Creagan with all the Sunday papers, was ensconced in his deepest leather armchair in front of a furnace of a fire, and was already looking forward to the first gin-and-tonic of the day.

He laid down the *Observer,* and looked up over his spectacles as Oliver came bounding up the stairs two at a time.

"Hello," he said. "I thought I'd been deserted."

"I had a phone call." Oliver came to sit in the chair opposite to Roddy, with his hands hanging loose between his bony knees.

Roddy sent him a keen look. He sensed the suppressed, secret excitement. "Good news, I hope."

"Yes. Good. It was my agent. It's all fixed. The new play's moving to London when it's finished the run at Bristol. Same cast, same producer, everything."

"Fantastic." Roddy dropped the paper to the floor, reached up a hand to pull off his spectacles. "My dear boy, that really is the most splendid news."

"There are other goodies in the pipeline as well, but those can wait till later. I mean, they're not actually signed and sealed yet."

"I couldn't be more pleased." Roddy glanced at his watch. "The sun's not over the yardarm yet, but I think this calls—"

But Oliver interrupted him. "There's just one thing. Would you mind if I left Victoria and Thomas with you for a couple of days? I have to go to London. I have to go tomorrow. Just for one night. There's a plane from Inverness about five o'clock in the evening. I wondered, too, if someone would be able to drive me over to catch it."

"But of course. You can leave them here as long as you like. And I'll take you over in the MG."

"It's only for two days. I'll be coming back the next day. And after that I'll pack the others up and we'll make our way back south in the car."

The very idea of them all leaving made Roddy feel miserable. He dreaded being on his own again, not simply because he loved to have young company about the place, but because with Oliver and Victoria and little Thomas gone, he knew that there would no longer be an excuse not to face up to facts. And the facts were cold. Jock was dead. John was going to sell Benchoile. Ties and traditions would be broken forever. It was the end of a way of life. This was the last house party.

He said, with the vague notion of putting off the evil moment, "You don't have to go. You know you don't have to go."

"You know that we have to. As it is, you've been more than kind and marvelously hospitable, but we can't stay forever. Anyway, fish and guests stink after three days, and we've been here three already, so tomorrow we're going to start stinking."

"I'll miss you. We all will. Ellen has lost her heart to Thomas. It won't seem the same without you all around."

"You'll still have John."

"John won't stay longer than he has to. He can't. He's got to get back to London."

"Victoria tells me that he's going to sell Benchoile."

Roddy was surprised. "I didn't realize he'd discussed it with Victoria."

"She told me last night."

"Yes. He's going to sell up. He really has no alternative. To be truthful, it's what I expected."

"What will happen to you?"

"It depends who buys the place. If it's a rich American with sporting instincts, perhaps I could get a job as ghillie. I rather see myself touching my cap and collecting massive tips."

"You should get married," said Oliver.

Roddy sent him another sharp look. "You're a fine one to be talking."

Oliver grinned. "I'm different," he said smugly. "I'm a different generation. I'm allowed to have a different set of morals and values."

"You certainly have those."

"Don't you approve?"

"It would make no difference whether I approved or not. I'm too idle a man to take up attitudes about matters which really don't concern me. Perhaps I was too idle to get married, because getting married was expected of me. I never really did anything that was expected of me. Not getting married was just part of the pattern. Like writing books and watching birds and drinking too much. My brother Jock despaired of me."

"I think it's a good way to be," said Oliver. "I suppose I've followed pretty much the same pattern myself."

"Yes," said Roddy, "but in my case I had a golden rule. I never got involved with anybody, because I knew that once I did I was in danger of hurting them."

Oliver looked at him, surprised. "You're talking about Victoria, aren't you?"

"She is very vulnerable."

"She is also intelligent."

"The heart and the head are two separate entities."

"Reason and emotion?"

"If you like."

Oliver said, "I can't be tied."

"You already are," Roddy pointed out. "You have the child."

Oliver reached for his cigarettes. He took one and lit it with a spill kindled from the fire. When it was alight, he tossed the spill onto the flames. He said, "In that case, isn't it a little late to start talking to me like a father?"

"It's never too late to rectify matters."

Across the hearthrug their eyes clashed, and Roddy recognized the coldness in Oliver's pale gaze. When he spoke, it was to change the subject. "Do you know where Victoria is?"

It was a sort of dismissal. Roddy sighed. "I think she took Thomas for a walk."

Oliver stood up. "In that case, I'd better go and find her. Tell her what's happening."

He went, running down the wooden staircase, and slamming the front door shut behind him. His footsteps rang across the cobbles of the stableyard. Roddy was left no wiser as to Oliver's intentions, suspecting that he had done more harm than good, and wishing that he had kept his mouth shut. After a little, he sighed again, hauled himself out of his chair and went to pour himself that longed-for gin-and-tonic.

Victoria, making her way back through the birch wood, saw Oliver emerge from beneath the stableyard archway, and walk out onto the gravel in front of the house. He was smoking a cigarette. She was about to call out to him, when he caught sight of her and Thomas, and came across the grass to meet them.

Thomas, whose legs had given out on him halfway home, was riding pickaback on Victoria's shoulders. When she saw Oliver coming towards them, Victoria bent down and let Thomas slip to the ground. He ran ahead of her and reached Oliver before she did, butting his father in the legs with his head and hobbling Oliver's knees with his arms.

Oliver did not pick him up, but stood there, penned, waiting until Victoria was within earshot.

"Where have you been?" he asked her.

"Just for a walk. We found another stream, but not as pretty as the waterfall." She reached his side. "What have you been doing?"

"Telephoning," he told her. The walk, the cold air, had brought color to her cheeks. Her pale hair was blowing and tousled. She had found, somewhere, a clump of yellow aconites, and had picked one or two and put them in the buttonhole of her jacket. Oliver pulled her into his arms and kissed her. She smelled cool and fresh, of apples and

the outdoors. Her lips were sweet and clean, her kiss tasted as innocent as clear water.

"Telephoning who?"

"I wasn't telephoning anybody. I was being telephoned."

"Who by?"

"My agent." He let her go, and stooped to disentangle Thomas
from his legs. They began to walk towards the house, but Thomas
protested, so Victoria went back to lift him up in her arms. When she
was alongside Oliver once more, she asked. "What did he say?"

"Good things. *Bent Penny*'s going to London."

She stopped dead. "*Oliver!* But that's *marvelous.*"

"And I'm going to London too, tomorrow." Her face dropped.
"I'm leaving you and Thomas behind."

"You can't mean it."

He laughed. "Don't look so tragic, you ninny. I'm coming back
the next day."

"But why can't we come with you?"

"What's the point of coming to London for one day? Anyway, I
can't talk business with you and Thomas under my feet all the time."

"But we can't stay here without you!"

"Why not?"

"I don't want to be left behind."

In a flash, Oliver became irritated. He stopped his good-natured
teasing, and said, in some exasperation, "I'm *not* leaving you behind.
I'm simply going to London for a night. I'm flying down and I'm
flying back. And when I get back, we're packing up and we're getting
into the car and we're all going south again. Together. Now, does
that make you happy?"

"But what am I going to do without you?"

"Exist, I imagine. It shouldn't be too difficult."

"I just feel it's so awful for Roddy. We dumped ourselves on him in
the first place, and now . . ."

"He's fine. He's delighted at the idea of having you and Thomas
to himself for a day or two. And as for dumping ourselves on him, he
doesn't want us to go. Once we've gone, he'll have to face reality,
and he doesn't relish that in the very least."

"That's a horrible thing to say about Roddy."

"OK, it's horrible, but it's true. OK, he's charming and amusing, a
character straight from the pages of some old nineteen-thirties

comedy. Rattigan, perhaps, at his most fresh-faced. But I doubt if he's ever faced an issue in his life."

"He was in the war. Anybody who went through the war was bound to face issues. That was what it was all about."

"I'm talking about personal issues. Not National Emergencies. You can't hide from a National Emergency by climbing behind a brandy and soda."

"Oh, *Oliver*. I hate it when you're like this. And I still don't want you to go and leave Thomas and me behind."

"Well, I'm going." She did not reply, and he put his arm around her, and bent and kissed the top of her head. "And you are not to sulk about it. And on Tuesday, when I fly back, you can jump into the Volvo and come and meet me. And if you're particularly charming, I shall take you out to dinner in Inverness. And we'll eat haggis and chips and join in the folk dancing. Can you think of anything more riveting?"

"I'd rather you didn't go." But she was beginning to smile.

"I have to. Duty calls. I'm a successful man. Leaving you behind is one of the prices I have to pay for being successful."

"Sometimes I wish you weren't."

He kissed her again. "You know what's wrong with you? You're never happy."

"That's not true."

He relented. "I know it isn't."

"I've been happy here," she told him, and she was suddenly shy. She hoped that Oliver would tell her that he had been happy too. But he did not say anything, and she heaved Thomas's weight from one arm to the other, and together, they walked back to the house.

13
MONDAY

───❦───

*R*oddy stood at the top of his staircase and called "Victoria!"

Victoria, who had spent the morning ironing shirts and hand-kerchiefs for Oliver, sorting out socks and sweaters, and finally packing a suitcase, straightened up from her task, pushed a lock of hair from her face, and went to open the bedroom door.

"I'm here!"

"John's here, and Oliver. Come and join us. We're having a drink."

It was nearly half past twelve, a bright, cold day and the sun was shining. Roddy and Oliver were leaving for the airport after lunch. A quarter of an hour previously, Ellen had appeared to take charge of Thomas and to get him ready for lunch, for lunch today was to be a substantial affair, cooked by Ellen and Jess Guthrie and eaten in the big dining room at Benchoile. This was Ellen's decision. She had always been of the opinion that no person should set out on a journey, however short, without a good meal inside him, and Oliver was, apparently, no exception. Accordingly, she and Jess had been busy all morning. Appetizing smells had wafted through from the big house, and there was a certain sense of occasion in the air, as though something important was happening, like a birthday, or the last day of the holidays.

Above her, in Roddy's sitting room, Victoria could hear the murmured conversation of the others. She closed the suitcase and
snapped shut the locks. She went to the mirror and combed her hair,
gave a final glance about the room to make sure that nothing had
been forgotten, and then went upstairs to join the rest of the party.

Because of the sunshine and the brightness of the day, she found
them gathered, not about the fireside, but at the huge window.
Oliver and Roddy sat on the window seat with their backs to the
view, and John Dunbeath on a chair that he had pulled back from the
desk. When Victoria appeared, Roddy said, "Here she is, come along,
we've been waiting for you," and John stood up and moved his chair
to one side in order to make space for her. "What'll you have to
drink?"

She considered this. "I don't think I really want a drink."

"Oh, come on," said Oliver. He held out a long arm, and drew
Victoria to his side. "Don't be prissy. You've been beavering around
all morning, being domestic. You deserve a drink."

"Oh, all right."

John said, "What would you like? I'll get it for you."

Still caught in the circle of Oliver's arm, she looked across at him.
"A lager, perhaps?" And he smiled, and went through to Roddy's
kitchen to collect her a can out of the fridge.

But there was scarcely time to open the can and pour the lager
before they were interrupted by the sound of the front door opening,
and Ellen's voice from the foot of the stairs, raised to tell them all that
lunch was ready, it was on the table, it would spoil if they didn't come
immediately.

Roddy said, sotto voce, "Drat the woman," but there was obviously nothing to be done about it, and so, carrying their various
glasses, they all got to their feet and made their way downstairs and
across the yard to the big house.

They found the dining room full of sunshine, the big table laid
with a white cloth. A roast of beef steamed on the sideboard, dishes
of hot vegetables stood on the hot plate, and Thomas was already
installed, hungry and feedered, in an ancient wooden high chair that
Jess Guthrie had brought down from the old nursery.

Ellen pottered to and fro on her unsteady legs, telling everybody
where they were to sit, complaining that the roast was getting cold,
and what was the point of cooking good meat if folks couldn't be on
time for their meals?

John said, good-naturedly, "Now come on, Ellen, that's not true. We were off our backside the moment you hollered up the stairs. Who's going to carve?"

"You," said Roddy instantly, and went to sit down with his back to the window, as far from the sideboard as possible. He had never been any good at carving. Jock had always done the carving.

John sharpened the horn-handled knife with all the élan of a master butcher, and got to work. Ellen took the first plate for Thomas, and herself dealt with it, cutting up the meat and squashing the vegetables and gravy into a mess like brown porridge.

"There he is, the wee man. You eat that up now, pet, and you'll turn into a great big boy."

"Not that we have too many problems," Roddy murmured when Ellen had departed and closed the door behind her, and everybody laughed because this morning Thomas's cheeks appeared to be fatter and rounder than ever.

They had finished their first course and were just starting in on Ellen's apple pie and baked custard, when the telephone started to ring. They all waited, as seemed to be the custom at Benchoile, for somebody else to go and answer it. Finally Roddy said, "Oh, damn."

Victoria took pity on him. "Shall I go?"

"No, don't bother." He took another leisurely mouthful of apple pie, and pushed back his chair and ambled from the room, still grumbling. "What a bloody stupid time to ring up." He had left the dining room door open, and they could hear his voice from the library. "Benchoile. Roddy Dunbeath here." Then a pause. "Who? What? Yes, of course. Hold on a moment and I'll go and get him." A moment later he reappeared, still holding the table napkin, which he had taken with him.

"Oliver, dear boy, it's for you."

Oliver looked up from his plate. "Me? Who is it?"

"No idea. Some man or other."

He returned to his apple pie, and Oliver pushed back his chair and went to take the call. "I can't think," said Roddy, "why they can't invent some device so that when you sit down to a meal, you can stop the telephone ringing."

"You could always take it off the hook," John suggested mildly.

"Yes, but then I'd forget to put it back again."

Thomas was beginning to be bored with his pudding. Victoria

picked up his spoon and began to help him. She said, "You could always just let it ring."

"I'm not strong-minded enough. I can let it ring for just so long, and then I can't bear it for another moment. I always imagine that someone is waiting to tell me something tremendously exciting, and I go cantering off to grab the receiver from the hook, only to find myself voice-to-voice as it were with the Inland revenue. Or else it's a wrong number."

John said, "If you're a wrong number, then why did you answer the phone?" which was somehow all the funnier, because he didn't often make jokes.

By the time Oliver returned, their meal was over. Roddy had lighted a cigar, and John brought the tray of coffee through from the kitchen. Victoria was peeling an orange for Thomas, because however much he ate, he always liked oranges more than anything. The orange was juicy and the task absorbed her, so that she did not look up when Oliver came back into the room.

"Good news, I hope," she heard Roddy say. The last of the peel fell away, and she broke the orange into sections and handed the first one to Thomas. Oliver did not reply. "Nothing serious?" Roddy now sounded concerned.

Still Oliver said nothing. The silence suddenly caught Victoria's attention. It grew longer, more strained. Even Thomas was stilled by it. He sat, with a piece of orange in his hand, and stared across the table at his father. Victoria's cheeks began to prickle. She realized that they were all looking at her. She looked at Roddy, and then up at Oliver. She saw his face, intensely pale, and his cold, unblinking eyes. She felt the blood drain from her own cheeks, and a reasonless sense of doom, like a sickness, knot her stomach.

She swallowed. "What is it?" Her voice sounded thin and insubstantial.

"Do you know who that was on the telephone?" Oliver asked her.

"I've no idea," but she could not keep her voice from trembling.

"It was Mr. Bloody Archer. Ringing up from Hampshire." *But I told her not to ring up. I said I'd write again. I explained about Oliver.* "You wrote to them."

"I . . ." Her mouth was dry, and she swallowed again. "I didn't write to him. I wrote to her."

Oliver advanced to the table, he laid the palms of his hands flat upon its surface, and leaned towards her.

"I told you not to write to her." Each word came out like a hammer blow. "I told you you were not to write to her, nor telephone her, to get in touch with her in any way at all."

"Oliver, I had to . . ."

"How did you know where to write, anyway?"

"I . . . I looked it up in the telephone directory."

"When did you write?"

"On Thursday . . . Friday . . ." She was beginning to be flustered. "I can't remember."

"What was I doing?"

"I . . . I think you were still asleep." It was beginning to sound so underhand, so secretive, that she was impelled to stand up her herself. "I *told* you I wanted to write to her. I couldn't bear her not knowing about Thomas . . . not knowing where he was." Oliver's expression softened not one whit. Victoria realized, with horror, that she was going to cry. She could feel her mouth shaking, the lump grow in her throat, her eyes begin to swim with terrible, shaming tears. In front of them all, she was going to start crying.

"She *knew* where he bloody was."

"No, she *didn't*."

"She knew he was with me. And that's all that bloody matters. He was with me and I am his father. What I do with him, and where I take him, is no concern of anyone else. Least of all, you."

Tears were now running down her face. "Well, I think—" she managed before he interrupted her.

"I never asked you to think. I simply told you to keep your stupid little mouth *shut*."

This was accompanied by Oliver's fist coming down in a massive blow on the dining room table. Everything on it shivered and bounced. Thomas, who had been stunned into silence by the unfamiliar violence of words that he did not know, but understood only too well, chose this moment to emulate Victoria, and burst into tears. His eyes screwed up, his mouth fell open, the remains of his half-chewed orange dribbled from his mouth down onto his feeder.

"Oh, for God's sake . . ."

"Oh, Oliver, *don't*." She sprang to her feet, her knees trembling, and tried to lift Thomas out of his chair, to comfort him. Thomas clung to her, burying his sticky face into her neck, trying to hide from the shouting. "Don't, in front of Thomas. *Stop!*"

But her anguished appeal was ignored. By now Oliver was past stopping. "You knew why I didn't want you to get in touch with the Archers. Because I guessed that as soon as they knew where we were, I'd be bombarded with maudlin appeals, and when they failed, threats. Which is precisely what has happened. The next thing we know, there'll be some black-coated little bastard on the doorstep delivering a letter from some lawyer or other . . ."

"But you said . . ." She couldn't remember what he had said. Her nose had started to run, and she could scarcely speak for crying. "I . . . I . . ." She scarcely knew what she was trying to say. *I'm sorry,* perhaps, but it was just as well that this final abasement was never uttered, because Oliver was in no mood to be placated by anything. Not his weeping son, nor his weeping mistress, nor all the apologies in the world.

"You know what you are? You're a deceitful little bitch."

And with this final broadside, Oliver straightened up from the table, and turned and stalked out of the room. Victoria was left, trapped by her own tears, with the weeping, hysterical child in her arms, with the appalled silence of the other two men, with the shambles of the ruined meal. Worst of all, with humiliation and shame.

Roddy said, "My dear," and got up from the table and came around to her side, and Victoria knew that she must stop crying, but she couldn't stop, or wipe away her tears, or even start looking for a handkerchief, while still burdened with the howling Thomas.

John Dunbeath said, "Here." He was beside her, lifting Thomas out of her arms and up against his broad shoulder. "Here, come along now, we'll go and find Ellen. She'll maybe have some candy for you to eat." Bearing Thomas with him, he made for the door. "Or a chocolate biscuit. Do you like chocolate biscuits?"

When they had gone," My dear," said Roddy again.

"I . . . I can't help it . . ." Victoria gasped.

He could bear it no longer. Streaming face, running nose, sobs and all, he pulled her into his arms and held her against him, cradling the back of her head with his gentle hand. After a little, he reached up and took the red and white handkerchief from the breast pocket of his aged tweed jacket, and gave it to her, and Victoria was able to blow her nose and wipe her eyes.

After that, things got a little better, and the nightmare scene started to be over.

*   *   *

She went in search of Oliver. There was nothing else to be done. She found him down by the edge of the loch, standing at the end of the jetty, smoking a cigarette. If he heard her coming across the grass, he gave no sign of it, for he never turned round.

She reached the jetty. She said his name. He hesitated for a moment, and then threw his half-smoked cigarette into the sun-dappled water, and turned to face her.

Victoria remembered him saying, *If you so much as pick up a telephone, I'll batter you black and blue.* But she hadn't really believed the threat, because in all the time that she had known him, she had never seen the true violence of Oliver's uncontrolled rage. Now, she knew, she had seen it. She wondered if his wife, Jeannette, had seen it. If that, perhaps, was one of the reasons why his marriage had lasted only a few months.

"Oliver."

His eyes rested on her face. She knew she looked hideous, still swollen from weeping, but even that didn't matter any longer. Nothing mattered except that the dreadful quarrel, for Thomas's sake, had to be patched up.

She said, "I really am sorry."

He still said nothing. After a little, he gave a long sigh, and then shrugged.

She went on, painfully. "It's difficult for you to understand. I know that. And I don't suppose I understood, either, because I'd never had a child of my own. But after I'd been with Thomas for a bit, I began to realize what it was like. I mean, having a little boy, and loving him." She wasn't doing it right at all. She was making it sound sentimental, and that wasn't what she was trying to be at all. "You get bound up with a child. Involved. As though it were part of you. You begin to feel that if anybody hurt it, or even threatened it, you could kill them."

"Do you imagine," said Oliver, "that Mrs. Archer was going to kill me?"

"No. But I did know that she was probably out of her mind with anxiety."

"She always hated me. They both did."

"Perhaps you didn't give them much reason to do anything else?"

"I married their daughter."

"And fathered their grandchild."

"He's my son."

"That's the whole point. Thomas is your son. You've told me over and over that the Archers have no legal claim on him. So how can it hurt you to be a little generous to them? He's all they have left of their daughter. Oh, Oliver, you must try to understand. You're perceptive and clever, you write plays that wring people's hearts. Why can't you come to terms with a situation that should be so close to your own heart?"

"Perhaps I haven't got a heart."

"You've got a heart." She began, tentatively, to smile. "I've heard it beating. Thump thump thump, all through the night."

It worked. His grim expression softened a little, as though the situation had, in its way, a wry humor. It wasn't much, but emboldened by this, Victoria went down the jetty to his side, she put her arms around his waist, beneath his jacket, and pressed her cheek against the front of his rough, thick sweater.

She said, "They don't matter anyway, the Archers. What they do can't make any difference."

His hands rubbed up and down her back, as though he were absently fondling a dog. "Any difference to what?"

"My loving you." It was said. Pride, self-esteem no longer mattered. Loving Oliver was their only talisman, all she had to hold onto. It was the key to the lock that held the two of them, and Thomas, together.

He said, "You must be mad."

He did not apologize for any of the searing remarks and accusations he had thrown at her down the length of the lunch table. She wondered if he would apologize to Roddy and John, and knew that he would not. Simply because he was Oliver Dobbs. But that didn't matter. Victoria had bridged the breach between them. The wound of the hideous scene was still open, and agonizing, but perhaps, in time, it would heal. She realized that it was always possible to pick yourself up and start again, however many times you fall.

She said, "Would you mind very much if I was?"

He did not reply. Presently he laid his hands on her shoulders and put her away from him. "I must go," he told her. "It's time I was going, or I'll miss my plane."

They went back to the Stable House and collected his suitcase, a couple of books. When they came out again, they saw Jock's old Daimler parked in front of the house, and Roddy and John standing beside it, waiting.

It seemed that everybody had decided to behave as though

nothing had happened. "I thought it would be better to take the big car," Roddy explained. "There's not much room for luggage in the MG."

His tone was quite matter-of-fact, and Victoria felt grateful to him.

"That's great," Oliver opened the back door and heaved his case in, and the books on top of it. "Well," he grinned, quite unrepentant, even perhaps a little amused by the lack of expression on John Dunbeath's face, "I'll say good-bye, John."

"I'll see you again," John told him. He did not hold out a hand. "I'm not leaving till Wednesday."

"That's great. Bye, Victoria," he stooped to kiss her cheek.

"Tomorrow," she said. "What time does your plane get in?"

"About seven-thirty."

"I'll be there to meet you."

"See you then."

They got into the car. Roddy started the engine. The Daimler moved away, ponderous and dignified, tires crunching on the gravel. Down through the rhododendrons, over the cattle grid, through the gate.

They had gone.

He was terribly afraid that now it was all over, now he was alone with her, she would start to cry again. It was not that he was afraid of tears, or would even be embarrassed by them. In fact, he would have almost welcomed them. But he knew, too, that this was not the right time to take her in his arms, to comfort her as Roddy had done.

She was standing with her back to him. She was done with waving good-bye. To John, her erect and slender back seemed immensely courageous. He saw the firm set of her shoulders under the thick sweater, the long silky tail of fair hair, and was reminded of a colt his father had reared, long ago, on the ranch back in Colorado. Once frightened by a clumsy hand, only the most patient and perceptive of handling had finally brought it back to anything approaching trust. But little by little, letting the colt take his own time, John himself had achieved this.

He knew that he had to be very careful. He waited. After a bit, perhaps realizing that he was not going to simply melt away and tactfully disappear, Victoria pushed her hair out of her face, and turned to face him. She was not crying. She was smiling. The sort of smile that lights up a face, but does not reach the eyes.

She said, briskly, "Well, that's that."

He said, "They've got a good day for a drive. It'll be very beautiful, going over Struie."

"Yes."

"Don't you think we ought to go for a drive, too?" Victoria's smile froze and became agonized, and he knew that this was what she had been dreading; he was sorry for her and so he was going to be kind to her. He went on, quickly, "I have to go to Creagan, anyway. I have to go to the chemist. I've run out of shaving soap. And I thought the newsagent might have a *Financial Times*. I haven't seen the market prices for three days." This was not true, but it was a face-saver, and as good an excuse as any.

Victoria said, "What about Thomas?"

"We'll leave Thomas here. He's happy with Ellen."

"I haven't taken Thomas to the beach yet. I've always meant to take him."

"You can take him another time. If you don't tell him where you're going, he won't want to come."

She considered this. She said at last, "Well . . . all right. But I must go and tell Ellen that we're going out."

That was good enough. "You'll find them out at the back, on the drying-green. I'll get the car and meet you here in a moment or two."

When he returned, at the wheel of the hired Ford, she was back on the steps by the front door, waiting for him. He knew that in Creagan it would be windswept and cold, and she was wearing no sort of coat, but there was a spare sweater of his own lying on the back seat of the car, and he did not want to put off any time. He drew up beside her, leaned across to open the passenger door, and let Victoria get in beside him. Then, with no more discussion, they were on their way.

He took it slowly. There was no hurry. The more leisurely their passage, the more relaxed he hoped she would become. He said, casually, "How was Thomas?"

"You were right. He and Ellen are perfectly happy. Ellen's taken a chair out into the sun, and she's doing her knitting, and Thomas and Piglet are playing with her clothes pegs." She added, a little wistfully, "They looked very peaceful."

He said, "Thomas isn't your child, is he?"

Victoria, beside him, was very still. She stared ahead at the convolutions of the narrow road. Her hands lay clasped in her lap. She said, "No."

"I don't know why, but I always imagined that he was. I suppose Roddy thought he was, too. At least, he never gave me any reason to suspect that he wasn't. And he looks like you. That's the extraordinary thing. A bit fatter, perhaps, but he really looks like you."

"He isn't my child. But he's Oliver's. Thomas's mother was called Jeannette Archer. Oliver married her, but then the marriage broke up and she was killed in an aircrash soon after."

"How do you come into it?"

"I've been in it for years . . ." Her voice began to shake. "I'm terribly sorry, but I think I'm going to start crying again."

"It doesn't matter."

"Don't you mind?" She sounded surprised.

"Why should I mind?" He leaned forward and opened the cubbyhole on the dashboard, and revealed an enormous box of Kleenex. "See? I'm even prepared."

"Americans always have paper handkerchiefs." She took one out and blew her nose. "Crying's horrible, isn't it? Once you start, it's like a terrible addiction. However many times you stop, you always start again. I don't usually ever cry."

But this brave assertion dissolved, even as she made it, into tears. John waited peacefully, taking no notice, saying nothing. After a little, when the sobs had reduced themselves to chokes and then to sniffs and she had blown her nose, determinedly, once more, he observed, "If a person wants to cry, I never see any reason why they shouldn't. I always cried when I was a kid and being sent back to Fessenden. And my father never tried to stop me nor tell me that it wasn't manly. In fact, he sometimes looked as though he were about to burst into tears himself."

Victoria smiled wanly, but made no comment on this, and John decided to leave it, and nothing more was said until they reached Creagan. The little town lay bathed in cold afternoon sunshine, its streets swept and empty of the modest throngs who would fill it later on in the year as the summer season swelled.

He drew up in front of the chemist. "Do you want to do any shopping?" he asked Victoria.

"No. I'm all right, thank you."

He left her and went into the shop and bought the shaving soap and some razor blades. Next to the chemist was a newsagent, so he went in there and asked for the *Financial Times,* but they didn't have one, so he bought a bag of peppermints instead, and bore these back to the car.

"Here." He tossed them into Victoria's lap. "If you don't like them, we'll give them to Thomas."

"Perhaps Ellen would like them. Old people always like peppermints."

"These are toffees. Ellen can't eat toffees on account of her false teeth. Now, what shall we do?"

"We could go back to Benchoile."

"Is that what you want to do? Don't you want to go for a walk or something? Don't you want to go to the beach?"

"Do you know the way?"

"Sure I know the way, I used to come here when I was knee-high to a bee."

"Haven't you anything else you'd rather do?"

"Not a mortal thing."

The beach at Creagan was divided from the town by the golf links, and there was no access by road to the sands, so John parked the car by the clubhouse. When he switched off the engine, they could hear the whine of the wind. The long pale grasses that flanked the fairways lay flat beneath its blast, and the brightly colored waterproof jackets of a couple of hardy golfers were filled with it, so that they resembled balloons. John pulled up the zipper of his old leather jacket, and reached back for the sweater that lay on the backseat.

It was blue and very thick with a tall polo neck. She pulled it over her head and the tight, ribbed collar dragged her hair. She flipped it free and shook it loose. The cuffs of the sweater covered her hands, the hem reached below her narrow hips.

They got out of the car, and the wind pounced on the open doors and it was a struggle to get them shut. A path, a right-of-way, led down towards the sea across the fairways. Wild thyme grew underfoot, and there were hazards of whin and gorse. Beyond the links lay dunes of coarse grass, "bents" they were called in this part of the world, and there was a little caravan site, and small, ramshackle edifices, which in summer would open their shutters and sell chocolate and fizzy drinks and ice creams. The dunes ended abruptly in a sloping cliff of sand. The tide was out. Now there was nothing but white beach and the distant sea. Far away, the rollers creamed in, crested with spray. There was not another soul about, not a dog, not a scampering child. Only the wheeling gulls hung overhead screaming their disdain at the world in general.

After the soft, dry, sand of the dunes, the beach seemed very flat and firm underfoot. They ran, trying to get warm. As they approached the sea, shallow pools, fed from some mysterious source, reflected the brightness of the sky, and there were immense quantities of shells. Victoria's attention was caught by these. She picked up one and then another, marveling at their size and unbroken state.

"They're so beautiful. I've never seen shells before that weren't all broken to bits. Why aren't these broken?"

"I suppose because this is a shallow, sandy shore." He joined in her ploy, grateful for any diversion that would take her mind off her woes. He found the skeleton of a starfish, the delicate fossilized claw of a miniature crab.

"What's this?" she asked him.

He inspected it. "A sand gaper. And the blue one is a common mussel."

"And this? It looks exactly like a very small baby's toenail."

"That's called a banded wedge."

"How do you know their names?"

"I used to come and collect shells when I was a boy, and Roddy gave me a book so that I'd learn to identify them."

They walked on in silence, and came at last to the sea. They stood, facing the wind, and watched the breakers pouring in. The waves rose and curled and broke and hissed in over the sand, and the water was clear and clean and the color of aquamarine.

The shell lay, just out of reach of the ebbing tide. John stooped and picked it up, and placed it, wet and shining, in the palm of Victoria's hand. It was the color of coral, with a sunburst of raised ribs, semispherical in shape, so that if it had still been attached to its twin they could have formed a whole roughly the size of a tennis ball.

"Now there's a prize," he said.

She was openmouthed. "Whatever is it?"

"That's a queen scallop, and what a size of one."

"I thought you only found shells like that in the West Indies."

"Well, now you know you can find them in Scotland."

She held it away from her, taking enormous pleasure in its shape, the very feel of the shell. She said, "I shall keep it for always. Just for an ornament."

"And a keepsake, perhaps."

Victoria looked at him, and he saw the beginnings of her first smile. "Yes. Perhaps as a keepsake too."

They turned their backs on the sea, and started on the long return journey. The sands stretched forever, and the dunes seemed very far away. By the time they had reached the steep cliff of sand down which they had tumbled so easily, Victoria was beginning to flag, and John had to take her hand, and pull her, floundering and slipping, to the top. Halfway up, she began to laugh, and when they finally reached the summit, they were both breathless. In wordless agreement, they collapsed, exhausted into a sheltered hollow, where the sand gave way to a thick, coarse grass, and the tussocks of bents protected them from the worst of the wind.

Here, there even seemed to be a little heat in the sun. John lay back on his elbows, and let its warmth generate through the thick, dark suede of his jacket. Victoria sat forward, her chin on her knees, still gloating over her shell. Her hair had parted at the back of her neck, and his enormous sweater made her look even thinner and frailer than she actually was.

After a bit, she said, "Perhaps I shouldn't keep it. Perhaps I should give it to Thomas."

"Thomas wouldn't appreciate it."

"He would, when he's older."

"You're very fond of Thomas, aren't you? Even though he isn't your child."

Victoria said, "Yes."

"Do you want to talk about it?"

"It's difficult to know where to begin. And you probably wouldn't understand anyway."

"You could try me."

"Well . . ." She took a deep breath. "The Archers are Thomas's grandparents."

"I gathered that."

"And they live in Hampshire. And Oliver was driving back from Bristol, and he passed near Woodbridge—that's where the Archers live . . ."

Slowly, hesitantly, the story unfolded. All the time she was speaking, Victoria kept her back turned to John, and he was forced to listen to the entire saga while staring at the back of her neck. He found this intensely frustrating.

". . . that night you brought me back from the Fairburns' party, and Thomas was crying—that was the evening they turned up."

He remembered that night, the evening before he had flown to Bahrain. The dark windy skies and the little house in the Mews; Victoria with her chin buried in the fur collar of her coat, and her eyes filled with apprehension and anxiety.

". . . and all come away for a little holiday. So we came to Benchoile on account of Oliver knowing Roddy. I told you about that."

"I take it you don't have a job to keep you in London?"

"Oh, yes I do. But I work in a dress shop in Beauchamp Place, and Sally, the girl I work for, wanted me to take a holiday anyway. So she said I could have a month off, and she's got a temporary girl in to help out till I get back again."

"And are you going back?"

"I don't know."

"Why don't you know?"

"I may just stay with Oliver."

This silenced John. He could not comprehend how any girl could want to stay with that raving egotist. Despite all his original and laudable intentions of keeping a fair and open mind, he found himself becoming slowly more and more incensed.

She was talking again. ". . . I knew how worried Mrs. Archer must be, so I said to Oliver that I thought I should write to her, and Oliver was furious because he didn't want them to know where we were. But I did write, although I explained to her about Oliver being so difficult, and I asked her not to get in touch, but I suppose Mr. Archer got hold of my letter."

Now that the telling was safely over, Victoria appeared to decide that the time had come to look John in the eye. She turned to face him, her attitude confiding, her weight resting on one hand, her long legs curled up beneath her.

"And it was he who rang up Oliver at lunchtime. So now you see why Oliver was so angry."

"Yes, I suppose I do see. But I still think it was a fairly gruesome scene."

"But you do understand?"

It was obviously important to her that he did. But for John understanding made things no better. In fact, if anything, a good deal worse, for his most pessimistic suspicions had proved themselves wellfounded. It was all in place now, the pieces of the jigsaw slotted together and the pattern clear. A person was selfish. Another person was greedy. Pride came into it, and resentment and even a sort of spite. Nobody came out of it well, and only the innocent suffered. The innocent. A noxious word, but how else to describe Victoria and Thomas?

He thought of Oliver. From the first encounter, there had been antipathy between the two men. Like dogs, they had circled each other, hackles bristling. John had told himself that this antipathy was reasonless, instinctive, and with the inbred good manners of a man staying in another man's house, had fallen over backwards in his efforts not to let it show. But the antipathy was obviously mutual and before long John found himself resenting Oliver's casual treatment of Victoria, his offhand attitude to Roddy, his lack of interest in his child. After a couple of days in Oliver's company he had to admit that he actively disliked him. Now, after the appalling scene over the lunch table, he knew that he detested him.

He said, "If you stay with Oliver, will you marry him?"

"I don't know."

"Do you mean you don't know if you'll marry him, or if he'll marry you?"

"I don't know." A flush crept up into her pale cheeks. "I don't know if he'll marry me. He's funny. He . . ."

All at once, John was filled with a boiling, unaccustomed rage. Brutally, he interrupted her. "Victoria, don't be a fool." She stared at him, her eyes enormous. "I mean that. Don't be a fool. You have a whole, wonderful life in front of you, and you talk about getting married to a guy, and you don't even know if he loves you enough to marry you. Marriage isn't a love affair. It isn't even a honeymoon. It's a job. A long hard job, at which both partners have to work, harder than they've worked at anything in their lives before. If it's a good marriage, it changes, it evolves, but it goes on getting better. I've seen it with my own mother and father. But a bad marriage can dissolve in a welter of resentment and acrimony. I've seen that, too, in my own miserable and disastrous attempt at making another person happy. And it's never one person's fault. It's the sum total of a thousand little irritations, disagreements, idiotic details that in a sound alliance would simply be disregarded, or forgotten in the healing act of making love. Divorce isn't a cure, it's a surgical operation, even if there are no children to consider. And you and Oliver already have a child. You have Thomas."

She said, "I can't go back."

"Sure you can."

"It's all very well for you to talk. Your marriage may have broken up, but you still have your parents, your job. You have Benchoile, too, whatever you decide to do with it. If I don't have Oliver and Thomas, then I don't have anything. Not anything really precious. Not anyone to belong to, not anyone to need me."

"You have yourself."

"Perhaps I'm not enough."

"In that case, you dismally underestimate yourself."

Victoria turned swiftly away from him, and John was presented once more with the back of her head. He realized that he had been shouting at her, and this astonished him, because it was the first time in many months that he had felt sufficiently involved or aroused to shout at anyone. He said, gruffly, "I'm sorry," and when she did not move or speak, he went on, more gently, "It's just that I hate to see someone like you make such a goddamn mess of her life."

She said, sounding sullen as a child, "You forget. It's still my life."

"It's Thomas's too," he reminded her. "And Oliver's." Still she did not move. He put his hand on her arm and pulled her around to face him. With an immense effort she met his eyes. He said, "You have to love Oliver very much. Much more than he loves you. To make it work, I mean."

"I know."

"In that case you're going into it with your eyes open."

"I know," she said again. Gently, she eased herself free of his grasp. "But you see, there was never anyone else. There was never anyone but Oliver."

14
TUESDAY

⸺◈⸺

*T*he wind, he thought, was the same wind that blew in Scotland, but in London it took on a different shape. It sneaked from around corners, it tore the first buds from the trees in the park, and littered the streets with torn scraps of paper. It was not a friend. People pressed against it, their faces agonized, their coats wrapped tight against them. The wind was an enemy, invading the city.

The rain came as the taxi, which had brought him out from Fulham, turned at last into the complexities of Heathrow Airport. It came through tunnels and circled rotaries, a tiny entity in an endless stream of traffic. Lights flashed, reflected in the wet roadways; overhead a jet droned, waiting to land. There was the heavy smell of petrol.

This taxi, in a long queue of taxis, drew in at last under the canopy of the terminal building. Oliver got out, pulled his suitcase after him, and stood at the pavement's edge feeling in his pocket for the fare. The driver, waiting, let his eyes move over his passenger, his passenger's luggage.

"Here." Oliver handed the notes over.

"Sure I've brought you to the right place, mate? This is domestic flights here. Terminal one."

"Yes, that's right."

"Just saw the label on your case. You ought to be over in international flights, terminal three."

"No. This is the one I want." He grinned. "Keep the change."

"Well, it's you who's traveling. You ought to know."

He picked up his case and went in through the glass doors, across the polished expanse of the great building, up the escalator, following the signs that led to domestic departures.

The departure hall was crowded as usual, every seat taken with travelers waiting for their various flights to be called. There was the smell of coffee, and cigarette smoke and humanity. Oliver moved slowly down the room, looking about him, like a man with a rendezvous. He saw the woman with her five exhausting children; a pair of nuns. He saw the man in the tweed overcoat and bowler hat, immersed in his newspaper. His briefcase stood on the floor between his legs. Oliver stopped before him.

"Excuse me."

Startled, the man looked up from his paper. He had a long, pale face, a neat collar, a dark tie. He wore spectacles. A lawyer, thought Oliver. A businessman. He said, "I *am* sorry, but I saw the label on your briefcase. Are you flying to Inverness?"

"Yes," said the man, sounding as though he did not think it was any of Oliver's business.

"On the five-thirty plane?"

"Yes."

"I wonder if you'd be very kind and deliver a letter for me." He reached into his pocket and took out the envelope. "The thing is, I'd arranged to catch this flight, but I'm not going to be able to make it after all, and there's someone meeting me at Inverness."

The man in spectacles continued to look unenthusiastic. He probably thought the envelope contained some sort of an explosive device, and that he and the rest of his fellow passengers were going to be blown to kingdom come whilst in transit over the Pennines.

"This has just all cropped up in the last couple of hours, and I can't telephone her—the girl who's meeting me, I mean—because she's driving to Inverness from Sutherland, and she'll have left by now."

The man in spectacles looked at the envelope and then back at Oliver. Oliver put on his sincere and open expression. The man laid down his newspaper.

"If I do take your letter, how shall I know the young lady?"

"Well, she's young, and she's got long fair hair, and she'll probably be wearing trousers. She's called Victoria Bradshaw." He added, as though it were a little lure, "She's very pretty."

But the other was not so easily seduced. "What shall I do if she isn't there?"

"She will be there. I promise you. She'll be there."

The man took the envelope at last, gingerly. "Wouldn't it be better to hand this over to the air hostess?"

"I suppose we could, but you know what they're like, always so busy giving people cups of tea. And anyway, I haven't got time to wait till she turns up, because I've got to get over to the international terminal and catch another plane."

"Very well," said the man at last. Having made the decision, he allowed a small smile to cross his chilly features. "You can leave it with me."

"Thank you," said Oliver. "Thank you very much. I'm really sorry to have bothered you. And I hope you have a good flight."

"The same to you," said the man in spectacles, and went back to his paper.

Oliver picked up his suitcase and turned away. He would go down the stairs and out of this building, and he would walk through the rain, over to terminal three, and check in to the New York flight, and after that he was on his own once more. He was on his way.

He was free. It was over. An interlude, a brief encounter finished. The actors had departed, and the stage lay empty. Like an untouched canvas, it waited for Oliver to inhabit it with his own people, his own private and absorbing world.

You're back then.

That's right.

She's gone, then.

Yes, she's gone.

You can tell. A house has got a funny feeling when the last child goes. You think they're there forever but they go. And there's nothing much left, really. Except the telly. There's always the telly.

"Oh, excuse me."

He had reached the top of the stairs. He turned and found himself face to face with the man in the bowler hat. It took an instant's mental reorganization before Oliver even recognized him. He carried his briefcase in one hand, and Oliver's letter in the other.

"I'm sorry, but the young lady I have to give this to, I can't remember what you said she was called. You've written it on the envelope, but your writing's not all that clear. Is it Miss Veronica Bradshaw?"

"No," said Oliver. "It's . . ." he hesitated, having to remember. "It's Victoria."

He supposed there came a time for starting to feel old. Not just mature, or experienced, or any of the other euphemisms. Just old. He was sixty. Jock had died at sixty-nine. If he, Roddy, were to die at sixty-nine, that meant that he had only nine years left to enjoy. Or did it mean that he had nine years to fill in before he was finally released? And if so, then how was he to fill them? He would not have Benchoile to cushion him against the cold winds of the outside world, and he knew—had known for some years—that to all intents and purposes he had outwritten himself. There was no longer a readable book inside his head, and scarcely the most banal of articles. His friends, his social life, which had once so satisfyingly filled his time, were fading. His contemporaries had started to die; and delightful women who had once charmed him were becoming grandmothers, unable to cope—as inflation swallowed everything and old servants went into retirement—with house parties and dinner parties and all the endless, pleasant diversions of former days.

Pouring his second drink of the evening, trying to cheer himself up, Roddy Dunbeath told himself that in many ways he was fortunate. He would become old and he would probably be lonely, but at least he would not be penniless. All right, so Benchoile was going to be sold, but Roddy Dunbeath was in a financial position that would allow him to buy, outright, some modest house in which to spend the rest of his days. Where this house was to be, he had not yet decided, but Ellen was another problem which loomed like a shadow at the back of his mind. There could be no question of abandoning Ellen. If none of her many relations could be persuaded to have the cantankerous old thing live with them, then Roddy would have to take her on himself. The very prospect of living in a small house with no one but Ellen Tarbat for company gave him the shivers. He prayed, fervently, that it would never have to happen.

It was eight o'clock in the evening, and he was alone in his house, and it was this very solitude that had brought on his gloomy mood. Oliver was in London, by now—Roddy glanced at his watch—by now probably on his way back to Scotland. Victoria had departed in that immense Volvo to meet him at the airport. Thomas was in the bedroom downstairs, asleep, having been bathed and put to bed by Ellen. John was over in the big house, doing God knew what. The whole business of Benchoile seemed to have got the boy down, for he had been going around all day with a face like a wet weekend and with scarcely a word for anybody. To put the final lid on things, the weather had degenerated dismally with sleet showers and a force eight gale, and the summits of the hills were once more blanketed in snow.

Where, Roddy asked himself, was the spring? On such an evening, in such a mood, it was possible to believe that it would never come again. There would be some freak in the cosmos, the stars would start clashing, earthquakes erupt and the planet Earth be trapped forever in the grip of eternal winter.

Enough. That was as far as a man's depression could be allowed to go. Supine in his chair, his slippered feet sharing the hearthrug with his old dog, Roddy decided that the time had come to take some positive step to raise his spirits. He looked once more at his watch. He would go over to the big house and take a drink with John. They would then eat dinner together, and later, when Oliver and Victoria returned from Inverness, would all sit around the fire and listen to Oliver's news.

This pleasant prospect stimulated him sufficiently to make the effort of pulling himself up out of his chair. The newspaper that he had been reading sometime before slipped from his knees. Outside, the wind howled, and an icy draught came up the stairs and stirred the rugs on the polished floor. The Stable House was unusually cozy, but no door or window built by man's hands could keep that north-west wind from penetrating. The room felt chilly. The fire was dying. He took logs from the basket, tossed them onto the dying embers, building up a good blaze that would still be alight when he returned later on in the evening.

He turned off the lamp and said, "Come along, Barney," and the old dog heaved himself up, obviously feeling, as Roddy was, his age. "You're not the only one," he told him, and he turned off the center light, and together, slowly, they started down the stairs.

Without occupants, the darkened room was still and quiet. The fire flickered. A log cracked and kindled into flame. There came a crack of splitting wood, and a shower of sparks erupted like fireworks, out onto the hearthrug. Unattended, they smoldered. Then a draught snaked in up the stairs, a spark flared for a second, and caught the corner of the abandoned newspaper. Tiny flames began to lick and then grew larger. They played up the leg of Roddy's chairside table, where he kept his books and his cigars and a pile of old magazines. They reached the tindery withies of the old basket where he kept his logs. Soon, the hem of the curtain had started to smolder.

John Dunbeath sat at the desk in the library, where he had spent most of the afternoon going through his uncle's papers, sorting out farm accounts from personal accounts, arranging neat piles for the attention of Robert McKenzie, for Jock's stockbroker in Edinburgh, for his accountant.

The old man had kept a neat and efficient tally of his affairs, and this task had not been complicated, but tedious and inevitably sad. For there were as well old diaries, dance cards, and faded photographs of people whom John had never known. Regimental groups taken in the Red Fort at Delhi; a snapshot of a party of guns in jungly surroundings gathered for what looked like a tiger shoot; a wedding. Some of the photographs were Benchoile. He recognized his father as a small boy, and Roddy, a slender stripling, wearing white flannels and looking as though he were about to burst into song, the juvenile lead in some prewar musical comedy.

The door opened and the present-day Roddy ambled in. John was pleased to see him and to have the excuse to stop working. He pushed his chair back from the desk and held up the photograph.

"Look what I've just found."

Roddy came to inspect it over John's shoulder. "Good God. Inside every fat man there's a thin man struggling to get out. Where did you find that?"

"Oh, put away with some other old papers. What time is it?" He looked at his watch. "A quarter past eight already? I didn't realize it was as late as that."

"Quarter past eight on a vile cold winter's evening." He shivered. "I was nearly blown away just coming across the yard."

"Let's have a drink."

"Splendid idea," said Roddy as though he had not thought of it himself. He headed over to the table where the bottles and glasses had already been set out by Ellen, and John wondered how many private Scotches his uncle had already consumed, and then told himself that it didn't matter anyway, and it was none of his business. He only knew that he felt tired, and the prospect of a restoring drink was all at once very welcome.

He got up and went to build up the fire, and to draw a chair close to the blaze, for Roddy. Roddy brought the drinks over, and handed John his, and then sank into the chair with what sounded like a sigh of relief. John remained standing, and the warmth of the flames crept up his back, and he realized that he was stiff and cold from sitting in the bay of the window.

"Slainthe," said Roddy, and they both drank. "When are the others getting back, do you know?"

"No idea," John's dark face was impassive. "Around ten, I guess. Depends on whether the plane's on time or not. This gale might delay them."

"Are you really going back to London tomorrow?"

"Yes, I should. I'll probably be back again, next week or the week after, but we've got this big thing going just now, and I should be around."

"It was good that you were able to come."

"I've liked it. I'm just sorry that it had to end this way. I'd have liked Benchoile to go on."

"Dear boy, nothing can go on forever, and we've had a good run for our money."

They started talking about the old days, and as they both relaxed in the warmth, and each other's companionship, the time slipped pleasantly by. They were on to their second drink (or John's second drink and Roddy's fourth) when there came a scuffling sound from outside the door, the door opened, and Ellen advanced into the room. Neither of the men were surprised by this sudden appearance, for Ellen had long since given up knocking on doors. She was looking tired and particularly old. The wind and the bitter cold were bad for her bones, and she had been on her feet most of the day. Her expression showed this. Her mouth was buttoned up. She seemed determined to be put upon.

"I don't know when you two are wanting your dinner, but you can have it anytime you like."

"Thank you, Ellen," said Roddy, with a mild sarcasm that was wasted upon her.

"And when the others are getting back from Inverness I do not know, but they'll just have to make do with a bowl of broth."

"That'll be all they want," John assured her, and added, with some idea of placating her, "We'll be in the dining room in a moment. We're just having a drink."

"So I can see for myself." She hovered for a moment, trying to think of some other fault to find. "Did you check on the little boy before you came across, Roddy?"

"Um?" Roddy frowned. "No, I didn't. Was I meant to?"

"It seems it might have been a sensible thing to do instead of just leaving the mite there, abandoned for the evening."

Roddy became exasperated. "Ellen, I've only just got over here. Anyway, we leave him happily every evening."

"Oh, well, never you mind. I'll go and look for myself."

She began to shuffle off, but seemed, in truth, so tired, so old, with her sticklike black legs and her trodden shoes that John couldn't bear it. He laid down his drink. "Here, Ellen, don't you worry. I'll go."

"It's no trouble."

"It's no trouble for me either. It'll take me one minute. And when I get back, we'll come and eat dinner, and then you can take yourself off to bed."

"Who said anything about bed?"

"I did. You're looking tired, and it's the best place for you."

"Well, I don't know . . ." Shaking her head, she made for the kitchen, and John started down the long flagged passages that led to the stableyard. Tonight they were as cold as dungeons, eerily lighted by naked bulbs which swung in the draughts. He seemed to be surrounded by looming shadows.

He opened the back door to the outside. The wind snatched at it and nearly blew it out of his hand, and for a second that seemed like forever, he stood there in the doorway.

For ahead of him, across the cobbles of the yard, every upstairs window of Roddy's house was filled with dancing orange light. Smoke and flames gushed from the roof, and above the wind's fury, he could hear the terrifying sounds of the fire, a roar like a furnace, the splinter and crack of wood, sharp as rifle fire. Even as he stood there, a window exploded into a shatter of glass as its frame disintegrated in the heat. Instantly, flames leaped from the empty void, and John felt the heat of them sear his face.

Thomas.

He was across the yard and had opened the door before he considered the consequences. The stairs were already alight, and the wind

caught the flames and the whole edifice turned into a sort of blast furnace from which he reeled. The smoke was suffocating. He turned
from it, and holding his arm up to his face, made his way down the
narrow passage and threw open the door of the first bedroom.

"Thomas!" He had no idea where Thomas was sleeping.
"Thomas!"

Now, he was directly under Roddy's sitting room, and the smoke
was blinding; his eyes began to stream and sting, he started to cough.

"Thomas!" His voice was a croak. He plunged on through the
smoke and found the other door, the other bedroom.

Here, mercifully, the air was a little clearer.

"Thomas!"

A wail answered him. There was no time to be relieved, to give
thanks that the child had not already died from asphyxiation, for it
was clear that the charred ceiling of the room was about to give way
at any moment. As John scooped Thomas up in his arms, there came
a great load of plaster and charred lathe, spilling down from above
and making a sound like falling rocks. He looked up, and saw the
ragged crater of the hole, the inferno beyond. Thomas let out a
scream, and John pressed the child's face against his shoulder and
stumbled from the room.

He was scarcely through the door before the remainder of the
ceiling collapsed, and the floor, the carpet, Thomas's bed, everything
was obliterated beneath an avalanche of burning debris.

The London plane, fifteen minutes late on account of head winds,
could be heard long before it was seen. The dark evening was stormy,
the cloud ceiling very low, and when the aircraft did appear, it was
with great suddenness, breaking through the murk at the end of the
runway as it came in to land on the black, puddled tarmac.

Soon after this, the usual small activities began to take place.
Trucks and tankers converged on the stationary plane. Steps were
wheeled up to its side by two men in black oilskins. Doors opened.
An air hostess appeared at the head of the steps. Slowly the passengers
began to alight, to walk across the windswept apron towards the terminal building. They struggled with cases and baskets and awkwardly
shaped parcels. The wind caught their clothes, they ducked their
heads against the rain. One woman's hat blew off.

Victoria, with her hands in the pockets of her coat, stood just
inside the plate glass doors and waited. One by one the other people,

who had waited with her, claimed their various friends and relations. "There you are, pet. And did you have a good flight?" Affectionate kisses. There were two nuns met by a priest in a black biretta. "I've got a car waiting," he told them matter-of-factly. A woman with far too many children and no husband to help her, a few businessmen with briefcases.

The straggle of passengers thinned. There was still no sign of Oliver. She imagined him still sitting in the aircraft, taking his time, waiting until the first ugly rush was over. Then he would unfold his long legs, reach for his coat, and make his own leisurely way down the aisle. He would probably stop to chat with the air hostess. Victoria found herself smiling wryly, because she knew him so well.

"Excuse me." The voice spoke from just behind her. Startled, she turned. She saw one of the businessmen, with his bowler hat and his stiff collar and his briefcase. "Are you by any chance Miss Victoria Bradshaw?" He held an envelope in his hand.

"Yes, I am."

"I thought you must be. This letter's for you. Your friend asked me to give it to you."

She did not take the letter. "My friend?"

"A young man with a beard. I'm afraid I never caught his name. He asked me to give you this."

"But isn't he on the plane?"

"No, he couldn't come. But I'm sure this will explain everything."

Victoria took her hand from her pocket and took the envelope. She saw Oliver's tightly formed black writing. Miss Victoria Bradshaw.

"But where is he?"

"He just said he couldn't make the flight, and he told me what you looked like and asked me to give you the letter."

"I see. Well, thank you. I . . . I'm sorry you were bothered with it."

"No bother. It was no bother at all," he assured her. "Well, I must be off. My wife's waiting in the car, and she'll wonder what's happened to me." He began to back away, eager to be off. He tipped his bowler hat. "I'll say good-bye."

"Good-bye."

She was alone. Everybody had gone. Only a few official looking people moved briskly about. A man in overalls wheeled a trolley of luggage. Shocked, confused, Victoria stood there, with Oliver's letter in her hand. She could not think what she was meant to do with it.

On the other side of the arrivals hall, she saw a small refreshment booth. She went across the polished floor and sat on one of the tall stools and asked for a cup of black coffee. A homely woman poured it for her from an urn.

"Do you take sugar?"

"No. No sugar, thank you."

She slit the envelope and took out the letter.

"It's a terrible night, isn't it?"

"Yes it is." She opened her bag and found her purse and paid for the coffee.

"Have you far to go?"

"Yes. I have to drive to Sutherland."

"Oh, my, what a way. Rather you than me."

She unfolded the letter. He had typed it, on his battered old type-writer. She was filled with cold apprehension. With her hand closed around the mug of hot coffee, she began to read.

Fulham
Tuesday
February 24.

Victoria,

If I were any other sort of man I should start this letter by telling you that it is a difficult one to write. But I'm not going to say that, because writing is the one thing I have never found difficult, even when it has to be a letter like this one.

I am not coming back to Scotland. I have spent most of the day with my agent, and he is very anxious that I should go to New York where a director called Sol Bernstein is already waiting to sign on the dotted line and to launch A Man In the Dark—with, I hope, a tremendous fanfare of trumpets—on Broadway.

So I am going, catching a plane out of Heathrow this evening.

But he can't do this to me.
Oh, yes he can. He has.

I don't know when I shall return. This year, next year, some-time, never. Certainly not in the foreseeable future. There is too much at stake for plans to be made. Too much to think about. Too much buzzing around in my head.

I haven't made this decision without thought of you. In fact, I thought about you most of last night. The night is a good time to get things sorted out. It's dark and quiet and the truth comes more clearly. It's easier to see.

And the truth is that I could never stay with you, because I could never stay with any woman. A long time ago, when I left you for the first time, I told you that I'd never loved anybody, and it's still the same way. I suppose what I feel for you is something rather special, but still the only thing that really turns me on is what goes on inside my head and somehow putting all that down on paper.

This decision had nothing to do with what happened when we were at Benchoile. It has nothing to do with the letter that you wrote the Archers, it really has nothing to do with you. The few days we spent together were unforgettable, and you gave me the closest thing to delight that I have ever known. But they were days stolen out of time and now I have to get back to reality.

There are things that you will have to do. You'll have to get Thomas back to the Archers for one, and hand him over once more to their loving care. I still resent their hold over him. I still curl up at the sort of conventional life they will undoubtedly map out for him, but it is obvious that this is just one of those things that I am going to have to accept.

The Volvo is another problem. You probably won't feel like driving it south by yourself. If this is the case, then ask Roddy if he will take it off your hands and perhaps find a buyer for it in Creagan. Tell him I shall be writing to him.

There is also the vexing problem of cash, but I have spoken to my agent and I will put his name and address at the bottom of this letter, so that if you get in touch with him when you get back to London, he will reimburse you and cover any expenses that you may have to incur.

So that's it. I did not mean to finish on such a mundane and mercenary note. I did not mean anything to finish quite this way. But happy endings are things that don't seem to be part of my life. I've never expected them, and in a funny way, I don't suppose I've ever wanted them.

She was crying. Now the words swam and shimmered before her eyes, and she could scarcely read them. Tears fell on the paper and blurred the handwritten signature.

Take care of yourself. I wish I could end by telling you that I loved you. Perhaps I do a little. But it could never begin to be enough, either for you or for me.
Oliver

Victoria folded the letter and put it back into the envelope. She fumbled in her bag and found a handkerchief. It wasn't any good crying. With a two-hour drive ahead of her through the stormy night, she had to stop crying. Otherwise she would drive into a ditch, or a river, or another car, and have to be dragged, mangled, from the wreckage of the Volvo, and then what would happen to Thomas?

After a little the kindly woman behind the bar, unable to ignore the obvious distress of her lonely customer, said, "Are you all right, dear?"

"Yes," lied Victoria.

"Was it bad news?"

"No, not really." She blew her nose again. She tried to smile. "I have to go." She got off the stool.

"Have another cup of coffee. Have a bite to eat."

"No, I'm all right. I'm really all right."

The Volvo stood lonely in the deserted car park. She found the key and got in behind the wheel. She fastened the seat belt. High above, a hidden plane droned, perhaps coming in to land. She thought of being in an airplane, going somewhere, anywhere. She thought of landing on some sunbaked airstrip surrounded by palm trees, in a place where nobody knew her, where she could lick her wounds and start again. Like a criminal, searching for a new life, a new identity.

Which was, of course, exactly what Oliver had done, settling his few affairs with a single letter, shedding his responsibilities like an old coat. By now he would be in the transatlantic plane, high over the ocean, Victoria and Thomas already fading into the past, into forgetfulness. Unimportant. Important was what lay ahead. She imagined him, drinking a highball, filled with anticipation for the excitement ahead. A new production. Probably a new play. New York.

Oliver Dobbs.

The only thing that really turns me on is what goes on inside my head.

This was the key to Oliver, his own personal, private key. And Victoria had never come near to understanding the private obsessions of his innermost mind. Perhaps if she had been his intellectual equal, a brilliant bluestocking with a university degree, it might have been different. Perhaps if she had known him longer, or closer; if she had been a stronger personality, able to stand up to his moods. Perhaps if she had not always been so dependent upon him, had been able to give him something in return.

But I gave him myself.

That wasn't enough.

I loved him.

But he never loved you.

I wanted to make a life for him. I wanted to make a life for Thomas.

She was back to Thomas. At the thought of Thomas, the old, ridiculous, protective tenderness took possession of her. For the time being Thomas still needed Victoria. For his sake, she would be efficient, calm, practical. Thomas must be delivered back to his grandparents with as little upheaval as possible. She was herself calmly packing, buying train tickets. Hiring a taxi, taking him to Woodbridge, finding the Archer's house, ringing the bell. She saw the door opening. . . .

But beyond that her imagination shied. Because once Thomas was gone from her life, then it really was the end. It would be all over. Not simply the reality, but the dream as well.

She started the car, switched on the headlights and the windscreen wipers and moved forward, away from the little airport and out onto the main road.

Two hours later she had reached Creagan, but it was not until she had turned into the single track road that led to Benchoile that she began to realize that something was wrong. The weather conditions, unpredictable as always, had begun to improve. The wind had dropped slightly, the clouds thinned, and as these were blown to rags across the night sky, the stars were revealed, and a pale new moon rose out of the east.

But it was not starlight that warmed the darkness ahead of her, and stained the sky like the glow from a whole city full of street lamps. It was not starlight that flickered and billowed and sent great storms of smoke up into the wind. She rolled down the window and smelled the reek of bonfires. Bonfires? More likely burning heather. Someone has started to burn heather, and it had got out of control and started a hill fire. But did one burn heather in February? And even if one did, surely the fire would have been extinguished by now.

Suddenly, she was afraid. She put her foot down on the accelerator, and the Volvo surged forward, swinging around the bends of the narrow road. The brightness of the fire seemed to grow no less. She had passed the Guthrie's house, she was coming at last to the final bend of the road. Then the house lay ahead of her, the gate and the pine trees, and she knew then that it was neither heather nor bonfires that burned, but Benchoile itself.

With a roar of its powerful engine, the Volvo racketed over the cattle grid and up the slope to the sweep in front of the house. The light of flames made all as bright as day. She saw the cars lined up at random, the fire engine, the huge snaking hosepipes. There seemed to be people everywhere, all grimed and red-eyed. A man ran across the beam of her headlights, shouting instructions to a colleague, and she saw, with a shock, that it was Davey Guthrie.

The big house was untouched, although lights blazed from every window. But the Stable House . . . She brought the Volvo to a screeching halt, struggled with her seat belt, the door handle, remembered the hand brake. Panic, like the worst sort of sickness, threatened to choke her.

Thomas.

The arch to the stableyard was there, but Roddy's house was almost gone. Only the stone gable end had withstood the onslaught of the flames; it loomed, stark as a ruin, the void where the window had been bright as an eye, with the glow of the conflagration that still raged beyond.

Thomas, in his room, on the ground floor, in his bed. She had to know, but there was no time to ask, no time to wait for answers. She began to walk towards the fire, to run. The smoke was acrid in her nostrils, and the heat was blown towards her on the great gusts of wind.

"Thomas!"

"Look out there . . ." a man shouted.

She had nearly reached the archway.

"Victoria!"

She heard the footsteps coming up behind her. Arms came around her, caught her, held her. She struggled to be free.

"Victoria."

It was John Dunbeath. Because she could not hit him with her hands, she kicked backwards at his shins with the heels of her boots. He swung her around to face him.

"Don't you understand?" she shouted into the blur that was John Dunbeath. "It's Thomas."

"Listen, stop . . ." She kicked him again, and he took her by the shoulders and shook her. "Thomas is all *right*. He's all *right*. He's *safe*."

She was still at last. She could hear her own breathing, labored, like a person on the point of death. When she felt strong enough, she looked up into his face. In the glow of the fire, she saw his dark eyes, red-rimmed and bloodshot, and there was dirt all over his face and down the front of his shirt.

She said, faintly, "He's not in there?"

"No. We got him out. He's fine. He's all right."

Relief made her weak as a kitten. She closed her eyes, afraid that she was either going to be sick or faint. She tried to tell John that her legs had started to feel like cooked spaghetti, but somehow could find neither the words nor the energy to speak them. By then it didn't matter anyway. Because by then John had already picked her up in his arms and was carrying her across the gravel and in through the front door of the big house of Benchoile.

By midnight it was more or less over. The fire was out, the ruin of the Stable House a still-smoking confusion of charred stone and fallen timber. The cars John had managed to rescue, backing them out of the garage onto the grass by the loch while Roddy telephoned the fire brigade. With them disposed of, and the cans of petrol that stood about, fuel for the motor mowers and the chain saws, he had felt a little easier in his mind for the safety of the big house. But even so, the garage roof had been swallowed and destroyed in the conflagration, and all that remained within it had gone as well.

And yet, the main house stood, miraculously unharmed. Within it, in various rooms, the survivors of the household were now bedded down. Thomas had wept, heartbreakingly, not from fear, but because he had lost Piglet. There was no way to tell him that Piglet was no more. Ellen had found him some other toy, a teddy bear that had once belonged to John's father, but at the very sight of this harmless, threadbare creature, Thomas had screamed more loudly than ever, and had finally gone to sleep with his arms wrapped around a wooden engine, the paint scarred and scratched and one of the wheels long since missing.

Ellen had come through it like the tough old thing she was. Only at the very end had she given way and started to tremble, and John had sat her down and given her a brandy, and Jess Guthrie had helped the old woman to bed. For Jess and Davey had been on the scene almost before Roddy had made his telephone call, and it was Davey who organized the team of fire fighters, and helped the men from Creagan—torn so abruptly from their own firesides—to set up the pumps and go about extinguishing the flames.

As for Victoria . . . As though he were controlling, reining-in a bolting horse, John's thoughts came to an abrupt halt. But one indisputable fact stood out. She had returned from Inverness alone, and nobody had had the time nor the inclination to ask her what had happened to Oliver. As far as John was concerned, her sudden reappearance in the midst of chaos, her mindless dash towards the holocaust which was all that remained of Roddy's house, had simply been the unthinkable climax of what had so nearly been a ghastly tragedy, and then he had had no thought in his head but to grab her back from the edge of the fire and carry her to safety.

He had taken her, for want of anywhere better, to his own bedroom, placed her on his own bed. She had opened her eyes and said once more, "Thomas is really safe, isn't he?" and he had time to do no more than reassure her before Jess Guthrie came bustling in to take over with soothing words and hot drinks. Now, presumably, Victoria was sleeping. With luck, she would sleep till the morning. In the morning there would be all the time in the world to talk.

So, it was midnight, and it was over. He stood at the edge of the loch, with his back to the water, staring up at the house. He realized that he was exhausted, drained of emotion and energy, and yet beneath this aching lassitude lay a calmness and a peace that he had not known for years.

Why he felt thus was a mystery. He only knew that Thomas was alive, and Oliver Dobbs had not come back from London. He sighed with an enormous content as though, single-handed, he had successfully achieved some impossible task.

Around him, the stormy evening was slipping into a peaceful night. The wind had dropped, the clouds thinned to a few sailing shreds, like billows of mist. Above, a sliver of moon hung in the sky, and the dark waters of the loch were touched with the silver of its reflection. A pair of ducks flew over. Mallards, he guessed. For an instant he glimpsed them, silhouetted against the sky, and then they were swallowed into the darkness and their cry faded to an immense silence.

But there came other sounds. The wind in the topmost branches of the pines, the whisper of water nudging against the wooden piles of the old jetty. He looked at the house and saw the comfort of lights in windows. He saw the dark swell of the hills that rose behind it.

His hills. Benchoile hills.

He stood there for a long time, his hands in his pockets, until a fit of the shivers made him realize that he was growing cold. He turned back for a final look at the loch, and then, slowly, made his way up the slope of the lawn and so indoors.

Roddy had not gone to bed. Roddy waited still in the library, slumped in Jock's old armchair by the dying fire. John's heart bled for his uncle. Of all of them, Roddy was the one to suffer most. Not simply because he had lost his house, his clothes, his books and papers, all the personal and cherished possessions of a lifetime, but because he blamed himself for what had happened.

"I should have *thought*," he had said, over and over again, his usual loquacity overwhelmed by the potential tragedy, by the ghastly realization of what could have happened to Thomas. "I simply never thought."

But he had always piled logs onto his open fireplace, carelessly trodden out the random sparks on his old hearthrug, never bothered about a fireguard. "One of the last things Jock ever said to me was that I should have a fireguard. But I never did. Put it off. Lazy, procrastinating bastard that I am. Simply put it off."

And then, again, "Suppose Ellen hadn't had the wit to think about the child. Supposing, John, you hadn't gone along then to check . . ." His voice trembled.

"Don't think about it," John had interrupted quickly, because it didn't bear contemplating. "She did have the sense, and I did go. Come to that, it should have occurred to me to go without Ellen's prompting. I'm just as much to blame as you are."

"No, I'm totally to blame. I should have thought . . ."

Now, John stood in the chilling room, looking down at his father's brother and filled with a sympathy and affection that were, for the time being, of little use to Roddy. He was inconsolable.

A log crumbled into the dying fire. The clock showed a quarter past twelve. John said, "Why don't you go to bed? Jess has made beds up for all of us. There's no point in staying down here."

Roddy rubbed a hand over his eyes. "No," he said at last. "I suppose there isn't. But I don't think I could sleep."

"In that case . . ." He did not finish the sentence. He stirred the ashes of the fire, and put on more wood. In a moment the flames began to lick up around the dry bark. Roddy stared at them morosely.

"It's over," John told him firmly. "Don't think about it anymore. It's over. And if it helps to lessen your guilt, just remember that you've lost everything you possess."

"That's of small account. Possessions have never mattered."

"Why don't you have a drink?"

"No. I don't want a drink."

John managed not to look surprised. "Do you mind if I do?"

"Help yourself."

He poured himself a small brandy and filled the glass up with soda. He sat, facing his uncle. He raised his glass. "Slainthe."

A spark of wry amusement glimmered in Roddy's eye. "What an old Scotsman you're becoming."

"I've always been one. Or half one, at any rate."

Roddy heaved himself up in the chair. He said, "Oliver didn't come back from London."

"Apparently not."

"Why not, I wonder?"

"I have no idea."

"Do you suppose he's coming?"

"Again, I have no idea. I simply dumped Victoria on my bed, and after that Jess took over. No doubt we'll hear about it tomorrow."

"He's a strange man," mused Roddy. "Clever, of course. Perhaps a little bit too clever." Across the fireside, their eyes met. "Too clever for that little girl."

"Yes, I guess you're right."

"Still, she has the child."

"I have news for you. Thomas is not her child."

Roddy raised his eyebrows. "Really? Now you do surprise me." He shook his head. "The world is full of surprises."

"I have more surprises up my sleeve."

"You do?"

"Do you want to hear about them?"

"What, now?"

"You've already told me you don't want to go to bed. If we're going to sit here for the rest of the night, we might as well talk."

"All right," said Roddy, and composed himself to listen. "Talk."

15
WEDNESDAY

◆◆◆

John Dunbeath, bearing a tray laid for breakfast, cautiously opened the kitchen door with the seat of his pants, and made his way across the hall and up the stairs. Outside a breeze, baby sister of last night's gale, stirred the pine trees and disturbed the surface of the loch, but already a cold and brazen sun, rising in a sky of frosty blue, was beginning to penetrate the house. Roddy's old Labrador had already found a bright lozenge of sunshine by the fireplace, and lay there, supine, basking in its frail warmth.

John crossed the landing and, carefully balancing the tray on one hand, knocked at the door of his own room. From within, Victoria's voice called, "Who is it?" and he said, "The floor waiter," and opened the door. "I've brought you your breakfast."

She was still in bed, but sitting up and looking quite alert, as though she had been awake for some time. The curtains had been drawn back, and the first oblique rays of sunshine touched a corner of the chest of drawers and lay like gold on the carpet. He said, "It's going to be a beautiful day," and set the tray, with something of a flourish, on her knees.

She said, "But I don't need breakfast in bed."

"You've got it. How did you sleep?"

"As though I'd been drugged. I was just going to come down. The thing is, I must have forgotten to wind my watch, and it's stopped, and I've no idea of the time."

"Nearly half past nine."

"You should have woken me before."

"I decided to let you sleep."

She wore a nightdress lent to her by Ellen. It was peach pink crepe de chine, much hemstitched and embroidered and had, in fact, once belonged to Lucy Dunbeath. Over this, in lieu of a dressing-gown, was wrapped a white Shetland shawl. Her hair, tangled from sleep, lay forward across one shoulder, and there were dark shadows, like bruises, beneath her eyes. She seemed to John, in that moment, intensely frail. As though, if he were to take her into his arms, she would break into pieces, as fragile as china. She looked about her. "This is your room, isn't it? When I woke up I couldn't think where I was. Is it your room?"

"It is. It was the only bed that happened to be made up at the time."

"Where did you sleep?"

"In Uncle Jock's dressing room."

"And Roddy?"

"In Jock's bedroom. He's still there. We sat up talking till four o'clock in the morning, and he's catching up on his beauty sleep."

"And . . . Thomas?" She sounded as though she could scarcely bring herself to say his name.

John pulled up a chair and settled himself, facing her, with his long legs stretched out in front of him, and his arms folded.

"Thomas is downstairs in the kitchen, being given breakfast by Ellen and Jess. So now, why don't you start eating *your* breakfast before it gets cold?"

Victoria unenthusiastically eyed the boiled egg and the toast and the coffeepot. She said, "I don't actually feel very hungry."

"Just eat it, anyway."

She began, half-heartedly, to take the top off the egg. Then she laid down the spoon again. "John, I don't even know how it happened. I mean, how the fire started."

"None of us do, for sure. We were having a drink in the library before dinner. But Roddy says he made up his fire before he came over. I suppose, as usual, the logs sparked all over the hearthrug, and there wasn't anybody there to put them out. Added to which, there was the hell of a wind blowing. Once it started, the whole room went up like a tinder box."

"But when did you first realize the house was on fire?"

"Ellen came to tell us supper was ready, and then she started fussing about Thomas being on his own. So I went along to check on him, and found the place blazing away like a bonfire."

She said, faintly, "I can't bear it. What *did* you do?"

He proceeded to tell her, playing down the circumstances as much as possible. He felt that Victoria had enough trouble on her mind as it was, without adding to it by graphic descriptions of the nightmare of Thomas's smoke-filled bedroom, the collapsing ceiling, the flaming crater, and the inferno overhead. He knew that the memory of that moment would return to haunt him, like some ghastly dream, for the rest of his life.

"Was he frightened?"

"Of course he was frightened. It was enough to frighten any man. But we got out all right, through one of the bedroom windows, and then we came back here, and Ellen took Thomas over, and Roddy rang the fire brigade in Creagan, and I went back to get the cars out of the garage before the petrol exploded and we were all blown to kingdom come."

"Did you manage to salvage anything from Roddy's house?"

"Not a thing. It all went. Everything in the world that he owned."

"Poor Roddy."

"Losing his possessions doesn't seem to bother him much. What bugs him is that he feels the fire was his fault. He says he should have been more careful, he should have had a fireguard, he should never have left Thomas alone in the house."

"I can't bear it for him."

"He's all right now, but that's why we sat up talking till four in the morning. And Thomas is all right too, except that he's lost Piglet. He spent last night with an old wooden engine in his arms. And of course, he's lost all his clothes as well. He's still wearing his pajamas, but this morning sometime Jess is going to take him into Creagan and buy him a new outfit."

Victoria said, "I thought he was still there. I mean, when I got back from the airport, and saw the fire. At first I thought it was a bonfire, and then I thought it was someone burning heather, and then I saw it was Roddy's house. And all I could think of was that Thomas was in the middle of it somewhere . . ."

Her voice had begun to shake. "But he wasn't," John said quietly. "He was safe."

Victoria took a deep breath. "I'd been thinking of him," she said and her voice was quite steady again. "All the way back from Inverness. The road seemed to go on forever, and I was thinking of Thomas all the way."

"Oliver didn't come back from London." He made it, not a question, but a statement of fact.

"No. He . . . he wasn't on the plane."

"Did he call you?"

"No. He sent a letter." With some determination, as if the time had come to put fancies aside, Victoria took up her spoon again and ate a mouthful or two of the boiled egg.

"How did he do that?"

"He gave a letter to one of the passengers. I suppose he told him what I looked like, or something. Anyway, the man delivered it to me. I was still waiting. I still thought Oliver was going to get off the plane."

"What did the letter say?"

She gave up the impossible task of eating breakfast and pushed the tray away from her. She leaned back on her pillows and closed her eyes. "He isn't coming back." She sounded exhausted. "He's going to New York. He's in New York now. He flew out yesterday evening. Some producer's going to put on his play, *A Man In The Dark,* and he's gone out to see about it."

Dreading the answer, it took a certain courage to ask the question. "Is he coming back?"

"I suppose he will one day. This year, next year, sometime, never." She opened her eyes. "That's what he said. Anyway, not in the foreseeable future." He waited and she finished, "He's left me, John," as though there could be any doubt still in his mind.

He did not say anything.

She went on, her voice inconsequent, trying to make what she was saying of small importance. "That makes it twice he's left me. It's almost becoming a habit." She tried to smile. "I know you said I was being a fool about Oliver, but this time I really, truly thought it would be different. I thought he would want the things he'd never wanted before. Like maybe buying a house and making a home for Thomas . . . and getting married, too. I thought he wanted the three of us to be together. To be a family."

John watched her face. Perhaps the abrupt disappearance of Oliver Dobbs, the paralyzing shock of the fire, had acted as a sort of catharsis. He only knew that the barriers between them, her frigid reserve, were tumbling at last. She was being, at the end of the day, honest with herself, and so had nothing left to shut away from him. He was filled with a marvelous sort of triumph, and recognized this as a carryover from his private elation of the previous night.

She said, "Yesterday, on the beach at Creagan, I wouldn't listen to you. But you were right, weren't you? You were right about Oliver."

"I wish I could say 'I wish I weren't.' But truthfully I can't."

"You're not going to say 'I told you so.' "

"I'd never say that in a thousand years."

"You see, the real trouble was that Oliver doesn't need anybody. That's what's wrong with him. He admitted as much in his letter. He told me that the only thing that turns him on is his writing." She managed a wry smile. "And that was a smack in the face. I'd been telling myself it was me."

"So what will you do now?"

Victoria shrugged. "I don't know. I don't know where to start. But Oliver says I have to take Thomas back to the Archers, and I've been trying to think how I'm going to do it. I don't even know where they live, and I certainly don't know what I'm going to say to them when I get there. And I don't want to lose Thomas, either. I don't want to have to say good-bye to him. It's going to be like being torn apart. And there's the business of the car. Oliver said that if I left the Volvo here, perhaps Roddy could sell it. He said that I could drive it south if I wanted to, but I really don't want to, not with Thomas. I suppose I could get a plane or a train from Inverness, but that means . . ."

John found that he could not stand it for another instant. Loudly he interrupted her, "Victoria, I don't want to hear another word."

Halted in mid-sentence, astonished at the roughness of his voice, Victoria stared open-mouthed. "But I have to talk about it. I have to do things . . ."

"No, you don't. You don't have to do anything. I shall see to it all. I shall arrange to get Thomas back to his grandparents . . ."

". . . but you have enough to think about . . ."

". . . I shall even placate them . . ."

". . . with the fire, and Roddy, and Benchoile . . ."

". . . though, from the sound of things they're going to require some placating. I shall take care of Thomas, and I shall take care of you, but as for Oliver's car, it can rot on a rubbish heap for all I care. And Oliver Dobbs, for all his genius and his sexual prowess and whatever it is that turns him on—can rot as well. And I never want to hear that self-centered son of a bitch's name again. Is that totally understood?"

Victoria considered this. Her face was serious. "You never really liked him did you?"

"It wasn't meant to show."

"It did, a little. Every now and again."

John grinned. "He was lucky not to get his nose punched in." He looked at his watch, stretched like a cat, and then pulled himself to his feet.

"Where are you going?" she asked him.

"Downstairs to the telephone. I have a million calls to make. So why don't you eat that breakfast now. There's nothing more to worry about."

"Yes, there is. I just thought of it."

"What's that?"

"My shell. My queen cockle. It was on the window ledge in my bedroom. In Roddy's house."

"We'll find another."

"I liked that one."

He went to open the door. He said, "The sea is full of gifts."

In the kitchen he found Jess Guthrie, peeling potatoes at the sink.

"Jess, where's Davey?"

"He's away up the hill this morning."

"Will you be seeing him?"

"Yes, he'll be down for his dinner at twelve."

"Ask him to come down and have a word with me, would you? This afternoon sometime. Say about half past two."

"I'll give him the message," she promised.

> *If my true love, she were gone*
> *I would surely find another,*
> *Where wild mountain thyme,*

Grows around the blooming heather,
Will ye go, lassie, go?

He went into the library, shut the door firmly behind him, built up the fire, sat at his uncle's desk, and settled down to a positive orgy of telephoning.

He rang the office in London. He spoke to his vice president, a couple of colleagues, and his secretary, Miss Ridgeway.

He rang directory inquiries and was told the Archers' address and telephone number in Woodbridge. He made the call and spoke, at some length, to them.

With this safely behind him, he called the station in Inverness, and booked three seats on the Clansman for the following day.

He rang the lawyers, McKenzie, Leith and Dudgeon. He spoke to Robert McKenzie, and then, later, to the insurance company about the fire damage.

By now it was nearly midday. John did a few swift time-lag calculations, put a call through to his father in Colorado, dragged that good man from his early morning sleep and talked to him for an hour or more.

Finally, at the very end, he rang up Tania Mansell, dialing her London telephone number from memory. But the line was engaged, and after waiting for a little, he rang off. He did not try the number again.

16
THURSDAY

*I*t did not take very long to pack for the simple reason that they had nothing to pack. Everything that Victoria and Thomas had brought to Benchoile with them had been lost in the fire. And so they left bearing only a paper carrier containing Thomas's pajamas and the old wooden engine, which Ellen said that he could keep.

Good-byes were brief and brisk, for the true Highlander is neither demonstrative nor sentimental. As well, there was little opportunity for prolonged farewells. No sooner had breakfast been eaten in the kitchen at Benchoile than it was time to be off. Before Thomas had finished munching his toast, John Dunbeath was behaving like a family man with a punctuality complex, rounding them up and insisting that it was time to leave.

For this Victoria was deeply grateful. She even suspected that he was overplaying his role a little. His car was parked and waiting in front of the door, already loaded with his own suitcase, and John himself appeared to have deliberately taken on a new image, for he had abandoned the casual and comfortable clothes in which they were used to seeing him, and appeared at breakfast in the formality of a dark suit and a tie. The different clothes changed him. Not just the way he looked, but his entire manner. He was no longer the amiable, easygoing houseguest of the last few days, but a man used to responsibility and authority. A man to be reckoned with. He was in charge, not aggressively, but comfortingly, so that Victoria was left with the good feeling that nothing would go wrong. They would not have a puncture, they would not lose their tickets, there would be porters and reserved seats, and they would not miss the train.

"It's time to go."

Ellen put the last finger of toast into Thomas's mouth, wiped it clean and lifted him from his high chair. He wore tartan dungarees and a blue sweater, chosen for him by Jess Guthrie in the small shop in Creagan that was owned by her sister-in-law, so Jess had got a discount. His new shoes were brown lace-ups, and there was a small blue anorak with red stripes to go on top. Ellen had brushed his red-gold hair flat to his head. She was wanting to kiss him good-bye, but decided not to with everybody watching. Her eyes had a way, these days, of filling with tears at the most inconvenient moments. Running, Ellen called it. "My eyes are starting to run," she would say, blaming the wind or the hay fever. She never cried. At times of great emotion, like anniversaries or weddings or funerals, she would shake a body's hand, but nothing more. So now, "There he is," she said, setting Thomas firmly down onto his feet. "Put your coat on." She picked up the new jacket, and stooped over him to help him with the zipper.

They were all on their feet. Victoria gulping the last mouthful of coffee. Roddy standing, scratching the back of his hand, but not looking as disconsolate as she had feared he might. He seemed to have recovered with amazing rapidity from the shock of the fire and losing everything he owned. Indeed he was really being quite organized; had spent most of yesterday with the man from the insurance company, and had already started to make a little nest for himself in the big house, sleeping in his brother's old bedroom and tossing logs as carelessly as ever onto the fire in the library. The library fire was surrounded by a hearth of stone flags and a huge club fender, but still, said Roddy, he would get a proper fireguard. One of those chain curtains. He had seen one advertised. Just as soon as he could find the advertisement, he would order one for Benchoile.

"We must go *now*," said John, so they all left the kitchen and the remains of breakfast and trooped out, across the hall and through the front door. Outside, it was cold again and frosty, but it was going to be fine. It was good-bye. To the garden, the loch, the hills beyond, sparkling in the crystal clear morning air. It was good-bye to the friendly, peaceful house, good-bye to the sad charred remains of what had once been Roddy's domain. It was good-bye, Victoria knew, to a dream. Or perhaps a nightmare. Only time would give the answer to that one.

"Oh, Roddy." He opened his arms and she went to him, and they hugged. "Come back again," he said. "Come back again and see us all." He kissed her on both cheeks and let her go. Thomas, with the cheerful prospect of a car ride in front of him, had already climbed, independent of anyone, onto the back seat, had taken his wooden engine out of the paper bag, and had started to play with it.

"Good-bye, Ellen."

"It's been nice to know you," said Ellen briskly and stuck out her gnarled, red hand to be shaken.

"You've been so endlessly kind. You and Jess. I can't thank you enough."

"Away with you," said Ellen, brisk and much embarrassed. "Into the car, and don't keep John waiting."

Only John was allowed to kiss her. She had to stand tiptoe in her flat old shoes to receive his kiss, and then she had to fumble up the sleeve of her dress for her handkerchief. "Oh, my, what an edge to that wind," she remarked to no one person in particular. "It fairly makes your eyes run."

"Roddy."

"Good-bye, John." They shook hands, smiling into each other's faces, two men who had come together through a bad time.

"I'll be back sometime, but I'll call you and let you know when."

"Anytime," said Roddy.

That was all. They got into the car, fastened the safety belts, John started up the engine and they were away. There was scarcely time for Victoria to turn in her seat and wave a last farewell—scarcely time for a final glimpse of the two of them, Roddy and Ellen, standing there on the gravel sweep in front of the house. Roddy was waving, and Ellen was waving too, her white handkerchief a tiny flag. And then they were hidden, gone, lost behind the curving bank of the rhododendrons.

"I hate saying good-bye," said Victoria.

John's eyes were on the road ahead. "Me too," he said. He was driving very fast.

Behind them Thomas rolled his three-wheeled engine up and down the seat. "Meh meh, meh," he intoned to himself.

*   *   *

He played with the engine for most of the day, taking time off to sleep, to look out the windows, to be taken down the corridor at decent, regular intervals, to be given lunch, to be given tea. As the train thundered south, the weather, disobliging, degenerated. They were no sooner across the border than thick clouds rolled up, obliterating the sky, and soon the rain started to fall. The hills were left behind them, the countryside became flat and incredibly dull, and watching acres of flat, wet plough wheel past the window, Victoria's own spirits sank accordingly.

She discovered that it was all very well being brisk and sensible about your future when you happened to be eight hundred miles from it, but now, with every moment and every turn of the wheel, it was drawing closer. She felt lamentably unprepared.

It was not just the distant prospect of the remainder of her own life, which would presumably fall into some pattern of its own. As for Oliver . . . she was not thinking about Oliver just now. Later, she told herself, she would find the necessary moral courage. When she was back in her own flat, with her own familiar possessions around her. Possessions helped, whatever anybody said. And friends. She thought of Sally. She would be able to talk to Sally about Oliver. Sally's robust attitudes, her impatience with the vagaries of the opposite sex in general, would swiftly cut the whole disastrous episode down to size.

No, worse was the immediate and dreaded ordeal of having to hand Thomas back to the Archers; of having to say good-bye to him forever. Victoria could not imagine what she was going to say to his grandparents. Unfortunately, without much difficulty, she could imagine what they might be going to say to Victoria in her role of Oliver's accomplice.

There were other hideous possibilities as well. Suppose Thomas did not want to return to them? Suppose he took one look at the Archers, and burst into tears and had hysterics and clung to Victoria!

He had adjusted so easily to her in two weeks, had been so happy and become so affectionate. She found that she was torn in two opposite directions where Thomas was concerned; one half of her wanting him to need her as much as she needed him, the other shying like a frightened horse at the idea of any sort of a scene.

She looked at Thomas. He was sitting on the opposite side of the first-class carriage, his legs sticking straight out in front of him, his head, tousled by now, leaning against John Dunbeath's arm. John was entertaining him by drawing pictures with a felt pen on the pink pages of the *Financial Times*. He had drawn a horse, a cow, a house, and now he was drawing a pig.

"He's got a big nose that sticks out in front. That's for snuffling with and finding stuff to eat. And he has a tail with a curl in it." He drew the tail. Thomas's face broke into a smile. He settled down more cosily. "More," he ordered, and plugged his mouth with his thumb.

Victoria closed her eyes and leaned her head against the rain-streaked window of the train. It was sometimes easier not to cry if you didn't keep your eyes open.

It was dark long before they reached Euston, and Thomas had gone to sleep again. When the train stopped, Victoria picked him up in her arms. His head lolled on her shoulder. John carried his suitcase, and the little party stepped out onto the dark platform, into the usual confusion of barging passengers, trolleys, porters, luggage and mail vans. Victoria, weighed down by Thomas's considerable weight, felt overwhelmed. She supposed they must now trudge the length of the platform, wait in a queue for a taxi . . .

But she supposed wrong, and realized that in this supposition she had totally underestimated John Dunbeath. For from the confusion emerged a figure, grey-suited, with a grey uniform cap.

"Good evening, Mr. Dunbeath."

"George, you're a wonder. How did you know where we'd be?"

"Had a word with the ticket collector, he said you'd probably be down this end." With no more fuss, he relieved John of his suitcase. John duly relieved Victoria of Thomas. They followed the neat, uniformed figure down the length of the platform.

"Who is he?" asked Victoria, having to run every now and then to keep up with John's long legs.

"He's the office driver. I told my secretary to send him to meet us."

"Has he brought a car?"

"I hope he's brought my car."

He had. Outside the station, they were left waiting for a moment or two while George disappeared into the rainy darkness. In no time he was back, at the wheel of John's Alfa-Romeo. He got out and they got in, Victoria with Thomas still sleeping on her shoulder.

"Thanks a lot George, that was very good of you. Now, how are you going to get back?"

"I'll pop into the tube, Mr. Dunbeath. Very handy."

"Well, thanks again, anyway."

"A pleasure Mr. Dunbeath."

"How nice," said Victoria.

"Nice of him?"

"Yes, nice of him, but nice to be met. Not to have to wait for a taxi, or wait for a bus, or fight your way down the underground. Just nice to have a friendly face on a station platform."

"It makes all the difference between traveling hopefully and arriving," said John.

She knew what he meant.

The car sped west down the rain-drenched motorway. Three-quarters of an hour later, they had turned off it, and down the side road that led to Woodbridge. Now, there were little fields and hedgerows, and water meadows fringed with willows. Lights shone, here and there, from the windows of small, red-brick houses. They came over a bridge, and a train screamed past beneath them.

John said, "That's lucky."

"What is?"

Going over a bridge the same time that the train's going under it."

"What else is lucky?" She needed luck.

"Letters crossing. If you write someone a letter, and he writes you and the letters cross, that's enormously lucky."

"I don't think it's ever happened to me."

"And black cats and picking up pins and new moons."

"There was a new moon the night of the fire."

"Disregard new moons, then."

At last, the lights of the village twinkled ahead of them. They passed the sign, WOODBRIDGE. The road swung around into a curve, and the long, wide main street sloped away before them. The car idled down to a gentle crawl. There were shops and a pub with a lighted sign. A church, set back behind a stone wall.

"We don't know where they live."

"Yes, we do. It's on the right hand side, and it's red brick, and it has a yellow door, and it's the only one in the street that is three stories high. There it is."

He drew up at the pavement's edge. Victoria saw the flight of steps that led up to the door from the pavement, the pretty fanlight, the tall lighted windows. She said, "How do you know this is the house?"

He switched off the engine. "Because I rang Mrs. Archer, and she told me.

"Did she sound furious?"

"No." He opened his door. "She sounded very nice."

Thomas, disturbed by the sudden cessation of movement, chose this moment to wake up. He yawned, bleary with sleep, rubbed his eyes, gazed about him with the confused expression of a person on whom some terrible trick has been played. He still held the wooden engine.

"You're home," Victoria told him gently. She smoothed down his hair with her hand, with some vague idea of tidying him up.

Thomas blinked. The word "home" apparently meant little to him. He gazed out at the darkness. Then John opened the door and lifted Thomas and his engine up and off Victoria's knee. She reached around into the back of the car, retrieved Thomas's paper carrier luggage, and followed them.

They stood in front of the yellow front door, and John rang the bell. Almost instantly, as though the person inside had been waiting for them, there was a footstep and the door was flung open. From the bright, warm hallway, light poured out upon the three of them, so that they were caught in its beam, like actors spotlighted upon a stage.

"Good evening," said John. "I'm John Dunbeath."

"Yes, of course." He looked nice. Sixtyish, grey-haired, not tall, nor particularly impressive, but nice. He did not try to snatch Thomas from John's arms. He simply looked at Thomas and said, "Hello, old boy," and then stepped back, and went on, "I think you should all come in."

They did so, and he closed the door behind them. John stooped and set Thomas on his feet.

"I'll just call my wife. I don't think she can have heard the bell . . ."

But she had heard it. From a door at the far end of the narrow hall, she appeared. She had curly white hair and the sort of complexion that would go on being young, even when she was in her eighties. She wore a blue skirt with a cardigan to match and a rose-pink shirt with a bow at the neck. In her hand she carried her spectacles.

Victoria imagined her, sitting in some chair, trying to read, or to do a crossword, anything to fill in the time while she waited for them to bring Thomas back to her.

There was a long silence. She and Thomas eyed each other down the length of the hall. Then she began to smile. She leaned forward, her hands on her knees. "And who is this," she asked him, "that Thomas has come home to?"

Victoria was frigid with anxiety, but she need not have had any worries. For Thomas, after an astonished silence, suddenly realized what was happening. Slowly, his rosy face became suffused by an expression of total, incredulous delight. He took a single enormous breath, and let it all come out in the first proper sentence that anyone had ever heard him utter.

"It my *Ganny*!"

He flung himself towards her, and was instantly swept up, lost in her embrace.

It was all very emotional. Mrs. Archer laughed, and cried, and then laughed again, and hugged her grandson. Mr. Archer took out his handkerchief and blew his nose. From upstairs, alerted by the noise, came running helter-skelter a young girl, round and plump and pretty as a milkmaid, and when Mrs. Archer could be persuaded to relinquish Thomas, he was engulfed in yet another pair of loving arms. Finally, he was set down and allowed to go to his grandfather, who had stopped blowing his nose, and who, in his turn, picked him up, and jigged him up and down, in a manly sort of way, which Thomas seemed to find wholly satisfactory.

While all this was happening, Victoria and John could do nothing but stand and watch. Victoria wanted to go, to get away while everyone was still happy and before any possible recriminations could set in, but it was hard to know how to achieve this without appearing rude.

It was Thomas who finally put an end to the great reunion scene. He wriggled himself down from his grandfather's arms, and with deadly determination made for the stairs that led to his nursery, where he remembered leaving a number of delightful toys. His grandparents sensibly let him go, and the little au pair girl went with him. As they disappeared around the bend in the staircase, Victoria took hold of John's sleeve and gave it a tug, but if Mrs. Archer noticed this, she showed no sign of it.

"I am sorry, keeping you standing there like that. But it's all just so . . ." She wiped away the last of her happy tears, and blew her nose on a lacy handkerchief. "You must come in and have a drink."

"We really ought to go . . ." Victoria began, but Mrs. Archer would have none of it.

"Of course you must stay, for just a moment. Come along in by the fire. Edward, I am sure Mr. Dunbeath would like a drink . . ."

There was nothing for it but to follow her, through a door that led into a pleasant, chintz-upholstered sitting room. A fire flickered pleasantly from an old-fashioned grate, there was a grand piano arrayed with family photographs, there were flowers, beautifully arranged, and the sort of cushions that looked as though nobody ever sat on them.

But it was warm and welcoming and under the influence of Mrs. Archer's obvious good intentions, her obvious gratitude, Victoria began to relax a little. The men had gone, presumably, to fetch the drinks, so she and Mrs. Archer were to be left alone together for a moment or two. Cautiously Victoria let herself down onto the sofa, and Mrs. Archer did not look disappointed about the cushions being squashed.

"Have a cigarette? You don't smoke. You must be tired. You've been traveling all day. And with a little boy, too. And I know how active Thomas can be."

Victoria realized that Mrs. Archer was just about as nervous as she was, and her manner was so different from the antagonistic reception that Victoria had anticipated that she felt totally confused.

She said, "He was good. He's always good. He's been good all the time we were away."

"It was you who wrote that kind letter, wasn't it? You're Victoria?"

"Yes."

"It was sweet of you. Very thoughtful."

"Oliver was furious."

"I wanted to apologize about that. I would never have tried to ring you or get in touch, but my husband read the letter, and he was so incensed by the whole business, that I could do nothing to stop him telephoning Benchoile and having it out with Oliver. Nothing. It isn't very often," she added, her sweet face concerned, "that I don't get my own way, but there was nothing I could do to stop Edward making that call."

"It didn't matter."

"I hope not. You see, Edward never liked Oliver, even when he was married to Jeannette. But he was very fond of Thomas. And when Oliver just walked into our house, out of the blue, and stole Thomas, you can imagine the scenes. It had Helga in hysterics, poor girl, as though it could possibly have been her fault. And Edward saying he was going to put the police onto Oliver, and all the time I had no idea where the little boy was. It was a nightmare."

"I do understand."

"Yes. I believe you do." Mrs. Archer cleared her throat. "Your . . . your friend, Mr. Dunbeath. He rang me up yesterday to say you were bringing Thomas back. He told me, too, that Oliver has gone to America."

"Yes."

"Something about a play?"

Victoria said, "Yes," again.

"Do you suppose he'll come back to this country?"

"Yes, I suppose he will. Sometime or other. But I don't think he'll ever bother with Thomas again. I don't mean that he wasn't fond of him, and very good to him, but being a father isn't exactly Oliver's scene."

Their eyes met. Victoria smiled. Mrs. Archer said, very gently, "Nor being a husband, my dear."

"No, I suppose not. I really wouldn't know."

"He's a destroyer," said Mrs. Archer.

Perhaps no other person could have told her. She knew it was true. She knew something else as well. "He hasn't destroyed me," she told Mrs. Archer.

The men returned, Mr. Archer bearing a tray with glasses and bottles, and John following with a soda syphon. The conversation turned to day-to-day matters. The weather in Scotland, the weather in Hampshire, the state of the stock market, the variable fluctuation of both dollar and pound. John, without waiting for her to ask for one, quietly handed Victoria a whisky and water. This small service filled her with gratitude. She seemed to spend her time being grateful to him for one reason or other. It occurred to her then that his perception was remarkable, all the more so because he seemed to achieve it with so little fuss. He was, perhaps, the kindest person she had ever known. She had never even heard him say an unkind thing about any person, except to call Oliver Dobbs a son of a bitch, and he hadn't done that until Oliver had taken himself off to America, and there was no point in prevaricating any longer.

Now, she watched him, deep in conversation with the Archers. She saw his heavy, serious face, which could light up so unexpectedly in a smile. The dark, close-cut hair, the intensely dark eyes. He had been traveling all day with a small child, and yet he gave no sign of the sort of exhaustion that Victoria felt. He appeared as fresh and alert as the moment they had set out from Benchoile, and it was this resilience that she so envied and admired, because she knew that it was lacking in herself.

She thought, nothing defeats him. His disastrous marriage had left behind no apparent trace of bitterness. Things will always go right for him, because he likes people, but mostly because people like him.

Even over the telephone, it seemed, this genuine benevolence came through, for how else had he contrived, in the short space of the trunk call he had put through to Mrs. Archer yesterday morning, to make everything all right for Victoria, to somehow condone the circumstances of Thomas's abduction, and to pave the way for Mrs. Archer's reunion with Thomas.

One thing, she thought, I haven't had time to start taking him for granted. Before she knew what was happening, they would be saying good-bye. He would drive her to London, and leave her at the door of Pendleton Mews. There wouldn't even be the excuse of carrying luggage to invite him in and up the stairs, because she had no luggage to carry. They would just say good-bye. Perhaps he would kiss her. He would say, "Take care now."

That would be the end. John Dunbeath would walk away from her, and be instantly absorbed back into that busy, important life about which Victoria knew nothing. She remembered the anonymous girlfriend who had not been able to come to the Fairburns' party with him. Probably the first thing John would do when he returned to the peaceful familiarity of his own flat would be to dial her number and tell her he was safely back in London, "How about dinner tomorrow night?" he would say, "And I'll give you all my news then." And her voice would float back at him over the line, "Darling, how heavenly." Victoria imagined her a little like Imogen Fairburn, beautiful, sophisticated, and knowing everybody.

"We really mustn't keep you." John's drink was finished. He stood up. "You'll be wanting to go and talk to Thomas before he goes to bed."

The Archers, too, rose to their feet. Victoria jerked back to reality, began to struggle up out of the deep sofa, but John took her empty glass from her, gave her his hand, and helped her.

"I feel," said Mrs. Archer, "that we should offer you something to eat."

"No, we really must get back to London. It's been a long day."

They all went out into the hall. Mrs. Archer said to Victoria, "Do you want to say good-bye to Thomas before you go?" But she said, "No." And then, because this sounded a little abrupt, she explained. "I mean, it wouldn't do any good, upsetting him again. Not that I think he would be upset, he's obviously so glad to be home, but . . . well, I'd rather just go, I think."

"I believe," said Mrs. Archer, "that you've become quite fond of Thomas."

"Yes." They were all looking at her. She wondered if she was going to start blushing. "Yes, I suppose . . ."

"Come along," said John, putting an end to all this by opening the front door. Victoria said good-bye, and was surprised when Mrs. Archer leaned forward to kiss her.

"You've looked after him so beautifully. I can't thank you enough. He looks rosy and well, and I'm sure the little experience has done him no harm at all."

"I hope not."

"Perhaps one weekend, when the weather is better, you'd like to come down one Sunday and see him. We could have lunch. You could take him for a walk." She looked at John, including him in this invitation. "You too, Mr. Dunbeath."

"That's very kind," said John.

"You're very quiet."

"I'm trying not to cry again."

"You know I don't mind if you do cry."

"In that case, I probably won't. Isn't it extraordinary if you know you can cry, and nobody is going to become upset or embarrassed about it, then you stop wanting to."

"Did you want to cry about anything in particular?"

"Thomas, I suppose. Thomas in particular."

"Thomas is fine. Thomas is nothing to cry about, except that you're going to miss him. Thomas has got a great home, and he's surrounded by people who love him. And what did you think of that welcome he gave his grandmother?"

"I nearly cried *then*."

"I have to admit to a lump in my throat myself. But you can see him anytime you want. Mrs. Archer liked you. It isn't good-bye to Thomas. You've got a standing invitation to go and see him."

"They were nice, weren't they?"

"Did you think they wouldn't be?"

"I don't know what I thought." She remembered something. "I didn't say anything to Mrs. Archer about the fire."

"I told Mr. Archer while we were in the dining room getting the glasses out of a cupboard. At least, I told him what had happened. I didn't enlarge too much on the possibility of Thomas being frizzled to a cinder."

"Oh, *don't*."

"I have to say things like that every now and then to lay my own private specter of what might have happened."

"But it didn't happen."

"No. It didn't happen."

They fell silent. The car nosed its way back along the narrow country road. A soft persistent rain blurred everything like mist. The windscreen wipers swung to and fro.

Victoria broke the silence at last. "I suppose," she said, "I could cry for Benchoile."

"What a girl you are for thinking of things to cry about."

"It's just that I so hated leaving it."

John made no comment on this. The car traveled on, swiftly, down the winding road, but they passed the sign of an approaching lay-by, and he began to slow down. Moments later they came to the lay-by itself, and here John drew off the road, pulled on the handbrake and turned off the engine.

The windscreen wipers ceased their demented dance. There was only the whisper of the rain, the ticking of the dashboard block.

Victoria looked at him. "What are we stopped for?"

He switched on the interior light and turned towards her. "It's all right," he reassured her. "I am not about to ravish you. It's just that I want to talk to you. Ask you some questions. And I want to see your face when you answer them. You see, before we go a step further, I have to be totally and absolutely certain about Oliver Dobbs."

"I thought you never wanted his name mentioned again."

"I didn't. This is the last time."

"Mrs. Archer was talking about him. She was very wise. I didn't realize that she would be such a wise person. She said that Oliver was a destroyer."

"What did you say to that?"

"I said that he hadn't destroyed me."

"Is that the truth?"

She hesitated for an instant before replying. Then "Yes," she said. She looked at John and smiled, and it felt as though his heart was turning over. "It is the truth. Perhaps I've always known it was the truth, but I wouldn't admit it even to myself. I suppose everybody has to have one great traumatic love affair in his life, and Oliver was mine."

"What about when he comes back from America?"

"Somehow, I don't think he'll ever come back . . ." She thought about this, and then went on, in tones of the greatest conviction, "And even if he did, I wouldn't want to see him."

"Because he hurt you, or because you've stopped loving him?"

"I think I stopped loving him when we were at Benchoile. I can't tell you the exact moment. It just happened gradually. Now . . ." She made a vague gesture with her hands. "I don't think I even like him any more."

"That makes two of us," said John. "And with Oliver Dobbs disposed of, we can now go on to talk of other things. Just before I stopped the car, you said that you supposed that if you needed something to cry about, you could cry about Benchoile. And I think that this is as good a time as any to tell you that you don't have to. You'll be able to go back there, any time, and see them all, because I'm not going to sell it. At least not just yet."

"But . . . you said . . ."

"I've changed my mind."

"Oh . . ." She looked as though she were going to burst into tears, but she didn't do this. She said "Oh, *John,*" and then she began to laugh, and finally she flung her arms around his neck and kissed him.

He was immensely gratified, but as well taken totally unawares by her spontaneous delight. He had known that she would be pleased, but scarcely expected this throttling embrace.

"Hey, you'll strangle me!" But she took no heed.

"You're not going to sell it! Oh, you marvelous man! You're going to keep Benchoile."

He put his arms around her and pulled her close. She felt small-boned and fragile, and her fair hair was soft against his cheek, and she rattled on, excited as a child. "You said it wasn't viable, it wasn't practical." She drew away from him but he still kept his arms about her.

"Without your Uncle Jock to run the place, you said that Benchoile would fall to pieces."

"Like I said, I changed my mind. I'm going to hang on to it, anyway for a year, till we see how things work out."

"What made you change your mind?"

"I don't know." He shook his head, a man still confused by the reasons for his sudden volte-face. "Perhaps it was the fire. Perhaps a man doesn't realize how much something means to him until he's in danger of losing it. That night, I had visions of the whole place going up. You weren't there, but it was only by the grace of God that the big house wasn't burnt to the ground with everything else. Late that night, I went out into the garden, and just stood there, and looked at it. And it was still standing, with the hills behind it, and I don't think I've ever been so grateful for anything in all my life."

"But who's going to run it?"

"Roddy and Davey Guthrie between them, and we're going to get another man in to help."

"Roddy?"

"Yes, Roddy. It was you who pointed out that Roddy is more informed and more interested in the land than any of us. He knows more about Benchoile than I could learn in a hundred years. The only reason that he's never become more actively involved before is because he's idle, and because there was always Jock there to do the thinking for him. I have a feeling that without Jock, and with a real job to do, Roddy has a good chance of laying off the booze and astonishing us all."

"Where will he live?"

"In the big house with Ellen. You see, all my problems have been solved by one inspired decision. They'll squabble like crazy, as they always have. But the big house is large enough to contain the two of them, without one murdering the other." He thought about this. "At least," he added, "I devoutly hope so."

"You really think it will work?"

"I told you, I'm going to give it a year. But, yes, I think it will work. And what is more, my father thinks so too."

"How do you know what your father thinks? He's in Colorado."

"I called him yesterday morning, we had a long talk about it all."

Victoria could only marvel. "What a morning you had on the telephone!"

"I'm used to it. In my office I'm on the phone most of the day."

"Even so," said Victoria, "I'd never think of calling someone up in Colorado."

"You should try it sometime."

So, at least, for a little longer, Benchoile would go on. And perhaps John was right, and Roddy would take on a new lease on life. He was, after all, only sixty. Perhaps he would turn into a tremendously keen outdoorsman, felling trees and climbing hills, losing weight and generally becoming tanned and fit. The image was not particularly convincing, but there was no denying that it had distinct possibilities. And, living in the big house, perhaps he would be persuaded to enliven his social life a little. Throw small dinner parties, and have people to stay. Ellen would take the dust covers off the furniture in the drawing room, and rehang the curtains. Someone would light a fire in the fireplace, and people in evening dress would dispose themselves about the room while Roddy played the piano to them, and sang his old songs.

She said, "I know it will work. It has to work."

"So. With Benchoile and Oliver Dobbs safely out of the way, we can now get on to much more important things."

"Like what?"

"Like you and me." Victoria's expression became wary, and before she could start protesting, he went firmly on. "I thought it might be an idea for us to start over, from the beginning. It seems to me that from the moment we first met, we set out on the wrong foot, and it's only now, after all this time, and so much happening, that we're finally fallen into step. And the first thing to be rectified is that I've never gotten around to taking you out for dinner. So I thought that when we get back to London, we might go out some place. If you want we can go straight there, and eat. Or you'd maybe want to wash up first and change your clothes, so I could take you to your flat, and then come around and pick you up later. Or we can both go straight to my flat and have a drink, and then go out to dinner from there. The permutations, as you will realize, are endless. The only constant is that I want to be with you. I don't want to say good-bye. Does that makes sense?"

"John, I don't want you to be sorry for me. And you don't have to go on being kind."

"In fact," he told her, "I'm not being kind. I'm being utterly selfish, because it's what I want more than anything else in the world. I always knew I'd fall in love again one day. I didn't think that it would happen just this way. I didn't even think that it would happen so soon. But what I don't want is for you to get tangled up in a new relationship until you've had time to take a deep breath and look around and generally get used to the idea."

I don't want to say good-bye.

She thought, if this were a movie, it's where they'd start playing the really soupy theme music. Or there'd be an explosion of stars, or shots of sun shining down through branches laden with apple blossoms. None of these things was happening. There was just the car, and the darkness beyond, and the man, with whom already she seemed to have come so far.

She said, thoughtfully, "You know, I don't think I ever met any person as nice as you."

"Well, that'll do for a start," he told her. They watched each other, and she began to smile, and he took her face between his hands, and bent his dark head and kissed her smiling mouth. When he had finished kissing her, he put her gently from him, turned back to the driving wheel, switched on the ignition, started up the powerful engine. The car moved forward. Soon they came to the junction that marked the end of the quiet country road and the beginning of the motorway. The car came through a tunnel and then swept up the curved ramp. They waited to filter into the three-lane of cars which poured east.

Victoria said, "When we were with the Archers, I suddenly realized that I didn't want to say good-bye to you. But I never imagined that you wouldn't want to say good-bye to me."

A gap appeared in the traffic. Smoothly John slipped the Alfa-Romeo into gear; the engine changed tune, and the car swept forward.

He said, "Perhaps not wanting to say good-bye is just another word for loving."

The wide, fast road curved ahead of them, leading to London.

FLOWERS IN THE RAIN AND OTHER STORIES

CONTENTS

Introduction

When I wrote the preface for Rosamunde Pilcher's first collection of stories, *The Blue Bedroom and Other Stories,* I knew *she* would be getting letters from readers. But to my surprise, I did too—letters from English students researching Rosamunde Pilcher for class papers, from *Good Housekeeping* readers who wanted to share how much it had meant to them to discover her in the magazine's pages, from longtime Pilcher fans who'd read every book she'd ever written and now wanted a copy of every story of hers *Good Housekeeping* had ever published.

I even got a letter from my Aunt Margaret, in Michigan, who wrote, "I bought a new book by my favorite writer today. When I saw that you wrote the preface, I almost swooned! I never realized your work connected you to the author who gave us Penelope Keeling. *The Shell Seekers* is one of the best novels I've ever read."

My aunt continued praising Rosamunde Pilcher's writing and naming other characters from other novels. "I feel like I know them all," she wrote.

With that she echoed the sentiment expressed by each correspondent. Countless readers, around the world and across generations, are struck by the recognizability, the believability of the people

Rosamunde Pilcher creates, by the impeccably conveyed emotion in situations from tragedy to triumph.

It is rewarding to be "connected" to such an author, a privilege I share with a network of publishing colleagues, all of whom, from the beginning, believed in Rosamunde Pilcher's talent and in helping her work reach the public.

Shortly after the phenomenal success of *The Shell Seekers*, Rosamunde Pilcher and I marveled together at the overwhelming acceptance that the novel was receiving. "It seems a lot of people like to read about the same kind of details in everyday lives that you and I do," she said.

Exactly so. And many of the stories that we liked so much in the early years of her career are contained in this marvelous collection. All readers, old and new, will find here the genesis of Rosamunde Pilcher's fictional world, the inviting surroundings richly described, the intelligent, likeable characters, and the ordinary events that become extraordinary in the hands of this master storyteller.

—LEE QUARFOOT
FICTION EDITOR
GOOD HOUSEKEEPING MAGAZINE

The Doll's House

—⟨∾⟩—

Opening his eyes, William recognized the feel of Saturday morning. A lightness in the atmosphere, an ambience of freedom. From downstairs came the smell of frying bacon, and outside in the garden Loden, the dog, began to bark. He heard his mother go to open the door and call him indoors. William stirred and reached for his wrist-watch. Eight o'clock.

Because there was no urgency to be up and about, he lay for a little, considering the day ahead. It was April, and a lozenge of sunlight lay across his carpet. The sky beyond the window was a pale, pellucid blue traversed by random, slow-moving clouds. A day to be spent out of doors; the sort of day when his father would have collected the family together with a shout and an exciting, impetuous plan, piling them all into the car and driving them to the seaside, or up onto the moors for a long hike.

Most of the time William tried not to think too much about his father, but every now and then memories would come surging back, like pictures, clean-cut, and with very sharp edges. Then he would see his father striding up a brackeny slope, with Miranda on his shoulders because the climb was too steep for her short fat legs. Or hear his deep voice, reading to them on winter evenings. Or see his clever hands, mending a bicycle, or doing intricate things with electric plugs and fuse-boxes.

He bit his lip and turned his head on the pillow, as though to turn from some unimaginable pain, but that was even worse, because now he was confronted by the object that stood, accusing, on his work-table at the other side of the room. Last night, when he had finished his homework, he had laboured over this thing for an hour or more, and had finally climbed into bed knowing that it had defeated him.

Now, it seemed to his imagination, it openly sneered at him.

You haven't a hope of enjoying yourself today. You're going to spend this Saturday wrestling with me. And you'll probably lose.

It was enough to make a strong man despair. Twenty pounds it had cost him, and all he had to show for it was something that looked more like an orange box than anything else.

After a bit, he got out of bed and went across the room to examine it more closely, hoping that it would look better than he remembered. It didn't. A floor, a back, two sides; a pile of small bits of wood about the size of nail-files, and a page of baffling, incomprehensible instructions.

Glue to scotia angle to the top front edge of the front panel.

Glue window jambs to inner head cills.

A doll's house. It was meant to be a doll's house. For Miranda's seventh birthday, two weeks away. It was a secret, even from his mother. And he couldn't finish it because he was too clumsy or too stupid or possibly both.

Miranda had always wanted a doll's house, had been asking for one for the past year. Their father had promised that she would get it for her birthday, and the fact that he was no longer there had made no difference to Miranda, who was too young to understand, too young to be told that she must learn to go without.

"I'm going to get a doll's house for my birthday," she boasted to her friends while they dressed up in tattered party clothes and old ostrich feathers and totter-heeled shoes sizes too big for them. "They promised."

William, worried by this, had a conference with his mother. This took place when they were alone together, eating supper. Before his father died, he used to have high tea with Miranda and then watch television for a bit, but now, at twelve years old, he had been promoted. So, over the chops and broccoli and mashed potatoes, William said, "She thinks she's getting that doll's house."

"Oh, darling."

"We must give her one."

"They're dreadfully expensive."

"Daddy promised."

"I know. And he'd have bought her a beauty, no expense spared. But now, we don't have that sort of money to spend on presents."

"What about a second-hand one?"

"Well . . . I'll look . . ."

She looked. She found one in the local antique shop, but it cost more than a hundred pounds. A second-hand dealer produced another, but it was so tatty and shabby that the thought of actually giving it to Miranda for her birthday was somehow an insult to the child's intelligence. Together, William and his mother cased the toy shops, but the doll's houses there were horrible plastic things with pretend doors and windows that didn't open.

"Perhaps we would wait another year," his mother suggested. "It would give us more time to save up . . ."

But William knew that it had to be this year. If they let Miranda down now, he knew that she would probably never trust an adult again. Besides, they owed it to his father.

And then, the answer came. By chance he saw the advertisement on the back page of the Sunday newspaper.

> *Build your own traditional doll's house from one of our kits. Full instructions, so simple a child could follow them. Special offer, open for only two weeks. £19.50, including post and packing.*

He read this, and then, more carefully, read it again. There were snags. For one thing, woodwork was not his strong point. Top of his class in English and history, he nevertheless found it well-nigh impossible to drive a straight screw. For another, there was the question of money. His pocket money had been severely cut since the death of his father, and this he was saving to buy a calculator.

But needs must when the devil drives. The instructions were so simple, a child could follow them. And he could probably manage for a bit longer without the calculator. He made up his mind; wrote out the order form, withdrew his savings from the bank, bought a postal order and sent away for the doll's-house kit.

He did not tell his mother what he had done. Each morning he got up early and went downstairs to intercept the postman before she should see the parcel. When at last it came, he carried it straight up to his bedroom and hid it under the wardrobe. That evening he shut himself away and ceremoniously unwrapped the package, to be faced with a confusion of oddly shaped pieces of board, a polythene bag filled with very small pieces of plywood, a tube of glue, some nails, and a closely typed instruction sheet. He took a deep breath, found a hammer, lighted his lamp and set to work.

To begin with it wasn't bad, and he got the main bits of the house together. But then the problems started. There was a diagram for fitting the windows into their apertures, but the instructions might have been written in double Dutch.

Glue jambs to inner head cills, making a complete L frame all around the window.

He made a sound of disgust. It was impossible. Before breakfast, it was even more impossible. William turned from the maddening object, got dressed, and went downstairs to find something to eat.

As he crossed the hall, the telephone rang, and as he happened to be alongside, he picked up the receiver.

"Hello."

"William."

"Yes." He made a private face. It was Arnold Ridgeway, and Arnold, he knew, rather fancied William's mother. Although William could understand this, he found Arnold's company fairly heavy weather. Arnold ran the big hotel on the far side of town, and he was a widower, and very cheerful and noisy in a hail-fellow-well-met sort of way. Lately, William had begun to suspect that Arnold had private plans to marry his mother, but he hoped very much that this would not happen. His mother did not love Arnold. There was a certain private look about her that only happened every now and then—a sort of secret radiance—and William had not seen this since his father had died. It was certainly never evident when she was in Arnold's company.

There was, however, always the possibility that Arnold might wear her down with the sheer force of his personality, and she would marry him for the comfort and security of his wordly goods. She would do such a thing for his sake and for Miranda's, he knew. For her children she would be prepared to make any sacrifice.

"Arnold here!" His voice fairly carolled over the phone. "How's your mother this morning?"

"I haven't seen her yet."

"Such a lovely day. Thought I might take you all out for lunch. Drive over to Cottescombe, have lunch in the Three Bells. We could go and look at the Game Park. How does that sound to you?"

"It sounds great, but I think I'd better get my mother." Then he remembered the doll's house. "But I don't think I can come. It's very kind of you, but I've got . . . well, lots of homework to do, and things like that."

"That's a pity. Never mind. Another time. Fetch your mother, like a good boy."

He put down the receiver and went into the kitchen.

"That's Arnold on the phone . . ."

She was sitting at the table, drinking coffee and reading the morning paper. She wore her old turquoise wool dressing-gown and her beautiful red hair lay like silk down to her shoulders.

"Oh, thank you, darling." She stood up, laying aside the paper, and brushed his head with her hand as she went out of the room.

Miranda, decked out as usual in beads and ear-rings, was eating her boiled egg.

"Hello, bootface," William greeted her and went to the hot drawer to find his breakfast. It was bacon and sausage and egg.

"What does Arnold want?" Miranda asked.

"Asking us all out for lunch."

She was immediately interested. "To a restaurant?" She was a social child, and loved eating out.

"That's the idea."

"Oh, good." When their mother returned, she asked at once, "Are we going?"

"If you'd like to, Miranda. Arnold thought Cottescombe would be fun."

William said shortly, "I can't come."

"Oh, darling, do. It's such a lovely day."

"I've got things I have to do. I'll be all right."

She did not argue. She knew, of course, that there was a secret up in his bedroom, but it was always carefully dust-sheeted when she went up to make his bed, and he knew that she was too highly principled ever to peep.

She sighed. "All right. We'll leave you behind. You can have a peaceful day on your own." She picked up the paper again. "The Manor House has been sold."

"How do you know?"

"It's here, in the paper. It's been bought by a man called Geoffrey Wray. He's the new manager of that electronics factory in Tryford. See for yourself . . ."

She handed the newspaper over to him, and William read the item with some interest. The Manor House used to belong to Miss Pritchett, and this house, the one in which William and his mother and Miranda lived, had once been the gate-lodge of the Manor, so whoever bought the big house would be their nearest neighbour.

Old Miss Pritchett had been an excellent neighbor, allowing them to use her garden as a short cut to the common and the hills beyond, and letting the children pick apples and plums in her orchard. But old Miss Pritchett had died three months ago, and since then the house had stood empty and sad.

But now . . . the manager of the electronics factory. William made a face.

His mother laughed. "What's that for?"

"Sounds a bit boring. Bet he looks like an adding machine."

"We'd better not go through the garden any longer. At least not until we're invited to."

"He probably won't ever invite us."

"You mustn't have preconceived ideas. He might have a wife and a lot of jolly children for you to make friends with."

But William only said, "I doubt it," and put down the newspaper and went on with his breakfast.

He worked all morning on the doll's house. At twelve o'clock, his mother tapped at his door, and he went out onto the landing, carefully closing the door behind him.

"We're just off, William." She wore her cord trousers and a big blanket coat and smelt of her best scent.

"Have a good time."

"There's a shepherd's pie in the oven for your lunch. And take Loden for a walk if you've time."

"I will."

"But don't go through the Manor House garden."

"I won't."

The front door closed and he was alone. Reluctantly he went back to his task. He had made the staircase, gluing each little tread carefully into place, but for some reason it was a fraction too wide for the space allotted to it and impossible to fit into place.

Perhaps he had done something wrong. He went back, for the thousandth time, to the instruction sheet.

Glue stair treads to base. Glue second mid-wall to base . . .

He had done all that. And still the stairs would not fit. If only he had someone to ask, but the only person he could think of was his woodwork teacher, whom he didn't much like anyway.

Suddenly, he longed for his father. His father would have known exactly what to do, would have taken over, reassured, explained, eased the little staircase into place with his clever fingers.

His father had always made everything so simple, so right. His father . . .

Horrified, unable to do anything about it, he felt the lump grow in his throat and the half-finished doll's house and all its attendant bits and pieces were dissolved, lost, in a flood of tears. He had not cried for years; could not remember when he had last cried, and was appalled at his own childishness. Thank goodness there was no person but himself in the house; no person to see or hear or come to comfort. He found a handkerchief and blew his nose, wiped away the shameful tears. Beyond the open window he saw the warm spring day beckoning to him. He stuffed the handkerchief into the pocket of his jeans, thought, oh, to hell with the doll's house, and was out of the room and down the stairs before he had even thought about it, whistling for Loden, bursting out of the front door, running as though he were competing in a vital race, with the cool air blowing into his face, and the black sheep-dog bounding delightedly at his heels.

After a bit, when he could run no farther, and was panting and gasping, and had a stitch, it was better. He felt released, refreshed. He bent double to relieve the stitch, to embrace Loden, and bury his face in the dog's thick, dark coat.

When he had got his breath back, he straightened up, and it was only then that he realized he had forgotten his mother's stricture, and that his feet, in their headlong escape, had carried him quite naturally through the gates of the Manor House and half-way up the drive. For a moment he hesitated, but the prospect of retracing his steps and going around by the road was too tedious for words. Besides, the house had only just been sold. There would be nobody there. Not yet.

He was wrong. As he came around the last curve of the lane, he saw the car parked in front of the house. The front door was open and a tall man was on the point of emerging, with a dog at his side. Immediately, all was lost. Miss Pritchett had not owned a dog, and Loden considered this his garden. He now let out a furious *woof* and all his hackles went up. The other dog sprang to instant attention, and William grabbed, just in time, for Loden's collar.

Dark mutterings sounded in Loden's throat. "For heaven's sake, Loden, behave yourself," William whispered desperately, but the other dog was already bounding towards them, a friendly-looking Labrador bitch, ready and waiting for a game.

Loden growled again. "Loden!" William jerked his collar. The growl changed to a whine. The Labrador approached and the dogs tentatively sniffed at each other. Loden's hackles subsided, his tail began to wag. Cautiously, William released him, and the two dogs began to romp. So that was all right. Now he had to deal with the Labrador's owner. He looked up. The man was coming towards him. A tall man, with a pleasantly weather-beaten look, as though he spent much time out of doors. The wind ruffled his greying hair, and he wore spectacles and a blue sweater. He carried a clipboard and a yardstick. He looked a bit like an architect. William hoped that he was.

He said, "Good morning."

The man looked at his wrist-watch. "Actually, it's good afternoon. Half past one."

"I didn't know it was so late."

"What are you doing?"

"I'm taking my dog for a walk. Going over the common and up onto the hill. I always used to come this way when Miss Pritchett was alive." He enlarged on this. "I live in the house at the bottom of the road."

"The lodge?"

"That's right."

"What's your name?"

"William Radlett. I saw in the paper this morning that this house has been sold, but I didn't think there'd be anybody here."

"Just looking around," said the man. "Taking a few measurements."

"Are you an architect?"

"No. My name's Geoffrey Wray."

"Oh, so *you* . . . ? He felt himself grow red in the face. "But

you . . ." He had almost said, *You don't look like an adding machine.*
"I . . . I'm afraid I'm trespassing," he finished at last, sounding feeble.

"No matter," said Mr. Wray. "I'm not living here yet. Like I said,
just taking a few measurements." He turned to look back at the worn
fabric face of the house. As though seeing it for the first time, William
noticed the rotting trellis that supported the upper balcony, the blis-
tered paintwork and broken guttering.

He said, "I suppose it will need a lot done to it. It's a bit old-
fashioned."

"Yes, but charming. And most of it I can do myself. It'll take time,
but that's half the fun." The two dogs were by now quite at ease with
each other, chasing around the rhododendron bushes and searching
for rabbits. "They've made friends," observed Mr. Wray.

"Yes."

"How about you? I was just going to have something to eat.
Brought a picnic with me. Like to share it?"

William remembered the shepherd's pie, uneaten, and realized that
he was ravenously hungry.

"Have you got enough?"

"I imagine so. Let's go and look."

He took a basket from the back seat of his car and carried this
to the wrought-iron garden seat that stood by the front door. In the
sun and out of the wind, it was quite warm. William accepted a ham
sandwich.

"I've only got lager to drink," said Mr. Wray. "Are you old enough
to drink lager?"

"I'm twelve."

"Old enough," decided Mr. Wray, and handed over a can. "And
there's a fruit-cake. My mother makes excellent fruit-cake."

"Did she make the sandwiches, too?"

"Yes."

"Do you live with her?"

"Just for the moment. Until I come to live here."

"Are you going to live here alone?"

"I haven't got a wife, if that's what you mean."

"My mother thought you might have a wife and a lot of jolly children for us to play with."

He smiled. "Who's us?"

"Miranda and me. She's nearly seven."

"And where is she today?"

"She and my mother have gone out for lunch."

"Have you always lived in the lodge?"

"Yes, always."

"Does your father work in the town?"

"I haven't got a father. He died about ten months ago."

"I am sorry." He looked and sounded both distressed and genu-
inely sympathetic, but, blessedly, not in the least embarrassed by
William's revelation. "I lost my father when I was about your age.
Nothing's ever quite the same again, is it?"

"No. No, it's not the same."

"How about a chocolate biscuit?" He held one out. William took
it and looked up, straight into Mr. Wray's eyes, and suddenly smiled,
for no particular reason except that he felt comforted and at ease, and
. . . last, but not least . . . not hungry any longer.

When they had finished the picnic they went indoors and all through
the house, room by room. Without furniture, smelling chill and
slightly damp, it could have been depressing, but it wasn't. On the
contrary, it was rather exciting, and flattering to be discussing plans as
though he were a grown-up man.

"I thought I'd take this wall down, make a big open-plan kitchen.
Fit an Aga in here, and build pine fitments around that corner."

His enthusiasm dispelled the gloom even of the old kitchen, which
smelt of stone floors and mice.

"And this old scullery I'll turn into a workshop, with the work-
bench here, under the window, and plenty of space for hanging tools
and storing stuff."

"My father had a workshop, but it was in a shed in the garden."

"I expect you use it now."

"No. I'm useless with my hands."

"It's amazing what you can do if you have to."

"That's what I thought," said William impulsively, and then
stopped.

"What did you think?" Mr. Wray prompted gently.

"I thought I could do something because I had to. But I can't. It's
too difficult."

"What would you be trying to do?"

"Build a doll's house. From a kit. For my sister's birthday."

"What's gone wrong?"

"Everything. I'm stuck. I can't get the staircase to fit, and I can't work out how to put the window-frames together. And the instructions are so *complicated*."

"I hope you don't mind my asking," said Mr. Wray politely, "but if you aren't a particularly handy chap, why did you embark on this in the first place?"

"Miranda was promised a doll's house, by my father. And they're too expensive to buy. I really thought I could do it." He added, making a clean breast of his own stupidity, "And it cost twenty pounds. I've wasted twenty pounds."

"Couldn't your mother help you?"

"I want it to be a surprise."

"Isn't there anyone you could ask?"

"Not really."

Mr. Wray turned and leaned against the old sink, his arms folded. "How about me?" he asked.

William looked up at him, frowning. "You?"

"Why not?"

"You'd help me?"

"If you want."

"This afternoon? Now?"

"Good a time as any."

He was flooded with gratitude. "Would you really? Just explain it to me. Show me what to do. It won't take long. No more than half an hour . . ."

But it took a good deal longer than half an hour. The instructions had to be carefully studied, the little staircase sandpapered down and fitted into place. (It looked splendid; really real.) Then, on a clean sheet of newspaper, Mr. Wray placed all the little bits of wood in order, arranged into five small window surrounds, ready to be glued.

"You fit the glass in first, and then the frames fit round it, and keep it in place. Just like an ordinary window."

"Oh, I *see*."

Like all things, once explained, it became marvellously simple.

"You'd better paint them first and let them dry before you fix them permanently. And then the roof goes like this; and the scotia angle gets glued along the top of the front panel, so . . ."

"I can do that."

"The hinges might be tricky. It's a question of getting them quite straight so that the front panel swings straight. You don't want any sag."

They worked on, companionably, and all became as clear as light. So preoccupied was William, so involved, that he did not hear the car coming up the road and stopping at the gate, and the first inkling that he had of his mother's return was the sound of the front door opening and her voice calling to him.

"William!"

She was back already. He looked at his watch and was astonished to see that it was nearly five o'clock. The hours had flown past like moments.

He sprang to his feet. "That's my mother."

Mr. Wray smiled. "So I guessed."

"We'd better go down. And, Mr. Wray, don't say anything."

"I won't."

"And thank you so much for helping me. I can't thank you enough."

He went from the room and hung over the landing banister. Mother and sister stood below him in the hall, their faces turned up towards him. His mother carried an enormous bunch of daffodils, wrapped in pale-blue tissue paper, and Miranda clutched a new and particularly hideous doll.

"Did you have a good time?" he asked.

"Lovely. William, there's a car outside with a dog in it."

"It's Mr. Wray's. He's here." He turned as Mr. Wray emerged from the bedroom, closing the door behind him, and came to stand beside William. "You know," William went on. "He's bought the Manor House."

His mother's smile became a little fixed, as she gazed in some astonishment at the tall stranger who had so unexpectedly appeared. William hastily filled in the ensuing silence with explanations. "We met this afternoon, and he came home with me to give me a hand with . . . well, with something . . ."

"Oh . . ." With a visible effort, she collected herself. "Mr. Wray . . . but how very kind . . ."

"Not at all, it's been a pleasure," he told her in his deep voice, and went down the stairs to meet her. "After all, we're going to be neighbours."

His hand was outstretched. "Yes. Yes, of course." Confused still, she juggled the daffodils into her left arm and took the prof-fered hand.

"And this must be Miranda?"

"Arnold bought me a new doll," Miranda told him. "She's called Priscilla."

"But . . ." William's mother had still not quite got the hang of the situation. ". . . how did you meet William?"

Before Mr. Wray had time to answer this, William began to explain. "I forgot about not going through the garden, and Mr. Wray was there. We ate his picnic lunch together."

"What happened to the shepherd's pie?"

"I forgot that too."

For some reason, this broke the ice, and suddenly they were all smiling.

"Well, have you had tea?" his mother asked. "No? Neither have we, and I'm longing for a cup. Come into the sitting-room, Mr. Wray, and I'll go and put the kettle on."

"But I'll do it," said William, running down the stairs. "I'll get the tea."

In the kitchen, he laid a tray, found some biscuits in a tin, filled the kettle. Waiting for this to boil, he went, with some satisfaction, over the events of the day. The problem of the doll's house was now solved, he knew what he had to do, and he would finish it in good time for Miranda's birthday. And Mr. Wray was coming to live at the Manor House, and he was not the walking adding machine that he had feared, but the nicest person William had met in years. As well, he was willing to bet, they would be allowed to walk through the garden, just as they had done in Miss Pritchett's day, and perhaps, when the autumn came and the leaves turned gold, to pick the fruit in the old orchard.

And so, with one thing and another, he felt better about life than he had for a long time. The kettle boiled and he filled the teapot and set it on the tray and carried it through to the sitting-room. From the playroom came the sound of the television, which Miranda was watching, and from the sitting-room a pleasant murmur of voices.

"When will you move in?"

"As soon as possible."

"You'll have a lot to do."

"There's a lot of time. All the time in the world."

He pushed the door open with his foot. The room was filled with evening sunlight and there was something in the air, so tangible it almost could be touched. Companionship, maybe. Ease. But excitement, too.

All the time in the world.

They stood by the fireplace, half turned towards the newly kindled flames, but he could see his mother's face reflected in the mirror that hung over the mantel-piece. Suddenly she laughed, though at what he could not guess, and tossed back her lovely red hair, and there was that look about her . . . the old glowing look that he had not seen since his father died.

His imagination bolted ahead, like a runaway horse, only to be reined firmly in and brought to a halt. It wasn't any good making plans. Things had to happen at their own speed, in their own time.

"Tea's ready," he told them and set down the tray. As he straightened up he caught sight of the daffodils, lying on the window-seat where his mother had tossed them down. The tissue paper was crushed and the delicate petals beginning to wilt, and William thought of Arnold, and had it in his heart to be very sorry for him.

Endings and Beginnings

*T*om said, without much hope, "You could come with me."

Elaine gave a derisory laugh, which sounded like a snort from her pretty nose. "Darling, can you see my freezing in a castle in Northumberland?"

"Not really," he admitted with honesty.

"Besides, I haven't been invited."

"That wouldn't matter. Aunt Mabel would love a new face around the place. Particularly one as attractive as yours."

Elaine tried hard not to look pleased. She adored compliments and soaked them up as blotting paper absorbs ink. "Flattery will get you nowhere," she told him. "And I'm cross. You were meant to be coming down to the Stainforths with me this weekend. What am I going to tell them?"

"Tell them the truth. That I've got to go north for my Aunt Mabel's seventy-fifth birthday ball."

"But *why* do you have to go?"

He explained again, patiently. "Because somebody's got to put in an appearance, and my parents are in Majorca, and my sister's living in Hong Kong with her husband. I've already told you that three times."

"I still don't see why you have to leave me in the lurch like this. I don't like being left in the lurch." She gave him one of her most persuasive smiles. "I'm not used to it."

"I wouldn't leave you in the lurch," he swore to her, "for anyone in the world but Aunt Mabel. But she's a very special old girl, and she doesn't have any children of her own, and she was always so marvelous to us when we were young. And she must have had to go to a lot of effort to organize any sort of a shindig. I think it's very plucky of her. It would be churlish if I made no sort of effort to turn up. Besides," he finished in truth, "I want to be there." He said again, "You could come with me."

"I shouldn't know anybody."

"You would, after you'd been there for five minutes."

"Anyway, I hate being cold."

He stopped trying to persuade her. It was always fun taking Elaine to places and introducing her around to his awe-struck acquaintances, because she was so sensational to look at that Tom's own self-esteem took a welcome boost. On the other hand, if she was not having a good time, she would make no effort to hide the fact. Staying with Aunt Mabel was always a bit dicey. One's well-being and comfort depended heavily on the state of the weather, and if the coming weekend turned chilly or damp, then Elaine, hothouse London flower that she was, might turn out to be the worst possible companion.

They had dined together in their favorite restaurant, just around the corner from Elaine's little flat in the King's Road. Now Tom reached across the table, around the coffee-cups, and put his hand over hers.

"All right," he said. "You don't have to come. I'll ring you when I get back and tell you all about it. And you'll just have to say I'm sorry to the Stainforths. Say I'll take a rain-check on that invitation."

The next day was Friday. Tom, who had already squared things with his boss, left the office at lunch-time and drove north, up the Motorway. It was April and showery weather, but the roads were clear and he was able to allow his thoughts a free rein. Inevitably, they chose to chew over the problem of Elaine.

He had known her now for three months, and despite the fact that she frequently exasperated him, she was nevertheless the most engaging person he had met in years. Her very unpredictability he found delightfully stimulating, and she never failed to make him laugh. Because of this, he had taken her home once or twice for long weekends, not anticipating that his mother would find Elaine just as attractive as he did. "She's perfectly charming," she kept saying, but she was a model mother and managed, with obvious effort, not to say more. Tom, however, knew very well what she was thinking. He was, after all, nearly thirty. It was time that he settled down, got himself married, provided his mother with the grandchildren that she craved. But did he want to marry Elaine? It was a dilemma that had been tearing him for some time. Perhaps getting away from it—and her— for a little while would be the best thing that could happen. He could view the problem at a distance, as though he were studying some complicated painting; get the details of their relationship into a true proportion. The best way to start doing this was to stop thinking about her, so he put visions of Elaine firmly out of his mind and concentrated instead on the weekend that lay ahead.

Northumberland. Kinton. Aunt Mabel's party. Who would be there? Tom was the sole representative of his particular family, but what about all the other cousins? All Ned's young relations, who had formed the larger part of that gang of children who had run wild at Kinton when they were young. He ran a mental finger down an imaginary list. Roger was a soldier. Anne married and with a family. Young Ned was in Australia. Kitty . . .

Putting on speed to pull out into the fast lane and pass a thundering lorry, Tom found himself smiling. Kitty. By some confusion of generations, Kitty was Ned's great-niece. Kitty had been the rebel, the one who led the way. Kitty who fell out of the tree-house. Kitty who organized the skating party the night the lake was frozen. Kitty who slept out on the battlements because one of the others had dared her, and because she thought that she might see a ghost.

The rest of them, over the years, had, more or less, conformed. Taken typing courses and become secretaries. Been articled to chartered accountants or lawyers and finally qualified. Joined the services. Kitty had conformed to nothing. In desperation her parents had sent her to a French family in Paris as an au-pair girl, but after Madame had found her in the passionate embrace of Monsieur, she was given—unfairly, everybody agreed—the sack.

"Come home," her frantic mother had cabled her, but Kitty hadn't. She had hitched a lift to the south of France, where she met up with a most unsuitable—everybody agreed again—man.

He was called Terence, a wild Irishman from County Cork, and he ran a yacht-charter service out of Saint-Tropez. For a bit Kitty chartered yachts with him, and then brought him back to England to meet her parents. The opposition to him had been so deadly and so absolute that the inevitable happened and Kitty married him.

"But why?" Tom asked his mother when he heard this incredible news. "He's a gruesome chap. He'll make a rotten husband. Why did she marry him?"

"I've no idea," said his mother. "You know Kitty better than I do."

"She was the sort of person," Tom told her, "that you could lead with a carrot, but you could never push with a goad."

"What a pity her parents never found that out," said his mother.

Once, on the way back to London after a weekend in Sussex, he had gone to see Kitty and her husband; they had a boat on the Hamble River and Kitty was pregnant. The boat, and Kitty, were both in such a state of shambles, that Tom, without having meant to, asked Kitty and her husband out for dinner. It was a disastrous evening. Terence had got drunk; Kitty had talked nonstop, as though she had been wound up; and Tom had said scarcely anything at all. He had simply listened, paid the bill, helped Kitty get Terence back on board, and flat on his back on his bunk. Then he had left her, got into his car, and driven back to London. Later he heard that the baby was a boy. He did not see her again. He did not see either of them. Mainly he did not want to become involved.

Once, when he was a young man, Mabel told Tom that he should marry Kitty. He had bucked from the very idea, partly because she was like a sister to him, and partly because he was embarrassed, at nineteen, even to be talking about such things as lasting love and matrimony.

"Why do you say that?" he had asked Mabel, nonplussed as to why she had boxed him into this uncomfortable corner.

"You're the only person she's ever taken any notice of. If you told her to do something, or not to do it, then she'd behave herself. Of course those parents of hers have never known how to deal with her. There's a lot going for Kitty, if only they'd let her do her own thing."

"She's so bouncy, she'd wear me out," Tom had said. He was just going to Cambridge and bouncy sixteen-year-olds had no place in his plans. He was into the older woman, the skinnier and sexier, the better.

"She won't always be bouncy," Aunt Mabel pointed out. "One day she'll be beautiful."

"I'll wait for that."

The road unrolled like a great grey ribbon behind him. He was through Newcastle and now deep into Northumberland. He left the Motorway and headed into the country, through hilly moorland and small stone villages, and down steep avenues of beech. By now it was late afternoon. The sun was setting in a blaze of pink, casting rosy shadows on the undersides of large, wet-looking clouds, and tinting the blue bits of sky that showed between them to an extraordinary, translucent aquamarine.

He came at last to Kinton, rounded the squat, square-towered church, and the main street of the village stretched before him. It was an unremarkable street. Two rows of small houses, little shops, a pub. It could have been anywhere. Except that, at the far end of this street, a cobbled ramp climbed a grassy slope and passed beneath the arch of a magnificent gatehouse. Beyond the gatehouse was a high-walled courtyard as big as a rugger pitch, and on the far side of this stood the castle. Four stories high, square and turreted with the pepper-pot towers; romantic, unexpected, incongruous.

This was the home of Tom's redoubtable Aunt Mabel.

The older sister of Tom's father, horse-mad, leathery, and down-to-earth, Mabel had never been expected to find a husband. But when she was approaching thirty, love—or something very much like it—had struck. At a horse show near Basingstoke, she had met Ned Kinnerton, allowed him to buy her a half-pint in the beer tent, and was married to him within the month.

Her family had been, by all accounts, torn between delight and horror. Telephones all over Hampshire had buzzed with speculation.

Isn't it marvellous that she's found a husband at last.

He's twice her age.

She's going to have to go and live in an enormous unheated castle in Northumberland.

It's his family home. It's belonged to the Kinnertons for generations.

Imagine the winters! Let's hope I'm never invited to stay.

But Mabel loved Kinton as much as Ned did. Their union was not blessed with children, which was sad because they would have made perfect parents, but, as though to make up for this slip of nature, a selection of nephews and nieces, as often as possible, descended from all quarters of the country upon Mabel and Ned for their school holidays, and more or less took the place over. Mabel never minded what anybody did, provided no one was ever unkind to an animal. So, unchecked, they climbed battlements, slept out in a makeshift tent beneath the cedar tree, poured make-believe boiling oil from the slit window over the massive front door, swam in the reedy lake that lay at the back of the castle, contrived bows and arrows, fell out of trees.

After Ned died, everyone imagined that Mabel would move out of Kinton. But the only male relation who might have been capable of shouldering the massive responsibility of the castle had already taken off for Australia and was making a good life for himself there, and so Mabel remained. *Don't need to heat all the rooms,* she pointed out and shut off the attics by means of draping old blankets across the tops of the circular stairs. *Nice to have a bit of space for friends to come and stay.* She moved the kitchen from the dungeonlike basement to the first floor and had installed a service lift that never worked, but apart from that, life carried on as before. Still housefuls of children—now in their teens and fast growing up. Still immense meals at the long mahogany dining-table. Still dogs everywhere, smouldering log fires, snapshots stuck into the frames of mirrors and left there forever, to grow dusty and curl at the corners.

Kinton. He had arrived. He eased the car gently up the cobbled ramp, passed beneath the shadowed arch of the gatehouse. There was a notice posted which read:

> *This is a private, occupied house. You are welcome to look at it, but please don't drive cars in and frighten the dogs.*

On the far side of the gatehouse was an immense ragged lawn. The road separated and ran around this on both sides, to meet again in front of the massive front door. The encircling walls were part of the most ancient remains of the castle, and the crevices between their stones sprouted with wild valerian and wallflowers that had seeded themselves and flowered every year.

There did not seem to be anybody about. Tom parked the car at the foot of the steps, turned off the engine and got out. The evening air smelt sweet and fresh—cold after London. He went up the steps and grappled with the huge wrought-iron latch of the front door and it swung slowly inwards, creaking slightly, like a door in a horror film. Inside, the high, unheated hallway struck with a damp chill. The floors were stone, an immense fireplace stood flanked by dusty armour and crowned with a ring of ancient swords. He crossed this hallway and went through another set of doors, and now it was as though he had left the Middle Ages behind and was stepping into a set for some film taking place in the Italian Renaissance.

When he had first come to Kinton as a small boy, expecting only spiral staircases and secret passages, and small, darkly panelled rooms, he had been flummoxed by all this opulence. He had looked forward to living in a medieval castle, and felt slightly cheated. But when questioned, Ned had explained to him that a Victorian forbear had taken as his wife a lady of great wealth, and one of her conditions for marrying him was that she should be allowed a free hand with the interior of the castle. So besotted was he with this lady that he agreed to her terms, and she had subsequently spent five years and a great deal of money in transforming Kinton to a show-piece of pseudo-Renaissance splendour.

Interior walls, as much as possible, were ripped away. Architects devised the enormous curving stairway, the wide panelled passage-ways, the delicately arched and pillared windows. Craftsmen were rounded up to work in wrought iron and marble, to carve mantel-pieces, and construct immense and beautiful double doors to all the main rooms.

An Italian was imported from Florence to design and paint the highly decorated ceilings and to transform the walls of the heiress's boudoir, by means of a trompe-l'oeil mural, into a Mediterranean ter-race, complete with plaster troughs of scarlet geraniums and views of an azure sea.

After all this structural work had been completed, it was still another six months before the young couple were able to take up resi-dence. Wallpapers were chosen, curtains hung, new carpets laid in all the rooms. Furniture, some old and some new, was carefully dis-posed. The Kinnerton portraits were hung on the dining-room walls. Family mementoes were displayed in glass-fronted cabinets. Sofas and chairs were upholstered, and scattered with cushions of embroidered Chinese silk.

But since those palmy days of mad extravagance, nothing very much had been done to Kinton. Nothing had been changed or renewed, although from time to time various articles might be glued or nailed together, mended, repainted, or patched. The same cur-tains, however, still hung, in tatters of faded red brocade. The same carpets lay threadbare down the long passages. The sofas wore sagging slip-covers of some indeterminate print, and were usually covered in dog hairs. Fires smouldered in the grates of sitting-rooms, but passages and bedrooms, dark and sunless, were apt to be piercingly cold. There was a monster boiler down in the basement, and sometimes, in midwinter, if Mabel was feeling extravagant, she would get this going, whereupon a thin warmth would emanate from the huge, bulky radiators. But most of the time they stood, jeering, cold as stone.

There was a smell; musty, familiar, dear. Tom ran up the curve of the staircase, taking the steps two at a time, his hand brushing lightly against the mahogany rail that had been polished to a sheen by generations of hands doing just this thing. At the top, he paused on the wide landing. He listened. There was no definite sound, but the old walls stirred and whispered about him, and he knew that Mabel would be somewhere around.

He called her name.

"Tom! I'm here!"

He found her in the library, wearing an apron and a hat, surrounded by the usual selection of old and faithful dogs, as well as a litter of newspaper and flower stalks. She was constructing, in a priceless Chinese bowl, an arrangement of white cherry, yellow forsythia, and enormous yellow trumpet daffodils.

"Oh, my dear."

She laid down her secateurs and enfolded him in her embrace, which was something of an experience, as she was as tall as Tom, and twice as wide. Then she stood back, holding him at arm's length, the better to savour the sight of him.

Her face, he had always thought, was a man's face; strong-featured, large-nosed, square-chinned. This masculinity was emphasized by her uncompromising coiffure, her grey hair drawn tightly back and screwed into a straggling bun, but belied by the generosity of her considerable bosom.

She said, "You're looking marvellous. Did you have a good journey? How splendid of you to come. Look at me, trying to make the place look presentable for tomorrow night. Can't describe to you what it's been like. Eustace—you remember my old gardener—he's been in, shoving furniture around, and his wife's polished everything in sight, including the dogs' bowls, and the kitchen's full of caterers. Hardly know my own house. How's your mother and father?"

She picked up her secateurs and went on with her task while Tom, leaning up against a table with his hands in his pockets, told her.

"Wretched creatures," she remarked, "going off to Majorca at a time like this. I really wanted them to be here. There!" She inserted the last daffodil and stood back to admire the finished result.

"Where's that going?" Tom asked her.

"I thought on the grand piano."

"Aunt Mabel, isn't all this a frightful lot of work for you?"

"No, not really. I just tell people to do things, and they do them. It's called delegating. And we're not having a proper orchestra. Not the kind I would have liked. But nobody knows how to waltz these days, so I've ordered something called a disco. Heaven knows what's going to happen."

"Rock music and strobe lights," Tom told her. "Where's the disco going to be?"

"In the old nursery. We emptied it of all the old toys and the doll's house and the books, and Kitty's decorating it to look like a jungle."

After a bit, Tom said, "Kitty?"

"Yes. Kitty. Ned's niece. Our Kitty."

"She's here?"

"Of course she's here. She couldn't be decorating the disco if she wasn't here."

"But . . . the last time I heard of her—the last time I saw her . . . she was living in a boat on the Hamble River."

"Oh, dear, you're very out of date. That marriage broke up. She got a divorce. I'm amazed you didn't know."

"I've been out of touch with Kitty. What happened to the dreaded Terence?"

"I think he went back to the south of France."

"And the little boy?"

"He's with Kitty."

"Is she staying here?"

"No. She lives in Caxford." Caxford was a village out on the moor a few miles from Kinton. "She came to stay with me after the divorce, and then she bought this derelict cottage. Heaven knows what with, she doesn't appear to have two brass farthings to rub together. Anyway, she bought it and told us all that she was going to do it up and live there. With that, the council slapped a preservation order on it. I thought that would be the end of it, but she managed to get quite a good grant, and she's been there ever since, living in a caravan with Crispin and working with the builders."

"Crispin?"

"The boy. He's four. Nice little chap."

Tom privately decided that only Kitty would have a son called Crispin.

"But what is she going to do with herself?"

"Oh, goodness knows. You remember what Kitty was like. Once she'd got the bit between her teeth, you could never get a word of sense out of her. Do you want a cup of tea?"

"No, I'm fine."

"I'll give you a drink later on." She began to clear up the litter of her flower arrangement, but as she did this, a knock came at the door, and an unknown head appeared around the edge of it.

"Mrs. Kinnerton, that's the man with the tumblers. Where do you want them to go?"

"Oh, dear life, if it isn't one thing, it's another. Tidy this up for me, would you, Tom, and put a log on the fire . . ." And she took herself off to deal with the problem of the tumblers, the dogs at her heels and the rubber soles of her sturdy shoes squeaking on the newly polished parquet.

Tom was left in the empty room. He dutifully threw a few dead flower stalks into the fire, added some logs, and then went off to find Kitty.

The old nursery at Kinton was situated at some distance from the main rooms, and shut off from them by a swinging, studded in red baize door. It was contained within the walls of one of the many towers, and so was round, with two low, arched windows, and this in itself had made it fascinatingly attractive to small children. Normally it contained a litter of old toys and some antique, broken-springed chairs, but now, when he opened the door he saw that it stood empty. The ceiling and the walls, however, had been draped with garden netting, suspended from a central fixture in the roof, and this netting was woven with long strands of trailing ivy and sprays of evergreen.

As well, there was a tall pair of steps, and on the top of these, with pliers gripped between her teeth and a ball of green string in her hands, was a tall and slender girl, her blonde hair scraped back into a pony-tail and a look of agonized concentration on her face as she struggled with a recalcitrant branch of spruce.

As he came into the room, she took the pliers from her mouth and, without looking at him, said, "If somebody would just get this bit of ivy out of my face . . ."

"Hello, Kitty," said Tom.

She turned, at some peril to her own safety, and looked down at him. The spruce branch fell to the floor and the ivy wound itself around her neck like some pagan wreath. After a bit, she said, "Tom."

"You seem to be having a good time."

"I'm having a miserable time. I can't get anything to stay in place, and I've got cramp in my fingers from tying knots."

"It looks fine to me."

Cautiously, she disentangled herself from the ivy, tucked it away in the folds of the netting, and then turned cautiously around and sat on the top step, facing him.

She said, "I knew you were coming. Mabel told me."

"I didn't know you were here."

"Nice surprise for you."

"You're thin."

"Last time you saw me, I was large with child."

"I don't mean that sort of thin. You're really thin. It suits you."

"That's all my hard work. Have you heard about my house?"

"Mabel just told me. She told me about the divorce too. I'm sorry."

"I'm not. The whole thing was a ghastly mistake, and one that I should never have made." She shrugged. "But you know me, Tom. If ever there was a stupid thing to do, then I did it."

"Where's your little boy?"

"Around the place somewhere. Probably eating sandwich crusts in the kitchen."

She was wearing a dirty old pair of jeans and blue canvas sneakers. Her sweater was so old as to be ragged. There was a hole in one sleeve, and Kitty's bony elbow protruded from this. Looking up at her, he realized how much she had changed. Where once cheeks had curved above that stubborn chin, bones and planes and angles now showed. There were lines about her mouth, but the shape of that mouth was the same, with laughter hovering, and a dimple that appeared when she smiled.

She smiled now. Her eyes were intensely blue. He dragged his gaze away from her and searched for other things to talk about. He saw the complicated contrivance of garden net and greenery. A jungle, Mabel had called it. "Did you do all this yourself?"

"Most of it. Eustace helped getting the netting up. It's going to be a disco. Isn't Mabel a marvel? Imagine having a disco at your seventy-fifth birthday ball."

"You've made a good job of it. It looks very night-clubby."

She said rather wistfully, "How's London?"

"Same as ever."

"Have you still got the same job? With the insurance people?"

"So far."

"So far, so good. And how's your love life? Isn't it time you were getting married? Not that I'm much of an example to follow."

"My love life is doing very nicely, thank you."

"I'm glad to hear it. Here!"

He caught the pliers that she threw to him, and the ball of string, and then went to hold the stepladder steady while Kitty descended.

"Are you stopping now?"

"Yes, there's nothing more I can do . . . It'll look all right when the lights are off; you won't be able to see all the knots."

"Tell me about your house."

"Nothing to tell, really. We're living in a caravan."

"Will you show me the house?"

"Of course I will. You can come and see me tomorrow. I'll probably give you a job of work to do." She yawned. "Do you think if we went and made the right sort of noises, somebody would give us a cup of tea?"

So they turned off the light and made their way back across the landing and through the big door that led to the kitchen. There a couple of stalwart ladies were engaged in every sort of culinary preparation for the party the following day. A roasted turkey was just coming out of the oven; egg whites were beating in an electric mixer; soup steamed in an enormous pan. In the middle of all this, on the table and eating pastry scraps, sat Crispin. He was amazingly like his mother to look at, and even dressed in the same style, with the additional garnish of chocolate-cake mixture around his mouth, and a pair of suspiciously sticky hands.

Kitty went to pick him off the table. He tried to wriggle out of her arms, but she kissed his chocolate mouth and then took him to the sink to wash his hands and wipe at the front of his jersey with a damp cloth. When she had dried him off with a handy tea-towel, she brought him back to be introduced to Tom.

"This is Tom, and he's a sort of cousin. I don't know whether you call him Tom or Uncle Tom or Cousin Tom or what."

"Just Tom."

"We live in a caravan," Crispin told him.

"I know. Your mother was saying."

"But we're going to live in a new house."

"I've been hearing about it. I'm going to come and see it."

"You're not allowed to walk on the floor because it's all sticky. Mummy's been varnishing it . . ."

"It'll be dry by now," Kitty told him. "Is there any tea going?" she asked one of the catering ladies, and was informed that a tray had already been taken into the library, so they all trooped off and found Aunt Mabel sitting by the fire, drinking tea from a mug with SNOOPY LOVES YOU written on the side, and sharing a large slice of ginger-bread with four slavering dogs.

He slept that night in a brass bedstead, in a bedroom that had only a single dim light hanging from the middle of the ceiling and a howling draught which whistled across the floor-board. Investigation dis-closed the fact that this was coming from a hole in the roof of an adjoining tower room, where a row of coat hooks and some wire hangers indicated that this was the closet where he was expected to dispose of his clothes. Tom, unpacking, did this, got into his pyjamas, and then made the long journey to the nearest bathroom in order to clean his teeth. Finally he got into bed. The sheets were linen, much darned and icy to touch, and the pillowcase was so heavily embroi-dered he knew that he would awake in the morning with the pattern embossed upon his cheek.

It rained in the night. He awoke and heard it and lay listening; first a patter of drops and then a steady drumming on the roof, and then, inevitably the drip, drip, drip of the leak in the turret room. He lay and thought about his dinner jacket hanging there, and wondered whether he should get up and rescue it, and then decided that he couldn't be bothered to leave his cosy bed. He thought about Mabel, and tried to imagine how much longer she could continue to live in this vast and primitive place. He thought about Kitty and Crispin and

wondered if this same rain was drumming on the roof of their caravan. He thought about Elaine, and was glad, under such circumstances, that she had decided not to accompany him. He thought
about Kitty again. That face . . . the mouth with the dimple when she
smiled. He rolled over on his side and, still thinking about Kitty, went
to sleep, lulled by the peaceful sound of the rain.

It had stopped by the morning. Tom awoke late and came downstairs
to find a plate of bacon and eggs kept warm in the oven, and a flurry
of domestic activity already in progress. Chairs were being shunted to
and fro, crates of glasses manhandled up the stairs, tables set out,
draped in immense damask cloths, unused for years. Small vans burst
into the forecourt through the arch of the gatehouse, to park at the
front door and unload pot plants, piles of plates, crates of wine, trays
of freshly baked rolls.

One particularly disreputable van disgorged two long-haired
young men and all the trappings of the disco. Tom showed them to
the jungly nursery and left them, twined about with electrical wires,
to set up their speakers and woofers and tweeters. Then, when he
asked for a job to do, he was given the task of humping sackfuls of
logs up the back stairs, as fuel for the many open fires that were going
to be lighted.

Mabel was everywhere, large-footed, wrapped in a hessian gardening apron, apparently tireless. On his fourth trip upstairs with a
sack of logs on his back, Tom came upon her on the kitchen landing,
peacefully mixing up the dogs' dinners in their various bowls, as
though it were the most important task of the day. Which, to her, it
probably was.

He set down his sack and straightened his aching shoulders.

"This is worse than the salt mines. How many more of these do I
have to bring up?"

"Oh, my darling, I'm sure you've brought enough. I didn't realize
you were still doing it. I thought you'd stopped."

He laughed. "Nobody told me to stop."

"Well, stop now. Stop doing anything. There's nothing more to
do, and if there is, somebody else can do it." She looked at the massive watch strapped to her wrist. "Go and buy yourself a drink in the
pub. And have something to eat as well. The caterer doesn't provide
luncheon, and I daren't go into the kitchen and cook for you, I'd be
turned out."

"I thought," said Tom, "I might go and see Kitty's house."

"What a good idea. You can take her out for lunch as well. I'm sure she never eats enough. I sometimes wonder if she ever eats anything. That's why she's got so thin. And as for that little Crispin, when he comes here, he never has his hand out of the biscuit tin. Starved, most likely," she added tranquilly, and beamed down at her drooling dogs. "Who's ready for their din-dins then? Who are Mummy's darling boys?"

So Tom unloaded the last sackful into an already brimming log basket, stuffed the empty sack behind a sofa because he could not face the thought of trudging back down to the basement, cleaned himself up and went off to visit Kitty.

Caxford lay on the edge of the moor, with a distant view of the North Sea and a small and beautiful church surrounded by trees that all leaned inland, away from the prevailing wind. Kitty's house lay at the far end of the main street, set away by itself, a little distant from the last struggling row of cottages. Tom drew up at the side of the road and got out of the car and smelt the peaty tang of the moor, and heard the distant baa-ing of sheep. He saw the little house, the old walls and the new roof, the chaos of building that had churned up what had once been a front garden. He opened a sagging gate and went up a path that led around the side of the house. At the back was a great deal more land. He looked about him with interest, and saw the border hedge of hawthorn, a line of derelict outbuildings that had probably once been piggeries; in front of these was parked Kitty's caravan and a battered old car, along with a cement mixer and a selection of shovels and wheelbarrows.

Picking his way across the churned mud, he now had a view of the back of the house, and saw that on this side a whole new extension had been constructed, the new roof tiles melding with the slope of the old. Planks led across pools of mud at the side of the house to the main door, at the front, which stood open. It was a very beautiful panelled door of stripped pine, and from beyond it came the cheerful sound of pop music.

He made his way across the plank and banged on the door.

"Kitty!"

The music stopped. She had switched off her transistor. A moment later she appeared at the door, looking much as she had yesterday except for a smear of brown varnish down one cheek.

"Tom. I didn't think you'd come."

"I said I would."

"I thought you'd be too busy helping Mabel."

"I've been working like a slave, but thank God she turned me out. She said I was to come and buy you lunch." He stepped through the door and looked about him with interest. "What are you doing?"

"I've just finished Crispin's bedroom floor."

"Where is he?"

"He's gone to spend the day with the schoolmaster's family. They're terribly kind. My best friends, really. The schoolmaster's wife is keeping him for tonight as well, and she says I can change for Mabel's party in her house, and have a bath. It's not very easy getting dressed for a dance if you're living in a caravan."

"No, I can see that. When are you moving in here?"

"It ought to be ready in about two weeks."

"Have you got any furniture?"

"Enough for just the two of us to start with. It's not a very big house. Just a cottage. Not very grand."

"It's got a frightfully grand front door."

Kitty looked delighted. "Isn't it beautiful? I got it from a scrap merchant. I got all the doors from scrap merchants or junk yards. You know, people pull down lovely old houses because they are falling to pieces or somebody wants to build a factory in the garden, and sometimes somebody has the wit to save all the doors and the window-frames and the shutters. This one was so handsome I made it my front door. I think it looks really impressive, don't you?"

"Who stripped the paint off?"

"I did. I've done a lot of other things as well. I mean the builders have done all the professional work, but they're terribly nice men, and they don't seem to mind having me under their feet all the time. And if you have to pay people to strip paint off doors, it costs the earth, and, you see, I haven't got very much money. Anyway, come and look round. This is the kitchen, and we're going to eat in here as well, so it's got to be a kitchen-dining-room . . ."

Slowly they inspected the house, going from room to room, and Tom's natural interest grew to a sort of amazed admiration, for Kitty had somehow managed to see in a derelict cottage the possibilities of creating a house that was quite unique. Every room had its charming, unexpected feature. An odd little window, a recess for books, a soaring tongue-and-grooved ceiling, a skylight.

The kitchen was flagged with red quarry tiles that she had found on a dump, painfully cleaned, one by one, and laid on the floor herself. From the kitchen an open stair rose to Crispin's attic bedroom, which had a long, low window where his bed would be, so that he could lie in the mornings and watch the sun rising.

The sitting-room had not only a small charming Victorian fireplace but a gallery as well, with access by means of a ladder that Kitty had had riveted to the wall.

"That's where Crispin can go to watch television. He can get away by himself and not have to talk to people."

A fire burnt cheerfully in the grate.

"I lit the fire to see if it would draw properly. And to dry the new plaster out a bit."

"Was the fireplace here?"

"No. I rescued that from a dump, too, and set the blue-and-white tile in around it. I think it looks just right, don't you?"

She showed him a pine dresser that she had bought and was going to fill with coloured china. She showed him a chair that she had made from a barrel sawn in two. She showed him her own bedroom, which was on the ground floor and had French windows leading out onto what would one day be a terrace.

He stood and looked out at the churned mud and the piles of bricks.

"Who's going to put the garden straight for you?"

"I'll do it myself. I'll have to dig it, because there are all sorts of hideous treasures buried there. Like old bedsteads. I thought of putting a cultivator through it, but I think a cultivator would be broken in a matter of minutes."

He said, "Are you going to live here with Crispin?"

"Of course. What else would I do?"

"Sell it. Make an enormous profit. Move on."

"I couldn't sell it. I've put too much of myself into it."

"It's very isolated."

"I like it."

"And Crispin? What will happen to him? Where will he go to school?"

"Right here. In the village."

He turned from the window and faced her. He said, "Kitty, are you sure you haven't taken on too much?"

For a moment she met his gaze. Her eyes were enormous in

her thin face, their very blueness startling. Then she turned away from him.

"Look, Tom, these are my fitted cupboards. See how huge they are. And I've only got one pair of jeans and a dress to put in them. But you see, we used old shutters for the doors. They're lovely, aren't they?" She laid her hand on the satiny honey-coloured wood, and it was like watching a person caress some living creature. "There's this pretty plaster moulding. At first I thought it was carved wood and I nearly rubbed it off . . ." He saw her hand, the nails broken, the skin roughened and ingrained with dirt.

"Kitty, is this what you really want?"

She did not at once reply to this. Her hand continued to stroke the wood. He waited, and after a little she said, "In a moment, Tom, you're going to say, 'Kitty, you don't want to live here.' It's what people have been saying to me all my life. Kitty, you don't want to ride that horse. Kitty, you don't want to wear that dreadful dress. Whatever I really wanted to do my parents always told me that I didn't. How could they know? It wasn't any good telling them that I didn't want to go to Paris and be an au-pair girl, but if I hadn't gone, then I'd have been sent to some dismal place to be taught how to cook or type or arrange flowers. I'm not that sort of person, Tom. That's why, when I got chucked out of that job in Paris—and it *wasn't* my fault, Monsieur was a sexy creep—I didn't come home. I knew that if I didn't escape then, then I never would. And as for Terence, . . . if only everybody had just left me alone, I know I'd never have married him. But it started right away, just as soon as they'd set eyes on him. 'Kitty, you don't want to have anything to do with a man like that. Kitty, you don't want to spend the rest of your life living on a boat. Kitty, you don't want to marry him.' So in the end, I did. It's as simple, and as stupid, as that."

Tom leaned his shoulders against the cold glass of the French windows, and put his hands in his pockets. He said cautiously, "I wouldn't ever tell you what you want. I wouldn't know what you want. I just don't want to see you make another mistake, get into a situation that's way over your head."

"I've been making mistakes all my life. Either that, or my horoscope's gone mad, and all my stars are in the wrong order. But still, I must be allowed to do my own thing. I must lead my own life. I've got Crispin and I don't need a lot of money. And I like it here in Caxford. I like being near Mabel, I like being near Kinton and remembering all the fun we had when we were children. That's why I came back to Northumberland, and that's why I want to stay here."

"I'm filled with admiration for you, and astonished at what you've achieved. I just can't bear to think of you struggling on on your own . . ."

"You mean the house? But that's been a sort of therapy. It's got me over a lump. It's got me over Terence."

"What's happened to Terence?"

"He's gone back to France." She closed the doors of her cupboards and turned the latch, as though she were shutting Terence away. "You know, Tom, when I knew that you were coming north this weekend, I wished that you weren't. I didn't want to be reminded of that terrible evening when you took us out for dinner and Terence got so drunk. I suppose it makes me feel embarrassed and ashamed. Nobody ever likes to feel ashamed. Or guilty."

"You have nothing to feel guilty about. I think you've come through a long dark tunnel, all on your own, and you're still in one piece, and you've still got Crispin. As for Terence, you can write him down to experience."

"Then you *don't* think this house is another mistake?"

"Someone who never made a mistake never made anything. And even if it is a mistake, it's a magnificent one. Like I said, I'm filled with admiration."

"You mustn't say that. You mustn't be too kind." He realized, with some surprise, that she was on the edge of tears. He could not remember, ever, having seen Kitty cry. "I'm . . . I'm not used to people being so kind . . ."

"Oh, Kitty . . ."

"It's just talking about it. Even Mabel thinks I'm insane. I haven't been able to talk to anybody. Not like this. Not to someone like you."

"You mustn't cry."

"I know I mustn't, but I can't help it."

She felt hopelessly for a handkerchief that did not materialize, and he gave her his own one and she blew her nose and wiped her eyes. "It's just that so many things have gone wrong, that sometimes—like this winter—when I'm tired and the car won't start, and the caravan's icy cold, and there's nowhere for Crispin to play . . . I lose confidence in myself and begin to wonder if I'm ever going to get anything right, if I'm really as irresponsible as everybody keeps telling me I am. 'Kitty, you don't want to bury yourself in Northumberland. Kitty, you must think of Crispin. Kitty, you're so selfish to cut yourself off from your family.' " The tears welled once more. " 'Kitty, what are you doing with your l-l-life?' "

Tom could bear it no longer. He crossed the floor and turned her towards him and pulled her into his arms. He could feel the skinny ribs beneath the wool of her sweater, and her thick hair was soft beneath his chin.

He said, "Don't cry. Don't cry any more. I don't associate you with tears and having you cry makes me feel that the world is coming to pieces."

"I don't mean to be so stupid."

"You're not stupid. I think you're fantastic. You're beautiful and you're still in one piece, and you've got your child. That's what I think. And I'll tell you something else as well. I'm hungry. And I need a drink. Let's go down to the pub and sit by the fire and talk about cheerful things, like summer coming and Mabel's party. And after we've had something to eat, I'll take you for a drive, and we'll go and walk on the moor; or we'll go down to the beach and throw pebbles into the sea, or we'll go to Alnwick and find an antique shop and I'll buy you something marvellous for your house. Whatever you'd like to do, Kitty. You only have to say. You only have to tell me . . ."

Dusk was falling as, that evening, he drove back to Kinton. The first of the lights came on as he turned the corner of the village street, and the castle loomed ahead of him, silhouetted against a turquoise sky.

It was odd to realize that tonight, perhaps for the last time ever, Kinton would be *en fête*. Lights would shine and music would play. Cars would roll up and through the arch of the gatehouse, their headlights flashing on the ancient walls. The old and shabby rooms, flower-filled and soft with candle-light, would ring with voices and laughter.

Never again, never again. It was a miracle that the old ways had endured so long. Kinton was a ridiculous, outdated anachronism, perhaps, but no more of an anachronism than Mabel herself. It was she who had achieved so much, by sticking to what she believed in; by knowing what she wanted out of life, by being prepared to pay for it. She had turned the castle into a home, filled it with other people's children, seen only beauty in the cold and lofty rooms. She had

tended her garden, walked her dogs, gathered friends around her fireside. She had, by some stubborn contrivance, managed to hold
together the tattered fabric of threadbare carpets and recalcitrant
boilers and crumbling walls. She had been, for so long, indomitable.

Driving slowly down the street, up the ramp and through the arch,
Tom thought about that word, indomitable. And it occurred to him,
then, that Kitty and Mabel had a lot in common. They were both
unconventional to the point of eccentricity, their actions incomprehensible to ordinary beings. But they were survivors, too. In one
way or another, whatever happened, he knew that they would both
survive.

He was in his cheerless bedroom, standing at his dressing-table and
trying to tie his bow-tie in the inadequate light, when there came a
tap at his door.

"Tom."

He turned. It was Mabel. She looked magnificent in a long brown
dress of old-fashioned cut, with inherited diamonds in her ears,
and the pearls that Ned had given her on her wedding day around
her neck.

He stopped struggling with his bow-tie. He said, "You look wonderful," and meant it.

She closed the door behind her and came towards him. "You
know, Tom, I feel rather wonderful. Quite youthful and festive. Do
you want me to help you with your tie? I always used to have to tie
Ned's for him, poor man, he was incapable of deciding which end was
which." Tom, who had already made this decision stood, obediently,
while she dealt with it for him. "There." She gave the finished effort a
little pat. "Perfect."

They stood looking at each other, smiling.

He said, "Perhaps this is as good a time as any to give you your
present." He went to take it from the top of the dressing-table, a
large, flat parcel, painstakingly wrapped in crisp white paper and tied
with a gold ribbon.

"Oh, Tom, you are a dear boy. You shouldn't have brought me
anything. Just having you here with me is gift enough."

But she carried it, in obvious pleasure and anticipation, to the bed,
where she sat herself down and proceeded to undo the wrappings. He
went to sit beside her. The ribbon and the paper fell away, and the
old print, mounted and framed, was revealed.

"Tom! Oh, Tom, it's Kinton. Where did you find a print of Kinton?"

"By some extraordinary chance, in an antique shop in Salisbury. There were two or three in a sort of job-lot and this was one of them." He recalled the pleasure he had had in buying it, in finding such a perfect present for Mabel; not flinching at the inflated sum the dealer was asking. "I took it back to London and got it mounted and framed there."

She peered at it short-sightedly, because, with her evening gown, she was not wearing her glasses. "It must be very old. At least two hundred years, I should think. How very kind of you. I shall take it with me . . ."

"Take it with you?"

"Yes." She laid the picture carefully on the bed beside her and turned to him. "I wasn't going to tell you tonight, but perhaps I will, after all. It's right that you should be the first to know. I'm going to leave Kinton. It's become, all at once, too much for me. Too big and too old." She laughed. "Rather like me."

"Where will you go?"

"There's a small house in the main street of the village. I've had my eye on it for a little while. I shall do it up and put in some central heating, and the dogs and I will move there just as soon as possible, and live out the rest of our lives with the pork-butcher on one side and the newsagent on the other."

Tom, picturing this, smiled. He said, "I'm not surprised, you know. Sorry, but not surprised. Coming home this evening, driving down the street, I saw the castle and I knew then that there was no way it could carry on for very much longer."

"I'd like to have died here. But then, I might have to be very ill and old first, and what a tiresome worry I should have been to all my good friends and relations."

"You've got years to go yet."

"I'm not sorry, you know. There comes a time to end everything; like leaving a party when you're really enjoying yourself. And we've had good times here, haven't we? It's so full of happy memories for me, and I would hate to sit around and grow old, and let them all turn stale."

"What will happen to Kinton?"

"I've no idea. Perhaps someone will want to buy it for a school or a hospital, or a remand home, but I doubt it. Perhaps the National Trust will take it over. Perhaps it will just crumble to bits. It's not far from that already. Dry rot in the basement. Death-watch beetle in the west tower." She laughed and struck him a loving blow on the knee. "Bats in the belfry."

Tom laughed with her. He said, "If you want to do up the house in the village, why don't you ask Kitty to help you?"

"Oh, yes," said Mabel. "I thought we'd come round to the subject of Kitty sooner or later."

"That little house of hers. I was wordless with admiration. The work she's put into it beggars belief."

"I know. She's a maddening, pig-headed child, but one has to take off one's hat to her."

"She's not as tough as she likes people to think."

"No. She's been through a bad time. After the divorce, I asked her and Crispin to live with me for a little, but she wouldn't. She said she had to sort her own mess out for herself." She fell silent. Tom could feel her eyes upon his face, and looking up, found himself on the receiving end of her thoughtful, calculating gaze.

Before he could speak, Mabel asked him, "What did you do today, you and Kitty?"

"Looked at the house. Had lunch in the Dog and Duck at Caxford, drove to Alnwick and did some shopping. I bought her some blue-and-white Spode plates for her dresser. Then I took her home. That's all."

"You were always very close to Kitty. I think perhaps you were always the only person who really understood her."

"You told me once that I should marry her."

"And you said that it would be incestuous."

"And you said that one day she would be beautiful."

"And you told me that you could wait."

"I've waited," said Tom.

Mabel sat, vastly patient, waiting to see if he was going to enlarge upon this. When he didn't, she simply said, "Don't wait too long."

From far away, in the depths of the castle, came the faint sound of music. They listened. As though in deference to the occasion of the party, the long-haired boys with the disco had chosen to start off the evening with a selection of Strauss waltzes.

Mabel was pleased. "How pretty! But I thought," she added, as

though the complicated stereo sytem were an instrument on which
the two young men were going to perform, "that they could only
play rock and roll."

He was about to explain, when there came yet another knock at
his door.

"Mabel."

"I'm in here, come along."

The door opened slowly, and Kitty's head appeared around the
edge of it. Tom got to his feet.

"Mabel, I've been looking for you everywhere. Eustace says the
first cars are beginning to arrive and you've got to be downstairs to
greet your guests."

"Heavens." Mabel heaved herself off the bed, tidied her bun,
smoothed down the brown lace-front of her skirt. "I had no idea it
was so late." She looked keenly at Kitty. "And when did you get
here?"

"About five minutes ago. I parked my car outside the back door,
it's so dirty I didn't have the nerve to put it out in the front. Oh,
Mabel, you look marvellous. But do hurry. You've got to be there."

"I'm on my way," said Mabel. She gathered up her picture and the
paper and the golden ribbon. She kissed Tom on the cheek and made
for the door, kissing Kitty *en passant* in an abstracted sort of way, and
then was gone, her back erect, her diamonds flashing, her brown lace
trailing on the threadbare carpet behind her.

Across the room, Tom and Kitty smiled at each other. Tom said,
"Mabel is not the only one who looks marvellous." Kitty wore a dress
so utterly romantic and feminine that she was, all at once, a totally
different person. Slipper satin, white and pale blue, with a skirt that
rustled when she moved, and a neckline cut low to reveal her delicate
shoulders, her vulnerable neck. Her pale, thick hair, clean and shining
and very fair, had been arranged in a formal chignon high on the back
of her head, and there were pearl studs in her ears and a tiny jewelled
watch around one narrow wrist.

"Where on earth did you get that lovely creation?"

"It's terribly old. I had it when I was eighteen and my mother was
trying to turn me into a deb. She sent it to me in a great big box. The
poor postman could scarcely carry it."

Tom smiled. "Come in and shut the door. I'm not ready yet, but I
won't be a moment."

She did as he said, coming to sit on the bed where Mabel had sat. She watched while he put on his shoes and tied the laces, picked up his jacket and put that on too, did up the buttons, disposed of money and keys and handkerchief in various pockets. She said, "What did you give Mabel for a birthday present?"

"A print of Kinton. She says she's going to take it with her."

"Where is she going to take it?"

"To a small house in the village. She's leaving the castle."

After a little, Kitty said, "I thought she might."

"I don't know whether I was meant to tell you or not. You don't need to say anything."

"I'm just full of wonder that she's stuck it out—living here, I mean—so long. I . . . I'm glad she's going."

"So am I. Like she said, it's best to leave a party while you're still enjoying yourself. And she doesn't want to become ill or infirm, and so an anxiety to all her friends."

"If she does become old and infirm," said Kitty, "then I shall look after her."

"Yes," said Tom. "Yes, I believe you will."

From below them, the music still played. But now, as well, there was the sound of cars approaching, of voices—Mabel's friends, forgathering from all over the county to celebrate her birthday.

He said, "We should go down. We should give Mabel some moral support."

"All right," said Kitty.

She stood up, smoothing down her skirts as Mabel had done, and Tom took her hand, and together they went out of the room and down the long passage to the head of the stairs. Now the music sounded clearly. "Tales from the Vienna Woods."

Side by side, they started down the stairs. But as they descended, rounding the curve beneath the beautiful arched window, the hall below them revealed itself. He saw it, candle-lit and fire-lit, the flickering flames reflected in the curved, bubblelike surfaces of dozens of champagne glasses lined up upon a table.

Suddenly, it was a moment so important that he wanted to savour it, to spin it out, to remember it for always.

He stopped, and held Kitty back. "Wait," he told her.

She turned to look at him. "Why, Tom?"

"There'll never be an instant quite like this again. You know that, don't you? We shouldn't hurry away from it."

"What should we do?"

"Enjoy it?"

He lowered himself down onto the wide lap of the stone stair and drew her down beside him. She sat, sinking down in a whisper of satin skirts, wrapping her arms about her knees. She was smiling at him, but he knew that she understood. A combination, perhaps, of everything that could fill him with pleasure and satisfaction. The time, the place, and the girl.

Kitty. Whom he had known for the best part of his life; and yet had never known at all. She was part of it all. Part of this evening, part of Kinton. He looked about him, at the painted ceiling, the perfectly proportioned curve of the stone staircase upon which they sat together. He looked into her lovely face, and all at once was filled with joy.

He said, "When are you going to move out of your caravan and into your house?"

Kitty began to laugh. "What's so funny?" Tom asked.

"You. I thought you were going to come out with something enormously flattering or romantic. And instead you ask me when I'm going to stop living in a caravan."

"I'm keeping the romance and the flattery for later on in the evening. This is the moment for humdrum affairs."

"All right. I told you, in about two weeks."

"I was thinking . . . if you could wait for a month, I'm due for a few days off. I thought I might go to Spain, but I'd much rather come to Northumberland and perhaps give you a hand with your move. That is . . . if you'd like me to."

Kitty had stopped laughing. Her eyes, unblinking, enormous, very blue, were on his face. She said, "Tom, you must never be sorry for me."

"I couldn't be sorry for a person like you. I might admire, or be envious, or even be maddened. But pity would never come into it."

"You don't think we've known each other for too long?"

"I don't think we've known each other nearly long enough."

"I've got Crispin."

"I know you have."

"If you did come and help me—and I can't think of anything I'd like more—and at the end of it you decided you'd had enough . . . I mean, I wouldn't want you to feel that I wasn't able to be on my own . . . be independent. Do things for myself . . ."

"You know something, Kitty? You're floundering."

"You don't understand."

"I understand perfectly." He took one of her hands and sat looking at it. He thought of Mabel and Kinton. Kinton a ruin, and Mabel and the dogs living in a small centrally heated house and probably warm for the first time in their lives. He remembered Kitty sleeping out on the battlements, stubborn and resolute and brave, and he thought of her son Crispin lying in his bed in Kitty's new house, and watching, through the window, the sun rise.

Kitty's hand was ingrained and rough and broken-nailed, but he thought it beautiful. He raised it to his lips and planted a kiss in her palm and folded her fingers over it as though he had given her a present.

"What's that for?" she asked him.

"Endings," he told her. "And beginnings. Perhaps we'd better move."

And so he stood, still holding her hand, and gently pulled Kitty to her feet. Then together, side by side, they went on down the stairs.

Flowers in the Rain

*T*hrough thick, wetting mist and a cold east wind, the slow, stopping country bus finally ground its way up the last incline towards the village. We had left Relkirk an hour before, and as the winding road climbed up into the hills, the weather had worsened, turning from an overcast, but dry afternoon, to this sodden, cheerless day.

"Aye, it's driech," the conductor commented, taking the fare from a fat country woman with a pair of carrier bags filled with her morning's shopping. And the very word, *driech*, took me back into the past, and made me feel that I was almost coming home.

I rubbed a patch of clear glass on the window and looked hopefully out. Saw stone walls, the vague shapes of silver birch and larch. Small turnings led to invisible farmsteads, lost in the murk, but by now I recognized the road, and knew that in a moment we should cross the bridge and draw, at last, into the main street of the village.

I was sitting by the window. "Excuse me," I said to the man next to me. "I have to get out at the next stop."

"Oh, aye." He heaved himself out of his seat and stood in the aisle to let me pass. "It's no' a very good day."

"No. It's horrible."

I made my way to the front of the bus. We crossed the bridge and the next moment were there, halted by the pavement in front of Mrs. McLaren's shop.

EFFIE MCLAREN
LACHLAN GENERAL STORES
POST OFFICE

The sign over her door read the same it had read ever since I could remember. The door of the bus opened. I thanked the conductor and stepped down, followed by one or two other passengers who were alighting.

"Aye, aye," we all agreed, "it is a terrible day."

They went their separate ways, but I stayed where I was, standing on the pavement by the bus-stop. I waited until the bus pulled out; until the sound of its grinding engine had died away, up and around the next bend in the road. The silence filled up with other sounds. The bubbling, watery chuckle of the river. The bleat of unseen sheep. The sough of wind through the pines on the hillside above me. All blessedly familiar. Unchanged.

I and my three brothers had first come to Lachlan, one Easter time, with our parents, when I was about ten. After that the holiday became an annual event. Our home was in Edinburgh, where my father was a schoolmaster, but both my parents loved fishing, and each year rented the same little cottage from Mrs. Farquhar, who lived in what was always known as the "Big Hoose."

They were wonderful times. While my mother and father flogged the river, or sat for hours in a boat in the middle of the loch, we children were left to our own devices, running wild over the heathery hillsides, swimming in icy pools, guddling for trout, or hiking, professionally haversacked, to some distant beauty spot. As well, we were absorbed into the local village life. My father sometimes played the harmonium in the Presbyterian church on Sunday mornings; my mother was asked to demonstrate Italian quilting to the Women's Rural Institute, and my brothers and I were included in school outings and concerts.

But the best—and this added real glamour to our yearly excursions—was the endless hospitality of Mrs. Farquhar herself. A widow, and quite elderly, she genuinely loved people, and there was always a selection of friends, their children, nephews and nieces, perhaps a godchild or two, staying in the house.

But only one grandson, the only son of Mrs. Farquhar's only son.

We were, from the first, automatically included in any ploy that might have been planned. Perhaps tennis, or a tea-party, or a paper-chase, or a picnic. I remembered how the front door of the Big House stood always open; the dining-room table laid for the next generous meal; the fire in her sitting-room always lighted, blazing and welcoming. I think of daffodils and I think of the Big House at Lachlan at Easter time. Drifts of them in the wild garden, bowlfuls of them indoors, filling the rooms with their heavy scent.

When I told my mother, over the telephone, that I was coming to Relkirk to work for a month, she had said at once, "I wonder if you'll be able to get up to Lachlan?"

"I'm sure they'll give me a day off. They'll have to, some time, or I'll collapse. I can catch a bus and make a visit. Go and see Mrs. Farquhar."

"Yes . . ." My mother didn't sound too sure about this.

"Why shouldn't I go and see her? Do you think she wouldn't remember us?"

"Darling, of course she would, and she'd adore to see you. It's just that I don't think she's been awfully well . . . I heard something about a stroke, or a heart attack. But perhaps she's better now. Anyway, you could always ring up first . . ."

But I hadn't rung up first. Presented with a day to myself, I had simply got myself to the bus-stop in Relkirk and boarded the country bus. And now I was here, standing like a lunatic in the driving rain and already drenched. I crossed the pavement and went into the post office, and the bell above the door went *ting*, and I was met by the familiar smell of paraffin mixed with oranges and cloves and the smell of sweets.

The shop was empty. It always was. It always had been empty, unless there was actually some customer there, buying stamps or chocolate, or cans of peaches, or button thread. Mrs. McLaren preferred to live in her back room, beyond the bead curtain, where she drank cups of tea and talked to her cat. I could hear her now. "Well, now, Tiddles, and who will that be?" A few shuffling steps, and she appeared through the beads, with her flowered pinafore, and her brown beret, worn well down over her eyebrows. We had never seen her without that beret. My brother Roger insisted that, underneath it, she had no hair, was as bald as Kojak.

"Well, and what a terrible day it's turned into. And what can I be doing for you?"

I said, "Hello, Mrs. McLaren."

She eyed me across the counter, frowning. I pulled off my woollen hat and shook out my hair and at once recognition dawned in her face. Her mouth opened in delight, her hands went up in the classic gesture of astonishment. "And if it isn't Lavinia Hunter! What a surprise. My, you've grown! However long is it since you were last here?"

"It must be five years."

"We've missed you all."

"We've missed coming, too. But my father died, and my mother went to live in Gloucestershire, near her sister. And my brothers seem to be living all over the world."

"I'm sorry to hear about your father. He was a dear man. And how about yourself? What are you doing?"

"I'm a nurse."

"But that's splendid. In a hospital?"

"No. I was in a hospital. But now I do private nursing. I'm with a family in Relkirk, just for a month, helping to look after two children and a new baby. I'd have been up to see you all before, but it's not very easy to get time off."

"No, no, you'll be busy."

"I . . . I thought I might go and see Mrs. Farquhar."

"Oh, dear." Mrs. McLaren's cheerful expression changed to one of sadness and gloom. "Poor Mrs. Farquhar. She had a wee stroke, and she's been going downhill, by all accounts, ever since. The house is changed now, not the way it used to be with all of you running around. Just the old lady upstairs in her bed, and two nurses, night and day. Mary and Sandy Reekie are still there, she doing the cooking and he taking care of the garden, but Mary says it's a chilling business cooking for just the nurses, for poor Mrs. Farquhar takes no more than a wee cup of baby food."

"Oh, I am sorry. You don't think there's any point my going up, then?"

"And why not? She might just be having a good day, and then, who knows the good it would do her to see a cheerful young face about the place."

"Doesn't anybody come to stay any more?" It was sad to think of the big house so bleak.

"Well, it wouldn't work, would it? Mary Reekie told me the one person Mrs. Farquhar wanted to see was Rory, and she told the minister, too, and he wrote to Rory, but Rory's in America and I don't know if there was ever any reply to the letter."

Rory. Mrs. Farquhar's grandson. What had prompted Mrs. McLaren to suddenly come out with his name? I looked at her across the counter and tried to detect some glimmer of unexplained Highland intuition. But her faded eyes remained innocent and met my own with an untroubled gaze. I told myself that she could not guess at the pounding that started up in the region of my heart at the very mention of his name. Rory Farquhar. I had always thought of him as Rory, and will write of him that way, but in fact his name was spelt, with Gaelic inconsistence, R-u-a-r-a-i-d-h.

I fell in love with Rory, one remembered sunny spring, when I was sixteen and he was twenty. I had never been in love before and it had the effect of making me, not dreamy, but intensely perceptive; so that objects, previously unnoticed, became beautiful; leaves and trees, flowers, chairs, dishes, firelight—everything was touched with the magic of a spell-binding novelty, as though I had never known any of these ordinary day-to-day things before.

There were many picnics that spring, and swimming in the loch and tennis parties, but the best was the idleness, the casual getting to know each other. Lying on the lawn in front of the Big House, watching some person practising his casting, with a scrap of sheep wool instead of a fly to weight the line. Or walking down to the farm in the evenings to fetch the milk, or helping the farmer's wife to bottle-feed the abandoned lamb who lived by her kitchen fireside.

At the end of those holidays Mrs. Farquhar arranged a little party. We cleared the old billiard-room of furniture and put on the record-player, and danced reels. And Rory wore his kilt and an old khaki shirt that had belonged to his father, and showed me the steps and spun me till I was breathless. It was at the end of that evening that he kissed me, but it didn't do much good because he was going back to London the next morning, and I could never be sure if it was a kiss of affection or a kiss of goodbye.

After he went, I lived in a fantasy world of getting letters and phone calls from him, and having him realize that he could not live without me. But all that happened was that he started working in London, with his father's firm, and after that he did not come back to Lachlan for Easter. If he did take a few days off in the spring, Mrs. Farquhar told me that he was going skiing, and I imagined rich and elegant girls in dashing ski-clothes and felt sick with jealousy.

Once I stole a photograph of Rory out of an old album I found in a bookcase in Mrs. Farquhar's library. It had come loose and fallen out of the shabby pages, so it wasn't really stealing. I picked it up and put it in my pocket and later between the pages of my diary. I always kept it, although I never saw Rory again, and since my father died and we stopped coming to Lachlan, I had heard no news of him.

And now Mrs. McLaren had said his name, and I remembered that young Rory, with his worn kilt and his brown face and dark hair.

I said, "What's he doing in America?"

"Oh, some business or other, in New York. *His* father died too, you know. I think that was the start of Mrs. Farquhar getting so ill. She never lost heart, but she aged a lot."

"I expect Rory's a married man now, with a string of children."

"No, no. Rory never married."

I said, lying, "I'd forgotten about Rory."

"Ah, you'll have other things to think about with your nursing and your fine job."

We talked a little longer, and then I bought some chocolate from her and said goodbye and went out of the shop and set off in the direction of the big house. I tore the paper from the chocolate and bit off a chunk. Eaten thus, in the open air, it tasted just the way it used to.

I'll just go and see, I told myself. *I'll just go and ring at the door, and if the nurse sends me packing, it won't matter.*

A woman was coming towards me down the street, carrying a shopping basket and dressed in the countrywoman's uniform of head-scarf, tweed skirt, and sleeveless quilted waistcoat in that horrible sludgy green colour.

I can't come all this way and not just try.

She stopped. "Lavinia."

I stopped, too. It was certainly a day for being recognized. My heart sank. "Hello, Mrs. Fellows."

I *would* meet her. Stella Fellows, the one woman in the village my mother could never bring herself to like. She and her husband, who had been a lawyer, had built themselves a house in Lachlan after his retirement and had settled permanently. He was a manic fisherman and always said "Tight Lines" instead of "Cheers" when he took a drink, and she was enormously efficient and spent most of her time trying to dragoon the village ladies into attending unsuitable Arts Council lectures, or involving them in money-making events for charity. The village ladies were polite and charming, but despite Stella Fellows's enthusiasm, the events were never very lucrative. She could never think why, and we were all far too kind to tell her.

"What a surprise! I couldn't believe it was you. What on earth are you doing here?"

I told her, as I had told Mrs. McLaren.

"But my dear, you must come and see us. Lionel would love to have a glimpse of you." *Tight Lines.* "Anyway, he's bored stiff today. He was meant to be fishing, but it was called off."

"It . . . it's very kind of you, but actually I'm on my way to see Mrs. Farquhar."

"Mrs. Farquhar!" Her voice rose an octave. "But hasn't anybody told you? She's dying."

I could have hit her.

"Had this appalling stroke a couple of months ago. My dear, nurses day and night. It's no good going to see her, she just lies like a log. We do what we can, of course, but I'm afraid social visiting is just a waste of time. So sad, when you remember how wonderful she was, and how much she's always done for the village. But of course, now that the house is no longer a free meal-ticket, none of her so-called friends come near her. And as for her family"—her mouth buttoned—"I could kill that Rory. There he is, sitting in New York, and he's never been to see her. You'd think, when he'll obviously inherit the place . . ."

I couldn't bear to listen to any person talking about Rory, and certainly not Stella Fellows.

I said, "I am sorry. I really must be on my way. I haven't much time before the last bus back to Relkirk."

"You're going to the Big House, then?" She made it sound as though I was deliberately defying her.

"Yes. I am."

"Oh, all right. But if you have a moment to spare before you do catch the bus, be sure to pop in . . ."

"Of course." I thought of their modern house, with the picture window framing the rain, and the switch-on logs in the grate. "So kind . . ."

"Lionel will give you a snifter . . ."

I backed away from her, and then turned and left her standing there, gazing after me as though I were mad. Which I probably was.

I wouldn't think about Rory, sitting in New York. If he hadn't come home, if he hadn't answered the minister's letter, there was probably some very good reason. I walked, in long, warming strides, on up the hill; along the narrow lane that led to the gates of the Big House. I came to them, and they loomed before me, standing open, and I did not walk up the drive, but took the short cut through the wild garden, through the sodden drifts of daffodils. They were still in bud, closed against the rain, their trumpets unopened. I went beneath the trees and opened the tall gate in the deer fence. Beyond lay the rough grass, the azaleas and the hybrid rhododendrons, and then the lawn, sloping up to the gravel terrace in front of the house.

Through the mist, the house took shape. The old, ugly red stone house with the conservatory tacked on to one side and the pepper-pot turret over the front door. The outer door stood open and I went up the slope of the grass, crossed the gravel, went into the porch and rang the bell. Then, with the jangling of the bell still sounding from the back regions, I opened the inner glass door and let myself in.

It was very quiet. Very tidy. No flowers stood upon the table in the hall; no dogs barked; no children's voices broke the quiet. There was the smell of pine and polish, and as well, a faint aura of disinfectant, nursing, hospitals, so familiar to me that I noticed it at once. I went into the centre of the hall and pulled off my hat. I looked up at the empty staircase. I said, not wanting to call too loudly, "Is anyone around?"

Out of the silence came footsteps along the upper passage. Not the quick, rubber-heeled tread of a professional nurse, but heavy, masculine footsteps. Sandy Reekie, I decided, upstairs to fill the log baskets for the invalid's fire. I waited.

The footsteps started downstairs. Reached the half-landing and stopped. He was silhouetted against the light of the stair window. Not Sandy Reekie, whom I remembered as wiry and stooped, but a tall man, dressed in a kilt and a thick sweater.

"Who is it?" he asked, and then he saw me, my face tilted up to his. Our eyes met. There was a long silence. Then, for the third time that day, someone said my name. "Lavinia."

And I simply replied, "Rory."

He came on down the stairs, his hand trailing on the banister. He crossed the hall and took my hand.

"I don't believe it," he said, and then he kissed my cheek.

"I don't believe it, either. Everybody tells me you're in New York."

"I flew over a couple of nights ago. I've been here a day."

"How is your grandmother?"

"She's dying." But he didn't say it the way Stella Fellows had said it. He made it sound rather peaceful and nice, as though he were telling me that Mrs. Farquhar was nearly asleep.

I said, "I came to see her."

"Where from? Where have you come from?"

"Relkirk. I'm working there, nursing for a month. I got a day off. I thought I'd come to Lachlan. My mother told me Mrs. Farquhar had been ill, but I thought perhaps she would be getting better."

"There are two nurses with her, around the clock. But the day nurse wanted to go and do some shopping in Relkirk, so I lent her the car and said I'd watch out for my grandmother." He paused, hesitating, and then said, "There's a fire on in the sitting-room. Let's go there. It'll be more cheerful. Besides, you're wet through."

It was more cheerful. He put logs onto the fire and the flames crackled up. I pulled off my wet anorak and warmed my swollen, scarlet hands at the blaze. He said, "Tell me about you all," so I told him, and by the time I had finished with all the family news, I was truly warm again, and the clock on the mantel-piece struck four, so he left me by the fire and went off to put the kettle on for a cup of tea. I sat by the fire, very cosy and happy, and waited for him. When he returned, with a tray and cups and a teapot and the heel of a gingerbread he had found in a tin, I said, "And what about you? I've told you all about our family. Now you've got to tell me about you."

"Not much to tell, really. Worked with my father for a bit, and then when he died, I went out and joined the American office. I was in San Francisco when my grandmother became so ill. That was why I've been so long in getting back."

"You had a letter from the minister."

I was pouring tea. He sat in an armchair and watched me, grinning. "Lachlan grape-vine never gets anything wrong. Who told you that?"

"Mrs. McLaren in the shop, and then Mrs. Fellows."

"That woman! She's been more trouble than she's worth. Endlessly telephoning and rubbing the nurses up the wrong way, organizing everybody, telling the Reekies what they ought to be doing. A nightmare."

"She told me that Mrs. Farquhar was lying like a log and there was no point in coming to see her."

"That's just because she hasn't been allowed near the house, and she's furiously jealous if anybody else is."

"I'm sure she means well. At least that's what my mother always used to say about her. Go on about America."

"Well, anyway, I had a letter from the minister. But I didn't get it until I returned to New York. I had a couple of days' work to get through, and then I lit out and came home. I've only got two or three days' leave and then I've got to get back again. I'll hate going, but I have to. I feel torn in half, with my loyalties pulled in two totally different directions. That's the worst of being the only, nearest, surviving relative."

"And if she . . . when she dies . . . what will happen to the house?"

"It'll come to me. And how fortunate I shall be. And what the hell am I going to do with it?"

"You could stop being a highly powered businessman and retire to the country and take up farming."

"Perhaps I'd end up like Lionel Fellows, saying 'Tight Lines' every time I took a drink."

I considered this. "No. I don't think you would."

He grinned again. "And farming is just about the most highly powered business that's going these days. I'd have to go back to college, start at the bottom, learn a whole new trade."

"Lots of people do that. You could go to Cirencester. Take what they call the Gin-and-Tonic course. That's what they mean by the course for mature students, retired army officers, those sort of people."

"How do you know so much about it?"

"My mother lives no more than five miles from Cirencester."

He laughed, and all at once looked just as young as I had remembered him. "And then I should be near you all again. That's just about the biggest carrot you could dangle in front of this old donkey. I shall have to think seriously about it." And then he became grave again. "I would rather hold on to this place than anything else in the world. What good times we used to have. What good times we could have again. Remember walking down for the milk? And how you fed the lamb from a bottle?"

"I was remembering that."

"And the evenings when we danced reels . . ."

We talked on, sharing memories, until the clock struck five. I could not believe the hour had passed so swiftly. I laid down my empty teacup and got to my feet. "Rory, I must go, or I'll miss my bus."

"I'd drive you back, only I have no car, and I can't leave my grandmother." He hesitated. "Do you want to come up and see her?"

I looked at him. I said, "I don't want to be like Stella Fellows. I just wanted to see her again. I wanted to talk to her. I suppose, now, I just want to say goodbye."

He took my hand. "Then come," he said.

We went out of the room and up the stairs, hand in hand. Along the passage. At the end of the passage a door stood open, and now the hospital smell was stronger. We went through the door, and into the big, pretty, faded bedroom, where Mrs. Farquhar had slept since coming to Lachlan as a bride. Even with the familiar evidences of professional nursing, it was still a warm and welcoming room, essentially feminine, with silver brushes on the dressing-table, photographs everywhere, frilled curtains drawn back from the long windows.

We went to the bedside. I saw her face, serene and beautiful still, the eyes closed, the wrinkled hand lying peacefully on the fold of the linen sheet. I took her hand in mine and it was warm, and I felt still that strong persistent throb of life. She wore a pale-pink Shetland bedjacket, lined with silk chiffon. A satin ribbon lay across her throat, provocative as if she had set it there herself.

Rory said, "Grandmother." I thought she was sleeping, but she opened her eyes and looked up at him, and then she turned her head and looked at me. For a moment, those blue eyes stayed puzzled and empty, and then, slowly, came alive. Recognition sparked. Her fingers closed upon mine, a smile touched her wrinkled mouth, and quietly, but quite distinctly, she said my name.

"Lavinia."

We stayed only for a moment. We spoke, exchanging a word or two, and then her eyes were closed once more. I bent quickly and kissed her. Her fingers loosened and I slipped my hand away and straightened up.

I said goodbye, but I didn't say it aloud. Then Rory put his arm around me, and turned me, and we went out of the room and left her by herself.

I was in tears. I couldn't find a handkerchief, but Rory had one and he mopped me up, and finally I managed to stop crying. We went downstairs and back into the sitting-room, and I picked up my anorak and put it on. I pulled on my woollen hat. I said, "Thank you for letting me see her."

"You mustn't be sad."

I said, "I have to go. I have to catch that bus."

"I have to go too. Back to New York."

"Let me know what you decide to do."

"I will. When I've decided."

We went out of the room and across the hall and out through the open door. It was colder and wetter than ever, but the air smelt of heather and peat, and across the sky, somewhere beyond the rain clouds, an invisible oyster-catcher flew, crying his lonely song.

"You'll be all right?" said Rory.

"Of course."

"You know the way?"

I smiled. "Of course." I put out my hand. "Goodbye, Rory."

He took my hand and pulled me close, and kissed me. "I'm not going to say goodbye," he told me. "I'm going to say what the Americans always do. Take care. It doesn't sound so final. Just take care."

I nodded. He let go of my hand, and I turned and walked away from him, down across the grass and into the misty tunnel beneath the trees, where the azaleas grew and the daffodils tossed their heads in the wind, waiting for the first of the sunshine, the first of the warmth.

Playing A Round
With Love

This, then, was the real beginning of their life together. The honeymoon was over and behind them. This morning Julian had returned to work in his London office, and now he was on his way home to Putney.

Feeling like an old married man, he found his latchkey, but Amanda opened the door before he had time to put it into the lock, and one of the best things that had ever happened to Julian was stepping inside his own house, shutting his own door behind him, and taking his own wife into his arms.

When she could speak, she said, "You haven't even taken off your coat yet."

"No time."

He could smell something delicious cooking. Over her shoulder he saw the table laid in the tiny hall that they used as a dining-room: the wedding-present glasses and table-mats, the silver that his mother had given them gleaming in the soft lighting . . .

"But, darling . . ."

He could feel Amanda's ribs, her narrow waist, the round curve of her neat behind. He said, "Be quiet. You have to realize I only have time to deal with essentials . . ."

The next morning in the office, Julian's telephone rang. It was Tommy Benham. "Nice to have you back in London again, Julian. Are you okay for Wentworth on Saturday? I've fixed Roger and Martin and we've got a starting time at ten."

Julian did not reply at once.

Amanda knew about Tommy and golf. Before they were engaged, and after, she had philosophically accepted the fact that Saturdays, and sometimes Sundays, too, belonged to the golf course. But this Saturday was the first of their real life together, and she might want to spend it with him.

"I'm . . . I'm not sure, Tommy."

Tommy was outraged. "What do you mean, you're not sure? You can't change your life-style just because you've got a wife! Besides, she's never minded before, why should she mind now?"

Now that was a point. "Perhaps I should have a word . . ."

"No discussions, therefore no arguments. Present it as a fait accompli. Can you be there by ten o'clock?"

"Yes, of course, but—"

"Fine, we'll see you. Till then." And Tommy rang off.

On his way home that evening, Julian stopped and bought his wife flowers.

She'll love them, he told himself smugly.

She'll smell a rat the moment she sees them, answered a sneering voice inside his head. Probably think you've been flirting with one of the typists.

That's ridiculous. She knows I play golf at the weekends. It's just that . . . well, this is the first time since we were married. And Tommy was right. Present it as a fait accompli. Getting married doesn't mean changing one's life-style. Compromises, okay, but not a total change of habits.

Who's going to make the compromises? sneered the voice. "Her or you?"

Julian didn't reply to that.

In the end he was completely honest. He found Amanda in the garden, mud-smeared and with her fair hair all over her face.

Julian produced the flowers, which he had been hiding behind his back, with the panache of a successful conjurer.

"I have bought them," he said, "because I feel a louse. Tommy rang up this morning, and I've said I'll play golf with him on Saturday and my conscience has been pricking ever since."

She had buried her face in the flower heads. Now she looked up, astonished and laughing. "But why should your conscience prick, darling?"

"You don't mind?"

"Well, you can't say it's the first time it's happened!"

He knew a great surge of love for her. He took her into his arms and kissed her passionately.

Saturday was a beautiful day. Wentworth basked in sunshine, the fairways rolled before them, inviting and velvety. Julian, partnering Tommy, could do no wrong all that day.

His mind was filled with pleasant and generous thoughts as he drove home. He decided that he would take Amanda out for dinner, but when he got in he found that she had already made her special moussaka, so he opened a bottle of wine and they had dinner at home.

Amanda wore a canary-yellow caftan which he had bought her on their honeymoon in New York and her hair lay over her shoulders like a curtain of pale silk.

She said, "Shall I make some coffee?"

He put out his hand and touched the ends of that fair hair.

"Later . . ."

He played golf again the next Saturday, and the next. The following weekend, the day was shifted to Sunday, but he accepted this arrangement light-heartedly.

"Not playing this Saturday," he told Amanda when he got home. "Playing on Sunday instead."

"On Sunday?"

"Yes." He poured drinks and flopped into the armchair with the evening paper.

"Why Sunday?"

Engrossed in the share prices, he missed a certain tone in her voice.

"Um? Oh, Tommy's tied up on Saturday."

"I did say we'd go down and see my parents on Sunday."

"What?" She was not angry in any way, just polite. "Oh, sorry. But they'll understand. Ring them and say we'll come down some other weekend." He went back to the share prices and Amanda said no more.

The Sunday was a failure. It rained non-stop, Tommy had a hangover from the previous evening, and Julian played the sort of golf that makes a man swear he will give away his precious golf clubs and take up some other sport. He returned home in a black and dismal mood which was not dispelled by finding his house empty.

He wandered about aimlessly and eventually went upstairs and had a bath. While he was soaking in the bath, Amanda returned.

"Where have you been?" he demanded angrily.

"I went home. I said I was going to."

"How did you get there? I mean, I had the car."

"I caught a train down and someone very kindly gave me a lift back here."

"I didn't know where you were."

"Well, now you know, don't you?" She kissed him unenthusiastically. "And don't tell me what sort of a day you've had, because I know. Dreadful."

He was indignant. "How can you tell?"

"Because there is no light in the eye, no frisking of the tail."

"What's for supper?"

"Scrambled eggs."

"Scrambled eggs? I'm starving. I only had a sandwich for lunch."

"I, on the other hand, had a full Sunday lunch, so I am not in the least hungry. Scrambled eggs," she said as she closed the door between them.

Julian supposed this was their first quarrel. Not even a quarrel, really, just a coolness. But it was enough to make him feel miserable and the next day he bought flowers once more on the way home, made love to her as soon as he got home, and then took her out for dinner afterwards.

Everything was all right again. When Tommy rang to fix the next Saturday's game, Julian joyfully agreed to play.

That evening he found Amanda perched on top of a step-ladder in the bathroom, painting the ceiling white.

"For heaven's sake, be careful."

"I'm all right." She leaned down for his kiss. "Don't you think it looks better?" Together, they stared at the ceiling. "And then I thought we'd have primrose walls to match the bath, and perhaps a new green carpet."

"A carpet?"

"Don't sound so horrified. We can get a cheap one. There's a sale on in the High Street; we can go and look on Saturday."

She went back to her painting. There was a long pause during which Julian, instantly defensive, took stock of the situation.

He said evenly, "I can't on Saturday. I'm playing golf."

"I thought you played golf on Sundays now."

"No. That was last week."

There was another pause. Amanda said, "I see."

She scarcely spoke to him again all that evening. And when she did, it was in the politest possible manner. After dinner they went into the sitting-room and she turned on the television. He turned it off and said, "Amanda."

"I want to watch it."

"Well, you can't watch it because you're going to talk to me."

"No, I'm not."

"Well, I'm going to talk to you. I am not about to become the sort of husband who shops with his wife on Saturday mornings and cuts the grass on Sunday afternoons. Is that quite clear?"

"I suppose I'm meant to do the shopping and cut the grass."

"You can do what you like. We see each other every day . . ."

"What do you suppose I do when you're at the office all day?"

"You don't need to do nothing. You had a marvellous job, but you chucked it up because you said you wanted to be a housewife."

"So what if I did? Does that mean I have to spend the rest of my life on my own, adapting my plans to your beastly golf?"

"Well, what do you want to do?"

"I don't care what I do—but I don't want to do it by myself. Do you understand that? I don't want to do it by myself!"

This time it was a real quarrel, sour and rancorous. By morning the rift was still between them. He kissed her goodbye, but she turned her head away and he went, furious, to work.

The long day droned on, irritating and bugged with frustrations. At the end of it he felt in need of some calm and understanding company. Someone old and wise who would reassure him.

There was one person who fitted this bill and Julian made his way to her. His godmother.

"Julian," she said. "What a wonderful surprise. Come in."

He looked at her with affection. Well into her sixties, she was as pretty and lively as ever. She had been a friend of his mother's and no relation at all, but he had always called her Aunt Nora. Nora Stockforth.

He told her about everything. The honeymoon in New York, the new house.

"And how is Amanda?"

"She's all right."

There was a small silence. Aunt Nora refilled his glass. As she sat down again, he looked up and caught her eye. She said gently, "You don't make it sound as though she's all right."

"She is all right. It's just that she . . ."

And then it all came out. He told her about Tommy and the weekly golf games. He told her about Amanda's always having known about this arrangement, and never minding. "But now . . ."

"Now she minds."

"It's so ridiculous. It's simply one day in the week. It isn't as though she wants to do anything in particular, it's just that she says she doesn't want to do it by herself."

Aunt Nora said, "I hope you're not asking me to make any sort of comment."

Julian frowned. "How do you mean?"

"I would never dream of taking sides. But I think you were right to come over and talk to me. Sometimes just talking about things helps to keep one's sense of proportion."

"You think I've lost mine?"

"No, I don't mean that at all. But I think you must take the long view. I always think a new marriage is a little like a baby. It needs to be cuddled and loved for the first two years, to be wrapped in security.

"Just now you and Amanda only have each other to think about. This is the time that you shape your life together so that when the bad times come—which they will—there'll be something there to remember, to hold you together."

"You think I'm being selfish?"

"I told you I wasn't going to comment."

"You think her complaints are justified?"

Aunt Nora laughed. "I think that if she's complaining, you haven't got too much to worry about. It's when she stops complaining that you have trouble on your hands."

He laid down his glass. "What sort of trouble?"

"I leave you to work that out for yourself. And now I think you should go, or Amanda will think you've had a terrible accident." They stood up. "Julian, do come again. But bring Amanda with you next time."

He was still in a thoughtful mood when he reached home. Amanda opened the door before he had time to find his keys and they stood eyeing each other, their faces solemn.

Then she smiled. "Hello."

It was all right. "Darling." He stepped indoors and kissed her. "I'm sorry about everything."

"Oh, Julian, I'm sorry, too. Did you have a good day?"

"No—but it's all right now. I'm a bit late because I called in to see Aunt Nora on the way back home. She sent you her love, of course."

Later, Amanda said casually, "Could I have the car tomorrow?"

"Yes, of course. Going somewhere special?"

"No," she said, not looking at him. "It's just that I might need it, that's all."

He waited for her to tell him more, but she didn't. Why did she want the car? Perhaps she was going to have lunch with a girl-friend in town.

The next evening when he got home, Amanda was in the sitting-room watching television, wearing her smartest clothes.

He said, "How did you get along?" and waited to be told all about her day.

But she only said, "All right."

"Would you like a drink?"

"No, thank you."

She seemed intent on the television, so he left her and went out into the kitchen to find himself a beer. As he opened the refrigerator door, he suddenly stopped dead. Aunt Nora's words came clear as a bell: 'It's when she stops complaining that you have trouble on your hands.'

Amanda had, it was obvious, stopped complaining. What was it about her that was different? And why those clothes?

Carefully testing the ground, he said, "Well, how's the bathroom going?"

"I haven't had a chance to get at it today."

"Do you still want to buy the carpet? I could probably call Tommy and he could get hold of someone else to play golf on Saturday."

Amanda laughed. "Oh, it doesn't matter that much. No point in changing any plans."

"But—"

"Anyway," she interrupted his self-sacrifice without even bothering to listen, "I shall probably be busy on Saturday myself." She looked at her watch. "When do you want to eat?"

He didn't want to eat. His stomach was a vacuum probed by ghastly suspicions. She didn't mind being left on her own any more. She had occupations of her own . . . appointments. Dates?

But she wouldn't . . . not Amanda.

But why not? She was young and attractive. Before Julian had finally pinned her down, there had been a horde of young men waiting to take her out.

"Julian, I asked you when you wanted to eat."

He gazed at her as though he had never seen her before. He managed to say, through an unexplained obstruction in his throat, "Any time."

He found himself longing for a cold, for flu—anything would do, provided it gave him a cast-iron excuse not to play golf at Wentworth on Saturday. But his health, perversely, remained unimpaired. When he left, Amanda was still in bed, which was quite out of character.

He played in a stupor. Eventually, Tommy was moved to ask, "Anything wrong?"

"Um? No, nothing."

"Just seem a bit preoccupied. We're seven down, you know."

They were, inevitably, beaten into the ground and Tommy was not pleased. He was even less pleased when Julian excused himself from playing a second round and said that he was going home.

"There *is* something wrong," said Tommy.

"Why should there be anything wrong?"

"Just thought you were beginning to look like a husband. Amanda's not creating, is she? You must assert yourself, you know, Julian."

Stupid fool, thought Julian, roaring back towards London. What does he know about it? Looking like a husband, indeed. What does he expect me to look like? Miss World?

But as he turned at last into their own little tree-lined street, all these bolstering blusterings collapsed about his ears. For the house was empty.

He looked at his watch. Four o'clock. What was she doing? Where was she? She might have left him a note, but there was nothing. Only the hum of the refrigerator, the smell of polish.

He thought, She's not coming back. The very prospect left him cold and trembling. No Amanda. No laughter, no digging in the garden, no arguments. No love. The end of love.

He had dropped his bag of clubs at the foot of the stairs. Now he stepped over them and settled himself on the bottom stair, because there didn't seem to be anywhere better to sit.

He thought back. That Sunday when she had gone to have lunch with her parents and had a lift home . . . Who had brought her? Julian had never got around to asking, but now he knew that it had been Guy Hanthorpe.

Guy Hanthorpe had been Amanda's most faithful boy-friend. He had known her all his life, for their parents were neighbours in the country. He was a stockbroker, successful and distinguished. Julian, who was stocky and dark, had disliked and resented the tall, fair Guy on sight.

Perhaps they had been meeting each other secretly ever since Julian had brought her back from New York.

He was still there, sitting in the dusk at the foot of the stairs, smoking himself silly and concocting heart-chilling fantasies, when he heard a car come up the road.

It stopped outside the house, doors opened and shut, he heard voices, footsteps on the path.

He got up and flung the door open.

It was Amanda. And with her was Guy.

"Darling, you're back!" Amanda looked amazed.

Julian said nothing. He simply stood and looked at Guy, aware of rage, like a vice, gripping his rib-cage. He thought of hitting Guy; saw himself doing it, like some violent film, slow-motion.

He saw his hand come up and smash itself into Guy's amiable face. Saw Guy go down, crumpled, insensible, hitting his head as he fell; lying unconscious on the paving, blood seeping from his mouth, from the ghastly wound in his head . . .

"Hello, Julian," said Guy and Julian blinked, surprised to find that he hadn't hit Guy after all.

"Where have you been?" he asked Amanda.

"Down at my mother's. And Guy was seeing *his* mother, so he gave me a lift home." Julian said nothing.

Irritated, Amanda continued. "Do you think we could come in? It's rather cool, and it's beginning to drizzle."

"Yes. Yes, of course."

He stood aside, but Guy said, "Actually, I won't, thank you." He glanced at his watch. "I'm going out for dinner tonight, and I must get back and get myself changed. So I'll say goodbye. 'Bye, Amanda." He gave her a peck on the cheek, raised a hand to Julian, and was off, plunging down the path on his long legs.

Amanda called, "Goodbye, and thanks for the lift."

She stood in the hall and looked at the bag of golf clubs at the foot of the stairs. At the undrawn curtains. At Julian.

She said, "Is anything wrong?"

"No," he said with fine bitterness. "Nothing. Just that I thought you weren't ever coming home again."

"Never coming . . . ? Have you gone out of your mind?"

"I thought you were with Guy."

"I was."

"I mean, all day."

She laughed and then stopped laughing. "Julian, I told you, I've been with my mother."

"You didn't tell me that this morning. And where were you the other day, when I came home and found you all dressed up and reeking of perfume?"

"If you're going to be like that, I shan't tell you."

"Oh, yes, you will!" he yelled.

After the yell, there was a terrible silence. Then Amanda said very quietly, "I have a feeling we should both take a deep breath and start at the beginning."

Julian took his deep breath. "Right," he said. "You start."

She said, "That day I went home for the day. I needed the car because I wanted to go and see the doctor. I'm still registered with my parents' doctor and I haven't got a doctor in London.

"And I dressed myself up because I'm sick of wearing paint-stained jeans and my mother likes to see me looking smart. And today I had to go back to see the doctor again, because he wanted to give me another check-up and be completely sure."

Was she going to die? "Completely sure of what?"

"And you had the car, so I had to go down by train, and Guy brought me back, very kindly, as he did the time before, and all you did was stand and glower at him. I've never been so ashamed."

"Amanda! What did the doctor say to you?"

"I'm going to have a baby, of course."

"A baby!" He searched for words. "But we've only just got married!"

"We've been married nearly four months. And we had a very long honeymoon . . ."

"But we never meant . . ."

"I know we never meant." She sounded near to tears. "But it's happened, and if you dare take that horrible tone of voice . . ."

"A baby." He said it again, but this time his voice was filled with wonder. "You're going to have a baby! Oh, my darling, you are the most wonderful girl."

"You don't mind?"

"Mind? I'm thrilled!" He was astonished to find that it was true. "I've never been so thrilled about anything."

"Will the house be big enough for three?"

"Of course it will."

"I don't want to have to move. Our little house . . ."

"We won't move. We'll stay here forever, and breed an enormous family and have rows of perambulators all the way up the garden path."

She said, "I didn't want to tell you about what I was doing, Julian, because I couldn't be sure myself, so I wanted to wait for a while."

"It doesn't matter. Nothing matters except this . . ."

And it didn't. That evening Julian cooked supper for Amanda, and they ate it off a tray in front of the fire, and she put her feet up on the sofa because he said that that was what all expectant mothers were meant to do.

When at last it was time to go to bed, Julian locked up the house, put his arm around his wife, and then led her gently towards the stairs.

His precious bag of golf clubs still lay where he had dropped it, but he shoved it out of the way with his foot and left it. There would be plenty of time to put it away safely . . .

Christabel

—◦◦◦—

Mrs. Lowyer awoke at her usual civilized hour of eight-thirty in the morning, to the hum of the combine harvester in the barley field. It was a good sound to wake up to on a late summer morning. She had always been very fond of this time of the year; loving the precious golden sunshine of Indian summers, the brilliance of laden rowan trees, the first taste of blackberries. She had been married—a long time ago—in September, and her only son Paul had been born a year later in the same month. And now *his* daughter was going to be married in a week's time. Mrs. Lowyer lay in bed and watched the sky through the open window (she had never been able to bear sleeping with drawn curtains) and saw it blue as a robin's egg between soft, slow-moving clouds.

After a little she got up, put on her dressing-gown and slippers, and went to the window to inspect the outside world. Her window was at the back of the little house, overlooking the scrap of garden. Beyond the fence was the great, golden field of barley, and beyond that again, Shadwell, the old house where her son and his wife now lived, and where Mrs. Lowyer had lived and brought up her family for more than thirty years.

The combine was moving across the farthest edge of the field. A huge scarlet monster, eating its way through the waist-high crop. It was too distant to see the driver, but she knew that it was Sam Crichtan. He ran the farm with only sporadic help, and he trusted no one but himself to work that precious, hideously expensive piece of equipment. She wondered how long he had been working. Probably since sun-up, and he would not stop until it was too dark to work any longer. He did this—seven days a week.

Mrs. Lowyer sighed. For Sam; for changed days; for the fact that at sixty-seven she was too old to go out and give him a hand. And for another, nebulous reason that had been at the back of her mind for some time now, but which she refused to take out and inspect. She shut the window firmly and went downstairs to put out her little dachshund, Lucy, for her morning excursion, and then to light the gas and fill her breakfast kettle.

By ten o'clock, dressed and breakfasted, she was out in her garden, snipping a few deadheads off the roses, pulling up a weed or two, staking a straggling clump of Michaelmas daisies. The combine now had cut a deep swath around the border of the field, and as she fiddled with scissors and string, it came surging up the slope towards the fence at the edge of her garden. She abandoned her flower-bed and went to wave as Sam passed. But he didn't pass. He switched off the engine and stopped the immense machine. All clanking and turning and grinding ceased. The morning was all at once blessedly still. Sam opened the door of the cab and climbed down, and came stiffly and tiredly across the stubble towards her.

She said, "I didn't mean you to stop, I was just waving hello."

"I'm sorry about that. I thought you were going to offer me a cup of tea. I forgot to fill a flask and my throat's as dry as the desert."

"Well, of course I'll give you a cup of tea." *And something to eat as well,* she decided privately, but she did not say this. "How will you get over the fence?"

"Easy," said Sam. He put a hand on the fence-post and vaulted lightly over. "Amazing what you can do if there's a cup of tea in the offing."

She smiled. She had always liked Sam. For ten years he had been tenant farmer at Shadwell, and she had watched him, by sheer determination and plodding hard work, turn what had been a neglected, run-down property, into a viable proposition. Steadings were repaired, fences mended, profits—and she knew that at first these had been sadly meagre—ploughed back, again and again, into the land.

She could not remember him ever taking a holiday, although in the early days he had had two men to help him. Now, with modern stream-lined methods and new machinery, he insisted on running the place more or less single-handed, and it was a constant wonder to Mrs. Lowyer that he didn't die of exhaustion or become embittered and dour. He had, however, done neither of these things, but he was terribly thin, and looked much older than his thirty-two years, and sometimes so tired that she expected him to fall asleep on his feet.

She said, "Come along then, and sit down for a minute."

"I can't stay more than ten. I've the whole field to finish before this evening. The forecast for tomorrow's not too good."

"Well, provided we have a good day next Saturday, a little rain won't do any harm."

"That's one of the reasons I'm cutting today. Paul wants to use the field as a car-park for the wedding. He's going to build a ramp up over the ha-ha so that the guests can walk from their cars up to the marquee . . ." They had reached the back door, and he paused to toe off his mud-caked wellington boots. There were holes in the toes of his socks, but she did not let on that she had noticed this. She led the way into her miniature kitchen and put on the kettle while Sam shrugged off his oil-stained jacket, pulled out a chair and settled himself with a sigh of relief at the kitchen table.

"What time were you up this morning?" she asked him.

"Six o'clock."

"You must feel as though you've done a day's work already." Without asking him, she took down the frying pan and opened the fridge to get out bacon and eggs and sausages. Behind her, he looked about him with appreciation.

"Best-designed little kitchen I've ever seen, this one. Like a ship's galley."

"It does very nicely for one person, but when I have guests to stay it does get a little overcrowded."

He lit himself, luxuriously, a briar pipe, as though it were one of the greatest treats in the world. Mrs. Lowyer found an ashtray and laid it on the table. The bacon began to sizzle in the pan.

Sam asked suddenly: "Didn't you mind coming to live here after Paul and Felicity moved into Shadwell?"

"No, I didn't mind. I was fortunate that there was a house available for me, even though it is so tiny. The only thing that made me sad was leaving most of my furniture behind, because there simply wasn't the space for it here. But I've got my favourite bits and pieces. And after all, what is furniture? Nothing worth breaking your heart over. And whenever I go up to the house, I'm able to see it and enjoy it. Felicity loves it too, and probably takes far better care of it than I ever did. She puts me to shame, she's so capable, and of course she's in her element now, planning Christabel's wedding. Lists everywhere, charts pinned up on the kitchen wall, all her girl-friends roped in to do the flowers for her."

Deftly, she broke an egg into the pan, looked at it, and then broke another. She knew, of old, that feeding Sam was like pouring water down a well. His appetite was enormous, but he never seemed to put on an ounce of weight.

He made no comment on this last remark. In order to keep the conversation going, she asked, "When is the marquee going up?"

"Tuesday, or Wednesday, depending on the weather."

"Are you going to be roped in to help with that?"

"No. I offered, but the hire firm do the whole thing. However, Felicity said she'd want furniture to be moved in the house, so doubtless I'll be there, heaving sofas as to the manner born."

"And you're going to the party tonight?"

Again, he did not reply. Mrs. Lowyer turned to look at him and saw him lean forward to tap out the pipe in the ashtray. He was looking down, his expression shuttered. She said in sudden concern, "You *have* been asked, haven't you?"

"Yes, and I said I'd go. But I don't know. I'll have to see."

"Sam, you have to go."

"Why?"

"Christabel would be so hurt if you weren't there."

"I don't suppose she'd even notice."

"Don't be so ridiculous, of course she'd notice. And of course she'd be hurt. Besides, you've never met Nigel. This is what the party's all about; so that everybody can meet Nigel before he's suddenly produced at the wedding. He's made a special trip up from London just for this occasion, and it would be very rude if we didn't all turn up." She put the bacon and eggs and the sausages onto a plate and set it, with a steaming mug of tea, on the table before him.

He looked at the spread with satisfaction and some surprise. "What's this? A second breakfast?"

"I'm quite sure you haven't even had a first breakfast." She pulled out a chair and sat down, facing him across the table.

"Well, no, I don't suppose I have." He began to eat.

"You're impossible. No man can do everything for himself, certainly not when he's working from dawn to dusk on the farm."

"I'm all right."

"But it must be so cheerless . . ."

"Aggie Watson comes in most mornings."

"And what does she do? Scrub a floor and peel a pot of potatoes? That's not what I'm talking about, Sam. You should get a housekeeper. Or a wife. It's time you were married."

He said, "I can't afford a housekeeper."

Mrs. Lowyer sighed. "And there's nobody you want to marry."

After a long pause, Sam said, "No."

"Nobody except Christabel," said Mrs. Lowyer. She said it very quickly, before she had time to think, before she lost the courage to go treading in where she was obviously not going to be welcome. But she knew that it had to be said. It had to come out into the open if Christabel's wedding day was not to be clouded in any way by any person.

He said, as she knew that he would, "What makes you think that?"

"I suppose I've always known."

"She's just a little girl."

"She was a little girl when you first knew her, but she's twenty now."

Their eyes met across the table. Sam's eyes were a very pale blue, like winter skies. When he was in a cheerful mood they sparkled with good humour, but now they were cold, guarded, giving nothing away.

He said, "She's getting married on Saturday," and went on with his meal.

It was as though he had slammed a door in her face, but Mrs. Lowyer knew that this was no time for moral cowardice. She said, "I think you've always loved her. I don't think there was a time when you didn't love her. And she was always so fond of you. I remember you helping her with her first pony, and the way she was always under your feet, trying to do things on the farm, holding the staples when you mended fences . . ."

"Losing the hammer . . ." said Sam.

"She was never remotely interested in any of the young boys who grew up with her. She even took your photograph when she went away to boarding-school. Did you know that?"

"Things change," said Sam.

"Do you mean that you've changed, or that Christabel's changed?"

"Both, I suppose. As I said, she was just a little girl. She grew up, and I grew older. Then she went away down to London, got a job, a flat of her own . . ."

"Met Nigel," finished Mrs. Lowyer.

"Yes. She met Nigel. And now she's going to marry him."

"Do you blame her?"

"I've never met him."

"He's a very nice, very suitable young man. Any sensible girl would have been a fool to turn him down."

"Christabel never was a fool."

"But I'm beginning to suspect that you are."

"Why?"

"Because it's patently obvious that you're in love with her. You've always loved her, but you've never asked her to marry you."

"I couldn't," said Sam.

"Why not, for heaven's sake?"

"For every reason. That's why not. For every reason. What did I have to offer her? A little farm that doesn't even belong to me. A little house with two bedrooms and no form of central heating. And what about money, material things, all the things that a girl like Christabel deserves? I could never give them to her."

"Did you ever ask her if she even wanted them?"

"No."

"But . . ."

Sam looked despairing. He pushed the empty plate away from him and leaned his arms on the table. He said, "Please. Don't go on about it."

"Oh, Sam." For a moment she wondered if she was going to cry. She hadn't cried for years. She laid her hand over his and felt the horny, calloused skin.

He said, "It's too late, anyway."

She knew that he was right. It was too late. She smiled firmly and gave his hand a little pat. "All right, I won't talk about it any more. But you must come to the party tonight. We're going to be given a buffet dinner, and then there is to be dancing. Disco, I think they call it."

He grinned. "Can you disco dance?"

"I don't know. I've never tried. But if anybody asks me, I shall have a good shot at it."

The day progressed, the morning taken up with small day-to-day chores. After lunch, Mrs. Lowyer got her modest car out of the garage and drove to the neighbourhood market town where she had her hair done at the only hairdresser's, which was called Huntleys of Mayfair. Miss Pickering, who owned this establishment, had never been near Mayfair in her life, and had chosen the name Huntley because she thought it added a touch of class. Here, Mrs. Lowyer endured being alternately frozen and scalded by a terrified junior and then had her hair wound around rollers, her scalp speared with plastic pins, and the torture finally rounded off by being put under a red-hot dryer which she was unable to make cooler, however much she turned the knob on the dial.

At last the ordeal was over. Feeling scarlet in the face and totally exhausted, she drove herself home. She would have a cup of tea and then go to bed for a couple of hours to relax before the evening's festivities. But no sooner had she been greeted by Lucy and put on the kettle than the back door opened, a voice said, "Granny," and it was Christabel herself.

"Darling," said Mrs. Lowyer, and kissed her.

"Are you making tea? Can I have some with you? Gosh, you're looking smashing. Miss Pickering's pulled out all the stops this time. Is there any fruit-cake?" She began opening her grandmother's cake tins, found a chocolate biscuit and started to eat it.

She was forever eating. Potato crisps, bars of chocolate, ice-cream in cones, snacking away on all the worst sort of junk food, but not a blemish marred her milky skin, and, if anything, she seemed to be more slender than ever. Today she wore her oldest jeans, scuffed cowboy boots, a sagging sweater with darns in the elbows. Her hair, that beautiful hair that was a shade somewhere between chestnut and chocolate, was braided tightly into two pigtails. Her face was innocent of make-up, and she looked like a leggy fifteen-year-old. Impossible, thought Mrs. Lowyer, to believe that next Saturday she was going to be married.

She said, "Has Nigel arrived yet?"

"Heavens, yes, he got here for lunch. He left London about four o'clock this morning. That wasn't bad going, was it?"

"Why isn't he with you now?"

"Oh, he and Pa are having a great crack about shooting pigeons and how many of Nigel's relations are coming to the wedding. You haven't seen Sam, have you?"

"I think he's still combining the barley field. Didn't you see him?"

"No, I went along by the river. There wasn't anybody at his house, not even Aggie."

"What did you want to see Sam about?"

"I wanted to thank him for my wedding present." She pulled out a chair and sat at the table, much as Sam had sat this morning. "Do you know what he gave me? It's simply beautiful and he made it all himself."

"No. What did he give you?"

"A walking-stick."

Mrs. Lowyer said faintly, "A walking-stick," and tried not to sound too astonished.

"Yes, and you know how he used to carve horn handles for walking-sticks. He hasn't done it for ages, poor man, because he hasn't had the time, but he's done one for me, and it's all carved with flowers and sheaves of wheat, and it's all polished and gorgeous. And then around the stick there's a little silver band with my name on. Don't you think that was the most lovely thing to give me?"

"Yes, darling, lovely," said Mrs. Lowyer, privately deciding that if Sam had considered the problem for a year, he could scarcely have given Christabel anything more unsuitable. A walking-stick, for a young girl, who was going to get married and go and live in a flat in London.

"I mean, it's so personal. Not just having my name on, but his making it for me with his own two hands."

"I must say, that does make it rather special."

"I hope he'll come tonight. That he won't go on combining after dark, or make some excuse."

"Of course he'll come. He was in this morning having a cup of tea with me, and he said he was coming."

"I can't tell you the spread Mother's laying on. She's put all the leaves in the dining-room table and pushed it against the wall of the dining-room, and there are the best white table-cloths, and so much to eat you just can't imagine."

Mrs. Lowyer smiled. "She's in her element," she told Christabel.

She found the cake tin with the fruit-cake in it, put the cake on a plate, and set the plate in front of Christabel. She poured tea for Christabel into her own mug, the blue-and-white-striped one that she had used whenever she came to tea, ever since she was a little girl.

"And we're going to have a disco. That was another thing Pa wanted Nigel to do—buff up the old playroom floor."

"I don't quite know what I'm meant to do in a disco."

"Oh, snake around, you know, like they do on the box."

"Couldn't I just sit and watch?"

"Oh, heavens, Granny, don't be so old-fashioned. Just get with it, man." She shrugged her shoulders, tossed her plaits, tilted her chin, looked cool.

"Is that what I'm meant to do?"

"Well, I'll tell you what," said Christabel, cutting a wedge out of the fruit-cake and beginning to eat it. "I'll make sure we have at least two Viennese waltzes, and you can whirl away to your heart's content with Colonel Foxton."

"Oh, really, Christabel . . ."

"Now, you know he's madly in love with you. I can't think why you don't marry him."

"What, go and live in that freezing house with all the pitch pine and stained glass?"

"He could come and live here."

"There wouldn't be room."

"You're terribly unkind about Colonel Foxton," Christabel told her. She had been teasing her grandmother about Colonel Foxton ever since the old gentleman had asked her to tea with him and had spent the time showing her his collection of photographs taken when he was a young subaltern in India. "After all, he's exactly the right age for you."

"No, he's not. If I were to marry someone exactly the right age for me, he'd be over a hundred."

"How do you work that out?"

"Because the perfect age for a marriage is for the girl to be half the man's age, plus seven years. So if the man is twenty, he marries a girl of seventeen. And if the girl is sixty-seven, then she would have to marry a man of . . . um . . ." Mrs. Lowyer's arithmetic had never been her strong point. "A hundred and twenty."

Christabel gazed at her. After a little she said, "But I'm twenty, and Nigel's only twenty-three. That's all wrong. I should be marrying somebody of twenty-six."

"Well, you'd better hurry up, because you've only got a week to find him."

"Do you really think twenty-three is too young for me?"

"No, I don't think it matters at all. It's just a stupid sort of joke people make. It doesn't matter what ages a man and a woman are, provided they are truly fond of each other and want to spend the rest of their lives together."

"You don't say love," said Christabel.

"Darling, I never talk about love at tea-time. And now eat up that cake and drink up that tea, because I'm going upstairs to have a rest before the party. I wonder what time I'm expected?"

"Oh, I should think about eight. Do you want someone to come and fetch you?"

"Of course not. It's going to be a beautiful, fine evening. I shall walk up the lane. And I shall enjoy seeing the house, all lit up and festive. There's something very romantic about a house all lit up for a party. Especially a party that's being given for such a happy reason."

"Yes," said Christabel. She did not sound very certain. "Yes, I suppose it is romantic."

At exactly five to eight, wearing her best sapphire-blue velvet dinner dress and a cashmere shawl over her shoulders, Mrs. Lowyer bid Lucy good night, turned off the lights, and made her way down the garden path and up the lane that led to her old house. There was a half-moon sailing high in the sky, and overhead the branches of the ancient beeches laced their arms together like the flying buttresses of some great cathedral. Ahead of her, lighted windows shone through the dusk, and the air was filled with the scent of dying leaves and moss, and the strains of music.

Already cars were arriving, parking on the gravel in front of the house, and as Mrs. Lowyer went up the stone steps to the open door, she was joined by other guests, the women holding up their long skirts, the men in black ties and dinner jackets.

"Oh, Mrs. Lowyer, how lovely to see you. Doesn't the house look pretty coming along the road, through the trees . . . ? How does Felicity manage even to arrange that the weather is perfect? It never seems to rain when she has a party."

"Let's hope her luck holds for next Saturday."

The hall was filled with people. Mrs. Lowyer kissed her son and her pretty daughter-in-law and then made her way upstairs to leave her shawl. She laid this on Felicity's bed and then went to the dressing-table to check that her coiffure was still a credit to Miss Pickering's hands. Her reflection gazed back at her from the antique triple mirror. It was the mirror that had always stood on that dressing-table—Mrs. Lowyer had inherited it from her own mother-in-law. She remembered reflections of herself as she had been, slender and shingle-headed. Now she saw, beneath the careful make-up, the wrinkles of age, the crêpey neck, the silver hair. Her hands, touching that hair, were the hands of an old lady. *I am a grandmother,* she told herself. *In a year or so, I may be a great-grandmother.* The prospect she found unalarming. If she had learned nothing else, she had learned that every age brings its own rewards.

"I've caught you preening!"

Mrs. Lowyer turned from the looking glass and saw Christabel behind her. She was laughing at her grandmother, her eyes sparkling with amusement.

"I'm not preening. I'm thinking how glad I am that I'm not young any more, that I don't have to worry if some man will dance with me. That I don't have to worry if my husband dances with some other pretty woman."

"I bet you never had any of those worries. And now you look gorgeous."

"Oh, darling, you look lovely too. Is that a new dress?"

"Yes." Christabel straightened up and whirled around to show off her finery. The dress was white, layers of soft, floating lawn. The neck was low, and her hair, released from the plaits of this afternoon, was romantically looped and swathed about her head. Her eyes swam and sparkled.

"Where did you get it?"

"In London. Mother saw it when we were trousseau shopping and said I had to have it. It's meant to be part of my trousseau, but I thought I'd wear it tonight."

Mrs. Lowyer gave her a kiss. "It's perfect. You look lovely."

* * *

From outside the open door, from the landing, a voice said, "Christabel!" Christabel went to open the door, and Nigel was revealed, standing outside, looking both embarrassed and faintly put out.

"What are you doing?" Christabel demanded. "Lurking around outside the ladies' room? You'll get a bad name for yourself."

He smiled, but not as though he thought the joke particularly funny. "I've been looking for you all over. Your mother's waiting for you. She sent me to find you."

"Granny and I are having a mutual-admiration session."

"Hello, Mrs. Lowyer."

"Nigel. How very nice to see you again." She went through the open door and planted a light kiss on his cheek. With his dark hair and his formal clothes, he looked, not sophisticated as he should have, but like a young boy dressed up for a party. "And I'm sorry Christabel and I have kept you all waiting. Perhaps now we should all go down and join the others."

It was not until halfway through the evening, when most of the guests had had supper, and the younger element had already taken themselves off to the disco, that Sam Crichtan appeared. Mrs. Lowyer, trapped in a corner by the fireplace with Colonel Foxton, saw him come into the room through the French windows, which had been left open for air, and she knew a rush of relief that he had kept his word to her.

It was a long time since she had seen him dressed for an evening out, and she decided, with private satisfaction, that his dark formal clothes became him. With his thin brown face and his neatly brushed hair, he looked more than presentable—distinguished, even.

". . . it's a funny thing," droned Colonel Foxton. "Damn' funny thing, the way some people can get planning permission. Wanted to renovate my gardener's cottage. Wasn't allowed to put a window in the roof. It's a funny . . ."

"I wonder, would you excuse me?" Gracefully, charmingly, Mrs. Lowyer got to her feet. "I have an urgent message for Sam, and I must give it to him before he gets swept out of my sight."

"What? Oh, yes. Sorry, my dear. Didn't realize how I'd been going on."

"I loved hearing about your gardener's cottage. You must tell me the rest of the story another time."

She made her way across the room. "Sam."

"Mrs. Lowyer."

"I am glad you came. Have you eaten?"

"No, I didn't really have time."

"I thought not. Then come with me right away, and before you do anything else you must have a drink, and some cold salmon and cold roast beef that is out of this world."

She led him through to the dining-room and found him a glass of whisky and a plate which she proceeded to heap with food.

"Have you seen Christabel?"

"I've only just got here."

"But you didn't see her this afternoon?"

"No."

"She was looking for you. To thank you for the walking-stick."

"I suppose you thought it was a pretty stupid present?"

"Yes." said Mrs. Lowyer, who had never believed in mincing words. "But a very special one. Christabel was not only delighted, she was touched. How about a baked potato with butter? Or even two?"

"You didn't tell her? What we talked about this morning?"

"Of course not. A roll?"

"I wouldn't want her to know."

"No," said Mrs. Lowyer. "Of course not." Across the room, through the open door, she could see Christabel and Nigel. He had his arm around her shoulder, her amazing hair glinted in the candle-light. "Nigel is a very nice young man. She is a very lucky girl."

Sam glanced up, saw that she was looking over his shoulder, and turned. Nigel bent and kissed the top of Christabel's head. Some-body made a remark, and everybody laughed. For a second Sam was still, and then he turned back to the table. He said, "And some of that mayonnaise, too, if I may. I was always very fond of Felicity's mayonnaise."

But, later again, taken to inspect the disco by her son, Mrs. Lowyer saw Christabel dancing with Sam. Everybody else on the floor appeared to be dancing by themselves, gyrating to the thumping music, grotesque in the whirling, flashing lights. Only Christabel and Sam seemed a couple. Moving together, their arms around each other, Christabel's head rested against Sam's shoulder.

Mrs. Lowyer hoped that her son had not seen. She put a hand on his arm. She said, "The noise is deafening. I'd rather go back to the drawing-room," and obediently, he led her away. But at the door Mrs. Lowyer looked back. It did not take a second to realize that in that instant, apparently without trace, Sam and Christabel had disappeared.

After that, she went home. Slipped away unnoticed, said good night to nobody. Wrapped in the familiar warmth of her shawl, she made her way down the lane. The sounds of music, the hum of conversation died away behind her, swallowed into the quiet of a country night. September. Her favourite month.

This is all a terrible mistake. She is marrying the wrong man.

Her house, dark and small and quiet, was a sanctuary. She lifted Lucy from her basket, put her out into the garden, got herself a cup of hot milk, let Lucy in again, carried the milk upstairs, slowly undressed, and put herself to bed. Through the open window, she saw the half-moon sickle from the sky. The world outside was filled with small night sounds. She longed for sleep.

It was four o'clock before the rattle of pebbles sounded like rain against her window-pane. At first she thought that she had imagined it, but it came again. And then, "Granny!"

She got out of bed, took up her dressing-gown, wrapped herself in it, tied the sash. She went to the open window. Below in the garden, she saw the blur of white. White as a ghost, a wraith.

"Granny."

"Christabel, what are you doing?"

"I want to talk to you."

She went downstairs, switching on lights. She opened the front door, and Christabel came in, shivering with cold, the white dress muddied at its hem.

"What about the party?"

"The party's nearly over. I wanted to talk to you. Everybody thinks I've gone to bed."

"Where's Nigel?"

"Having a second supper."

"And Sam?"

"He went home."

In silence Mrs. Lowyer looked into her granddaughter's eyes. They were bright with unshed tears. "Come upstairs," she said.

* * *

They went back to her room, her own pretty, fragrant bedroom. Mrs. Lowyer got into bed, and Christabel slid in beside her, beneath the eiderdown. Mrs. Lowyer could feel the coldness of Christabel's arms, the bony young rib-cage, the beat of Christabel's heart.

Christabel said, "I'm afraid."

"What are you afraid of?"

"Everything. Getting married. Being trapped. Doors closing in on me."

"That's what being married is all about," said Mrs. Lowyer. "Being trapped. All that matters is that you're trapped with the right person."

"Oh, Granny, why can't everything be easy?"

"Nothing is ever easy," said Mrs. Lowyer. Her hand moved against Christabel's shoulder. "Being born isn't easy. Growing up isn't easy. Getting married isn't easy. Having children can be murder. Growing old is just as bad."

"I think . . . I think I don't want to marry Nigel."

"Why not?"

"I don't know."

"Aren't you in love with him?"

"I was. Terribly. Really terribly in love. But . . . I don't know. I don't want to live in London. I don't like being in a flat. I feel as though I'm going to have to live in a box. And . . . there's another thing. I don't like his friends very much. I don't feel I have anything in common with them. Does that matter? Does it matter terribly?"

"Yes," said Mrs. Lowyer. "Yes, I think it probably does."

"It's called wedding nerves, isn't it?"

"It is, sometimes."

"Do you think it is this time?"

Mrs. Lowyer answered this with another question. "Where did you go with Sam?"

"Into the garden. We just went and sat on the seat under the beech tree. It was quite harmless."

"And then you said good night and he went home?"

"Yes."

"He loves you. You know that, don't you?"

"I hoped he would say that. But he didn't say anything."

"He thinks he has nothing to offer you. He's very proud."

"Why didn't he tell me?"

"Oh, Christabel. Use your imagination."

"I wouldn't mind being poor. I wouldn't mind helping him on the farm. I wouldn't even mind living in that cold little house; I know I could make it bright and comfortable. Nothing would matter provided I was with Sam."

"You'll have to convince him."

"But Granny, the wedding. The marquee and the arrangements and the presents and the invitations. It's all costing so much, and . . ."

"It can be put off," said Mrs. Lowyer. "The last thing that your mother and father would want would be for you to marry a man whom you didn't truly love. If you want Sam, you're going to have to go and tell him. You must tell him what you've told me—that you don't mind about his being poor and hard-working and living in that funny little farmhouse. You must tell him that he is the only man in your life that you have ever truly loved."

"You've always known, haven't you?"

"Yes."

"How?"

"I'm old. I'm experienced. I've seen it all happen before."

"When shall I tell him?"

"Now. Go to his house now. You can borrow my car so that you don't get your feet wet. And I'll lend you a cardigan to keep you warm. And if he's asleep, wake him up, get him out of bed. Just tell him. Be truthful to him, but most important of all, be truthful to yourself."

"But Mother and Pa . . . I'll never have the nerve to tell them. I've been so stupid . . ."

"I shall tell them."

"And Nigel . . . ?"

"I shall tell Nigel as well. He's young. He'll be hurt, but he'll recover. Nothing could be worse for him than a half-hearted marriage." She kissed her granddaughter, her heart filled with sympathy and love. "Now off you go, my darling, and good luck. And, Christabel . . ."

"Yes, Granny."

"My dearest love to Sam."

She heard Christabel go. Heard her get the little car out of the garage and drive away down the rutted farm lane that led to Sam Crichtan's house. It was now five o'clock in the morning. *What am I thinking of?* Mrs. Lowyer asked herself. *What in the name of goodness have I done?*

But she could not make herself feel repentant. It had gone, that anxiety which she had been too afraid to take out and examine. She had always known about Sam and Christabel. She had told herself that their destiny was of no concern to her. But now their destiny had been put into her hands, and she had made her decision. Right or wrong, there could be no going back.

She lay sleepless until full light. At eight-thirty, she awoke from a doze, got out of bed and put on her dressing-gown and went to shut the window. The barley field lay shorn and gold under a watery sky. She knew that Sam and Christabel were right for each other. She thought of Paul and Felicity and Nigel. She dressed and went downstairs; said good morning to Lucy and put her out into the garden, cooked her own breakfast, drank her coffee. Then she put on her coat and, taking Lucy with her, let herself out of the house. It was a sweet, damp morning. Mrs. Lowyer went down the path and through the gate, and then, briskly, set off up the lane towards the big house, with her little dog at her heels.

The Blackberry Day

*T*he night train moved out of Euston Station, headed north. Claudia, already changed into her night-gown and robe, pulled up the blind and sat on the edge of the narrow bunk, watching the city slip away, lights and dim streets and high-rise flats wheeling off into the past. It was a cloudy evening, the clouds stained bronze by a million street lamps, but as she watched, the clouds parted for a moment and a moon sailed into view, a full moon, round and shining as a polished silver plate.

She turned off the lights, got into the bunk, with its cotton sheets all crisp and tight as a hospital bed, and lay and watched the moon, lulled by the smooth, gathering speed of the train. Inevitably, she recalled other, long-ago journeys, and for the first time, she thought of tomorrow and felt a mild stirring of excitement. It was as though what she was doing had become a positive action, not simply a compromise. Not simply the next-best thing.

This did something to bolster her bruised pride and enabled her to bundle, for the moment, anxious uncertainties out of her mind. They were still there, and would remain so, lurking around the edge of her subconscious, but for the time being she allowed herself the luxury of knowing that, at the end of the day, she had taken the right course.

She was immensely tired. The moon shone into her eyes. She turned on her side, away from its disturbing brilliance, buried her face in the pillow, and, surprisingly, slept.

At Inverness Claudia alighted from the train into a climate so different that the night train could have carried her not only north, but abroad. The day was Saturday, the month September, and she had left London on an evening warm as June, the air muggy and stale, the sky overcast. But now she walked out into a world that glittered in the early light, and was arched by a high and cloudless sky of pale and pristine blue. It was much colder. There was the nip of frost in the air, and leaves on trees were already turning autumn gold.

Here, she had an hour or two to wait for the small stopping train that would carry her, through the morning, even farther north. She filled this in by going to the nearest hotel and eating breakfast, and then walked back to the station. The news-stand had opened, so she bought a magazine and made her way to the platform where the smaller train waited, already gradually filling with passengers. She found a seat, stowed her luggage, and was almost at once joined by a pleasant-faced woman who settled herself across the table in the seat opposite. She wore a tweed coat with a cairngorm brooch in the lapel and a furry green felt hat, and, as well as her zipped overnight bag, was burdened by a number of plastic shopping bags, one of which contained what looked like a hefty picnic.

Their eyes met across the table. Claudia smiled politely. The woman said, "Oh, my, what a cold morning. I had to wait for the bus. My feet turned to stone."

"Yes, but it's lovely."

"Oh, ay, good and fine. Anything's better than the rain, I always say." A whistle blew, doors slammed. "There we are, we're off. Sharp on time, too. Are you going far?"

Claudia, who had picked up her magazine, resigned herself to conversation, and laid it down again.

"Lossdale."

"That's where I'm bound, too. I've been down for a night or two, staying with my sister. For the shopping, you know. They've a lovely Marks and Spencers. Bought a shirt for my husband. Are you staying in Lossdale?"

She was not curious, simply interested. Claudia told her, "Yes, just for a week." And then, because it was obvious that she would be asked, she volunteered the information. "At Inverloss, with my cousin Jennifer Drysdale."

"Jennifer! Oh, I know her well, we're on the Rural together. Stitching new kneelers for the kirk. Funny she never mentioned the fact that you were coming."

"It was very much a last-minute arrangement."

"Is this your first visit?"

"No. I used to come up every summer when I was young. When her parents were alive, and before Jennifer inherited the farm."

"You live in the south?"

"Yes, in London."

"I thought so. By your clothes." The train was rattling over the bridge, the firth spread below them, stretching from the far western hills to the sea. She saw small boats going about their business, delectable houses facing out over the water, with gardens sloping down to the shore. "I came up last night on the sleeper."

"That's a long journey, but better than driving a car. My man will scarcely go on the main roads these days, the traffic goes so fast. Like taking your life in your hands. But then he was always slow. It's his nature. Goes with his job."

Claudia smiled. "What is his job?"

"He's a shepherd. And his mind on not much else but his sheep. I just hope he remembers to come and pick me up at the station. I left a note over the cooker to remind him, but that's no certainty that he'll remember." She was not complaining. In fact, she looked quite smug about her husband's shortcomings, as though they made him special. "And is Jennifer coming to meet you?"

"She said she would."

"She's a busy girl, with the farm and the animals and the children. They're lovely bairns."

"I've only seen photographs. I haven't been to Inverloss for twenty years. Jennifer wasn't even married then."

"Well, she's got a lovely man in Ronnie. Mind, he comes from south of the border, but for all that he's a good farmer. Just as well, with that great place to run."

The conversation lapsed. Claudia gazed from the window. They were into the hills now, snaking away into a country desolate save for isolated farmsteads and flocks of sheep, and rivers flowing through wide green straths. The sun rose in the sky, and long shadows grew shorter. Claudia's companion opened her picnic bag, poured tea into a plastic mug, munched genteelly on a ham sandwich.

The small stations came and went, the train idling for moments while passengers alighted or climbed aboard. They passed the time of day, and dogs barked, and porters trundled trolleys of parcels. Nobody hurried. It was as though there was all the time in the world.

The journey progressed, and Claudia began to count the stops, as once she used to. Three more to go. Two more. One more. Nearly there. The train ran alongside the sea. She saw ebb-tide beaches and distant breakers. The shepherd's wife packed up her picnic, dusted shortbread crumbs from her pouter-pigeon bosom, rummaged in her capacious handbag for her ticket.

The train slowed, and the sign LOSSDALE sailed past the window. The two women stood, gathered up their belongings, stepped down onto the platform. The shepherd was there, with his dog. He had not forgotten, but greeted his wife with little fuss. "You're here," he told her unnecessarily, took her bag from her, and strode away. She followed him, turning back to wave at Claudia. "See you around, maybe."

No sign of Jennifer. The train drew away, and Claudia was left alone on the platform. She stood by her suitcase in her London suit and decided that there is nothing more letting down than to have no person to meet one at the end of a journey. She determined not to become impatient. There was no hurry, no pressing appointment. Jennifer had just been held up . . .

"Claudia!"

A man's voice. Startled, she turned, full into the sun, needing to shade her eyes. She saw him, coming at her out of the dazzle, unrecognized for an instant, and then, astonishingly, familiar.

Magnus Ballater. The last person she had ever expected to see. Not forgotten, but out of mind for longer than Claudia cared to think about. Magnus, in dark corduroys and a hugely patterned sweater; taller and more heftily built than she remembered, with a head of unfashionably long, dark, thick hair, and that old irrepressible grin on his sun-tanned, weather-seamed face.

"Claudia."

She knew that she was gaping, and had to laugh at her own amazement. "Magnus. For heaven's sake. What are *you* doing?"

"Come to meet you. Jennifer's been held up at Inverloss. Something about the boiler. She gave me a ring and asked me to come and collect you." He stood there, looking down at her. "Do I get a kiss?"

Claudia reached up and planted a peck on his cold cheek. "I didn't know you'd be around."

"Oh, yes, I'm around. A local inhabitant now. Is this all your luggage?" He swept it up. "Come along now."

She followed him, almost running to keep up with his long legs, through the gate, and out into the station yard, where a large battered car awaited them. A dog looked out of the back window. Its nose had made smeary marks on the glass. Magnus flung open the boot and tossed Claudia's suitcase in with the dog, and then came around to open the front door for her. She got in. The car smelled of dog, and the inside looked as though it hadn't been cleaned out for months, but Magnus made no apologies as he settled himself beside her, slammed the door and started up the engine. Gravel shot from behind the back wheels and they were away. She remembered that he had never been a man to waste time.

She said, "But what do you do here?"

"I run my father's old woollen mill."

"But you always swore you'd never do that. You were going to be independent, go out on your own."

"And so I was for a bit. Worked in the Borders, and then Yorkshire. Then I went to Germany for a couple of years, and ended up in New York as a wool broker. But then my father died, the mill started running down, and it was going to be sold, so I came home."

There was an air of tremendous confidence about him. She said, and it was a statement and not a question, "And pulled it all together."

"Tried to. At least we're out of the red now, and we've got some important orders coming in. Doubled the work-force. You must come and see it. See if you approve of our end product."

"And what is that?"

"Tweeds, but much finer than the ones my father used to make. Closer weaves, lighter weights. Hard-wearing, but not hard. Malleable, I think the word is. And some amazing colours."

"Are you designing?"

"Yes."

"And where are the important orders coming from?"

"All over the world."

"That's marvellous. And where do you live?"

"In Pa's old house."

Old Mr. Ballater's house. Claudia remembered it, built high on the hill, above the town. It had a large garden and a tennis court, and many energetic afternoons had been spent there, for Magnus, a year or so older than Claudia and Jennifer, had been one of a pack of youngsters who had spent all their time together. Leaving school, he had studied textile design, and that last summer of all, he was already a first-year student.

That had been a special summer, for a number of reasons. The weather was one of them, for it had been exceptionally warm and dry, and the long, light northern evenings had seen many fishing expeditions, walks up the river bank, and quiet hours spent casting for trout. The social life was another. They were all grown up now, and never had there been such an endless round of picnics and golf matches and tennis tournaments and reel parties and midnight barbecues on the beach. But Magnus, perhaps, had been the most important reason of all, for his enormous energy and his appetite for new diversions had swept them all up in his wake. A young man who never tired, was never bored nor out of humour, who owned his own car, and generally gave the impression that never for one moment did he doubt that life was living and every day to be filled with enjoyment.

"But tell me about yourself." Driving at an alarming rate, they were already through the little town, and out into the countryside beyond. "Jennifer says you haven't been north for twenty years. How could you stay out of touch for so long?"

"We weren't out of touch. We've always written to each other, and telephoned, and every now and then Jennifer comes to London for a day or two and stays with me, and we go shopping and to the theatre . . ."

"But twenty *years*. So long since we were all together. What times those were." He turned to smile at her, and Claudia prayed that a car was not bombing towards them around the curve of the road. "Why didn't you come? Were you too busy?"

"Like you. Learning a trade. Getting experience. Starting a business."

"Interior designing. Jennifer told me. Where do you operate?"

"London. The Kings Road. I've got a shop, and my own workrooms. Lots of commissions; too many sometimes."

"Who runs it while you're away?"

"I have an assistant."

"You sound successful."

Claudia thought about this. "I suppose I am."

His eyes were back on the road. He said, "You never married."

"I suppose Jennifer told you that as well."

"Of course. I found it hard to believe."

Claudia knew a stirring of feminine irritation. Her voice was cool. "I suppose you imagined that my only potential was a house, a husband, and children."

"No," Magnus replied calmly, "I didn't imagine anything of the sort. I was just surprised that a girl so beautiful hadn't been snapped up years ago."

He spoke so naturally, so reasonably, that Claudia was ashamed of her own thoughtless words. She said, "I'm doing what I want to," but thought of Giles, and then did not think of Giles, because Giles was in America, and this place and this moment and this man beside her had no part of Giles. "I am being independent."

"May I say that it suits you?"

She was touched. "Yes, I should like that very much." She smiled, and smoothly changed the direction of the conversation. "And you, Magnus? A wife?"

"Still unresolved."

"What does that mean?"

"That I never actually gathered up the courage to make the great commitment. A certain amount of dabbling has taken place, of course, but not the dreaded plunge." Once more, he turned his head to look into her face, and his blue eyes gleamed with amusement. "It would appear that we are birds of a feather."

Claudia turned away, making no comment. She knew that he was mistaken, and they were not birds of a feather, but she wasn't going to tell him so. *A certain amount of dabbling has taken place.* It was not difficult to imagine the extent of these dabblings, for he was, and always had been, an extremely attractive man. But she had not followed suit. Since meeting Giles eight years ago, she had remained constant to him; seen him through an unsatisfactory marriage and an acrimonious divorce, and, staunchly, been around ever since. And Magnus's dreaded plunge, the final commitment of marriage, she did not fear, but longed for.

Inverloss lay back from the road, reached by a rutted track, and sheltered by a stand of ancient beeches and oaks. Bumping down the lane, Claudia looked for change, and was grateful to see little. A new barn had been built, and there was a cattle-grid between the road and the garden, but otherwise all was just the same. Beyond the cattle-grid, sea pebbles did duty as gravel, and approaching the house had always sounded just like driving across a beach. Magnus put the heel of his hand on the horn in a long blast, and before Claudia could open the door of the car, Jennifer was there, erupting out of the house with dogs at her heels and a toddler on her hip. She wore jeans and a sweat-shirt, and her freckled face shone with good health. Her hair was a curly mop, and she looked no different from the tomboy teenager she had once been.

"Oh, Jennifer . . ."

Jennifer set the toddler down, and they hugged. All the dogs, including Magnus's, began to bark, and the child's face crumpled and he began to howl, so Jennifer picked him up again, and he gazed at Claudia with baleful, tear-brimmed eyes.

"I'm sorry I couldn't get to meet you, but Ronnie's fishing, and the man came to see about the boiler. We've been waiting for days, and he had to come on a Saturday!"

"No problem. I'm here."

"Magnus, you are a saint. Stay and have lunch with us. It's such a gorgeous day, we're going to go blackberrying. We decided this morning that this is going to be our blackberry day. Jane and Rory are riding their ponies, but they'll be back soon."

There had always, every year, as far back as Claudia could remember, been a blackberry day. A traditional expedition to pick the dark fruit for a twelve months' supply of jellies and jams.

She said, "Are we going to Creagan Hill?"

"But of course. Where else. Do come, Magnus. We can always do with an extra pair of hands."

"All right. But I have to go back to the mill first, there are a few things I have to sort out. What time's lunch?"

"Around one."

"I'll be there."

The inside of the house was no different. Such comfort. It smelt the same, a little musky and smoky and peaty, and there were worn bits on the carpets, and grubby marks on the wallpaper, just the height of children's hands.

"Isn't it great that Magnus has come back to Lossdale to live? It's like old times. He and Ronnie are tremendous buddies, and he's doing wonders at the mill. Were you surprised to see him?" Jennifer, hefting her baby, led the way upstairs, and Claudia, carrying her suitcase, followed. They crossed the wide landing, Jennifer flung open a door, and they walked into the sunlight beyond.

"I put you in here, it's the room you always had . . ." Claudia went to lay her suitcase across the seat of a chair. "Don't you adore the new bedspreads? I found them in a trunk in the attic. You must be longing to get out of your trainy clothes. I can't wait to introduce you to Ronnie; I can't *believe* you've never met him. And Jane and Rory. This one's called Geordie." She set him on his feet and sat herself down on the edge of the bed. Geordie, tottering slightly, made his way to the chest of drawers, thumped down on his bottom, and began to play with one of the brass handles. "He's such a love."

Claudia was at the window, standing with her back to her cousin, looking down over the fields to the distant sea. She said, "I was so afraid everything would be changed, but it isn't." She turned back to smile at Jennifer. "Nor have you. You never do."

"You've changed," said Jennifer bluntly. "You've lost weight. You're dreadfully thin."

"That's just London. And we're both thirty-seven now. Not girls any longer."

"I didn't say you looked old. Just thin. And sort of polished." Jennifer's gaze was steady and unblinking. "Why did you suddenly decide to come, at a day's notice? Or don't you want to talk about it?" There had never been secrets between them. Claudia lowered her head and began to unbutton the jacket of her suit. "It's Giles, isn't it?"

And it was a relief to hear her say his name; to have it said, so that it did not have to hang, like a spectre, between them.

Jennifer knew about Giles. Had gleaned what she could from letters, and had met him once in London, when Giles took the pair of them out for dinner. At that time he had been divorced for nearly a year. "Is he going to marry you?" Jennifer had asked, but Claudia had laughed, and told her that it was not like that at all, they were simply good friends.

Giles. Handsome, successful, charming, but paranoiacally elusive. He and Claudia each kept their separate establishments, but they were lovers. They were a pair, accepted as a couple, and when asked away for country weekends, went together and stayed together.

But Giles's job as a money-broker was far-reaching. Much of his time he spent in New York, where he had an apartment in the city, and often he was away for three or four months at a time. She did not know when he was returning until he called her. "I am back," he would say. "I am here." Whereupon, as if their separation had never taken place, the pattern of a shared life was taken up again: the dinner party in Giles's house, which Claudia was glad to organize; the contacting of mutual friends; the intimate evenings in their favourite Italian restaurant; the magic nights, their love shared in Claudia's huge, downy bed.

And life changed colour, and became vital, with energies to spare so that the day-to-day demands of home and job and business presented no problems, rather were a challenge that Claudia gladly met. She felt fulfilled, each tomorrow bright with promise—so much so, that it was hard to believe that it was not the same for Giles. One day, she told herself, tomorrow, he will discover that he cannot exist without me. But then that tomorrow would bring a telephone call to let her know that Giles was once more on his way, his flight dictated by the vagaries of his job. And he would be gone, across the Atlantic, leaving her alone, to get on as best she could with her single, lonely existence.

Jennifer was waiting. She said at last, "Yes, it's Giles. We were going to Spain with a party of friends. Everything booked. But he's been held up in New York and we had to cancel. I could have gone, but it would have been pointless on my own."

"How long has he been away this time?"

"A few months. He was due back three days ago."

"How *mean*."

Claudia sprang to Giles's defence. "It's not his fault."

"You make excuses for him. Does he ever write to you? Is he ever in touch?"

"He telephones. Sometimes. He's a busy man."

"More excuses. I suppose you love him. Would you marry him?"

"I . . ." Claudia sought for the right words. "Yes. Yes, I do. I mean, I want to be married. I want to have children. Everybody thinks I'm a dedicated career woman, but I would love to have children. Soon I'll be too old."

"Are you certain," Jennifer asked with disconcerting frankness, "that you are not simply his London lady?"

The feared, unacknowledged suspicion. As she had always done, Claudia shrugged it away. "There's a possibility, I suppose."

"Do you trust him?"

"I don't think about trust."

"But Claudia, trust is the most important thing of all. Don't *waste* your life."

"How could I walk away from Giles? It's too big a decision. I can't handle it. He's part of me now; I've loved him for too long."

"Yes. Too long. Cut loose."

Claudia said, "I can't."

They fell silent. This silence was shattered by doors opening and slamming shut, footsteps, high-pitched voices calling up the stairs. "Mummy! We're back. We're *starving*."

Jennifer sighed. She got to her feet and went to gather Geordie up into her arms. She said, "I must go and see to lunch. We'll talk some more."

She went. Claudia, alone, unpacked and changed into old jeans and trainers. She cleaned her face, brushed her hair. As she did this, she heard a car drawing up outside the front door, and looking from the window, saw Magnus, returned from his mill. He got out of the car and started towards the house. Claudia watched him, but as though she had called out his name, he suddenly stopped and looked up and saw her there, framed in the upstairs window.

He said, "Are you not ready yet, for lunch?"

"Yes, I'm ready. On my way."

Creagan Hill lay three miles from Inverloss, on the far side of the little town. From a rounded summit, crowned with scree and rock, it swept down, heather-clad, to the coastal plain, there giving way to a scattering of small drystone-diked fields, where bracken grew and sheep grazed. Narrow lanes wound around the margins of these fields, sheltered from the prevailing wind and in the full face of the sun. Here were the bramble thickets, and the fat, dark blackberries, clustered, ripening, upon the thorny stems.

The prospect of the expedition filled Jennifer's children with unsophisticated anticipation.

"We go *every* year," Jane explained through a mouthful of cottage pie. "And we get absolutely filthy, and the person who's picked the most gets a prize. I got it last year . . ."

"You stole some of mine," Rory pointed out. He was a stolid child, with blue eyes and his mother's hair.

"I didn't, you gave them to me."

"I'd filled my bucket. I didn't have any more room."

Magnus tactfully intervened. "Never mind. Perhaps this year everybody will get a prize."

"Even Geordie?"

"Why not?"

"He'll just be a nuisance and get under everybody's feet, and eat berries. He'll probably make himself sick."

Geordie banged a spoon on his high chair, and when they all looked at him, dissolved into delighted laughter.

"In fact," Jennifer said, when they had all stopped laughing at Geordie, "Jane's got a point. Geordie certainly won't last the whole afternoon. So I think we should take two cars, and then I can bring him home when he starts to flag."

"I want to go with Magnus," Jane announced. "I'm going in his car."

Rory was not to be outdone. "Me too."

Their mother sighed. "I don't mind who goes with who, but how about getting the plates into the dishwasher, and then we can make a start."

And so Claudia found herself once more seated beside Magnus in his car, with Rory and Jane on the back seat, and Magnus's dog in the boot. The expression on the dog's face was long-suffering, and Claudia did not blame him. Jennifer went ahead, the baby strapped into his chair behind her, and Magnus, at a more prudent speed than their drive of the morning, brought up the rear of the little procession.

The afternoon fulfilled the promise of the early morning and remained incredibly bright and clear and warm. Once they had left the town behind them, Claudia saw the shape of the hills, the brilliance of the sea. Sunlight streamed down over tawny bracken and the plum-bloom of the heather. They turned off the road and plunged into a maze of small lanes, headed away from the sea. Creagan Hill reared up before them, so steeply that the summit was lost from view.

Rory and Jane were asking riddles.

What's green and goes at a hundred miles an hour?

A ton-up gooseberry.

Why did the razorbill raise 'er bill?

Because she wanted the sea urchin to see 'er chin. Get it, Rory? See 'er chin.

Screams of laughter.

Claudia opened her window and let the wind blow in on her face. It was cold and smelt of grass and moss and seaweed, and she thought of Spain, and was, quite suddenly, glad that she was here and not there.

They reached the chosen spot at last, spilled out of the cars and set to work. Ranged along the roadside, scrambling over dykes into the fields, they picked busily all afternoon. The plastic buckets were slowly filled with the dark fruit. Mouths and fingers were stained purple, sweaters snagged, jeans torn, shoes coated with mud. By four o'clock little Geordie had had enough, and Jennifer decided that it was time to take him home.

"He's been so good, sitting in that nice bit of bog and looking for ladybirds, haven't you, my poppet?" She kissed his filthy face. "Anyway, I've got to get back and do something about dinner. Come and eat dinner with us, Magnus."

"You've already fed me."

"We'll feed you again. No problem. And Ronnie will want to tell you all about the fish he didn't catch. Who's coming with me?"

Jane and Rory debated, and finally decided to go with their mother. They were sated with blackberries, and there was a television programme they wanted to watch.

"How about you two?"

Claudia put her heavy bucket of berries into the boot of Jennifer's car and stretched her aching arms and shoulders. "It's such a beautiful day, I can't bear to waste a moment of it." She looked at Magnus. "Perhaps we could take your dog for a walk? So far, he seems to have had a fairly boring time."

Magnus was easy. "Whatever. We could climb the hill. Look at the view. Would you like that?"

It was exactly what she had been wanting to do all afternoon. She said, "Yes, I'd love it."

Jennifer departed, the children waving from the open windows of the car as though they were saying goodbye forever. When they were gone, Magnus turned to Claudia.

"So. What are we waiting for?"

They set off. Up through the fields, up the gradually steepening slope; through broken gateways and knee-high bracken, and on, up again, until they were surrounded by heather. The dog, delighted at last to have some attention paid to it, raced ahead, scenting rabbits, his great tail pluming. A few old sheep, seeing them approach, ceased their grazing and stared. Now, Claudia could feel the wind on her cheeks and was grateful for its coolness, and was grateful too for the path that stretched ahead, for the firmness of the close-cropped turf, which made for pleasant walking. She could feel the stretch and pull of the muscles in her legs, and her lungs were filled with air as pure and as cold as fresh spring water.

About half-way up the hill, they came upon a grassy corrie cleft by a tiny burn, miniature waterfalls bubbling down over a bed of white pebbles. Claudia was thirsty. She knelt and scooped water up in her palm and drank it. It tasted of peat. She sat then, with her back to the hill and her eyes, for the first time, turned upon the view.

"I had no idea that we had come so far, and climbed so high."

"You've done well." He settled himself beside her, his knees drawn up. He shaded his eyes with his hand. "No need to climb further. We won't get a better sighting than this."

He was right. A spectacular view, remembered from years back, but always breath-taking. It took in the curve of the coastline, the fields and the farms and the inland lochs. All was spread before them like some giant-sized map. So clear was the air that the mountains, some fifty miles to the south, showed themselves, their peaks frosted with the first snows of the winter. And ahead was the sea, on this day blue as the Mediterranean, the wine-dark seas of Homer's Greece.

And the silence. Only the wind, the song of a lark, the long sad call of a curlew. Sitting still, they were soon chilled by the wind. Claudia, who had taken off her sweater and tied the arms around her waist, now undid the knot, and pulled the sweater on again.

He said, "You mustn't get cold."

"I'm all right. And it's good for the soul just to look at a view like that on a day like this. How fortunate we are. You in particular, because now you live here *all* the time."

"I know what you mean. It gets everything into proportion."

"It makes me feel like an ant."

"An *ant?*"

"Tiny. Insignificant. Unimportant."

But not just she herself. All of life, with its problems: working, making money, loving. Up here, so high above the world, was like seeing the day-to-day rat race through the wrong end of a telescope, so that all became diminished, weightless, and trivial. And if Claudia was an ant, then the Atlantic was no more than a pond, and New York a dot on the globe, yet alive with the millions of teeming insects which peopled that teeming glut of humanity. Giles was one of them.

Magnus said, "Would you actually want to live here all the time?"

"I've never thought about it. But there is Jennifer, so happy. With her husband and her farm and her children. Yet I don't suppose it would ever do for me."

"Life is strange. All of us scattered, all over the place, and then after all these years . . . Why should you and I, of all people, find ourselves here and now, half-way up Creagan Hill and on a God-given day to boot?"

"I have no idea, Magnus."

He said, "I wonder if you have any idea of how much I was in love with you."

Claudia, frowning, turned to gaze at him in total puzzlement. His profile was sombre. She could see the lines around his mouth, the crow's feet, the strands of grey in his thick dark hair. Then he turned and looked into her face, and she saw his eyes, and for once there was no laughter in them.

She said, "You can't be serious."

"You had no idea?"

"I was seventeen."

"You were amazing. So beautiful that I was scared of how I felt because I was so certain that wanting you was unattainable."

"You never said . . ."

"Nor let it show."

"But why? Why not?"

"It wasn't the time. We were too young. Scarcely out of school, with all our lives in front of us. Everything to be learned, to be done. The world our oyster, filled with people waiting to love. And all we wanted was to get out and discover it for ourselves. I had a photograph of you. I used to carry it round and show it to my mates. 'This is my first love,' I would say. I didn't say, 'my only love.' That's what I should have said."

"Why do you tell me now?"

"Because I am too old for pride."

Simply spoken. Claudia dropped her eyes, not wishing him to read her thoughts. I am too old for pride as well, but I've hung on to it, because as far as Giles is concerned, it seems to be the only way I can hold on to him. Bleak knowledge. She thought about opening her heart to Magnus and telling him about Giles. Explaining, trying to make him understand. But she knew that she could never inflict such pain. Not now, not while she was in such a confused and distressed state of mind. Giles was her life and her love, but also her problem, and not one to be unloaded onto this man, this old friend, who had just declared his own undying love for her.

No. It must be kept inconsequent, light-hearted. She smiled. She said, "Pride is a nuisance anyway. It just gets between people."

"Yes. And then you say nothing until it is too late. Better, perhaps, not to say anything at all."

"Don't feel that." The afternoon was dying, the sun sinking behind them, the last of its rays casting long shadows. The wind, rising, bent the long grasses that grew on the banks of the little burn. Claudia shivered. She said, "It's getting cold." And then, because he looked so much in need of comfort, she leaned forward and kissed his mouth. "It's time we went home, Magnus."

After that, it was all right again. He grinned, ruefully, but still, it was a smile of sorts, and got to his feet, and held out a hand to help Claudia up. Then he whistled for his dog, and they set off. The downward slope was easy going, and by the time they reached the car, he was his old cheerful self again, full of plans for the evening ahead.

". . . I must buy some wine for Ronnie. Do you mind if we stop off in the town for a moment while I do a quick bit of shopping? I'm out of bacon as well, and I need a bag of dog biscuits."

In the last golden light of the afternoon, the main street of Inverloss bustled with the last activities of the day. The shops were still open; the butcher, the greengrocer, the fishing-tackle shop. The Italian café spilled neon light out onto the pavement, and from its interior came the sound of pop music and the evocative smell of frying fish and chips. Girls hung around outside the café, giggling in their Saturday finery, tight jeans and ear-rings, and the young men sat across the road, outside the pub, and eyed them.

Magnus drew up by the newsagent. "I won't be long."

He disappeared inside, and emerged almost immediately with a newspaper. Through the open window, he dropped it onto her lap. "This'll keep you amused."

He strode off.

It was this morning's paper he had brought her, a national tabloid printed in London. She cast her eye over the screaming headlines and then slowly scanned the rest of the paper, glancing at items, photographs, advertisements. She turned to the Social Diary. And saw the picture of Giles.

It was neither a very large nor a very good photograph, but it jumped at her as a known name will leap from a column of newsprint. He stood with a girl on his arm. A fair-haired girl, with a long cascade of hair. She wore a low-necked dress, her arms were bare. She carried a small bunch of flowers. Giles was smiling, showing his teeth. He looked overweight, a bit ponderous. He was sporting a tremendously spotted tie.

The caption: "Giles Savours with his young bride Debbie Peyton. See Column 4."

Her first instinctive thought was *It can't be true. It's a ghastly mistake. They've got it all wrong.* Quite suddenly, she felt dreadfully cold, her lips frozen, her mouth dry. *It can't be true.*

Column 4.

The headline in thick black type. BUSINESS AS USUAL FOR GILES AND DEBBIE. And then the story.

> *There will be no immediate honeymoon for London business man Giles Savours (forty-four), who was married this week in the Church of St. Michael, Brewsville, New York State. Giles, a partner with the City firm Wolfson-Rilke, has work aplenty to keep him at his desk in his New York office, but plans to jet to Barbados for Christmas.*
>
> *His lovely bride Debbie Peyton (twenty-two) is the only daughter of Charlie D. Peyton, of Consolidated Aluminium. A petite five feet two, she met Savours for the first time only three months ago, but their whirlwind courtship has not gone unobserved by Giles's New York colleagues. This is his second time around—his previous wife was Lady Priscilla Rolands—and his friends were beginning to doubt if he would ever take the plunge again . . .*

She could not read any more. The light was too dim, the newsprint wavered, the words blurred together. Giles—married. She thought of his voice, over the transatlantic telephone lines, easy as ever, ripe with reasonable excuses. "Terribly sorry. Something's come up. No possibility of my getting back to London in time for Spain. I know you'll understand. Why don't you go without me? You'll have a great time. Yes, of course. Just as soon as I can . . ."

And so on. The same voice, the same old let-down. Nothing new. Except this time he hadn't even had the courage to tell her that he was going to be married to another woman. A girl. Young enough to be his daughter. He was married. It was over.

She still felt numb with cold. She thought, I am numb with shock. She sat in Magnus's car and waited for her reactions to make themselves evident. For rage. Perhaps screams of fury. For furious tears of rank humiliation. For a terrible sense of loss. But none of these things happened, and after a bit, she realized that they would not.

Instead, she discovered that she was experiencing the most unexpected emotions of all. Relief, and a sort of gratitude. Relief because all decision had been taken out of her hands, and gratitude because perhaps this was the last and the best thing that Giles could have done for her.

"Sorry I've been so long." Magnus was back. He hurled a paper sack of dog meal over onto the back seat and then got in behind the wheel, placing a grocer's carrier bag on the floor between them. Claudia heard the clank of bottles. He slammed the door shut.

"I got the wine and some sweets for the children. I remembered, just in time, I'd promised them *all* prizes for blackberry-picking . . ."

Claudia said nothing. She did not turn to look at him, but felt his eyes on her face.

"Claudia?" And then: "Is something wrong?"

After a bit, she shook her head.

"Something is wrong."

She stared at the newspaper. Gently he reached over and took it from her. "What is it?"

"Just a man I know."

"What's happened to him?" He obviously feared the worst.

"He's not dead or anything. Just married."

"This guy here? Giles Savours?"

Claudia nodded.

"An old friend?"

"Yes."

"A lover?"

"Yes."

"How long have you known him?"

"Eight years."

A long pause, while Magnus read what Claudia had already read. "Why are ages and measurements always so vital on these bloody pages?" He folded the newspaper with some force and dropped it on the floor. Then he did a kindly thing. He reached out and took her hand in his own. He said, "Do you want to tell me about it?"

"Nothing to tell. Nothing and everything. It would take too long. But Giles is the reason that I am here. Because we were going to Spain together, and he cried off at the last moment. He didn't tell me why, just said that something had come up."

"Didn't you know about this other girl?"

"No. I didn't know anything about her. I suppose because I didn't want to. I wouldn't let myself think about anybody but myself. There is nothing more unattractive than a suspicious woman, and I knew that if I said anything to Giles, what existed between us would all be spoiled."

"That's not much of a basis for a relationship. You deserve better than that."

"No. It was my own fault. But it would have been more dignified for both of us had he found the courage to tell me himself. In a way I'm rather sorry for him. It must be dreadful to have so little moral courage."

"I'm not sorry for him. I think he sounds a cruel bastard."

"No. Not cruel, Magnus. One of us had to finish it . . . it's limped along for long enough. And you mustn't be sorry for me. You think I've been abandoned, but I think I feel as though I'd been set free."

Her hand still lay in his. For the first time, she turned her head and looked full into his face, and this time, it was he who kissed her.

He said, "It has been, to put it mildly, a remarkable day. And what is more, it is the first day of the rest of your life. So what do you say? Shall we nail our flags to the mast, and make what remains of it just as memorable? After all, we have wine and we have women, and I can always oblige with a song."

Despite everything, she found herself laughing at him. She said,

"I'm glad you were the person who was with me. I'm glad that you were the person I was able to tell."

"I'm glad too," said Magnus.

And that was all. He started up the engine and the car moved forward, down the street and out into the dusky countryside beyond. Claudia looked out over the sea and saw the moon rising up over the horizon and felt comforted, and she smiled into its silvery face as though she were greeting an old friend.

The Red Dress

A month after old Dr. Haliday's funeral, Mr. Jenkins, the gardener, sought out Abigail, and with a long face and much scratching of his head, gave in his notice.

Abigail had been half-expecting this for some time. Mr. Jenkins was well over seventy. He had gardened for her father for nearly forty years. But still nothing could assuage her dismay.

She thought of the beautiful garden, now with nobody to tend it. She had frightening visions of herself, single-handed, having to mow lawns, dig potatoes, weed flower-beds. She saw herself being overwhelmed by it all, letting the garden go to seed. She saw nettles, brambles, groundsel slowly encroaching, taking over. She thought in a panic, What on earth am I going to do without him?

She said this: "Mr. Jenkins, what am I going to do without you?"

"Perhaps," said Mr. Jenkins after a long, ruminative pause, "you could find somebody else?"

"I suppose I'll just have to try." She felt defeated, inadequate. "But you know how difficult it is even to find an odd-job man. Unless . . ." But she was without much hope. "Unless you know somebody?"

Mr. Jenkins shook his head slowly, from side to side, like an old horse bothered by flies. "It's difficult," he admitted. "And I don't like to leave you. But somehow, without the Doctor, I don't have the heart to go on. We made it together, him and me. Besides, I'm getting a bit beyond it, and the wet weather does play up my rheumatics. Mrs. Jenkins, now, she's been on at me the past year or two to hand in my notice, but I didn't want to leave the Doctor . . ."

He looked more anguished than ever. Abigail's tender heart went out to him. She put out a hand and laid it on his arm. "Of course you must retire. You've worked all your life. It's time you took things more easily. But . . . I will miss you. It's not just the garden. You've been a friend for so long . . ."

Mr. Jenkins mumbled something embarrassed and took himself off. A month later he departed for the last time, weaving down the lane on his ancient bicycle. It was the end of an era. Worse, Abigail had still found no one to take his place.

"I'll put a notice in the post-office window," Mrs. Midgeley had suggested, and together she and Abigail had drafted the wording of a little card. All that came of this, however, was a shifty-eyed boy on a motorcycle, who looked so untrustworthy that Abigail did not even let him into the kitchen. Too frightened to say that she didn't like the look of him, she told a lie and said that she had already found somebody else. He had then turned quite unpleasant and given Abigail one or two pieces of his meagre mind before roaring away with an offensive blast of smelly exhaust-pipes.

"Why don't you get in touch with a gardening contractor?" Yvonne had asked. Yvonne was Abigail's friend, married to Maurice, who commuted daily to the City. Yvonne preferred horses to gardening. She spent her life ferrying her children and their ponies to and from gymkhanas and meets, and when she wasn't doing this she was either mucking out, heaving hay bales, cleaning tack, grooming, plaiting manes, or ringing up the vet. "Maurice got fed up with these casual men who never come, so he made a deal with a contractor, and now a team comes once a week, and we never even pull up a weed."

But Yvonne's garden was simply a lawn, some beech hedges, and a few daffodils. It never looked anything but starkly neat, and bore no relation at all to the beautiful garden which was one of the nicest things old Dr. Haliday had bequeathed to his daughter Abigail. She didn't want it licked over once a week by a team of stout, heartless men. She wanted somebody who would not only work in the garden, but would love it as well.

"It would help," said Mrs. Brewer, who came in two mornings a week to do for Abigail, "it would help if you had a cottage to offer. Easy to get help if you can offer a house with the job."

"But I haven't got a cottage. And there's no room to build a cottage. And even if there was, I couldn't afford it."

"Makes a difference, having a little cottage," Mrs. Brewer said again. She went on saying it, at intervals, all through the morning, but did nothing to help the situation.

For six weeks Abigail toiled on her own. The weather was fine and this made things worse, because it meant that she never stopped working out of doors until it was almost too dark to see. But despite this, she saw the slow rot already begin. Things became untidy. Chickweed and couch-grass crept in from the neighbouring wood. Dead leaves revealed themselves, skulking beneath the lavender hedge, blown into dismal heaps behind the sundial. The vegetable garden, dug by Mr. Jenkins, lay dark and sullen, waiting for the drills which she had no time to make, for the seeds which she had no time to sow.

"Perhaps," she said to Mrs. Brewer, "I should forget about vegetables. Perhaps I should just sow it all out in grass."

"That would be a crying shame," said Mrs. Brewer sternly. "Took years to make, that asparagus bed. And think of those parsnips Mr. Jenkins used to bring in. Could make a meal of them, I used to say. That's what I used to say. Could make a meal of them."

A wind blew, and one of the gates swung open and broke its hinge. The clematis Montana needed to be pruned, but Abigail was frightened of ladders. She knew that she should order peat for the azaleas. She wondered if the motor mower had been serviced.

She met Yvonne in the village. Yvonne said, "Darling, you're beginning to look exhausted. Don't tell me you're trying to cope with that garden on your own?"

"What else can I do?"

"Life is too short to kill yourself over a garden. You've just got to face facts. Your father and Mr. Jenkins were unique. Now, you'll have to simplify things. You've got to have some sort of a life of your own."

"Yes," said Abigail, knowing that this was true. She walked home with her basket of groceries and tried to decide what she should do. She thought, I am forty, and this gave her a shock as it always did. What had happened to the dreams of youth? They were gone, slipped away with the years. Years spent working in London, and then coming back to Brookleigh to take care of her father after her mother died. To keep herself busy, she had taken a job in the local library, but six months ago, when the Doctor had had a minor stroke, she had given this up as well, and devoted all her time and energy to keeping an eye on the active and determined old man.

And now he was dead, and Abigail was forty. What did one do at forty? Did one stop wearing jeans, buying pretty clothes, feeling cheerful in the sunshine? Did one become a career woman, or did one simply vegetate, moving, without visible effort, from one day to another, until one was fifty, and then sixty. She thought, I don't feel forty. It was nearly middle-aged, and sometimes Abigail felt as though she were still eighteen.

These baffling reflections lasted her all the way home. She came up the lane, and around the corner of the privet hedge, and saw the bicycle. It was a blue bicycle, very spindly and old, with the most uncomfortable-looking seat. An unfamiliar bicycle. Whose?

There was nobody in sight. But, as Abigail approached her back door, a figure came around the house from the front garden and said, "Good morning," and so amazing was his appearance that for an instant Abigail could only stare. He had a great deal of hair and a large, shaggy brown beard. On top of the hair was a knitted hat with a red tassel. Below the beard came a sagging sweater, which reached almost to the man's knees. Then stained corduroys and old-fashioned lace-up boots.

He came towards her. "That's my bicycle." She saw that he was quite young; his eyes, in all that mass of hair, a remarkable blue.

"Oh, yes," said Abigail.

"I heard you were wanting a gardener."

Abigail played for time. "Who told you?"

"The wife went to the post office, and the lady there told her." They gazed at each other. He added simply, "I'm needing a job."

"You're new here, aren't you?"

"Yes. We hail from Yorkshire."

"How long have you been in Brookleigh?"

"About two months now. We're living in the Quarry Cottage."

"The Quarry Cottage . . ." Abigail's voice was dismayed. "I thought that had been condemned."

The man grinned. White teeth, very straight and shining, gleamed through the undergrowth of his beard. "It should have been. But at least it's a roof over our heads."

"What brought you to Brookleigh?"

"I'm an artist." He went to lean, gracefully, against the kitchen window-sill, his hands in his pockets. "I've been teaching in a secondary school in Leeds for the past five years, but I decided that if I didn't chuck it up and try to make something of my painting now, then I never would. I talked it over with Poppy—she's my wife—and we decided to give it a try. And I came here because I wanted to be near London. But I've got a couple of kids and they have to be fed, so I need a part-time job."

There was something very disarming about him, with his bright blue eyes and his extraordinary clothes and his composed manner. After a little, Abigail said, "Do you know anything about gardening?"

"Yes. I'm a good gardener. My father had a little plot when I was a boy. I used to garden with him."

"There's a lot to be done here."

"I know," he answered coolly. "I was having a look around. It's time you got your vegetables in, and that climbing rose on the front of the house needs to be cut back . . ."

"I really meant that it's quite a big garden. A lot of work."

"But it's beautiful. It would be a pity to let it go."

"Yes," said Abigail, and her heart warmed to him.

There was another small pause while they eyed each other. He asked, "Have I got the job?"

"How much time can you give me?"

"I could come three days a week."

"Three days isn't very much in a garden this size."

He smiled again. "I have to keep time for my painting," he insisted, politely but firmly. "And in three days I can do a right load of work."

Abigail hesitated only a moment longer. And then, impulsively, she made up her mind. "All right. It's a deal. And you can start on Monday morning."

"Eight o'clock, I'll be here." He picked up his bicycle and swung a leg over that dreadful saddle.

"I don't know your name," said Abigail.

"It's Tammy," he told her. "Tammy Hoadey." And with that he was away, pedalling down the drive, with the tassel on his hat blown backwards in the breeze.

*   *   *

The village, when they heard the news, were much concerned. Tammy Hoadey was not a local man. He came from "up north," nobody knew anything about him. He had set up house in the derelict cottage by the old quarry. His wife looked like a gypsy. Was Abigail sure of what she was doing?

Abigail assured the village that she was quite sure.

Mrs. Brewer was more horrified than most. "Not a bit like old Mr. Jenkins. Gives me quite a turn seeing him working away with that beard. And the other day, he ate his lunch by the sundial. Sitting in the sun, he was, cool as a cucumber, just eating his sandwich."

Abigail had already noticed this breach of etiquette but had not remarked upon it. After all, just because old Mr. Jenkins had incarcerated himself each day in the dank tool-shed, to sit on an upturned bucket, eat his lunch and read the racing page of the daily paper, there was no reason why Tammy should be expected to do the same. And if a man worked in a garden, why should he not enjoy it as well? She said as much, in her usual diffident manner, to Mrs. Brewer, who sniffed and was silenced, but continued to disapprove of Tammy.

For two months all went well. The gate was mended, the lily-pool cleaned, the vegetable garden planted. The grass began to grow, and Tammy rode up and down the sloping lawn on the motor mower. He barrowed manure, tied up the clematis, weeded the borders, shifted a straggling rhododendron. And all the time, as he worked, he whistled. Whole arias and cantatas complete with trills and arpeggios. Strains of Mozart and Vivaldi pierced the air, mingling with bird-song. It was like having one's own private flautist.

And then, in the middle of July, he came to Abigail and told her that he was going to be off for two months. She was both hurt and angry. "But, Tammy, you can't leave me without warning. There's the grass, and the fruit to pick, and *everything*."

"You'll manage," he told her calmly.

"But *why* are you going?"

"I'm going to work at the potatoes for a contractor. It's good money. I want to get all my pictures framed, and that costs a bomb. If they're framed I can try to get them into some exhibition. Unless I exhibit, I'm never going to sell anything."

"Have you ever exhibited?"

"Yes, once, in Leeds. A couple of pictures." He added, with no false modesty, "They both sold."

"I still think it's very unfair of you to walk out on me."

"I'll be back," he told her. "In September."

There was obviously nothing to be done. Tammy duly went, leaving Abigail with no hope of finding, in midsummer, a replacement. No hope, even, of hiring some odd-job man to see her over the crisis. Besides, after her fury had died down and she was able to view the situation in comparative calm, she realized that she did not want another gardener. No man worked harder than Tammy Hoadey, but what was most important was that Abigail liked him. It was a bore, but the two months would pass. She would wait for him to return.

Which he did. Unchanged, still wearing the same bizarre clothes, thinner, perhaps, but as cheerful as ever. Whistling, he began to sweep up the first of the leaves. Now, it was the Rodrigo Guitar Concerto. Abigail, in jeans and a scarlet sweater, went out to help him. They built a fire and pale smoke rose, a grey plume, up into the still, early-autumn air. Tammy stepped back from the bonfire and leaned on his broom. Across the fire and the smoke their eyes met. He smiled at Abigail. He said, "You look really nice in red. Never seen you wear red before."

She was embarrassed, but gratified as well. It was years since she had been paid such a warm and spontaneous compliment.

"It . . . it's only an old jersey."

"It's a good colour."

The compliment stayed with her, warming her, all through the next day. That morning, she walked to the village to do her shopping. Next door to the chemist was a small boutique, recently opened. In the window was a dress. A silk dress, very simple, neatly belted, the skirt a fan of deep pleats. The dress was red. Without allowing herself a second thought, Abigail walked into the shop, tried on the dress and bought it.

She did not tell Yvonne the reason she had been so impulsive. "Red?" said Yvonne. "But, darling, you never wear red."

Abigail bit her lip. "You don't think it's too bright? Too young?"

"No, of course I don't. I'm just astonished at your doing something so out of character. But I'm pleased, too. You can't go on mouldering around in dun-coloured clothes forever. Anyway, I had a great-aunt who lived to be eighty-four, and she always went to funerals in a sapphire-blue hat with feathers."

"What's that got to do with my red dress?"

"Nothing, I suppose." They began to laugh together, like school-girls. "I'm glad you bought it. I'll have to throw a party, so that you can wear it."

But, in October, the cheerful whistling suddenly stopped. Tammy came to work silent and uncommunicative. Abigail, terrified that he was going to hand in his notice, gathered up her courage and asked him if anything was the matter. He said yes, everything. Poppy had left him. She had taken the children and gone to her mother in Leeds.

Abigail was devastated. She sat on the edge of the cucumber frame and said, "For good?"

"No, not for good. Just for a visit, she says. But we had a row. She's so fed up with Quarry Cottage, and I can't really blame her. She's scared the kids'll fall down the quarry bank, and the little one's been coughing at nights. She says it's the damp."

"What are you going to do?"

He said, "I can't go back to Leeds. I can't go back to living in a city. Not after all this." A tired gesture somehow involved the garden, the wood, the flaming borders, the golden oak leaves.

"But she's your wife. And your children . . ."

"She'll come back," said Tammy, but he did not sound convinced. Abigail ached with sympathy for him. At lunchtime, when he settled down to his meagre snack, she filled a bowl with soup and carried it out to where he slumped, despondent, by the greenhouse.

"If your wife isn't here to take care of you, then I must," she told him, and he smiled gratefully, and took the soup.

Unbelievably, Poppy and the children returned, but the tuneful whistling was not resumed. Abigail felt herself caught up in some television soap opera: "The Continuing Saga of Tammy Hoadey." She told herself the problems were between Tammy and Poppy, husband and wife. It was no concern of Abigail's. She would not interfere.

But remaining a bystander was not to be possible. A week or so later, Tammy sought her out and said that he wanted to ask a favour of her. The favour was that Abigail should buy one of Tammy's pictures.

She said, "But I've never seen any of your pictures."

"I brought one with me. On the back of the bike. It's framed." She stared at him, trapped in embarrassment, and he went off and returned with a large parcel wrapped in crumpled brown paper and tied up with binder twine. He undid the knots and held the picture out for Abigail to inspect.

She saw the silvered frame, the bright colours, the upside-down procession of odd little people, and felt total incomprehension of this new form of art. It was so out of her league, so foreign to any of Dr. Haliday's pictures, that she could think of nothing to say. She started to blush. Tammy stayed silent. At last Abigail blurted out, "How much do you want for it?"

"A hundred and fifty pounds."

"A hundred and fifty? Tammy, I haven't got a hundred and fifty pounds to spend on a picture."

"Have you got fifty?"

"Well . . . yes . . ." Cornered, she was driven to cruel truth. "But . . . well, it's just not my sort of picture. I mean, I would *never* buy a picture like that."

He was undeflected by this. "Well, would you lend me fifty pounds? Just for a bit? You can have the picture as surety."

"But I thought you'd earned so much on the potatoes?"

"It all went in framing. And it's my little boy's birthday next week, and we owe the grocer. Poppy's come to the end of her rope. She says if I don't start selling pictures and making money, she's going back to her mother for good." He sounded desperate. "Like I said, I don't blame her. It's a hard deal for her."

Abigail looked again at the picture. The colours, at least, were bright. She took it from Tammy. She said, "I'll keep it for you. I'll keep it safely." And she went indoors and up to her bedroom and found her bag, and took from it five crisp ten-pound notes.

"This," she told herself, "is probably the stupidest thing I've ever done in my life." But she closed her handbag and went downstairs and gave the money to Tammy.

He said, "I can never thank you enough."

"I trust you," Abigail told him. "I know you won't let me down."

At lunchtime that day Yvonne called. "Darling, it's dreadfully short notice, but would you come and have dinner with us tonight? Maurice has just phoned from the office, and he's bringing a business friend back for the night, and I thought it would be nice if you'd come and help me entertain him."

Abigail did not really want to go. She felt depressed by Tammy's problems, and not in the mood for a party. She began to make unenthusiastic noises, but Yvonne thought she was being stupid, and told her so. "You're getting terribly old-maidish. What's happened to all that impulsive spirit? Of course you're coming. It'll do you good and you can wear your new red dress."

But Abigail did not wear the red dress. She was keeping the dress for . . . something. Some person. Some special day. She put on, instead, a brown dress that Yvonne had seen a dozen times before. She arranged her hair, made up her face, went downstairs. In the hall, Tammy's picture, still in its untidy wrappings, lay on the chest by the telephone. Its presence was somehow pathetic, like a cry for help. *Unless I exhibit, I'm never going to sell anything.* Unless people saw his extraordinary pictures, he was never going to hope to get started. An idea occurred to Abigail. Perhaps Yvonne and Maurice would be interested. Perhaps they would like it so much that they would buy a picture of Tammy's for themselves. And they would hang it in their sitting-room, and other people would see it and ask about him.

It was a faint hope. Maurice and Yvonne did not go in for patronage of the arts. But still, it was worth a try. Decisively, Abigail pulled on her coat, did up the buttons, gathered up the parcel, and set off.

Maurice's friend was called Martin York. He was a very large man, taller than Maurice, and extremely fat. His head was bald, fringed with greying hair. He had come down from Glasgow for a meeting, he told Abigail over sherry, and had actually booked into a London hotel, but Maurice had persuaded him to cancel the booking and instead to spend the night at his home in Brookleigh.

"A charming little village. You live here?"

"Yes, I've lived here all my life, on and off."

Maurice chipped into the conversation. "She's got the prettiest house in the village. And quite the most enviable garden. How's the new gardener doing, Abigail?"

"Well, he's not so new now. He's been working for me for some months." She explained about Tammy to Martin York. ". . . he's really an artist—a painter." This seemed as good a moment as any to broach the subject of the picture. "As a matter of fact, I brought one of his paintings with me. I . . . I bought it from him. I thought you might be interested . . ."

Yvonne came through from the kitchen and caught the tail end of this remark. "Who, me? Darling, I never bought a picture in my life."

"But we could look at it," said Maurice quickly. He was a kind man and always ready to make amends for his wife's forthright remarks.

"Oh, I'd like to *look* at it . . ."

So Abigail set down her sherry glass and went out to the hall where she had left Tammy's picture along with her coat. She brought the parcel into the sitting-room and untied the binder twine and pulled aside the paper. She handed the picture to Maurice, who set it up on the seat of a chair, and then stood back, the better to inspect it.

The other two also arranged themselves, standing around in a half-circle. Nobody said anything. Abigail found that she was as nervous of their reaction as if she had herself been responsible for creating those little figures, that brilliant mosaic of colour. She wanted desperately for them all to admire and covet it. It was as though she were the mother of a cherished child being examined, and found wanting.

Yvonne broke the silence at last. "But it's all upside down!"

"Yes, I know."

"Darling, did you *really* buy it from Tammy Hoadey?"

"Yes," lied Abigail, not having the nerve to disclose the arrangement she had made with Tammy.

"However much did you give him for it?"

"Yvonne!" her husband remonstrated sharply.

"Abigail doesn't mind, do you, Abigail?"

"Fifty pounds," Abigail told them, trying to sound cool.

"But you could have got something really good for fifty pounds!"

"I think it *is* really good," said Abigail defiantly.

There was another long pause. Martin York had still said nothing. But he had taken out his spectacles and put them on, the better to inspect the picture. Abigail, unable to bear the silence a moment longer, turned to him.

"Do you like it?"

He took his spectacles off. "It's full of innocence and vitality. And I love the colour. It's like the work of a very sophisticated child. I am sure you will have great enjoyment from it."

Abigail could have wept with gratitude. "I'm sure I will," she told him. She went to rescue Tammy's work from the others' unappreciative gaze, to bundle it back into its crumpled wrapping.

"What did you say his name was?"

"Tammy Hoadey," said Abigail. Maurice passed around the sherry decanter once more, and Yvonne started to talk about some new pony. Tammy was not mentioned again, and Abigail knew that her first tentative attempt at patronage had been a dismal failure.

The next Monday Tammy did not turn up for work. At the end of the week, Abigail made a few discreet inquiries. Nobody in the village had seen the Hoadeys. She let another day or two pass before getting out the car and driving down the rutted, rubbish-strewn lane which led to the old quarry. The dismal cottage lay by the lip of the cliff. No smoke rose from the chimney. The windows were shuttered, the door locked. In the trodden garden lay a child's abandoned toy, a plastic tractor missing a wheel. Rooks cawed overhead, a thin wind stirred the black water at the base of the quarry.

"I know you won't let me down."

But he had gone, back to Leeds with his wife and children. To start teaching again, and to forget his dreams of becoming an artist. He had gone, taking Abigail's fifty pounds with him, and she would never see him again.

She went home and took his picture from its wrapping and carried it into the sitting-room. She laid it on a chair, and went, with care, to take down the heavy canvas of some Highland glen that had hung forever above the mantel-piece. Its departure revealed a plethora of dust and cobwebs. She fetched a duster, cleaned these up, and then hung Tammy's picture. She stood back and surveyed it: the pure, clean colours, the little procession of figures, walking up the walls of the canvas and across the top, like those old Hollywood musicals when people danced on the ceiling. She found herself smiling. The whole room felt different, as though a lively and entertaining person had just walked into it. Enjoyment. That was the word that Maurice's friend had used. Tammy had gone, but he had left part of his engaging self behind.

Now it was nearly a month later. The autumn was truly here, cold winds and showers of rain, the beginning of frosts at night. After lunch Abigail, bundled against the cold, went out to tidy the rose-beds, dead-head the frosted blossoms, cut out the dead wood. She was wheeling a barrow of rubbish towards the compost heap when she heard the sound of an approaching car and saw a long, sleek black saloon come quietly around the curve of the lane and draw up at the side of the house. The door opened and a man got out. A tall stranger, silvery-haired, bespectacled, wearing a formal, dark overcoat. He looked almost as distinguished as his car. Abigail set down the wheel-barrow and went to meet him.

"Good afternoon," he said. "I'm so sorry to disturb you, but I'm looking for Tammy Hoadey and I was told in the village that you might be able to help me."

"No, he isn't here. He used to work for me, but he's gone. I think he's gone back to Leeds. With his wife and children."

"You haven't any idea how I could get in touch with him?"

"I'm afraid not." She took off a gardening glove and tried to push a stray lock of hair under her headscarf. "He didn't leave any address."

"And he's not coming back?"

"I'm not expecting him."

"Oh, dear." He smiled. It was a rueful smile, but all at once he looked much younger and not nearly so intimidating. "Perhaps I should explain. My name is Geoffrey Arland . . ." He felt inside his coat and produced, from an inner breast pocket, a business card. Abigail took it in her earthy hand. *Geoffrey Arland Galeries,* she read, and beneath this a prestigious Bond Street address. "As you can see, I'm an art dealer . . ."

"Yes," said Abigail. "I know. I came to your gallery about four years ago. With my father. You had an exhibition of Victorian flower paintings."

"You came to that? How very nice. It was a delightful collection."

"Yes, we enjoyed it so much."

"I . . ."

But the wind had blown a dark shower cloud over the sun, and now it started, suddenly, to rain.

"I think," said Abigail, "it would be better if we went indoors." And she led the way into the house, through the garden door, directly into the sitting-room. It looked pretty and fresh, the fire flickering in the grate, an arrangement of dahlias on the piano, and over the mantel-piece, the brilliant mosaic of Tammy's picture.

Coming behind her, he saw this at once. "Now, that's Hoadey's work."

"Yes." Abigail closed the glass door behind them and unknotted her headscarf. "I bought it from him. He needed the money. He and his family lived in a gruesome cottage down by the quarry. It was all he could find. They were always on the breadline. It seemed a dreadfully hand-to-mouth existence."

"Is this the only picture you have?"

"Yes."

"Is this the one you showed to Martin York?"

Abigail frowned. "Do you know Martin York?"

"Yes, he's a good friend of mine." Geoffrey Arland turned to face Abigail. "He told me about Tammy Hoadey because he thought I would be interested. What he didn't know was that I've been interested in Hoadey's work ever since I caught sight of a couple of his pictures in an exhibition in Leeds some time ago. But they were both sold, and for some reason I was never able to make contact with Hoadey. He seems to be an elusive sort of man."

Abigail said, "He gardened for me."

"It's a beautiful garden."

"It was. My father made it. But he died at the beginning of spring and our old gardener didn't have the heart to go on without him."

"I'm sorry."

"Yes," said Abigail inadequately.

"So now you live alone?"

"For the moment I do."

He said, "Decisions are difficult at such a time . . . I mean, when you lose someone close to you. My wife died about two years ago, and I've only just had the courage to up sticks and move. Not very far, admittedly. Just from a house in St. John's Wood to a flat in Chelsea. But still, it was something of an upheaval."

"If I can't find another gardener, I suppose I shall have to move. I couldn't bear to stay here and watch it all go to rack and ruin, and it's too big for me to manage on my own."

They smiled at each other, understanding. She said, "I could make you a cup of coffee."

"No, really, I must be on my way. I've got to get back to London, preferably before the rush-hour. If he does come back, you could get in touch with me?"

"Of course."

The rain had stopped. Abigail opened the door and they moved back out onto the terrace. The flagstones shone wet, the rain clouds had been blown away, and now the garden was suffused in misty golden sunlight.

"Do you ever come up to London?"

"Yes, sometimes. To see the dentist or something boring like that."

"Next time you come to the dentist, I hope you'll visit my gallery again."

"Yes. Perhaps. And I'm sorry about Tammy."

"I'm sorry too," said Geoffrey Arland.

November passed and then it was December. The garden lay grey and bare beneath the dark wintry skies. Abigail abandoned the garden and moved indoors, to write the first of the Christmas cards, do her tapestry, watch television. For the first time since her father died, she knew loneliness. Next year, she told herself, I shall be forty-one. Next year I will be decisive and competent. I must find a job, make new friends, have people for dinner. No one could do any of these things except herself, and she knew this, but at the moment she had hardly the heart to walk up to the village. She certainly hadn't the energy to undertake a trip to London. Geoffrey Arland's card remained, just as she had left it, tucked into the frame of Tammy's picture. But it was beginning to grow dusty, to curl at the corners, and soon, she knew, she would throw it into the fire.

Her low spirits turned out, inevitably, to be the onset of a bad cold and she was forced to spend two gloomy days in bed. On the third morning she awoke late. She knew it was late, because she could hear sounds of the vacuum cleaner from downstairs, which meant that Mrs. Brewer had let herself in with her latchkey and started work. Beyond Abigail's open curtains the sky was filling with light, turning from early grey to a pale, pristine, wintry blue. The hours stretched ahead of her like an empty void. Then Mrs. Brewer turned off the vacuum cleaner, and Abigail heard the bird singing.

A bird? She listened more intently. It was not a bird. It was a person whistling Mozart. *Eine Kleine Nachtmusik.* Abigail sprang from her bed and ran to the window, holding back the curtains with both hands. And saw, below her in the garden, the familiar figure; the red-tasseled cap, the long green pullover, the boots. He had his spade over his shoulder; he was heading for the vegetable garden, his feet making tracks on the frosty lawn. She threw up the sash, regardless of the fact that she was wearing only her night-dress.

"Tammy!"

He stopped short, turned, his face tilted up towards her. He grinned. He said, "Hello, there."

She bundled herself into the nearest clothes to hand and ran downstairs and out of doors. He was waiting for her by the back door, grinning sheepishly.

"Tammy, what are you *doing* here?"

"I've come back."

"All of you? Poppy and the children too?"

"No, they're still in Leeds. I've gone back to teaching again. But it's the school holidays, so I'm here now on my own. I'm back in the Quarry Cottage." Abigail stared in puzzlement. "I've come to work off that fifty pounds I owe you."

"You don't owe me anything. I bought the picture. I'm going to keep it."

"I'm glad of that, but even so I want to work off my debt." He scratched the back of his neck. "You thought I'd forgotten, didn't you? Or scarpered with your money? I'm sorry I went off like that, without letting you know. But the little boy got worse, he got flu and Poppy was frightened of pneumonia. His temperature was up, so we took him away from that house; it wasn't healthy. We went back to Poppy's mother. He was very ill for a bit, but he's all right now. Anyway, a teaching job came up. They're hard to get nowadays, so I thought I'd better grab the chance."

"You should have *told* me."

"I'm not much of a one at writing letters and the local telephone-box was always being vandalized. But I told Poppy that these holidays I'd be coming back to Brookleigh."

"But what about your painting?"

"I've put that behind me . . ."

"But . . ."

"The children come first. Poppy and the children. I see that now."

"But, Tammy . . ."

He said, "Your telephone's ringing."

Abigail listened. It was, too. She said, "Mrs. Brewer will answer it." But it kept on ringing, so she left Tammy standing there and went back into the house.

"Hello?"

"Miss Haliday?"

"Yes."

"This is Geoffrey Arland speaking . . ."

Geoffrey Arland. Abigail felt her mouth drop in astonishment at the extraordinariness of the coincidence. Naturally unaware of her gaping amazement, he went on, "I'm very sorry to ring you so early in the morning, but I have rather a busy day ahead of me, and I thought I'd have a better chance of getting hold of you now rather than later. I wondered if there was any hope of you getting up to town between now and Christmas. We're mounting an exhibition which I would particularly like to show you. And I thought we could perhaps have lunch together? Almost any day would suit me, but . . ."

Abigail found her voice at last. She said, "Tammy's back!"

Geoffrey Arland, interrupted in mid-flow, was naturally disconcerted. "I beg your pardon?"

"Tammy's back. Tammy Hoadey. The artist you came to look for."

"He's back with you?" Geoffrey Arland's voice was at once quite different, imperative, and businesslike.

"Yes. He turned up today, this very morning."

"Did you tell him I'd been to Brookleigh?"

"I haven't had the chance."

"I want to see him."

"I'll bring him up to London," said Abigail. "I'll drive him up in my car."

"When?"

"Tomorrow if you like."

"Has he got any work to show me?"

"I'll ask him."

"Bring anything he's got. And if he hasn't got any work at Brookleigh, then just bring him."

"I'll do that."

"I'll expect you in the morning. Come straight to the galleries. We'll have a talk with him and I'll take you both out for lunch."

"We should be with you about eleven."

For a moment neither of them said anything. And then, "What a miracle," said Geoffrey Arland and he did not sound businesslike any longer, but pleased and grateful.

"They happen." Abigail was smiling so widely, her face felt quite strange. "I am so *glad* you called."

"I'm glad too. For all sorts of reasons."

He rang off, and after a while Abigail put down her receiver. She stood by the telephone and hugged herself. Nothing had changed and everything had changed. Upstairs, Mrs. Brewer continued to move ponderously about behind her vacuum cleaner, but tomorrow Abigail and Tammy were driving to London to see Geoffrey Arland; to show him all Tammy's pictures; to be taken out for lunch. Abigail would wear her red dress. And Tammy? What would Tammy wear?

He was waiting for her, just as she had left him when the telephone started to ring. He was leaning on his spade, filling his pipe, waiting for her to return. As she appeared, he looked up and said, "I thought I'd start in on the digging . . ."

She very nearly said, *To hell with the garden.* "Tammy, did you take your pictures with you, when you went back to Leeds?"

"No, I left them behind. They're still at Quarry Cottage."

"How many?"

"A dozen or so."

"And there's something else I must ask you. Have you—have you got a suit?"

He looked as though he thought she had gone mad. But, "Yes," he said. "It was my father's. I wear it to funerals."

"Perfect," said Abigail. "And now don't talk for at least ten minutes because I've got an awful lot to tell you."

Mrs. Brewer hoped that Miss Haliday was giving Tammy Hoadey his notice. She had seen him coming up the lane on his bicycle, cool as a cucumber, without so much as a word of warning or explanation. Cheeky devil, she had thought, turning up out of the blue just as though he had never been away.

Now at the sink, filling the kettle for her morning cup of tea, she watched them at it: Miss Haliday talking nineteen to the dozen (and that wasn't her usual way) and Tammy just standing there like an idiot. She's giving him a piece of her mind at last, Mrs. Brewer told herself with satisfaction. It's what he's been needing, all these months. A piece of her mind.

But she was wrong. For when Miss Haliday stopped talking, nothing happened at all. She and Tammy just stood, quite still, staring at each other. And then Tammy Hoadey let his spade fall to the ground, tossed his pipe into the air, flung wide his arms and wrapped Miss Haliday in a bearlike embrace. And Miss Haliday, far from resisting such impudent goings-on, put her arms around his neck and hugged Tammy, right there in front of Mrs. Brewer's eyes, and took her feet off the ground, and was swung into the air, careless and graceless as some flighty teen-age girl.

Well, whatever next? Mrs. Brewer asked herself as the stream of water filled the kettle and overflowed, unheeded, into the sink. Whatever next?

A Girl I Used
to Know

The cable-car, at ten o'clock in the morning, was as crammed with humanity as a London bus at rush-hour. Grinding, swaying slightly, it mounted, with hideous steadiness, up into the clear, blindingly bright air, high over the snow-fields and scattered chalets of the valley. Behind them, the village sank away—houses, shops, hotels clustered around the main street. Far below lay great tracts of glittering snow, blue-shadowed beneath random stands of fir. Ahead and above it climbed—it gave Jeannie vertigo just to think about it—towards the distant peak piercing the dark-blue sky like a needle of ice . . .

The peak. The Kreisler. Just below it stood the sturdy wooden buildings of the upper cable station, the complex of the restaurant. The face of this edifice was one enormous window, flashing signals of reflected sunshine, and overhead fluttered the flags of many nations. Both the cable-car station and the restaurant had seemed, from the village, as distant as the moon, but now, with every moment, they drew closer.

Jeannie swallowed. Her mouth felt dry, her stomach tight with apprehension. Pressed into a corner of the cable-car, she turned her head to look for Alistair, but he and Anne and Colin had become separated from her in the rush to get on board, and he was away over on the other side. Easy to spot, because he was so tall, his profile blunt and handsome. She willed him to turn and catch her eye, to give her a smile of reassurance, but all his concentration was for the mountain, for the morning's run down the Kreisler and back into the village.

Last night, as the four of them had sat in the bar of the hotel, she had said, "I won't come." There was dancing going on and a jolly band in lederhosen.

"But of course you must. That was the whole point of your coming on holiday, so that we could all ski together. It's no fun if you spend the whole time rabbiting around on the nursery slopes."

"I'm not good enough."

"It's not difficult. Just long. We'll take it at your speed."

That was even worse. "I'll hold you back."

"Don't be so self-abasing."

"I don't want to come."

"You're not frightened, are you?"

She was, but she said, "Not really. Just frightened of spoiling it for you."

"You won't spoil it." He sounded marvellously certain of this, just as he was marvellously certain of himself. He seemed not to know the meaning of physical fear, and so was unable to recognize it in another person.

"But . . ."

"Don't argue any more. Don't talk about it. Come and dance."

Now, crammed into a corner of the cable-car, she decided that he had forgotten her existence. She sighed, and turned back to the window to view the void, the impossible, dizzying height. Far, far below, the skiers were already moving down the pistes, tiny antlike creatures drawing trails in the virgin snow, flying down the slopes back to the village. It looked so easy. That was the horrible thing, it looked so easy. But for Jeannie it was almost impossibly difficult. *Bend the knees,* the instructor had told her. *Weight on the outside leg.*

Weight on the outside leg. I mustn't forget. Weight on the outside leg. I can do it. I have to do it. Relax. Bend the knees. Weight on the outside leg.

They had arrived. One moment swinging in the clear air and the brilliant sunshine, the next clanking into the shadowed gloom of the cable-car terminal. They stopped with a jerk. The doors opened, everybody flooded out. Up here it was degrees colder. Icicles festooned the exit door, and there was the crunch of frozen snow underfoot. Jeannie was the last to emerge, and by the time she did this, the first ones out were already away, down the mountain, anxious not to waste a moment of the morning, reluctant to spend even five minutes in the warmth of the restaurant, with a mug of hot chocolate or a steaming glass of glühwein.

"Come on, Jeannie."

Alistair and Colin and Anne already had their skis on, their goggles pulled down over their eyes, the three of them itching to be off. Her feet felt like lead in the heavy boots, slipping and stumbling across the snow. The cold stung her cheeks, filled her lungs with painfully icy air.

"Here, come on, I'll help you."

Somehow, she reached Alistair's side, dropped her skis. He stooped to help her, snapping on the bindings. Lumbered with the weight of the skis she felt even more incapable, helpless.

"All right?"

She could not even speak. Colin and Anne, taking her silence for assent, smiled cheerfully, gave her a wave with their ski poles, and were gone. A smooth push sent them over the brow of the slope, and they disappeared, with a hiss of snow, into the glittering infinity of space that lay beyond.

"Just follow me," Alistair told her. "It'll be fine." And then he, too, was gone.

Just follow me. It was Alistair, and she would have followed him anywhere, but this was an impossibility. Impossible to do anything but simply stand there, quaking. In her wildest imaginings she had never thought up such horror as this. Shivering with cold and fright, there was a moment when she wondered if she was actually going to be sick. But the moment passed, and she was still standing there, and in place of panic came, slowly, a calm resolution.

She was not going to ski down the Kreisler. She was going to take off her skis and go into the restaurant and sit down and get warm and have a hot drink. Then, like any old lady, she would clamber into the cable-car and go back that way, on her own, to the village. Alistair would be furious, but she was beyond caring. The others would think nothing of her, but that had ceased to matter. She was hopeless. A funk. She couldn't ski and never would. At the first possible opportunity, she would get herself to Zurich, get herself on a plane, and go home.

Having faced up to this, everything suddenly became quite easy. She took off her skis and carried them back to the restaurant and stuck them in the snow, along with the ski poles. She went up the wooden steps and through the heavy glass doors. Here was warmth, the smell of pine and wood-smoke and cigars and coffee. She bought herself a cup of coffee and took it to an empty table and sat down. The coffee steamed, fragrant and comforting. She pulled off her woollen hat and shook out her hair and felt as though she were taking off some hideous disguise and was herself again. Putting her hands around the blissful warmth of the coffee mug, she decided that she would concentrate on this moment of total relief and not think one moment ahead. Most specially, she would not think about Alistair. She would not think about losing him . . .

"Is anybody joining you?"

The question came out of nowhere. Startled, Jeannie looked up, saw the man standing across the table from her, and realized, after a second's blankness, that he was talking to her.

"No. Nobody."

"Then would you mind if I did?"

She was astonished, but endeavored to hide her astonishment. "No . . . of course not . . ." There was no question of being chatted up, because he was a quite elderly man, obviously British, and perfectly presentable. Which made his unexpected appearance all the more surprising.

He too had a cup of coffee in his hand. He set it down on the table and pulled out a chair and settled himself. She saw his very blue eyes, his thinning grey hair. He wore a navy-blue anorak with a scarlet sweater beneath it. His skin was very brown, netted with wrinkles, and he had the weather-beaten appearance of a man who has spent most of his life in the open air.

He said, "It's a beautiful morning."

"Yes."

"There was a fall of snow at two o'clock in the morning. Quite a heavy one. Did you know that?"

She shook her head. "No. I didn't know."

He watched her, his bright eyes unblinking. He said, "I've been sitting by the table in the window. I saw what happened."

Jeannie's heart sank. "I . . . I don't understand." But of course, she understood only too well.

"Your friends went off without you." He made it sound like an accusation, and Jeannie instantly sprang to their defence.

"They didn't mean to. They thought I was going to follow."

"Why didn't you?"

A number of likely fibs sprang to mind. *I like to ski alone. I wanted a cup of coffee. I'm waiting till they come up again on the cable-car, and then we'll all go down together in time for lunch.*

But those blue eyes were not to be lied to. She said, "I'm afraid."

"Of what?"

"Of heights. Of skiing. Of making a fool of myself. Of spoiling their fun for them."

"Haven't you skied before?"

"Not before this holiday. We've been here for a week and I've spent all that time on the nursery slopes with an instructor, trying to get the hang of it."

"And have you?"

"Sort of. But I think I'm uncoordinated or something. Or else just plain chicken. I mean, I can get down the slopes and turn corners and stop, and things like that, but I'm never sure when I'm not going to fall flat on my back, and then I get nervous and I tense up, and then of course I usually do fall. It's a vicious circle. And I'm frightened of heights as well. Even coming up on the cable-car I found terrifying."

He did not comment on this. "Your friends, I take it, are all fairly expert?"

"Yes, they've been skiing together for a long time. Alistair used to come out here with his parents when he was a little boy. He loves the village, and he knows all the runs like the back of his hand."

"Is Alistair *your* friend?"

She felt embarrassed. "Yes."

"Is he the reason you came in the first place?"

"Yes." He smiled. Suddenly, it was easy to talk, as it is easy to confide in a stranger met by chance in a train, knowing that you will never see that particular stranger again. "It's funny, we have everything in common, and we get on so well, and we laugh at the same things . . . but now there's this. I always knew that if I really wanted to be with him, and part of his life, I'd have to ski, because it's the one thing he really loves to do. And I've always been apprehensive about it, because, like I said, I'm the most uncoordinated person in the world. I used to go to dancing classes when I was a little girl, and I could never even tell my left foot from my right. But I thought perhaps skiing would be different, and that it would be something I'd be able to do. So when Alistair suggested we all come out together, I jumped at the chance to prove that I *could*. And I thought it would be fun . . . like the advertisements for winter holidays. You know, jolly fun in the snow, and the whole business not much more demanding than a game of tennis. I never imagined being put on a mountain the height of this one, and being expected to actually ski down it."

"Does Alistair know how you feel about all this?"

"It's hard to make him understand. And I don't want him to think that I'm not enjoying myself."

"But you're not."

"No. I'm hating it. Even the evenings and the fun we have then are spoiled, because all the time I'm thinking about what I've got to make myself do the next day."

"When you've finished that cup of coffee, how are you going to get back to the village?"

"I thought on the cable-car."

"I see." He considered this, and then said, "Let's both have another cup of coffee and talk things over."

Jeannie couldn't think what there could possibly be to talk over, but the idea of another cup of coffee was a good one, and so she said, "All right."

He took their cups and went to the bar, and came back with them, steaming and refilled. As he sat again, he said, "You know, you remind me, quite extraordinarily, of a girl I used to know. She looked rather like you, and she talked with your voice. And she was just as frightened as you were."

"What happened to her?" Stirring her coffee, Jeannie tried to turn the whole thing into a joke. "Did she go down in the cable-car, and then fly home in disgrace? Because I think that's what's going to happen to me."

"No, she didn't do that. She found someone who understood and was prepared to give her a little help and encouragement."

"I need more than that. I need a miracle."

"Don't underestimate yourself."

"I'm a coward."

"That's nothing to be ashamed of. It isn't brave to do something that you're not afraid of. But it's very brave to face up to something which frightens you paralytic."

As he was saying this, the door of the restaurant opened and a man appeared, looked about him, and then came across the room towards them. Reaching their table, he stopped, respectfully removing his woollen hat.

"Herr Commander Manleigh."

"Hans! What can I do for you?"

The man spoke in German, and Jeannie's companion replied in the same language. They talked for a moment, and then the problem, whatever it was, was apparently solved. The man bowed to Jeannie, made his farewells, and took himself off.

"What was all that about?" she asked.

"That's Hans from the cable-car. Your young man telephoned up from the village to find out what had happened to you. He thought you might have had a fall. Hans came to find you, he recognized you from your friend's description."

"What did you say?"

"I said to tell him not to worry. We'll be down in our own time."

"We?"

"You and I. But not in the cable-car. We're doing the Kreisler run together."

"I can't."

He did not contradict her. Instead, after a thoughtful pause, he asked, "Are you in love with this young man?"

She had never actually considered this before. Not seriously. But all at once, faced with the question, she knew the truth. "Yes," she told him.

"Do you want to lose him?"

"No."

"Then come with me. Now. Right away. Before either of us has time to change our minds."

Outside again, it was still just as cold, but the sun was climbing into the sky, and the icicles that festooned the balcony of the restaurant and the doorways of the cable house were already beginning to thaw and drip. Jeannie pulled on her hat and her gloves, retrieved her skis, fastened the bindings, took a ski pole in either hand. Her new friend was ready before her, and waiting, and together they moved across the beaten, rutted snow to the verge of the slope where the piste, like a silver ribbon, wound away down the snow-fields before them. The village, reduced by distance to toy size, lay deep in the valley, and beyond again, the further mountains, ranges of them, shone and glittered like glass.

She said, for the first time, "It's so beautiful."

"Enjoy the beauty. That is one of the joys of skiing. Having time to stop and stare. And this is a magical day. Now. Are you ready to go?"

"As ready as I'll ever be."

"Then shall we make a start?"

"Before we do, can I ask you one thing?"

"What's that?"

"The girl you told me about. The one who was as scared as I am. What happened to her?"

He smiled. "I married her," he said, and then he was gone, gently, smoothly, down the slope, traversing a ridge, turning, sailing away in the other direction.

Jeannie took a deep breath, set her teeth, pushed with her ski poles and followed him.

At first, she was as stiff and awkward as she had ever been, but every moment that passed increased her confidence. Three turns and she hadn't fallen. Her blood quickened, her body warmed, she could actually feel her muscles relax. There was sunshine on her face and the cool rush of clean air, sparkling, crisp as chilled wine. There was the sweet hiss of her own skis in the snow, the gathering sense of speed, the rasp of steel edges on ice as she manoeuvred a tricky corner.

He was never far ahead. Every so often, he would stop to wait for her and let her get her breath. Sometimes the way ahead needed a little explanation. "It's a narrow track through the woods," he would say. "Let your skis run in the tracks that other skiers have made, and then you'll be quite safe." Or, "The piste circles the edge of the mountain here, but it's not as dangerous as it looks."

He made her feel that nothing could be too difficult or frightening if he was there, leading the way. As they sank down into the valley, the terrain altered. There were bridges to be crossed, and open farm gateways through which they hurtled.

And then, all at once, long before she had expected it, they were in familiar territory, at the top of the nursery slopes, and so the finish of the run was child's play compared with what had gone before.

Jeannie came down these slopes, on which she had unhappily struggled for seven solid days, with a flourish of speed, and a sensation of
elation and achievement that she had never known before in her life.
She had done it. She had come down the Kreisler. She had done it.

It was over. The slope levelled out by the ski-school hut and the
little café where she had gone each day for a comforting mug of hot
chocolate. Here, he waited for her, relaxed and smiling, delighted as
she was, and yet obviously amused by her own delight.

She stopped alongside him, pushed up her goggles and laughed
up into his face. "I thought it was going to be horrible and it was
heavenly."

"You did very well."

"I didn't fall once. I don't understand it."

"You only fell because you were nervous. Now you will never fall
for that reason again."

"I can't thank you enough."

"You don't have to thank me. I enjoyed it. And if I'm not mistaken, I think that's your young man come to claim you."

Jeannie turned and saw that it was indeed Alistair, emerging from
the door of the café, down the wooden steps and across the snow
towards them. His face was filled with a marvellous relief, and the
smile he had for her, a congratulation in itself.

"You made it, Jeannie. Well done, my darling." He enfolded her in
a huge bear-hug. "I watched you coming down the last bit of the
nursery slope, and you were really good." And then, across her head,
his eyes met those of the man who had come to her rescue. Jeannie
looked up and saw another expression cross his handsome features—
the same respect and reverence that had shown on the face of the
cable-car man when he had come to deliver Alistair's message.

"Commander Manleigh." If he had been wearing a hat, he would
surely have removed it. "I didn't realize it was you. I didn't even
know you were out here." The two men shook hands. "How are you,
sir?"

"All the better for having met your charming young lady. I'm
sorry, I don't know your name."

"Alistair Hansen. I used to watch you skiing when I was a boy. I
had great photographs of you pinned up all over my bedroom walls."

"Well, it's very nice to meet you."

"It was good of you to come down with Jeannie."

"Hans at the cable-car station gave me your message."

"I was half-way down the piste before I realized that she wasn't behind me, and by then it was too late to make my way back."

"I found her in the restaurant. She was feeling a bit cold, so she went to get herself a hot drink. We got talking."

"I was afraid she'd fallen. Had visions of her coming down the mountain on the blood-wagon."

Commander Manleigh stooped and loosened his bindings and stepped out of his skis. Shouldering them, he stood erect. He smiled. "Given a little encouragement, young man, she won't let you down. Now I must be off. Goodbye, Jeannie, and good luck."

"Goodbye, and thank you again for being so kind."

He slapped Alistair across the shoulder. "Take good care of her," he told him, and then turned and walked away from them, a tall grey-haired man on his own. A strangely solitary figure in the crowded street.

Jeannie was taking off her own skis. "Who is he?" she wanted to know.

"Bill Manleigh. Come on, let's go and have a drink."

"But who's Bill Manleigh?"

"I can't believe you've never heard of him. A famous fellow. One of the best skiers we've ever produced. When he grew too old to race, he became a coach for the Olympic team. So you see, my darling, you came down the Kreisler with a champion."

"I didn't know that. I only know that he was terribly kind. And Alistair, it wasn't because I was cold that I went into the restaurant, it was because I was too frightened to follow you. You might as well know."

"You should have told me."

"I couldn't. I just stood there, being terrified, and then I knew I hadn't the nerve to make the run. And I was drinking coffee and he came and talked to me. And he didn't tell me anything about himself at all. Not at all." She thought about this. "Except that he was married."

Alistair lifted her skis onto his shoulder, and took her hand in his other hand. Together, they made their way towards the little café. "Yes, he was," he told her. "To a lovely girl. I used to watch them ski together, and think that they must be the most glamorous couple in the world. They were always such good friends, always laughing together. As though they didn't need anybody but each other."

"You talk as though it's all in the past."

"It is." They had reached the wooden building, and Alistair paused to ram her skis into the snow. "She died last summer. She was drowned. I read about it in the papers. They were sailing with friends in Greece, and there was some ghastly misadventure. He was devastated, and now he must be so lonely without her." Jeannie looked down the street, the way that he had gone, but he had been swallowed up in the cheerful crowds of holiday-makers, and there was no sign of him. *He must be so lonely.* For a terrible moment, she thought that she was going to cry. A lump swelled in her throat, and her eyes misted with ridiculous tears. Such a kind man. She would probably never see him again, and yet she owed him an immeasurable debt. She would never forget him. "But I don't suppose," Alistair went on, "that he would have said anything to you about that."

You remind me, quite extraordinarily, of a girl I used to know.

Going hand in hand with him up the wooden steps that led to the café door, she realized that she wasn't going to cry after all. "No," she said. "No, he didn't say anything."

The Watershed

———◦◦◦◦———

"Can you manage, now, Mrs. Harley?"

"Yes, of course." Edwina slung her handbag over one arm, the bulging basket over the other, and, with some effort, heaved the box laden with groceries off the counter. The bag of tomatoes at the top teetered dangerously, so she steadied it with her chin. "If you could just open the door."

"Your car there, is it?"

"Yes, right outside."

"Cheerio, then, Mrs. Harley."

"Goodbye."

She emerged from the doorway of the village shop and stepped out into the chill February sunshine, crossed the cobbled pavement in a couple of steps, dumped the box onto the hood of her car, put the basket alongside, and went around to the back to open the trunk.

As this was Friday, and so shopping morning, the trunk was already half-full. A large parcel from the butcher's; Henry's shoes, picked up from the cobbler; clean sheets collected from the laundry; and the garden shears, newly sharpened and oiled by the local blacksmith. She lifted the grocery box and basket into the trunk, then found that it would not close, and so did a bit of rearranging and finally got it shut.

Finished. All done. No reason now not to drive straight home. Yet she hesitated, standing there by her car in the middle of the small Scottish village, to turn her attention to the stone house which stood across the street. A house with a face as symmetrical as a child's drawing, and a roof tiled with a grey slate. A narrow strip of garden, a white wooden gate, and a clipped privet hedge separated it from the pavement. Its curtains were drawn.

Old Mrs. Titchfield's house. Empty, because two weeks ago Mrs. Titchfield had died in the local hospital.

Edwina knew the house. Had known Mrs. Titchfield for years. Had sometimes called to collect a pie for the church sale, or to deliver a Christmas card and a fruit-cake, and be asked indoors to sit by the fire with a cup of tea.

She knew the tiny rooms and the narrow stairway, the garden at the back with its Albertine roses and the clothesline strung between two apple trees . . .

"Edwina!" She had neither heard nor seen the other car draw up in the space behind her own. But here was Rosemary Turner approaching; Rosemary, with her shopping basket and her neat, grey hair and her fat, white peke on a scarlet leash. Rosemary was one of Edwina's closest friends. Her husband, James, played golf with Henry, and Rosemary was godmother to Edwina's oldest child. "What are you doing, standing there, gazing into space?" Rosemary asked.

"Just that."

"Poor old Mrs. Titchfield. Never mind—she had a good, long life. Seems funny though, doesn't it, not to see her puttering about in that strip of garden? It must have been the best-weeded plot in the county. Have you done your shopping?"

"Yes. Just on my way home."

"I'm going to get some biscuits for Hi-Fi. Are you in a mad hurry?"

"No. Henry's out for lunch today."

"In that case, why don't we live dangerously and go and have a cup of coffee in Ye Olde Thatched Café? I haven't seen you for ages. Masses of things to talk about."

Edwina smiled. "All right."

"Hold Hi-Fi for me, then. He hates going into the shop because the cat always spits at him."

Edwina took the leash and, waiting, leaned against her car. Her eyes drifted back to Mrs. Titchfield's house. She had an idea, but knew that Henry would hate it, and the prospect of heated discussion filled her with dismay. She sighed, feeling tired and old. Probably, at the end of the day, she would take the easy way out and say nothing.

The little café was cramped and dark and old. But the china was pretty, there were fresh flowers on the tables, and the coffee, when it arrived, was fragrant and strong.

Edwina took a sustaining mouthful. "I needed that."

"I thought you looked a bit washed out. Are you feeling all right?"

"Yes. Just overwhelmed by the tedium of shopping. Why does it always have to be such a boring routine?"

"I suppose, after years of marriage, we've become programmed. Like computers. Where's Henry having lunch?"

"With Kate and Tony. He and Tony have spent the morning having horrible financial discussions."

Kate was Henry's sister. Her husband, Tony, was Henry's accountant, and his office was walking distance from Edwina and Henry's spacious home in Relkirk.

"Does Henry like being retired?"

"I think so. He always seems to be occupied."

"Do you find him getting under your feet? I nearly went crazy when James first retired. He kept coming into the kitchen and switching off my radio and asking me questions."

"What sort of questions?"

"Oh, the usual. 'Have you seen my calculator?' 'What do you want done with the lawn mower?' 'What time is lunch?' Who was it who said that you marry a man for better, for worse, but not for lunch?"

"The Duchess of Windsor."

Rosemary laughed. Across the table, their eyes met. Her laughter died. "So what's the problem? You're not usually so down in the mouth."

Edwina heaved her shoulders and sighed. "I don't know . . . Yes, I do. I looked in my diary this morning and realized that next month Henry and I will have been married for thirty years."

"So you will! A pearl anniversary. Is it really five years since your silver? How splendid! Another excuse for a lovely party."

"There's no point in having a party if the children can't be there."

"Why can't they be there?"

"Because Rodney's with his ship, patrolling the Straits of Hormuz. And Priscilla's in Sussex, totally occupied with Bob and the two babies. And Tessa's finally found herself a job in London, but she scarcely earns enough to keep body and soul together, so even if she could get the time off, she wouldn't be able to afford the train fare home. Besides, thirty years doesn't seem to be anything to celebrate. To me it feels uncomfortably like a watershed . . . you know, from now on it's downhill all the way . . ."

"Don't *say* such depressing things!"

". . . and at the end of the day, what has one achieved? I don't feel I've got anything to show for it all."

Rosemary, with characteristic good sense, made no comment on this lament. Instead, stirring her coffee, she turned the conversation to another tack.

"Were you gazing at Mrs. Titchfield's house for any particular reason?"

"In a way . . . It's suddenly come home to me that I'm fifty-two and Henry's sixty-seven, and that the day will come when, physically, we won't be able to live at Hill House any longer. As it is, we rattle around like a couple of dried peas, and every spare moment is spent trying to keep the garden the way it's always looked."

"Beautiful."

"Yes, it's a beautiful garden, and we love it, and we love the house. But it was always too big for us, even with the three children living at home."

"If you're thinking of moving, you're going to have difficulty persuading Henry."

"You don't have to tell me that." Henry had inherited Hill House from his parents. He had lived there all his life, and remembered the days when there were a large indoor staff and two gardeners. Now there was just Bessie Digley, and she could only manage three mornings a week.

"I can't bear the thought of you not living there. Aren't you jumping the gun? After all, you're not *old*—you've years and years ahead of you. And what about having the grandchildren visit? You'll need space for them."

"I've thought of that. But isn't it better to make a move before you're too old to enjoy it? Think of the poor old Perrys. They clung on to the manor until they were so decrepit, they simply had to sell. And then they bought that dreadful little house, and Mrs. Perry fell down the stairs and broke her hip, and that was the end of both of them. Suppose Henry and I bought Mrs. Titchfield's house? Wouldn't it be fun, doing it up together? Redecorating, and replanning the garden? I know it's tiny, but it's in the village. I wouldn't have to drive seven miles every time I want to buy a loaf of bread or a pound of sausage. And we'd be able to keep it really warm, and never be snowed in in the winter. And the children wouldn't worry about us."

"Do they worry now?"

"No, but they will."

Rosemary laughed. "You know what I think is wrong with you? You're missing those children. They've all fled the nest, even little Tessa, and you miss them. But that's no reason to make a momentous decision about moving. You'll just have to find something else to fill your life. Make Henry take you on a cruise."

"I don't want to go on a cruise."

"Then take up yoga. Do something."

They finally parted and Edwina drove the seven winding miles back to Hill House. She came to the white gate, opened it, and drove up the steep driveway between the tall beeches and the thick clumps of rhododendron. Beyond the trees was the lawn, which, in spring, would be a riot of yellow daffodils. Beyond it was the big old Georgian house, its windows blinking in the low February sunshine.

Parking the car in the stable yard, Edwina carried the groceries indoors. The kitchen was huge and homey, with a dresser stacked with ironstone china, a basket of laundry waiting to be ironed, and the two Labradors waiting to be taken for a walk.

Without Henry, the house always felt strangely empty. She was suddenly aware, with piercing intensity, of the deserted rooms above and about her. The dust-sheeted drawing-room; the great Victorian dining-room, scene of countless cheerful family meals, but now scarcely used, for she and Henry always ate in the kitchen. Like a ghost, her imagination wandered up the stairs to the wide landing and the doors leading off it, into the spacious bedrooms where once the children had slept, or where visitors, often entire families, had stayed; down the passage to the white-painted nurseries, the linen room, the cavernous bathrooms; up to the attic, where the household staff had long ago slept, and where she had stored the outgrown bicycles and perambulators and doll's houses.

The house was a monument to family life. To a family of children who were children no longer. How had the years swept by so swiftly?

There was no answer to this. The dogs demanded her attention, so she left the groceries on the kitchen table, pulled on her green Wellingtons, and set off, with the dogs at her heels, for a long walk.

That evening over supper, emboldened by a glass of wine, Edwina broached the subject of Mrs. Titchfield's house.

"I expect it will be coming up for sale."

"I expect it will."

"You don't think we should buy it?"

Henry raised his handsome white head to stare at her in disbelief. "*Buy* it? For heaven's sake, why?"

Edwina gathered her courage about her. "To live in."

"But we live here."

"We're getting older. And Hill House seems to be getting bigger."

"We're not that old."

"I just feel we ought to be sensible."

"And what do you intend doing with this house?"

"Well . . . if Rodney wants it one day, we could rent it. And if he doesn't, we could sell it."

At this he laid down his knife and fork and reached for his Scotch and soda. She watched him. He set down the glass, then asked, "When did you get this brilliant idea?"

"Today. No, not today. It's been in the back of my mind for some time. I love Hill House, Henry, just the way you do. But face it, the children are gone. They have their own lives to live. And we're not going to be able to stay here forever . . ."

"I can't see why not."

"But there's so much to look after. The garden . . ."

"If I didn't have the garden, what would I do with myself? Imagine me in Mrs. Titchfield's house, banging my head every time I went through a door. If I didn't die of brain damage, I'd go dotty with claustrophobia. Probably end my days as one of those seedy old men you see ambling down to the pub at midday and not emerging until closing time. Besides, this is our home."

"I just feel . . . perhaps . . . that we should look ahead."

"I look ahead all the time. To the spring, and the bulbs coming up. To the summer, and seeing my new rose-bed bloom. I'm looking ahead to Rodney finding himself a wife, and Tessa getting married in this house. I'm looking forward to having them all back to stay, with their families. We've survived the traumas of raising them; now let's allow ourselves to reap some of the rewards."

After a bit, Edwina said, "Yes."

"You sound unconvinced."

"You're right, of course. But I think I'm right, too." He reached across the table and laid his hand on hers. She said, "I miss the children."

He did not argue with this. "Wherever we lived, we'd miss them."

Two weeks later, Rosemary called. "Edwina, it's about your wedding anniversary. Come and have dinner with James and me, and we'll have a little celebration. That's Saturday in two weeks' time. Shall we say seven-thirty?"

"Oh, Rosemary, you *are* sweet."

"It's settled, then. If I don't see you before, I'll see you then."

That evening, Edwina's sister-in-law, Kate, called. "Edwina, what are you doing about your thirtieth wedding anniversary?" she asked.

"I didn't think you'd remember."

"Of course I remember. How could I forget?"

"Well, actually, we're going to have dinner with James and Rosemary. She asked us this morning."

"Splendid. I imagined you and Henry eating a chop in the kitchen and none of us doing anything to mark the occasion. But I'll worry no longer. See you sometime. 'Bye."

Thirty years. She awoke to rain pouring down the window-panes and splashing sounds from the bathroom, which meant that Henry was taking his morning shower. She lay and watched the rain, and thought, "I have been married for thirty years." She tried to remember that day thirty years ago and scarcely remembered anything, except that her younger sister had tried to iron her wedding-dress petticoat and had scorched the white silk. And everybody had carried on as though it were a total disaster, when, in fact, it hadn't mattered at all. She turned her head on the pillow and called "Henry!" and after a moment, he appeared through the open door, with his hair on end and a bath towel tied around his waist.

She said, "Happy day," and he came to kiss her, damply and fragrantly, and produced a small box. She unwrapped it, and there was a red-leather jewel box and, inside, a pair of ear-rings: small, gold leaves, each set with a pearl.

"Oh, they're so pretty!" She sat up, and he brought her a hand mirror so she could put them on and admire herself. Kissing her again, he went off to get dressed, and she went downstairs to cook breakfast. While they were eating, the postman came, and there was a cable from Rodney and cards from Priscilla and Tessa. "Thinking of you today," they said. "Wish we could be with you." "Happy anniversary," they said, "and lots and lots of love."

"Well, that's very gratifying," Henry said. "At least they remembered."

Edwina read Rodney's cable for the fourth time. "Yes."

He looked anxious. "Being married to me for thirty years doesn't make you feel old, does it?"

She knew that he was thinking of Mrs. Titchfield's house, although they had not spoken of it again. But the idea still hung about at the back of her mind, and she had watched the For Sale sign being put up. So far, no one had bought the house.

She said, "No." Just empty and deserted like the rooms upstairs.

"Good. I don't like you feeling old. Because you don't look old. In fact, you look more beautiful than ever."

"That's because of my beautiful ear-rings."

"I don't think so."

It rained most of the day. Edwina spent it making marmalade, and, because they were going out for dinner, did not light the fire in the little sitting-room. By the time the marmalade had set and been stowed away in the storeroom, it was time to go upstairs and change. She made up her face, fixed her hair, and put on her black velvet dress and a great deal of perfume. Then she helped Henry with his cuff links and gave his best grey flannel suit a brush.

"It smells of mothballs," she told him.

"All the best suits smell of mothballs."

Wearing it, he looked handsome and very distinguished. They turned off the lights and went downstairs. They locked the front door, said goodbye to the dogs, locked the back door, and scurried through the rain and into the car. They drove down the hill, leaving the house, dark, cold, and deserted, behind them.

The Turners lived ten miles on the other side of the village. Their front door opened as Henry and Edwina alighted from the car, and light streamed out, turning the rain to a shimmer of silver. Rosemary and James were waiting for them.

"Happy anniversary! Congratulations!" There were kisses and

hugs, warmth and brightness. They took off their raincoats and went into Rosemary's sitting room, where a log fire burned and the white peke sat on her cushion and yapped. There was a present, too, a new rose-bush for the garden.

"Wonderful," Edwina told them. "That's something we can both enjoy."

Then James opened a bottle of champagne, and after he had raised his glass to them both and made a little speech, they all settled by the fireside in Rosemary's marvellously comfortable chairs, and chatted in the easy manner of four mature people who have been friends for a long time. Their glasses emptied. James refilled them. Henry stole a furtive glance at his watch. It was ten minutes to eight. He cleared his throat. "James, I'm not complaining, but are we to be the only guests this evening?" he asked.

James looked at his wife. She said, "No, but we're not having dinner here. Just a drink."

"Where are we eating?"

"Out."

"I see," said Henry, not sounding as though he saw at all.

"But where are we going?" Edwina asked.

"Wait and see."

Mysterious, but rather exciting. Perhaps they were going to be taken to the new and expensive French restaurant in Relkirk. A pleasing possibility, because Edwina had never been there. Her spirits rose in cautious anticipation.

At a quarter past eight. James set down his glass. "Time to leave." So they all got up, and climbed into their coats, and went out into the rainy darkness. "Edwina, you come with me, and Henry can drive Rosemary. I'll lead the way, Henry."

They set off. James began to tell her about how well old Henry was playing golf these days. She sat beside him, her chin deep in the collar of her coat, watching the headlights probe the winding road ahead. "It's his swing. His swing has really improved since that chat with the pro." In the village she thought he would turn right and head for the road leading to the French restaurant. But he did not do this, and she was mildly disappointed.

"Extraordinary what bad habits one can get into with golf," he was saying. "Sometimes all you need is a little objective advice."

"We seem to be going towards Hill House," she said.

"Edwina, Hill House is not the only establishment in this part of the world."

She fell silent, gazing from the window, trying to get her bearings. Then the car swung around a steep corner, and she saw lights. They were above her, shining out over the dark countryside, dazzling as a fireworks display. But where were they? Listening to James, she had become disoriented. The lights grew larger, brighter. Then they came to a crossroads with two cottages, a familiar landmark, and she realized she had been right all along, the lights were the lights of Hill House, and James was driving her home.

To a house that they had left deserted and dark. A house now with every light on, and every window blazing a welcome.

"James, what's *happening?*"

But James did not answer. He turned the car in through the gates and roared up the hill. The trees lining the driveway opened out, and the lawn lay illuminated as though floodlit. The front door was open, and the dogs came belting out, barking a welcome, and there were two people standing there, a man and a woman. At first she thought it couldn't be true, but it *was* true. It was Priscilla. Priscilla and Bob.

Almost before the car had stopped, she was out of it, for once ignoring her precious dogs, running across the gravel through the rain, heedless of her hair and her high-heeled satin shoes.

"Hello, Mummy!"

"Oh, Priscilla! Oh, darling!" They hugged enormously. "But what are you *doing?* What are you *doing* here?"

"We've come for your anniversary," her son-in-law told her. He was grinning from ear to ear, and she embraced him lovingly, and then turned back to Priscilla. "But the children? What have you done with the babies?"

"Left them with my darling neighbour. It's all been the most tremendous conspiracy." The other car had by now arrived, disgorging Henry, who appeared to be poleaxed with astonishment. "Hello, Dad! Surprise, surprise!"

"What the hell is happening?" was all he seemed to be able to say.

Priscilla took his hand. "Come indoors, and we'll show you."

Bemused, they followed her. As they stood in the middle of the hall, a voice floated down from upstairs. "Happy anniversary, you darling old things." They looked up, and there was Tessa, running down the stairs, with her long, silky mane of hair flying behind. She took the last three steps in a single leap, the way she had always done, and Henry scooped her up into his arms and swung her off her feet.

"You monkey! Where did you spring from?"

"From London, where else? Oh, Mum, darling, aren't you looking gorgeous! Isn't this the best surprise ever? No, it isn't the best surprise, there's more . . . come with me!"

"It's worse than 'This Is Your Life,' " Henry said, but Tessa was not listening. She grasped her mother's wrist, and Edwina found herself being dragged across the hall and through the open door which led into the big drawing-room. The dust sheets were gone, the fire had been lighted, and there were flowers everywhere. Kate and Tony were there, standing with their backs to the fire, along with a young man with a deeply tanned face and hair bleached blond by the tropic sun. It was Rodney.

"There!" said Tessa and let go of her wrist.

"Happy anniversary, Ma," said Rodney.

"But how did you do it?" Edwina asked, walking into his arms. "How did you arrange everything?"

"It was a conspiracy. Aunt Kate and Uncle Tony were in on it— and Rosemary and James as well, and Bessie Digley. We all met up in London yesterday and flew north together."

"But Rodney, how did you get leave?"

"I was due some anyway. Been saving it up."

"But I got a cable this morning, from your ship."

"I got the first lieutenant to send it for me."

She turned to her daughters. "And your cards . . ."

"Red herrings," Tessa told her. "To allay any suspicions you might have had. And of course, we're all having dinner here, in the dining-room. Priscilla and I cooked it in Aunt Kate's kitchen, and we brought it all over in the trunk of their car."

"But . . . the fire. This room. The flowers. Everything . . ."

"Rodney and Uncle Tony did all that while we flew around setting the table. And Bob went around turning on every single light."

"It was so funny," Priscilla chimed in. "When you left for Rose-mary's, we were all waiting in two cars at the bottom of the drive, with everything switched off so you wouldn't see us. Just like playing hide and seek. Then, as soon as you were safely on your way, we shot up the drive and set to work."

"And how did you get in?" Henry wanted to know.

"Tessa still has her key. And Bessie Digley's here. She's going to make up all our beds. You don't mind if we stay the weekend, do you? Rodney can stay longer, of course, because he's got two weeks' leave, but I can't leave the children too long, and Tessa has to get back to work."

Champagne corks had been popping. Somebody handed Edwina a glass. She hadn't even taken off her coat yet, and she had never felt so happy in her whole life.

A little later, Edwina slipped away from the laughter and talk and champagne. She looked into the dining-room and saw that here, too, the fire had been lighted, and the great mahogany table laid as though for a royal banquet. She moved towards the kitchen and looked in around the door. Bessie Digley turned from the stove. "Now this was a good surprise," she said, with a smile that Edwina had never seen on her dour face.

She went upstairs. On the landing every bedroom door was ajar, and every light blazed. She glimpsed open suitcases and clothes lying about in a heartwarming muddle. In her own room, she took off her coat and laid it across the bed. She thought about drawing the curtains, then decided against it. Let the whole world see and guess what was happening! She stood with her back to the window and surveyed her large, familiar, faintly shabby bedroom. Her dressing-table, the huge double bed, the towering Victorian wardrobe, her desk. She saw the plethora of photographs, which seemed to cover every surface. The children at all stages and ages, and now grandchildren, too, and dogs and picnics and reunions and celebrations.

A thousand memories.

After a little while, she went to the mirror, fixed her hair, and powdered her nose. It was time to join the others. But at the top of the stairs, she paused. From the drawing room, voices and laughter floated upward, filling the air with happy sounds. Her children were here. They had come to tear the dust sheets from the empty rooms, and fill the vacant bedrooms. Henry had been right. There were still years of life to be lived in this house. It was too soon to be thinking of leaving. Too soon to be thinking of growing old.

Thirty years. She touched her new ear-rings, found herself smiling, and ran downstairs, excited as a bride.

Marigold Garden

*J*He had not planned to go to Brookfield. It lay deep in the Hampshire countryside, fifteen miles from the motorway between Southampton and London, and he had seen himself simply speeding past the turn-off, without, as it were, a sideways glance.

But somehow—perhaps by memory, perhaps by the familiar countryside drowsing in the afternoon sunshine—he was seduced, beguiled. After all, now it was over. Finished. Julia and her new husband would still be away on their honeymoon, basking in the nailing heat of the Mediterranean, or sailing some boat across turquoise-blue, glass-clear West Indian waters. She was now out of his reach. It was over.

The huge road curved ahead of him, poured behind. On either side villages, orchards, farms, sliced in two by progress, lay untouched, unchanged. Cows stood in the shade beneath clumps of trees, and fields were thick and yellow with ripening corn.

The sign came up at him. *Lamington. Hartston. Brookfield.* Miles eased his foot from the accelerator. The needle on the dashboard dropped from seventy to sixty to fifty. *What the hell am I doing?* But the image of the old red brick house smothered in wisteria, the lawn sloping down to the river, the heady scent of roses, pulled him like a magnet. He knew that he had to go back. Now he saw the turn-off, the bridge across the motorway. He glanced into his driving-mirror to check the traffic behind him, and then, inexorably, slid across into the slow lane, and so up onto the ramp.

He grinned at himself wryly. *Perhaps you always meant to do this.* But why not? It was too late for memories. Ten days too late.

Out of sight and sound of the motorway, the surroundings were, almost at once, familiar. He knew this road, that village; had drunk beer in that pub after a cricket match; had once been to a party in the house that lay beyond a pair of impressive gates. It was four years ago when he had first made this journey, but, idling along the country lanes, he could remember every moment, every nuance of that drive. Excited he had been, and a little anxious, because he was fresh out of Agricultural College and going to an interview for his first job, as manager of Brookfield Farm, working for Mrs. Hawthorne.

When they eventually met, she explained her position. Her husband had recently died. Her son, who would one day take over the farm, had taken a short service commission in the Army, and was at present stationed in Hong Kong.

". . . but when he leaves the Army, he plans to go to agricultural college, but meantime I must have somebody to help me . . . just to keep things going until Derek's ready to come home again . . ."

Privately Miles decided that she looked far too young to have a grown-up son, but he said nothing, because this was a business matter, and no time for personal compliments.

". . . so you can see, I must have a manager. Now, why don't we go and have a look around?"

They had spent the day inspecting the farm. There were good out-buildings, a tarmacadamed yard, well-kept cattle-courts, modern tractors. Beyond lay fields of arable land, some stock, sheep and cattle. In a little paddock horses grazed.

"Do you ride?" he asked Mrs. Hawthorne.

"No. Julia's the horsy one in our family."

"Your daughter?"

"Yes. She's got a job in Hartston; she works in an antique shop there. It's nice for me, because she lives at home, but I expect before long she'll get restless and go and find herself a flat in London. That's what all her friends seem to be doing."

"Yes, I suppose they do."

She smiled. "You never wanted to work in London?"

"No. I never wanted to do anything except farm."

She showed him the house where he would live, a brick cottage with a small and totally unkempt garden. "I'm afraid it's rather a mess . . ."

He eyed it. "It wouldn't take long to get straight."

"Are you a keen gardener?"

"Put it this way: I don't like weeds."

She laughed at that. "I know. I spend most of my time pulling the beastly things up."

"My mother does that too." They looked at each other, smiling. It was the beginning of friendship, of liking.

Finally, they were back indoors, in the house, in the farm office that had been her husband's. She did not sit in the impressive leather chair, but leaned against the desk, with her hands deep in the pockets of her cardigan, and turned to face Miles.

"The job is yours if you want it," she told him.

Against all sense, because he wanted to work there more than anything else in the world, he heard himself suggesting that perhaps she would be better off with a man older than himself, someone with more experience. But she had thrown back her head and laughed, and said "Oh, heavens, I'd be terrified of someone like that. It would end up with *him* telling *me* what to do."

"In that case," said Miles, "it's a deal."

He stayed at Brookfield for a year. He would have stayed longer if it had not been for Julia. He was twenty-three. He had never seriously considered meeting a person, and falling in love, and wanting to spend the rest of his life with her. It happened, he knew, to other men. It had already happened to several of his friends. But somehow he had always imagined that, for himself, such an occurrence was a long way off—he would be thirty, or more. The time would be ripe, he would have made his way, built for himself a solid future, which he would then offer to some suitable female, as though he were giving her a present which he had made himself.

But Julia was suddenly there, in his life, and all his pre-conceived ideas, floating like soap bubbles around the back of his mind, instantly burst and disappeared forever. Why did it have to be Julia? What was it about her that was different? What was it about her that made everything magic? He had heard a word, "propinquity," and he looked it up in the dictionary, and it said *nearness in place; close kinship.*

They were indeed near. He saw her, if only briefly, every day. Helped her start her little car on frosty mornings; rode with her on April Sundays; swam with her in the river, when the leaves were thick and heavy overhead, and the brown, slow-moving water danced with sun-shafts and midges. They swept leaves together in the autumn, and built bonfires fragrant with wood-smoke. He remembered her at haymaking time, wearing a tattered old straw hat like a hobo, and with her arms sunburnt and her face running with sweat. He remembered her at Christmas, in a holly-red dress, her eyes as bright as an excited child's.

And as for kinship . . . if that meant laughter and companionship and keeping silence without constraint, then they had been kin. If it meant going to a party with her and glowing with pride because she was more attractive than any other girl in the room, then that was kin. If it meant not minding whom she danced with, because, inevitably, it was always Miles who drove her home; slowly, dawdling down the dark lanes, discussing, like an old married couple, everything that had happened—then that was kin.

Propinquity. It was he who had ruined it all. He thought of the old Frank Sinatra song. "And then I have to spoil it all by saying something stupid like I love you."

It was a Sunday evening. Warm and dusky, and they were sitting down by the river. The sound of church-bells, ringing for evensong, reached them from far across the meadows.

"I love you."

She had said, "I don't want you to love me."

"Why not?"

"Because I don't. Because you're not that sort of a person."

"What sort of a person am I?"

"You're Miles."

"Is Miles so different from other men?"

"Yes, and a thousand times nicer."

"If you say you think of me as a brother, then I shall strangle you."

"I have a brother. I don't need another."

"A dog, then. A faithful hound."

"That's a horrible thing to say."

"What do you want me to say? We can't go on like this forever."

"I just don't want it to be any other way than this."

"Julia, grow up. Nothing can stay the same."

"Why *me?* Why do you have to be in love with *me?*"

"I didn't, actually, organize it."

"I'm not ready for falling in love. I'm not ready for getting married and white wedding dresses and setting up house and having babies."

"What are you ready for, then?"

"I don't know. Change, perhaps, but not marriage."

"What sort of change?"

She looked away from him. A lock of dark hair fell forward and hid her face. "I can't stay home forever. I could go to London, perhaps. Sukie Robins . . . you know, you met her at that party. We were at school together. She's getting a flat in Wandsworth—she wants someone to share it with her." Miles did not say anything to this shattering revelation, and Julia suddenly turned and faced him in a sort of rage, but whether it was at him or herself, he could not guess. "Oh, Miles, it's all right for you. You're doing what you want, you don't want to do anything else. You haven't any doubts. You're on your way, you've made your decisions. But I'm twenty-one and I don't *know.* I haven't *done* anything . . ."

He could think of no response to this outburst. "What about your mother?" he asked at last.

"I adore my mother. I adore her. You know that. But she would be the last person to want to pin me down, to be possessive."

"Is that what you think I'm doing?"

"I don't know. I only know that I don't want to get married for years. Years and years. There are a thousand things I want to do before that happens and I want to start doing them *now.*"

After a little he said, "I shan't always be a farm manager, you know. One day I'll have a farm of my own. I'll be self-supporting, independent. I won't always be like this."

"You mean money? You think I don't want you because you haven't got any money? How can you think anything so horrible?"

"Being practical isn't horrible."

"That doesn't come into it."

"We'll see."

"You can't have a very high opinion of me to say a thing like that. I never thought you could be so materialistic."

"Julia—I love you very much."

"Then I'm sorry. I'm *sorry!*" With that, she burst into tears, springing to her feet. "I'm sorry for you and I'm sorry for me. But I don't want to be like . . . like a dead butterfly, pinned to a bit of cork . . ." And with this extraordinary statement, she fled from him, away up the lawn towards the house.

And Miles sat on, alone, bitten to death by midges, and not caring; because he had spoiled everything, and nothing could ever be the same again.

He lived with it for a week, and then he went to Mrs. Hawthorne and gave in his notice. She was not a stupid woman and he respected her for her outspokenness.

"Oh, Miles. It's Julia, isn't it?"

As well, he respected her too much to lie. He said, "Yes."

"You're in love with her."

"I think I always have been. From the first moment I set eyes on her."

"I was so afraid that something like this had happened. Julia's going to London. She's got a flat, and she's going to get a job there. She told me last night. So there is no reason that you have to go too."

"I must."

"Yes. I can see that. I'm sorry. I've been dreading this, and yet I wanted it too. I've grown so fond of you. I had silly dreams, like any sentimental mother. But I wouldn't be any use as a parent if I tried to influence Julia."

"I . . . I never meant it to happen."

"You're not to blame. Nobody is to blame."

"I'll stay, of course. Until you find somebody to take over my job."

"And you?"

"I'll find another job."

He did, too. In Scotland, with the Forestry Commission. When he told Mrs. Hawthorne, she smiled wryly. "It could scarcely be further away," she said.

"Perhaps that's what I need. Perhaps that's what we all need."

"Oh, Miles. Dear Miles. How much I shall miss you."

"I'll come back," he promised her.

But he did not come back. He moved forward, to a new life in more senses than one. He went to solitude as he had never known it before, to a small granite house in heathery hills that stretched forever. He went to new attitudes, new problems, new solutions. He made, gradually, new friends. Learned to drive thirty or forty miles for any sort of social contact. Lived with bitter cold and wide skies, endless rain and drifting snow. He planted trees, and brushed trees and felled trees; ploughed land that had never known anything but heather and ling and the cries of grouse and curlew. He learned to melt ice when the water from the tap trickled to a standstill, learned to fish for salmon, to dance an eightsome reel. He learned to live alone.

He worked, sometimes seven days a week, using self-imposed labour as a sedative, numbing his memories and his heartache. Sometimes there was leisure to read a book or a paper. One morning, more than two years after he had said goodbye to Brookfield, he went the twenty miles to Relkirk for Market Day, and along with a few crates of necessary groceries, he bought a *Times*. In it, he read the announcement of Julia's engagement to a man called Humphrey Fleet. He had meant to drive straight home, but instead took himself into the nearest pub with the intention—for the first time in his life—of getting slowly, systematically drunk.

He did not. Because in the pub he met an old friend from Agricultural College, and with this extraordinary coincidence, the whole course of his life took a new turning.

And now the road ran downhill and Brookfield lay below him in the valley, a cluster of cottages around a crossroads, surrounded by farmland and shallow hills. He came to the vicarage and the church, passed the Flower in Hand, the grocer's shop that sold everything from frozen scampi to floor polish. He came to the oak copse, the white gates standing open, the cattle-grid. Brookfield Farm. He went through the gates and up between the white-painted fences and over the little bridge, and the house revealed itself, rose-red brick smothered in wisteria, the garden concealed by banks of rhododendrons.

He drew up at the back of the house, stopped the car and turned off the engine. He could smell the rich, sweet fragrance of the farmyard, heard the soft, contented squawks of Mrs. Hawthorne's free-range hens. He got out of the car and opened the back gate and made his way down to the house and through the open kitchen door. The Aga hummed companionably. There were roses in a lustre jug in the middle of the scrubbed pine table, and all the old lustre plates still ranged upon the open shelves of the dresser.

"Mrs. Hawthorne?"

No sound. No reply. He went through the kitchen and into the hall, and the door to the garden was open to the warm afternoon, and beyond it lay the terrace and the long lawn, sloping down to the river. A wheelbarrow stood in the middle of the grass, and he stepped out into the sunshine, and there was Mrs. Hawthorne, on her hands and knees, peacefully weeding her border.

He walked across the grass towards her. She did not hear him, but suddenly became aware that she was not alone. She turned her head, putting up a muddy gloved hand to push back her hair with her wrist.

He said, "Hello."

"Miles!" Astonishment, delight filled her face. She dropped her weeding fork and got to her feet. "Oh, Miles."

They had never been on kissing terms, but he kissed her now, and she put her arms around him to give him a hug, and then held him off in order to gaze into his face.

"What a wonderful surprise. Where have you sprung from?"

"I was on my way to London from Southampton. I thought I had to call in and see you."

"And I thought you were in Scotland."

"Yes, I am. I'm still working there, but I've been on holiday with some friends, they've got a cottage in the Dordogne. Now I'm on my way back. I'm putting the car on the Motorail to Inverness this evening. It saves a long drive."

"But how wonderful that you came. I am touched." She pulled off her gloves and dropped them onto the grass. "Let's go and sit in the shade. Would you like a drink? How about some lemonade?"

"That would be delicious."

She led the way back to the house and he watched her go and thought that the years had still not touched her. She remained as slim as a girl, her fair, greying hair cut casually short, her step long-legged and supple. She disappeared indoors for a moment, and then returned with a tray, a jug of lemonade clinking with ice, and two tumblers. She put this down on a battered table that had seen many such al-fresco occasions.

"Don't look too closely at the garden, Miles. I've been so busy, there's been no time to tie things up or get rid of the weeds."

He turned from his contemplation of the familiar view and came to sit beside her.

"How's the farm going?" he asked.

"Splendidly." She poured him a glass of lemonade, picked it up and handed it to him. "Derek's out of the Army, finished with

Cirencester, and now he's in charge. So far everything seems to be going according to plan, but I'm afraid you won't meet him, because he's gone over to Salisbury today, to see about a new tractor."

"And the farm manager who took over when I left?"

"A great success. He's moved on to work for some friends of ours who farm near Newbury. The only thing was that he wasn't as keen a gardener as you were, and I'm afraid your little garden at the cottage has gone back to rack and ruin again."

"There's nobody living in that house, then?"

"No. Derek thought we'd maybe let it. He hasn't decided yet. Now, tell me about you. Tell me about everything you've been doing. Are you still with the Forestry Commission?"

"No. No, I'm not. I've gone into partnership with a chap called Charlie Westwell. We were at Cirencester together, and I met up with him again in a pub in Relkirk, quite by chance. He'd come north to look at a farm that was for sale, but he couldn't raise sufficient capital to buy it on his own. So, right then and there, we went off together to look at the place. It's a good farm, in the Vale of Strathmore, south-facing, incredibly fertile. The sort of place I've always dreamed about. I rang my father that evening, and put the scheme to him, and he came up trumps with just about enough cash for the half-share, and a long-suffering bank manager lent me the balance. We've been working together now for four months, and I think it's going to work out." He grinned. "The best thing about having a partner is that you can sometimes take a holiday. This is the first one I've had in years."

"And I'm sure you needed it! He sounds a good friend to have met again. Do you share a house?"

"No. Charlie's married, you see. He and Jenny live in the farm-house and I've got the grieve's cottage. It's actually quite a big house, with a new kitchen and central heating and all sorts of luxuries. I scarcely know myself."

"And you . . ." She smiled at him. "You never married?"

"No."

"You should be, Miles."

He took a long drink of the lemonade. It was sour and refreshing and the ice clinked against the glass, and touched his mouth. When he had drained it, he set down the empty tumbler and said, as casually as he could, "How did the wedding go?"

She said, "It didn't." Miles looked up quickly, and her blue gaze met his own.

"You mean, it didn't go well?"

"No, I don't mean that. I mean it didn't happen. Five days before the wedding was due to take place, Humphrey and Julia came to me and said that they had decided they didn't want to get married after all. We put an announcement in the paper, but of course, if you were in the Dordogne, you wouldn't have seen it."

"Dear heaven," said Miles.

His voice sounded quite ordinary and calm, but inside he felt as though he had been kicked in the stomach, knocked to the ground, left in some gutter, bruised and incapable. A sort of panic knocked in his chest, and it was a second or two before he realized that it was simply the beating of his own heart.

"Luckily," Mrs. Hawthorne's gentle voice went on, "they at least came out with this before the marquee went up. So I was able to cancel that. But it took a good deal of organization to put off the caterers and the guests and the lady who was going to do the flowers; and the man with the crates of champagne, and the poor vicar."

He said, "But *why?*"

She shrugged and sighed deeply. "I don't know. I simply don't know. They neither of them were able to find any particular reason."

"Did you imagine that this was going to happen?"

"No, I didn't."

"Did you like him?"

"Yes. Yes, really, I did. Very much. He was a very nice young man. Really, everything any mother could wish for. Nice-looking, plenty of money, a good job. I always thought, perhaps, that Julia was more in love with him than he was with her, but you know what sort of a person she is. Demonstrative and outgoing. She was never any good at hiding her feelings. I think he had learned to be a little bit more reserved."

"Is Julia back in London?"

"No. She'd given up her flat, given up her job. She's still here. She won't see anybody. She's very unhappy." Once more their eyes met and held. "I don't suppose," said Mrs. Hawthorne, "that you would want to see her."

"What you mean is, that Julia wouldn't want to see me."

"Oh, dear Miles. I don't know what I mean."

She looked, he thought, all at once exhausted and distraught. As though, suddenly, she felt that she could let down her defences, and stop pretending to be practical and strong.

"It's such a mess," she admitted. "Derek was furious with her. He'd bought himself a new morning coat. He said that if he was going to give his sister away, he couldn't do it in a hired outfit from Moss Brothers. He kept saying, 'And I've bought myself a bloody morning coat,' as though that were really all that mattered. Poor man, he's been a tower of strength to me, but he doesn't seem to be able to do anything for Julia."

"Where is she now?"

"Do you remember the raspberry canes you planted at the back of the cottage when you were living here? I don't think you stayed long enough to harvest the fruit, but they produce the most beautiful berries. Julia went down there to see if she could find a bowlful for our supper. Perhaps . . . perhaps if you're not in too much of a hurry, you could go and help her . . . ?"

It was a humble plea from the heart, and Miles recognized it as such.

He said, "You know, if I'd known what had happened, I mean, about the wedding being called off, I don't think I'd have turned off the Motorway today. I'd have just bombed on to London."

"Then I'm glad you didn't know."

"I don't want to start anything up . . . the same way. I wouldn't want it to end all over again."

"If I didn't know you better, I'd say that was a selfish thing to say. Julia doesn't need a love affair. But she certainly needs every friend she's got. You were always such good friends . . ."

"Until I had to spoil it all by saying something stupid like 'I love you.' "

"It wasn't stupid. I never thought it was stupid. It was just ill-timed."

The bumpy lane led from the back of the house, down between stone walls smothered in convolvulus. The cottage, where he had lived for those twelve, never-to-be-forgotten months, nestled in the lea of its own garden wall. The little gate had come off its hinges and now hung lopsidedly, and beyond it the weeds had taken over. Where once had grown cabbages, potatoes, carrots was a riot of groundsel and waist-high grass. Only the raspberry canes bravely raised their heads above the jungle. There was no sign of Julia.

The back door of the cottage was closed and locked. He went around the flagged path, ducking long thorny branches of bramble and pushing aside the tall spires of purple willow-herb. At the front of the house, he had once grown flowers and had planted a little lawn. The lawn had disappeared, and the flowers were buried in weed. Only the orange marigolds had somehow survived, seeding themselves to spread all over, a carpet of bitter-smelling sun daisies.

She was there; not picking raspberries, not doing anything. Just sitting waist-deep in fiery flower heads. Her dark hair was bundled carelessly up at the back of her head; one or two fronds had escaped and fell across her face. She looked very thin. He did not remember her being so thin. She did not hear his footsteps, and when he said her name, she looked up vaguely, like a person awakened from a dream.

"Julia," he repeated, and crossed what had once been his garden towards her.

She pushed a lock of hair away from her eyes and stared at him. *"Miles."*

"Surprise," he said, smiling and squatting beside her. "I thought you were meant to be picking raspberries."

"What are you doing here?"

He explained, simply and briefly.

"Have you seen my mother?"

"Yes, I found her gardening." He settled himself beside her, crushing the flowers beneath his weight. "But she stopped and gave me a glass of lemonade, and we caught up on all the news."

"She told you."

"Yes."

Julia's eyes dropped. She picked a marigold head and began to tear it apart, petal by petal. She said, "You must think I'm mad or something." She sounded as though she was on the verge of tears. He was not surprised. He imagined that she had spent most of the last couple of weeks in floods of weeping. She had always cried easily. For ridiculous reasons, like seeing beautiful sunsets, or hearing choirboys sing "Oh, for the Wings of a Dove." It was one of the things about her that he had most loved.

He said, "Not at all. I think you were very brave. It takes a lot of courage to call off a wedding at the last moment. But it was right. It was the right thing to do, if you didn't believe yourself that it was right."

She said, "It was all too awful even to think about. Mother was marvellous, but Derek was furious with me. He kept saying I was selfish, that I wasn't considering anybody but myself . . ."

"Perhaps you were considering Humphrey."

"I tried to tell Derek that."

"If you truly love a person, sometimes the best thing you can do for them is to gently let them go."

"I did love him, Miles. I wouldn't have said I'd marry him if I hadn't truly wanted to. He was everything I'd ever imagined and never thought would happen to me. When I met him in London, I couldn't believe he'd even notice me. There seemed to be so many other girls. But then he asked me out one evening, and after that it all just got better and better. It was like living in a whole new world. As though everything was brighter, and had sharper edges. And then when he asked me to marry him I said yes very quickly, in case he should change his mind. That was how it was. The sort of relationship that doesn't often happen. It couldn't."

"But at the end of the day, you decided not to go through with it."

She looked away from him, out over the little garden, the crumbling wall, to the pastoral scene that lay beyond. Shallow hills and stands of trees, with peaceful cattle gathered in the shade around the edge of the river.

He said, "Things pass, you know. You have to remember that."

"It was the most dreadful thing I've ever had to do. I felt so conscience-stricken about my mother. She'd been working so hard for months, and all for me. And the vicar, and the reception, and all the guests had to be told. Goodness knows what everybody thought. It was a nightmare."

"Your mother understood."

"I almost wanted her to be angry, too. I was so ashamed."

"Moral courage is nothing to be ashamed about."

She said nothing to this. He went on, finding it hard to find the right words, but knowing that somehow he had to.

"Things pass, like I said. Time heals. All the old clichés, but they're true, or they wouldn't be clichés in the first place. The important thing is that you're still yourself. Julia. A person. An identity. That's what you have to hang on to."

She stayed silent, motionless, and he ploughed on, talking to the back of her head, wondering if she even heard what he said.

"The worst of it is over now. From now on, I'm sure, things can only get better."

"I can't believe they'll ever get better . . ." Suddenly she turned to him, and for an instant he saw her face, streaming with tears, before she flung herself into his arms. "He . . . he wanted people to think that it was a decision that we made together . . ." It was hard to hear what she was trying to tell him, so closely was her face pressed to his shoulder. "But really it was Humphrey who all at once didn't want any of it to happen. He said he didn't love me enough . . . not to give up his freedom. He didn't w-want me any more . . ."

A lump filled his throat, and he was suffused with tenderness. He held her very close, his chin against the top of her head, his arms tight around her sob-racked body. He could feel her ribs through the thin stuff of her dress, and her tears were soaking the front of his shirt.

"It's all right." He couldn't think of anything else to say. "It's all right. It's over now."

"I don't know what I'm going to do . . ."

"Do you want me to tell you?"

There were a few more sniffs and sobs, and then Julia drew away from him, turned up her streaming face to look into his own. Her eyes were swollen with weeping. He thought that he had never seen her look so beautiful.

She tried to brush away her tears with her hands, and he took out his own clean handkerchief and gave it to her.

"What am I going to do?" she asked him.

"If I told you I had a good idea, would you listen?"

She appeared to consider this. She blew her nose. She said, "Yes."

"Well, I think you should get right away, have a holiday, meet new people, see new places, get everything that happened into perspective."

"But where would I go?"

He told her about Scotland. About his farm. About Charlie and Jenny and his own little house. "It's got a honeysuckle growing over the gate, and a marvellous view of the Sidlaws, and there is everything in the world to be done to it."

"What sort of everything?"

"Making curtains, mowing the grass, building fences, feeding my hens. Having fun."

She blew her nose again, and pushed her hair back from a face that by now was becoming less woeful by the minute.

"Oh, Miles, you were always good for me. I always used to feel that nothing too ghastly could happen if you were around. And I know I made you unhappy. Then, I didn't know how unhappy one person could make another."

"I'm sorry you had to find out the hard way."

"I can't think why you came back to Brookfield. Why you turned off the Motorway."

"I think it was like swimming, and being caught in a strong current. Perhaps I couldn't have stopped myself. Perhaps love is more of a constant emotion than I'd ever realized. It becomes part of you. A heartbeat; a nerve end."

"When are you going back to Scotland?"

"Tonight, on the Motorail."

"Could I come with you?"

"If you want to. If you don't take too long to pack."

"I have to pick raspberries for supper."

"I'll help you."

"It's . . . it's just a holiday, isn't it? Nothing more."

"You come home to Hampshire whenever you want."

"We won't fall in love. We won't hurt each other."

"I don't think so. And I'm not having all my friends saying I caught you on the rebound."

She suddenly leaned forward and kissed him, briefly, softly on his cheek. She said, "I think I'd forgotten how nice you are. And comfortable. It's like being with the other half of myself."

He did not kiss her back. He said, "For a start, that's quite a good way to feel."

For a start. He knew that events had gone full circle, and now they were both back at the beginning again. Except that now they had both grown up, and were ready and able to cope with all the problems of the old—and yet new—relationship. He thought of the farm, of his future, of all the work that waited to be accomplished. He thought of Charlie and Jenny, and was filled with impatience, as though he could not wait to get home again, to start work, to start building that future that some day he would offer to Julia, like some marvellous present that he had made for her, himself.

Weekend

~~~

*I*t was a truce weekend. Not a truce from quarrelling, because in the two years that they had known each other they had never quarrelled. And maybe it was not so much a truce as a gentleman's agreement— that Tony should not ask Eleanor to marry him, backing up this suggestion with a string of sound reasons why she should; and that Eleanor should not say no to him, backing up her refusal with a string of sound reasons why she should not.

He had telephoned her three or four days previously. "I've just been told I've got a few days' leave coming to me. If I got into the car, took myself out of London, away from the rat race, and headed for the country, would you be able to come with me?"

Eleanor, snowed under with printer's galley proofs, a crammed engagement diary, and a potential author playing hard to get, was taken unawares. "Oh, Tony I don't know. I don't think I can. I mean . . ."

"Try," he interrupted her. "Just try. Speak to that editor-in-chief of yours and tell him you've got a sick auntie who has to have her pillow smoothed."

"It's not as easy as that . . ." She pushed her enormous spectacles up onto her forehead and gazed at her work-piled desk.

"Then let's just make it a weekend. We'll go on Friday after you've finished work, and get back to London on Sunday evening."

"Where did you think of going?"

"I'd like it to be the south of France, but I don't think there's time for that. We could go to Gloucestershire. To Brandon Manor."

"You mean, where you used to work?"

"That's right. Wouldn't you like to see for yourself the hotel where I learned how to decorate function rooms and flambé the larks' tongues in aspic?"

"I thought only millionaires could afford to go there."

"Millionaires and employees of the Triangle Hotel Group, of which I am one. I can get a cut-rate deal. Say yes, and I'll telephone and see if they have an empty room or two."

"You're boxing me into a corner."

"I only wish I could. Say you'll come."

Eleanor sighed and thought about it. She was tempted. It was the month of May and she was beginning to feel tired. A weekend in the country, in comfort and quiet, seemed very attractive. The trees would be bursting into leaf, the grass turning green, the birds beginning to sing. Perhaps the sun would shine, it would be warm.

"You won't . . ." she started to say, and then stopped. In the corner of the office her little secretary was putting letters into envelopes and trying to look as though she weren't listening.

"I mean, we aren't going to . . ." She stopped again.

"No," said Tony after a little, "we aren't going to argue. The subject of wedding rings, wedding bells, any sort of permanence shall be strictly taboo. Let's just get away from everybody and simply enjoy ourselves."

Eleanor began to smile. "It sounds," she told him, "almost irresistible."

"Only almost?"

"Irresistible, then."

"If I picked you up at the office about five o'clock Friday evening, would you be ready?"

"Yes, I'll be ready."

"Packed and waiting."

"I'll pack on Thursday evening, and bring my case into work."

"What about your car?"

"I'll leave it in the underground garage."

He said, "I love you."

"Tony, you promised."

"No, I didn't. I only said I wouldn't ask you to marry me. The two things, as we already know, seem to have nothing to do with each other." But he was smiling. She knew from his voice that he was smiling. "See you on Friday."

And so now they were nearly there, the long drive behind them, the agonizing crawl out of the city, choked in with weekend commuting traffic. Then the motorway, and the sudden, startling emergence into the country. It had been a fine day, warm and dry, with the first scent of summer in the air. In London, awnings had started to appear, and there were the first roses on the flower stalls. But in the country the signs of the approaching season were less sophisticated. Orchards of fruit trees were awash with tender pink blossoms and cottage gardens bright with forsythia and neat borders of velvety polyanthus. In the Cotswolds, villages and farms drowsed peacefully in the thin evening sunshine, golden stone buildings sheltered by coppices of oak and beech. The road wound ahead of them to the edge of the hills, and then there came a break in the trees, and the view was spread before their eyes, the great flat vale of Evesham, the distant Malvern Hills grey with haze.

"We would go on forever," said Eleanor. "On and on, till we came to Wales and then to the sea."

"But we're not. We're going to Brandon, and we're very nearly there." He changed down, and the car nosed its way down the steep and winding hill, and at the bottom was the scattering of picture-book houses that made up the village. A bridge over a rush-bordered river, water-meadows, more trees, and then the famous gatehouse, the winding drive beyond. She saw the white-painted fence, the horses in the park. A glimpse of a distant lake, the undulations of a small nine-hole golf course. They came around a corner and the old house lay ahead of them, low and rambling, with mullioned windows and steeply sloping roofs of dark slate.

"It's beautiful," was all she could think of to say.

"I didn't bang on about how beautiful it was because I didn't want you to be disappointed."

"How long did you work here?"

"About four years. I was assistant undermanager, which means general dogsbody, but I learned everything I know behind those ancient walls."

"How long has it been a hotel?"

"The family who owned it sold up after the war. Their only son had been killed and there was no one to inherit. Poor things, I suppose they lost heart. It's been a hotel ever since. A great favourite with visiting Americans, and honeymooners. It's even got a honeymoon suite." Gravel crunched as they drew up on the sweep outside the enormous stone porch of the front door. Tony turned off the engine, loosened his seat-belt, and turned to smile at Eleanor. "But don't worry. We're not going to be sleeping in it."

"I didn't for a moment imagine that we were."

"Not that I don't think it would have been a splendid idea."

"Tony." Her voice was full of stern warning. "You promised."

"What, that I wouldn't talk about the honeymoon suite?"

"That you wouldn't mention anything even remotely connected with honeymoons."

"It's such a romantic spot, I'm going to find it very difficult."

"In that case, you'll have to spend the whole three days playing golf."

"Will you come and caddy for me?"

"No, I shall find some nice unattached spinster like myself and sit and talk knitting patterns with her."

Tony began to laugh. "What an unusual weekend we're going to have." Unexpectedly, he leaned forward and quickly kissed her mouth. "I love you even more when you try to look cross. Now come along, don't let's hang around. We'll go and see if they've got a porter to carry our bags."

They got out of the car and crossed the gravel, and passed under the dark lintel of the porch and through a pair of inner glass doors. Inside was the hall, stone-flagged. The walls were panelled; a square Elizabethan staircase led to the upper floors. In a cavernous fireplace a fire of logs burned in a bed of grey ash. The flicker of this fire and the ticking of a grandfather clock were the only sounds.

Beneath the turn of the stairs had been discreetly infiltrated a reception desk. Behind it a man in a dark coat stood with his back to them, sorting some mail. He had not heard them come in and did not turn until Tony, coming up behind him across the thick rug, said his name.

"Alistair."

Surprised, he swung round. There was a moment's astonished

silence, and then his face broke into an incredulous but delighted smile.

"Tony!"

"Hello, Alistair."

"My dear man, what are you doing here?"

"Come to stay. Didn't you see my name in the book?"

"Yes, of course I did. Talbot. But I had no idea it was you. The receptionist took the booking . . ." He gave Tony a friendly bang on the shoulder. "What a marvellous surprise."

Eleanor was standing a little behind Tony. Now he moved aside and put out a hand to draw her forward. "This is Eleanor Crane."

"Hello, Eleanor."

"Hello." They shook hands across the polished counter.

"Alistair and I did our training together when we were mere lads. In Switzerland."

"Did you know he was working here?" Eleanor wanted to know.

"Yes, of course I did. One of the reasons we came."

"You're in London, aren't you?" said Alistair.

"That's right. The Crown, in St. James. But I've been given a few days off, so I thought I'd come back and see what sort of a job you're making of this place." He looked about him in a deprecating sort of fashion. "Doesn't look too bad. No stained table-cloths, no dirty ash-trays, no piped music. Doing well, are you?"

"Booked to the hilt for most of the year."

"Brisk trade in the honeymoon suite?"

"Well, it's certainly been taken this weekend." A grin crept into Alistair's face. "Why? Did you have designs on it?"

"Heavens, no. None of that sort of rubbish for Eleanor and me."

Alistair laughed and rang the bell. "I'll get the porter to bring your stuff in." He lifted the flap of the counter and came out to join them. "What would you like in the way of refreshment?"

"I'd love a cup of tea," Eleanor told him.

"I'll have it sent up."

It was, Eleanor decided, exactly like staying in the very nicest sort of private house, except that one knew one was not going to have to help with the washing-up. All those years ago, when the family who had lived in and loved this house, had finally, sadly, had to leave, they had left behind not only their beautiful furniture, but, as well, a sort of ambience that was hard to define. It was as though they had all gone away for a little while, but would soon be back. So cleverly had the house been altered, adapted, and redecorated that the modern improvements did nothing to detract from this atmosphere, but rather added to it.

The bedrooms were wallpapered in designs that might have been created especially for the small, oddly shaped rooms. Crisp cotton curtains framed the deep-silled, leaded windows, and although now each room had its own modern bathroom, there were still the original bathrooms to be found down the crooked passages, with marvellous mahogany-encased tubs and great brass taps.

Downstairs, the same inspired touch was evident. The lounge had once been the drawing-room of the old house, with French windows that led down a flight of steps to a terrace and then onto the lawns of the garden. The dining-room had been the great hall, with an oriel window that reached to the ceiling, and the bar discreetly had been contrived within some smaller downstairs apartment, perhaps a sewing-room or a morning-room, and in no way detracted from the dignified and yet homely feel of the rest of the hotel.

That evening, Tony was bathed and changed for dinner before Eleanor had even made up her face. Waiting, he came to sit on the edge of her bed, looking impatient, but as well looking tall and suave and exactly right in a dark blazer and a fresh shirt and tie.

She said, "You smell delicious. I do like men who smell delicious. All clean and spicy."

"I smell delicious, but I'm in need of a drink."

"Go down and get yourself one, and I'll join you later. In the bar. I shan't be more than ten minutes."

So he got to his feet and left her, and she was alone. She began to brush her long pale hair and then met her own eyes in the mirror, and slowly, the long strokes ceased. She gazed at herself—not admiring the reflection that gazed back at her, but almost despising it. Despising the girl who sat there, in the loose frilled gown, its neckline open to her waist, exposing the curve of her breast, the lacy edge of her bra.

What do you want? she asked that girl, with her pale, unpainted face, her long hair a silky curve from the crown of her head to her shoulders. What do you really want?

To know, was the answer. To know that I can give myself to this relationship and yet not be submerged by it. To be loved and not overwhelmed. To give love, but to keep something back for myself.

You want everything. You can't have your cake and eat it.

I know that.

You have to make up your mind. You're not being fair to Tony.

I know that too.

I wish, she thought, I could find someone to talk to. Someone who isn't Tony. Someone who would understand. Slowly, she began to brush her hair again, to cream her face, reach for her eye-shadow. Behind her, the little bedroom, flower-dappled and fresh with white paint, appeared secure as a Victorian nursery. It would be nice to have been a child in this house. Children had been happy in this house. It would be nice, perhaps, to be a child again. With everything arranged for one and no decisions to make.

But she was not a child. She was Eleanor Crane, Editor of Children's Books with the publishing firm of Parker and Passmore, twenty-eight years old, successful and efficient. She was Eleanor Crane—and far beyond the age of being sentimentally nostalgic for long-gone days. Briskly, she finished her face, sprayed on some scent, stepped out of her dressing-gown, and zipped herself into a brilliantly casual but sophisticated dress. She slid her feet into soft leather pumps, picked up her handbag, turned off the lights, and went from the room without so much as a backward glance towards the girl reflected in the mirror.

She found Tony in the bar, sitting at a table near the fire, with a whisky and soda and a dish of nuts in front of him. When she joined him he went to get her the glass of wine that she asked for, and then settled himself once more and picked up his glass.

The bar was busy, all the little tables occupied by various residents, attired in various degrees of formality. Some had obviously come for a weekend of golf. There were one or two elderly single ladies, a party of Americans. As well, some younger people, perhaps just dinner guests, treating themselves to a night out.

When they had finished their drinks, Tony and Eleanor stood up and went down the thickly carpeted passage to the dining-room, where three-quarters of the tables were already occupied and dinner was in full swing.

"Do they ever," Eleanor wanted to know, when they had ordered from the menu and were waiting for the wine list, "have a time when they aren't full up?"

"No, not really. There are only twenty bedrooms, and it's not the sort of place that is affected by the seasons. I mean, even if you don't play golf, there's always something to do or to look at, at all times of the year. People make pilgrimages to Stratford, or to Wells and Bath. They go to Broadway, and explore the Cotswolds. Then there's always a dinner dance on Saturday nights, and special festivities at Christmas and Easter."

"Christmas must be perfect. It's a house made for Christmas."

The wine list was produced. Tony put on his horn-rimmed spectacles, inspected it, and ordered a bottle. When the waiter had gone, he took off his glasses and leaned across the table on folded arms.

"I'll play a guessing game with you. Which, of all the people in this room, are shacked up in the honeymoon suite?"

His eyes were dancing with amusement. What was so funny? Eleanor, puzzled, looked casually around the room. The young couple, perhaps, in the corner? No, they didn't look nearly opulent enough. The tall, bored-looking pair over by the window? The woman was gazing into space, like a highly bred horse, and the man wore an expression of agonized boredom. One somehow couldn't imagine them having got to the lengths of getting married, let alone going on a honeymoon. Or was it the young golfing Americans, she with her tan, and he immaculate in his maroon blazer and tartan trousers . . . ?

Her eyes came back to Tony's face. "I haven't the faintest idea."

He gave a tiny inclination of his hand. "The couple by the fireplace."

Eleanor looked over his shoulder. Saw them, old enough to be her parents, or even her grandparents. The woman was silvery-headed, her shining white hair swept up into a casual knot at the back of her head; the man quite portly, moustached and balding. She wore an unexciting, comfortable-looking dress, and he was in a dark suit and a formal tie. Just an ordinary elderly couple. And yet they weren't ordinary, because they were having such a good time, chatting and laughing away together, with eyes for no one but each other.

Amazed, Eleanor looked back at Tony. "Are you *sure?*"

"Yes. Sure. Mr. and Mrs. Renwick. Honeymoon suite."

"You mean they've just got married?"

"They must have. That's what honeymoons are all about."

Cautiously, Eleanor looked at them again. The woman was talking, the man listening, sitting there, holding his glass of wine. Perhaps she was telling him a joke, because he suddenly let out a great guffaw of laughter. It was fascinating.

"Perhaps," said Eleanor, "they've been friends for years, and then her husband died, and his wife died, and they decided to marry each other."

"Perhaps."

"Or perhaps she never married, and when his wife died, he was able to confess to her that he'd secretly loved her all his life."

"Perhaps."

"Or perhaps they met on a cruise, and his fancy was caught by the fetching figure she cut playing shuffleboard."

"It's possible."

"Can't you find out? I long to know."

"I thought they would intrigue you."

The honeymoon suite. She looked at them again, charmed by their obvious delight in each other. Mr. and Mrs. Renwick.

"Do you think," asked Tony, "that seeing them will help you change your mind, or make up your mind, or whatever it is you're trying to do? About us, I mean."

Eleanor looked down at the table-cloth. Carefully, as though it mattered, she altered the position of her knife. She said, "You promised. You mustn't break your promise."

Their wine arrived; was poured, tasted, the bottle left upon the table.

"Who shall we drink to?" Tony asked.

"Not you and me."

"The newly-weds, perhaps. And a long and happy life to them."

"Why not?" They drank. Over the rim of her glass, their eyes met. I love him, Eleanor told herself. I have faith in him. Why can't I have faith in myself?

In the morning, after a late breakfast, they went out for a walk. The weather, obligingly, was perfect. Eleanor wore white jeans and a pullover over her shirt, and when they had explored the gardens and looked at the massive tithe barn which stood a little way from the house, they wandered down to the lake and found a sheltered hollow by the reedy bank where the wind could not reach them. The grass was thick and green, starred with the first daisies, and they lay and watched random clouds sail across the pristine blueness of the sky, and were so still and quiet that a couple of inquisitive swans slid across the lake to inspect these strangers to their remote and watery world.

"How wonderful it must have been," said Eleanor, "to own all this. To be a child here, and take it all for granted. To be a man, and know that it was part of you. Part of your life and the person you were."

"But there were responsibilities, too," Tony pointed out. "People to work for you, yes, but people to take care of, too. When a man or a woman grew old, you had to watch out for them, see they had a roof over their heads, coal for their fire, food in the larder. The land was their responsibility as well; there were buildings to keep up, and the church to sustain. These old boys were great churchmen. Whether or not they believed in God was never totally certain, but they were always fairly sure that God believed in them."

"They must have been nice, the family who lived here. The house is fairly buzzing with good vibes. Benevolent. Did you like working here?"

"Yes," said Tony, "but after a bit I felt I was becoming drowned in some gorgeous backwater. Not enough stimulation."

"Aren't people enough stimulation?"

"For me, not entirely."

She said, "If we got married, do you think we should begin to feel we were becoming drowned in some gorgeous backwater?"

Tony opened his eyes, and raised his head and looked at her in some surprise. "I thought we weren't going to talk about getting married."

"We seem to be talking about it all the time, without actually saying anything. Perhaps it would be better if we forgot about promises and brought it all out into the open. It's just that I don't want to start an argument."

"We don't have to argue. There's nothing to argue about. I want to get married and you don't. It's as simple as that."

"That makes me sound cold and heartless."

"I know you're not, so it doesn't matter how it sounds. Look . . ." He raised himself up on an elbow. "Look, my darling Eleanor, we've known each other for two years. We've proved, to ourselves and the rest of the world, that this is a good thing we're on to. It isn't just some wild infatuation, a fly-by-night affair that's going to turn sour the moment we commit ourselves." He grinned. Even when they were at odds with each other, he never lost his good humour. "After all, we're neither of us in what you might call the first flush of careless youth. I don't want to be like Mr. and Mrs. Renwick and miss all the fun of growing old together."

"Nor I, Tony. But I don't want it to go wrong."

"You mean, like my parents."

His mother and father had had a rancorous divorce when Tony was fifteen, and then gone their separate ways. He never spoke about this traumatic experience, and Eleanor had not met his parents. He went on, "No marriage can be perfect. And mistakes don't have to be inherited. Besides, your parents were happy. They lasted the course."

"Yes, they were happy." She turned away from him, pulling absently at a tuft of grass. "But my mother was only fifty when my father died."

Tony put a hand on her shoulder and turned her to face him. He said, "I can't promise to live forever, but I'll do my best."

Despite herself, Eleanor smiled. "I believe you would."

"We've talked about it, then. Cleared the air, like you said. Now we can go on enjoying ourselves." He looked at his watch. "Just about time for lunch. And this afternoon I shall take you to Broadway in the car and buy you a cream tea, and this evening we shall dress up in our smartest togs and do our best to dance to the local band. Give the residents something to talk about."

On the Sunday morning, like any husband, Tony decided to take himself off and see if he could find some man prepared to play a round of golf with him. Eleanor was invited to accompany him, but she declined and had her breakfast in bed, blanketed in newsprint and all the Sunday papers. About eleven o'clock, she got up and had a bath and got dressed and went downstairs and out of doors. It was still sunny, though not as warm as the previous day, and she set off briskly in the direction of the little golf pavilion, with the intention of walking out over the course and meeting Tony on his way in.

When she reached the pavilion she stopped, hesitating because she was uncertain as to the layout of the course, and not sure in which direction she should head. She was trying to make up her mind when a voice behind her said, "Good morning," and she turned and saw, sitting in the sheltered veranda that fronted the pavilion, none other than the honeymooner, Mrs. Renwick. Mrs. Renwick wore a tweed skirt and a thick knitted jacket, and looked content and comfortable in a basket chair, warm in a patch of sunshine, and out of the wind.

Eleanor smiled. "Good morning." Slowly, she went to join the older woman. "I thought I might walk out, but I don't know which way to go."

"My husband's playing golf too. I think they come from that direction, but I decided it was more pleasant to sit than to walk. Why don't you join me?"

Eleanor hesitated, and then succumbed. She pulled up another of the basket chairs and settled herself beside Mrs. Renwick, stretching out her legs and turning up her face to the sun.

"This is nice."

"Much nicer than walking in that chilly wind! What time did your husband go out?"

"A couple of hours ago. And he's not my husband."

"Oh, dear, I am sorry. How mistaken can one be? We'd made up our minds that you were married, and even possibly on your honeymoon."

It was amusing to realize that the Renwicks had discussed her and Tony, just as they had speculated about them.

"No, I'm afraid not." She glanced at Mrs. Renwick's left hand, expecting to see a sparkling engagement ring, and a shining gold wedding ring as well. But there was no flash of diamonds, and Mrs. Renwick's wedding ring was as thin and worn as the hand that wore it. Puzzled, Eleanor frowned, and Mrs. Renwick saw this.

"What's wrong?"

"Nothing. It's just that . . . well, we thought you and your husband were on *your* honeymoon."

Mrs. Renwick threw back her head and gave a peal of quite girlish laughter. "What a compliment. I suppose you found out we were in the honeymoon suite!"

"Well . . ." Eleanor felt embarrassed, as though they had been prying. "It's just that Tony works for the Triangle Hotel Group, and he and the manager are old friends."

"I see. Well, I'll put your mind at rest. We've been married for forty years. This is our ruby wedding, and a weekend at Brandon is my husband's little treat instead of throwing a party. You see, we came to Brandon for our honeymoon . . . we could only afford to stay for two days, but we always promised ourselves that one day we'd come back. And it's just as lovely as ever!" She laughed again. "Fancy you thinking we were newly-weds. You must have wondered what on earth a couple of old fogies like us were up to."

"No," said Eleanor, "we didn't. You looked perfectly believable. Laughing and talking and looking as though you'd just met each other and fallen madly in love."

"An even nicer compliment. And we've been watching you. Last night, when you were dancing together, my husband said he'd never seen a better-looking couple." She hesitated for a moment, and then went on, her manner now very down-to-earth. "Have you known each other long?"

"Yes," said Eleanor. "Quite long. Two years."

Mrs. Renwick considered this. "Yes," she said thoughtfully. "That is quite a long time. I'm afraid nowadays men are very spoilt. They seem to get all the advantages of married life, handed to them on a plate, without having to bother about any of the responsibilities."

Eleanor said, "It's my fault. Tony isn't like that. He wants to get married."

Mrs. Renwick smiled tranquilly. "He obviously loves you," she said.

"Yes," said Eleanor faintly. She looked at the older woman, sitting there in the pale sunshine, her expression kindly and her eyes wise. A stranger; but all at once Eleanor knew that she could confide in her.

She said, "I don't know what to do."

"Is there any reason why you shouldn't marry him?"

"No concrete reason. I mean, we're both free; we neither of us have other commitments. Except our jobs."

"And what are those?"

"Tony's manager of the Crown Hotel in St. James. And I work for a publishing company."

"Perhaps your career is important to you?"

"Yes, it is. But not that important. I mean, I could go on working after I was married. At least, until I started to have children."

"Perhaps . . . you don't feel prepared to spend the rest of your life with him."

"But I want to. That's what's so frightening. This thing of becoming part of another person. Losing oneself. Tony's parents never made it. They divorced when he was a boy. But my parents did everything together, they lived for each other. When they were away from each other, they used to telephone every day. And then my father had a heart attack and died, and my mother was alone. She was only fifty. She'd always been such a marvellous person, and a tower of strength to her family and her friends, and she simply . . . went to pieces. We thought that when she'd stopped grieving, she'd pick up and start again, but she never did. Her life simply stopped when my father died. I love her very much, but I simply can't go on being unhappy with her."

"Has she met your Tony? Does she like him?"

"Yes. And yes, she does like him. She's a little disconcerted by the fact that he's in the hotel business. Once we went home for the weekend, and Mother was rather tired, and Tony offered to cook the dinner. It really threw her. She was all embarrassed and flustered. Like a hen. Afterwards she said to me, 'Your father would never have done that.' Everything harks back to my father. Not in a happy way, but almost resentfully, as though he had no right to go without her."

"I am sorry," said Mrs. Renwick. "It's difficult for you and so very sad for her. But I'm afraid the final parting comes to all of us. I'm sixty now, and my husband is seventy-five. It would be foolish to pretend we have many years left to us, and by the law of averages, he will probably die before me and I shall be left on my own. But I shall have marvellous memories, and being on my own has never frightened me. I am, after all, myself. I always have been. I adore Arnold, but I never wanted to be with him all the time. That's why I'm sitting here now, and not trudging down the fairway feeling martyred, and watching him miss all his putts."

"You never played golf?"

"Heavens, no. I could never make contact with any sort of a ball. But I'm lucky, because when I was a child I was taught to play the piano. I was never very good. Not good enough to become a professional. But I used to play in our local orchestra, and sometimes for dancing classes and that sort of thing. But mostly I played for myself. It was my private thing. My time on my own. Restoring when I was tired. Comforting when I was anxious. It has sustained me all my life, and will continue to do so, whatever happens."

"My mother doesn't play the piano. She doesn't even want to garden any longer, because my father isn't there to garden with her."

"Like I said, I was lucky. But there are other things. I have a friend who has no particular talents. But she goes out every afternoon for a walk with her dog. She walks by herself, rain or shine, for an hour. Nobody is ever allowed to accompany her. She assures me that more than once it has saved her reason."

Eleanor said, "If I knew I could be like that . . . Not like my mother. I'm so afraid of being like my mother."

Mrs. Renwick sent her a long, measuring look. "You want to marry this young man?" After a little, Eleanor nodded. "Then marry him! You're far too intelligent to let yourself be overwhelmed by any man, let alone that charming-looking creature who obviously adores you." She leaned forward and laid her hand over Eleanor's. "Just remember. A private world of your own. An independence of spirit. He will respect you for it, and thank you for it, and it will make your life together infinitely more interesting and worthwhile."

"Like your life," said Eleanor.

"You know nothing about my life."

"You've been married for forty years, and you still laugh with your husband."

"Is that what you want?" asked Mrs. Renwick.

After a little, "Yes," said Eleanor.

"Then why don't you go and get it? Grasp it with both your hands. I think I can see your Tony now, at the very end of the fairway. Why don't you walk out and meet him?"

Eleanor looked. Saw the two distant figures walking in—one of them, unmistakably, Tony. A ridiculous excitement filled her heart.

"Perhaps I will," she said.

She stood up and then hesitated, and turned back to Mrs. Renwick. She put her hands on Mrs. Renwick's shoulders and stooped to kiss her cheek. "Thank you," she said.

She left Mrs. Renwick sitting there in the basket chair. She went down the steps of the pavilion and across the gravel and onto the springy turf of the fairway. In the far distance Tony, seeing her, waved. She waved back and then began to run, as though, even if they were going to spend the rest of their lifetimes together, there was no longer a single second to be wasted.

A Walk in the Snow

—⟨⟩—

Waking to darkness, Antonia, drowsy with half-sleep, at first thought herself back in the flat in London. But then consciousness stirred. No sound of traffic, no pale light seeping through curtains that had never properly fitted, no bundling of a duvet up to her ears. Instead the darkness; silence; extreme cold. Linen sheets, tightly tucked. The smell of lavender. And she knew that it was a Saturday morning at the end of January, and she was not in London, but home, in the country, for the weekend.

Her mother had sounded a little surprised when she had telephoned to say that she was coming.

"Darling, heaven to see you." Mrs. Ramsay adored it when Antonia came home. "But won't it be dreadfully dull? Not a thing going on and the weather's appalling. Terrible gales and bitterly cold. I'm sure we're in for snow."

"It doesn't matter." Without David, nothing mattered. She only knew that the prospect of a weekend alone in London was unbearable. "I'll take the train if Pa could meet me at the station."

"Of course he will . . . usual time. I'll race upstairs now and make your bed."

Mrs. Ramsay was right about the weather. The snow had begun to fall as the train made its way from Paddington Station and out into the country. By the time they reached Cheltenham, the railway platform was two inches deep in snow, and Antonia's father, come to meet her, wore rubber boots and the very old tweed coat, rabbit-lined, that had once belonged to his grandfather and only came into its own in the most bitter of weather. The drive home had been dicey, with frozen ruts in the road and the occasional skid, but they made it safely and duly arrived, only to be plunged in darkness just as they sat down to supper. Antonia's father, after lighting candles, had telephoned the authorities and been told that a main cable was down, but repair-men were, at that moment, setting out to find the fault. And so they had spent the evening by firelight and candle-light, struggling with the crossword, and grateful for the Aga, which simmered comfortingly on, allowing them to boil kettles for hot-water bottles and make warm bedtime drinks.

And now, the next morning . . . still darkness, silence, and cold. Antonia reached out a chilly hand and tried to switch on the bedside lamp, but nothing happened. There was no alternative but to sit up, grope for matches and light the stub of the candle that had seen her to bed, and it was astonishing to see, by its pale flame-light, that it was past nine o'clock. With a sort of puny courage, she threw back the covers and stepped out into the icy cold. Drawing back the curtains, she saw the whiteness of snow, black trees etched against the half-light, no glimmer of sunlight. A rabbit had made its way across the lawn, leaving a trail of footmarks like sewing-machine stitches. Shivering, Antonia pulled on the warmest garments she could lay hands on, brushed her hair by candle-light, cleaned her teeth and went downstairs.

The house felt deserted. No sound disturbed the quiet. No washing machine, no dishwasher, no vacuum cleaner, no floor polisher. But someone had lighted a coal-fire in the hall fireplace, and it flickered in a welcome fashion and smelt comforting.

Looking for company, Antonia made her way to the kitchen, where she found comparative warmth and her mother, sitting at the kitchen table, which she had spread with newspapers, and where she was about to embark on the tedious task of plucking a pair of pheasants.

A small and slender woman with a mop of curly grey hair, she looked up as Antonia appeared through the door.

"Darling! Isn't this terrible? We still haven't got any power. Did you have a good sleep?"

"I've only just woken up. It's so dark and so quiet. Like the North Pole. Do you suppose I'll ever get back to London?"

"Oh, yes, you'll be all right. We listened to the weather forecast and the worst seems to be over. Make yourself some breakfast."

"I'll just have some coffee . . ." She poured herself a mugful from the jug that stood at the back of the stove.

"You should have a proper breakfast in weather like this. Are you sure you eat enough? You're dreadfully thin . . ."

"That's just London life. You mustn't start making noises like a mother." She opened the fridge for milk, and it was queer having no light go on. "Where is everybody?"

"Mrs. Hawkins is snowed up. She rang me up about an hour ago. She can't even get her bike out of the shed. I told her not to bother to come, because without any power, there's not a lot she can do."

"And Pa?"

"He walked over to the farm to get some milk and eggs. He had to walk, because the gale we had yesterday blew down one of the Dixons' beech trees, and the lane's blocked. Was it windy in London?"

"Yes, but somehow in London it's different. Just piercingly cold, and rubbish and stuff flying around. You don't think about trees blowing down." She sat at the table and watched her mother, busy at work with deft fingers. Soft-grey and brown feathers drifted into the air. "Why are you plucking pheasants? I thought Pa always did that for you."

"Yes, he does, and we're having them for dinner tonight, but after he'd gone and I'd washed up the breakfast dishes I simply couldn't think what to do next. Without electricity, I mean. In the end I decided it was either plucking pheasants or cleaning silver, and I hate cleaning silver so much, I plumped for the pheasants."

Antonia set down her mug and reached for the cock pheasant. "I'll help you." Its body was cold and solid, the feathers on its well-fed breast thick and downy, but those at its neck blue as peacock eyes, bright as jewels.

She held the bird, spreading its wing like a fan. "I always feel guilty pulling such a beautiful creature to pieces."

"I know. I do too. That's why your father always does them for me. And yet there's something comfortingly timeless about plucking birds. You think of generations of country women—doing just this thing, sitting in their kitchens, and talking to their daughters.

Probably saving all the down feathers for stuffing pillows and quilts. Anyway, we mustn't be sentimental. The poor birds are already dead, and just think of delicious roast pheasant for dinner. I've asked the Dixons and Tom to come and eat them with us." She reached down for a large plastic dustbin bag and bundled the first of the feathers into it. "I thought," she went on with elaborate casualness, "that David might have been here too."

David. Mrs. Ramsay was a perceptive woman, and Antonia knew that this gentle probing was a tentative invitation for confidences. But somehow, Antonia could not talk about David. She had come this weekend because she was lonely and desperately unhappy, but she could not bring herself to talk about it.

The reason that his name had come so easily into the conversation was because David and Tom Dixon were brothers, and the family were friends and neighbours of a lifetime to the Ramsays. Mr. Dixon ran his farm, and Mr. Ramsay ran the local bank, but when they could they played golf together, and sometimes escaped for a week's fishing. Mrs. Ramsay and Mrs. Dixon were equally close, stalwart supporters of the local Women's Rural and members of the same little bridge club. Tom . . . the older brother . . . worked now with his father. He had always seemed to Antonia very adult and remote, a responsible sort of person, useful at mending bikes and building rafts, but never a close friend. Not like David. David and Antonia, only a couple of years apart in age, were inseparable.

Like brother and sister, everybody said, but it had been more than that. There had never been anybody but David. Going away to school, to college, their ways separating and their lives widening, it was natural to expect that their fondness for each other would mature into simple friendship, but somehow the very opposite happened. Being apart only served to fan the flame of their affection, so that each reunion, each coming together, was more satisfying and exciting than the time before. For Antonia there were other boys, and then other men, but none of them ever stood a chance, because in comparison to David they seemed dull, or plain, or so demanding that she was sickened by them.

David was her yardstick. He made her laugh. With David, she could talk about anything, because everything important in her life she had shared with him, and if she hadn't, then he knew all about it anyway.

As well, he was the best-looking man she knew . . . had grown from a handsome boy to an attractive adult without any of the usual uncomfortable stages in between. Everything was easy for David. Making friends, playing games, passing exams, getting to University, finding a job.

"I'm coming to London," he told her.

Antonia had already been there for a year, working for the owner of a bookshop in Walton Street, and sharing a flat with an old school friend.

"David, that's marvellous."

"Got a job with Sandberg Harpers."

She had been terrified that he would go abroad, or to the north of Scotland or somewhere remote where she would never see him. Now, they could do things together. She imagined little dinners in Italian restaurants, trips down the river, the Tate Gallery on bright cold winter afternoons. "Have you got somewhere to live?"

"I'm going to move in with Nigel Crawston; he's living in his mother's house in Pelham Crescent. He says I can have the attics."

Antonia had never met Nigel Crawston, but when she went to the house in Pelham Crescent, she knew the first stirrings of unease. Because Nigel was a young man of much sophistication, and the house was beautiful, quite beyond the style of Antonia's little flat. It was a proper grown-up house, filled with lovely things, and David's attics proved to be a self-contained flat, with a bathroom that looked like an advertisement for high-quality plumbing.

As if all this were not enough, Nigel, as well, had a sister. She was called Samantha, and she used the house as a sort of pied-à-terre in between sorties to ski in Switzerland, or to join friends on some yacht in the Mediterranean. The Crawstons were those sort of people. Sometimes, when she was in London, she would take some undemanding job, just to fill in time, but there seemed no question of having to earn a living. As well, she was almost unbearably glamorous, thin as a rail and with long, straight fair hair that never looked anything but immaculate.

Antonia did her best, but she found the Crawstons heavy going. Once, they all went out to dinner together, to a restaurant so expensive that she could scarcely bear to watch David forking out his half of the bill.

Afterwards, she said, "You can't take me to places like that. You must have spent at least a week's salary on just one meal."

He was annoyed. "What's it got to do with you?"

He had never spoken that way to her before, and Antonia felt as if she had been slapped in the face. "It's just . . . well, it's just a waste."

"A waste of what?"

"Well . . . money."

"How I spend my money is my own concern. Your opinion doesn't interest me."

"But—"

"Don't ever interfere again."

It was their first-ever real quarrel. That night, she cried herself to sleep, hating herself for having been so stupid. The next morning, she rang at his office to apologize, but the girl on the switchboard said that he wasn't available, and after that Antonia lost her nerve, and it was nearly five days before David called her.

They made it up, and Antonia told herself that everything was the way it had always been, but in her heart of hearts, she knew that it wasn't. At Christmas, they drove back to Gloucestershire together, in David's car, with the back seat piled with presents for their assorted families. But even Christmas provided its own problems. The holiday, traditionally, is a time for engagements, and, for the first time, Antonia felt that friends and family expected some sort of an announcement. One or two coy ladies, the vicar's wife and Mrs. Trumper from The Hall, even went so far as to make an arch reference or two, heavily veiled, but unmistakable. Ultra-sensitive, Antonia was certain that their beady eyes wandered to her left hand, as though expecting to spy some enormous diamond ring.

It was horrible. In the old days, she would have confided in David, and they could have laughed about it together, but somehow now that was impossible.

From this situation she was rescued, oddly enough, by none other than Tom. Tom, uncharacteristically, all at once elected to throw a party in his barn. It was on Boxing Night, and he hired a disco and asked everybody in the neighborhood under the age of twenty-five. The dancing and merriment went on until five in the morning and caused such a stir that people stopped speculating about Antonia and David and discussed the party instead. With the pressure off, things were easier, and at the end of the holiday she and David returned to London together.

Nothing had changed; nothing was settled; nothing had even been discussed, but she wanted it no other way. She wanted, simply, not to lose him. He had been part of her life for so long that losing him would be like losing part of herself, and the prospect filled her with such desolation that it didn't bear imagining. Shamingly, she pretended to herself that it would never happen.

But David was stronger than she. One evening, soon after Christmas, he called and suggested coming round to her flat for a meal. Antonia's flat-mate tactfully took herself off, and Antonia made a spaghetti bolognese and went around the corner to the off-licence for an affordable bottle of wine. When the doorbell sounded, she ran down the stairs to let him in, but as soon as she saw the expression on his handsome face, all self-deception and reasonless hope seeped away and she knew that he was going to tell her something terrible.

David.

I thought that David might have been here too.

Antonia began to tear at the breast feathers of the cock pheasant.

"No . . . he's staying in London this weekend."

"Oh, well," said her mother calmly. "There probably wouldn't have been enough for us all anyway." She smiled. "You know," she went on, "being like this, without electricity, and forced onto our own resources, reminds me so much of when I was little. I've been sitting here wallowing in memories, and all of them so vivid and clear."

Mrs. Ramsay had been brought up, one of five children, in a remote area of Wales. Her mother, Antonia's grandmother, lived there yet, independent and wiry, keeping hens, preserving fruit, digging in her vegetable garden, and, when forced by darkness or inclement weather to retreat indoors, knitting large knobbly sweaters for all her grandchildren. Going to stay with her had always been a treat and something of an adventure. You never knew what was going to happen next, and the old lady had passed on much of her enthusiasm and energy for life to her daughter.

"Tell me," said Antonia, partly because she wanted to hear, but mostly because she hoped to get off the subject of David.

Mrs. Ramsay shook her head. "Oh, I don't know. Just being without any appliances or labour-saving devices. The smell of a coal-fire, and the iciness of bedrooms. We had a range in the kitchen, and that heated the bath-water, but all the washing had to be done, once a week, in a huge boiler in the scullery. We all used to help, pegging out lines of sheets, and then, when they were dry, turning the handle of the old mangle. And in winter it was so cold that we all used to dress ourselves in the airing cupboard, because that was the only spot that was remotely warm."

"But Granny has electricity now."

"Yes, but it was a long time coming to the village. The main street was lit by lamps, but once you'd passed the last house, that was it. I had a great friend, the vicar's daughter, and if I had tea with her, I always had to walk home by myself. Most times I didn't mind, but sometimes it was dark and windy and wet, and then I used to imagine every sort of spook, and by the time I reached home I'd be running as though there were monsters at my heels. Mother knew that I was frightened, but she said I must learn to be self-reliant. And when I complained about the spooks and monsters she said the thing to do was to walk slowly, looking up at the trees and the infinity of the sky. Then, she said, I would realize how infinitesimal I was, how pointless and puny my tiny fears. And the funny thing was, it really worked."

As she spoke, she had concentrated on the task in hand, but now she looked up and across the littered, feathery table, and her eyes met Antonia's. She said, "I still do it. If I'm miserable or worried. I take myself out and go somewhere peaceful and quiet and look up at the trees and the sky. And after a bit, things do get better. I suppose it's a question of getting your values straight. Keeping a sense of proportion."

A sense of proportion. Antonia knew then that her mother knew that there was something horribly wrong between herself and David. She knew, and was offering no form of comfort. Simply advice. Face up to the spooks of loneliness, the monsters of jealousy and hurt. Be self-reliant. And don't run away.

By afternoon, the electric power still had not come on. When the lunch dishes were tidied away, Antonia pulled on boots and a sheepskin coat and persuaded her father's old spaniel to come out for a walk. The dog, having already been exercised, was reluctant to leave the fire, but once out of doors, forgot his misgivings and behaved like a puppy, bounding through the snow and chasing interesting rabbit smells.

The snow was deep, the sky low and grey as ever; the air still, the countryside blanketed and soundless. Antonia followed the track that climbed the hill behind the house. Every now and then there came the clatter of wings in the still air as a pheasant, disturbed, shouted warning, got up and sailed away through the trees. As she climbed, she stopped feeling cold, and by the time she reached the top of the hill was warm enough to clear the snow from a tree-stump and sit there, looking at the great spread of the familiar view.

The valley wound away into the hills. She saw the white fields, the stark trees, the silver river. Far below, the village, darkened by the power cut, lay clustered around the single street; smoke from chimneys rose straight into the motionless air. The silence was immense, broken only now and then by the whine of the chain-saw slicing the crystal quiet, and she guessed that Tom Dixon and one of the farm workers were still dealing with the fallen beech.

The hill sloped gently down towards the wood. On this hill, she and David had sledged as children; in the wood, they had, one summer, built a camp, and baked potatoes in the ashes of their fire. Where the river curved into the Dixons' land, they had fished for trout, and on hot days bathed in the clear shallows. It seemed that the whole of this small world was littered with memories of David.

David. That last evening. "You're saying that you don't want to see me any more." Angry, and hurt, she had finally blurted it out.

"Oh, Antonia, I'm being honest. Without meaning to hurt you. I can't go on pretending. I can't lie to you. We can't go on like this. It's not fair for either of us, and it's not fair to our families."

"I suppose you're in love with Samantha."

"I'm not in love with anybody. I don't want to be. I don't want to settle down. I don't want to commit myself. I'm twenty-two and you're twenty. Let's learn to live without each other, and be ourselves."

"I am myself."

"No, you're not. You're part of me. Somehow, you're all entangled with me. It's a good thing, but it's a bad thing, too, because we've neither of us ever been free."

Free. He called it being free, but for Antonia, it meant being alone. On the other hand, as her mother had said, you couldn't be self-reliant until you'd learned to live with yourself. She tipped back her head and looked up through the black winter branches of the overhead trees, to grey and comfortless sky beyond.

You hold most fast to the people you love by gently letting them go. Long ago, some person had said this to her—or she had read it. The source of wisdom was forgotten, but the words suddenly, out of nowhere, resurfaced. If she loved David enough to let him go, then, that way, he would never be wholly lost to her. And she had already had so much of him . . . it was greedy to yearn for more.

Besides—and this was a surprising, cool-headed revelation, and something of a shock—she didn't want to get married any more than he did. She didn't want to get engaged, have a wedding, settle down forever. The world spread far beyond this valley, beyond London, beyond the bounds of her own imagination. Out there, it waited for her, filled with people she had yet to meet and things that she had yet to do. David had known this. This was what he had been trying to tell her.

A sense of proportion. Relative values. Once you had got these worked out, things didn't look so bleak after all. In fact, a number of interesting possibilities began to present themselves. Perhaps she had worked for too long in the bookshop. Perhaps it was time to move on—go abroad, even. She could be a cook on a Mediterranean yacht, or look after some Parisian child and learn to speak really good French; or . . .

A cold nose nuzzled her hand. She looked down and the old dog stared plaintively up at her, telling her, with large brown eyes, that he was sick of sitting there in the snow, and wanted to get on with his walk, chase some more rabbits. Antonia realized that she too had grown chill. She got up off the stump and they started for home, not retracing their steps, but setting off down the snow-deep fields towards the wood. After a little, she began to run, not simply because she was cold, but with something of the high spirits of childhood.

She came to the wood, and then to the track that led through the trees to the Dixons' farm. She came to the clearing where the beech had fallen. Already its immense trunk had been sliced into lengths by the chain-saw, and a way cleared, but devastation lay all about, along with the smell of newly sawn timber, and the fragrance of wood-smoke from a smouldering fire. There was nobody about, but as she stood there, mourning the demise of the noble tree, she heard a tractor coming down the road from the farm, and the next moment it appeared around the bend of the lane, with Tom at the wheel. Reaching the clearing, he killed the engine and climbed down out of the cab. He wore dungarees and an old sweater and a donkey jacket, but, despite the cold, was bareheaded.

"Antonia."

"Hello, Tom."

"What are you doing here?"

"Just out for a walk. I heard the saw going."

"We've been at it most of the afternoon."

He was older than David and neither so tall nor so handsome. His weather-beaten face did not often smile, but this seriousness was belied by his amused pale eyes, which always seemed to brim with incipient laughter. "Got rid of the worst of it now." He went to the smouldering bonfire and kicked the grey ashes into life. "At least we won't need to worry about firewood for a month or two. And how are things with you?"

"All right."

He looked up, and across the little flames and the sweet plume of smoke, their eyes met. "How's David?"

"He's all right, too."

"He didn't come with you?"

"No, he stayed in London." She buried her hands deep into the pockets of the sheepskin coat, and said, as she had not been able to say to her mother, "He's going skiing next week with the Crawstons. Didn't you know that?"

"I think my mother said something about it."

"They've taken a villa in Val d'Isère. They asked him to go with them."

"Didn't they ask you?"

"No. Nigel Crawston's got a girl of his own."

"Is Samantha Crawston David's girl now?"

Antonia met his steady gaze. She said, "Yes. For the moment."

Tom stooped, gathered up another branch and threw it onto the fire. "Does that worry you?" he asked her.

"It did, but not any more."

"When did all this happen?"

"It's been happening for some time, only I didn't want to admit it."

"Are you unhappy?"

"I was. But not any longer. David says we each have to live our own lives. And he's right. We've been close for too long."

"Were you hurt?"

"A bit," she admitted. "But I don't own David. I don't possess him."

Tom was silent for a moment. "That's a pretty grown-up thing to say," he observed then.

"But it's true, isn't it, Tom. And at least now we know where we stand. Not just David and me, but all of us."

"I know what you mean. It certainly makes things easier." He tossed another armful of branches onto the flames, and there was the sizzling sound of melting snow. "There was, without any doubt, a certain amount of covert expectation at Christmas about what the pair of you were up to."

Antonia was surprised. "You felt that too? I thought I was the only one. I kept telling myself I was over-reacting."

"Even my mother, who's the most sensible of women, caught the bug, and started hinting at Christmas engagements and June weddings."

"It was awful."

"I guessed it was awful." He grinned. "I was very sorry for you."

Watching him, a thought occurred to Antonia. "Was it because of that . . . that you threw your party?"

"Well, anything was better than having everybody sitting around speculating. Waiting for you and David to come prancing in, all bright-eyed and bushy-tailed, saying, 'Listen, listen to our news; we have an announcement to make." He said this in a ridiculous voice, and Antonia began to laugh, filled with grateful affection.

"Oh, Tom, you are marvellous. You really took the pressure off. You saved my life."

"Well, I don't know. I've been mending your bicycles and building you tree-houses for long enough. I thought it was time I did something a bit more constructive."

"You've never been anything else. Always. I can't thank you enough."

"You don't have to thank me."

He went on working. "I've got to get the worst of this cleared before dark."

She remembered something. "You're coming to dinner tonight. Did you know that?"

"Am I?"

"Well, you've been invited. You must come. I've been plucking pheasants all morning, and if you aren't there to eat them, I'll feel the entire effort's been wasted."

"In that case," said Tom, "I'll be there."

* * *

She stayed with him for a little, helping with his task, and then, as the midwinter afternoon slipped into dusk, she left him, still at it, and set off for home. Walking, she realized that the air had gentled and a soft westerly wind was stirring in the trees. Branches that had been frozen in snow were starting to drip. Overhead, the clouds were parting, revealing glimpses of a pale evening sky the colour of aquamarines. As she came through the gate that stood at the end of the Dixons' lane, she looked up the hill towards home and saw the lights shining out from the uncurtained windows.

So things were looking up. The power failure was over. And living without David was not going to be impossible after all. She decided that when she got home, she would ring him up and tell him this, putting his mind at rest, and leaving him free to make his plans for Val d'Isère without any guilty backward glances over his shoulder.

And it had started to thaw. Tomorrow it might even be a beautiful day.

And Tom was coming for dinner.

Cousin Dorothy

———

Mary Burn awoke early on a fine bright morning in May. She was in her own deliciously comfortable bed, in her own flower-sprigged room, and with all her pretty and personal possessions about her. The sun was shining and the birds were singing, but even before she opened her eyes, she knew that something was wrong. The black anxiety, the worry that she had taken to bed with her, had not retreated. It had probably spent the entire night sitting on her pillow.

She turned over, shut her eyes, and longed for Harry to be there; to say, "It's all right, it doesn't matter. I'll see to it." But Harry wasn't there, because he was dead. He had died five years ago, and their daughter Vicky was getting married in a week's time, and Mary was at her wit's end, because the wedding dress still had not materialized.

She didn't know what to do, and Harry would have. For, with his going, Mary had lost not only lover and dearest friend, but a competent and kindly husband who dealt with every problem.

Mary, happily content with the day-to-day demands of house, garden, and one small child, had been delighted to let him. Organization, she was the first to admit, was not her strong point. She was useless on committees, and frequently forgot when it was her Sunday for doing the flowers in church. It was Harry who arranged holidays, ordered coal, interviewed headmistresses, coped with horrible things like Income Tax, filled the cars with petrol, and when door handles fell off, was there with a screwdriver to screw them on again.

As well, he handled the problem of Vicky. As a small girl, she had been loving and warm-hearted, a delightful little female companion, happy with her mother, content to make doll's clothes and bake gingerbread men and dig her own private patch of garden. But, at around age twelve, she had changed. Overnight, it seemed, she was no longer the biddable and responsive little girl, but a prickly adolescent, stubborn and contrary. And everything, from the wrong sort of shoes to bad marks for her homework, was her mother's fault.

Mary was both hurt and baffled by this hateful metamorphosis. "What on earth is wrong with her?" she whispered furiously to Harry after a particularly painful exchange with Vicky, concluding with a furiously slammed door. "I don't think she even *likes* me any more. Nobody could behave like that to someone they *liked*."

"She adores you. She's growing up. Asserting herself. She's probably jealous of you because you're beautiful and young-looking instead of being fat and old."

"Perhaps I should put on weight and stop using lipstick."

"Don't you dare. It's just a stage. It'll pass. Daughters are often jealous of their mothers."

"How do you know? You never had a sister. You've only got Cousin Dorothy."

"Now, don't start in on her."

As much as there could be a bone of contention between them, Harry's cousin Dorothy was it. She was a good ten years older than Mary, and in every way, immensely superior. Unmarried, she had made her career in the Civil Service, attached, for some years, to the Foreign Office. She spoke three languages and worked for some Under-Secretary of State, with whom she was constantly being sent abroad on important missions. When she wasn't either in Geneva or Brussels or stalking the corridors of power at Whitehall, she lived in a service flat in the neighbourhood of Harrods, where she did her grocery-shopping and had her hair done. Mary had never seen her when her hair was not immaculate. Her clothes were the same, and she always wore very beautiful, expensive shoes, and carried a leather handbag large as a briefcase, bulging, one was certain, with immensely important State Secrets.

"I'm not starting in on her. It's just that I can't imagine Dorothy being a tedious teenager, or falling in love, or suffering from any sort of emotion. Admit it, Harry, she is fairly awe-inspiring. She must think I'm the most boring little housewife, because whenever I meet her, I clam up and can't think of a word to say."

"Never mind. Your paths don't often cross."

"No. But she is your cousin. It would be nice to be friends."

Vicky was seventeen when Harry died. By then, one would have thought, the teen-age antagonism between mother and daughter would have burnt itself out, but it had simply faded to embers, which, under stress, flamed up again into a blaze of meaningless resentment, and when they should have been able to comfort each other, they seemed to do nothing but quarrel.

It was a terrible time. Coping with grief and loss and all the painful formalities of death had been bad enough, but learning to live without Harry was worse. Over the months, through sheer necessity, Mary taught herself to be practical. Learned to make lists, write important dates on the calendar, use a calculator. By trial and error she finally managed to get the motor mower started. She found out where to put the oil in the car, to interpret the incomprehensible forms sent in by the Inland Revenue, and how to change the plug on the electric kettle.

Vicky, however, was another matter altogether. Vicky was lost and hurt and angry because her father was gone, and Mary understood this and was deeply sympathetic, but still found herself wishing that Vicky did not find it necessary to take this anger out on her mother. Their arguments—usually about something utterly trivial—invariably ended in floods of tears, or doors being slammed in Mary's face. The problem was that Mary couldn't reach her. She understood exactly what poor Vicky was going through and yet she couldn't reach Vicky to comfort her. And she knew that there was nothing she could do, because whatever she said would automatically, inevitably, be wrong.

The worst was having no person to confide in. There were many friends, of course, in the little Wiltshire village where she had lived all through her married life, but you couldn't confide in friends about your daughter's shortcomings. It would be too disloyal.

And as for family, there was only Harry's cousin Dorothy. Retired now from the Foreign Office, she had left London and moved to the country, to live not ten miles away, run the local Red Cross and play a great deal of golf. Sometimes, she and Mary met for a formal lunch, but it was difficult to think of things to talk about. And Vicky was a touchy subject, for Dorothy had never shown much fondness for Vicky. "She's a spoilt brat," she had told Harry more than once. "Only child, of course. You've never learned to say no to her. You'll regret it, of course. You'll live to regret it."

The last thing Mary wanted was to give Dorothy the opportunity to say "I told you so."

Altogether, life went through a phase of being almost impossibly difficult, but just when Mary was deciding she couldn't carry on for another moment, Vicky herself, cool as ever, came up with the solution. At breakfast one morning, she announced that it was pointless hanging around at home, doing nothing. So why didn't she go to London and learn to cook?

Mary's first, thoughtless reaction was to say, "But, darling, you're a marvellous cook." Which Vicky was, and had turned out many a delicious meal when she was feeling in a good humour and ready to be helpful.

"Oh, *yes.*" Vicky was scornful. "Shepherd's pie and cauliflower cheese. But if I do this course, I'll get a degree. I'll be a professional. And then I can stay in London and earn my own living and be independent."

She was just eighteen. Mary carefully set down her coffee cup. "Where did you think you might do this training?"

Vicky told her. "Sarah Abbey went there. You remember, she was at school with me. She's living in her own flat now and earning a bomb doing director's lunches. She says I could stay with her. She's got a spare bed in the flat."

Mary, presented with this *fait accompli,* weakly said that she would look into it. But Vicky, it appeared, already had. In fact she had already put her name down for the next term. The course cost an arm and a leg, but Mary meekly supposed she would find the money somewhere and agreed to the arrangement. There wasn't much else she could do.

When the time came to put Vicky on the train for London, she was torn by two conflicting emotions. Losing her only child, knowing that Vicky was virtually leaving home for good, caused a lump to come into her throat and her eyes fill with stupid tears, which she had some difficulty in concealing. And yet, as well, there was some relief in returning to her quiet and empty house, where she could be herself, alone and peaceful, and subjected no longer to Vicky's casually hurtful remarks, her disparagement, or, worst of all, her baffling, brooding silences.

She'll be better on her own, she told herself robustly, and went upstairs to change into old jeans and a sweater that had once belonged to Harry. *Eighteen's adult nowadays. Vicky's got her feet on the ground.* She went out into the garden to do some weeding. *She won't do anything stupid.*

But Vicky, true to form, proceeded to do everything possible that would fill her mother's heart with alarm. She moved in with Sarah Abbey, the old school friend, stayed a month, and then moved out. To give her her due, she called Mary on the telephone and told her what was happening.

"But, Vicky, I thought you liked her."

"Mummy, she's turned into the most frightful bore. I'm going to live with another girl, who's in the course with me. And two chaps. They all share this house in Fulham. It's going to be much more fun."

Mary swallowed. "Yes, I see . . ."

"Look, here's my address . . ." Mary grabbed a pad and pencil and wrote it down. "Got it? Great. Look, I must fly."

"Vicky . . . ?"

"What is it?"

"How's everything going?" She amended this hastily. "The course, I mean."

"Oh, like a breeze. Dead easy. I'll do you a crown of lamb next time I come down."

"When . . . ?"

"Oh, soon. A weekend some time . . ."

She came and had changed, and wore extraordinary clothes that looked as though they had been bought at a jumble sale or a flea market. Which they had. She came again with a young man, whom she had met, she explained, at a disco. He wore a crumpled mauve linen suit and spent the entire weekend plugged into his Sony Walkman. He even wore it when Vicky took him for a country walk, as if determined not to hear a single thrush go tweet.

The cooking course lasted a year. At the end of it, Vicky passed all her examinations with flying colours and instantly set about finding work. She bought herself a second-hand Mini and in no time at all was busy as a bee, driving herself around London with pots and pans, cooking knives and liquidizers all piled up on the back seat. She cooked for dinner parties, filled deep-freezes, catered for wedding receptions, and concocted enormous luncheons for prestigious board meetings.

With evidence of such industry and success, it was pointless to go on worrying about the child, and so Mary stopped, but still could find no good excuse to explain away Vicky's quite extraordinary friends. They were brought to Wiltshire at regular intervals, and each was odder than the last, but quite the strangest was a girl called Regina French, who looked like a very thin, young witch, and would eat nothing but raw oatmeal and nuts.

Mary made these friends all welcome and entertained them and fed them, and made certain that they had enough to drink, but she found them all peculiar. There must be, she told herself, some perfectly pleasant, normal young people living in London. Why didn't Vicky ever meet them? And if she did meet them, why didn't she like them? Was she trying to prove something? Was she reacting against her own conventional upbringing?

There didn't seem to be any answers.

Dorothy rang.

"Mary?"

"Yes. Dorothy. How are you?"

"My dear, I just had to ask. I was in London yesterday in Harrods and I saw Vicky. At least, I think I did. But she's dyed her hair. It's bright yellow."

"Well, at least it isn't pink."

"What's she doing with herself? Has she got a job, or is she on the dole?"

"No, she is not on the dole." Mary was indignant. "She's started her own little catering business. She's working very hard."

"Well, she looks extraordinary. I'm amazed any person employs her to boil so much as an egg."

"How she looks is her affair."

"I'd be concerned if I were you."

"I am not concerned."

"Oh, well, she's your daughter."

"Yes," said Mary firmly. "She is my daughter."

It was the first time she had ever stood up to Dorothy. It made her feel quite good.

And then, out of the blue, the unimaginable happened. Vicky went to Scotland for a fortnight, to cook for some fishing party in a remote Highland village that had a name like a sneeze. There, she met a man called Hector Harding. Before long, his name was being mentioned with monotonous frequency and slipped into the conversation on the slenderest of excuses.

Mary's attention was caught. "Who is Hector, Vicky?"

"Oh, just a chap I met in Scotland. I . . . I've been seeing quite a lot of him."

"What does he do?"

"He's an architect."

An architect. This was breaking new ground. There had never been an architect before. Hope stirred. But she had learned to keep her counsel, and silence was rewarded. Hector Harding was invited to Wiltshire for the weekend.

Just another friend, Mary told herself firmly, and made no special preparations, but yet, when the car came trundling up to the front door on Friday evening, she could not suppress a flutter of curiosity as she went out to meet them. They had come, not in Vicky's Mini, but in Hector's car, which meant, at least, that he had some possession of his own, and that she had not had to do the driving. He climbed out from behind the wheel, unfolding very long blue-jeaned legs, and came at once to shake his hostess by the hand. He was immensely tall and thin, wore horn-rimmed spectacles, and had a lot of wild and untidy brown hair. Not particularly good-looking; not particularly anything, really. Just ordinary. And terribly nice. On the Saturday morning, he cut the grass and mended the electric toaster, which had been behaving oddly for weeks. That afternoon, he and Vicky took themselves off for a long walk. They returned at five o'clock looking faintly bemused. Later, over drinks before dinner, they told Mary that they wanted to get married.

Dorothy rang.

"Mary, I've just opened the *Daily Telegraph,* and read the announcement of Vicky's engagement. When did this happen?"

Mary told her.

"Who is he?"

"He's an architect."

"Do you like him?"

"Very much. And Harry would have liked him, too."

"What a stroke of good fortune! I was perfectly certain that Vicky would end her days with some appalling hippie. When's the wedding?"

"In May."

"Soon as that? Registry office, I suppose."

"No. The village church, and a party here afterwards. Not a big, elaborate wedding. Just their friends."

"Even so, you'll have your work cut out."

"Vicky's coming home to help me. And like I said, it's all going to be very simple."

But she was wrong, because it wasn't. Vicky, as always, had a mind of her own.

"We'll have to get invitations printed and make out a guest list."

"Hector and I don't want more than fifty people. Just our close friends. No old relations we don't know."

"But some relations will have to be asked. Cousin Dorothy, for instance."

"Why do I have to have Cousin Dorothy at my wedding? She's never been able to stand the sight of me. I saw her in Harrods one day, and I shot off, through the soft furnishings, before she could buttonhole me. I knew she'd fix me with that beady eye of hers and ask a lot of probing questions."

Mary was sympathetic. "I know. She puts my back up too, some-times. But I still think she must be asked."

"Oh, all right," Vicky conceded ungraciously. "She can always sit in a corner and chat to Hector's old granny. *She's* ninety-two and uses an ear-trumpet."

Which dealt with Dorothy. But there were other considerations.

The catering?

Vicky would do that herself. Concoct an enormous cold luncheon and put it all in the deep-freeze.

Champagne?

No, not champagne. Far too expensive. They would give the guests white wine. Vicky knew a man who would let her have it wholesale.

A photographer?

They would ask the nice man in the village.

Flowers?

Mary could do the flowers. She was better at doing flowers than any florist.

Bridesmaids?

No. No bridesmaids. Vicky was quite firm on this point.

Finally, the most important question of all.

"What about a wedding dress?"

"What about it?"

"Well, you'll have to wear something."

"Actually," said Vicky. "I've seen a picture in a magazine."

A picture in a magazine. It sounded quite hopeful. Mary tentatively imagined white lace and a veil. She might have saved herself the bother. Presented with the periodical, she gazed, wordless, at the picture. The model in the photograph was not unlike Vicky, with a short blonde thatch of hair and long skinny legs. The dress resembled a T-shirt, with a cotton skirt attached. The skirt fell in points, like handkerchiefs hung out to dry. The model wore ankle socks and tennis shoes.

Vicky broke the silence. "Don't you think it's smashing?"

"It costs three hundred and twenty pounds," was all her mother could think of to say.

"Oh, I wouldn't buy it. I'd get it copied. Have it made. You remember Regina French? I brought her down to stay once, ages ago." Mary remembered Regina, munching her nuts. "She dressmakes."

"Professionally?"

"No. Just as a hobby. I'll ask her to do it for me."

"Vicky . . ." It had to be said. "Are you sure she'd be good enough? I don't mind what we have to pay."

"Of course she's good enough."

"Would she get it done in *time?*"

"Why shouldn't she?"

"Yes. Well." Mary took a last look at the frightful picture of the frightful dress and laid it down on the table. It was, after all, Vicky's wedding. "Perhaps you'd better get in touch with her right away. Make sure she can do it. After all, we haven't got that much time."

Vicky went off to telephone. But she couldn't get through to Regina, so she rang Hector instead and talked for an hour. Mary, washing up the breakfast dishes, was filled with foreboding. She yearned for her dear, dead husband. She felt very alone.

Her foreboding had been well grounded. Regina French was not a girl upon whom one could rely. Each time Vicky went up to London to see how she was getting on, or telephoned the wretched female, there was always some excuse. The material had not come. Her sewing machine was on the blink. She had to go to Devon to look after somebody's baby. But not to worry, not to worry, it would all be all right on the night.

Not to worry. Mary opened her eyes. Saw her own flower-sprigged room, and all her own pretty and personal possessions around her. The wedding was a week away and still the wedding dress had not come. She got out of bed, dressed and went downstairs, only to discover Vicky down before her, sitting at the kitchen table and drinking coffee out of a Wedgwood mug. The post had arrived.

"Anything from Regina?"

Vicky said, "Yes." She would not look at her mother. Mary glanced around in the hopes of seeing a large parcel that might contain a wedding dress. There was none. "A letter," Vicky enlarged, and held it out. With a sinking heart, Mary took it from her. She put on her spectacles and read it.

> *Dear Vicky. Terribly sorry, have been stricken with measles. Can't even reach a telephone. Sorry about the dress, can't possibly cope with it now. Hope you have a lovely wedding. Love, Regina.*

She felt her knees turn to water. Reached for a chair and sat down. Across the table, mother and daughter eyed each other.

Vicky spoke first. "If you say 'I told you so,' I shall scream."

"I wasn't going to say anything of the sort."

"Well, you're thinking it. You always thought Regina would be a dead loss. Admit it."

"Well, I don't know . . . she did seem a bit . . . fey. Rather vague. And now she's got measles." She added, for form's sake, "Poor girl."

"I'm not in the least sorry for her. If she'd got on with my dress when she said she would, it would have been finished, and hanging in my cupboard by now."

"Well, at least we know where we stand."

"Yes. Stark naked. Without a thing to wear."

Mary told herself that she must keep calm. "Shall we go to London? Now. Today. And see if we can buy something?"

"I'll never find one I like. I know I won't." Vicky's voice rose. She was beginning to sound hysterical. "And I am not going to get married in a crinoline with frills of lace, looking like something off a tea-cosy."

"Darling, there are places you can *hire* dresses. They might have more choice. Or second-hand shops . . . ?"

"We haven't got time to go browsing around all the second-hand shops . . . We've only got a *week* . . ."

"Vicky, I know that—"

"If I don't get the sort of dress I want, then I'll get married in a boiler suit . . ."

"Oh, darling, don't get worked up . . ."

Vicky sprang to her feet. "What else is there to do? I wish it was all over. I wish Hector and I could just run away . . . I'd like to cancel the whole beastly affair . . ."

"Oh, Vicky . . ."

"And not get married *at all*."

The kitchen door slammed shut between them. Vicky's footsteps fled upstairs. Then her bedroom door was slammed. Then silence.

For a moment Mary sat where she was. To begin with, she thought that she was going to cry. And then, perhaps, scream. She then decided that she was about to become so angry that she would not be able to answer for her actions. That decided it. Before she should break something, or dash upstairs after Vicky and hit her, or say something unforgivable that could never be unsaid, she picked up her bag, walked out of the house, got into her car, and drove the ten miles to Dorothy's house.

She found Dorothy gardening. Even when she gardened, Dorothy looked neat, in well-cut slacks and a net over her white hair. She was forking over her rose border, but when she saw Mary approach across the grass, she instantly laid down the fork and came to meet her, stripping off her canvas gloves.

"My dear." Her face was all concern. I must look truly frightful, Mary told herself. She tried to speak, but before she could say a word, had burst into tears.

Dorothy was very kind. She led her gently indoors, settled her in a chair in the sitting-room, and tactfully disappeared. The sitting-room was cool and orderly and smelt of polish and linen loose covers. The window was open, the morning air fanned the crisp chintz curtains. Gradually soothed by this calm ambience, Mary controlled her weeping. She found a handkerchief and blew her nose. Dorothy returned, bearing, not coffee, but a small glass of brandy.

"Drink this."

"But Dorothy, it's not ten o'clock yet."

"Medicinal." Dorothy sat down in the other armchair. "You look totally shattered. Drink it up."

Mary did so. The brandy hit the back of her throat and descended warmingly into her stomach. She at once felt stronger. She even managed a weak smile.

"I am sorry. It's just that everything's so awful and I knew I had to get out of the house and talk to someone. And you were the only person I could think of."

"Is it Vicky?"

"Well . . . yes. In a way. It's not her fault. She's really helped me get this wedding together, and I began to think we were going to be able to do it without a single row." She laid down the empty glass. "I know you always thought Harry and I spoilt her, and perhaps we did, but the truth is that Vicky and I are very different people. I don't seem to have anything in common with her; not even friends. And I think I irritate her most dreadfully. It's all right when we're not living together, and it's all right when things are going smoothly, but this morning . . ."

She related the disastrous saga of the wedding dress.

"But it's not your fault," Dorothy pointed out when she had finished.

"I know. I think perhaps it might be easier if it was. But Vicky knows she's made a fool of herself, insisting on that idiot Regina making her dress, trusting her to have it finished in time. And now, of course, we've only got a week to find another. And Vicky's got such violent ideas about what she's going to wear. She won't even agree to try the shops, or the hire-firms, and she says she's going to wear a boiler suit, or run away with Hector, or even not get married at all."

Dorothy listened to all this, and then shook her head. "It sounds to me like a clear case of wedding nerves. For both of you. A wedding is twice as much work when you haven't got your husband to help you. In fact, I've been on the point of ringing you up, more than once, to suggest I lend a hand with the organization, but I was frightened you'd think I was interfering. And as for Vicky, you've been splendid with her. It can't have been easy without Harry. She is, after all, your only child. And you let her go off on her own to London, and make her own way, and never tried to stop her. I really admired you for that."

To be admired by Dorothy was an entirely new sensation.

"I always thought you thought I was a fool."

"Oh, my dear. Never that."

A silence fell between them. It was not a difficult one nor strained in any way. Mary had never felt so at ease with Dorothy before. She smiled and put her handkerchief away. She glanced at the clock. She said, "I feel better now. I just needed to talk. I should be getting home."

"What are you going to do about the dress?"

"I have no idea."

Dorothy said, "I have a wedding dress."

Mary drove home at a tremendous speed, feeling ridiculously light-hearted. The garden, as she came up the drive, had never looked so dear or so pretty, and the climbing rose that smothered the front porch was covered with tight pale-pink buds. She got out of the car, took the huge old-fashioned cardboard dress-box off the back seat, carried it indoors and upstairs to her bedroom. She laid the box on her bed (still unmade) and sat at her dressing-table to do something about her face. Crying when you were fifty-six was really most unbecoming.

"Mummy?" The door opened and Vicky appeared. "Are you all right?"

Mary did not turn. "Yes, of course I am." She smothered creamy moisturizer onto her cheeks.

"I couldn't think where you'd gone." Vicky came from behind her, put her arms around Mary's neck, and bent to kiss her. "I'm sorry," she said to Mary's reflection. "For flying off the handle like that. It's entirely my own fault that I haven't got a stitch to wear, and I shouldn't have taken it out on you."

"Oh, darling."

"Where did you go? I thought I'd been so beastly, I'd made you run away from home."

"Just to see Dorothy." Vicky went and sat on the bed. Mary reached for her foundation cream.

"Dorothy? Why did you go and see *her?"*

"I had a sudden, irresistible urge to get out of the house and go and talk to somebody sane. And she is the sanest woman I know. It worked. She gave me brandy and she gave me a wedding dress."

"You have to be joking."

"I'm not. It's in that box."

"But whose wedding dress is it?"

"Dorothy's own." She set down the jar of Elizabeth Arden and turned to face her daughter. "We all think we know so much about other people, and we don't know anything at all. When Dorothy was nineteen, she was engaged to a young naval officer. The wedding was to be in September 1939, but then war broke out and it was post-poned. He went to sea, and was almost at once lost with the sub-marine *Thetis.* So that's why Dorothy never married."

"But why didn't we know about this before? Why didn't Daddy know?"

"Harry was just a little boy of nine, away at boarding-school. I don't suppose he ever realized it happened."

"Oh, dear, how dreadfully sad. It doesn't bear thinking about. And then she went on to make such a terrific life for herself. And we all thought she was so frigid and tough."

"I know. It makes me feel a bit red in the face. But that's not the point. The point is that she says that if you like it, you can have her dress. Circa 1939. A real museum piece, and it's never even been worn."

"Have you seen it?"

"No. She just gave me the box."

"Let's look."

They sat together on the bed and untied the knot of the string and took off the lid of the box and folded aside the sheets of tissue paper. Standing, Vicky carefully lifted the dress out, to hold up in front of her. Folds of pure silk satin whispered to the floor; a flowing skirt out of the bias, puff sleeves, the shoulders padded, the neckline low and square and embroidered in pearls. There was a faint smell, sweet and musty, like old bowls of potpourri.

"Oh, Mummy, it's blissful."

"It is rather lovely. But the shoulder pads . . . ?"

"They're high fashion. I think it's perfect."

"It'll be too long."

"You and I can hem it up. Dorothy wouldn't mind, would she?"

"She doesn't want it back. She says you can keep it forever. Try it on."

Vicky did so, tearing off shirt and jeans and slipping the soft silk over her head. It slipped into place, and Mary did up the dozens of tiny buttons that ran down the back.

"They only had zips for suitcases in those days, not for wedding dresses."

Vicky moved to the long mirror. Aside from the fact that it was far too long, the dress might have been made for her. She touched her hair into place, turned to see her own back view, to admire the cunningly cut skirt, which fanned out into a fish-tail of silk to form a little train.

"It's beautiful," she breathed. "I'm going to wear it. I couldn't have found anything so beautiful if I'd looked for a hundred years. How kind of Dorothy. I can't think why she should be so kind . . ."

They undid all the buttons again and Vicky took the dress off. Then Mary put it on a padded hanger and hung it on the door of her wardrobe, where it looked impressively rich and significant.

"Goodness, Mummy, what a stroke of luck. It's like a miracle. I must go and ring Hector and tell him. No, I'm not going to. I'm going to surprise him. I'll ring Dorothy instead. Right away. How could I have been so horrible about asking her to the wedding? You didn't tell her I was horrible, did you?"

"No, of course I didn't."

Vicky hauled on her jeans. "You were right." She zipped them up. "We think we know so much about people and we don't know anything at all." She buttoned up her shirt and hugged her mother. "And as for you, you've been a veritable saint."

She took herself off. Moments later, she could be heard speaking to Dorothy, her voice loud with delight and gratitude. Mary shut the bedroom door and sat down once more at her dressing-table. She looked at the dress, and knew that, for once in her life, Vicky would allow herself to look truly beautiful. She thought about the wedding, in just a week's time, and for the first time found herself looking forward to it. She thought about dear Hector, who was going to become her son-in-law, and she thought about Dorothy, and it was like having just met and made a new friend. Soon, after the wedding, they would lunch together. There was much that they had to talk about.

She thought about Harry. Amongst the bottles and jars on her dressing-table stood a photograph of him, in a heavy silver frame. She smiled at it. *You don't have to worry about a thing, Harry.* She felt full of confidence. *"It's all going to be all right."*

She looked at her own reflection; powdered her face, and then, feeling light-hearted as the girl she had once been, reached for her lipstick.

Whistle for the Wind

*I*t was Saturday morning. Blinks of golden light lit the trees, and cloud shadows raced across the face of the hills, chasing each other out to the distant blue line of the sea.

Jenny Fairburn, heading home for lunch after a walk with the two family dogs, was pleasantly tired because she had been a long way—right around the loch and back by the rutted, winding farm road. Home lay ahead, an old Manse alongside a ruined church. It was sheltered from the north by a stand of pines, and the south-facing windows flashed in the sunlight as though sending out signals of welcome. Jenny thought about lunch, because she was hungry as well as tired. She knew that it was roast lamb, and her mouth watered, like a hungry child's.

She was, in fact, twenty, a tall, thin girl with the reddish blonde hair and pale skin that she had inherited from her father's mother, a true Highlander. Her eyes were dark, her nose narrow and tip-tilted, and her mouth wide and expressive. When she smiled, it lit up her face, but she knew that when she was feeling cross or depressed she could look sulky and plain.

In the back porch, she gave the panting dogs a drink and then toed off her muddy boots. From the kitchen she could hear her mother's voice, presumably chatting on the telephone, because Jenny's father had spent the morning on the golf-course and his car was still not back in the garage.

In stockinged feet, she let herself into the kitchen, and smelt the roasting lamb and the sharpness of mint sauce.

". . . how very kind of you," her mother was saying. She turned, saw Jenny and smiled in an abstracted sort of way. "Yes. Yes. About six-thirty? All of us. Well, we'll look forward to that. 'Bye." She put down the receiver and smiled at her daughter. "Did you have a nice walk?"

She sounded a little too bright. Jenny frowned. "Who was that on the telephone?"

Mrs. Fairburn was stooping to open the oven door and inspect the lamb. A fragrant gust of heat escaped into the kitchen.

"Just Daphne Fenton."

"What does she want?"

Mrs. Fairburn shut the oven door and straightened up. Her face was pink, but perhaps that was just the heat. "She's asked us all for a drink this evening."

"What's the celebration?"

"No celebration. Fergus is home for the weekend, and Daphne's asked a few people in for a drink. She particularly wants you to come."

Jenny said, "I don't want to come."

"Oh, darling, you must."

"You can say I'm doing something else."

Her mother came over to Jenny's side. "Look, I know you were hurt, and I know how much you loved Fergus, but it's over. He's marrying Rose next month. At some point you've got to let everybody see that you've accepted this."

"I think I will once they're married. But they're not yet, and I don't like Rose."

They gazed hopelessly at each other, then they heard Mr. Fairburn's car coming up the road, turning into the gate.

"There's your father. He'll be starving." Mrs. Fairburn gave Jenny's hand a loving pat. "I must make the gravy."

After lunch, with the dishes washed and the kitchen tidy, they dispersed on their various ploys. Mr. Fairburn changed into his gardening clothes (in which no self-respecting gardener would be seen dead) and went out to sweep leaves; Mrs. Fairburn disappeared to work on the new sitting-room curtains which she had been trying to finish for a month; Jenny decided to go fishing. She collected her rod and her fishing bag, pulled on her father's old shooting jacket and the rubber boots, and firmly told the dogs that this time they couldn't come.

"Is it all right if I borrow your car?" she asked her mother. "I'm going up to the loch to see if I can catch anything."

"Catch at least three trout. Then we can have them for supper."

As Jenny came to the loch, she saw the stillness of the brown water, scarcely touched now by the breeze. "Too still for fish," Fergus would have said. "We'll need to whistle for the wind."

About a mile down the loch, a grassy track led off the road and down towards the water. Jenny took this, letting the small, battered car bump and bounce its way over tussocks of turf and heather. She parked a few feet from the shore, collected her rod and the bag, and made her way down to where the little rowing boat was pulled up on a sickle of shingle.

But she didn't get into it at once. Instead, she sat on the bank, and listened to the silence, which was not a silence at all but a stirring and murmuring of tiny sounds. The buzz of a bee, the distant baa-ing of sheep, the sigh of a breeze, the whisper of water against pebbles.

"We'll need to whistle for the wind."

Fergus . . . What could you do about a man who had been part of your life since you were a little girl? A boy in patched jeans, collecting shells on the beach. A young man in a worn kilt, walking the hill. A grown man, immensely sophisticated and attractive, with a smooth dark head and eyes as blue as the loch on a summer day. What could you do about someone with whom you had quarrelled and laughed, who had always been your friend and your rival and finally turned out to be—she knew—the only man she could ever love?

He was six years older than Jenny, which made him now twenty-six, and the son of her parents' friends, the Fentons, who farmed Inverbruie, two miles down the road.

"He's like a brother," people used to say to Jenny who was an only child. But she knew that it had never been like that. For what brother would spend patient hours teaching a small girl how to fish? What brother would dance with a gangling teenager at parties, when the room was filled with older, more charming and prettier girls?

And when Jenny, sent to boarding-school in Kent, hated being away from Scotland so much that every letter home begged to be allowed to return, it was Fergus who eventually persuaded her parents that Jenny would do just as well, and be a thousand times happier, at the local Creagan High School.

"One day," she had promised herself, "I shall marry him. He will fall in love with me and I shall marry him, and I'll move down the road to Inverbruie and be the young farmer's wife."

But this happy prospect was slightly dimmed by Fergus deciding that he did not want to follow his father into farming, but would go to Edinburgh to learn how to be a chartered accountant.

So what. Jenny's private schemes for the two of them did a quick change of direction. "One day he will fall in love with me and I shall marry him, and go with him to live in Edinburgh and we'll have a little house in Ann Street and go to symphony concerts together."

The thought of living in Edinburgh was, truth be told, fairly daunting. Jenny hated towns but perhaps Edinburgh wouldn't be too bad. They could come home for weekends.

But Fergus did not stay in Edinburgh. After he qualified, he was offered a transfer to the main office of his firm, and moved to London. London? For the first time Jenny knew a nudge of doubt. London. Could she bear to go so far away from her beloved hills and loch?

"Why don't you go to London?" her mother asked when Jenny finally left school. "You could go to college there. Perhaps share a little flat!"

"I couldn't bear it. It would be worse than Kent."

"Edinburgh, then? You ought to get away from home for a bit."

So Jenny went to Edinburgh and learned shorthand and typing, studied French and went to art galleries, and when she became home-sick, climbed Arthur's Seat and pretended she was on the top of Ben Creagan. By Easter, she had finished the course and been duly presented with a Certificate, and it was time to go home. Fergus would probably be home for Easter as well and she wondered if he would notice a change in her.

He would probably look at her, like people did in books, as though seeing her for the first time, and perhaps then he would recognize what Jenny had known for years. That they were made for each other. And at last all those elusive day-dreams would come true. It would, of course, mean living in London, but by now Jenny knew that living anywhere without Fergus was no fun at all.

As her train drew into Creagan, she hung out of the window and saw her mother waiting for her, which was odd, because usually it was her father who met her.

"Darling!" They hugged and kissed, and there was the business of getting cases off the train and making their way out into the yard where the car waited. It was now nearly dark, street lights were on, and the air smelt of hills and peat.

They came through the little town and turned on to the side road which led to home. They passed Inverbruie.

"Is Fergus back?"

"Yes. He's home." Jenny hugged herself. "He's—he's brought a friend with him."

Jenny turned her head and looked at her mother's neat profile. "A friend?"

"Yes. A girl called Rose. You may have seen her on television. She's an actress." A friend. A girl. An actress? "He met her a couple of months ago."

"H—have you met her?"

"No, but we've all been invited to a party there tomorrow night."

"But—but—" There didn't seem to be any words for the shock and the desolation which she felt. Mrs. Fairburn stopped the car and turned to Jenny. "This is why I came to meet you at the station. I knew you'd be upset. I wanted to talk it over."

"I just—I just don't want him to bring anyone here to Creagan." Even to herself this sounded pathetically juvenile.

"Jenny, you don't own Fergus. He has a perfect right to make new friends. He's a grown man with his own life to live. Just as you have a life to make for yourself. You can't spend it looking over your shoulder and mourning for childhood fancies."

The worst bit was not that she actually said this, but that she had been so perceptive in the first place.

"I—I really do love him."

"I know. It's agony. First love is always agony. But you'll have to grit your teeth and see it through. And don't let anybody see how much you mind." They sat in silence for a bit. Then, "All right?" her mother asked, and Jenny nodded. Mrs. Fairburn started the car up again, and they moved on.

"Do you think he'll marry her?"

"I've no idea. But from what Daphne Fenton tells me, it sounds perfectly possible. She says he's bought himself a flat in Wandsworth and Rose is making his loose covers."

"Do you think that's a bad sign?"

"Not bad, exactly. But indicative."

Jenny fell silent. But as they turned into the gates of the Manse, she stirred herself. "Perhaps I shall like her."

"Yes," said Mrs. Fairburn. "Perhaps you will."

And she did try to like Rose. But it was difficult, because, without realizing it, she had seen Rose on television, in a hospital drama, where Rose had played a nurse. Even then Jenny had thought that she was a bore, with her heart-shaped face struggling with a variety of emotions, and unbearable distress being conveyed by a slight tremor in her well-bred voice.

In real life, Rose was pretty enough.

Her hair was silky black, loose and curly around her shoulders, and she wore a low-waisted dress with unexpected bits of beading and glitter stitched to its loose folds.

"Fergus has told me so much about you," she said to Jenny when they were introduced at Inverbruie. "He says you were practically brought up together. Is your father a farmer too?"

"No, he's the bank manager in Creagan."

"And you've always lived here?"

"Born and bred. I even went to school here. I was in Edinburgh for the winter, but it's heaven to be back."

"Don't you get—er—rather bored in such a desolate spot?"

"No."

"What are you going to do now?"

"I don't know."

"Come to London. Nowhere else on earth to live, I always say to Fergy. Come to London and we'll keep an eye on you—" She reached out and closed her fingers around Fergus' arm. Fergus was at that moment engaged, happily, in conversation with somebody else, but she drew him physically away from this person and back to herself. "Darling, I was just saying, Jenny must come to London."

Fergus and Jenny looked into each other's eyes: Jenny smiled and found to her surprise that it was remarkably easy.

Fergus said, "Jenny doesn't like city life."

Jenny shrugged. "It's a matter of taste."

"But you can't stay here always." Rose sounded incredulous.

"I will for the summer." She had not, in fact, thought about it, but now discovered, in an instant, that her decision was made. "I'll get a holiday job in Creagan, I expect." She decided to change the subject. "My mother was telling me about the flat in Wandsworth."

"Yes . . ." Fergus began, but that was as far as he got because Rose took over.

"It's heavenly. Not very big, but full of sunshine. Just a few little touches and it will be quite perfect."

"Has it got a garden?" Jenny asked.

"No. But there's a window-box or two. I thought we could plant geraniums. Real scarlet ones. Then we can pretend we're in Majorca or Greece. Can't we, darling?"

"Whatever you say," said Fergus.

Scarlet geraniums. Dear heaven, thought Jenny, he really is in love with her. And suddenly she couldn't bear to stand there any longer, watching them. She made her excuses and turned away. She did not speak to either Rose or Fergus for the rest of the evening.

But she could not escape Fergus, because he sought her out the very next day, spring-cleaning the summer-house.

"Jenny."

She was actually shaking dust out of a rush mat when he appeared, unexpectedly, around the side of the summer-house, and for an instant she was startled into immobility.

"What do you want?" she managed at last.

"I've come to see you."

"How nice. Where's Rose?"

"She's at home. She's washing her hair."

"It looked perfectly clean to me."

"Jenny, are you going to listen to me?"

She sighed noisily and looked resigned. "It depends on what you've got to say."

"I just want you to understand. To understand the way things are. I want you not to be angry. I want to feel that we can still at least talk to each other. And be friends."

"Well, we're talking, aren't we?"

"And friends?"

"Oh, friends. Always friends. Friends whatever we do to each other."

"And what have I done?"

She glared at him accusingly, and then threw down the rush mat.

"All right, so you don't like Rose. You might as well admit it," he said.

"I don't feel about Rose one way or the other. I don't know Rose."

"Then isn't it a little unfair—on both Rose and myself—to make a snap judgement?"

"I just don't feel I have anything in common with her."

"That's just because she told you that you ought to get away from Creagan."

"And what possible business is it of hers?"

Now his temper was rising to match her own. She saw his jaw muscles tighten, a familiar sign, and she was pleased because she had made him angry. It somehow eased the hurt inside her.

"Jenny, you stay here for the rest of your life, and you'll end up a country bumpkin in a seated tweed skirt with nothing to talk about except dogs and fishing."

She turned on him. "You know something? I'd rather be that than a third-rate actress with a mouth like a button."

He laughed, but he was laughing at Jenny and not with her. He said unforgivably, "I do believe you're jealous. You always could be quite impossible!"

"And you, perhaps, could always be a fool, but I never realized it until now."

Fergus turned on his heel and walked away, across the lawn. Jenny watched his progress, her temper dying as swiftly as it had blown up. Words spoken in heat and haste were all very well, but they could never be taken back. Nothing could ever be the same again.

Jenny found a job in Creagan, working in a shop which sold Shetland pullovers and pebble-jewellery to tourists. Around July, she was told by her mother that Fergus and Rose were engaged, and were to be married in September in London where Rose's parents lived. Just a quiet wedding, with a few of their close London friends. But meantime, they had returned to Inverbruie and there was to be another little party and Jenny could not find the courage to go. After they were married, she told herself again, it would be different. She would become dynamic; go abroad perhaps; get a job in the French Alps as a chalet girl, or be a cook on a yacht. However, she was growing cold and there were trout to be caught for supper. She stood up, clam-

bered down the heathery bank, untied the painter, pushed the boat
out into the water and began to row.

Fishing was special, because when you fished you thought about
nothing else. She took the boat a long way up the loch and then
shipped the oars and let the wind drift her back towards the shore.
Now, there was enough breeze to stir the surface of the water, and
she began casting.

She heard the car coming up the road, but was too engrossed to
pay attention to it. There was another bite or two, and then at last she
hooked a fish, and concentrating on nothing else, began gently to
reel it in. She netted it out of the water, and dropped it in the bottom
of the boat.

As if on cue, she heard a voice say, "Well done."

Startled by this interruption from the business in hand, she looked
up and saw, all at once, a number of surprising things. She had,
without realizing it, drifted to within yards of the shore; the car she
had heard on the road had stopped and was now parked a little way
off; and Fergus, a solitary figure, stood on the bank and watched her.

He was bare-headed, the wind ruffling his dark hair. He wore a
tweed jacket and a pair of corduroys, tucked into green rubber boots.
Not dressed for fishing. Jenny sat in the rocking boat and looked at
him, and wondered if he had come upon her by chance, or if, in fact,
he had come looking, to ask why she had refused to come to the
party, to try to persuade her to change her mind. If he did this, then
they would have another argument, another row, and she knew that
rather than repeat their last painful set-to, she would prefer never to
have to speak to him again.

He grinned. He said again, "Well done. You handled that very
neatly. I couldn't have done better myself."

Jenny did not reply. Instead, she busied herself in reeling in the
loose line, securing the barbed fly. With care, she laid down the rod,
and then looked up again at Fergus.

She said, "How long have you been there?"

"Ten minutes or more." He put his hands in his jacket pockets. "I
came to find you. Your mother told me you'd come up here. I want
to talk to you."

"What about?"

"Jenny, don't get your hackles up. Let's call it pax."

It seemed only fair. "All right."

"Come and get me then."

Jenny made no move to do this, but even as they spoke she was being blown inshore, and as she hesitated, she felt the first bump as the keel touched stone. Before she realized what was happening, Fergus had waded out and grabbed the bow, thrown one long leg over the gunwale and was aboard.

"Now," he said, "give me the oars."

There didn't seem to be very much alternative. With a couple of clean strokes, he had turned the light craft, and then they were headed back out into the middle of the loch. It was ten minutes or so before he looked about him, decided they had come far enough, shipped the oars, and turned up the collar of his jacket against the cold edge of the wind.

"Now," he said, "we're going to talk."

It seemed sensible to take the initiative. "I suppose my mother told you that I didn't want to come tonight. I suppose that's what it's all about."

"Yes, it's about that. And other things, too."

She waited for him to enlarge on this, but he did not continue. Across the thwarts, they looked at each other, and then suddenly smiled. And all at once Jenny was filled with a curious contentment and peace. It was a long time since she'd sat in a boat with Fergus, in the middle of the loch, with the familiar hills folding away on all sides and the sky arched above them, and have him smile at her like that. It made it easier to be honest, not only with him, but with herself.

"It's just that I don't want to come. I don't want to see Rose again. It'll be different when you're married to her. But now . . ." She shrugged. "It's cowardice, I suppose," she finally admitted.

"That doesn't sound like you."

"Perhaps it isn't me. Perhaps I'm all twisted and back to front. You said that day by the summer-house that I was jealous, and, of course, you were quite right. I suppose I always thought of you as my property, but that's wrong, isn't it? No person can ever belong to another person, even after they're married."

"No man is an island."

"I always thought that bits of a man had to be an island. You can't creep inside somebody else's head."

"No. You can't do that."

"Just like you can't go on being a child. You have to grow up whether you want to or not."

He said. "Did you get that job in Creagan?"

"Yes, but it folds up in October when the shop closes down for the winter. I've decided that then I shall be enormously enterprising and find myself an occupation that's very well paid and miles away. Like America or Switzerland." She smiled, wryly. "Rose would approve of that."

Fergus stayed silent. His eyes, watching her, were unblinking, intensely blue.

"And how," she asked politely, "is Rose?"

"I don't know."

Jenny frowned. "But you have to know. She's at Inverbruie."

"She's not at Inverbruie."

"She's not . . . ?" A curlew flew overhead, its cry mournful, and the water slapped and whispered against the planking of the boat. "But Mother said . . ."

"She got it wrong. My mother didn't say anything about Rose being here; your mother just took it for granted that Rose was with me. We're not going to get married. The engagement's off."

"Off? You mean—? But why didn't Mother tell me?"

"She didn't know. I haven't got around to telling my own parents yet. I wanted to tell you before I told anyone else."

For some reason, this was so touching that Jenny wondered if she were about to burst into tears. "But, why? Why, Fergus?"

"You just said it. No person can belong to another person."

"Didn't—didn't you love her?"

"Yes, I did. I loved her very much." He could say that, and she didn't feel jealous in the least, just sad for him because it hadn't worked out. "But you marry a life as well as a person, and Rose's life and mine seemed to run along parallel lines, like railway tracks, without ever actually touching."

"When did all this happen?"

"A couple of weeks ago. That's why I came north for the weekend; I wanted to explain it to my parents, and let my mother see I wasn't dying of a broken heart."

"And aren't you?"

"Perhaps a little bit, but not enough to show."

"Rose loved you."

"For a bit she did, yes."

Jenny hesitated, and then said it, *"I love you."*

* * *

It was Fergus's turn to look as though he were about to burst into tears. "Oh, Jenny."

"You might as well know. You've probably always known. I never thought I could say that to anybody, least of all to you, but for some reason it seems to be quite easy. I mean, you don't have to do anything about it, but you might as well know. It doesn't change anything. I shall still find that marvellous job and winkle myself away from Creagan into the wide, wide world."

She smiled, expecting him to smile back at her, approving of this sensible, mature scheme. But he did not smile. For a long moment he simply looked at her, and she felt her own smile die beneath the sadness in his face. Then he said, "Don't."

Jenny frowned. "But, Fergus, I thought that was what you wanted. For me to get away from Creagan, and stand on my own feet."

"I couldn't bear you to go away and stand on your own feet," he told her bluntly.

"Well, whose feet am I going to stand on?"

The absurdity of her question somehow made everything all right again. He was caught unawares by this absurdity, and despite himself, began to laugh, wryly, as much at himself as at her. "I don't know. I suppose mine. The truth is, that you've been part of my life for so long that I don't think I can bear the thought of your going away and leaving us all. Leaving me. Life would be so dreadfully dull. There'd be nobody to argue with. Nobody to yell at. Nobody to make me laugh."

Jenny thought about this. She said, "You know, if I had an ounce of pride, I would go away. I'd be the sort of girl who didn't want to be loved on the rebound from some other person."

"If you had an ounce of pride, you wouldn't have told me that you loved me."

"You must have known."

"I only know that you were there long before Rose."

"So what was Rose?"

Fergus fell silent. Then he said tentatively, "A pause in the conversation?"

"Oh, Fergus."

"I—I think I'm asking you to marry me. We've wasted enough time as it is. Perhaps I should have had the sense to do it a long time ago."

"No." She was suddenly very wise. "A long time ago would have been too soon. I thought you belonged to me then. But now, like I said, I know that nobody can ever belong to anybody else. Not totally. And yet, it's only when you think that you're going to lose something that you realize how precious it is."

"I found that out too," said Fergus. "What a very good thing that we both found it out at the same time."

Out in the middle of the water, it was becoming chilly. Jenny, despite herself, shivered.

"You're cold," said Fergus. "I'll take you back." He reached for the oars, took his bearings with a glance over his shoulder and turned the little boat.

Jenny suddenly remembered. "But I can't go back yet, Fergus. I've only caught one trout and we'll need three for supper."

"To hell with supper. We'll go out. We'll take all the parents and I'll stand the lot of you dinner at the Creagan Arms. We might even rustle up some champagne and it can be an engagement party—if you like!"

Now they were heading home, back towards the mooring, the little craft skimming across the choppy waters of the loch. The wind blew from behind her. She turned up the collar of her jacket and dug her hands deep into its capacious pockets. She smiled at her love. She said, "I like."

Last Morning

Laura Prentiss woke to the unfamiliar hotel bedroom and the sounds of her husband making shaving noises from beyond the open bathroom door. Perhaps out of deference to his sleeping wife, Roger had left the bedroom curtains closed, and when Laura groped first for her spectacles and then for her watch, she saw, with some surprise, that it was already half past eight.

"Roger."

He appeared, in his pyjama trousers and a face half-covered in lather.

"Good morning."

"I'm afraid to look. What sort of a day is it?"

"Fine."

"Thank heavens for that."

"Cold, with a bit of wind. But fine."

"Draw the curtains and let me look at it."

He did this with difficulty, first trying to pull the curtains manually, as he did at home, and then realizing there was a gadget involved, a string with a handle that was meant to be employed. Roger was not good with gadgets. He tugged at it and was finally successful.

The sky beyond the glass was a pale, clear blue, swept with long, thin fine-weather clouds, and when Laura sat up she could see the sea; dark blue and flecked with white horses.

She said, "I hope Virginia's veil doesn't blow off."

"Even if it does, she's not your daughter, so you don't need to feel any responsibility."

Laura leaned back on her pillow, took off her spectacles and smiled at him gratefully. He had always been a comfortably practical man, and this morning was obviously treating the day as though it were a perfectly ordinary one, getting up, shaving, going down to eat his breakfast.

He disappeared back into the bathroom and, through the open door, they continued their conversation.

"What are you going to do this morning?" she asked.

"Play golf," said Roger.

She should have known. The hotel had a fine links on its doorstep.

"You won't be late?"

"Am I likely to be?"

"And leave plenty of time to change. It will take such ages to get you into your morning suit." She might have added. "Specially since you've put on weight," but she didn't, because Roger was sensitive about his mildly expanding waistline, and had decided to ignore the small insert which the tailor had been forced to let into the back of his trousers.

"Stop worrying about details," said Roger. He appeared once more in the doorway, smelling of after-shave. "Stop worrying about anything. You're a guest at this wedding. You've got nothing to plan, nothing to agonize over, nothing to do. Enjoy it."

"Yes. You're quite right. I will."

She got up, pulled on her dressing-gown and went to the window. She opened it and leaned out. The air was icy and smelt of salt and seaweed. Already there was a single golfer, in a red sweater, out on the fairway. Below her, in the hotel grounds, lay the little pitch-and-putt course, and she remembered, long ago, bringing the children to this very hotel for a summer holiday. Tom had been six, Rose three, and Becky a fat baby in a pram, and the weather had been terrible, nothing but rain and wind. They had passed the time playing card games in the leaden sun porch, and every time the rain stopped had dashed across the links to the beach, where the children had crouched, sweatered and chapped of cheek, and built sand castles of dark, sodden sand.

But some time during that holiday Tom had been introduced to the pitch-and-putt course and the fascinating frustrations of golf, and after that he was out by himself in all weathers, his small form bent against the wind, and golf-balls and divots of turf flying in all directions.

Remembering the small boy he had been, she felt sad, thinking, Where have all the years gone? and immediately was annoyed with herself for being a typical, doting, cliché-ridden mother.

She shut the window when Roger came back into the room. She said, "I thought Tom would have liked a game this morning. Keep his mind off this afternoon."

"I thought of that, too, and I asked him, but he said he had other things to do."

"You mean like recovering from last night's party?"

Roger grinned. "Maybe."

Tom had gone out on a traditional bachelor's spree with one or two of his friends who'd come up for the wedding. Laura hoped, for Virginia's sake, that the party had not been too rowdy. Nothing in this world could be more unattractive than a sheepish and hung-over bridegroom.

"I wonder what he's planning to do."

"No idea," said Roger. He came over to kiss her. "What about breakfast?" he asked.

"What about it?"

"Do you want it up here? You only have to call Room Service."

She must have looked agonized, because he grinned, recognizing her horror of asking anybody to do anything for her, and went over to the telephone and ordered her breakfast for her, without asking her what she wanted because, after twenty-seven years of married life, he knew. Orange juice, a boiled egg, coffee. When he put the receiver down, she smiled at him gratefully across the room, and he sat on the edge of the bed and smiled back at her, and she had the good feeling that the momentous day had started well.

While she was eating breakfast, propped up with Roger's pillows as well as her own, her two daughters burst in upon her, talking nineteen to the dozen as usual, and come to find out how she was going to spend the morning.

They both had long mouse-coloured hair and clean shining faces naked of make-up except sooty smudges of eye-shadow and mascara. They wore their usual bizarre uniform of jeans and sneakers, long-sleeved blouses and short-sleeved sweaters, and carried sacklike hand-bags with dangling fringes. Laura thought they were both beautiful.

They sat on the foot of her bed and ate the bits of toast that had been sent up on the breakfast tray, loading them with butter and mar-malade and munching as though they had not seen food for a week.

"It was a super party last night . . ."

"I thought it was meant to be a bachelor party?"

". . . well, of course it started out as one, but this is such a tiny place that in the end we all met up and joined forces. He's terrific, that friend of Tom's . . . what's his name? Mike, or something . . ."

"Yes, he plays the guitar like a dream. Super songs, the kind we all know. Everybody joined in, even quite prim-looking people."

"Did Tom come home with you?"

"No, but he wasn't far behind. We heard him come in. Have no fears, Ma. Did you think he was going to die of drink in some Scot-tish ditch? I say, is there any coffee left in that pot?"

Laura pushed the tray towards them, leaning back, watching them chattering. Why did they have to grow up and get jobs in London and leave home forever?

In the middle of a sentence Rose suddenly caught sight of her watch. "Gosh, look at the time! We must go."

"Where are you going?"

"There's a beauty salon in the village, believe it or not. We found out last night. We're going to go so that we'll stun all Virginia's smart friends this afternoon, and not be a cause of shame to our brother. Why don't you come too? We can ring up and fix a time for you."

Laura's hair was short and inclined to curl. She had it cut once a month, then dealt with it herself. The thought of spending a morning being rolled and bouffed and sprayed with lacquer, today of all days, was almost more than she could bear. She said, "I don't think I will."

"Your hair looks super anyway. I'm glad we haven't got curly hair, but I must say when one gets a bit long in the tooth, there's nothing more charming."

Laura laughed. "Thank you *very* much."

"That was meant as a terrific compliment. Come on, we must go."

They collected their handbags and climbed off the bed, slim and long-legged and graceful. As they made for the door, their mother said, "You'll get back in plenty of time to get changed, won't you? We really mustn't be late today."

They smiled. "We will," they promised. Rose was going to wear trousers, and Becky a long granny-type dress in prune-coloured cotton, with hand-crocheted lace at wrist and throat. To complement this outfit she had chosen an enormous natural-straw hat, which looked to Laura as though the brim had started to unravel. But on making a few tactful inquiries, she had been assured that this was half its charm.

When the girls had gone, Laura stayed where she was for a little, trying to decide what to do next. She thought of Virginia, waking up in her parents' house only two miles away. She wondered if Virginia had had breakfast in bed too; whether she was feeling nervous. But no, one could not imagine Virginia nervous about anything. She was probably calming down the rest of her family, coping serenely with all the last-minute details.

And Laura tried to conjure up her own wedding morning, but it was too long ago and she discovered that she could remember very little about it, except that the wedding dress had been very slightly too large, and Laura's Aunt Mary, ever-present in times of crisis, had got on her knees with needle and thread, making the waistline fit.

Getting up and bathed and dressed took, for some reason, much longer than it did at home. Analysing this, Laura discovered that she was putting off time. Was, in fact, fearful of going downstairs and getting involved with Aunt Lucy and Uncle George, and Tom's godmother and her husband, and the Richard cousins who had come, unexpectedly, all the way north from darkest Somerset to be present at Tom's wedding. It was not that she did not dearly love all these people, but this morning she wanted to be alone. She wanted to go out into that miraculous fresh morning and walk, and sort herself out and not talk to anybody.

She put on a tweed coat, tied a scarf over her head, cautiously let herself out of her room, and went down the wide staircase to the lobby. Thankfully, she realized there did not seem to be anybody about, and she made for the main door, but as she passed the glass doors of the dining-room she stopped, for there, in solitary state, sat her son, eating a large, late breakfast, and reading the newspaper.

And at once, as though feeling her eyes upon him, he looked up, saw her and smiled. She went through the doors and across the room to join him, regarding him anxiously, searching for bloodshot eyes, bad colour; but her eldest child, much to her relief, seemed to be in the best of health.

He pulled out a chair for her and she sat down.

"How was the party?"

"Great."

"The girls told me you'd all met up . . ."

"Yes, by the end it was a free-for-all; half the local inhabitants joined in as far as I could see." He folded the newspaper. "You look as though you're planning a little outdoor exercise."

"Yes, I thought I'd go out for a walk."

"I'll come with you," said Tom.

"But . . ."

"But what? Don't you want me?"

"Yes, of course. It's just that I thought you'd have a million other things to do."

"Such as?"

"I can't think of one, but I'm sure there must be something."

"Neither can I." He got up. "Come on, let's go."

He wore a thick cardigan and did not seem to feel the need for a jacket. With no more ado, they went together out of the dining-room, and out through the door. The wind had an edge to it like a knife, but the turf of the little pitch-and-putt course was green as velvet from the shower of rain that had fallen during the night, and all the flags on the greens blew straight and perky.

"Isn't it strange," said Tom as they set off at a spanking pace, heading for the right-of-way that led across the golf-links to the beach, "that the girl I should marry should come from this part of the world, and we should all come back to stay in this hotel? Do you remember that holiday?"

"I'll never forget it. I shall always remember the rain."

"I don't remember the rain. I only remember trying to teach myself how to play golf." He stopped and took a stance and swung an imaginary club. "That was a good shot. A hole in one."

"I should have thought you'd have wanted to play with your father this morning."

"He asked me, but somehow it didn't seem quite the right thing to do on one's wedding morning. Anyway, if I had I should have missed out on this nice little walk with you."

He grinned down at her. He was fair like his mother, with the slightly curly hair that he had inherited from her. The shining commas of hair lay thick and close to his skull. Otherwise he resembled his father, except, in the disconcerting fashion of modern children, he had grown to be four inches taller than Roger, and was brawny to match.

She remembered the tough, peppery little boy, pitting himself against the complexities of golf, just as he had always flung himself head first at any problem, not always with felicitous results. But he had never been discouraged, and had finally got his quick temper under control; and somehow that little boy had turned into this shrewd, amiable young man who had finally got himself engaged, and today would be married, to Virginia.

Virginia was, Laura often thought, a match for Tom: intelligent, capable, amusing, and pretty to boot. If they had been less in love, she might have had reservations about two such positive people deciding to spend their lives together. "There is not room," Laura's wise old grandmother had once said, "for more than one born leader in a family." But perhaps if the two born leaders loved each other sufficiently to take turns standing aside, then it would be all right. She stole a glance at Tom, striding out beside her, and he caught this anxious glance and grinned reassuringly, and she thought, Yes, it will be all right.

The path led over the dunes and down to the sand which was at first soft and dry, and then firm where the high tides had washed it flat. There was a line of seaweed and flotsam from passing ships. An old boot, a blue detergent bottle, a wrecked crate.

"Do you remember," said Tom, "reading *Ring of Bright Water* to me when I had that knee operation, and how we liked the idea of Gavin Maxwell making all his furniture out of old herring-boxes that had been washed up on the beach?" He stooped and picked up a ragged slat with a nail protruding from it. "Perhaps I should emulate him. Think of the money I'd save on three-piece suits. What could I turn this into?"

Laura considered it. "The leg of an elegant coffee-table, perhaps?" she suggested.

"Good idea." He leaned back, then flung the piece of wood far out to sea. They walked on.

*   *   *

Ring of Bright Water had been only one of many books that she had read aloud to Tom during the tedious weeks after the operation. His knee had been injured playing football; he had torn a ligament and a blood clot had formed, but the operation to clear this had been as delicate as a cartilage removal, and he had lain on his back for six weeks while his mother played games with him, read to him, watched television or solved crosswords with him, anything to stop his getting bored. Both of them were devilled by the unspoken fear that Tom would never be able to play football again, and for Laura it had been a particularly anxious time, and yet, looking back, she remembered it only with pleasure and gratitude. Pleasure at having him to herself, rediscovering with him all the books that she had loved at his age, and gratitude at being given time, like an unexpected present, really to get to know her son, to discover him as a person.

Tom, too, had been thinking about that time, for he suddenly said, "You read aloud so well. Some people are awful at it. You used to do different voices for different people. It made it all come real."

"Oh, Tom, it was about the only thing I could do."

"What do you mean?"

"Well, I was always so useless at anything physical, where you were meant to hit a ball. I could never play tennis and I was hopeless at skiing . . . And when I came to watch school rugger matches, everything always had to be explained to me, and I could never get the hang of the game."

"The great thing was you used to come and watch."

"Yes, but I always felt so inadequate. And whenever I tried to plan something really exciting, it always went wrong. I mean, that holiday we had here, it was meant to be all bathing and picnics and sand-castles, and all we did was play Racing Demon in the sun lounge and wait for the rain to stop."

"I liked that holiday."

"And that terrible time I took you three with the Richard family to Norway to ski. We got caught in a blizzard before we'd even got to the airport, and we missed the plane, and your father had to telegraph us enough money to spend the night in a hotel and wait for a flight the next day."

"That was an adventure. And it wasn't your fault."

"And the time I took you all to the Hebrides, and it was April and the boat hit the worst storm of the winter, and we got marooned on Tiree with a lot of hungry cattle. The awful things always happened when your father wasn't there. When he was with us, everything went on oiled wheels. No snowstorms, no shipwrecks, and the sun always shone."

"I think you're underestimating yourself," said Tom.

They were alone on the beach now, away from everybody, out in a world of rushing air and flattened grass and blown sand. They came to a breakwater and Tom said, "Let's sit down for a bit," so they did, sheltered from the wind, and in the full beneficence of the sun. Suddenly it felt quite warm. The sun burnt comfortingly through Laura's coat and warmed her knees. It was companionable, just the two of them tucked into the shelter of the breakwater, with only the wind and the gulls for company.

After a little, Tom said, "You didn't really think I wanted a hockey-playing mother, did you?"

Laura's thoughts had already strayed from this line of conversation, and she was surprised to find that Tom still wanted to continue it.

"Not hockey . . . but something, perhaps. Think what fun you're going to have with Virginia. You can do so much together. You both swim and play tennis, you'll probably find her beating you at golf one day. It makes life so much more . . . I don't know . . . complete, I suppose. It makes for friendship. And in a marriage that's almost as important as love."

"You never did anything sporty with Dad, and you don't seem to have managed too badly."

"No. But we raised a family together; perhaps that was enough."

"Only if you're pleased with the results."

"You wouldn't, by any chance, be fishing for a compliment?"

"No, I'm just trying to pay you one."

"I don't understand."

"Just that the results may not be all that outstanding, but the job you did certainly was."

"I still don't understand."

"You always treated us like people. I never appreciated this till I went to school and realized that not everybody was as lucky as me. And you never laughed at us."

"Was that so important?"

"More important than anything. We were allowed to preserve our dignity."

Laura frowned, determined to keep sentimentality at bay. "It's funny, growing older. You try to do all the right things, and you think it's going to last forever, and suddenly it's all over. You are twenty-five and getting married today, and the girls are living in London and I scarcely see them . . ."

"But they come home. And when they do, the three of you start gossiping and giggling just the way you've always done."

"Perhaps I should try to be more detached."

"Don't try to be anything. Just go on being nice you, and you'll end up the bonniest granny a baby ever had."

She began to laugh at the thought, then pulled back the cuff of her coat to look at her watch. "You know, we shouldn't dawdle. Time's getting on."

They got to their feet and climbed back over the breakwater and headed back for the distant hotel. Tom found for her a pair of tiny yellow shells, still joined so that they looked like a butterfly, and Laura put them in her glove for safety, and thought that when she got home she would put them with her other small mementoes.

With the wind against them there was no breath to spare for conversation, so they trudged in silence, each busy with his own thoughts. As they crossed the links, they saw Roger coming down the fairway towards them. And all at once Laura was caught up in a gust of real excitement, the first she had felt all day. They were all converging, heading for the hotel, to change into their finery, and to drive to the little church where Tom and Virginia were going to be married. The day that they had all looked forward to for so long was finally here, and although she loved her son and knew that she was losing him, she could not feel any regret. He was simply stepping on and out, as they had always encouraged him to do, and she was filled with the deepest thankfulness at the way everything had turned out.

They reached the hotel porch at last, glad to be out of the buffeting wind. They faced each other surrounded by folded sun umbrellas and deck-chairs. Laura said, "That was a lovely walk. The best. Thank you for coming."

"Thank you."

"I . . . I'll say goodbye now, Tom. I hate saying it in front of people. And, darling"—she took his hand—"you've been so clever to find Virginia. She's exactly right for you, and you're going to have a great time together."

He said, "Yes, I know. And I know why. It's because, basically, she's like you."

"Me?" The very idea was ridiculous. No two women had ever been more different. "Virginia like me?"

"Yes, you. You see, beneath the capability and the brightness, and the very pretty face, she's gentle and she's wise."

To hear her down-to-earth Tom come out with this brought a sudden lump to Laura's throat. Surely she was not going to cry? For a terrible second her eyes pricked and she could feel the tears rising, but she fought them back, and the little crisis was over. She was able to smile and reach up to kiss him. "That was a nice thing to tell me, Tom. Goodbye."

"Goodbye, Mummy."

The baby name for her came naturally, although he had not used it for years. She let go of his hand and went ahead of him through the door, and into the carpeted interior of the hotel.

Gentle and wise. The old-fashioned words filled her with warmth. Gentle and wise. Perhaps she hadn't done so badly after all.

She headed for the staircase and went up, two steps at a time, to get changed for Tom's wedding.

Skates

~~~~~~

Jenny Peters, ten years old, opened the door of Mr. Sims's ironmongery store and went inside. It was four o'clock in the afternoon, already dark, and bitterly cold, but Mr. Sims's shop was cosy with the smell of his paraffin heater, and all was adorned for Christmas. He had put a notice on his counter, USEFUL AND ACCEPTABLE GIFTS FOR THE FESTIVE SEASON, and to prove his point, tied a red tinsel bow around the handle of a formidable claw hammer.

"Hello there, Jenny."

"Hello, Mr. Sims."

"What can I do for you?"

She told him what she needed, not certain whether he would be able to help her. ". . . they have to be little lights, like the ones inside the fridge. And then clips. Like bulldog clips. To fasten them onto the edge of a box . . ."

Mr. Sims considered the problem, gazing at Jenny over the top of his spectacles. "Do you want batteries?" he asked.

"No. I've got a long lead that plugs into the wall socket."

"Sounds like you're going to be electrocuting yourself."

"I won't do that."

"Well. Wait a moment . . ."

He disappeared. She took her purse out of her coat pocket and counted out the last few notes and coins of her Christmas spending money. She hoped that there would be enough. If not, Mr. Sims would probably let her have credit until next week's pocket money came in.

After a bit, he came back with the makings of exactly what she needed. He opened the boxes, and put all the bits together. There was a little adaptor plug and a couple of yards of flex. The clips were meant for bigger lights, but that didn't matter.

"That's perfect, Mr. Sims. Thank you. How much is it going to cost?"

He smiled, reaching for a stout paper bag into which he put her purchases. "Cash down, you get ten per cent discount. That's, let's see . . ." He did a sum with a stubby pencil on the corner of the bag. "One pound eighty-five pence."

Relief. She had enough. She handed over two pound notes and was solemnly given change. But Mr. Sims could not contain his curiosity. "What's all this for, then?"

"It's Natasha's Christmas present. It's a secret."

"Say no more. Spending Christmas at home?"

"Yes. Granny's staying. Dad fetched her from the station last night."

"That's nice." He handed over the bag. "Too busy to go skating, are you?"

Jenny said, "Yes." And then, in truth, added, "I can't skate."

"Bet you never even tried."

"Yes, I did. I borrowed an old pair of Natasha's boots. But they were too big and I kept falling over."

"Just a knack," said Mr. Sims. "Like riding a bicycle."

"Yes," said Jenny. "I suppose so." She took the bulky bag. "Thank you, Mr. Sims, and have a lovely Christmas."

Outside, the cold hit her like a solid thing. A bit like walking into a deep-freeze. But it was not dark, because the street lights were on, and the floodlights which Tommy Bright, who ran the Bramley Arms, had set up in the forecourt of his pub, poured out, like spotlights in a theatre, over the flooded frozen skating rink which the village green had become. For this gratuitous service he was rewarded by a packed bar every evening, and the constant ringing of his till.

The village lay in a bowl of countryside with a line of hills to the south. Houses, church, shops, and pub were grouped around the green, and a small river, hardly more than a stream, flowed through the middle of it. It was this river which had burst its banks. For most of November, it had rained, and the beginning of December had brought the first snows. Old people said that they had never known such weather. The river had steadily risen and finally, unable to contain itself, overflowed and flooded the green. Then the temperature dropped abruptly, the night frosts were cruel, and all was frozen hard as iron.

A skating rink. The ice had held for a week, and now it was Christmas Eve, and if the forecasts were to be believed, looked as though it was going to go on holding.

Standing outside Mr. Sims's shop, Jenny paused to watch the carnival scene. The skaters, the sledges, the clumsy games of hockey. There were shrieks and shouts of revelry, and whole families had turned out to enjoy the fun, pulling bundled babies on toboggans or skating hand in hand.

She looked for her sister Natasha and saw her almost at once, for she stood out in her bright pink track suit. Natasha skated the way she did everything, with consummate expertise and grace. She was tall and slender, with blonde hair and endless legs, and took any sort of physical activity in her easy stride. Captain of the junior tennis at school and in the gymnastic team as well, but her great passion in life was dancing. She had been attending classes since she was five and had already won a number of medals and prizes. Her single-minded ambition was to be a ballerina.

Jenny, smaller, younger, and a great deal more dumpy, trailed in this brilliant sister's wake. She went to dancing class as well, but never progressed further than "The Sailors Hornpipe," or some middle-European polkas. The trouble was, she had difficulty remembering which was her left foot and which her right. Games were little better, and when it came to leaping over the horse at gym, she nearly always ended up the same side that she had started off.

She did not like going to dancing class, but complied with the arrangement, because it was about the only thing that the two sisters did together. Sometimes she dreamed about devoting her energies to something entirely different. Like learning the piano. There was a piano in the dining-room at home, and the frustration of knowing that it stood there, filled with music which she was unable to release, was a constant reminder of her own inadequacies. But piano lessons were expensive. Much more costly than the communal dancing class, and she was too diffident to suggest them to her parents. Perhaps, for her birthday, she could ask for piano lessons. But her birthday wasn't until next summer. It was all very difficult.

"Jenny!" It was Natasha, sailing by, hand-in-hand with another girl. "Come on. Have another try."

Jenny waved, but they had already gone, floating away to the far side of the ice. It looked so easy, but she had discovered that it was the most impossible thing in the world. Wearing Natasha's old boots, she *had* tried. But every step was agony, and her feet and legs had shot in all directions, and finally, she had fallen and hurt herself quite badly. But being hurt was not as painful as the knowledge that, yet again, she had made a fool of herself.

She sighed, turned, and set off for home. It was nice walking, with the Christmasy feeling all about her, and people's windows bright with the lights of their trees, shining out into frozen gardens. Her own house had a Christmas tree too, in the dining-room window, but the curtains of the sitting-room were drawn. Indoors, she opened the sitting-room door and put her head around the edge of it. Mum and Dad and Granny were having tea by the fire, and Granny was knitting. They all looked up, and smiled.

"Do you want a cup of tea, darling? Or shall I make you some hot chocolate?"

"No, thank you. I'm just going upstairs to my room."

Upstairs, she turned on her light, and drew the curtains. It wasn't a very large room, but all her own. A good deal of it was taken up with her work-table, which is where she did her homework, and her drawing, and set up her little sewing machine when she felt in the mood for making things. Now, however, it was littered with all the bits and pieces needed to make Natasha's present. Pots of paint, and tubes of glue and bits of cotton wool, and pipe cleaners and scraps of ribbon. The present stood, shrouded under a dust sheet. It had stayed hidden all the time Jenny was working on it, and she had enough respect for her mother to know that under no circumstances would she ever take so much as a single peep.

Now, she lifted off the dust sheet, and stood, staring at it, trying to see it with Natasha's critical eyes.

It was a miniature stage-set of a ballet. An empty wooden wine crate had given her the idea, and her father had helped her adapt it, so that she was left with a floor and three sides. Two of these sides she had painted green, but the backdrop was a reproduction of an old painting which she had found in a junk shop, and which, with a bit of trimming, fitted exactly. A pastoral scene, wintry and bright, with farm animals about the place and a man in a red cloak pulling a sledge laden with logs.

The floor she had painted with glue and sprinkled with sawdust, and in the middle had fixed a round mirror, from an old handbag, to make a frozen lake.

There were trees as well, twigs of evergreen fixed into old cotton reels, and they sparkled frostily because she had sprinkled them with Christmas glitter. For the dancers she had made tiny people out of pipe cleaners and cotton wool, and dressed them in bright snippets of ribbon, and scraps of white net. Making the dancers had taken ages, because they were fiddley, with their tiny painted features and embroidered hair.

But it was done. Finished. Only the lights to fix. She opened the bag, and carefully assembled all the bits and pieces that Mr. Sims had so kindly found for her. This took some time, and necessitated a journey downstairs to look for a screwdriver. When all was finally accomplished, she fastened the lights with their clips on either side of the little theatre, and then plugged the long flex into the socket of her bedside lamp. She pressed the switch, and the little lights came on. But they scarcely showed, so she turned off the main light, and in the darkness turned to see the full effect.

Better than she had ever expected. Perfect. So real, you could imagine the tiny floodlit figures were about to spring into dance, twirling fouettés across the sawdust floor.

Surely, Natasha would love it.

After a bit, she put everything away, covered the theatre with the dust sheet, adjusted the expression on her face, and went downstairs.

"All right, darling?" said her mother.

"Yes. All right," Jenny replied, at her most unconcerned, and went to cut herself a slice of cake.

The best of Christmas was that it was always the same. Carols after supper on Christmas Eve, with Granny playing the piano for all of them, and then bed, and hanging up stockings, and thinking that you would never go to sleep. And then, when you stopped trying, finding yourself awake again, and the clock pointing to half past seven, and the stocking bulging at the end of the bed.

Christmas was the smell of newly peeled tangerines, and bacon and eggs for breakfast. It was walking to church in the bitter, frosty air, and singing "Hark the Herald Angels Sing," which was Jenny's favourite. And talking to people outside the church, after the service, and rushing home to see to the turkey and light all the fires.

And then, when everything was ready, Dad said, "Ready, steady, go," and that was when they were allowed to fall on the presents piled beneath the tree.

Natasha's present had posed something of a problem—how to wrap up a theatre. In the end, Jenny had made a sort of tea-cosy of holly paper, put this over the theatre and carried it carefully downstairs, then placed it on the sideboard where nobody would walk on it.

But, for the moment, she forgot about the theatre in the excitement of her own presents. A new lamp for her bicycle, a Shetland sweater in pinks and blues, and a pair of black patent shoes that she had been yearning for for weeks. From Natasha, a book. From her god-mother a china mug with her name in gold. And from Granny . . . a large square parcel, wrapped in red-and-white-striped paper. Sitting on the floor, surrounded by the detritus of ribbons and packages and cards, Jenny undid it. The paper fell away, disclosing a large white box. More tissue paper. Skating boots.

Beautiful, new, white skating boots, the blades shining steel, and exactly the right size. Jenny gazed at them with a mixture of delight, because they were so fantastic, and apprehension at the thought of what she was expected to do with them.

"Oh. *Granny.*"

Granny was watching her. Jenny scrambled up off the floor to go and hug her. "They're . . . they're *wonderful.*"

Granny's eyes met her own. Granny's eyes were old but very bright. They never missed a trick. Granny said, "You can't possibly skate in boots that don't fit you. I bought them yesterday, because I couldn't bear to think of you missing all the fun."

"We'll go skating this afternoon," Natasha announced firmly. "You've *got* to give it another try."

"Yes," said Jenny meekly. And at that moment remembered the theatre, the only gift still unopened. "But now you've got to open your present from me."

The grown-ups sat back in some anticipation. In truth, they could scarcely wait to see what Jenny had been constructing in the secrecy of her bedroom over the last few weeks.

Crouching, Jenny put the plug into the hot-plate socket. "Now,

Natasha, you've got to take the paper off the *moment* I turn on the switch, otherwise it might catch fire."

"Heavens," said Granny in some dismay. "Do you suppose it's a volcano?"

"Now," said Jenny, and turned on the switch. Natasha whisked off the paper tea-cosy, and there it was. With the lights twinkling on all the sparkley bits of glitter; shining back from the mirror pond, gleaming on the satin-ribbon skirts of the miniature ballerinas.

For a satisfactory space of time there was total silence. Then Natasha said, "I don't believe it," and everybody started to exclaim.

"Oh, darling. It's the cleverest thing. The prettiest . . ."

"Never seen anything so enchanting . . ."

"Is *that* what you wanted the wine box for?"

They rose from their chairs, came to inspect, to stand back, to wonder and admire. No audience could have been more appreciative. As for Natasha, for once she seemed to be lost for words. Finally, she turned to her sister and hugged her. ". . . I shall keep it, always and always."

"It's not a real ballet. I mean it's not *La Fille Mal Gardée,* or anything like that."

"I like it better that way. My very own winter ballet. I simply love it. Oh, thank you, Jenny. Thank you."

By four o'clock Christmas dinner was finished, and finally cleared away. Over for another year. The crackers pulled, the nuts cracked. Jenny's parents and her grandmother were in the sitting-room, enjoying coffee before taking a little necessary exercise in the outdoor air. Natasha had already gone, her skates in her hand.

"Come on, Jenny. I'm ready," she had called up the stairs.

"I'll be there in a moment."

"What are you *doing?*"

Jenny was sitting on her bed. "Just tidying up."

"Shall I wait?"

"No. I'll be there in a moment."

"Promise?"

"Yes. I promise. I'll come."

"All right, then. See you later!"

The door banged shut, and she had gone, running down the path to the gate. Jenny was alone. She had been given skates, and she wished she hadn't been, because she couldn't skate. It wasn't that she didn't *want* to, but she was frightened. Not so much of falling and hurting herself, but of making an idiot of herself; of other people laughing at her; of having to come home and admit the usual utter failure.

I want to be like Natasha, she thought. But she knew that this was impossible, because she could never be like Natasha. I want to float over the ice, and have long blonde hair and long slender legs and have everybody admire me, and want to skate with me.

But *poor old Jenny* they would say, as she hit the ice yet another time. *Bad luck. Have another go.*

She would have given her soul simply to stay where she was; to curl up on her bed and read the new book that Natasha had given her. But she had promised. She picked up the skates and went out of her room and down the stairs, slowly, one step at a time, as though she had only just learned how to walk.

They were talking in the sitting-room. She heard Granny's voice, quite clearly, through the closed door.

". . . such a talented child. The hours she must have spent constructing that little masterpiece. And the thought and invention that went into it."

"She's always been good with her hands. Creative." That was Dad. And they were talking about her. "Perhaps she should have been born a boy."

"Oh, really, John, what a thing to say." Granny sounded quite irritated by him. "Why shouldn't girls be good with their hands?"

"It's funny . . ." Jenny's mother, now, sounding thoughtful. "That two daughters should be so different. Natasha finding everything so easy. And Jenny . . ." Her voice trailed to nothing.

"Natasha finds everything easy to do that she *wants* to do." Granny again, at her most brisk. "Jenny is not Natasha. She is a different child. I think that you should respect that, and treat her as such. After all, they're not a pair of identical twins. Why should Jenny have to dance, just because Natasha sees herself as a budding ballerina? Why should she even have to go to dancing classes? I think that you should let her talents lead her in her *own* direction."

"Now, what do you mean by that, Mamma?"

"I listened to her when we were singing carols last night. It seems to me that she has almost perfect pitch. I think she is musical. It is strange that her teachers at school have not already realized this. Have you ever thought of piano lessons?"

There was a long pause, and then Jenny's father said, "No." He didn't say it crossly, rather as though he had never thought of such a thing, but couldn't think why he hadn't.

"Dancing, Jenny will never do more than galumph about with a tambourine. Let her learn the piano, see how she does."

"You think she'd like that? You think she'd be good at it?"

"A child so talented could do anything she tried if she set her heart to it. She just needs confidence. I think, if you change your tack with her, she'll surprise us all."

The voices stopped. A silence fell. At any moment, her mother would start setting the empty coffee-cups on the tray. Not wishing to be discovered, Jenny tip-toed down the last of the stairs, and let herself out through the front door, making no sound. Down the path, through the gate, out onto the road.

She paused.

Have you ever thought of piano lessons? Let her learn the piano.

No more dancing classes. Just herself, on her own, making music.

A child so talented could do anything she tried if she set her heart to it.

If Granny thought she was as clever as that, perhaps she could. As well, she had gone to much trouble and expense to buy Jenny the skating boots for Christmas. The least Jenny could do was to have another try.

The orange sun was dipping down over the rim of the hills. From afar, across the frosty stillness of Christmas afternoon, she could hear the laughter and the voices from the village green. She began to walk.

When she got there, she didn't look for Natasha. She knew what she had to do, and she wanted to do it on her own.

"Hello, Jenny. Happy Christmas."

It was a school friend, with a sledge. Jenny borrowed the sledge to sit on. She took off her rubber boots and put on the beautiful new white skating boots. They felt soft and supple, and when she laced them, hugged her ankles like old friends. She stood up, on the frozen grass, and took a step or two. No wobbles. She reached the ice.

Remembered Natasha's instructions. *Put your feet in third position, and push off.* A bit unsteady, but she kept her balance. Now. Third position. A big breath for courage. She could do anything if she set her heart to it. Push. All right. Now the other foot . . .

It worked. She was away. She wasn't falling or waving her arms about. One, two. One, two. She was skating.

"You're doing it! You've got it." Natasha, all at once, materialized at her side. "No, don't look at me, keep concentrating. You mustn't fall over. Look, take my hands and we'll go together. Well done! You remembered what I told you to do. It's easy. The only reason you couldn't do it before was because of those stupid old boots . . ."

They were skating together. Two sisters, with hands clasped and the icy air burning their cheeks. Sailing over the ice. It was like having wings on your feet. The sun was gone, but over in the east, like a pale eyelash, hung the crescent of a young new moon.

"The present you gave me was the best I had," Natasha told her. "What was your best present?"

But Jenny couldn't tell her. Partly because she hadn't the breath to talk, and partly because she hadn't had time to work it out for herself yet. She only knew that it had not come in a package wrapped in holly paper, and that it was something she was going to be able to keep for the rest of her life.

ABOUT THE AUTHOR

Rosamunde Pilcher has had a long and distinguished career as a novelist and short story writer, but it was her phenomenally successful novel *The Shell Seekers* that captured the hearts of all who read it and won her international recognition as one of the most-loved storytellers of our time. She lives in the countryside near Dundee, Scotland, with her husband, Graham.